Archaeologist and anthropologist STEVEN ERIKSON is a graduate of the celebrated Iowa Writers' Workshop. His first fantasy novel, the critically acclaimed *Gardens of the Moon*, marked the opening chapter in his epic *The Malazan Book of the Fallen* sequence and was nominated for a World Fantasy Award. *Deadhouse Gates* is the second thrilling instalment in this remarkable story and the third book, *Memories of Ice*, is now available in Bantam Press trade paperback. Steven Erikson lives in Canada.

Acclaim for Steven Erikson and *Deadhouse Gates*:

'Steven Erikson afflicts me with awe . . . vast in scope, almost frighteningly fecund in imagination, and rich in sympathy, his work does something that only the rarest of books can manage: it alters the reader's perceptions of reality' **Stephen R. Donaldson**

'In the course of this vast and complex novel, there is enough intrigue, magic and warfare to keep even the most hardcore fantasy fans salivating, and enough solid characterization to make sure we care. This is very memorable fantasy fare, with some cool ideas and imagery . . . Sit up and pay attention. You'll be glad you did' **Neil Walsh, *SF Site* 'Best Fantasy Books of the Year'**

'Rare is the writer who so fluidly combines a sense of mythic power and depth of world, with fully realized characters and thrilling action, but Steven Erikson manages it spectacularly. The books are reminiscent of Tolkien's scope, Zelazny's cleverness and wit, and Donaldson's brooding atmospherics; yet all combined with dazzling talent into a narrative flow that keeps the reader turning pages. Some writers open windows on worlds, Erikson opens worlds and makes them so real, so magickal, you're not sure if you can escape – and I don't want to' **Michael A. Stackpole**

'Such is the impact of the first book in Erikson's monumental Malazan saga, *Gardens of the Moon*, that the achievement of this sequel is doubly surprising. Not only is the vigour and sweep of the earlier book effortlessly recaptured, the complex plot is simultaneously deepened and accelerated, with a grasp of tempo that has the reader inexorably gripped . . . Roll on, book three!' ***The Good Book Guide***

www.booksattransworld.co.uk

'Wondrous voyages, demons and gods abound . . . dense and complex . . . ultimately rewarding' *Locus* **magazine**

'One of the most promising new writers of the past few years, and has more than proved his right to A-list status' ***Bookseller***

. . .and *Gardens of the Moon*:

'Steven Erikson is an extraordinary writer . . . I would be hard pressed to decide what I enjoyed more: the richly and ominously magical world of Malaz and Genabackis; the large cast of sympathetically rendered characters; or the way the story accumulates to a climax that hits like machinegun fire. My advice to anyone who might listen to me is, treat yourself to *Gardens of the Moon*' **Stephen R.Donaldson**

'Steven Erikson . . . is able to create a world that is both absorbing on a human level and full of magical sublimity, and, above all, he can write . . . A wonderfully grand conception . . . splendidly written . . . fiendishly readable' **Adam Roberts,** *amazon.co.uk*

'Erikson's style is no-nonsense, and his military campaigns have a reality to them that's often lacking in fantasy . . . complex, challenging . . . Erikson's strengths are his grown-up characters and his ability to create a world every bit as intricate and messy as our own' **J. V. Jones,** *SFX*

'Erikson . . . has created a fantasy world as rich and detailed as any you're likely to encounter. It's a world you'll be glad you weren't born into, but one that is so engrossing you'll be hard pressed to set it aside . . . an astounding début' *SF Site*

'Complex and powerful . . . the best fantasy novel I've read since George R. R. Martin's *A Game of Thrones*, bar none . . . Superb stuff' **Waterstone's** *The Alien Has Landed*

'One of those rare fantasy books that not only attempts to be huge in scope, but actually succeeds in being so' *Vector* **magazine**

DEADHOUSE GATES

A Tale of the
Malazan Book of the Fallen

STEVEN ERIKSON

BANTAM BOOKS

London • New York • Toronto • Sydney • Auckland

DEADHOUSE GATES
A BANTAM BOOK : 0553 813110

Originally published in Great Britain by Bantam Press,
a division of Transworld Publishers

PRINTING HISTORY
Bantam Press edition published 2000
Bantam Books edition published 2001

1 3 5 7 9 10 8 6 4 2

Set in 10/12pt Goudy by
Falcon Oast Graphic Art Ltd

Bantam Books are published by Transworld Publishers,
61–63 Uxbridge Road, London W5 5SA,
a division of The Random House Group Ltd,
in Australia by Random House Australia (Pty) Ltd,
20 Alfred Street, Milsons Point, Sydney, NSW 2061, Australia,
in New Zealand by Random House New Zealand Ltd,
18 Poland Road, Glenfield, Auckland 10, New Zealand
and in South Africa by Random House (Pty) Ltd,
Endulini, 5a Jubilee Road, Parktown 2193, South Africa.

Printed and bound in Great Britain by
Cox & Wyman Ltd, Reading, Berkshire.

This novel is dedicated to two gentlemen: David Thomas Jr, who welcomed me to England with an introduction to a certain agent; and Patrick Walsh, the agent he introduced me to. There has been a lot of faith shown over the years, and I thank you both.

Acknowledgements

With deepest gratitude I acknowledge the
following for their support: The staff at Café
Rouge, Dorking (keep the coffees coming . . .);
the folks at Psion, whose extraordinary 5
Series was home to this novel's first draft;
Daryl and crew at Café Hosete; and, of course,
Simon Taylor and the rest at Transworld.
For my family and friends, thank you for
your faith and encouragement, without which
all that I achieve means little.
Thanks also to Stephen and Ross
Donaldson for their kind words, James Barclay,
Sean Russell and Ariel. Finally, a big thank
you to those readers who took time to write
their comments on various websites – writing
is a solitary, isolating activity, but you have
made it less so.

Contents

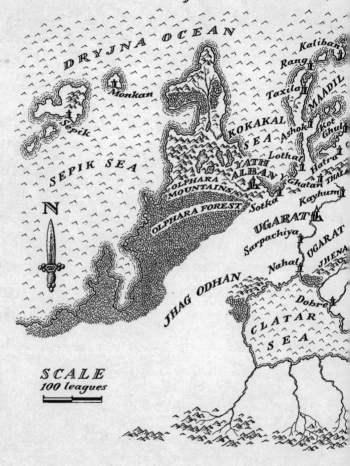

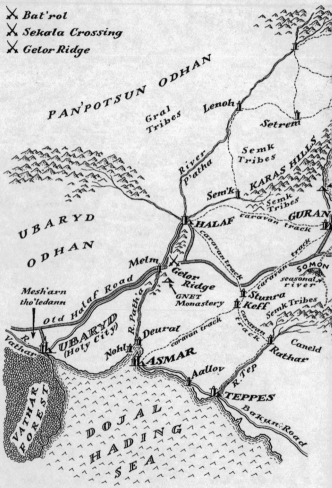

CHAIN of DOGS
COLTAINE'S MARCH The FIRST HALF

- ✘ Bat'rol
- ✘ Sekala Crossing
- ✘ Gelor Ridge

PAN'POTSUN ODHAN

Gral Tribes

Lenoh

Setrem

River P'atha

Semk Tribes

KARAS HILLS

Sem'k

Semk Tribes

caravan track

GURAN

HALAF

caravan track

UBARYD

ODHAN

Melm

Gelor Ridge

GNET Monastery

Slunra

Keff

caravan track

SOMON

seasonal river

Semk Tribes

Old Halaf Road

Mesh'arn tho'ledann

R. P'atha

Nohla

Deural

caravan track

caravan track

Caneld

Rathar

R. Vathar

UBARYD (Holy City)

ASMAR

Aallov

R. Tep

TEPPES

Bakun Road

VATHAR FOREST

DOJAL HADING SEA

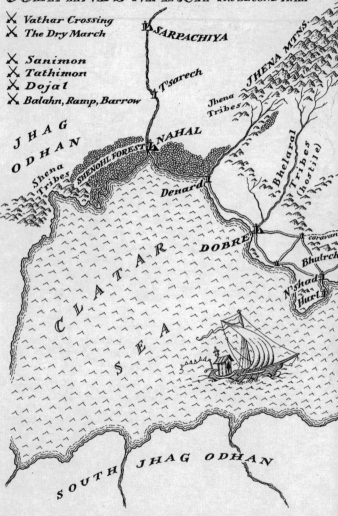

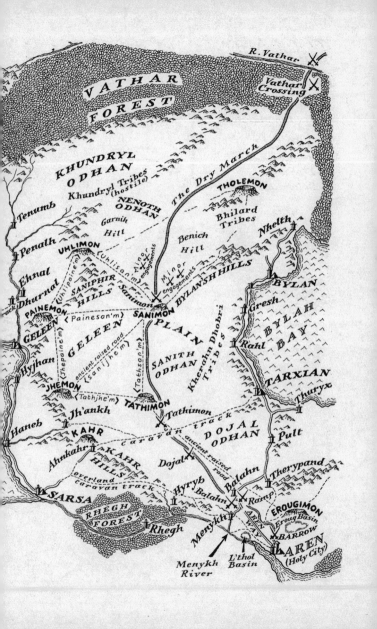

DRAMATIS PERSONAE

ON THE PATH OF THE HAND

Icarium, a mixed-blood Jaghut wanderer
Mappo, his Trell companion
Iskaral Pust, a High Priest of Shadow
Ryllandaras, the White Jackal, a D'ivers
Messremb, a Soletaken
Gryllen, a D'ivers
Mogora, a D'ivers

THE MALAZANS

Felisin, youngest daughter of House Paran
Heboric Light Touch, exiled historian and ex-priest of Fener
Baudin, companion to Felisin and Heboric
Fiddler, 9th Squad, Bridgeburners
Crokus, a visitor from Darujhistan
Apsalar, 9th Squad, Bridgeburners
Kalam, a corporal in the 9th Squad, Bridgeburners
Duiker, Imperial Historian
Kulp, cadre mage, 7th Army
Mallick Rel, chief adviser to the High Fist of the Seven Cities
Sawark, commander of the guard in the Otataral mining camp, Skullcup
Pella, a soldier stationed at Skullcup
Pormqual, High Fist of the Seven Cities, in Aren
Blistig, Commander of Aren Guard
Topper, Commander of the Claw
Lull, a captain in the Sialk Marines

17

Chenned, a captain in the 7th Army
Sulmar, a captain in the 7th Army
List, a corporal in the 7th Army
Mincer, a sapper
Cuttle, a sapper
Gesler, a corporal in the Coastal Guard
Stormy, a soldier in the Coastal Guard
Truth, a recruit in the Coastal Guard
Squint, a bowman
Pearl, a Claw
Captain Keneb, a refugee
Selv, Keneb's wife
Minala, Selv's sister
Kesen, Keneb and Selv's first-born son
Vaneb, Keneb and Selv's second-born son
Captain, owner and commander of the trader craft *Ragstopper*
Bent, a Wickan cattle-dog
Roach, a Hengese lapdog

WICKANS

Coltaine, Fist, 7th Army
Temul, a young lancer
Sormo E'nath, a warlock
Nil, a warlock
Nether, a warlock
Bult, a veteran commander and Coltaine's uncle

THE RED BLADES

Baria Setral (Dosin Pali)
Mesker Setral, his brother (Dosin Pali)

Tene Baralta (Ehrlitan)
Aralt Arpat (Ehrlitan)
Lostara Yil (Ehrlitan)

NOBLES ON THE CHAIN OF DOGS (MALAZAN)

Nethpara
Lenestro
Pullyk Alar
Tumlit

FOLLOWERS OF THE APOCALYPSE

Sha'ik, leader of the rebellion
Leoman, captain in the Raraku Apocalypse
Toblakai, a bodyguard and warrior in the Raraku Apocalypse
Febryl, a mage and elder adviser to Sha'ik
Korbolo Dom, renegade Fist leading the Odhan army
Kamist Reloe, High Mage with the Odhan army
L'oric, a mage with the Raraku Apocalypse
Bidithal, a mage with the Raraku Apocalypse
Mebra, a spy in Ehrlitan

OTHERS

Salk Elan, a traveller on the seas
Shan, a Hound of Shadow
Gear, a Hound of Shadow
Blind, a Hound of Shadow
Baran, a Hound of Shadow
Rood, a Hound of Shadow

Moby, a familiar
Hentos Ilm, a T'lan Imass Bonecaster
Legana Breed, a T'lan Imass
Olar Ethil, a T'lan Imass Bonecaster
Kimloc, a Tanno Spiritwalker
Beneth, a crime lord
Irp, a small servant
Rudd, an equally small servant
Apt, an aptorian demon
Panek, a child
Karpolan Demesand, a merchant
Bula, an innkeeper
Cotillion, patron god of assassins
Shadowthrone, Ruler of High House Shadow
Rellock, a servant

PROLOGUE

What see you in the horizon's bruised smear
That cannot be blotted out
By your raised hand?

The Bridgeburners
Toc the Younger

1163rd Year of Burn's Sleep
Ninth Year of the Rule of Empress Laseen
Year of the Cull

He came shambling into Judgement's Round from the Avenue of Souls, a misshapen mass of flies. Seething lumps crawled on his body in mindless migration, black and glittering and occasionally falling away in frenzied clumps that exploded into fragmented flight as they struck the cobbles.

The Thirsting Hour was coming to a close and the priest staggered in its wake, blind, deaf and silent. Honouring his god on this day, the servant of Hood, Lord of Death, had joined his companions in stripping naked and smearing himself in the blood of executed murderers, blood that was stored in giant amphorae lining the walls of the temple's nave. The brothers had then moved in procession out onto the streets of Unta to greet the god's sprites, enjoining the mortal dance that marked the Season of Rot's last day.

The guards lining the Round parted to let the priest pass, then parted further for the spinning, buzzing cloud that trailed him. The sky over Unta was still more grey than blue, as the flies that had swept at dawn into the capital of the Malazan Empire now rose, slowly winging out over the bay towards the salt marshes and sunken islands beyond the reef. Pestilence came with the Season of Rot, and the Season had come an unprecedented three times in the past ten years.

The air of the Round still buzzed, was still speckled as if filled with flying grit. Somewhere in the streets beyond a dog yelped like a thing near death but not near enough, and close to the Round's central fountain the abandoned mule that had collapsed earlier still kicked feebly in the air. Flies had crawled into the beast through every orifice and it was now bloated with gases. The animal, stubborn by its breed, was now over an hour in dying. As the priest staggered sightlessly past, flies rose

23

from the mule in a swift curtain to join those already enshrouding him.

It was clear to Felisin from where she and the others waited that the priest of Hood was striding directly towards her. His eyes were ten thousand eyes, but she was certain they were all fixed on her. Yet even this growing horror did little to stir the numbness that lay like a smothering blanket over her mind; she was aware of it rising inside but the awareness seemed more a memory of fear than fear now alive within her.

She barely recalled the first Season of Rot she'd lived through, but had clear memories of the second one. Just under three years ago, she had witnessed this day secure in the family estate, in a solid house with its windows shuttered and cloth-sealed, with the braziers set outside the doors and on the courtyard's high, broken-glass-rimmed walls billowing the acrid smoke of istaarl leaves. The last day of the Season and its Thirsting Hour had been a time of remote revulsion for her, irritating and inconvenient but nothing more. Then she'd given little thought to the city's countless beggars and the stray animals bereft of shelter, or even to the poorer residents who were subsequently press-ganged into cleanup crews for days afterwards.

The same city, but a different world.

Felisin wondered if the guards would make any move towards the priest as he came closer to the Cull's victims. She and the others in the line were the charges of the Empress now – Laseen's responsibility – and the priest's path could be seen as blind and random, the imminent collision one of chance rather than design, although in her bones Felisin knew differently. Would the helmed guards step forward, seek to guide the priest to one side, lead him safely through the Round?

'I think not,' said the man squatting on her right. His half-closed eyes, buried deep in their sockets, flashed with something that might have been amusement. 'Seen you flicking your gaze, guards to priest, priest to guards.'

The big, silent man on her left slowly rose to his feet, pulling the chain with him. Felisin winced as the shackle yanked at her when the man folded his arms across his bare, scarred chest. He glared at the approaching priest but said nothing.

'What does he want with me?' Felisin asked in a whisper. 'What have I done to earn a priest of Hood's attention?'

The squatting man rocked back on his heels, tilting his face into the late afternoon sun. 'Queen of Dreams, is this self-centred youth I hear from those full, sweet lips? Or just the usual stance of noble blood around which the universe revolves? Answer me, I pray, fickle Queen!'

Felisin scowled. 'I felt better when I thought you asleep – or dead.'

'Dead men do not squat, lass, they sprawl. Hood's priest comes not for you but for me.'

She faced him then, the chain rattling between them. He looked more of a sunken-eyed toad than a man. He was bald, his face webbed in tattooing, minute, black, square-etched symbols hidden within an overall pattern covering skin like a wrinkled scroll. He was naked but for a ragged loincloth, its dye a faded red. Flies crawled all over him; reluctant to leave they danced on – but not, Felisin realized, to Hood's bleak orchestration. The tattooed pattern covered the man – the boar's face overlying his own, the intricate maze of script-threaded, curled fur winding down his arms, covering his exposed thighs and shins, and the detailed hooves etched into the skin of his feet. Felisin had until now been too self-absorbed, too numb with shock to pay any attention to her companions in the chain line: this man was a priest of Fener, the Boar of Summer, and the flies seemed to know it, under-stand it enough to alter their frenzied motion. She watched with morbid fascination as they gathered at the stumps at the ends of the man's wrists, the old scar tissue the only place on him unclaimed by Fener, but the paths the sprites took to those stumps touched not a single tattooed line. The flies danced a dance of avoidance – but for all that, they were eager to dance.

The priest of Fener had been ankle-shackled last in the line. Everyone else had the narrow iron bands fastened around their wrists. His feet were wet with blood and the flies hovered there but did not land. She saw his eyes flick open as the sun's light was suddenly blocked.

Hood's priest had arrived. Chain stirred as the man on Felisin's left drew back as far as the links allowed. The wall at her back felt hot, the tiles – painted with scenes of imperial pageantry – now slick through the thin weave of her slave tunic. Felisin stared at the fly-shrouded creature standing wordless before the squatting priest of Fener. She could see no exposed flesh, nothing of the man himself – the flies had claimed all of him and beneath them he lived in darkness where even the sun's heat could not touch him. The cloud around him spread out now and Felisin shrank back as count- less cold insect legs touched her legs, crawling swiftly up her thighs – she pulled her tunic's hem close around her, clamping her legs tight.

The priest of Fener spoke, his wide face split into a humour- less grin. 'The Thirsting Hour's well past, Acolyte. Go back to your temple.'

Hood's servant made no reply but it seemed the buzzing changed pitch, until the music of the wings vibrated in Felisin's bones.

The priest's deep eyes narrowed and his tone shifted. 'Ah, well now. Indeed I was once a servant of Fener but no longer, not for years – Fener's touch cannot be scrubbed from my skin. Yet it seems that while the Boar of Summer has no love for me, he has even less for you.'

Felisin felt something shiver in her soul as the buzzing rapidly shifted, forming words that she could understand. 'Secret . . . to show . . . now . . .'

'Go on then,' the one-time servant of Fener growled, 'show me.'

Perhaps Fener acted then, the swatting hand of a furious god – Felisin would remember the moment and think on it often – or the secret was the mocking of immortals, a joke far beyond her understanding, but at that moment the rising tide of horror within her broke free, the numbness of her soul seared away as the flies exploded outward, dispersing in all directions to reveal . . . no-one.

The former priest of Fener flinched as if struck, his eyes wide. From across the Round half a dozen guards cried out, wordless sounds punched from their throats. Chains snapped as others in the line jolted as if to flee. The iron loops set in the wall snatched taut, but the loops held as did the chains. The guards rushed forward and the line shrank back into submission.

'Now that,' the tattooed man shakily muttered, 'was uncalled for.'

An hour passed, an hour in which the mystery, shock and horror of Hood's priest sank down within Felisin to become but one more layer, the latest but not the last in what had become an unending nightmare. An acolyte of Hood . . . who was not there. The buzzing of wings that formed words. *Was that Hood himself? Had the Lord of Death come to walk among mortals? And why stand before a once-priest of Fener – what was the message behind the revelation?*

But slowly the questions faded in her mind, the numbness seeping back, the return of cold despair. The Empress had culled the nobility, stripped the Houses and families of their wealth followed by a summary accusation and conviction of treason that had ended in chains. As for the ex-priest on her right and the huge, bestial man with all the makings of a common criminal on her left, clearly neither one could claim noble blood.

She laughed softly, startling both men.

'Has Hood's secret revealed itself to you, then, lass?' the ex-priest asked.

'No.'

'What do you find so amusing?'

She shook her head. *I had expected to find myself in good company, how's that for an upturned thought? There you have it, the very attitude the peasants hungered to tear down, the very same fuel the Empress has touched to flame—*

'Child!'

The voice was that of an aged woman, still haughty but with an air of desperate yearning. Felisin closed her eyes briefly, then straightened and looked along the line to the gaunt old woman beyond the thug. The woman was wearing her night-clothes, torn and smeared. *With noble blood, no less.* 'Lady Gaesen.'

The old woman reached out a shaking hand. 'Yes! Wife to Lord Hilrac! I am Lady Gaesen . . .' The words came as if she'd forgotten who she was, and now she frowned through the cracked make-up covering her wrinkles and her red-shot eyes fixed on Felisin. 'I know you,' she hissed. 'House of Paran. Youngest daughter. Felisin!'

Felisin went cold. She turned away and stared straight ahead, out into the compound where the guards stood leaning on pikes passing flasks of ale between them and waving away the last of the flies. A cart had arrived for the mule, four ash-smeared men clambering down from its bed with ropes and gaffs. Beyond the walls encircling the Round rose Unta's painted spires and domes. She longed for the shadowed streets between them, longed for the pampered life of a week ago, Sebry barking harsh commands at her as she led her favourite mare through her paces. And she would look up as she guided the mare in a delicate, precise turn, to see the row of green-leafed leadwoods separating the riding ground from the family vineyards.

Beside her the thug grunted. 'Hood's feet, the bitch has some sense of humour.'

Which bitch? Felisin wondered, but she managed to hold her expression even as she lost the comfort of her memories.

The ex-priest stirred. 'Sisterly spat, is it?' He paused, then dryly added, 'Seems a bit extreme.'

The thug grunted again and leaned forward, his shadow draping Felisin. 'Defrocked priest, are you? Not like the Empress to do any temples a favour.'

'She didn't. My loss of piety was long ago. I'm sure the Empress would rather I'd stayed in the cloister.'

'As if she'd care,' the thug said derisively as he settled back into his pose.

Lady Gaesen rattled, 'You must speak with *her*, Felisin! An appeal! I have rich friends—'

The thug's grunt turned into a bark. 'Farther up the line, hag, that's where you'll find your rich friends!'

Felisin just shook her head. *Speak with her, it's been months. Not even when Father died.*

A silence followed, dragging on, approaching the silence that had existed before this spate of babble, but then the ex-priest cleared his throat, spat and muttered, 'Not worth looking for salvation in a woman who's just following orders, Lady, never mind that one being this girl's sister—'

Felisin winced, then glared at the ex-priest. 'You presume—'

'He ain't presuming nothing,' growled the thug. 'Forget what's in the blood, what's supposed to be in it by your slant on things. This is the work of the Empress. Maybe you think it's personal, maybe you have to think that, being what you are . . .'

'What I am?' Felisin laughed harshly. 'What House claims you as kin?'

The thug grinned. 'The House of Shame. What of it? Yours ain't looking any less shabby.'

'As I thought,' Felisin said, ignoring the truth of his last observation with difficulty. She glowered at the guards. 'What's happening? Why are we just sitting here?'

The ex-priest spat again. 'The Thirsting Hour's past. The mob outside needs organizing.' He glanced up at her from under the shelf of his brows. 'The peasants need to be roused. We're the first, girl, and the example's got to be established. What happens here in Unta is going to rattle every nobleborn in the Empire.'

'Nonsense!' Lady Gaesen snapped. 'We shall be well treated. The Empress shall have to treat us well—'

The thug grunted a third time – what passed for laughter, Felisin realized – and said, 'If stupidity was a crime, lady, you would've been arrested years ago. The ogre's right. Not many of us are going to make it to the slave ships. This parade down Colonnade Avenue is going to be one long bloodbath. Mind you,' he added, eyes narrowing on the guards, 'old Baudin ain't going to be torn apart by any mob of peasants . . .'

Felisin felt real fear stirring in her stomach. She fought off a shiver. 'Mind if I stay in your shadow, Baudin?'

The man looked down at her. 'You're a bit plump for my tastes.' He turned away, then added, 'But you do what you like.'

The ex-priest leaned close. 'Thinking on it, girl, this rivalry of yours ain't in the league of tattle-tails and scratch-fights. Likely your sister wants to be sure you—'

'She's Adjunct Tavore,' Felisin cut in. 'She's not my sister any more. She renounced our House at the call of the Empress.'

'Even so, I've an inkling it's still personal.'

Felisin scowled. 'How would you know anything about it?'

The man made a slight, ironic bow. 'Thief once, then priest, now historian. I well know the tense position the nobility finds itself in.'

Felisin's eyes slowly widened and she cursed herself for her stupidity. Even Baudin – who could not have helped over-hearing – leaned forward for a searching stare. 'Heboric,' he said. 'Heboric Light Touch.'

Heboric raised his arms. 'As light as ever.'

'You wrote that revised history,' Felisin said. 'Committed treason—'

Heboric's wiry brows rose in mock alarm. 'Gods forbid! A philosophic divergence of opinions, nothing more! Duiker's own words at the trial – in my defence, Fener bless him.'

'But the Empress wasn't listening,' Baudin said, grinning. 'After all, you called her a murderer, and then had the gall to say she bungled the job!'

'Found an illicit copy, did you?'

Baudin blinked.

'In any case,' Heboric continued to Felisin, 'it's my guess your sister the Adjunct plans on your getting to the slave ships in one piece. Your brother disappearing on Genabackis took the life out of your father . . . so I've heard,' he added, grinning. 'But it was the rumours of treason that put spurs to your sister, wasn't it? Clearing the family name and all that—'

'You make it sound reasonable, Heboric,' Felisin said, hearing the bitterness in her voice but not caring any more. 'We differed in our opinions, Tavore and I, and now you see the result.'

'Your opinions of what, precisely?'

She did not reply.

There was a sudden stirring in the line. The guards straightened and swung to face the Round's West Gate. Felisin paled as she saw her sister – *Adjunct* Tavore now, heir to Lorn who'd died in Darujhistan – ride up on her stallion, a beast bred out of Paran stables, no less. Beside her was the ever-present T'amber, a beautiful young woman whose long, tawny mane gave substance to her name. Where she'd come from was any-one's guess, but she was now Tavore's personal aide. Behind these two rode a score of officers and a company of heavy cavalry, the soldiers looking exotic, foreign.

'Touch of irony,' Heboric muttered, eyeing the horsesoldiers.

Baudin jutted his head forward and spat. 'Red Swords, the bloodless bastards.'

The historian threw the man an amused glance. 'Travelled well in your profession, Baudin? Seen the sea walls of Aren, have you?'

The man shifted uneasily, then shrugged. 'Stood a deck or two in my time, ogre. Besides,' he added, 'the rumour of them's been in the city a week or more.'

There was a stirring from the Red Sword troop, and Felisin saw mailed hands close on weapon grips, peaked helms turning as one towards the Adjunct. *Sister Tavore, did our brother's disappearance cut you so deep? How great his failing you must imagine, to seek this recompense . . . and then, to make your loyalty absolute, you chose between me and Mother for the symbolic sacrifice. Didn't you realize that Hood stood on the side of both choices? At least Mother is with her beloved husband now . . .* She watched as Tavore scanned her guard briefly, then said something to T'amber, who edged her own mount towards the East Gate.

Baudin grunted one more time. 'Look lively. The endless hour's about to begin.'

It was one thing to accuse the Empress of murder, it was quite another to predict her next move. *If only they'd heeded my warning.* Heboric winced as they shuffled forward, the shackles cutting hard against his ankles.

People of civilized countenance made much of exposing the soft underbellies of their psyche – effete and sensitive were the brands of finer breeding. It was easy for them, safe, and that was the whole point, after all: a statement of coddled opulence that burned the throats of the poor more than any ostentatious show of wealth.

Heboric had said as much in his treatise, and could now admit a bitter admiration for the Empress and for Adjunct Tavore, Laseen's instrument in this. The excessive brutality of the midnight arrests – doors battered down, families dragged from their beds amidst wailing servants – provided the first layer of shock. Dazed by sleep deprivation, the nobles were trussed up and shackled, forced to stand before a drunken magistrate and a jury of beggars dragged in from the streets. It was a sour and obvious mockery of justice that stripped away the few remaining expectations of civil behaviour – stripped away civilization itself, leaving nothing but the chaos of savagery.

Shock layered on shock, a rending of those fine underbellies. Tavore knew her own kind, knew their weaknesses and was ruthless in exploiting them. What could drive a person to such viciousness?

The poor folk mobbed the streets when they heard the details, screaming adoration for their Empress. Carefully triggered riots, looting and slaughter followed, raging through the Noble District, hunting down those few selected highborns who hadn't been arrested – enough of them to whet the mob's bloodlust, give them faces to focus on with rage and hate. Then followed the reimposition of order, lest the city take flame.

The Empress made few mistakes. She'd used the opportunity to round up malcontents and unaligned academics, to close the fist of military presence on the capital, drumming the need for more troops, more recruits, more protection against the treasonous scheming of the noble class. The seized assets paid for this martial expansion. An exquisite move even if forewarned, rippling out with the force of Imperial Decree through the Empire, the cruel rage now sweeping through each city.

Bitter admiration. Heboric kept finding the need to spit, something he hadn't done since his cut-purse days in the Mouse Quarter of Malaz City. He could see the shock written on most of the faces in the chain line. Faces above nightclothes mostly, grimy and filthy from the pits, leaving their wearers bereft of even the social armour of regular clothing. Dishevelled hair, stunned expressions, broken poses – everything the mob beyond the Round lusted to see, hungered to flail—

Welcome to the streets, Heboric thought to himself as the guards prodded the line into motion, the Adjunct looking on, straight in her high saddle, her thin face drawn in until nothing but lines remained – the slit of her eyes, the brackets around her uncurved, almost lipless mouth – *damn, but she wasn't born with much, was she?* The looks went to her young sister, to the lass stumbling a step ahead of him.

Heboric's eyes fixed on Adjunct Tavore, curious, seeking something – a flicker of malicious pleasure, maybe – as her icy gaze swept the line and lingered for the briefest of moments on her sister. But the pause was all she revealed, a recognition acknowledged, nothing more. The gaze swept on.

The guards opened the East Gate two hundred paces ahead, near the front of the chained line. A roar poured through that ancient arched passageway, a wave of sound that buffeted soldier and prisoner alike, bouncing off the high walls and rising up amidst an explosion of terrified pigeons from the upper eaves. The sound of flapping wings drifted down like polite applause, although to Heboric it seemed that he alone appreciated that ironic touch of the gods. Not to be denied a gesture, he managed a slight bow.

Hood keep his damned secrets. Here, Fener you old sow, it's that itch I could never scratch. Look on, now, closely, see what becomes of your wayward son.

Some part of Felisin's mind held on to sanity, held with a brutal grip in the face of a maelstrom. Soldiers lined Colonnade Avenue in ranks three deep, but again and again the mob seemed to find weak spots in that bristling line. She found herself observing, clinically, even as hands tore at her, fists pummelled her, blurred faces lunged at her with gobs of spit. And even as sanity held within her, so too a pair of steady arms encircled her – arms without hands, the ends scarred and suppurating, arms that pushed her forward, ever forward. No-one touched the priest. No-one dared. While ahead was Baudin – more horrifying than the mob itself.

He killed effortlessly. He tossed bodies aside with contempt, roaring, gesturing, beckoning. Even the soldiers stared beneath their ridged helmets, heads turning at his taunts, hands tightening on pike or sword hilt.

Baudin, laughing Baudin, his nose smashed by a well-flung brick, stones bouncing from him, his slave tunic in rags and soaked with blood and spit. Every body that darted within his reach he grasped, twisted, bent and broke. The only pause in his stride came when something happened ahead, some breach in the soldiery – or when Lady Gaesen faltered. He'd grasp her arms under the shoulders, none too gently, then propel her forward, swearing all the while.

A wave of fear swept ahead of him, a touch of the terror inflicted turning back on the mob. The number of attackers diminished, although the bricks flew in a constant barrage, some hitting, most missing.

The march through the city continued. Felisin's ears rang painfully. She heard everything through a daze of sound, but her eyes saw clearly, seeking and finding – all too often – images she would never forget.

The gates were in sight when the most savage breach occurred. The soldiers seemed to melt away, and the tide of fierce hunger swept into the street, engulfing the prisoners.

Felisin caught Heboric's grunting words close behind her as he shoved hard: 'This is the one, then.'

Baudin roared. Bodies crowded in, hands tearing, nails clawing. Felisin's last shreds of clothing were torn away. A hand closed on a fistful of her hair, yanked savagely, twisting her head around, seeking the crack of vertebrae. She heard screaming and realized it came from her own throat. A bestial snarl sounded behind her and she felt the hand clench spasmodically, then it was gone. More screaming filled her ears.

A strong momentum caught them, pulling or pushing – she couldn't tell – and Heboric's face came into view, spitting bloody skin from his mouth. All at once a space cleared around Baudin. He crouched, a torrent of dock curses bellowing from his mashed lips. His right ear had been torn off, taking with it hair, skin and flesh. The bone of his temple glistened wetly. Broken bodies lay around him, few moving. At his feet was Lady Gaesen. Baudin held her by the hair, pulling her face into view. The moment seemed to freeze, the world closing in to this single place.

Baudin bared his teeth and laughed. 'I'm no whimpering noble,' he growled, facing the crowd. 'What do want? You want the blood of a noblewoman?'

The mob screamed, reaching out eager hands. Baudin laughed again. 'We pass through, you hear me?' He straightened, dragging Lady Gaesen's head upward.

Felisin couldn't tell if the old woman was conscious. Her eyes were closed, the expression peaceful – almost youthful – beneath the smeared dirt and bruises. Perhaps she was dead. Felisin prayed that it was so. Something was about to happen, something to condense this nightmare into a single image. Tension held the air.

'She's yours!' Baudin screamed. With his other hand grasping the Lady's chin, he twisted her head around. The neck snapped and the body sagged, twitching. Baudin wrapped a length of chain around her neck. He pulled it taut, then began sawing. Blood showed, making the chain look like a mangled scarf.

Felisin stared in horror.

'Fener have mercy,' Heboric breathed.

The crowd was stunned silent, withdrawing even in their bloodlust, shrinking back. A soldier appeared, helmetless, his young face white, his eyes fixed on Baudin, his steps ceasing. Beyond him the glistening peaked helms and broad blades of the Red Swords flashed above the crowd as the horsemen slowly pushed their way towards the scene.

No movement save the sawing chain. No breath save Baudin's grunting snorts. Whatever riot continued to rage beyond this place, it seemed a thousand leagues away.

Felisin watched the woman's head jerk back and forth, a mockery of life's animation. She remembered Lady Gaesen, haughty, imperious, beyond her years of beauty and seeking stature in its stead. What other choice? Many, but it didn't matter now. Had she been a gentle, kindly grandmother, it would not have mattered, would not have changed the mind-numbing horror of this moment.

The head came away with a sobbing sound. Baudin's teeth glimmered as he stared at the crowd. 'We had a deal,' he grated. 'Here's what you want, something to remember this day by.' He flung Lady Gaesen's head into the mob, a whirl of hair and threads of blood. Screams answered its unseen landing.

More soldiers appeared – backed by the Red Swords – moving slowly, pushing at the still-silent onlookers. Peace was being restored, all along the line – in all places but this one violently, without quarter. As people began to die under sword strokes, the rest fled.

The prisoners who had filed out of the arena had numbered around three hundred. Felisin, looking up the line, had her first sight of what remained. Some shackles held only forearms, others were completely empty. Under a hundred prisoners remained on their feet. Many on the paving stones writhed, screaming in pain; the rest did not move at all.

Baudin glared at the nearest knot of soldiers. 'Likely timing, tin-heads.'

Heboric spat heavily, his face twisting as he glared at the thug. 'Imagined you'd buy your way out, did you, Baudin? Give them what they want. But it was wasted, wasn't it? The soldiers were coming. She could have lived—'

Baudin slowly turned, his face a sheet of blood. 'To what end, priest?'

'Was that your line of reasoning? She would've died in the hold anyway?'

Baudin showed his teeth and said slowly, 'I just hate making deals with bastards.'

Felisin stared at the three-foot length of chain between herself and Baudin. A thousand thoughts could have followed, link by link – what she had been, what she was now; the prison she'd discovered, inside and out, merged as vivid memory – but all she thought, all she said, was this: 'Don't make any more deals, Baudin.'

His eyes narrowed on her, her words and tone reaching him, somehow, some way.

Heboric straightened, a hard look in his eyes as he studied her. Felisin turned away, half in defiance, half in shame.

A moment later the soldiers – having cleared the line of the dead – pushed them along, out through the gate, onto the East Road towards the pier town called Luckless. Where Adjunct Tavore and her retinue waited, as did the slave ships of Aren.

Farmers and peasants lined the road, displaying nothing of the frenzy that had gripped their cousins in the city. Felisin saw in their faces a dull sorrow, a passion born of different scars. She could not understand where it came from, and she knew that her ignorance was the difference between her and them. She also knew, in her bruises, scratches and helpless nakedness, that her lessons had begun.

BOOK ONE

RARAKU

He swam at my feet,
Powerful arms in broad strokes
Sweeping the sand.
So I asked this man,
What seas do you swim?
And to this he answered,
'I have seen shells and the like
On this desert floor,
So I swim this land's memory
Thus honouring its past,'
Is the journey far, queried I.
'I cannot say,' he replied,
'For I shall drown long before
I am done.'

Sayings of the Fool
Thenys Bule

CHAPTER ONE

And all came to imprint
Their passage
On the path,
To scent the dry winds
Their cloying claim
To ascendancy

The Path of Hands
Messremb

1164th Year of Burn's Sleep
Tenth Year of the Rule of Empress Laseen
The Sixth in the Seven Years of Dryjhna, the Apocalyptic

A corkscrew plume of dust raced across the basin, heading deeper into the trackless desert of the Pan'potsun Odhan. Though less than two thousand paces away, it seemed a plume born of nothing.

From his perch on the mesa's wind-scarred edge, Mappo Runt followed it with relentless eyes the colour of sand, eyes set deep in a robustly boned, pallid face. He held a wedge of emrag cactus in his bristle-backed hand, unmindful of the envenomed spikes as he bit into it. Juices dribbled down his chin, staining it blue. He chewed slowly, thoughtfully.

Beside him Icarium flicked a pebble over the cliff edge. It clicked and clattered on its way down to the boulder-strewn base. Under the ragged Spiritwalker robe – its orange faded to dusty rust beneath the endless sun – his grey skin had darkened into olive green, as if his father's blood had answered this wasteland's ancient call. His long, braided black hair dripped black sweat onto the bleached rock.

Mappo pulled a mangled thorn from between his front teeth. 'Your dye's running,' he observed, eyeing the cactus blade a moment before taking another bite.

Icarium shrugged. 'Doesn't matter any more. Not out here.'

'My blind grandmother wouldn't have swallowed your disguise. There were narrow eyes on us in Ehrlitan. I felt them crawling on my back day and night. Tannos are mostly short and bow-legged, after all.' Mappo pulled his gaze away from the dust cloud and studied his friend. 'Next time,' he grunted, 'try belonging to a tribe where everyone's seven foot tall.'

Icarium's lined, weather-worn face twitched into something like a smile, just a hint, before resuming its placid expression. 'Those who would know of us in Seven Cities, surely know of us now. Those who would not might wonder at us, but that is all they will do.' Squinting against the glare, he nodded at the plume. 'What do you see, Mappo?'

'Flat head, long neck, black and hairy all over. If just that, I might be describing one of my uncles.'

'But there's more.'

'One leg up front and two in back.'

Icarium tapped the bridge of his nose, thinking. 'So, not one of your uncles. An aptorian?'

Mappo slowly nodded. 'The convergence is months away. I'd guess Shadowthrone caught a whiff of what's coming, sent out a few scouts . . .'

'And this one?'

Mappo grinned, exposing massive canines. 'A tad too far

afield. Sha'ik's pet now.' He finished off the cactus, wiped his spatulate hands, then rose from his crouch. Arching his back, he winced. There had been, unaccountably, a mass of roots beneath the sand under his bedroll the night just past, and now the muscles to either side of his spine matched every knot and twist of those treeless bones. He rubbed at his eyes. A quick scan down the length of his body displayed for him the tattered, dirt-crusted state of his clothes. He sighed. 'It's said there's a waterhole out there, somewhere—'

'With Sha'ik's army camped around it.'

Mappo grunted.

Icarium also straightened, noting once again the sheer mass of his companion – big even for a Trell – the shoulders broad and maned in black hair, the sinewy muscles of his long arms, and the thousand years that capered like a gleeful goat behind Mappo's eyes. 'Can you track it?'

'If you like.'

Icarium grimaced. 'How long have we known each other, friend?'

Mappo's glance was sharp, then he shrugged. 'Long. Why do you ask?'

'I know reluctance when I hear it. The prospect disturbs you?'

'Any potential brush with demons disturbs me, Icarium. Shy as a hare is Mappo Trell.'

'I am driven by curiosity.'

'I know.'

The unlikely pair turned back to their small campsite, tucked between two towering spires of wind-sculpted rock. There was no hurry. Icarium sat down on a flat rock and proceeded to oil his longbow, striving to keep the hornwood from drying out. Once satisfied with the weapon's condition, he turned to his single-edged long sword, sliding the ancient weapon from its bronze-banded boiled-leather scabbard, then setting an oiled whetstone to its notched edge.

Mappo struck the hide tent, folding it haphazardly before stuffing it into his large leather bag. Cooking utensils followed, as did the bedding. He tied the drawstrings and hefted the bag over one shoulder, then glanced to where Icarium waited – bow rewrapped and slung across his back.

Icarium nodded, and the two of them, half-blood Jaghut and full-blooded Trell, began on the path leading down into the basin.

Overhead the stars hung radiant, casting enough light down onto the basin to tinge its cracked pan silver. The bloodflies had passed with the vanishing of the day's heat, leaving the night to the occasional swarm of capemoths and the batlike rhizan lizards that fed on them.

Mappo and Icarium paused for a rest in the courtyard of some ruins. The mudbrick walls had all but eroded away, leaving nothing but shin-high ridges laid out in a geometric pattern around an old, dried-up well. The sand covering the courtyard's tiles was fine and windblown and seemed to glow faintly to Mappo's eyes. Twisted brush clung with fisted roots along its edges.

The Pan'potsun Odhan and the Holy Desert Raraku that flanked it to the west were both home to countless such remnants from long-dead civilizations. In their travels Mappo and Icarium had found high tels – flat-topped hills built up of layer upon layer of city – situated in a rough procession over a distance of fifty leagues between the hills and the desert, clear evidence that a rich and thriving people had once lived in what was now dry, wind-blasted wasteland. From the Holy Desert had emerged the legend of Dryjhna the Apocalyptic. Mappo wondered if the calamity that had befallen the city-dwellers in this region had in some way contributed to the myth of a time of devastation and death. Apart from the

44

occasional abandoned estate such as the one they now rested in, many ruins showed signs of a violent end.

His thoughts finding familiar ruts, Mappo grimaced. *Not all pasts can be laid at our feet, and we are no closer here and now than we've ever been. Nor have I any reason to disbelieve my own words.* He turned away from those thoughts as well.

Near the courtyard's centre stood a single column of pink marble, pitted and grooved on one side where the winds born out in Raraku blew unceasingly towards the Pan'potsun Hills. The pillar's opposite side still retained the spiral patterning carved there by long-dead artisans.

Upon entering the courtyard Icarium had walked directly to the six-foot-high column, examining its sides. His grunt told Mappo he'd found what he had been looking for.

'And this one?' the Trell asked, setting his leather sack down.

Icarium came over, wiping dust from his hands. 'Down near the base, a scattering of tiny clawed hands – the seekers are on the Trail.'

'Rats? More than one set?'

'D'ivers,' Icarium agreed, nodding.

'Now who might that be, I wonder?'

'Probably Gryllen.'

'Mhm, unpleasant.'

Icarium studied the flat plain stretching into the west. 'There will be others. Soletaken and D'ivers both. Those who feel near to Ascendancy, and those who are not, yet seek the Path nonetheless.'

Mappo sighed, studying his old friend. Faint dread stirred within him. *D'ivers and Soletaken, the twin curses of shapeshifting, the fever for which there is no cure. Gathering . . . here, in this place.* 'Is this wise, Icarium?' he asked softly. 'In seeking your eternal goal, we find ourselves walking into a most disagreeable convergence. Should the gates open, we shall find our passage

45

contested by a host of blood-thirsty individuals all eager in their belief that the gates offer Ascendancy.'

'If such a pathway exists,' Icarium said, his eyes still on the horizon, 'then perhaps I shall find my answers there as well.'

Answers are no benediction, friend. Trust me in this. Please. 'You have still not explained to me what you will do once you have found them.'

Icarium turned to him with a faint smile. 'I am my own curse, Mappo. I have lived centuries, yet what do I know of my own past? Where are my memories? How can I judge my own life without such knowledge?'

'Some would consider your curse a gift,' Mappo said, a flicker of sadness passing across his features.

'I do not. I view this convergence as an opportunity. It might well provide me with answers. To achieve them, I hope to avoid drawing my weapons, but I shall if I must.'

The Trell sighed a second time and rose from his crouch. 'You may be tested in that resolve soon, friend.' He faced southwest. 'There are six desert wolves on our trail.'

Icarium unwrapped his antlered bow and strung it in a swift, fluid motion. 'Desert wolves never hunt people.'

'No,' Mappo agreed. It was another hour before the moon would rise. He watched Icarium lay out six long, stone-tipped arrows, then squinted out into the darkness. Cold fear crept along the nape of his neck. The wolves were not yet visible, but he felt them all the same. 'They are six, but they are one. D'ivers.' *Better it would have been a Soletaken. Veering into a single beast is unpleasant enough, but into many . . .*

Icarium frowned. 'One of power, then, to achieve the shape of six wolves. Do you know who it might be?'

'I have a suspicion,' Mappo said quietly.

They fell silent, waiting.

Half a dozen tawny shapes appeared out of a gloom that seemed of its own making, less than thirty strides away. At

46

twenty paces the wolves spread out into an open half-circle facing Mappo and Icarium. The spicy scent of D'ivers filled the still night air. One of the lithe beasts edged forward, then stopped as Icarium raised his bow.

'Not six,' Icarium muttered, 'but one.'

'I know him,' Mappo said. 'A shame he can't say the same of us. He is uncertain, but he's taken a blood-spilling form. Tonight, Ryllandaras hunts in the desert. Does he hunt us or something else, I wonder?'

Icarium shrugged. 'Who shall speak first, Mappo?'

'Me,' the Trell replied, taking a step forward. This would require guile and cunning. A mistake would prove deadly. He pitched his voice low and wry. 'Long way from home, aren't we. Your brother Treach had it in mind that he killed you. Where was that chasm? Dal Hon? Or was it Li Heng? You were D'ivers jackals then, I seem to recall.'

Ryllandaras spoke inside their minds, a voice cracking and halting with disuse. *I am tempted to match wits with you, N'Trell, before killing you.*

'Might not be worth it,' Mappo replied easily. 'With the company I've been keeping, I'm as out of practice as you, Ryllandaras.'

The lead wolf's bright blue eyes flicked to Icarium.

'I have little wits to match,' the Jaghut half-blood said softly, his voice barely carrying. 'And I am losing patience.'

Foolish. Charm is all that can save you. Tell me, bowman, do you surrender your life to your companion's wiles?

Icarium shook his head. 'Of course not. I share his opinion of himself.'

Ryllandaras seemed confused. *A matter of expedience then, the two of you travelling together. Companions without trust, without confidence in each other. The stakes must be high.*

'I am getting bored, Mappo,' Icarium said.

The six wolves stiffened as one, half flinching. *Mappo Runt*

47

and Icarium. Ah, we see. Know that we've no quarrel with you.

'Wits matched,' Mappo said, his grin broadening a moment before disappearing entirely. 'Hunt elsewhere, Ryllandaras, before Icarium does Treach a favour.' *Before you unleash all that I am sworn to prevent.* 'Am I understood?'

Our trail . . . converges, the D'ivers said, *upon the spoor of a demon of Shadow.*

'Not Shadow any longer,' Mappo replied. 'Sha'ik's. The Holy Desert no longer sleeps.'

So it seems. Do you forbid us our hunt?

Mappo glanced at Icarium, who lowered his bow and shrugged. 'If you wish to lock jaws with an aptorian, that is your choice. Our interest was only passing.'

Then indeed shall our jaws close upon the throat of the demon.

'You would make Sha'ik your enemy?' Mappo asked.

The lead wolf cocked its head. *The name means nothing to me.*

The two travellers watched as the wolves padded off, vanishing once again into a gloom of sorcery. Mappo showed his teeth, then sighed, and Icarium nodded, giving voice to their shared thought. 'It will, soon.'

The Wickan horsesoldiers loosed fierce cries of exultation as they led their broad-backed horses down the transport's gangplanks. The scene at the quayside of Hissar's Imperial Harbour was chaotic, a mass of unruly tribesmen and women, the flash of iron-headed lances rippling over black braided hair and spiked skullcaps. From his position on the harbour-entrance tower parapet, Duiker looked down on the wild outland company with more than a little scepticism, and with growing trepidation.

Beside the Imperial Historian stood the High Fist's representative, Mallick Rel, his fat, soft hands folded together and resting on his paunch, his skin the colour of oiled leather and smelling of Aren perfumes. Mallick Rel looked nothing like the chief adviser to the Seven Cities' commander of the Malazan armies. A Jhistal priest of the Elder god of the seas, Mael, his presence here to officially convey the High Fist's welcome to the new Fist of the 7th Army was precisely what it appeared to be: a calculated insult. Although, Duiker amended silently, the man at his side had, in a very short time, risen to a position of power among the Imperial players on this continent. A thousand rumours rode the tongues of the soldiers about the smooth, soft-spoken priest and whatever weapon he held over High Fist Pormqual – each and every rumour no louder than a whisper, for Mallick Rel's path to Pormqual's side was a tale of mysterious misfortune befalling everyone who stood in his way, and fatal misfortune at that.

The political mire among the Malazan occupiers in Seven Cities was as obscure as it was potentially deadly. Duiker suspected that the new Fist would understand little of veiled gestures of contempt, lacking as he did the more civilized nuances of the Empire's tamed citizens. The question that remained for the historian, then, was how long Coltaine of the Crow Clan would survive his new appointment.

Mallick Rel pursed his full lips and slowly exhaled. 'Historian,' he said softly, his Gedorian Falari accent faint in its sibilant roll. 'Pleased by your presence. Curious as well. Long from Aren court, now . . .' He smiled, not showing his green-dyed teeth. 'Caution bred of distant culling?'

Words like the lap of waves, the god Mael's formless affectation and insidious patience. This, my fourth conversation with Rel. Oh, how I dislike this creature! Duiker cleared his throat. 'The Empress takes little heed of me, Jhistal . . .'

Mallick Rel's soft laugh was like the rattle of a snake's tail. 'Unheeded historian or unheeding of history? Hint of bitterness at advice rejected or worse, ignored. Be calmed, no crimes winging back from Unta's towers.'

'Pleased to hear it,' Duiker muttered, wondering at the priest's source. 'I remain in Hissar as a matter of research,' he explained after a moment. 'The precedent of shipping prisoners to the Otataral mines on the island reaches back to the Emperor's time, although he generally reserved that fate for mages.'

'Mages? Ah, ah.'

Duiker nodded. 'Effective, yes, although unpredictable. The specific properties of Otataral as a magic-deadening ore remain largely mysterious. Even so, madness claimed most of those sorcerers, although it is not known if that was the result of exposure to the ore dust, or the deprivation from their Warrens.'

'Some mages among the next slave shipment?'

'Some.'

'Question soon answered, then.'

'Soon,' Duiker agreed.

The T-shaped quay was now a maelstrom of belligerent Wickans, frightened dock porters and short-tempered warhorses. A cordon of Hissar Guard provided the stopper to the bottleneck at the dock's end where it opened out onto the cobbled half-round. Of Seven Cities blood, the Guards had hitched their round shields and unsheathed their tulwars, waving the broad, curving blades threateningly at the Wickans, who answered with barking challenges.

Two men arrived on the parapet. Duiker nodded greetings. Mallick Rel did not deign to acknowledge either of them – a rough captain and the 7th's lone surviving cadre mage, both men clearly ranked too low for any worthwhile cultivation by the priest.

'Well, Kulp,' Duiker said to the squat, white-haired wizard, 'your arrival may prove timely.'

Kulp's narrow, sunburned face twisted into a sour scowl. 'Came up here to keep my bones and flesh intact, Duiker. I'm not interested in becoming Coltaine's lumpy carpet in his step up to the post. They're *his* people, after all. That he hasn't done a damned thing to quell this brewing riot doesn't bode well, I'd say.'

The captain at his side grunted agreement. 'Sticks in the throat,' he growled. 'Half the officers here saw their first blood facing that bastard Coltaine, and now here he is, about to take command. Hood's knuckles,' he spat, 'won't be any tears spilled if the Hissar Guard cuts down Coltaine and every one of his Wickan savages right here at the Quay. The Seventh don't need them.'

'Truth,' Mallick Rel said to Duiker with veiled eyes, 'behind the threat of uprisings. Continent here a viper nest. Coltaine an odd choice—'

'Not so odd,' Duiker said, shrugging. He returned his attention to the scene below. The Wickans closest to the Hissar Guard had begun strutting back and forth in front of the armoured line. The situation was but moments away from a full-scale battle – the bottleneck was about to become a killing ground. The historian felt something cold clutch his stomach at seeing horn bows now strung among the Wickan soldiers. Another company of guards appeared from the avenue to the right of the main colonnade, bristling with pikes.

'Can you explain that?' Kulp asked.

Duiker turned and was surprised to see all three men staring at him. He thought back to his last comment, then shrugged again. 'Coltaine united the Wickan clans in an uprising against the Empire. The Emperor had a hard time bringing him to heel – as some of you know first-hand. True to the Emperor's style, he acquired Coltaine's loyalty—'

'How?' Kulp barked.

'No one knows.' Duiker smiled. 'The Emperor rarely explained his successes. In any case, since Empress Laseen held no affection for her predecessor's chosen commanders,

Coltaine was left to rot in some backwater on Quon Tali. Then the situation changed. Adjunct Lorn is killed in Darujhistan, High Fist Dujek and his army turn renegade, effectively surrendering the entire Genabackan Campaign, and the Year of Dryjhna approaches here in Seven Cities, prophesied as the year of rebellion. Laseen needs able commanders before it all slips from her grasp. The new Adjunct Tavore is untested. So . . .'

'Coltaine,' the captain nodded, his scowl deepening. 'Sent here to take command of the Seventh and put down the rebellion—'

'After all,' Duiker said dryly, 'who better to deal with insurrection than a warrior who led one himself?'

'If mutiny occurs, scant his chances,' Mallick Rel said, his eyes on the scene below.

Duiker saw half a dozen tulwars flash, watched the Wickans recoil and then unsheathe their own long-knives. They seemed to have found a leader, a tall, fierce-looking warrior with fetishes in his long braids, who now bellowed encouragement, waving his own weapon over his head. 'Hood!' the historian swore. 'Where on earth is Coltaine?'

The captain laughed. 'The tall one with the lone long-knife.'

Duiker's eyes widened. *That madman is Coltaine? The Seventh's new Fist?*

'Ain't changed at all, I see,' the captain continued. 'If you're going to keep your head as leader of all the clans, you'd better be nastier than all the rest put together. Why'd you think the old Emperor liked him so much?'

'Beru fend,' Duiker whispered, appalled.

In the next breath an ululating scream from Coltaine brought sudden silence from the Wickan company. Weapons slid back into their sheaths, bows were lowered, arrows returned to their quivers. Even the bucking, snapping horses fell still, heads raised and ears pricked. A space cleared around Coltaine, who had turned his back on the guards. The tall warrior gestured and the four men on the parapet watched in silence as with absolute precision every horse was saddled. Less than a minute later the horsesoldiers were mounted, guiding their horses into a close parade formation that would rival the Imperial elites.

'That,' Duiker said, 'was superbly done.'

A soft sigh escaped Mallick Rel. 'Savage timing, a beast's sense of challenge, then contempt. Statement for the guards. For us as well?'

'Coltaine's a snake,' the captain said, 'if that's what you're asking. If the High Command at Aren thinks they can dance around him, they're in for a nasty surprise.'

'Generous advice,' Rel acknowledged.

The captain looked as if he'd just swallowed something sharp, and Duiker realized that the man had spoken without thought as to the priest's place in the High Command.

Kulp cleared his throat. 'He's got them in troop formation – guess the ride to the barracks will be peaceful after all.'

'I admit,' Duiker said wryly, 'that I look forward to meeting the Seventh's new Fist.'

His heavy-lidded eyes on the scene below, Rel nodded. 'Agreed.'

Leaving behind the Skara Isles on a heading due south, the fisherboat set out into the Kansu Sea, its triangular sail creaking and straining. If the gale held, they would reach the Ehrlitan coast in four hours. Fiddler's scowl deepened. *The Ehrlitan coast, Seven Cities. I hate this damned continent. Hated it the first time, hate it even more now.* He leaned over the gunnel and spat acrid bile into the warm, green waves.

'Feeling any better?' Crokus asked from the prow, his tanned young face creased with genuine concern.

The old saboteur wanted to punch that face; instead he just growled and hunched down deeper against the barque's hull.

Kalam's laugh rumbled from where he sat at the tiller. 'Fiddler and water don't mix, lad. Look at him, he's greener than that damned winged monkey of yours.'

A sympathetic snuffling sound breathed against Fiddler's cheek. He pried open one bloodshot eye to find a tiny, wizened face staring at him. 'Go away, Moby,' Fiddler croaked. The familiar, once servant to Crokus's uncle Mammot, seemed to have adopted the sapper, the way stray dogs and cats often did. Kalam would say it was the other way around, of course. 'A lie,' Fiddler whispered. 'Kalam's good at those—' *like lounging around in Rutu Jelba for a whole damn week on the off-chance that a Skrae trader would come in.* 'Book passage in comfort, eh, Fid?' *Not like the damned ocean crossing, oh no – and that one was supposed to have been in comfort, too. A whole week in Rutu Jelba, a lizard-infested, orange-bricked cesspool of a city, then what? Eight jakatas for this rag-stoppered sawed-in-half ale casket.*

The steady rise and fall lulled Fiddler as the hours passed. His mind drifted back to the appallingly long journey that had brought them thus far, then to the appallingly long journey that lay ahead. *We never do things the easy way, do we?*

He would rather that every sea dried up. *Men got feet, not flippers. Even so, we're about to cross overland – over a fly-infested, waterless waste, where people smile only to announce they're about to kill you.*

The day dragged on, green-tinged and shaky.

He thought back to the companions he'd left behind on Genabackis, wishing he could be marching alongside them. *Into a religious war. Don't forget that, Fid. Religious wars are no fun.* The faculty of reasoning that permitted surrender did not apply in such instances. Still, the squad was all he'd known for years. He felt bereft out of its shadows. *Just Kalam for old company, and he calls that land ahead home. And he smiles before he kills. And what's he and Quick Ben got planned they ain't told me about yet?*

'There's more of those flying fish,' Apsalar said, her voice identifying the soft hand that had found its way to his shoulder. 'Hundreds of them!'

'Something big from the deep is chasing them,' Kalam said.

Groaning, Fiddler pushed himself upright. Moby took the opportunity to reveal its motivation behind the day's cooing and crawled into the sapper's lap, curling up and closing its yellow eyes. Fiddler gripped the gunnel and joined his three companions in studying the school of flying fish a hundred yards off the starboard side. The length of a man's arm, the milky white fish were clearing the waves, sailing thirty feet or so, then slipping back under the surface. In the Kansu Sea flying fish hunted like sharks, the schools capable of shredding a bull whale down to bones in minutes. They used their ability to fly to launch themselves onto the back of a whale when it broke for air. 'What in Mael's name is hunting *them?*'

Kalam was frowning. 'Shouldn't be anything here in the Kansu. Out in Seeker's Deep there's dhenrabi, of course.'

'Dhenrabi! Oh, that comforts me, Kalam. Oh yes indeed!'

'Some kind of sea serpent?' Crokus asked.

'Think of a centipede eighty paces long,' Fiddler answered. 'Wraps up whales and ships alike, blows out all the air under its armoured skin and sinks like a stone, taking its prey with it.'

'They're rare,' Kalam said, 'and never seen in shallow water.'

'Until now,' Crokus said, his voice rising in alarm.

The dhenrabi broke the surface in the midst of the flying fish, thrashing its head side to side, a wide razorlike mouth flensing prey by the score. The width of the creature's head was immense, as many as ten arm-spans. Its segmented armour was deep green under the encrusted barnacles, each segment revealing long chitinous limbs.

55

'Eighty paces long?' Fiddler hissed. 'Not unless it's been cut in half!'

Kalam rose at the tiller. 'Ready with the sail, Crokus. We're going to run. Westerly.'

Fiddler pushed a squawking Moby from his lap and opened his backpack, fumbling to unwrap his crossbow. 'If it decides we look tasty, Kalam . . .'

'I know,' the assassin rumbled.

Quickly assembling the huge iron weapon, Fiddler glanced up and met Apsalar's wide eyes. Her face was white. The sapper winked. 'Got a surprise if it comes for us, girl.'

She nodded. 'I remember . . .'

The dhenrabi had seen them. Veering from the school of flying fish, it was now cutting sinuously through the waves towards them.

'That's no ordinary beast,' Kalam muttered. 'You smelling what I'm smelling, Fiddler?'

Spicy, bitter. 'Hood's breath, that's a Soletaken!'

'A what?' Crokus asked.

'Shapeshifter,' Kalam said.

A rasping voice filled Fiddler's mind – and the expressions on his companions' faces told him they heard as well – *Mortals, unfortunate for you to witness my passage.*

The sapper grunted. The creature did not sound at all regretful.

It continued, *For this you must all die, though I shall not dishonour your flesh by eating you.*

'Kind of you,' Fiddler muttered, setting a solid quarrel in the crossbow's slot. The iron head had been replaced with a grapefruit-sized clay ball.

Another fisherboat mysteriously lost, the Soletaken mused ironically. *Alas.*

Fiddler scrambled to the stern, crouching down beside Kalam. The assassin straightened to face the dhenrabi, one hand on the tiller. 'Soletaken! Be on your way – we care nothing for your passage!'

I shall be merciful when killing you. The creature rushed the barque from directly astern, cutting through the water like a sharp-hulled ship. Its jaws opened wide.

'You were warned,' Fiddler said as he raised the crossbow, aimed and fired. The quarrel sped for the beast's open mouth. Lightning fast, the dhenrabi snapped at the shaft, its thin, saw-edged teeth slicing through the quarrel and shattering the clay ball, releasing to the air the powdery mixture within the ball. The contact resulted in an instantaneous explosion that blew the Soletaken's head apart.

Fragments of skull and grey flesh raked the water on all sides. The incendiary powder continued to burn fiercely all it clung to, sending up hissing steam. Momentum carried the headless body to within four spans of the barque's stern before it dipped down and slid smoothly out of sight even as the last echoes of the detonation faded. Smoke drifted sideways over the waves.

'You picked the wrong fishermen,' Fiddler said, lowering his weapon.

Kalam settled back at the tiller, returning the craft to a southerly course. A strange stillness hung in the air. Fiddler disassembled his crossbow and repacked it in oilcloth. As he resumed his seat amidships, Moby crawled back into his lap. Sighing, he scratched it behind an ear. 'Well, Kalam?'

'I'm not sure,' the assassin admitted. 'What brought a Soletaken into the Kansu Sea? Why did it want its passage secret?'

'If Quick Ben was here . . .'

'But he isn't, Fid. It's a mystery we'll have to live with, and hopefully we won't run into any more.'

'Do you think it's related to . . . ?'

Kalam scowled. 'No.'

'Related to what?' Crokus demanded. 'What are you two going on about?'

'Just musing,' Fiddler said. 'The Soletaken was heading south. Like us.'

'So?'

Fiddler shrugged. 'So . . . nothing. Just that.' He spat again over the side and slumped down. 'The excitement made me forget my seasickness. Now the excitement's faded, dammit.'

Everyone fell silent, though the frown on the face of Crokus told the sapper that the boy wasn't about to let the issue rest for long.

The gale remained steady, pushing them hard southward. Less than three hours after that Apsalar announced that she could see land ahead, and forty minutes later Kalam directed the craft parallel to the Ehrlitan coastline half a league off-shore. They tacked west, following the cedar-lined ridge as the day slowly died.

'I think I see horsemen,' Apsalar said.

Fiddler raised his head, joining the others in studying the line of riders following a coastal track along the ridge.

'I make them six in all,' Kalam said. 'Second rider's—'

'Got an Imperial pennon,' Fiddler finished, his face twisting at the taste in his mouth. 'Messenger and Lancer guard—'

'Heading for Ehrlitan,' Kalam added.

Fiddler turned in his seat and met his corporal's dark eyes. *Trouble?*

Maybe.

The exchange was silent, a product of years fighting side by side.

Crokus asked, 'Something wrong? Kalam? Fiddler?'

The boy's sharp. 'Hard to say,' Fiddler muttered. 'They've seen us but what have they seen? Four fisherfolk in a barque, some Skrae family headed into the port for a taste of civilization.'

'There's a village just south of the tree-line,' Kalam said. 'Keep an eye out for a creek mouth, Crokus, and a beach with no driftwood – the houses will be tucked leeward of the ridge, meaning inland. How's my memory, Fid?'

'Good enough for a native, which is what you are. How long out of the city?'

'Ten hours on foot.'

'That close?'

'That close.'

Fiddler fell silent. The Imperial messenger and his horse guard had moved out of sight, leaving the ridge as they swung south towards Ehrlitan. The plan had been to sail right into the Holy City's ancient, crowded harbour, arriving anonymously. It was likely that the messenger was delivering information that had nothing to do with them – they'd given nothing away since reaching the Imperial port of Karakarang from Genabackis, arriving on a Moranth Blue trader having paid passage as crew. The overland journey from Karakarang across the Talgai Mountains and down to Rutu Jelba had been on the Tano pilgrim route – a common enough journey. And the week in Rutu Jelba had been spent inconspicuously lying low, with only Kalam making nightly excursions to the wharf district, seeking passage across the Otataral Sea to the mainland.

At worst, a report might have reached someone official, somewhere, that two possible deserters, accompanied by a Genabackan and a woman, had arrived on Malazan territory – hardly news to shake the Imperial wasp nest all the way to Ehrlitan. So, likely Kalam was being his usual paranoid self.

'I see the stream mouth,' Crokus said, pointing to a place on the shore.

Fiddler glanced back at Kalam. *Hostile land, how low do we crawl?*

Looking up at grasshoppers, Fid.

Hood's breath. He looked back to the shore. 'I hate Seven Cities,' he whispered. In his lap, Moby yawned, revealing a mouth bristling with needlelike fangs. Fiddler blanched. 'Cuddle up whenever you want, pup,' he said, shivering.

Kalam angled the tiller. Crokus worked the sail, deft enough after a two-month voyage across Seeker's Deep to let the barque slip easily into the wind, the tattered sail barely raising a luff. Apsalar shifted on the seat, stretched her arms and flashed Fiddler a smile. The sapper scowled and looked away. *Burn shake me, I've got to keep my jaw from dropping every time she does that. She was another woman, once. A killer, the knife of a god. She did things . . . Besides, she's with Crokus, ain't she. The boy's got all the luck and the whores in Karakarang looked like poxed sisters from some gigantic poxed family and all those poxed babies on their hips . . .* He shook himself. *Oh, Fiddler, too long at sea, way too long!*

'I don't see any boats,' Crokus said.

'Up the creek,' Fiddler mumbled, dragging a nail through his beard in pursuit of a nit. After a moment he plucked it out and flicked it over the side. *Ten hours on foot, then Ehrlitan, and a bath and a shave and a Kansuan girl with a saw-comb and the whole night free afterward.*

Crokus nudged him. 'Getting excited, Fiddler?'

'You don't know the half of it.'

'You were here during the conquest, weren't you? Back when Kalam was fighting for the other side – for the Seven Holy Falah'dan – and the T'lan Imass marched for the Emperor and—'

'Enough,' Fiddler waved a hand. 'I don't need reminding, and neither does Kalam. All wars are ugly, but that one was uglier than most.'

'Is it true that you were in the company that chased Quick Ben across the Holy Desert Raraku, and that Kalam was your guide, only he and Quick were planning on betraying you all, but Whiskeyjack had already worked that out—'

Fiddler turned a glare on Kalam. 'One night in Rutu Jelba with a jug of Falari rum, and this boy knows more than any Imperial historian still breathing.' He swung back to Crokus. 'Listen, son, best you forget everything that drunken lout told you that night. The past is already hunting our tails – no point in making it any easier.'

Crokus ran a hand through his long black hair. 'Well,' he said softly, 'if Seven Cities is so dangerous, why didn't we just head straight down to Quon Tali, to where Apsalar lived, so we can find her father? Why all this sneaking around – and on the wrong continent at that?'

'It's not that simple,' Kalam growled.

'Why? I thought that was the reason for this whole journey.' Crokus reached for Apsalar's hand and clasped it in both of his, but saved his hard expression for Kalam and Fiddler. 'You both said you owed it to her. It wasn't right and you wanted to put it right. But now I'm thinking it's only part of the reason, I'm thinking that you two have something else planned – that taking Apsalar back home was just an excuse to come back to your Empire, even though you're officially outlawed. And whatever it is you're planning, it's meant coming here, to Seven Cities, and it's also meant we have to sneak around, terrified of everything, jumping at shadows, as if the whole Malazan army was after us.' He paused, drew a deep breath, then continued. 'We have a right to know the truth, because you're putting us in danger and we don't even know what kind, or why, or anything. So out with it. Now.'

Fiddler leaned back on the gunnel. He looked over at Kalam and raised an eyebrow. 'Well, Corporal? It's your call.'

'Give me a list, Fiddler,' Kalam said.

'The Empress wants Darujhistan,' The sapper met Crokus's steady gaze. 'Agreed?'

The boy hesitated, then nodded.

Fiddler continued. 'What she wants she usually gets sooner or later. Call it precedent. Now, she's tried to take your city once, right, Crokus? And it cost her Adjunct Lorn, two Imperial demons, and High Fist Dujek's loyalty, not to mention the loss of the Bridgeburners. Enough to make anyone sting.'

'Fine. But what's that got to do—'

'Don't interrupt. Corporal said make a list. I'm making it. You've followed me so far? Good. Darujhistan eluded her once – but she'll make certain next time. Assuming there is a next time.'

'Well,' Crokus was scowling, 'why wouldn't there be? You said she gets what she wants.'

'And you're loyal to your city, Crokus?'

'Of course—'

'So you'd do anything you could to prevent the Empress from conquering it?'

'Well, yes but—'

'Sir?' Fiddler turned back to Kalam.

The burly black-skinned man looked out over the waves, sighed, then nodded to himself. He faced Crokus. 'It's this, lad. Time's come. I'm going after her.'

The Daru boy's expression was blank, but Fiddler saw Apsalar's eyes widen, her face losing its colour. She sat back suddenly, then half-smiled – and Fiddler went cold upon seeing it.

'I don't know what you mean,' Crokus said. 'After who? The Empress? How?'

'He means,' Apsalar said, still smiling a smile that had belonged to her once, long ago, when she'd been . . . *someone else*, 'that he's going to try and kill her.'

'What?' Crokus stood, almost pitching himself over the side. 'You? You and a seasick sapper with a broken fiddle strapped to his back? Do you think we're going to help you in this insane, suicidal—'

'I remember,' Apsalar said suddenly, her eyes narrowing on Kalam.

Crokus turned to her. 'Remember what?'

'Kalam. He was a Falah'dan's Dagger, and the Claw gave him command of a Hand. Kalam's a master assassin, Crokus. And Quick Ben—'

'Is three thousand leagues away!' Crokus shouted. 'He's a squad mage, for Hood's sake! That's it, a squalid little squad mage!'

'Not quite,' Fiddler said. 'And being so far away doesn't mean a thing, son. Quick Ben's our shaved knuckle in the hole.'

'Your what in the where?'

'Shaved knuckle, as in the game of knuckles – a good gambler's usually using a shaved knuckle, as in cheating in the casts, if you know what I mean. As for "hole", that'd be Quick Ben's Warren – the one that can put him at Kalam's side in the space of a heartbeat, no matter how far away he happens to be. So, Crokus, there you have it: Kalam's going to give it a try, but it's going to take some planning, preparation. And that starts here, in Seven Cities. You want Darujhistan free for ever more? The Empress Laseen must die.'

Crokus slowly sat back down. 'But why Seven Cities? Isn't the Empress in Quon Tali?'

'Because,' Kalam said as he angled the fisherboat into the creek mouth and the oppressive heat of the land rose around them, 'because, lad, Seven Cities is about to rise.'

'What do you mean?'

The assassin bared his teeth. 'Rebellion.'

Fiddler swung around and scanned the fetid undergrowth lining the banks. *And that,* he said to himself with a chill clutching his stomach, *is the part of this plan that I hate the most. Chasing one of Quick Ben's wild ideas with the whole countryside going up in flames.*

A minute later they rounded a bend and the village appeared, a scattering of wattle-and-daub huts in a broken half-circle facing a line of skiffs pulled onto a sandy beach. Kalam nudged the tiller and the fisherboat drifted towards the strand. As the keel scraped bottom, Fiddler clambered over the gunnel and stepped onto dry land, Moby now awake and clinging with all fours to the front of his tunic. Ignoring the squawking creature, Fiddler slowly straightened. 'Well,' he sighed as the first of the village's mongrel dogs announced their arrival, 'it's begun.'

CHAPTER TWO

To this day it remains easy to ignore the fact that
the Aren High Command was rife with treachery,
dissension, rivalry and malice . . . The assertion
that [the Aren High Command] was ignorant of
the undercurrents in the countryside is, at best
naive, at worst cynical in the extreme . . .

The Sha'ik Rebellion
Cullaran

The red ochre handprint on the wall was dissolving in
the rain, trickling roots down along the mortar
between the fired mudbricks. Hunched against the
unseasonal downpour, Duiker watched as the print slowly disappeared, wishing that the day had broken dry, that he could
have come upon the sign before the rain obscured it, that he
could then have gained a sense of the hand that had made its
mark here, on the outer wall of the old Falah'd Palace in the
heart of Hissar.

The many cultures of Seven Cities seethed with symbols, a
secret pictographic language of oblique references that carried
portentous weight among the natives. Such symbols formed a
complex dialogue that no Malazan could understand. Slowly,
during his many months resident here, Duiker had come to
realize the danger behind their ignorance. As the Year of

65

Dryjhna approached, such symbols blossomed in chaotic profusion, every wall in every city a scroll of secret code. Wind, sun and rain assured impermanence, wiping clean the slate in readiness for the next exchange.

And it seems they have a lot to say these days.

Duiker shook himself, trying to loosen the tension in his neck and shoulders. His warnings to the High Command seemed to be falling on deaf ears. There were patterns in these symbols, and it seemed that he alone among all the Malazans had any interest in breaking the code, or even in recognizing the risks of maintaining an outsider's indifference.

He pulled his cowl further over his head in an effort to keep his face dry, feeling water trickle on his forearms as the wide cuffs of his telaba cloak briefly opened to the rain. The last of the print had washed away. Duiker pushed himself into motion, resuming his journey.

Water ran in ankle-deep torrents down the cobbled slopes beneath the palace walls, gushing down into the gutters bisecting each alley and causeway in the city. Opposite the immense palace wall, awnings sagged precariously above closet-sized shops. In the chill shadows of the holes that passed for storefronts, dour-faced merchants watched Duiker as he passed by.

Apart from miserable donkeys and the occasional swaybacked horse, the streets were mostly empty of pedestrian traffic. Even with the rare wayward current from the Sahul Sea, Hissar was a city born of inland drylands and deserts. Though a port and now a central landing for the Empire, the city and its people lived with a spiritual back to the sea.

Duiker left behind the close ring of ancient buildings and narrow alleys surrounding the palace wall, coming to the Dryjhna Colonnade that ran straight as a spear through Hissar's heart. The guldindha trees lining the colonnade's carriage track swam with blurred motion as the rain pelted down on their ochre leaves. Estate gardens, most of them unwalled and open to public admiration, stretched green on either side. The downpour had stripped flowers from their shrubs and dwarf trees, turning the cobbled walkways white, red and pink.

The historian ducked as a gusting wind pressed his cloak tight against his right side. The water on his lips tasted of salt, the only indication of the angry sea a thousand paces to his right. Where the street named after the Storm of the Apocalypse narrowed suddenly, the carriage path became a muddy track of broken cobbles and shattered pottery, the tall, once royal nut trees giving way to desert scrub. The change was so abrupt that Duiker found himself up to his shins in dung-stained water before he realized he'd come to the city's edge. Squinting against the rain, he looked up.

Off to his left, hazy behind the sheets of water, ran the stone wall of the Imperial Compound. Smoke struggled upward from beyond the wall's fortified height. On his right and much closer was a chaotic knot of hide tents, horses and camels and carts – a trader camp, newly arrived from the Sialk Odhan.

Drawing his cloak tighter against the wind, Duiker swung to the right and made for the encampment. The rain was heavy enough to mask the sound of his approach from the tribe's dogs as he entered the narrow, mud-choked pathway between the sprawling tents. Duiker paused at an intersection. Opposite was a large copper-stained tent, its walls profusely cluttered with painted symbols. Smoke drifted from the entrance flap. He crossed the intersection, hesitating only a moment before drawing the flap to one side and entering.

A roar of sound, carried on waves of hot, steam-laden air buffeted the historian as he paused to shake the water from his cloak. Voices shouting, cursing, laughing on all sides, the air filled with durhang smoke and incense, roasting meats, sour wine and sweet ale, closed in around Duiker as he took in the scene. Coins rattled and spun in pots where a score of gamblers had gathered off to his left; in front of him a tapu weaved swiftly through the crowd, a four-foot-long iron skewer of roasted meats and fruit in each hand. Duiker shouted the tapu over, raising a hand to catch the man's eye. The hawker quickly approached.

'Goat, I swear!' the tapu exclaimed in the coastal Debrahl language. 'Goat, not dog, Dosii! Smell for yourself, and only a clipping to pay for such delicious fare! Would you pay so little in Dosin Pali?'

Born on the plains of Dal Hon, Duiker's dark skin matched that of the local Debrahl; he was wearing the telaba sea cloak of a merchant trader from the island city of Dosin Pali, and spoke the language without hint of an accent. To the tapu's claim Duiker grinned. 'For dog I would, Tapuharal.' He fished out two local crescents – the equivalent of a base 'clipping' of the Imperial silver jakata. 'And if you imagine the Mezla are freer with their silver on the island, you are a fool and worse!'

Looking nervous, the tapu slid a chunk of dripping meat and two soft amber globes of fruit from one of the skewers, wrapping them in leaves. 'Beware Mezla spies, Dosii,' he muttered. 'Words can be twisted.'

'Words are their only language,' Duiker replied with contempt as he accepted the food. 'Is it true then that a scarred barbarian now commands the Mezla army?'

'A man with a demon's face, Dosii.' The tapu wagged his head. 'Even the Mezla fear him.' Pocketing the crescents he moved off, raising the skewers once more over his head. 'Goat, not dog!'

Duiker found a tent wall to put his back against and watched the crowd as he ate his meal in local fashion, swiftly, messily. *Every meal is your last* encompassed an entire Seven Cities philosophy. Grease smeared on his face and dripping from his fingers, the historian dropped the leaves to the muddy floor at his feet, then ritually touched his forehead in a now outlawed gesture of gratitude to a Falah'd whose bones were rotting in the silty mud of Hissar Bay. The historian's eyes focused on a ring of old men beyond the gamblers and he walked over to it, wiping his hands on his thighs.

The gathering marked a Circle of Seasons, wherein two seers faced one another and spoke a symbolic language of divination in a complicated dance of gestures. As he pushed into a place among the ring of onlookers, Duiker saw the seers within the circle, an ancient shaman whose silver-barbed, skin-threaded face marked him as from the Semk tribe, far inland, and opposite him a boy of about fifteen. Where the boy's eyes should have been were two gouged pits of badly healed scar tissue. His thin limbs and bloated belly revealed an advanced stage of malnutrition. Duiker realized instinctively that the boy had lost his family during the Malazan conquest and now lived in the alleys and streets of Hissar. He had been found by the Circle's organizers, for it was well known that the gods spoke through such suffering souls.

The tense silence among the onlookers told the historian that there was power in this divination. Though blind, the boy moved to keep himself face to face with the Semk seer, who himself slowly danced across a floor of white sand in absolute silence. They held out their hands towards each other, inscribing patterns in the air between them.

Duiker nudged the man beside him. 'What has been foreseen?' he whispered.

The man, a squat local with the scars of an old Hissar regiment poorly obscured by mutilating burns on his cheeks, hissed warningly through his stained teeth. 'Nothing less than the spirit of Dryjhna, whose outline was mapped by their hands – a spirit seen by all here, a ghostly promise of fire.'

Duiker sighed. 'Would that I had witnessed that . . .'

'You shall – see? It comes again!'

The historian watched as the weaving hands seemed to

contact an invisible figure, leaving a smear of reddish light that flickered in their wake. The glow suggested a human shape, and that shape slowly grew more defined. A woman whose flesh was fire. She raised her arms and something like iron flashed at her wrists and the dancers became three as she spun and writhed between the seers.

The boy suddenly threw back his head, words coming from his throat like the grinding of stones. 'Two fountains of raging blood! Face to face. The blood is the same, the two are the same and salty waves shall wash the shores of Raraku. The Holy Desert remembers its past!'

The female apparition vanished. The boy toppled forward, thumping stiff as a board onto the sand. The Semk seer crouched down, resting a hand on the boy's head. 'He is returned to his family,' the old shaman said in the silence of the circle. 'The mercy of Dryjhna, the rarest of gifts, granted to this child.'

Hardened tribesmen began weeping, others falling to their knees. Shaken, Duiker pulled back as the ring slowly contracted. He blinked sweat from his eyes, sensing that someone was watching him. He looked around. Across from him stood a figure shrouded in black hides, a goat's-head hood pulled up, leaving the face in shadow. A moment later the figure looked away. Duiker quickly moved from the stranger's line of sight.

He made for the tent flap.

Seven Cities was an ancient civilization, steeped in the power of antiquity, where Ascendants once walked on every trader track, every footpath, every lost road between forgotten places. It was said the sands hoarded power within their susurrating currents, that every stone had soaked up sorcery like blood, and that beneath every city lay the ruins of countless other cities, older cities, cities that went back to the First Empire itself. It was said each city rose on the backs of ghosts, the substance of spirits thick like layers of crushed bone; that each city forever wept beneath the streets, forever laughed, shouted, hawked wares and bartered and prayed and drew first breaths that brought life and the last breaths that announced death. Beneath the streets there were dreams, wisdom, foolishness, fears, rage, grief, lust and love and bitter hatred.

The historian stepped outside into the rain, drawing in lungfuls of clean, cool air as he once more wrapped cloak about him.

Conquerors could overrun a city's walls, could kill every living soul within it, fill every estate and every house and every store with its own people, yet rule nothing but the city's thin surface, the skin of the present, and would one day be brought down by the spirits below, until they themselves were but one momentary layer among many. *This is an enemy we can never defeat*, Duiker believed. *Yet history tells the stories of those who would challenge that enemy, again and again. Perhaps victory is not achieved by overcoming that enemy, but by joining it, becoming one with it.*

The Empress has sent a new Fist to batter down the restless centuries of this land. Had she abandoned Coltaine as I'd suggested to Mallick Rel? Or had she just held him back in readiness, like a weapon forged and honed for one specific task?

Duiker left the encampment, once more hunched beneath the driving rain. Ahead loomed the gates of the Imperial Compound. He might well find some answers to his questions within the next hour, as he came face to face with Coltaine of the Crow Clan.

He crossed the rutted track, sloshing through the murky puddles filling the horse and wagon ruts, then ascended the muddy slope towards the gatehouse.

Two cowled guards stepped into view as he reached the gate's narrow side passage.

'No petitions today, Dosii,' one of the Malazan soldiers said. 'Try tomorrow.'

Duiker unclasped the cloak, opened it to reveal the Imperial diadem pinned to his tunic. 'The Fist has called a council, has he not?'

Both soldiers saluted and stepped back. The one who'd spoken earlier smiled apologetically. 'Didn't know you were with the other one,' he said.

'What other one?'

'He came in just a few minutes ago, historian.'

'Yes, of course.' Duiker nodded to the two men, then passed within. The stone floor of the passage bore the muddy tracks of a pair of moccasins. Frowning, he continued on, coming to the inside compound. A roofed causeway followed the wall to his left, leading eventually to the side postern of the squat, unimaginative headquarters building. Already wet, Duiker ignored it, electing to cross the compound directly towards the building's main entrance. In passing he noticed that the man who had preceded him had done the same. The pooled prints of his steps betrayed a bowlegged gait. The historian's frown deepened.

He came to the entrance, where another guard appeared, who directed Duiker to the council room. As he approached the room's double doors, he checked for his predecessor's footprints, but there were none. Evidently he'd gone to some other chamber within the building. Shrugging, Duiker opened the doors.

The council room was low-ceilinged, its stone walls unplastered but washed in white paint. A long marble table dominated, looking strangely incomplete in the absence of chairs. Already present were Mallick Rel, Kulp, Coltaine and another Wickan officer. They all turned at the historian's entrance, Rel's brows lifting in mild surprise. Clearly, he'd been unaware that Coltaine had extended to Duiker an invitation. Had it been the new Fist's intention to unbalance the priest, a deliberate exclusion? After a moment the historian dismissed the thought. More likely the result of a disorganized new command.

The chairs had been specifically removed for this council, as was evident in the tracks their legs had left through the white dust on the floor. The discomfort of not knowing where to stand or how to position oneself was evident in both Mallick Rel and Kulp. The Jhistal priest of Mael was shifting weight from one foot to the other, sweat on his brow reflecting the harsh glare of the lanterns set on the tabletop, his hands folded into his sleeves. Kulp looked in need of a wall to lean against, but was clearly uncertain how the Wickans would view such a casual posture.

Inwardly smiling, Duiker removed his dripping cloak, hanging it from an old torch bracket beside the doors. He then turned about and presented himself before the new Fist, who stood at the nearest end of the table, his officer on his left – a scowling veteran whose wide, flat face seemed to fold in on itself diagonally in a scar from right jawline to left brow.

'I am Duiker,' the historian said. 'Imperial Historian of the Empire.' He half bowed. 'Welcome to Hissar, Fist.' Up close, he could see that the warleader of the Crow Clan showed the weathering of forty years on the north Wickan Plains of Quon Tali. His lean, expressionless face was lined, deep brackets around the thin, wide mouth, and squint tracks at the corners of his dark, deep-set eyes. Oiled braids hung down past his shoulders, knotted with crow-feather fetishes. He was tall, wearing a battered vest of chain over a hide shirt, a crow-feather cloak hanging from his broad shoulders down to the backs of his knees. He wore a rider's leggings, laced with gut up the outer sides to his hips. A single horn-handled long-knife jutted out from under his left arm.

In answer to Duiker's words he cocked his head. 'When I last saw you,' he said in his harsh Wickan accent, 'you lay in fever on the Emperor's own cot, about to rise and walk through the Hooded One's Gates.' He paused. 'Bult was the young

73

warrior whose lance ripped you open and for his effort a soldier named Dujek kissed Bult's face with his sword.' Coltaine slowly turned to smile at the scarred Wickan at his side.

The grizzled horseman's scowl remained unchanged as he glared at Duiker. After a moment he shook his head and swelled his chest. 'I remember an unarmed man. The lack of weapons in his hands turned my lance at the last moment. I remember Dujek's sword that stole my beauty even as my horse bit his arm crushing bone. I remember that Dujek lost that arm to the surgeons, fouled as it was with my horse's breath. Between us, I lost the exchange, for the loss of an arm did nothing to damage Dujek's glorious career, while the loss of my beauty left me with but the one wife that I already had.'

'And was she not your sister, Bult?'

'She was, Coltaine. And blind.'

Both Wickans fell silent, the one frowning and the other scowling.

Off to one side Kulp voiced something like a strangled grunt. Duiker slowly raised an eyebrow. 'I am sorry, Bult,' he said. 'Although I was at the battle, I never saw Coltaine, nor you. In any case, I had not noticed any particular loss of your beauty.'

The veteran nodded. 'One must look carefully, it's true.'

'Perhaps,' Mallick Rel said, 'time to dispense with the pleasantries, entertaining as they are, and begin this council.'

'When I'm ready,' Coltaine said casually, still studying Duiker.

Bult grunted. 'Tell me, Historian, what inspired you to enter battle without weapons?'

'Perhaps I lost them in the melee.'

'But you did not. You wore no belt, no scabbard, you carried no shield.'

Duiker shrugged. 'If I am to record the events of this Empire, I must be in their midst, sir.'

74

'Shall you display such reckless zeal in recording the events of Coltaine's command?'

'Zeal? Oh yes, sir. As for reckless,' he sighed, 'alas, my courage is not as it once was. These days I wear armour when attending battle, and a short sword and shield. And helm. Surrounded by bodyguards, and at least a league away from the heart of the fighting.'

'The years have brought you wisdom,' Bult said.

'In some things, I am afraid,' Duiker said slowly, 'not enough.' He faced Coltaine. 'I would be bold enough to advise you, Fist, at this council.'

Coltaine's gaze slid to Mallick Rel as he spoke, 'And you fear the presumption, for you will say things I will not appreciate. Perhaps, in hearing such things, I shall command Bult to complete the task of killing you. This tells me much,' he continued, 'of the situation at Aren.'

'I know little of that,' Duiker said, feeling sweat trickle beneath his tunic. 'But even less of you, Fist.'

Coltaine's expression did not change. Duiker was reminded of a cobra slowly rising before him, unblinking, cold.

'Question,' Mallick Rel said. 'Has the council begun?'

'Not yet,' Coltaine said slowly. 'We await my warlock.'

The priest of Mael drew a sharp breath at that. Off to one side, Kulp took a step forward.

Duiker found his throat suddenly dry. Clearing it, he said, 'Was it not at the command of the Empress – in her first year on the throne – that all Wickan warlocks be, uh, rooted out? Was there not a subsequent mass execution? I have a memory of seeing Unta's outer walls . . .'

'They took many days to die,' Bult said. 'Hung from spikes of iron until the crows came to collect their souls. We brought our children to the city walls, to look upon the tribal elders whose lives were taken from us by the short-haired woman's command. We gave them memory scars, to keep the truth alive.'

'An Empress,' Duiker said, watching Coltaine's face, 'whom you now serve.'

'The short-haired woman knows nothing of Wickan ways,' Bult said. 'The crows that carried within them the greatest of the warlock souls returned to our people to await each new birth, and so the power of our elders returned to us.'

A side entrance Duiker had not noticed before slid open. A tall, bow-legged figure stepped into the room, face hidden in the shadow of a goat's-head cowl, which he now pulled back, revealing the smooth visage of a boy no more than ten years old. The youth's dark eyes met the historian's.

'This is Sormo E'nath,' Coltaine said.

'Sormo E'nath – an old man – was executed at Unta,' Kulp snapped. 'He was the most powerful of the warlocks – the Empress made sure of him. It's said he took eleven days on the wall to die. This one is not Sormo E'nath. This is a boy.'

'Eleven days,' Bult grunted. 'No single crow could hold all of his soul. Each day there came another, until he was all gone. Eleven days, eleven crows. Such was Sormo's power, his life will, and such was the honour accorded him by the black-winged spirits. Eleven came to him. *Eleven.*'

'Elder sorcery,' Mallick Rel whispered. 'Most ancient scrolls hint at such things. This boy is named Sormo E'nath. Truly the warlock reborn?'

'The Rhivi of Genabackis have similar beliefs,' Duiker said. 'A newborn child can become the vessel of a soul that has not passed through Hood's Gates.'

The boy spoke, his voice reedy but breaking, on the edge of manhood. 'I am Sormo E'nath, who carries in his breastbone the memory of an iron spike. Eleven crows attended my birth.' He hitched his cloak behind his shoulders. 'This day I came upon a ritual of divination and saw there among the crowd the historian Duiker. Together we witnessed a vision sent by a spirit of great power, a spirit whose face is one among many. This spirit promised armageddon.'

'I saw as he did,' Duiker said. 'A trader caravan has camped outside the city.'

'You were not discovered as a Malazan?' Mallick asked.

'He speaks the tribal language well,' Sormo said. 'And makes gestures announcing his hatred of the Empire. Well enough of countenance and in action to deceive the natives. Tell me, Historian, have you seen such divinations before?'

'None so . . . obvious,' Duiker admitted. 'But I have seen enough signs to sense the growing momentum. The new year will bring rebellion.'

'Bold assertion,' Mallick Rel said. He sighed, clearly uncomfortable with standing. 'The new Fist would do well to regard with caution such claims. Many are the prophecies of this land, as many as there are people, it seems. Such multitudes diminish the veracity of each. Rebellion has been promised in Seven Cities each year since the Malazan conquest. What has come of them? Naught.'

'The priest has hidden motives,' Sormo said.

Duiker found himself holding his breath.

Mallick Rel's round, sweat-sheened face went white.

'All men have hidden motives,' Coltaine said, as if dismissing his warlock's claim. 'I hear counsel of warning and counsel of caution. A good balance. These are my words. The mage who yearns to lean against walls of stone views me as an adder in his bedroll. His fear of me speaks for every soldier in the Seventh Army.' The Fist spat on the floor, his face twisting. 'I care nothing for their sentiments. If they obey my commands I in turn will serve them. If they do not, I will tear their hearts from their chests. Do you hear my words, Cadre Mage?'

Kulp was scowling. 'I hear them.'

'I am here,' Rel's voice was almost shrill, 'to convey the commands of High Fist Pormqual—'

'Before or after the High Fist's official welcome?' Even as he spoke Duiker regretted his words, despite Bult's bark of laughter.

In response, Mallick Rel straightened. 'High Fist Pormqual welcomes Fist Coltaine to Seven Cities, and wishes him well in his new command. The Seventh Army remains as one of the three original armies of the Malazan Empire, and the High Fist is confident that Fist Coltaine will honour their commendable history.'

'I care nothing for reputations,' Coltaine said. 'They shall be judged by their actions. Go on.'

Trembling, Rel continued, 'The High Fist Pormqual has asked me to convey his orders to High Fist Coltaine. Admiral Nok is to leave Hissar Harbour and proceed to Aren as soon as his ships are resupplied. High Fist Coltaine is to begin preparations for marching the Seventh overland . . . to Aren. It is the High Fist's desire to review the Seventh prior to its final stationing.' The priest produced a sealed scroll from his robes and set it on the tabletop. 'Such are the High Fist's commands.'

A look of disgust darkened Coltaine's features. He crossed his arms and deliberately turned his back on Mallick Rel.

Bult laughed without humour. 'The High Fist wishes to review the army. Presumably the High Fist has an attendant High Mage, perhaps a Hand of the Claw as well? If he wishes to review Coltaine's troops he can come here by Warren. The Fist has no intention of outfitting this army to march four hundred leagues so that Pormqual can frown at the dust on their boots. Such a move will leave the eastern provinces of Seven Cities without an occupying army. At this time of unrest it would be viewed as a retreat, especially when accompanied by the withdrawal of the Sahul Fleet. This land cannot be governed from behind the walls of Aren.'

'Defying the High Fist's command?' Rel asked in a whisper, eyes glittering like blooded diamonds on Coltaine's broad back.

The Fist whirled. 'I am counselling a change of those commands,' he said, 'and now await a reply.'

'Reply I shall give you,' the priest rasped.

Coltaine sneered.

Bult said, 'You? You are a priest, not a soldier, not a governor. You are not even recognized as a member of the High Command.'

Rel's glare flicked from Fist to veteran. 'I am not? Indeed—'

'Not by Empress Laseen,' Bult cut in. 'She knows nothing of you, priest, apart from the High Fist's reports. Understand that the Empress does not convey power upon people whom she does not know. High Fist Pormqual employed you as his messenger boy and that is how the Fist shall treat you. You command nothing. Not Coltaine, not me, not even a lowly mess cook of the Seventh.'

'I shall convey these words and sentiments to the High Fist.'

'No doubt. You may go now.'

Rel's jaw dropped. 'Go?'

'We are done with you. Leave.'

In silence they watched the priest depart. As soon as the doors closed Duiker turned to Coltaine. 'That may not have been wise, Fist.'

Coltaine's eyes looked sleepy. 'Bult spoke, not I.'

Duiker glanced at the veteran. The scarred Wickan was grinning.

'Tell me of Pormqual,' Coltaine said. 'You have met him?'

The historian swung back to the Fist. 'I have.'

'Does he govern well?'

'As far as I have been able to determine,' Duiker said, 'he does not govern at all. Most edicts are issued by the man you – Bult – just expelled from this council. There are a host of others behind the curtain, mostly nobleborn wealthy merchants. They are the ones primarily responsible for the cuts in duty taxation on imported goods, and the corresponding increases in local taxes on production and exports – with exemptions, of course, in whatever export they themselves are engaged in. The Imperial occupation is managed by Malazan merchants, a situation unchanged since Pormqual assumed the title of High Fist four years ago.'

Bult asked, 'Who was High Fist before him?'

'Cartheron Crust, who drowned one night in Aren Harbour.'

Kulp snorted. 'Crust could swim drunk through a hurricane, but then he went and drowned just like his brother Urko. Neither body was ever found, of course.'

'Meaning?'

Kulp grinned at Bult, but said nothing.

'Both Crust and Urko were the Emperor's men,' Duiker explained. 'It seems they shared the same fate as most of Kellanved's companions, including Toc the Elder and Ameron. None of *their* bodies were ever found, either.' The historian shrugged. 'Old history now. Forbidden history, in fact.'

'You assume they were murdered at Laseen's command,' Bult said, baring his jagged teeth. 'But imagine a circumstance where the Empress's most able commanders simply . . . disappeared. Leaving her isolated, desperate for able people. You forget, Historian, that before Laseen became Empress, she was close companions with Crust, Urko, Ameron, Dassem and the others. Imagine her now alone, still feeling the wounds of abandonment.'

'And her murder of the other close companions – Kellanved and Dancer – was not something she imagined would affect her friendship with those commanders?' Duiker shook his head, aware of the bitterness in his voice. *They were my companions, too.*

'Some errors in judgement can never be undone,' Bult said. 'The Emperor and Dancer were able conquerors, but were they able rulers?'

'We'll never know,' Duiker snapped.

The Wickan's sigh was almost a snort. 'No, but if there was one person close to the throne capable of seeing what was to come, it was Laseen.'

Coltaine spat on the floor once again. 'That is all to say on the matter, Historian. Record the words that have been uttered here, if you do not find them too sour a taste.' He glanced over at a silent Sormo E'nath, frowning as he studied his warlock.

'Even if I choked on them,' Duiker replied, 'I would recount them nonetheless. I could not call myself a historian if it were otherwise.'

'Very well, then.' The Fist's gaze remained on Sormo E'nath. 'Tell me, Historian, what hold does Mallick Rel have over Pormqual?'

'I wish I knew, Fist.'

'Find out.'

'You are asking me to become a spy.'

Coltaine turned to him with a faint smile. 'And what were you in the trader's tent, Duiker?'

Duiker grimaced. 'I would have to go to Aren. I do not think Mallick Rel would welcome me to inner councils any more. Not after witnessing his humiliation here. In fact, I warrant he has marked me as an enemy now, and his enemies have a habit of disappearing.'

'I shall not disappear,' Coltaine said. He stepped closer, reached out and gripped the historian's shoulder. 'We shall disregard Mallick Rel, then. You will be attached to my staff.'

'As you command, Fist,' Duiker said.

'This council is ended.' Coltaine spun to his warlock. 'Sormo, you shall recount for me this morning's adventure . . . later.'

The warlock bowed.

Duiker retrieved his cloak and, followed by Kulp, left the chamber. As the doors closed behind them, the historian plucked at the cadre mage's sleeve. 'A word with you. In private.'

'My thoughts exactly,' Kulp replied.

They found a room further down the hallway, cluttered with broken furniture but otherwise unoccupied. Kulp shut and locked the door, then faced Duiker, his eyes savage. 'He's not a man at all – he's an animal and he sees things like an animal. And Bult – Bult reads his master's snarling and raised hackles and puts it all into words – I've never heard such a talkative Wickan as that mangled old man.'

'Evidently,' Duiker said dryly, 'Coltaine had a lot to say.'

'I suspect even now the priest of Mael is planning his revenge.'

'Aye. But it was Bult's defence of the Empress that shook me.'

'Do you countenance his argument?'

Duiker sighed. 'That she regrets her actions and now feels, in full, the solitude of power? Possibly. Interesting, but its relevance is long past.'

'Has Laseen confided in these Wickan savages, do you think?'

'Coltaine was summoned to an audience with the Empress, and I'd guess that Bult is as much as sewn to his master's side – but what occurred between them in Laseen's private chambers remains unknown.' The historian shrugged. 'They were prepared for Mallick Rel, that much seems clear. And you, Kulp, what of this young warlock?'

'Young?' The cadre mage scowled. 'That boy has the aura of an ancient man. I could smell on him the ritual drinking of mare's blood, and that ritual marks a warlock's Time of Iron – his last few years of life, the greatest flowering of his power. Did you see him? He fired a dart at the priest, then stood silent, watching its effect.'

'Yet you claimed it was all a lie.'

'No need to let Sormo know how sensitive my nose is, and I'll continue treating him as if he was a boy, an impostor. If I'm lucky he'll ignore me.'

Duiker hesitated. The air in the room was stale, tasting of dust when he drew breath. 'Kulp,' he finally said.

'Aye, Historian, what do you ask of me?'

'It has nothing to do with Coltaine, or Mallick Rel or Sormo E'nath. I require your assistance.'

'In what?'

'I wish to free a prisoner.'

The cadre mage's brows rose. 'In Hissar's gaol? Historian, I have no clout with the Hissar Guard—'

'No, not in the city gaol. This is a prisoner of the Empire.'

'Where is this prisoner kept?'

'He was sold into slavery, Kulp. He's in the Otataral mines.'

The cadre mage stared. 'Hood's breath, Duiker, you're asking the help of a *mage*? You imagine I would willingly go anywhere near those mines? Otataral destroys sorcery, drives mages insane—'

'No closer than a dory off the island's coast,' Duiker cut in. 'I promise that, Kulp.'

'To collect the prisoner, and then what, rowing like a fiend with a Dosii war galley in hot pursuit?'

Duiker grinned. 'Something like that.'

Kulp glanced at the closed door, then studied the wreckage in the room as if he had not noticed it before. 'What chamber was this?'

'Fist Torlom's office,' Duiker answered. 'Where the Dryjhnii assassin found her that night.'

Kulp slowly nodded. 'And was our choosing it an accident?'

'I certainly hope so.'

'So do I, Historian.'

'Will you help me?'

'This prisoner . . . who?'

'Heboric Light Touch.'

Kulp slowly nodded a second time. 'Let me think on it, Duiker.'

'May I ask what gives you pause?'

Kulp scowled. 'The thought of another traitorous historian loose in the world, what else?'

The Holy City of Ehrlitan was a city of white stone, rising from the harbour to surround and engulf a vast, flat-topped hill known as Jen'rahb. It was believed that one of the world's first cities was buried within Jen'rahb, and that in the compacted rubble waited the Throne of the Seven Protectors which legend held was not a throne at all, but a chamber housing a ring of seven raised daises, each sanctified by one of the Ascendants who set out to found Seven Cities. Ehrlitan was a thousand years old, but Jen'rahb the ancient city, now a hill of crushed stone, was believed to be nine times that.

An early Falah'd of Ehrlitan had begun extensive and ambitious building on the flat top of Jen'rahb, to honour the city buried beneath the streets. The quarries along the north coast were gutted, whole hillsides carved out, the ten-tonne white blocks of marble dressed and transported by ship to Ehrlitan's harbour, then pulled through the lower districts to the ramps leading to the hill's summit. Temples, estates, gardens, domes, towers and the Falah'd palace rose like the gems of a virgin crown on Jen'rahb.

Three years after the last block had been nudged into place, the ancient buried city . . . shrugged. Subterranean archways collapsed beneath the immense strains of the Falah'd Crown, walls folded, foundation stones slid sideways into streets packed solid with dust. Beneath the surface the dust behaved like water, racing down streets and alleys, into gaping doorways, beneath floors – all unseen in the unrelieved darkness of Jen'rahb. On the surface, on a bright dawn marking an

84

anniversary of the Falah'd rule, the Crown sagged, towers toppled, domes split in clouds of white marble dust, and the palace dropped unevenly, in some places no more than a few feet, in others over twenty arm-spans down into flowing rivers of dust.

Observers in the Lower City described the event. It was as if a giant invisible hand had reached down to the Crown, closing to gather in every building, crushing them all while pushing down into the hill. The cloud of dust that rose turned the sun into a copper disc for days afterwards.

Over thirty thousand people died that day, including the Falah'd himself, and of the three thousand who dwelt and worked within the Palace, but one survived: a young cook's helper who was convinced that the beaker he had dropped on the floor a moment before the earthquake was to blame for the entire catastrophe. Driven mad with guilt, he stabbed himself in the heart while standing in the Lower City's Merykra Round, his blood flowing down to drench the paving stones where Fiddler now stood.

His blue eyes narrowed, the sapper watched a troop of Red Swords ride hard through a scattering crowd on the other side of the Round.

Swathed in thin bleached linen robes, the hood pulled up and over his head in the manner of a Gral tribesman, he stood motionless on the sacred paving stone with its faded commemorative script, wondering if the rapid thumping of his heart was loud enough to be heard by the crowds moving nervously around him. He cursed himself for risking a wander through the ancient city, then he cursed Kalam for delaying their departure until he'd managed to make contact with one of his old agents in the city.

'*Mezla'ebdin!*' a voice near him hissed.

Malazan lapdogs was an accurate enough translation. The Red Swords were born of Seven Cities, yet avowed absolute loyalty to the Empress. Rare – if at the moment unwelcome – pragmatists in a land of fanatical dreamers, the Red Swords had just begun an independent crackdown on the followers of Dryjhna in their typical fashion: with sword edge and lance.

Half a dozen victims lay unmoving on the bleached stones of the Round, amidst scattered baskets, bundles of cloth, and food. Two small girls crouched beside a woman's body near the dried-up fountain. Sprays of blood decorated nearby walls. From a few streets away the alarms of the Ehrlitan Guard were ringing, the city's Fist having just been informed that the Red Swords were once again defying his inept rule.

The savage riders continued their impromptu, indiscriminate slaughter up a main avenue leading off from the Round, and were soon out of sight. Beggars and thieves swooped in on the felled bodies, even as the air filled with wailing voices. A hunchbacked pimp gathered up the two girls and hobbled out of sight up an alleyway.

A few minutes earlier Fiddler had come near to having his skull split wide open upon entering the Round and finding himself in the path of a charging Red Sword. His soldier's experience launched him across the horse's path, forcing the warrior to swing his blade to his shield side, and a final duck beneath the swishing sword took the sapper past and out of reach. The Red Sword had not bothered pursuing him, turning instead to behead the next hapless citizen, a woman desperately dragging two children from the horse's path.

Fiddler shook himself, breathing a silent curse. Pushing through the jostling crowd, he made for the alley the pimp had used. The tall, leaning buildings to either side shrouded the narrow passage in shadow. Rotting food and something dead filled the air with a thick stench. There was no-one in sight as Fiddler cautiously padded along. He came to a side track between two high walls, barely wide enough for a mule and shin-deep in dry palm leaves. Behind each high wall was a garden, the tall palm trees entwining their fronds like a roof twenty feet overhead. Thirty paces on the passage came to a dead end, and there crouched the pimp, one knee holding down the youngest girl while he pressed the other girl against the wall, fumbling at her leggings.

The pimp's head turned at the sound of Fiddler striding through the dried leaves. He had the white skin of a Skrae and showed blackened teeth in a knowing grin. 'Gral, she's yours for a half jakata, once I've broken her skin. The other will cost you more, being younger.'

Fiddler stepped up to the man. 'I buy,' he said. 'Make wives. Two jakatas.'

The pimp snorted. 'I'll make twice that in a week. Sixteen jakatas.'

Fiddler drew the Gral long-knife he'd purchased an hour earlier and pressed the edge against the pimp's throat. 'Two jakatas and my mercy, simharal.'

'Done, Gral,' the pimp grated, eyes wide. 'Done, by the Hooded One!'

Fiddler drew two coins from his belt and tossed them into the leaves. Then he stepped back. 'I take them now.'

The simharal fell to his knees, scrabbling through the dried fronds. 'Take them, Gral, take them.'

Fiddler grunted, sheathing the knife and gathering one girl under each arm. Turning his back on the pimp, he walked out of the alley. The likelihood that the man would attempt any treachery was virtually nonexistent. Gral tribesmen often begged for insults to give cause for their favourite activity: pursuing vendettas. And it was reputedly impossible to sneak up on one from behind, so none dared try. For all that, Fiddler was thankful for the thick carpet of leaves between him and the pimp.

He exited the alleyway. The girls hung like oversized dolls in his arms, still numbed with shock. He glanced down at the

87

face of the older one. Nine, maybe ten years of age, she stared up at him with wide, dark eyes. 'Safe now,' he said. 'If I set you down, can you walk? Can you show me where you live?'

After a long moment, she nodded.

They had reached one of the tortuous tracks that passed for a street in the Lower City. Fiddler set the girl down, cradling the other in the crook of his arm – she seemed to have fallen asleep. The older child immediately grasped his robes to keep from being pushed away by the jostling crowd, then began tugging him along.

'Home?' Fiddler asked.

'Home,' she replied.

Ten minutes later they passed beyond the market district and entered a quieter residential area, the dwellings modest but clean. The girl guided Fiddler towards a side street. As soon as they reached it, children appeared, shouting and rushing to gather around them. A moment later three armed men burst from a garden gate. They confronted Fiddler with tulwars raised as the crowd of children dispersed on all sides, suddenly silent and watchful.

'Nahal Gral,' Fiddler growled. 'The woman fell to a Red Sword. A simharal took these two. I bought them. Unbroken. Three jakatas.'

'Two,' corrected one of the men, spitting on the cobbles at Fiddler's feet. 'We found the simharal.'

'Two to buy. One more to deliver. Unbroken. Three.' Fiddler gave them a hard grin. 'Fair price, cheap for Gral honour. Cheap for Gral protection.'

A fourth man spoke from behind Fiddler. 'Pay the Gral, you fools. A hundred gold jakatas would not be too much. The nurse and the children were under your protection, yet you fled when the Red Swords came. If this Gral had not come upon the children and purchased them, they would now be broken. Pay the coin, and bless this Gral with the Queen of Dreams' favour, bless him and his family for all time.' The man slowly stepped around. He wore the armour of a private guard, with a captain's insignia. His lean face was scarred with the hatched symbol of a veteran of Y'ghatan and on the backs of his hands were the pitted tracks of incendiary scars. His hard eyes held Fiddler's. 'I ask for your trader name, Gral, so that we may honour you in our prayers.'

Fiddler hesitated, then gave the captain his true name, the name he had been born with, long ago.

The man frowned upon hearing it, but made no comment.

One of the guards approached with coins in hand. Fiddler offered the sleeping child to the captain. 'It is wrong that she sleeps,' he said.

The grizzled veteran received the child with gentle care. 'We shall have the House Healer attend to her.'

Fiddler glanced around. Clearly the children belonged to a rich, powerful family, yet the abodes within sight were all relatively small, the homes of minor merchants and craftworkers.

'Will you share a meal with us, Gral?' the captain asked. 'The children's grandfather will wish to see you.'

Curious, Fiddler nodded. The captain led him to a low postern gate in a garden wall. The three guardsmen moved ahead to open it. The young girl was the first through.

The gate opened into a surprisingly spacious garden, the air cool and damp with the breath of an unseen stream trickling through the lush undergrowth. Old fruit and nut trees canopied the stone-lined path. On the other side rose a high wall constructed entirely of murky glass. Rainbow patterns glistened on the panes, beaded with moisture and mottled with mineral stains. Fiddler had never before seen so much glass in one place. A lone door was set in the wall, made of bleached linen stretched over a thin iron frame. Before it stood an old man dressed in a wrinkled orange robe. The deep, rich ochre of his skin was set off by a shock of white hair. The girl ran up to embrace the man. His amber eyes held steadily on Fiddler.

The sapper dropped to one knee. 'I beg your blessing, Spiritwalker,' he said in his harshest Gral accent.

The Tano priest's laughter was like blowing sand. 'I cannot bless what you are not, sir,' he said quietly. 'But please, join me and Captain Turqa in a private repast. I trust these guardians will prove eager to regain their courage in taking care of the children, here within the garden's confines.' He laid a weathered hand on the sleeping child's forehead. 'Selal protects herself in her own way. Captain, tell the Healer she must be drawn back to this world, gently.'

The captain handed the child over to one of the guards. 'You heard the Master. Quickly now.'

Both children were taken through the linen door. Gesturing, the Tano Spiritwalker led Fiddler and Turqa to the same door at a more sedate pace.

Inside the glass-walled room squatted a low iron table with shin-high hide-bound chairs around it. On the table were bowls holding fruit and chilled meats stained red with spices. A crystal carafe of pale yellow wine had been unstoppered and left to air. At the carafe's base the wine's sediment was two fingers thick: desert flower buds and the carcasses of white honey bees. The wine's cool sweet scent permeated the chamber.

The inner door was solid wood, set in a marble wall. Small alcoves set within that wall held lit candles displaying flames of assorted colours. Their flickering reflections danced hypnotically on the facing glass.

The priest sat down and indicated the other chairs. 'Please be seated. I am surprised that a Malazan spy would so jeopardize his disguise by saving the lives of two Ehrlii children. Do you now seek to glean valuable information from a family overwhelmed by gratitude?'

Fiddler drew his hood back, sighing. 'I am Malazan,' he

acknowledged. 'But not a spy. I am disguised to avoid discovery . . . by Malazans.'

The old priest poured the wine and handed the sapper a goblet. 'You are a soldier.'

'I am.'

'A deserter?'

Fiddler winced. 'Not by choice. The Empress saw fit to outlaw my regiment.' He sipped the flowery sweet wine.

Captain Turqa hissed. 'A Bridgeburner. A soldier of Onearm's Host.'

'You are well informed, sir.'

The Tano Spiritwalker gestured towards the bowls. 'Please. If, after so many years of war, you are seeking a place of peace, you have made a grave error in coming to Seven Cities.'

'So I gathered,' Fiddler said, helping himself to some fruit. 'Which is why I am hoping to book passage to Quon Tali as soon as possible.'

'The Kansu Fleet has left Ehrlitan,' the captain said. 'Few are the trader ships setting forth on oceanic voyages these days. High taxes—'

'And the prospect of riches that will come with a civil war,' Fiddler said, nodding. 'Thus, it must be overland, at least down to Aren.'

'Unwise,' the old priest said.

'I know.'

But the Tano Spiritwalker was shaking his head. 'Not simply the coming war. To travel to Aren, you must cross the Pan'potsun Odhan, skirting the Holy Desert Raraku. From Raraku the whirlwind of the Apocalypse will come forth. And more, there will be a convergence.'

Fiddler's eyes narrowed. *The Soletaken dhenrabi.* 'As in a drawing-together of Ascendant powers?'

'Just so.'

'What will draw them?'

'A gate. The Prophecy of the Path of Hands. Soletaken and D'ivers. A gate promising ... something. They are drawn as moths to a flame.'

'Why would shapeshifters have any interest in a warren's gate? They are hardly a brotherhood, nor are they users of sorcery, at least not in any sophisticated sense.'

'Surprising depth of knowledge for a soldier.'

Fiddler scowled. 'Soldiers are always underestimated,' he said. 'I've not spent fifteen years fighting Imperial wars with my eyes closed. The Emperor clashed with both Treach and Ryllandaras outside Li Heng. I was there.'

The Tano Spiritwalker bowed his head in apology. 'I have no answers to your questions,' he said quietly. 'Indeed, I do not think even the Soletaken and D'ivers are fully aware of what they seek. Like salmon returning to the waters where they were born, they act on instinct, a visceral yearning and a promise only sensed.' He folded his hands together. 'There is no unification among shapeshifters. Each stands alone. This Path of Hands –' he hesitated, then continued – 'is perhaps a means to Ascendancy – for the victor.'

Fiddler drew a slow, unsteady breath. 'Ascendancy means power. Power means control.' He met the Spiritwalker's tawny eyes. 'Should one shapeshifter attain Ascendancy—'

'Domination of its own kind, yes. Such an event would have ... repercussions. In any case, friend, the wastelands could never be called safe, but the months to come shall turn the Odhan into a place of savage horror, this much I know with certainty.'

'Thank you for the warning.'

'Yet it shall not deter you.'

'I am afraid not.'

'Then it befalls me to offer you some protection for your journey. Captain, if you would be so kind?'

The veteran rose and departed.

'An outlawed soldier,' the old priest said after a moment, 'who will risk his life to return to the heart of the Empire that has sentenced him to death. The need must be great.'

Fiddler shrugged.

'The Bridgeburners are remembered here in Seven Cities. A name that is cursed, yet admired all the same. You were honourable soldiers fighting in a dishonourable war. It is said the regiment was honed in the heat and scorched rock of the Holy Desert Raraku, in pursuit of a Falah'd company of wizards. That is a story I would like to hear some time, so that it may be shaped into song.'

Fiddler's eyes widened. A Spiritwalker's sorcery was sung, no other rituals were required. Although devoted to peace, the power in a Tano song was said to be immense. The sapper wondered what such a creation would do to the Bridgeburners.

The Tano Spiritwalker seemed to understand the question, for he smiled. 'Such a song has never before been attempted. There is in a Tano song the potential for Ascendancy, but can an entire regiment ascend? Truly a question deserving an answer.'

Fiddler sighed. 'Had I the time, I would give you that story.'

'It would take but a moment.'

'What do you mean?'

The old priest raised a long-fingered, wrinkled hand. 'If you were to let me touch you, I would know your history.'

The sapper recoiled.

'Ah,' the Tano Spiritwalker sighed, 'you fear I would be careless with your secrets.'

'I fear that your possessing them would endanger your life. Nor are all of my memories honourable.'

The old man tilted his head back and laughed. 'If they were all honourable, friend, you would be more deserving of this robe than I. Forgive me my bold request, then.'

Captain Turqa returned, carrying a small chest of weathered

wood the colour of sand. He set it down on the table before his master, who raised the lid and reached inside. 'Raraku was once a sea,' the Tano said. He withdrew a bleached white conch shell. 'Such remnants can be found in the Holy Desert, provided you know the location of the ancient shores. In addition to the memory song contained within it, of that inland sea, other songs have been invested.' He glanced up, meeting Fiddler's eyes. 'My own songs of power. Please accept this gift, in gratitude for saving the lives and honour of my granddaughters.'

Fiddler bowed as the old priest set the conch shell into his hands. 'Thank you, Tano Spiritwalker. Your gift offers protection, then?'

'Of a sort,' the priest said, smiling. After a moment he rose from his seat. 'We shall not keep you any longer, Bridgeburner.'

Fiddler quickly stood.

'Captain Turqa will see you out.' He stepped close and laid a hand on Fiddler's shoulder. 'Kimloc Spiritwalker thanks you.'

The conch shell in his hands, the sapper was ushered from the priest's presence. Outside in the garden the water-cooled air plucked at the sweat on Fiddler's brow. 'Kimloc,' he muttered under his breath.

Turqa grunted beside him as they walked the path to the back gate. 'His first guest in eleven years. Do you comprehend the honour bestowed upon you, Bridgeburner?'

'Clearly,' Fiddler said dryly, 'he values his granddaughters. Eleven years, you say? Then his last guest would have been . . .'

'High Fist Dujek Onearm, of the Malazan Empire.'

'Negotiating the peaceful surrender of Karakarang, the Holy City of the Tano cult. Kimloc claimed he could destroy the Malazan armies. Utterly. Yet he capitulated and his name is now legendary for empty threats.'

Turqa snorted. 'He opened the gates of his city because he values life above all things. He took the measure of your

Empire and realized that the death of thousands meant nothing to it. Malaz would have what it desired, and what it desired was Karakarang.'

Fiddler grimaced. With heavy sarcasm he said, 'And if that meant bringing the T'lan Imass to the Holy City – to do to it what they did to Aren – then we would have done just that. I doubt even Kimloc's sorcery could hold back the T'lan Imass.'

They stood at the gate. Turqa swung it open, old pain in his dark eyes. 'As did Kimloc,' he said. 'The slaughter at Aren revealed the Empire's madness—'

'What happened during the Aren Rebellion was a mistake,' Fiddler snapped. 'No command was ever given to the Logros T'lan Imass.'

Turqa's only reply was a sour, bitter grin as he gestured to the street beyond. 'Go in peace, Bridgeburner.'

Irritated, Fiddler left.

Moby squealed in delight, launching itself across the narrow room to collide with Fiddler's chest in a frenzied flap of wings and clutching limbs. Swearing and pushing the familiar away as it attempted a throat-crushing embrace, the sapper crossed the threshold, closing the door behind him.

'I was starting to get worried,' Kalam rumbled from the shadows filling the room's far end.

'Got distracted,' Fiddler said.

'Trouble?'

He shrugged, stripping off his outer cloak to reveal the leather-bound chain surcoat beneath. 'Where are the others?'

'In the garden,' Kalam replied wryly.

On his way over Fiddler stopped by his backpack. He crouched and set the Tano shell inside, pushing it into the bundle of a spare shirt.

Kalam poured him a jug of watered wine as the sapper joined him at the small table, then refilled his own. 'Well?'

'A cusser in an eggshell,' Fiddler said, drinking deep before continuing. 'The walls are crowded with symbols. I'd guess no more than a week, then the streets run red.'

'We've horses, mules and supplies. We should be nearing the Odhan by then. Safer out there.'

Fiddler eyed his companion. Kalam's dark, bearish face glistened in the faint daylight from the cloth-covered window. A brace of knives rested on the pitted tabletop in front of the assassin, a whetstone beside them. 'Maybe. Maybe not.'

'The hands on the walls?'

Fiddler grunted. 'You noticed them.'

'Symbols of insurrection aplenty, meeting places announced, rituals to Dryjhna advertised – I can read all of that as well as any other native. But those unhuman hand-prints are something else entirely.' Kalam leaned forward, picking up a knife in each hand. He idly crossed the blued blades. 'They seem to indicate a direction. South.'

'Pan'potsun Odhan,' Fiddler said. 'It's a convergence.'

The assassin went still, his dark eyes on the blades crossed before him. 'That's not a rumour I've heard yet.'

'It's Kimloc's belief.'

'Kimloc!' Kalam cursed. 'He's in the city?'

'So it's said.' Fiddler took another mouthful of wine. Telling the assassin of his adventures – and his meeting with the Spiritwalker – would send Kalam out through the door. *And Kimloc to Hood's Gates. Kimloc, his family, his guards. Everyone.* The man sitting across from him would take no chances. *Another gift to you, Kimloc . . . my silence.*

Footsteps sounded in the back hallway and a moment later Crokus appeared. 'It's as dark as a cave in here,' he complained.

'Where's Apsalar?' Fiddler demanded.

'In the garden – where else?' the Daru thief snapped back.

The sapper subsided. Remnants of his old unease still clung to him. *When she was out of sight, trouble would come from it.*

When she was out of sight you watched your back. It was still hard to accept that the girl was no longer what she'd been. *Besides, if the Patron of Assassins chose once more to possess her, the first warning we'd get would be a knife blade across the throat.* He kneaded the taut muscles of his neck, sighing.

Crokus dragged a chair to the table, dropped into it and reached for the wine. 'We're tired of waiting,' he pronounced. 'If we have to cross this damned land, then let's do it. There's a steaming pile of rubbish behind the garden wall, clogging up the sewage gutter. Crawling with rats. The air's hot and so thick with flies you can barely breathe. We'll catch a plague if we stay here much longer.'

'Let's hope it's the bluetongue, then,' Kalam said.

'What's that?'

'Your tongue swells up and turns blue,' Fiddler explained.

'What's so good about that?'

'You can't talk.'

The stars bristled overhead, the moon yet to rise as Kalam made his way towards Jen'rahb. The old ramps climbed to the hill's summit like a giant's stairs, gap-toothed where the chiselled blocks of stone had been removed for use in other parts of Ehrlitan. Tangled scrub filled the gaps, long, wiry roots anchored deep in the slope's fill.

The assassin scrambled lithely over the rubble, staying low so that he would make little outline against the sky, should anyone glance up from the streets below. The city was quiet, its silence unnatural. The few patrols of Malazan soldiery found themselves virtually alone, as if assigned to guard a necropolis, the haunt of ghosts and scant else. Their unease had made them loud as they walked the alleys and Kalam had been able to avoid them with little effort.

He reached the crest, slipping in between two large lime-stone blocks that had once formed part of the summit's outer wall. He paused, breathing deep the dusty night air, and looked down on the streets of Ehrlitan. The Fist's Keep, once the home of the city's Holy Falah'd, rose dark and misshapen above a well-lit compound, like a clenched hand rising from a bed of coals. Yet within that stone edifice the military governor of the Malazan Empire cowered, shutting his ears to the heated warnings of the Red Blades and whatever Malazan spies and sympathizers had not yet been driven out or murdered. The entire occupying regiment was holed up in the Keep's own barracks, having been called in from the outlying garrison forts strategically placed around Ehrlitan's circumference. The Keep could not accommodate such numbers – the well was already foul, and soldiers slept on the bailey's flagstones under the stars. In the harbour two ancient Falari triremes were moored-off the Malazan mole and a lone undermanned company of marines held the Imperial Docks. The Malazans were under siege with not a hand yet raised against them.

Kalam found within himself conflicting loyalties. By birth he was among the occupied, but he had by choice fought under the standards of the Empire. He'd fought for Emperor Kellanved. *And Dassem Ultor, and Whiskeyjack, and Dujek Onearm. But not Laseen. Betrayal cut those bonds long ago.* The Emperor would have cut the heart out of this rebellion with its first beat. A short but unremitting bloodbath, followed by a long peace. But Laseen had left the old wounds to fester, and what was coming would silence Hood himself.

Kalam swung back from the hill's crest. The landscape before him was a tumbled maze of shattered limestone and bricks, sinkholes and knotted shrubs. Clouds of insects hovered over black pools. Bats and rhizan darted among them.

Near the centre rose the first three levels of a tower, tilted with roots snaking down from a drought-twisted tree on its top. The maw of a doorway was visible at its base.

Kalam studied it for a time, then finally approached. He was ten paces from the opening when he saw a flicker of light within. The assassin withdrew a knife, tapped the pommel twice against a block, then crossed to the doorway. A voice from its darkness stopped him.

'No closer, Kalam Mekhar.'

Kalam spat loudly. 'Mebra, you think I don't recognize your voice? Vile rhizan like you never wander far from their nest, which is what made you so easy to find, and following you here was even easier.'

'I have important business to attend to,' Mebra growled. 'Why have you returned? What do you want of me? My debt was with the Bridgeburners, but they are no more.'

'Your debt was with me,' Kalam said.

'And when the next Malazan dog with the sigil of a burning bridge finds me, he can claim the debt as well? And the next, and the next after that? Oh no, Kal—'

The assassin was at the doorway before Mebra realized it, lunging into the darkness, a hand flashing out unerringly to grip the spy by the throat. The man squawked, dragged from his feet as Kalam lifted him and threw him against a wall. The assassin held him there, a knife point pricking the hollow above his breastbone. Something the spy had been clutching to his chest fell, slipping between them to thud heavily at their feet. Kalam did not spare it a glance; his eyes fixed on Mebra's own.

'The debt,' he said.

'Mebra is an honourable man,' the spy gasped. 'Pays every debt! Pays yours!'

Kalam grinned. 'The hand you've just closed on that dagger at your belt had best remain where it is, Mebra. I see all that you plan. There in your eyes. Now look into mine. What do you see?'

Mebra's breath quickened. Sweat trickled down his brow. 'Mercy,' he said.

Kalam's brows rose. 'A fatal misreading—'

'No, no! I ask for mercy, Kalam! In your eyes I see only death! Mebra's death! I shall repay the debt, my old friend. I know much, all that the Fist needs to know! I can deliver Ehrlitan into his hands—'

'No doubt,' Kalam said, releasing his grip on the man's throat and stepping back. Mebra slid down the wall into a feeble crouch. 'But leave the Fist to his fate.'

The spy looked up, in his eyes a sudden cunning. 'You are outlawed. With no wish to return to the Malazan fold. You are Seven Cities once again! Kalam, may the Seven bless you!'

'I need the signs, Mebra. Safe passage through the Odhan.'

'You know them—'

'The symbols have bred. I know the *old* ones, and those will get me killed by the first tribe that finds me.'

'Passage is yours with but one symbol, Kalam. Across the breadth of Seven Cities, I swear it.'

The assassin stepped back. 'What is it?'

'You are Dryjhna's child, a soldier of the Apocalypse. Make the whirlwind gesture – do you recall it?'

Suspicious, Kalam slowly nodded. 'Yet I have seen so many more, so many new symbols. What of them?'

'Amidst the cloud of locusts there is but one,' Mebra said. 'How best to keep the Red Blades blind? Please, Kalam, you must go. I have repaid the debt . . .'

'If you have betrayed me, Adaephon Ben Delat shall know of it. Tell me, could you escape Quick Ben with his warrens unveiled?'

Mute, his face pale as the moonlight, Mebra shook his head.

'The whirlwind.'

'Yes, I swear by the Seven.'

'Do not move,' Kalam commanded. One hand on the long-knife at his belt, the assassin stepped forward, crouched and collected the object that Mebra had dropped earlier. He heard the spy's breath catch and smiled. 'Perhaps I will take this with me, as guarantee.'

'Please, Kalam—'

'Silence.' The assassin found himself holding a muslin-wrapped book. He pulled the dirt-stained cloth away. 'Hood's breath!' he whispered. 'From the High Fist's vaults at Aren . . . into the hands of an Ehrlii spy.' He looked up and met Mebra's eyes. 'Does Pormqual know of the theft of that which is to unleash the Apocalypse?'

The little man grinned, displaying a row of sharp silver-capped teeth. 'The fool could have his silk pillow stolen from under him and would not know it. You see, Kalam, if you take this as guarantee, every warrior of the Apocalypse will be hunting you. The Holy Book of Dryjhna has been freed and must return to Raraku, where the Seeress—'

'Will raise the Whirlwind,' Kalam finished. The ancient tome felt heavy as a slab of granite in his hands. Its bhederin-hide binding was stained and scarred, the lambskin pages within smelling of lanolin and bloodberry ink. And on those pages . . . *words of madness, and in the Holy Desert waits Sha'ik, the Seeress, the rebellion's promised leader . . .* 'You shall tell me the final secret, Mebra, the one the carrier of this Book must know.'

The spy's eyes widened with alarm. 'This cannot be your hostage, Kalam! Take me in its stead, I beg you!'

'I shall deliver it into the Holy Desert Raraku,' Kalam said. 'Into Sha'ik's own hands, and this shall purchase my passage, Mebra. And should I detect any treachery, should I see any single soldier of the Apocalypse on my trail, the Book is destroyed. Do you understand me?'

Mebra blinked sweat from his eyes, then jerked a nod. 'You must ride a stallion the colour of sand, your bloods blended. You must wear a telaba of red. Each night you must face your trail, on your knees, and unwrap the Book and call upon

101

Dryjhna – that, and no more, not another word, for the Whirlwind goddess shall hear and obey – and all signs of your trail shall be obliterated. You must wait an hour in silence, then wrap the Book once again. It must never be exposed to sunlight, for the time of the Book's awakening belongs to Sha'ik. I shall now repeat those instructions—'

'No need,' Kalam growled.

'Are you truly an outlaw?'

'Is this not proof enough?'

'Deliver into Sha'ik's hands the Book of Dryjhna, and your name shall be sung to the heavens for all time, Kalam. Betray the cause, and your name shall ride spit into the dust.'

The assassin shrouded the Book once more in its muslin wrap, then tucked it into the folds of his tunic. 'Our words are done.'

'Blessings of the Seven, Kalam Mekhar.'

With a grunt his only reply, Kalam moved to the doorway, pausing to scan outside. Seeing no-one under the moonlight, he slipped through the opening.

Still crouched against the wall, Mebra watched the assassin leave. He strained to hear telltale sounds of Kalam crossing the rocks, bricks and rubble, but heard nothing. The spy wiped sweat from his brow, tilted his head back against the cool stone and closed his eyes.

A few minutes later he heard the rustle of armour at the tower's entrance. 'You saw him?' Mebra asked, eyes still shut.

A low voice rumbled in reply. 'Lostara follows him. He has the Book?'

Mebra's thin mouth widened in a smile. 'Not the visitor I anticipated. Oh no, I could never have imagined such a fortuitous guest. That was Kalam Mekhar.'

'The Bridgeburner? Kiss of Hood, Mebra, had I known, we would have cut him down before he'd taken a step from this tower.'

102

'Had you tried,' Mebra said, 'you and Aralt and Lostara would now be feeding your blood to Jen'rahb's thirsty roots.'

The large warrior barked a laugh, stepping inside. Behind him, as the spy had guessed, loomed Aralt Arpat, guarding the entrance, tall and wide enough to block most of the moonlight.

Tene Baralta rested his gauntleted hands on the sword pommels on either side of his hips. 'What of the man you first approached?'

Mebra sighed. 'As I told you, we would likely have needed a dozen nights such as this one. The man took fright and is probably halfway to G'danisban by now. He . . . reconsidered, as any reasonable man would.' The spy rose to his feet, brushing the dust from his telaba. 'I cannot believe our luck, Baralta—'

Tene Baralta's mailed hand was a blur as it flashed out and struck Mebra, the spurred links raking deep gashes across the man's face. Blood spattered the wall. The spy reeled back, hands to his torn face.

'You are too familiar,' Baralta said calmly. 'You have prepared Kalam, I take it? The proper . . . instructions?'

Mebra spat blood, then nodded. 'You shall be able to trail him unerringly, Commander.'

'All the way to Sha'ik's camp?'

'Yes. But I beg you, be careful, sir. If Kalam senses you, he will destroy the Book. Stay a day behind him, even more.'

Tene Baralta removed a fragment of bhederin hide from a pouch at his belt. 'The calf yearns for its mother,' he said.

'And seeks her without fail,' Mebra finished. 'To kill Sha'ik, you shall need an army, Commander.'

The Red Blade smiled. 'That is our concern, Mebra.'

Mebra drew a deep breath, hesitating, then said, 'I ask only one thing, sir.'

'You ask?'

'I beg, Commander.'

'What is it?'

'Kalam lives.'

'Your wounds are uneven, Mebra. Allow me to caress the other side of your face.'

'Hear me out, Commander! The Bridgeburner has returned to Seven Cities. He claims himself a soldier of the Apocalypse. Yet is Kalam one to join Sha'ik's camp? Can a man born to lead content himself to follow?'

'What is your point?'

'Kalam is here for another reason, Commander. He sought only safe passage across the Pan'potsun Odhan. He takes the Book because to do so will ensure that passage. The assassin is heading south. Why? I think that is something the Red Blades – and the Empire – would know. And such knowledge can only be gained while he yet breathes.'

'You have suspicions.'

'Aren.'

Tene Baralta snorted. 'To slip a blade between Pormqual's ribs? We would all bless that, Mebra.'

'Kalam cares nothing for the High Fist.'

'Then what does he seek at Aren?'

'I can think of only one thing, Commander. A ship bound for Malaz.' Hunched, his face pulsing with pain, Mebra watched with hooded eyes as his words sank roots into the Red Blade commander's mind.

After a long moment, Tene Baralta asked in a low voice, 'What do you plan?'

Although it cost him, Mebra smiled.

Like massive limestone slabs each resting against the other, the cliffs rose from the desert floor the height of four hundred arm-spans. Gouged across the weathered face were deep fissures, and tucked inside the largest of these, a hundred and fifty arm-spans above the sands, was a tower.

A single arched window showed black against the bricks.

Mappo sighed shakily. 'I see no obvious approach, but there must be one.' He shot a glance back at his companion. 'You believe it is occupied.'

Icarium rubbed the crusted blood from his brow, then nodded. He half slid the sword from its sheath, frowning at the fragments of flesh still snagged on the notched edge.

The D'ivers had caught them unawares, a dozen leopards the colour of sand, streaming from a gully bed less than ten paces to their right as the two travellers prepared to make camp. One of the beasts had leapt onto Mappo's back, jaws closing on the nape of his neck, the fangs punching through the Trell's tough hide. It had attacked him as if he was an antelope, seeking to bite down on his windpipe as it dragged him down, but Mappo was no antelope. Though the canines sank deep, they found only muscle. Enraged, the Trell had reached over his head and torn the animal from his shoulders. Gripping the snarling leopard by its skin at neck and hips, he had slammed it hard against a boulder, shattering its skull.

The other eleven had closed in on Icarium. Even as Mappo flung his attacker's body aside and whirled, he saw four of the beasts lying motionless around the half-blood Jaghut. Fear gripped the Trell suddenly as his gaze fell on Icarium. *How far? How far has the Jhag gone? Beru bless us, please*.

One of the other beasts had wrapped its jaws around Icarium's left thigh and Mappo watched the warrior's ancient sword chop downward, decapitating the leopard. In a macabre detail, the head held on briefly, a blood-gushing lump protruding from the warrior's leg.

The surviving cats circled.

Mappo lunged forward, hands closing on a lashing tail. He bellowed as he swung the squalling creature through the air. Writhing, the leopard sailed seven or eight paces until it struck a rock wall, snapping its spine.

It was already too late for the D'ivers. Realizing its error, it tried to pull away, but Icarium was unrelenting. Giving voice to a keening hum, the Jhag plunged among the five remaining leopards. They scattered but not quickly enough. Blood fountained, sheared flesh thudded into the sand. Within moments five more bodies lay still on the ground.

Icarium whirled, seeking more victims, and the Trell took half a step forward. After a moment Icarium's high-pitched keening fell away and he slowly straightened from his crouch. His stony gaze found the Trell, and he frowned.

Mappo saw the beads of blood on Icarium's brow. The eerie sound was gone. *Not too far. Safe. Gods below, this path . . . I am a fool to follow. Close, all too close.*

The scent of D'ivers blood so copiously spilled would draw others. The two had quickly repacked their camp gear and set off at a swift pace. Before leaving, Icarium withdrew a single arrow from his quiver, which he stabbed into the sand in full view.

They travelled at a dogtrot through the night. Neither was driven by fear of dying; for both of them, it was killing that brought a greater dread. Mappo prayed that Icarium's arrow would prove sufficient warning.

Dawn brought them to the eastern escarpment. Beyond the cliffs rose the range of weathered mountains that divided Raraku from the Pan'potsun Odhan.

Something had ignored the arrow and was trailing them, perhaps a league behind. The Trell had sensed it an hour earlier, a Soletaken, and the form it had taken was huge.

'Find us the ascent,' Icarium said, stringing his bow. He set out his remaining arrows, squinting back along their trail. After a hundred paces the shimmering heat that rose like a curtain obscured everything beyond. If the Soletaken came into view and charged, the Jhag had time to loose half a dozen arrows. The warrens carved into their shafts could bring down a dragon, but Icarium's expression made it clear he was sickened by the thought.

Mappo probed at the puncture wounds on the back of his neck. The torn flesh was hot, septic and crawling with flies. The muscles ached with a deep throb. He pulled a blade of jegura cactus from his pack and squeezed its juices onto the wounds. Numbness spread, allowing him to move his arms without the stabbing agony that had had him bathed in sweat over the last few hours. The Trell shivered with sudden chill. The cactus juice was so powerful it could be used only once a day, lest the numbing effect spread to the heart and lungs. And if anything, it would make the flies thirstier.

He approached the cleft in the rockface. Trell were plains dwellers. Mappo had no special skill in climbing, and he was not looking forward to the task ahead. The fissure was deep enough to swallow the sun's morning light, and narrow at the base, barely the width of his shoulders. Ducking, he slipped inside, the cool, musty air triggering another wave of shivering. His eyes quickly adjusting, he made out the fissure's back wall six paces away. There were no stairs, no handholds. Tilting his head, he looked up. The cleft widened higher up but was unrelieved until it reached what he took to be the base of the tower. Nothing so simple as a dangling knotted rope. Growling in frustration, Mappo stepped back into the sunlight.

Icarium stood facing their trail with arrow nocked and bow raised. Thirty paces from him was a massive brown bear, down on all fours, swaying, nose lifted and testing the wind. The Soletaken had arrived.

Mappo joined his companion. 'This one is known to me,' he said quietly.

The Jhag lowered his weapon, releasing the bowstring's tension. 'He is sembling,' he said.

The bear lurched forward.

Mappo blinked against the sudden blurring of his vision. He

tasted grit, nostrils twitching at the strong spicy smell that came with the change. He felt an instinctive wave of fear, a dusty dryness making swallowing difficult. A moment later the sembling was complete, and a man now strode towards them, naked and pale under the harsh sunlight.

Mappo slowly shook his head. When masked, the Soletaken was huge, powerful, a mass of muscle – yet now, in his human form, Messremb stood no more than five feet in height, was almost hairless and thin to the point of emaciation, narrow-faced and shovel-toothed. His small eyes, the colour of garnet, shone within wrinkled nests of humour that drew his mouth into a grin.

'Mappo Trell, my nose told me it was you!'

'It's been a long time, Messremb.'

The Soletaken was eyeing the Jhag. 'Aye, north of Nemil it was.'

'Those unbroken pine forests better suited you, I think,' Mappo said, his memories drawn back to that time for a moment, those freer days of massive Trellish caravans and the great journeys undertaken.

The man's grin fell away. 'That it did. And you, sir, must be Icarium, maker of mechanisms and now the bane of D'ivers and Soletaken. Know that I am greatly relieved you have lowered your bow – there was racing thunder in my chest when I watched you take aim.'

Icarium was frowning. 'I would be bane to no-one, were the choice mine,' he said. 'We were attacked without warning,' he added, the words sounding strangely uncertain.

'Meaning you had no chance to warn the hapless creature. Pity the pieces of his soul. I, however, am anything but precipitous. Cursed only with a curious nose. What scent is joined with the Trell's, I wondered, so close to Jaghut blood, yet different? Now that my eyes have given me answer I can resume the Path.'

108

'Do you know where it takes you?' Mappo asked.

Messremb stiffened. 'You have seen the gates?'

'No. What do you expect to find there?'

'Answers, old friend. Now I shall spare you the taste of my veering by putting some distance between us. Do you wish me well, Mappo?'

'I do, Messremb. And add a warning: we crossed paths with Ryllandaras four nights ago. Be careful.'

Something of the savage bear glittered in the Soletaken's eyes. 'I shall look out for him.'

Mappo and Icarium watched the man walk away, disappearing behind an outcrop of rock. 'Madness lurked within him,' Icarium said.

The Trell flinched at those words. 'Within them all,' he sighed. 'I've yet to find an ascent, by the way. The cave reveals nothing.'

The sound of shod hooves reached them, slow and plodding. From a trail paralleling the cliff face, a man on a black mule appeared. He sat cross-legged on a high wood saddle, shrouded in a ragged, dirt-stained telaba. His hands, which rested on the ornate saddlehorn, were the colour of rust. A hood hid his features. The mule was a strange-looking beast, its muzzle black, the skin of its ears black, as were its eyes. No lightening of its ebon hue was anywhere visible with the exception of dust and spatters of what might have been dried blood.

The man swayed on the saddle as they approached. 'No way in,' he hissed, 'but the way out. It's not yet the hour. A life given for a life taken, remember those words, remember them. You are wounded. You are bright with infection. My servant will tend to you. A caring man with salty hands, one wrinkled, one pink – do you grasp the significance of that? Not yet. Not yet. So few . . . guests. But I have been expecting you.'

The mule stopped opposite the cleft, swinging a mournful gaze on the two travellers as its rider struggled to pull his legs from their crossed position. Whimpers of pain accompanied the effort, until his frantic attempts overwhelmed his balance and, with a squeal of dismay, the man toppled, thumping into the dust.

Seeing crimson red bloom through the telaba's weave, Mappo stepped forward. 'You bear your own wounds, sir!'

The man writhed on the ground like an upended tortoise, his legs still trapped in their crossed position. His hood fell back, revealing a large hawk nose, tufts of wiry grey beard, a tattooed bald pate and skin like dark honey. A row of perfect white teeth showed in his grimace.

Mappo knelt beside him, squinting to see signs of the wound that had spilled so much blood. A smell of iron was pungent in the Trell's nose. After a moment he reached under the man's cloak and withdrew an unstoppered bladder. Grunting, he glanced over at Icarium. 'Not blood. Paint. Red ochre paint.'

'Help me, you oaf!' the man snapped. 'My legs!'

Bemused, Mappo helped the man unlock his legs, every move eliciting moans. As soon as they were free the man sat up and started beating his own thighs. 'Servant! Wine! Wine, damn your wood-rotted brain!'

'I am not your servant,' Mappo said coolly, stepping back. 'Nor do I carry wine when crossing a desert.'

'Not you, barbarian!' The man glared about. 'Where is he?'

'Who?'

'Servant, of course. He thinks carrying me about is his only task – ah, there!'

Following the man's gaze, the Trell frowned. 'That is a mule, sir. I doubt he could manage a wineskin well enough to fill a cup.' Mappo grinned at Icarium, but the Jhag was paying no attention to the proceedings: he had unstrung his bow and now sat on a boulder, cleaning his sword.

Still sitting on the ground, the man collected a handful of

sand and flung it at the mule. Startled, the beast brayed and bolted towards the cleft, disappearing into the cave. With a grunt the man clambered to his feet and stood wobbling, hands held before him plucking at each other in some kind of nervous tic. 'Mostly rude greeting of guests,' he said, attempting a smile. 'Most. *Most* rude greeting, was meant. Meaningless apologies and kindly gestures very important. I am so sorry for temporary collapse of hospitality. Oh yes, I am. I would have more practice if I wasn't the master of this temple. An acolyte is obliged to fawn and scrape. Later to mutter and gripe with his comrades in misery. Ah, here comes Servant.'

A wide-shouldered, bow-legged man in black robes had emerged from the cave, carrying a tray bearing a jug and clay cups. He wore a servant's veil over his features, with only a thin slit for his eyes, which were deep brown.

'Lazy fool! Did you see any cobwebs?'

Servant's accent caught Mappo by surprise. It was Malazan. 'None, Iskaral.'

'Call me by my title!'

'High Priest—'

'Wrong!'

'High Priest Iskaral Pust of the Tesem Temple of Shadow—'

'Idiot! You are Servant! Which makes me . . .'

'Master.'

'Indeed.' Iskaral turned to Mappo. 'We rarely talk,' he explained.

Icarium joined them. 'This is Tesem, then. I was led to believe it was a monastery, sanctified to the Queen of Dreams—'

'They left,' Iskaral snapped. 'Took their lanterns with them, leaving only . . .'

'Shadows.'

'Clever Jhag, but I was warned of that, oh yes. You two are sick as undercooked pigs. Servant has prepared your chambers.

And broths of healing herbs, roots, potions and elixirs. White Paralt, emulor, tralb—'

'Those are poisons,' Mappo pointed out.

'Are they? No wonder the pig died. It's almost time, shall we prepare to ascend?'

'Lead the way,' Icarium invited.

'A life given for a life taken. Follow me. None can outwit Iskaral Pust.' The High Priest faced the cleft with a fierce squint.

They waited, for what Mappo had no idea. After a few minutes the Trell cleared his throat. 'Will your acolytes send down a ladder?'

'Acolytes? I have no acolytes. No opportunity for tyranny. Very sad, no muttering and grumbling behind my back, few satisfying rewards for this High Priest. If not for my god's whispering, I wouldn't bother, be assured of that, and I trust you will take that into account with all I have done and am about to do.'

'I see movement in the fissure,' Icarium said.

Iskaral grunted. 'Bhok'arala, they nest on this cliffside. Foul mewling beasts, always interfering, sniffing at this and that, pissing on the altar, defecating on my pillow. They are my plague, they have singled me out, and why? I've not skinned a single one, nor cooked their brains to scoop out of their skulls in civilized repast. No snares, no traps, no poison, yet still they pursue me. There is no answer to this. I despair.'

As the sun sank further the bhok'arala grew bolder, flapping from perch to perch high on the cliff wall, scampering with their hands and feet along cracks in the stone, seeking the rhizan as the small flying lizards emerged for their night-feeding. Small and simian, the bhok'arala were winged like bats, tailless with hides mottled tan and brown. Apart from long canines, their faces were remarkably human.

From the tower's lone window a knotted rope tumbled

down. A tiny round head poked out to peer down at them.

'Of course,' Iskaral added, 'a few of them have proved useful.'

Mappo sighed. He'd been hoping for some sorcerous means of ascent to appear, something worthy of a High Priest of Shadow. 'So now we climb.'

'Most certainly not,' Iskaral replied with indignation. 'Servant climbs, then pulls us up.'

'He would be a man of formidable strength to manage me,' the Trell said. 'And Icarium, too.'

Servant set down the tray he had been holding, spat on his hands and walked over to the rope. He launched himself upward with surprising agility. Iskaral crouched by the tray and poured wine into the three cups.

'Servant's half bhokar'al. Long arms. Muscles like iron. Makes friends with them, probable source of all my ills.' Iskaral collected a cup for himself and gestured down at the tray as he straightened. 'Fortunate for Servant I am such a gentle and patient master.' He swung to check on the man's climb. 'Hurry, you snub-tailed dog!'

Servant had already reached the window and was now clambering through it and out of sight.

'Ammanas's gift, is Servant. A life given for a life taken. One hand old, one hand new. This is true remorse. You'll see.'

The rope twitched. The High Priest quaffed down the last of his wine, flung the cup away and scrambled towards the rope. 'Too long exposed! Vulnerable. Quickly now!' He wrapped his hands around a knot, set his feet atop another. 'Pull! Are you deaf? Pull!'

Iskaral shot upward.

'Pulleys,' Icarium said. 'Too fast to be otherwise.'

The pain returning to his shoulders, Mappo winced, then said, 'Not what you were expecting, I take it.'

'Tesem,' Icarium said, watching the priest vanish through

113

the window. 'A place of healing. Solitary reflection, repository of scrolls and tomes, and insatiable nuns . . .'

'Insatiable?'

The Jhag glanced at his friend, an eyebrow rising. 'Indeed.'

'Oh, sad demise.'

'Very.'

'In this instance,' Mappo said as the rope tumbled back down, 'I think solitary reflection has addled a brain. Battling wits with bhok'arala and the whisperings of a god most hold as himself insane . . .'

'Yet there is power here, Mappo,' Icarium said in a low voice.

'Aye,' the Trell agreed as he approached the rope. 'A warren opened in the cave when the mule entered.'

'Then why does the High Priest not use it?'

'I doubt we'll find easy answers to Iskaral Pust, friend.'

'Best hold tight, Mappo.'

'Aye.'

Icarium reached out suddenly, rested a hand on Mappo's shoulder. 'Friend.'

'Aye?'

The Jhag was frowning. 'I am missing an arrow, Mappo. More, there is blood on my sword, and I see upon you dreadful wounds. Tell me, did we fight? I recall . . . nothing.'

The Trell was silent a long moment, then he said, 'I was beset by a leopard while you slept, Icarium. Made some use of your weapons. I did not think it worthy of mention.'

Icarium's frown deepened. 'Once again,' he slowly whispered, 'I have lost time.'

'Nothing of worth, friend.'

'You would tell me otherwise?' There was a look of desperate pleading in the Jhag's grey eyes.

'Why would I not, Icarium?'

CHAPTER THREE

The Red Blades were, at this time, pre-eminent among those
pro-Malazan organizations that arose in occupied territories.
Viewing themselves as progressive in their embrace of the
values of imperial unification, this quasi-military cult became
infamous with their brutal pragmatism when dealing with
dissenting kin . . .

Lives of the Conquered
Ilem Trauth

Felisin lay unmoving beneath Beneth until, with a final
shudder, he was done. He pushed himself off and grabbed
a handful of her hair. His face was flushed under the
grime and his eyes gleamed in the lamp glow. 'You'll learn to
like it, girl,' he said.

The edge of something savage always rose closer to the
surface immediately after he'd lain with her. She knew it would
pass. 'I will,' she said. 'Does he get a day of rest?'

Beneth's grip tightened momentarily, then relaxed. 'Aye,
he does.' He moved away, began tying up his breeches.
'Though I don't much see the point. The old man won't
last another month.' He paused, his breath harsh as he
studied her. 'Hood's breath, girl, but you're beautiful. Show
me some life next time. I'll treat you right. Get you soap,
a new comb, lousebane. You'll work here in Twistings,

that's a promise. Show pleasure, girl, that's all I ask.'

'Soon,' she said. 'Once it stops hurting.'

The day's eleventh bell had sounded. They were in the third reach off Twistings Far shaft. The reach had been gouged out by the Rotlegs and was barely high enough to crawl for most of its quarter-mile length. The air was close and stank of Otataral dust and sweating rock.

Virtually everyone else would have reached Nearlight by now, but Beneth moved in Captain Sawark's shadow and could do as he pleased. He had claimed the abandoned reach as his own. It was Felisin's third visit. The first time had been the hardest. Beneth had picked her within hours of her arrival at Skullcup, the mining camp in the Dosin Pit. He was a big man, bigger than Baudin and though a slave himself he was master of every other slave, the guards' inside man, cruel and dangerous. He was also astonishingly handsome.

Felisin had learned fast on the slave ship. She had nothing but her body to sell, but it had proved a valuable currency. Giving herself to the ship guards had been repaid with more food for herself, Heboric and Baudin. By opening her legs to the right men she had managed to get herself and her two companions chained on the keel ramp rather than in the sewage-filled water that sloshed shin-deep beneath the hold's walkway. Others had rotted in that water. Some had drowned when starvation and sickness so weakened them that they could not stay above it.

Heboric's grief and anger at the price she paid had at first been difficult to ignore, filling her with shame. But it had paid for their lives, and that was a truth that could not be questioned. Baudin's only reaction had been – and continued to be – a regard without expression. He watched her as would a stranger unable to decide who or what she was. Yet he had held to her side, and now stood close to Beneth as well. Some kind of arrangement had been made between them. When Beneth was not there to protect her, Baudin was.

On the ship she had learned well the tastes of men, as well as those of the few women guards who'd taken her to their bunks. She'd thought she'd be prepared for Beneth, and in most ways she was. *Everything but his size.*

Wincing, Felisin pulled on her slave tunic.

Beneth watched her, his high cheekbones harsh ridges beneath his eyes, his long, curly black hair glistening with whale oil. 'I'll give the old man Deepsoil if you like,' he said.

'You'd do that?'

He nodded. 'For you I'll change things. I won't take any other woman. I'm king of Skullcup, you'll be my queen. Baudin will be your personal guard – I trust him.'

'And Heboric?'

Beneth shrugged. 'Him I don't trust. And he's not much use. Pulling the carts is about all he can do. The carts, or a plough at Deepsoil.' His gaze flickered at her. 'But he's your friend, so I'll find something for him.'

Felisin dragged her fingers through her hair. 'It's the carts that are killing him. If you've sent him to Deepsoil just to pull a plough, it's not much of a favour—'

Beneth's scowl made her wonder if she'd pushed too far. 'You've never pulled a cart full of stone, girl. Pulled one of those up through half a league of tunnels, then going back down and pulling another one, three, four times a day. Compare that to dragging a plough through soft, broken soil? Dammit, girl, if I'm to move the man off the carts, I've got to justify it. Everyone works in Skullcup.'

'That's not the whole story, is it?'

He turned his back on her in answer, and began crawling up the reach. 'I've Kanese wine awaiting us, and fresh bread and cheese. Bula's made a stew for the guards and we've got a bowl each.'

Felisin followed. The thought of food made her mouth water. If there was enough cheese and bread she could save some for Heboric, though he insisted that it was fruit and meat that was needed. But both were worth their weight in gold, and just as rare in Skullcup. He'd be grateful enough for what she brought him, she knew.

It was clear that Sawark had received orders to see the historian dead. Nothing so overt as murder – the political risks were too great for that – rather, the slow, wasting death of poor diet and overwork. That he had no hands gave the Pit Captain sufficient reason to assign Heboric to the carts. Daily he struggled at his harness, hauling hundreds of pounds of broken rock up the Deep Mine to the shaft's Nearlight. In every other harness was an ox. The beasts each hauled three carts, while Heboric pulled but one: the only acknowledgement the guards made to his humanity.

Beneth was aware of Sawark's instructions, Felisin was certain of that. The 'king' of Skullcup had limits to his power, for all his claims otherwise.

Once they reached the main shaft, it was four hundred paces to Twistings' Nearlight. Unlike Deep Mine, with its thick, rich and straight vein of Otataral running far under the hills, Twistings followed a folded vein, rising and diving, buckling and turning through the limestone.

Unlike the iron mines on the mainland, Otataral never ran down into true bedrock. Found only in limestone, the veins ran shallow and long, like rivers of rust between compacted beds filled with fossil plants and shellfish.

Limestone is just the bones of things once living, Heboric had said their second night in the hovel they'd claimed off Spit Row – before Beneth had moved them to the more privileged neighbourhood behind Bula's Inn. *I'd read that theory before and am now myself convinced. So now I'm led to believe that Otataral is not a natural ore.*

That's important? Baudin had asked.

If not natural, then what? Heboric grinned. *Otataral, the bane*

118

*of magic, was born of magic. If I was less scrupulous a scholar, I'd
write a treatise on that.*

What do you mean? Felisin asked.

He means, Baudin said, *he'd be inviting alchemists and mages
to experiment in making their own Otataral.*

Is that a problem?

Those veins we dig, Heboric explained, *they're like a layer of once
melted fat, a deep river of it sandwiched between layers of limestone.
This whole island had to melt to make those veins. Whatever sorcery
created Otataral proved beyond controlling. I would not want to be
responsible for unleashing such an event all over again.*

A single Malazan guard waited at Nearlight's gate. Beyond
him stretched the raised road that led into the pit town. At the
far end, the sun was just setting beyond the pit's ridge line,
leaving Skullcup in its early shadow, a pocket of gloom that
brought blessed relief from the day's heat.

The guard was young, resting his vambraced forearms on the
cross blades of his pike.

Beneth grunted. 'Where's your mate, Pella?'

'The Dosii pig wandered off, Beneth. Maybe you can tune
Sawark's ear – Hood knows he's not hearing us. The Dosii
regulars have lost all discipline. They ignore the duty rosters,
spend all their time tossing coins at Bula's. There's seventy-five
of us and over two hundred of them, Beneth, and all this
talk of rebellion . . . explain it to Sawark—'

'You don't know your history,' Beneth said. 'The Dosii have
been on their knees for three hundred years. They don't know
any other way to live. First it was mainlanders, then Falari
colonists, now you Malazans. Calm yourself, boy, before you
lose face.'

'"History comforts the dull-witted,"' the young Malazan
said.

Beneth barked a laugh as he reached the gate. 'And whose
words are those, Pella? Not yours.'

119

The guard's brows rose, then he shrugged. 'I forget you're Korelri sometimes, Beneth. Those words? Emperor Kellanved.' Pella's gaze slid to Felisin with a hint of sharpness. 'Duiker's *Imperial Campaigns, Volume One*. You're Malazan, Felisin, do you recall what comes next?'

She shook her head, bemused by the young man's veiled intensity. *I've learned to read faces – Beneth senses nothing.* 'I'm not that familiar with Duiker's works, Pella.'

'Worth learning,' the guard said with a smile.

Sensing Beneth's growing impatience at the gate, Felisin stepped past Pella. 'I doubt there's a single scroll in Skullcup,' she said.

'Maybe you'll find someone's memory worth dragging a net through, eh?'

Felisin glanced back with a frown.

'The boy flirting with you?' Beneth asked from the ramp. 'Be gentle, girl.'

'I'll think on that,' Felisin told Pella in a low voice before resuming her walk through the Twistings Gate. Joining Beneth on the raised road, she smiled up at him. 'I don't like nervous types.'

He laughed. 'That puts me at ease.'

Blessed Queen of Dreams, make that true.

Rubble-filled pits lined the raised road until it joined the other two roads at the Three Fates crossing, a broad fork that was flanked by two squat Dosii guardhouses. North of Twistings Road, and on their right as they approached the forks, was Deep Mine Road; to the south and on their left ran Shaft Road, leading to a worked-out mine where the dead were disposed of each dusk.

The body wagon was nowhere to be seen, meaning it had been held up on its route through the pit town, with more than the usual number of bodies being brought out and tossed onto its bed.

They crossed the fork and continued on to Work Road. Past the north Dosii guardhouse was Sinker Lake, a deep pool of turquoise-coloured water stretching all the way to the north pit wall. It was said the water was cursed and to dive into it was to disappear. Some believed a demon lived in its depths. Heboric asserted that the lack of buoyancy was a quality of the lime-saturated water itself. In any case, few slaves were foolish enough to try an escape in that direction, for the pit wall was as sheer on the north side as it was on the others, forever weeping water over a skin of deposits that glimmered like wet, polished bone.

Heboric had asked Felisin to keep an eye on Sinker Lake's water level in any case, now that the dry season had come, and as they walked Work Road, she studied the far side as best she could in the dim light. A line of crust was visible a hand's span above the surface. The news would please him, though she had no idea why. The notion of escape was absurd. Beyond the pit was lifeless desert and withered rock, with no drinkable water in any direction for days. Those slaves who somehow made it up to the pit edge, and then eluded the patrols on Beetle Road, the track that surrounded the pit, had left their bones in the desert's red sands. Few got that far, and the spikes named Salvation Row on the sheer wall of the Tower at Rust Ramp displayed their failure for all to see. Not a week went past without a new victim appearing on the Tower wall. Most died before the first day was through, but some lingered longer.

Work Road ran its worn cobbles past Bula's Inn on the right and the row of brothels on the left before opening out into Rathole Round. In the round's centre rose Sawark's Keep, a hexagonal tower of cut limestone three storeys high. Only Beneth among all the slaves had ever been inside.

Twelve thousand slaves lived in Skullcup, the vast mining pit thirty leagues north of the island's lone city on the south coast, Dosin Pali. In addition to them and the three hundred guards there were locals: prostitutes for the brothels, serving staff for Bula's Inn and the gambling halls, a caste of servants who had bound their lives and the lives of their families to the Malazan soldiery, hawkers for the struggling market that filled Rathole Round on Rest Day, and a scattering of the banished, the destitute and the lost who'd chosen a pit town over the rotting alleyways of Dosin Pali.

'The stew will be cold,' Beneth muttered as they approached Bula's Inn.

Felisin wiped sweat from her brow. 'That will be a relief.'

'You're not yet used to the heat. In a month or two you'll feel the chill of night just like everyone else.'

'These early hours still hold the day's memory. I feel the cold of midnight and the hours beyond, Beneth.'

'Move in with me, girl. I'll keep you warm enough.'

He was already on the edge of one of his sudden dark moods. She said nothing, hoping he would let it go for the moment.

'Be careful of what you refuse,' Beneth rumbled.

'Bula would take me to her bed,' she said. 'You could watch, perhaps join in. She'd be sure to warm the bowls for us. Even second helpings.'

'She's old enough to be your mother,' Beneth growled.

And you my father. But she heard his breathing change. 'She's round and soft and warm, Beneth. Think on that.'

She knew he would, and the subject of moving in with him would drift away. *For this night, at least. Heboric's wrong. There's no point in thinking about tomorrow. Just the next hour, each hour. Stay alive, Felisin, and live well if you can. One day you'll find yourself face to face with your sister, and an ocean of blood pouring from Tavore's veins won't be enough, though all they hold will suffice. Stay alive, girl, that's all you must do. Survive each hour, the next hour . . .*

She slipped her hand into Beneth's as they reached the inn's door, and felt in it the sweat born of the visions she had given him.

One day, face to face, sister.

Heboric was still awake, bundled in blankets and crouched beside the hearthfire. He glanced up as Felisin climbed into the room and locked the floor hatch. She collected a sheepskin wrap from a chest and pulled it around her shoulders.

'Would you have me believe you've come to enjoy the life you've chosen, girl? Nights like these and I wonder.'

'I thought you'd be tired of judgements by now, Heboric,' Felisin said as she collected a wineskin from a peg and picked through a pile of gourd shells seeking a clean one. 'I take it Baudin's not back yet. Seems even the minor chore of cleaning our cups is beyond him.' She found one that would pass without too close an inspection and squeezed wine into it.

'That will dry you out,' Heboric observed. 'Not your first of the night either, I'd wager.'

'Don't father me, old man.'

The tattooed man sighed. 'Hood take your sister anyway,' he muttered. 'She wasn't satisfied with seeing you dead. She'd rather turn her fourteen-year-old sister into a whore. If Fener has heard my prayers, Tavore's fate will exceed her crimes.'

Felisin drained half the cup, her eyes veiled as she studied Heboric. 'I entered my sixteenth year last month,' she said.

His eyes looked suddenly very old as he met her gaze for a moment before returning his attention to the hearth.

Felisin refilled the cup, then joined Heboric at the square, raised fireplace. The burning dung in the groundstone basin was almost smokeless. The pedestal the basin sat on was glazed and filled with water. Kept hot by the fire, the water was used for washing and bathing, while the pedestal radiated enough heat to keep the night's chill from the single room. Fragments of Dosii spun rug and reed mats cushioned the floorboards. The entire dwelling was raised on stilts five feet above the sands.

Sitting down on a low wooden stool, Felisin pushed her chilled feet close to the pedestal. 'I saw you at the carts today,' she said, her words slightly slurred. 'Gunnip walked beside you with a switch.'

Heboric grunted. 'That amused them all day, Gunnip telling his guards he was swatting flies.'

'Did he break skin?'

'Aye, but Fener's tracks heal me well, you know that.'

'The wounds, yes, but not the pain – I can see, Heboric.'

His glance was wry. 'Surprised you can see anything, lass. Is that durhang I smell, too? Careful with that, the smoke will pull you into a deeper and darker shaft than Deep Mine could ever reach.'

Felisin held out a pebble-sized black button. 'I deal with my pain, you deal with yours.'

He shook his head. 'I appreciate the offer, but not this time. You hold there in your hand a month's pay for a Dosii guard. I'd advise you to use it in trade.'

She shrugged, returning the durhang to the pouch at her belt. 'I've nothing I need that Beneth won't give me already. All I need do is ask.'

'And you imagine he gives it to you freely.'

She drank. 'As good as. You're being moved, Heboric. To Deepsoil. Starting tomorrow. No more Gunnip and his switch.'

He closed his eyes. 'Why does thanking you leave such a bitter taste in my mouth?'

'My wine-soaked brain whispers *hypocrisy*.'

She watched the colour leave his face. *Oh, Felisin, too much durhang, too much wine! Do I only do good for Heboric to give me salt for his wounds? I've no wish to be so cruel.* She withdrew from beneath her tunic the food she had saved for him, leaned forward and placed the small wrapped bundle in his lap. 'Sinker Lake has dropped another hand's width.'

He said nothing, eyes on the stumps at the ends of his wrists.

Felisin frowned. There was something else she wanted to tell him, but her memory failed her. She finished the wine and straightened, running both hands back through her hair. Her scalp felt numb. She paused, seeing Heboric surreptitiously glance at her breasts, round and full under the stretched tunic. She held the pose a moment longer than was necessary, then slowly lowered her arms. 'Bula has fantasies of you,' she said slowly. 'It's the . . . possibilities . . . that intrigue her. It would do you some good, Heboric.'

He spun away off the stool, the untouched food bundle falling to the floor. 'Hood's breath, girl!'

She laughed, watching him sweep aside the hanging that separated his cot from the rest of the room, then clumsily yank it back behind him. After a moment her laughter fell away, and she listened to the old man climb onto his cot. *I'd hoped to make you smile, Heboric,* she wanted to explain. *And I didn't want my laughter to sound so . . . hard. I'm not what you think I am.*

Am I?

She retrieved the wrapped food and placed it on the shelf above the basin.

An hour later, with Felisin lying awake on her cot and Heboric on his, Baudin returned. He stoked up the hearth, moving about quietly. Not drunk. She wondered where he'd been. She wondered where he went every night. It would not be worth asking him. Baudin had few words for anyone, and even fewer for her.

After a moment she was forced to reconsider, as she heard the man flick a finger against Heboric's divider. He responded promptly with low words she could not make out, and Baudin whispered something back. The conversation continued a minute longer, then Baudin softly grunted his laugh-grunt and moved off to his own bed.

The two were planning something, but it was not this that shook her. It was that she was being excluded. A flash of anger followed this realization. *I've kept them alive! I've made their lives easier – since the transport ship! Bula's right, every man's a bastard, good enough only to be used. Very well, see for yourselves what Skullcup is for everyone else, I'm done with favours. I'll see you back on the carts, old man, I swear it.* She found herself fighting tears, and knew she would do nothing of the sort. She needed Beneth, that was true enough, and she'd pay to keep him. But she needed Heboric and Baudin as well, and a part of her clung to them as a child to parents, denying the hardness that everywhere else filled her world. To lose that – to lose them – would be to lose . . . *everything.*

Clearly, they thought that she'd sell their trust as readily as she did her own body, but it wasn't true. *I swear it's not true.*

Felisin stared up into the darkness, tears streaming from her eyes. *I'm alone. There's just Beneth now. Beneth and his wine and his durhang and his body.* She still ached between her legs from when Beneth had finally joined her and Bula on the innkeeper's huge bed.

It was, she told herself, simply a matter of will to turn pain into pleasure.

Survive each hour.

The quayside market had begun drawing the morning crowds, reinforcing the illusion that this day was no different from any other. Chilled with a fear that even the rising sun could not master, Duiker sat cross-legged on the sea wall, his gaze travelling out over the bay into Sahul Sea, willing the return of Admiral Nok and the fleet.

But those were orders even Coltaine could not countermand. The Wickan had no authority over the Malazan warships, and Pormqual's recall had seen the Sahul Fleet depart Hissar's harbour this very morning for the month-long journey to Aren.

For all the pretence of normality, the departure had not gone unnoticed by Hissar's citizens, and the morning market was increasingly shrill with laughter and excited voices. The oppressed had won their first victory, and all that would distinguish it from those to follow was its bloodlessness. Or so ran the sentiment.

The only consolation Duiker could consider was that the Jhistal High Priest Mallick Rel had departed with the fleet. It was not a difficult thing, however, to imagine the report the man would prepare for Pormqual.

A Malazan sail in the strait caught his eye, a small transport coming in from the northeast. *Dosin Pali on the island, perhaps, or from farther up the coast.* It would be an unscheduled arrival, making Duiker curious.

He felt a presence at his side and glanced over to see Kulp clambering up onto the wide, low wall, dangling his legs down to the cloudy water ten paces below. 'It's done,' he said, as if the admission amounted to a confession of foul murder. 'Word has been sent in. Assuming your friend is still alive, he'll receive his instructions.'

'Thank you, Kulp.'

The mage shifted uneasily. He rubbed at his face, squinting at the transport ship as it entered the harbour. A patrol dory approached the craft as the crew struck the lone sail. Two men in glinting armour stood on deck, watching as the dory came alongside.

One of the armoured men leaned over the gunwale and addressed the harbour official. A moment later the dory's oarsmen were swinging the craft around with obvious haste.

Duiker grunted. 'Did you see that?'

'Aye,' Kulp growled.

The transport glided towards the Imperial Pier, pushed along by a low bank of oars that had appeared close to the hull's waterline. A moment later the pier-side oars withdrew back into the ship. Dockmen scrambled to receive the cast lines. A broad gangplank was being readied and horses were now visible on the deck.

'Red Blades,' Duiker said as more armoured men appeared on the transport, standing alongside their mounts.

'From Dosin Pali,' Kulp said. 'I recognize the first two: Baria Setral and his brother Mesker. They have another brother, Orto. He commands the Aren Company.'

'The Red Blades,' the historian mused. 'They've no illusions about the state of affairs. Word's come they are attempting to assert control in other cities, and here we are to witness a doubling of their presence in Hissar.'

'I wonder if Coltaine knows.'

A new tension filled the market; heads had turned and eyes now observed as Baria and Mesker led their troops onto the pier. The Red Blades were equipped and presented for war. They bristled with weapons, with full chain leggings and the slitted visors on their helms lowered. Bows were strung, arrows loosened in their quivers. The horse-blades were unsheathed and jutting from their mounts' forelegs.

Kulp spat nervously. 'Don't like the look of this,' he muttered.

'It looks as if—'

'They intend to attack the market,' Kulp said. 'This isn't just for show, Duiker. Fener's hoof!'

The historian glanced at Kulp, his mouth dry. 'You've opened your warren.'

Not replying, the mage slid off the sea wall, eyes on the Red Blades who were now mounted and lining up at pier's end, facing five hundred citizens who had fallen silent and were now backing away, filling the aisles between the carts and awnings. The contraction of the crowd would trigger panic, which was precisely what the Red Blades intended.

Lances dangling from loops of rawhide around their wrists,

128

the Red Blades nocked arrows, the horses quivering under them but otherwise motionless.

The crowd seemed to shiver in places, as if the ground was shifting beneath it. Duiker saw figures moving, not away, but towards the facing line.

Kulp took half a dozen steps towards the Red Blades.

The figures pushed through the last of the crowd, pulling away their telaba cloaks and hoods, revealing leather armour with stitched black iron scales. Long-knives flashed in gloved hands. Dark eyes in tanned, tattooed Wickan faces held cold and firm on Baria and Mesker Setral and their warriors.

Ten Wickans now faced the forty-odd Red Blades, the crowd behind them as silent and as motionless as statues.

'Stand aside!' Baria bellowed, his face dark with fury. 'Or die!'

The Wickans laughed with fearless derision.

Pushing himself forward, Duiker followed Kulp as the mage strode hurriedly towards the Red Blades.

Mesker snapped out a curse upon seeing Kulp approach. His brother glanced over, scowling.

'Don't be a fool, Baria!' the mage hissed.

The commander's eyes narrowed. 'Fling magic at me and I'll cut you down,' he said.

Now at closer range, Duiker saw the Otataral links interwoven in Baria's chain armour.

'We shall cut this handful of barbarians down,' Mesker growled, 'then properly announce our arrival in Hissar . . . with the blood of traitors.'

'And five thousand Wickans will avenge the deaths of their kin,' Kulp said. 'And not with quick sword strokes. No, you'll be hung still alive from the sea-wall spikes. For the seagulls to play with. Coltaine's not yet your enemy, Baria. Sheathe your weapons and report to the new Fist, Commander. To do otherwise will be to sacrifice your life and the lives of your soldiers.'

'You ignore me,' Mesker said. 'Baria is not my keeper, Mage.'

Kulp sneered. 'Be silent, pup. Where Baria leads, Mesker follows, or will you now cross blades with your brother?'

'Enough, Mesker,' Baria rumbled.

His brother's tulwar rasped from its scabbard. 'You dare command me!'

The Wickans shouted encouragement. A few brave souls in the crowd behind them laughed.

Mesker's face was sickly with rage.

Baria sighed. 'Brother, this is not the time.'

A mounted troop of Hissar Guard appeared above the heads of the crowd, pushing along the aisles between the market stalls. A chorus of hoots sounded to their left and Duiker and the others turned to see three score Wickan bowmen with arrows nocked and bows drawn on the Red Blades.

Baria slowly raised his left hand, making a twisting gesture. His warriors lowered their own weapons.

Snarling with disgust, Mesker slammed his tulwar back into its wooden scabbard.

'Your escort has arrived,' Kulp said dryly. 'It seems the Fist has been expecting you.'

Duiker stood at the mage's side and watched as Baria led the Red Blades forward to meet the Hissari troop. The historian shook himself. 'Hood's breath, Kulp, that was a chancy cast of the knuckles!'

The man grunted. 'You can always count on Mesker Setral,' he said. 'As brainless as a cat and just as easy to distract. For a moment there I was hoping Baria would accept the challenge – whatever the outcome, there'd be one less Setral, and that's an opportunity missed.'

'Those disguised Wickans,' Duiker said, 'were not part of any official welcome. Coltaine had infiltrated the market.'

'A cunning dog, is Coltaine.'

Duiker shook his head. 'They've shown themselves now.'

'Aye, and showed as well they were ready to lay down their lives to protect the citizens of Hissar.'

'Had Coltaine been here, I doubt he would have ordered those warriors forward, Kulp. Those Wickans were eager for a fight. Defending the market mob had nothing to do with it.'

The mage rubbed his face. 'Best hope the Hissari believe otherwise.'

'Come,' Duiker said, 'let us take wine – I know a place in Imperial Square, and on the way you can tell me how the Seventh has warmed to their new Fist.'

Kulp barked a laugh as they began walking. 'Respect maybe, but no warmth. He's completely changed the drills. We've done one battlefield formation since he arrived, and that was the day he took command.'

Duiker frowned. 'I'd heard that he was working the soldiers to exhaustion, that he didn't even need to enforce the curfew since everyone was so eager for sleep and the barracks were silent as tombs by the eighth bell. If not practising wheels and turtles and shield-walls, then what?'

'The ruined monastery on the hill south of the city – you know the one? Just foundations left except for the central temple, but the chest-high walls cover the entire hilltop like a small city. The sappers have built them up, roofed some of them over. It was a maze of alleys and cul-de-sacs to begin with, but Coltaine had the sappers turn it into a nightmare. I'd wager there's soldiers still wandering around lost in there. The Wickan has us there every afternoon, mock battles, street control, assaulting buildings, break-out tactics, retrieving wounded. Coltaine's warriors act the part of rioting mobs and looters, and I tell you, historian, they were born to it.' He paused for breath. 'Every day . . . we bake under the sun on that bone-bleached hill, broken down to squad level, each squad assigned impossible objectives.' He grimaced. 'Under this new Fist, each soldier of the Seventh has died a dozen times or more in mock battle. Corporal List has been killed in every exercise so far, the poor boy's Hood-addled, and through it all those Wickan savages hoot and howl.'

Duiker said nothing as they continued on their way to Imperial Square. When they entered the Malazan Quarter, the historian finally spoke. 'Something of a rivalry, then, between the Seventh and the Wickan Regiment.'

'Oh, aye, that tactic's obvious enough, but it's going too far, I think. We'll see in a few days' time, when we start getting Wickan Lancer support. There'll be double-crossing, mark my words.'

They strode into the square. 'And you?' Duiker asked. 'What task has Coltaine given the Seventh's last cadre mage?'

'Folly. I conjure illusions all day until my skull's ready to burst.'

'Illusions? In the mock battles?'

'Aye, and it's what makes the objectives so impossible. Believe me, there's been more than one curse thrown my way, Duiker. More than one.'

'What do you conjure, dragons?'

'I wish. I create Malazan refugees, historian. By the hundred. A thousand weighted scarecrows for the soldiers to drag around aren't sufficient for Coltaine, the ones he has me create flee the wrong way, or refuse to leave their homes, or drag furniture and other possessions. Coltaine's orders – my refugees create chaos, and so far cost more lives than any other element in the exercises. I'm not a popular man, Duiker.'

'What of Sormo E'nath?' the historian asked, his mouth suddenly dry.

'The warlock? Nowhere to be seen.'

Duiker nodded to himself. He'd already guessed Kulp's answer to that question. *You're busy reading the stones in the sand, Sormo. Aren't you? While Coltaine hammers the Seventh into shape as guardians to Malazan refugees.* 'Mage,' he said.

'Aye?'

'Dying a dozen times in mock battle is nothing. When it's for real you die but once. Push the Seventh, Kulp. Any way you can. Show Coltaine what the Seventh's capable of – talk it over with the squad leaders. Tonight. Come tomorrow, win your objectives, and I'll talk to Coltaine about a day of rest. Show him, and he'll give it.'

'What makes you so certain?'

Because time's running out and he needs you. He needs you sharp. 'Win your objectives. Leave the Fist to me.'

'Very well, I'll see what I can do.'

Corporal List died within the first few minutes of the mock engagement. Bult, commanding a howling mob of Wickans rampaging down the ruin's main avenue, had personally clouted the hapless Malazan on the side of his head, hard enough to leave the boy sprawled unconscious in the dust. The veteran warrior had then thrown List over one shoulder and carried him from the battle.

Grinning, Bult jogged up the dusty track to the rise from which the new Fist and a few of his officers observed the engagement, and dropped the corporal into the dust at Coltaine's feet. Duiker sighed.

Coltaine glanced around. 'Healer! Attend the boy!'

One of the Seventh's cutters appeared, crouching at the corporal's side.

Coltaine's slitted eyes found Duiker. 'I see no change in this day's proceedings, Historian.'

'It is early yet, Fist.'

The Wickan grunted, returning his attention to the dust-filled ruins. Soldiers were emerging from the chaos, fighters from the Seventh and Wickans, staggering with minor wounds and broken limbs.

Readying his cudgel, Bult scowled. 'You spoke too soon,

133

Coltaine,' he said. 'This one's different.'

There were, Duiker saw, more Wickans among the victims than soldiers of the Seventh, and the ratio was widening with every passing moment. Somewhere in the chaotic clouds of dust, the tide had turned.

Coltaine called for his horse. He swung himself into the saddle and shot Bult a glare. 'Stay here, Uncle. Where are my Lancers?' He waited impatiently as forty horsemen rode onto the rise. Their lances were blunted with bundled strips of leather. For all that, Duiker knew, anything more than a glancing blow from them was likely to break bones.

Coltaine led them at a canter towards the ruins.

Bult spat dust. 'It's about time,' he said.

'What is?' Duiker asked.

'The Seventh's finally earned Lancer support. It's been a week overdue, Historian. Coltaine had expected a toughening, but all we got was a wilting. Who's given them new spines, then? You? Careful or Coltaine'll make you a captain.'

'As much as I'd like to take credit,' Duiker said, 'this is the work of Kulp and the squad sergeants.'

'Kulp's making things easier, then? No wonder they've turned the battle.'

The historian shook his head. 'Kulp follows Coltaine's orders, Bult. If you're looking for a reason to explain your Wickans' defeat, you'll have to look elsewhere. You might start with the Seventh showing their true mettle.'

'Perhaps I shall,' the veteran mused, a glint in his small dark eyes.

'The Fist called you Uncle.'

'Aye.'

'Well? Are you?'

'Am I what?'

Duiker gave up. He was coming to understand the Wickan sense of humour. No doubt there would be another half a dozen or so brisk exchanges before Bult finally relented with an answer. *I could play it through. Or I could let the bastard wait . . . wait for ever, in fact.*

From the dust clouds a score of refugees appeared, wavering strangely as they walked, each of them burdened with impossible possessions – massive dressers, chests, larder-packed cupboards, candlesticks and antique armour. Flanking the mob in a protective cordon were soldiers of the Seventh, laughing and shouting and beating swords on shields as they made good their withdrawal.

Bult barked a laugh. 'My compliments to Kulp when you see him, Historian.'

'The Seventh's earned a day of rest,' Duiker said.

The Wickan raised his hairless brows. 'For one victory?'

'They need to savour it, Commander. Besides, the healers will be busy enough mending bones – you don't want them with exhausted warrens at the wrong time.'

'And the wrong time is soon, is it?'

'I am sure,' Duiker said slowly, 'Sormo E'nath would agree with me.'

Bult spat again. 'My nephew approaches.'

Coltaine and his Lancers had appeared, providing cover for the soldiers, many of whom dragged or carried the scarecrow refugees. The sheer numbers made it clear that victory for the Seventh had been absolute.

'Is that a smile on Coltaine's face?' Duiker asked. 'Just for a moment, I thought I saw . . .'

'Mistaken, no doubt,' Bult growled, but Duiker was coming to know these Wickans, and he detected a hint of humour in the veteran's voice. After a moment Bult continued, 'Take word to the Seventh, Historian. They've earned their day.'

Fiddler sat in darkness. The overgrown garden had closed in around the well and its crescent-shaped stone bench. Above the sapper only a small patch of starlit sky was visible. There was no moon. After a moment he cocked his head. 'You move quietly, lad, I'll give you that.'

Crokus hesitated behind Fiddler, then joined him on the bench. 'Guess you never expected him to pull rank on you like that,' the young man said.

'Is that what it was?'

'That's what it seemed like.'

Fiddler made no reply. The occasional rhizan flitted through the clearing in pursuit of the capemoths hovering above the well-mouth. The cool night air was rank with rotting refuse from beyond the back wall.

'She's upset,' Crokus said.

The sapper shook his head. Upset. 'It was an argument, we weren't torturing prisoners.'

'Apsalar doesn't remember any of that.'

'I do, lad, and those are hard memories to shake.'

'She's just a fishergirl.'

'Most of the time,' Fiddler said. 'But sometimes . . .' He shook his head.

Crokus sighed, then changed the subject. 'So it wasn't part of the plan, then, Kalam going off on his own?'

'Old blood calls, lad. Kalam's Seven Cities born and raised. Besides, he wants to meet this Sha'ik, this desert witch, the Hand of Dryjhna.'

'Now you're taking his side,' Crokus said in quiet exasperation. 'A tenth of a bell ago you nearly accused him of being a traitor . . .'

Fiddler grimaced. 'Confusing times for us all. We've been outlawed by Laseen, but does that make us any less soldiers of the Empire? Malaz isn't the Empress and the Empress isn't Malaz—'

'A moot distinction, I'd say.'

The sapper glanced over. 'Would you now? Ask the girl, maybe she'll explain it.'

'But you're expecting the rebellion. In fact, you're counting on it—'

'Don't mean we have to be the ones who trigger the Whirlwind, though, does it? Kalam wants to be at the heart of things. It's always been his way. This time, the chance literally fell into his lap. The Book of Dryjhna holds the heart of the Whirlwind Goddess – to begin the Apocalypse it needs to be opened, by the Seeress and no-one else. Kalam knows it might well be suicidal, but he'll deliver that Hood-cursed book into Sha'ik's hands, and so add another crack in Laseen's crumbling control. Give him credit for insisting on keeping the rest of us out of it.'

'There you go again, defending him. The plan was to assassinate Laseen, not get caught up in this uprising. It still doesn't make any sense coming to this continent—'

Fiddler straightened, eyes on the stars glittering overhead. Desert stars, sharp diamonds that ever seemed eager to draw blood. 'There's more than one road to Unta, lad. We're here to find one that's probably never been used before and may not even work, but we'll look for it anyway, with Kalam or without him. Hood knows, it might be Kalam's taking the wiser path, overland, down to Aren, by mundane ship back to Quon Tali. Maybe dividing our paths will prove the wisest decision of all, increasing our chances that one of us at least will make it through.'

'Right,' Crokus snapped, 'and if Kalam doesn't make it? You'll go after Laseen yourself? A glorified ditch-digger, and long in the tooth at that. You hardly inspire confidence, Fiddler. We're still supposed to be taking Apsalar home.'

Fiddler's voice was cold. 'Don't push me, lad. A few years pilfering purses on Darujhistan's streets don't qualify you to cast judgement on me.'

Branches thrashed in the tree opposite the two men, and Moby appeared, hanging one-armed, a rhizan struggling its jaws. The familiar's eyes glittered as bones crunched. Fiddler grunted. 'Back in Quon Tali,' he said slowly, 'we'll find more supporters than you might imagine. No-one's indispensable, nor should anyone be dismissed as useless. Like it or not, lad, you've some growing up to do.'

'You think me stupid but you're wrong. You think I'm blind to the fact that you're thinking you've got *another* shaved knuckle in the hole and I don't mean Quick Ben. Kalam's an assassin who just might be good enough to get to Laseen. But if he doesn't, there's another one who just might still have in her the skills of a god – but not any old god, no, the *Patron* of Assassins, the one you call the Rope. So you keep prodding her – you're taking her home because she isn't what she once was, but the truth is, you *want the old one back*.'

Fiddler was silent for a long time, watching Moby eating the rhizan. When it finally swallowed down the last of the winged lizard, the sapper cleared his throat. 'I don't think that deep,' he said. 'I run on instinct.'

'Are you telling me that using Apsalar didn't occur to you?'

'Not to me, no . . .'

'But Kalam . . .'

Fiddler resisted, then shrugged. 'If he didn't think of it, Quick Ben would have.'

Crokus's hiss was triumphant. 'I knew it. I'm no fool—'

'Oh, Hood's breath, lad, that you're not.'

'I won't let it happen, Fiddler.'

'This bhok'aral of your uncle's,' the sapper said, nodding at Moby, 'it's truly a familiar, a servant to a sorcerer? But if Mammot is dead, why is it still here? I'm no mage, but I thought such familiars were magically . . . fused to their masters.'

'I don't know,' Crokus admitted, his tone retaining an edge that told Fiddler the lad was entirely aware of the sapper's line of thinking. 'Maybe he's just a pet. You'd better pray it's so. I said I wouldn't let you use Apsalar. If Moby's a true familiar, it won't just be me you'll have to get past.'

'I won't be trying anything, Crokus,' Fiddler said. 'But I still say you've some growing up to do. Sooner or later it will occur to you that you can't speak for Apsalar. She'll do what she decides, like it or not. The possession may be over, but the god's skills remain in her bones.' He slowly turned and faced the boy. 'What if she decides to put those skills to use?'

'She won't,' Crokus said, but the assurance was gone from his voice. He gestured and Moby flapped sloppily into his arms. 'What did you call him – a bhoka . . . ?'

'Bhok'aral. They're native to this land.'

'Oh.'

'Get some sleep, lad, we're leaving tomorrow.'

'So is Kalam.'

'Aye, but we won't be in each other's company. Parallel paths southward, at least to start with.'

He watched Crokus head back inside, Moby clinging to the lad like a child. *Hood's breath, I'm not looking forward to this journey.*

A hundred paces inside the Caravan Gate was a square in which the land traders assembled before leaving Ehrlitan. Most would strike south along the raised coastal road, following the line of the bay. Villages and outposts were numerous on this route, and the Malazan-built cobble road itself was well patrolled, or, rather, would have been had not the city's Fist recalled the garrisons.

As far as Fiddler could learn in speaking with various merchants and caravan guards, few bandits had yet to take advantage of the troop withdrawal, but from the swollen ranks among the mercenary guards accompanying each caravan, it was clear to the sapper that the merchants were taking no chances.

It would have been fruitless for the three Malazans to disguise themselves as merchants on their journey south; they had neither the coin nor the equipment to carry out such a masquerade. With travel between cities as risky as it now was, they had chosen to travel in the guise of pilgrims. To the most devout, the Path of the Seven – pilgrimage to each of the seven Holy Cities – was a respected display of faith. Pilgrimage was at the heart of this land's tradition, impervious to the threat of bandits, or war.

Fiddler retained his Gral disguise, playing the role of guardian and guide to Crokus and Apsalar – two young, newly married believers embarking on a journey that would bless their union under the Seven Heavens. Each would be mounted, Fiddler on a Gral-bred horse disdainful of the sapper's imposture and viciously tempered, Crokus and Apsalar on well-bred mounts purchased from one of the better stables outside Ehrlitan. Three spare horses and four mules completed the train.

Kalam had left with the dawn, offering Fiddler and the others only a terse farewell. The words that had been exchanged the night before sullied the moment of departure. The sapper understood Kalam's hunger to wound Laseen through the blood spilled by rebellion, but the potential damage to the Empire – and to whoever assumed the throne following Laseen's fall – was, to Fiddler's mind, too great a risk. They'd clashed hard, then, and Fiddler was left feeling nicked and blunted by the exchange.

There was pathos in that parting, Fiddler belatedly realized, for it seemed that the duty that once bound him and Kalam together, to a single cause which was as much friendship as anything else, had been sundered. And for the moment, at least, there was nothing to take its place within Fiddler. He was left feeling lost, more alone than he had been in years.

They would be among the last of the trains to leave through Caravan Gate. As Fiddler checked the girth straps on the mules one final time, the sound of galloping horses drew his attention.

A troop of six Red Blades had arrived, slowing their mounts as they entered the square. Fiddler glanced over to where Crokus and Apsalar stood beside their horses. Catching the lad's eye, he shook his head, resumed adjusting the mule's girth strap.

The soldiers were looking for someone. The troop split, a rider each heading for one of the remaining trains. Fiddler heard hoofs clumping on cobbles behind him, forced himself to remain calm.

'Gral!'

Pausing to spit as a tribesman would at the accosting of a Malazan lapdog, he slowly turned.

Beneath the helm's rim, the Red Blade's dark face had tightened in response to the gesture. 'One day the Red Blades will cleanse the hills of Gral,' he promised, his smile revealing dull grey teeth.

Fiddler's only reply was a snort. 'If you have something worthy of being said, Red Blade, speak. Our shadows are already too short for the leagues we travel this day.'

'A measure of your incompetence, Gral. I have but one question to ask. Answer truthfully, for I shall know if you lie. We would know if a man on a roan stallion rode out alone this morning, through Caravan Gate.'

'I saw no such man,' Fiddler replied, 'but I now wish him well. May the Seven Spirits guard him for all his days.'

The Red Blade snarled. 'I warn you, your blood is no armour against me, Gral. You were here with the dawn?'

Fiddler returned to the mules. 'One question,' he grated. 'You pay for more with coin, Red Blade.'

The soldier spat at Fiddler's feet, jerked his mount's head around and rode to rejoin the troop.

Beneath his desert veil, Fiddler allowed himself a thin smile. Crokus appeared beside him.

'What was that about?' he demanded in a hiss.

The sapper shrugged. 'The Red Blades are hunting someone. Not anything to do with us. Get back to your horse, lad. We're leaving.'

'Kalam?'

His forearms resting on the mule's back, Fiddler hesitated, squinting against the glare bouncing from the bleached cobbles. 'It may have reached them that the holy tome's no longer in Aren. And someone's delivering it to Sha'ik. No-one knows Kalam is here.'

Crokus looked unconvinced. 'He met someone last night, Fiddler.'

'An old contact who owes him.'

'Giving him reason to betray Kalam. No-one likes being reminded of debts.'

Fiddler said nothing. After a moment he patted the mule's back, raising a faint puff of dust, then went to his horse. The Gral gelding showed its teeth as he reached for the reins. He gripped the bridle under the animal's chin. It tried tossing its head but he held firm, leaned close. 'Show some manners, you ugly bastard, or you'll live to regret it.' Gathering the reins, he pulled himself up into the high-backed saddle.

Beyond Caravan Gate the coastal road stretched south-ward, level despite the gentle rise and fall of the sandstone cliffs that overlooked the bay on the west side. On their left and a league inland ran the Arifal Hills. The jagged serrations of Arifal would follow them all the way to the Eb River, thirty-six leagues to the south. Barely tamed tribes dwelt in those hills, pre-eminent among them the Gral. Fiddler's greatest worry was running into a real Gral tribesman. The chance of that was diminished somewhat given the season, for the Gral would be driving their goats deep into the range, where both shade and water could be found.

They nudged their mounts into a canter and rode past a merchant's train to avoid the trailing dust clouds, then Fiddler settled them back into a slow trot. The day's heat was already building. Their destination was a small village called Salik, a little over eight leagues distant, where they would stop to eat the midday meal and wait out the hottest hours before continuing on to the Trob River.

If all went well, they would reach G'danisban in a week's time. Fiddler expected Kalam to be two, maybe even three days ahead of them by then. Beyond G'danisban was the Pan'potsun Odhan, a sparsely populated wasteland of desiccated hills, the skeletal ruins of long-dead cities, poisonous snakes, biting flies and – he recalled the Spiritwalker Kimloc's words – the potential of something far deadlier. *A convergence. Togg's feet, I don't like that thought at all.* He thought about the conch shell in his leather pack. Carrying an item of power was never a wise thing. *Probably more trouble than it's worth. What if some Soletaken sniffs it out, decides it wants it for its collection?* He scowled. *A collection easily built on with one conch shell and three shiny skulls.*

The more he thought on it, the more uneasy he became. *Better to sell it to some merchant in G'danisban. The extra coin could prove useful.* The thought settled him. He would sell the conch, be rid of it. While no-one would deny a Spiritwalker's power, it was likely dangerous to lean too heavily on it. The Tano priests gave up their lives in the name of peace. *Or worse. Kimloc surrendered his honour. Better to rely on the Moranth incendiaries in my pack than on any mysterious shell. A Flamer will burn a Soletaken as easily as anyone else.*

Crokus rode up alongside the sapper. 'What are you thinking, Fiddler?'

'Nothing. Where's that bhok'aral of yours?'

The young man frowned. 'I don't know. I guess he was just a pet after all. Went off last night and never came back.' He wiped the back of his hand across his face and Fiddler saw smeared tears on his cheeks. 'I sort of felt Mammot was with me, with Moby.'

'Was your uncle a good man, before the Jaghut Tyrant took him?'

Crokus nodded.

Fiddler grunted. 'Then he's with you still. Moby probably sniffed kin in the air. More than a few highborn keep bhok'ar-ala as pets in the city. Just a pet after all.'

'I suppose you're right. For most of my life I thought of Mammot as just a scholar, an old man always scribbling on scrolls. My uncle. But then I found out he was a High Priest. Important, with powerful friends like Baruk. But before I could even come to terms with that, he was dead. Destroyed by your squad—'

'Hold on there, lad! What we killed wasn't your uncle. Not any more.'

'I know. In killing him you saved Darujhistan. I know, Fiddler . . .'

'It's done, Crokus. And you should realize, an uncle who took care of you and loved you is more important than his being a High Priest. And he would have told you the same, I imagine, if he'd had the chance.'

'But don't you see? He had *power*, Fiddler, but he didn't do a damn thing with it! Just hid in his tiny room in a crumbling tenement! He could have owned an estate, sat on the Council, made a difference . . .'

Fiddler wasn't ready to take on that argument. He'd never had any skill with counsel. *Got no advice worth giving anyway.* 'Did she kick you up here for being so moody, lad?'

Crokus's face darkened, then he spurred forward, taking point position.

Sighing, Fiddler twisted in the saddle and eyed Apsalar, riding a few paces behind. 'Lovers' spat, is it?'

She blinked owlishly.

Fiddler swung back, settling in the saddle. 'Hood's balls,' he muttered under his breath.

Iskaral Pust poked the broom farther up the chimney and frantically scrubbed. Black clouds descended onto the hearth-stone and settled on the High Priest's grey robes.

'You have wood?' Mappo asked from the raised stone platform he had been using as a bed and was now sitting on.

Iskaral paused. 'Wood? Wood's better than a broom?'

'For a fire,' the Trell said. 'To take out the chill of this chamber.'

'Wood! No, of course not. But dung, oh yes, plenty of dung. A fire! Excellent. Burn them into a crisp! Are Trell known for cunning? No recollection of that, none among the rare mention of Trell this, Trell that. Finding writings on an illiterate people very difficult. Hmm.'

'Trell are quite literate,' Mappo said. 'Have been for some time. Seven, eight centuries, in fact.'

'Must update my library, an expensive proposition. Raising shadows to pillage great libraries of the world.' He squatted down at the fireplace, frowning through the soot covering his face.

Mappo cleared his throat. 'Burn what into a crisp, High Priest?'

'Spiders, of course. This temple is rotten with spiders. Kill them on sight, Trell. Use those thick-soled feet, those leathery hands. Kill them all, do you understand?'

Nodding, Mappo pulled the fur blanket closer around him, wincing only slightly as the hide brushed the puckered wounds on the back of his neck. The fever had broken, as much due to his own reserves as, he suspected, the dubious medicines

145

applied by Iskaral's silent servant. The fangs and claws of D'ivers and Soletaken bred a singularly virulent sickness, often culminating in hallucinations, bestial madness, then death. For many who survived, the madness remained, reappearing on a regular basis for one or two nights nine or ten times each year. It was a madness often characterized by murder.

Iskaral Pust believed Mappo had escaped that fate, but the Trell would not himself be confident of that until at least two cycles of the moon had passed without sign of any symptoms. He did not like to think what he would be capable of when gripped in a murderous rage. Many years ago among the warband ravaging the Jhag Odhan, Mappo had willed himself into such a state, as warriors often did, and his memories of the deaths he delivered remained with him and always would.

If the Soletaken's poison was alive within him, Mappo would take his own life rather than unleash its will.

Iskaral Pust stabbed the broom into each corner of the small mendicant's chamber that was the Trell's quarters, then reached up to the ceiling corners to do the same. 'Kill what bites, kill what stings, this sacred precinct of Shadow must be pristine! Kill all that slithers, all that scuttles. You were examined for vermin, the both of you, oh yes. No unwelcome visitors permitted. Lye baths were prepared, but nothing on either of you. I remain suspicious, of course.'

'Have you resided here long, High Priest?'

'No idea. Irrelevant. Importance lies solely in the deeds done, the goals achieved. Time is preparation, nothing more. One prepares for as long as is required. To do this is to accept that planning begins at birth. You are born and before all else you are plunged into shadow, wrapped inside the holy ambivalence, there to suckle sweet sustenance. I live to prepare, Trell, and the preparations are nearly complete.'

'Where is Icarium?'

'A life given for a life taken, tell him that. In the library.

146

The nuns left but a handful of books. Tomes devoted to pleasuring themselves. Best read in bed, I find. The rest of the material is mine, a scant collection, dreadful paucity, I am embarrassed. Hungry?'

Mappo shook himself. The High Priest's rambles had a hypnotic quality. Each question the Trell voiced was answered with a bizarre rambling monologue that seemed to drain him of will beyond the utterance of yet another question. True to his assertions, Iskaral Pust could make the passing of time meaningless. 'Hungry? Aye.'

'Servant prepares food.'

'Can he bring it to the library?'

The High Priest scowled. 'Collapse of etiquette. But if you insist.'

The Trell pushed himself upright. 'Where is the library?'

'Turn right, proceed thirty-four paces, turn right again, twelve paces, then through door on the right, thirty-five paces, through archway on right another eleven paces, turn right one last time, fifteen paces, enter the door on the right.'

Mappo stared at Iskaral Pust.

The High Priest shifted nervously.

'Or,' the Trell said, eyes narrowed, 'turn left, nineteen paces.'

'Aye,' Iskaral muttered.

Mappo strode to the door. 'I shall take the short route, then.'

'If you must,' the High Priest growled as he bent to close examination of the broom's ragged end.

The breach of etiquette was explained when, upon entering the library, Mappo saw that the squat chamber also served as kitchen. Icarium sat at a robust black-stained table a few paces to the Trell's right, while Servant hunched over a cauldron suspended by chain over a hearth a pace to Mappo's left. Servant's head was almost invisible inside a cloud of steam, drenched in condensation and dripping into the cauldron as he worked a wooden ladle in slow, turgid circles.

'I shall pass on the soup, I think,' Mappo said to the man.

'These books are rotting,' Icarium said, leaning back and eyeing Mappo. 'You are recovered?'

'So it seems.'

Still studying the Trell, Icarium frowned. 'Soup? Ah,' his expression cleared, 'not soup. Laundry. You'll find more palatable fare on the carving table.' He gestured to the wall behind Servant, then returned to the mouldering pages of an ancient book opened before him. 'This is astonishing, Mappo . . .'

'Given how isolated those nuns were,' Mappo said as he approached the carving table, 'I'm surprised you're astonished.'

'Not those books, friend. Iskaral's own. There are works here whose existence was but the faintest rumour. And some – like this one – that I have never heard of before. *A Treatise on Irrigation Planning in the Fifth Millennium of Ararkal*, by no fewer than four authors.'

Returning to the library table with a pewter plate piled high with bread and cheese, Mappo leant over his friend's shoulder to examine the detailed drawings on the book's vellum pages, then the strange, braided script. The Trell grunted. Mouth suddenly dry, he managed to mutter, 'What is so astonishing about that?'

Icarium leaned back. 'The sheer . . . frivolity, Mappo. The materials alone for this tome are a craftsman's annual wage. No scholar in their right mind would waste such resources – never mind their time – on such a pointless, trite subject. And this is not the only example. Look, *Seed Dispersal Patterns of the Purille Flower on the Skar Archipelago*, and here, *Diseases of White-Rimmed Clams of Lekoor Bay*. And I am convinced that these works are thousands of years old. Thousands.'

And in a language I never knew you would recognize, much less understand. He recalled when he'd last seen such a script, beneath a hide canopy on a hill that marked his tribe's northernmost border. He'd been among a handful of guards escorting the tribe's elders to what would prove a fateful summons.

Autumn rains drumming overhead, they had squatted in a half-circle, facing north, and watched as seven robed and hooded figures approached. Each held a staff, and as they strode beneath the canopy and stood in silence before the elders, Mappo saw, with a shiver, how those staves seemed to writhe before his eyes, the wood like serpentine roots, or perhaps those parasitic trees that entwined the boles of others, choking the life from them. Then he realized that the twisted madness of the shafts was in fact runic etching, ever changing, as if unseen hands continually carved words anew with every breath's span.

Then one among them withdrew its hood, and so began the moment that would change Mappo's future path. His thoughts jerked away from the memory.

Trembling, the Trell sat down, clearing a space for his plate. 'Is all this important, Icarium?'

'Significant, Mappo. The civilization that brought forth these works must have been appallingly rich. The language is clearly related to modern Seven Cities dialects, although in some ways more sophisticated. And see this symbol, here in the spine of each such tome? A twisted staff. I have seen that symbol before, friend. I am certain of it.'

'Rich, you said?' The Trell struggled to drag the conversation away from what he knew to be a looming precipice. 'More like mired in minutiae. Probably explains why it's dust and ashes. Arguing over seeds in the wind while barbarians batter down the gates. Indolence takes many forms, but it comes to every civilization that has outlived its will. You know that as well as I. In this case it was an indolence characterized by a pursuit of knowledge, a frenzied search for answers to everything, no matter the value of such answers. A civilization can as easily drown in what it knows as in what it doesn't know. Consider,' he continued, 'Gothos's Folly. Gothos's curse was in being too aware – of everything. Every permutation, every potential. Enough to poison every scan he cast on the world. It availed him naught, and worse, he was aware of even that.'

'You must be feeling better,' Icarium said wryly. 'Your pessimism has revived. In any case, these works support my belief that the many ruins in Raraku and the Pan'potsun Odhan are evidence that a thriving civilization once existed here. Indeed, perhaps the first true human civilization, from which all others were born.'

Leave this path of thought, Icarium. Leave it now. 'And how does this knowledge avail us in our present situation?'

Icarium's expression soured slightly. 'My obsession with time, of course. Writing replaces memory, you see, and the language itself changes because of it. Think of my mechanisms, in which I seek to measure the passage of hours, days, years. Such measurings are by nature cyclic, repetitive. Words and sentences once possessed the same rhythms, and could thus be locked into one's mind and later recalled with absolute precision. Perhaps,' he mused after a moment, 'if I was illiterate I would not be so forgetful.' He sighed, forced a smile. 'Besides, I was but passing time, Mappo.'

The Trell tapped one blunt, wrinkled finger on the open book. 'I imagine the authors of this would have defended their efforts with the same words, friend. I have a more pressing concern.'

The Jhag's expression was cool, not completely masking amusement. 'And that is?'

Mappo gestured. 'This place. Shadow does not list among my favourite cults. Nest of assassins and worse. Illusion and deceit and betrayal. Iskaral Pust affects a harmless façade, but I

150

am not fooled. He was clearly expecting us, and anticipates our involvement in whatever schemes he plans. We risk much in lingering here.'

'But Mappo,' Icarium said slowly, 'it is precisely here, in this place, that my goal shall be achieved.'

The Trell winced. 'I feared you would say that. Now you shall have to explain it to me.'

'I cannot, friend. Not yet. What I hold are suspicions, nothing more. When I am certain, I shall feel confident enough to explain. Can you be patient with me?'

In his mind's eye he saw another face, this one human, thin and pale, raindrops tracking runnels down the withered cheeks. Flat, grey eyes reaching up, finding Mappo's own beyond the rim of elders. 'Do you know us?' The voice was a rasp of rough leather.

An elder had nodded. 'We know you as the Nameless Ones.'

'It is well,' the man replied, eyes still fixed on Mappo's own. 'The Nameless Ones, who think not in years, but in centuries. Chosen warrior,' he continued, addressing Mappo, 'what can you learn of patience?'

Like rooks bursting from a copse, the memories fled. Staring at Icarium, Mappo managed a smile, revealing his gleaming canines. 'Patient? I can be nothing else with you. Nonetheless, I do not trust Iskaral Pust.'

Servant began removing sopping clothes and bedding from the cauldron, using his bare hands as he squeezed steaming water from the bundles. Watching him, the Trell frowned. One of Servant's arms was strangely pink, unweathered, almost youthful. The other more befitted the man's evident age, thickly muscled, hairy and tanned.

'Servant?'

The man did not look up.

'Can you speak?' Mappo continued.

'It seems,' Icarium said when Servant made no response,

'that he's turned a deaf ear to us, by his Master's command, I'd warrant. Shall we explore this temple, Mappo? Bearing in mind that every shadow is likely to echo our words as a whisper in the High Priest's ears.'

'Well,' the Trell growled as he rose, 'it is of little concern to me that Iskaral knows of my distrust.'

'He surely knows more of us than we do of him,' Icarium said, also rising.

As they left, Servant was still twisting water from the cloth with something like savage joy, the veins thick on his massive forearms.

CHAPTER FOUR

In a land where
Seven cities rose in gold,
Even the dust has eyes

Debrahl Saying

A crowd of dusty, sweat-smeared men gathered around as the last of the bodies were removed. The dust cloud hung unmoving over the mine entrance as it had for most of the morning, since the collapse of the reach at the far end of Deep Mine. Under Beneth's command the slaves had worked frantically to retrieve the thirty-odd companions buried in the fall.

None had survived. Expressionless, Felisin watched with a dozen other slaves from the rest ramp at Twistings Mouth while they awaited the arrival of refilled water casks. The heat had turned even the deepest reaches of the mines into sweltering, dripping ovens. Slaves were collapsing by the score every hour below ground.

On the other side of the pit, Heboric tilled the parched earth of Deepsoil. It was his second week there and the cleaner air and the relief from pulling stone carts had improved his health. A shipment of limes delivered at Beneth's command had helped as well.

Had she not seen to his transfer, Heboric would now be

dead, his body crushed under tons of rock. He owed her his life.

The realization brought Felisin little satisfaction. They rarely spoke to each other any more. Head clouded with durhang smoke, it was all Felisin could do to drag herself home from Bula's each night. She slept long hours but gained no rest. The days working in Twistings passed in a long, numb haze. Even Beneth had complained that her lovemaking had become . . . torpid.

The thuds and grunts of the water carts on the pitted work road grew louder, but Felisin could not pull her gaze from the rescuers as they laid out the mangled corpses to await the body wagon. A faint residue of pity clung to what she could see of the scene, but even that seemed too much of an effort, never mind pulling away her eyes.

For all her dulled responses, she went to Beneth, wanting to be used, more and more often. She sought him out when he was drunk, weaving and generous, when he offered her to his friends, to Bula and to other women.

You're numb, girl, Heboric had said one of the few times he'd addressed her. *Yet your thirst for feeling grows, until even pain will do. But you're looking in the wrong places.*

Wrong places. What did he know of wrong places? The far reach of Deep Mine was a wrong place. The Shaft, where the bodies would be dumped, that was a wrong place. *Everywhere else is just a shade of good enough.*

She was ready to move in with Beneth, punctuating the choices she'd made. In a few days, perhaps. Next week. Soon. She'd made such an issue of her own independence, but it was proving not so great a task to surrender it after all.

'Lass.'

Blinking, Felisin looked up. It was the young Malazan guard, the one who'd warned Beneth once . . . *long ago.*

The soldier grinned. 'Find the quote yet?'

'What?'

154

'From Kellanved's writings, girl.' The boy was frowning now. 'I suggested you find someone who knew the rest of the passage I quoted.'

'I don't know what you're talking about.'

He reached down, the calluses ridging the index finger and thumb of his sword hand scraping her chin and jawline as he raised her face. She winced in the bright light when he pushed her hair back. 'Durhang,' he whispered. 'Queen's heart, girl, you look ten years older than the last time I saw you, and when was that? Two weeks back.'

'Ask Beneth,' she mumbled, pulling her head away from his touch.

'Ask him what?'

'For me. In your bed. He'll say yes, but only if he's drunk. He'll be drunk tonight. He grieves for the dead with a jug. Or two. Touch me then.'

He straightened. 'Where's Heboric?'

'Heboric? Deepsoil.' She thought to ask why he wanted him instead of her, but the question drifted away. He could touch her tonight. She'd grown to like calluses.

Beneth was paying Captain Sawark a visit and he'd decided to take her with him. He was looking to make a deal, Felisin belatedly realized, and he'd offer her to the captain as an incentive.

They approached Rathole Round from Work Road, passing Bula's Inn where half a dozen off-duty Dosii guards lounged around the front door, their bored gazes tracking them.

'Walk a straight line, lass,' Beneth grumbled, taking her arm. 'And stop dragging your feet. It's what you like, isn't it? Always wanting more.'

An undercurrent of disgust had come to his tone when he spoke to her. He'd stopped making promises. *I'll make you my own, girl. Move in with me. We won't need anyone else.* Those gruff, whispered assurances had vanished. The realization did not bother Felisin. She'd never really believed Beneth anyway.

Directly ahead, Sawark's Keep rose squat from the centre of Rathole Round, its huge, rough-cut blocks of stone stained from the greasy smoke that never really left Skullcup. A lone guard stood outside the entrance, a pike held loosely in one hand. 'Hard luck,' he said once they were near.

'What is?' Beneth demanded.

The soldier shrugged. 'This morning's cave-in, what else?'

'We might've saved some,' Beneth said, 'if Sawark had sent us some help.'

'Saved some? What's the point? Sawark's not in the mood if you've come here to complain.' The man's flat eyes flicked to Felisin. 'If you're here with a gift, that would be another matter.' The guard opened the heavy door. 'He's in the office.'

Beneth grunted. Tugging at Felisin's arm, he dragged her through the portal. The ground floor was an armoury, weapons lining the walls in locked racks. A table and three chairs were off to one side, the leavings of the guards' breakfast crowding the small tabletop. Up from the room's centre rose an iron staircase.

They ascended a single flight to Sawark's office. The captain sat behind a desk that seemed cobbled together from driftwood. His chair was plushly padded with a high back. A large, leather-bound tally book was opened before him. Sawark set down his quill and leaned back.

Felisin could not recall ever having seen the captain before. He made a point of remaining aloof, isolated here within his tower. The man was thin, devoid of fat, the muscles on his bared forearms like twisted cables under pale skin. Against the present fashion, he was bearded, the wiry black ringlets oiled and scented. The hair on his head was cut short. Watery green eyes glittered from a permanent squint above high cheekbones. His wide mouth was bracketed in deep downturned lines. He stared steadily at Beneth, ignoring Felisin as if she was not there.

Beneth pushed her down in a chair close to one wall, on Sawark's left, then sat himself down in the lone chair directly facing the captain. 'Ugly rumours, Sawark. Want to hear them?'

The captain's voice was soft. 'What will that cost me?'

'Nothing. These are free.'

'Go on, then.'

'The Dosii are talking loud at Bula's. Promising the Whirlwind.'

Sawark scowled. 'More of that nonsense. No wonder you give me this news free, Beneth, it's worthless.'

'So I too thought at the beginning, but—'

'What else have you to tell me?'

Beneth's eyes dropped to the ledger on the desk. 'You've tallied this morning's dead? Did you find the name you sought?'

'I sought no particular name, Beneth. You think you've guessed something, but there's nothing there. I'm losing patience.'

'There were four mages among the victims—'

'Enough! Why are you here?'

Beneth shrugged, as if tossing away whatever suspicions he held. 'A gift,' he said, gesturing to Felisin. 'Very young. Docile, but ever eager. No spirit to resist – do whatever you want, Sawark.'

The captain's scowl darkened.

'In exchange,' Beneth continued, 'I wish the answer to a single question. The slave Baudin was arrested this morning – why?'

Felisin blinked. Baudin? She shook her head, trying to clear it of the fog that marked her waking hours. Was this important?

'Arrested in Whipcord Lane after curfew. He got away but

one of my men recognized him and so the arrest was effected this morning.' Sawark's watery gaze finally swung to Felisin. 'Very young, you said? Eighteen, nineteen? You're getting old, Beneth, if you call that very young.'

She felt his eyes exploring her like ghost hands. This time, the sensation was anything but pleasing. She fought back a shiver.

'She's fifteen, Sawark. But experienced. Arrived but two transports ago.'

The captain's eyes sharpened on her, and she watched, wondering, as all the blood drained from his face.

Beneth surged to his feet. 'I'll send another. Two young girls from the last shipment.' He stepped close to Felisin and pulled her upright. 'I guarantee your satisfaction, Captain. They'll be here within the hour—'

'Beneth.' Sawark's voice was soft. 'Baudin works for you, does he not?'

'An acquaintance, Sawark. Not one of my trusted ones. I asked because he's on my reach crew. One less strong man will slow us if you're still holding him tomorrow.'

'Live with it, Beneth.'

Neither one believes the other. The thought was like a glimmer of long-lost awareness in Felisin. She drew a deep breath. *Something's happening. I need to think about it. I need to be listening. Listening, right now.*

In answer to Sawark's suggestion, Beneth sighed heavily. 'I shall have to do just that, then. Until later, Captain.'

Felisin did not resist as Beneth propelled her towards the stairs. Once outside he pulled her across the Round, not answering the Keep guard as the man said something in a sneering tone. Breathing hard, Beneth dragged her into the shadows of an alley, then swung her around.

His voice was a harsh rasp. 'Who are you, girl, his long-lost daughter? Hood's breath! Clear your wits! Tell me what happened just now in that office! Baudin? What's Baudin to you? Answer me!'

'He's – he's nothing—'

The back of his hand when it struck her face was like a sack of rocks. Light exploded behind Felisin's eyes as she sprawled sideways. Blood streamed from her nose as she lay unmoving in the alley's rotting refuse. Staring dumbly at the ground six inches away, she watched the red pool spread in the dust.

Beneth dragged her upright and threw her up against a wood-slatted wall. 'Your full name, lass. Tell me!'

'Felisin,' she mumbled. 'Just that—'

Snarling, he raised his hand again.

She stared at the marks her teeth had left just above the knuckles. 'No! I swear it! I was a foundling—'

Disbelief crazed his eyes. 'A *what?*'

'Found outside the Fener Monastery on Malaz Island – the Empress made accusations – followers of Fener. Heboric—'

'Your ship came from Unta, lass. What do you take me for? You're nobleborn—'

'No! Only well cared for. Please, Beneth, I'm not lying. I don't understand Sawark. Maybe Baudin spun a tale, a lie to save his own skin—'

'Your ship sailed from Unta. You've never even been to Malaz Island. This monastery, near which city?'

'Jakata. There's only two cities on the island. The other's Malaz City, I was sent there for a summer. Schooling. I was in training to be a priestess. Ask Heboric, Beneth. Please.'

'Name me the poorest quarter of Malaz City.'

'Poorest?'

'Name it!'

'I don't know! The Fener Temple is in Dockfront! Is it the poorest? There were slums outside the city, lining the Jakata Road. I was there for but a season, Beneth! And I hardly saw Jakata – we weren't allowed! Please, Beneth, I don't understand any of this! Why are you hurting me? I've done everything you wanted me to do – I slept with your friends, I let you trade me, I made myself *valuable*—'

He struck her again, no longer seeking answers or a way through her frantic lies – a new reason had appeared in his eyes, birthing a bright rage. He beat her systematically, in silent, cold fury. After the first few blows, Felisin curled herself tight around the pain, the shadow-cooled alley dust feeling like a balm where her flesh lay upon it. She struggled to concentrate on her breathing, closing in on that one task, drawing the air in, fighting the waves of agony that came with the effort, then releasing it slowly, a steady stream that carried the pain away.

Eventually she realized that Beneth had stopped, that perhaps he'd only struck her a few times, and that he had left. She was alone in the alley, the thin strip of sky overhead darkening with dusk. She heard occasional voices in the street beyond, but no-one approached the narrow aisle she huddled in.

She woke again later. Apparently she had passed out while crawling towards the alley mouth. The torchlit Work Road was a dozen paces away. Figures ran through her line of sight. Through the constant ringing in her ears, she heard shouts and screams. The air stank of smoke. She thought to resume crawling, then consciousness slipped away again.

Cool cloth brushed her brow. Felisin opened her eyes.

Heboric was bending over her and seemed to be studying her pupils, each in turn. 'You with us, lass?'

Her jaw ached, her lips were crusted together with scabs. She nodded, only now realizing that she was lying in her own bed.

'I'm going to rub some oil on your lips, see if we can prise them open without it hurting too much. You need water.'

She nodded again, and steeled herself against the pain of his ministrations as he dabbed at her mouth with the oil-soaked cloth strapped onto the stub of his left arm. He spoke as he worked. 'Eventful night for us all. Baudin escaped the gaol, lighting a few buildings to flame for diversion. He's hiding somewhere here in Skullcup. No-one tried the cliff walls or Sinker Lake – the cordon of guards lining Beetle Road up top reported no attempts to breach, in any case. Sawark's posted a reward – wants the bastard alive, not least because Baudin went and killed three of his men. I suspect there's more to the tale, what do you think? Then Beneth reports you missing from the Twistings work line this morning, starts me wondering. So I go to talk to him at the midday break – says he last saw you at Bula's last night, says he's cut you loose because you're all used up, sucking more smoke into your lungs than air, as if he ain't to blame for that. But all the while he's talking, I'm studying those cut marks on his knuckles. Beneth was in a fight last night, I see, and the only damage he's sporting is what was done by somebody's teeth. Well, the weeding's done and nobody's keeping an eye on old Heboric, so I spend the afternoon looking, checking alleys, expecting the worst I admit—'

Felisin pushed his arm away. Slowly she opened her mouth, wincing at the pain and feeling the cool prick of reopened gashes. 'Beneth,' she managed. Her chest hurt with every breath.

Heboric's eyes were hard. 'What of him?'

'Tell him . . . from me . . . tell him I'm . . . sorry.'

The old man slowly leaned back.

'I want him . . . to take me back. Tell him. Please.'

Heboric rose. 'Get some rest,' he said in a strangely flat voice as he moved out of her line of sight.

'Water.'

'Coming up, then you sleep.'

'Can't,' she said.

'Why not?'

'Can't sleep . . . without a pipe. Can't.'

She sensed him staring at her. 'Your lungs are bruised. You've some cracked ribs. Will tea do? Durhang tea.'

'Make it strong.'

Hearing him fill a cup of water from the cask, she closed her eyes.

'Clever story, lass,' Heboric said. 'A foundling. Lucky for you I'm quick. I'd say there's a good chance Beneth believes you now.'

'Why? Why do you tell me this?'

'To put you at ease. I guess what I mean is –' he approached with the cup of water between his forearms '– he just might take you back, lass.'

'Oh. I . . . I don't understand you, Heboric.'

He watched her raise the clay cup to her lips. 'No,' he said, 'you do not.'

Like an enormous wall, the sandstorm descended down the west slope of the Estara Hills and approached the coastal road with a deathly moan. While such inland storms were rare on the peninsula, Kalam had faced their wrath before. His first task was to leave the road. It ran too close to the sea cliff in places, and such cliffs were known to collapse.

The stallion complained as he angled him down the road's scree bank. For a thick-muscled, vicious beast, the horse was overfond of comforts. The sands were hot, the footing treacherous with hidden sinkholes. Ignoring the stallion's neck tugs and head-tossing, he drove him down and onto the basin, then kicked the animal into a canter.

A league and a half ahead was Ladro Landing, and beyond that, on the banks of a seasonal river, Ladro Keep. Kalam did not plan on staying there if he could help it. The Keep's commander was Malazan, and so too were his guards. If he could, the assassin would outrun the worst of the storm, hoping to regain the coastal road beyond the Keep, then continue on south to the village of Intesarm.

Keening, the ochre wall drew the horizon on Kalam's left ever closer. The hills had vanished. A turgid gloom curtained the sky. The flap and skitter of fleeing rhizan surrounded him. Hissing a curse, the assassin spurred the stallion into a gallop.

As much as he detested horses in principle, the animal was magnificent when in full stride, seeming to flow effortlessly over the ground with a rhythm forgiving of Kalam's modest skills. He would come no closer to admitting a growing affection towards the stallion.

As he rode, he glanced to see the edge of the storm less than a hundred paces away. There would be no outrunning it. A swirling breaker of whipped sand marked where the wind met the ground. Kalam saw fist-sized rocks in that rolling surf. The wall would crash over them within minutes. Its roar filled the air.

Slightly ahead and on a course that would intercept them, Kalam saw within the ochre cloud a grey stain. He threw himself back in the saddle, sawing the reins. The stallion shrilled, broken out of his rhythm, slewing with his hooves as he stumbled to a stop.

'You'd thank me if you had half a brain,' Kalam snarled. The grey stain was a swarm of chigger fleas. The voracious insects waited for storms like this one, then rode the winds in search of prey. The worst of it was, one could not see them straight on; only from the side were they visible.

As the swarm swept past ahead of them, the storm struck.

The stallion staggered when the wall rolled over them. The world vanished inside a shrieking, whirling ochre haze. Stones and gravel pelted them, drawing flinches from the stallion and grunts of pain from Kalam. The assassin ducked his hooded head and leaned into the wind. Through the slit in his telaba scarf, he squinted ahead, nudging his mount forward at a walk.

He leaned down over the animal's neck, reached out one gloved hand and cupped it over the stallion's left eye to shield it from flying stones and grit. For being out here, the assassin owed him that much.

They continued on for another ten minutes, seeing nothing through the cloak of flying sand. Then the stallion snorted, rearing. Snapping and crunching sounds rose from beneath them. Kalam squinted down. Bones, on all sides. The storm had blown out a graveyard – a common enough occurrence. The assassin regained control of his mount, then tried to pierce the ochre gloom. Ladro Landing was nearby, but he could see nothing. He nudged the stallion forward, the animal stepping daintily around the skeletal clumps.

The coastal road appeared ahead, along with guardhouses flanking what had to be the bridge. The village must be on his right – *if the damned thing hasn't blown away*. Beyond the bridge, then, he would find Ladro Keep.

The single-person guardhouses both gaped empty, like sockets in a massive geometric skull.

His horse stabled, Kalam crossed the compound, leaning against the wind and wincing at the ache in his legs as he approached the keep's gatehouse entrance. Ducking within the alcove, he found himself beyond the storm's howl for the first time in hours. Drifts of fine sand filled the gatehouse's corners, but the dusty air was calm. No guardsman held the post: the lone stone bench was vacant.

Kalam raised the heavy iron ring on the wood door, slamming it down hard. He waited. Eventually he heard the bars being drawn on the other side. The door swung back with a grating sound. An old kitchen servant regarded him with his one good eye.

'Inside, then,' he grumbled. 'Join the others.'

Kalam edged past the old man and found himself in a large

common room. Faces had turned with his entrance. At the far end of the main table, which ran the length of the rectangular chamber, sat four of the keep's guardsmen, Malazans, looking foul-tempered. Three jugs squatted in puddles of wine on the tabletop. To one side, next along the table, was a wiry, sunken-eyed woman, her face painted in a style best left to young maidens. At her side was an Ehrlii merchant, probably the woman's husband.

Kalam bowed to the group, then approached the table. Another servant, this one younger than the doorman by only a few years, appeared with a fresh jug and a goblet, hesitating until the assassin settled on where he would sit – opposite the merchant couple. He set the goblet down and poured Kalam a half-measure, then backed away.

The merchant showed durhang-stained teeth in a welcoming smile. 'Down from the north, then?'

The wine was some kind of herbal concoction, too sweet and cloying for the climate. Kalam set the goblet down, scowling. 'No beer in this hold?'

The merchant's head bobbed. 'Aye, and chilled at that. Alas, only the wine is free, courtesy of our host.'

'Not surprised it's free,' the assassin muttered. He gestured to the servant. 'A tankard of beer, if you please.'

'Costs a sliver,' the servant said.

'Highway robbery, but my thirst is master.' He found a clipped Jakata and set it on the table.

'Has the village fallen into the sea, then?' the merchant asked. 'On your way down from Ehrlitan, how stands the bridge?'

Kalam saw a small velvet bag on the tabletop in front of the merchant's wife. Glancing up, he met her pitted eyes. She gave him a ghastly wink.

'He'll not add to your gossip, Berkru darling. A stranger come in from the storm, is all you'll learn from this one.'

One of the guardsmen raised his head. 'Got something to hide, have ya? Not guarding a caravan, just riding alone? Deserting the Ehrlitan Guard, or maybe spreading the word of Dryjhna, or both. Now here ya come, expecting the hospitality of the Master – Malazan born and bred.'

Kalam eyed the men. Four belligerent faces. Any denial of the sergeant's accusations would not be believed. The guards had decided he belonged in the dungeon for the night at least, something to break the boredom. Yet the assassin was not interested in shedding blood. He laid his hands flat on the table, slowly rose. 'A word with you, Sergeant,' he said. 'In private.'

The man's dark face turned ugly. 'So you can slit my throat?'

'You believe me capable of that?' Kalam asked in surprise. 'You wear chain, you've a sword at your belt. You've three companions who no doubt will stay close – if only to eavesdrop on the words we exchange between us.'

The sergeant rose. 'I can handle you well enough on my own,' he growled. He strode to the back wall.

Kalam followed. He withdrew a small pendant from under his telaba and held it up. 'Do you recognize this, Sergeant?' he asked softly.

Cautiously, the man leaned forward to study the symbol etched on the pendant's flat surface. Recognition paled his features as he involuntarily mouthed, 'Clawmaster.'

'An end to your questions and accusations, Sergeant. Do not reveal what you now know to your men – at least until after I am gone. Understood?'

The sergeant nodded. 'Pardon, sir,' he whispered.

Kalam hooked a half-smile. 'Your unease is earned. Hood's about to stride this land, and you and I both know it. You erred today, but do not relax your mistrust. Does the Keep Commander understand the situation beyond these walls?'

'Aye, he does.'

The assassin sighed. 'Makes you and your squad among the lucky ones, Sergeant.'

'Aye.'

'Shall we return to the table now?'

The sergeant simply shook his head in answer to his squad's querying expressions.

As Kalam returned to his beer, the merchant's wife reached for the velvet bag. 'The soldiers have each requested a reading of their futures,' she said, revealing a Deck of Dragons. She held the deck in both hands, her unblinking eyes on the assassin. 'And you? Would you know of your future, stranger? Which gods smile upon you, which gods frown—'

'The gods have little time or inclination to spare us any note,' Kalam said with contempt. 'Leave me out of your games, woman.'

'So you cow the sergeant,' she said, smiling, 'and now seek to cow me. See the fear your words have wrought in me? I shake with terror.'

With a disgusted snort, Kalam slid his gaze away.

The common room boomed as the front door was assailed.

'More mysterious travellers!' the woman cackled.

Everyone watched as the doorman reappeared from a side chamber and shuffled towards the door. Whoever waited outside was impatient – thunder rang imperiously through the room even as the old man reached for the bar.

As soon as the bar cleared the latch, the door was pushed hard. The doorman stumbled back. Two armoured figures appeared, the first one a woman. Metal rustled and boots thumped as she strode into the centre of the chamber. Flat eyes surveyed the guards and the other guests, held briefly on each of them before continuing on. Kalam saw no special attention accorded him.

The woman had once held rank – perhaps she still did, although her accoutrements and colours announced no present status; nor was the man behind her wearing anything like a uniform.

Kalam saw weals on both their faces and smiled to himself. They'd run into chigger fleas, and neither looked too pleased about it. The man jerked suddenly as one bit him somewhere beneath his hauberk, cursing, he began loosening the armour's straps.

'No,' the woman snapped.

The man stopped.

She was Pardu, a southern plains tribe; her companion had the look of a northerner – possibly Ehrlii. His dusky skin was a shade paler than the woman's and bare of any tribal tattooing.

'Hood's breath!' the sergeant snarled at the woman. 'Not another step closer! You're both crawling with chiggers. Take the far end of the table. One of the servants will prepare a cedar-chip bath – though that will cost you.'

For a moment the woman seemed ready to resist, but then she gestured to the unoccupied end of the table with one gloved hand and her companion responded by pulling two chairs back before seating himself stiffly in one of them. The Pardu took the other. 'A flagon of beer,' she said.

'The Master charges for that,' Kalam said, giving her a wry smile.

'The Seven's fate! The cheap bastard – you, servant! Bring me a tankard and I'll judge if it's worth any coin. Quickly now!'

'The woman thinks this a tavern,' one of the guards said.

The sergeant spoke. 'You're here by the grace of this Keep's commander. You'll pay for the beer, you'll pay for the bath, and you'll pay for sleeping on this floor.'

'And this is grace?'

The sergeant's expression darkened – he was Malazan, and he shared the room with a Clawmaster. 'The four walls, the ceiling, the hearth and the use of the stables are free, woman.

Yet you complain like a virgin princess – accept the hospitality or be gone.'

The woman's eyes narrowed, then she removed a handful of jakatas from a belt pouch and slammed them on the tabletop. 'I gather,' she said smoothly, 'that your gracious master charges even *you* for beer, Sergeant. So be it, I've no choice but to buy everyone here a tankard.'

'Generous,' the sergeant said with a stiff nod.

'The future shall now be prised loose,' the merchant's wife said, trimming the Deck.

Kalam saw the Pardu flinch upon seeing the cards.

'Spare us,' the assassin said. 'There's nothing to be gained from seeing what's to come, assuming you've any talent at all, which I doubt. Save us all from the embarrassment of your performance.'

Ignoring him, the old woman angled herself to face the guardsmen. 'All your fates rest upon . . . this!' She laid out the first card.

Kalam barked a laugh.

'Which one is that?' one of the guards demanded.

'Obelisk,' Kalam said. 'The woman's a fake. As any seer of talent would know, that card's inactive in Seven Cities.'

'An expert in divination, are you?' the old woman snapped.

'I visit a worthy seer before any overland journey,' Kalam replied. 'It would be foolish to do otherwise. I know the Deck, and I've seen when the reading was true, when power showed the hand. No doubt you intended to charge these guardsmen once the reading was done, once you'd told them how rich they were going to become, how they'd live to ripe old ages, fathering heroes by the score—'

Her expression unveiling the charade's end, the old woman screamed with rage and flung the Deck at Kalam. It struck him on the chest, cards clattering on the tabletop in a wild scatter – which settled into a pattern.

The breath hissed from the Pardu woman, the only sound to be heard within the common room.

Suddenly sweating, Kalam looked down at the cards. Six surrounded a single, and that single card – he knew with certainty – was his. *The Rope, Assassin of Shadow*. The six cards encircling it were all of one House. *King, Herald, Mason, Spinner, Knight, Queen . . . High House Death, Hood's House all arrayed . . . around the one who carries the Holy Book of Dryjhna*. 'Ah, well,' Kalam sighed, glancing up at the Pardu woman, 'I guess I sleep alone tonight.'

The Red Blade Captain Lostara Yil and her companion soldier were the last to leave Ladro Keep, over an hour after their target had departed on his stallion, riding south through the dusty wake of the sandstorm.

The forced proximity with Kalam had been unavoidable, but just as he was skilled at deception, so too was Lostara. Bluster could be its own disguise, arrogance a mask hiding an altogether deadlier assurance.

The Deck of Dragons' unexpected fielding had revealed much to Lostara, not only about Kalam and his mission. The Keep's sergeant had shown himself by his expression to have been a co-conspirator – yet another Malazan soldier prepared to betray his Empress. Evidently, Kalam's stop at the Keep had not been as accidental as it appeared.

Checking their horses, Lostara turned as her companion emerged from the Keep. The Red Blade grinned up at her. 'You were thorough, as always,' he said. 'The commander led me a merry chase, however. I found him in the crypt, struggling to climb into a fifty-year-old suit of armour. He was much thinner in his youth, it seems.'

Lostara swung herself into the saddle. 'None still breathing? You're certain you checked them all? What of the servants in the back hallway – I went through them perhaps too quickly.'

'You left not a single heart still beating, Captain.'

'Very good. Mount up. That horse of the assassin's is killing these ones – we shall acquire fresh horses in Intesarm.'

'Assuming Baralta got around to arranging them.'

Lostara eyed her companion. 'Trust Baralta,' she said coolly. 'And be glad that – this time – I shall not report your scepticism.'

Tight-lipped, the man nodded. 'Thank you, Captain.'

The two rode down the keep road, turning south on the coastal road.

The entire main floor of the monastery radiated in a circular pattern around a single room that was occupied by a circular staircase of stone leading down into darkness. Mappo crouched beside it.

'This would, I imagine, lead down to the crypt.'

'If I recall correctly,' Icarium said from where he stood near the room's entrance, 'when nuns of the Queen of Dreams die the bodies are simply wrapped in linen and placed on recessed ledges in the crypt walls. Have you an interest in perusing corpses?'

'Not generally, no,' the Trell said, straightening with a soft grunt. 'It's just that the stone changes as soon the stairs descend below floor level.'

Icarium raised a brow. 'It does?'

'The level we're on is carved from living rock – the cliff's limestone. It's rather soft. But beneath it there are cut granite blocks. I believe the crypt beneath us is an older construct. Either that or the nuns and their cult hold that a crypt's walls and approach must be dressed, whereas living chambers need not be.'

The Jhag shook his head, approaching. 'I would be surprised. The Queen of Dreams is Life-aspected. Very well, shall we explore?'

Mappo descended first. Neither had much need for artificial light, the darkness below offering no obstacle. The spiral steps showed the vestiges of marble tiling, but the passage of many feet long ago had worn most of them away. Beneath, the hard granite defied all evidence of erosion.

The stairs continued down, and down. At the seventieth step they ended in the centre of an octagonally walled chamber. Friezes decorated each wall, the colours hinted at in the many shades of grey. Beyond the staircase's landing, the floor was honeycombed with rectangular pits, cut down through the tiles and the granite blocks beneath removed. These blocks were now stacked over what was obviously a portalway. Within each pit was a shrouded corpse.

The air was dry, scentless.

'These paintings do not belong to the cult of the Queen,' Mappo said, stating the obvious, for the scenes on the walls revealed a dark mythos. Thick fir trees reared black, moss-stained boles on all sides. The effect created was of standing in a glade deep in an ancient forest. Between the trunks here and there was the hint of hulking, four-legged beasts, their eyes glowing as if in reflected moonlight.

Icarium crouched down, running a hand over the remaining tiles. 'This floor held a pattern,' he said, 'before the nuns' workers cut graves in it. Pity.'

Mappo glanced at the blocked doorway. 'If answers to the mysteries here exist, they lie beyond that barricade.'

'Recovered your strength, friend?'

'Well enough.' The Trell went to the barrier, pulled down the highest block. As he tipped it down into his arms, he staggered, voicing a savage grunt. Icarium rushed to help him lower the granite block to the floor. 'Hood's breath! Heavier than I'd expected.'

'I'd gathered that. Shall we work together, then?'

Twenty minutes later they had cleared sufficient blocks to

permit their passage into the hallway beyond. The final five minutes they had an audience, as a squall of bhok'aral appeared on the staircase, silently watching their efforts from where they clung from the railings. When first Mappo and then Icarium clambered through the opening, however, the bhok'arala did not follow.

The hallway stretched away before them, a wide colonnade lined by twin columns that were nothing less than the trunks of cedars. Each bole was at least an arm-span in diameter. The shaggy, gouged bark remained, although most of it had fallen away and now lay scattered over the floor.

Mappo laid a hand on one wooden pillar. 'Imagine the effort of bringing these down here.'

'Warren,' Icarium said, sniffing. 'The residue remains, even after all these centuries.'

'After *centuries*? Can you sense which warren, Icarium?'

'Kurald Galain. Elder, the Warren of Darkness.'

'Tiste Andii? In all the histories of Seven Cities that I am aware of, I've never heard mention of Tiste Andii present on this continent. Nor in my homeland, on the other side of the Jhag Odhan. Are you certain? This does not make sense.'

'I am *not* certain, Mappo. It has the feel of Kurald Galain, that is all. The *feel* of Dark. It is not Omtose Phellack nor Tellann. Not Starvald Demelain. I know of no other Elder Warrens.'

'Nor I.'

Without another word the three began walking.

By Mappo's count, the hallway ended three hundred and thirty paces later, opening out into another octagonal chamber, this one with its floor raised a hand's width higher than that of the hallway. Each flagstone was also octagonal, and on each of them images had been intricately carved, then defaced with gouges and scoring in what seemed entirely random, frenzied destruction.

The Trell felt his hackles stiffening into a ridge on his neck as he stood at the room's threshold. Icarium was beside him.

'I do not,' the Jhag said, 'suggest we enter this chamber.'

Mappo grunted agreement. The air stank of sorcery, old, stale and clammy and dense with power. Like waves of heat, magic bled from the flagstones, from the images carved upon them and the wounds many of those images now bore.

Icarium was shaking his head. 'If this is Kurald Galain, its flavour is unknown to me. It is . . . corrupted.'

'By the defilement?'

'Possibly. Yet the stench from those claw marks differs from what rises from the flagstones themselves. Is it familiar to you? By Dessembrae's mortal tears it should be, Mappo.'

The Trell squinted down at the nearest flagstone bearing scars. His nostrils flared. 'Soletaken. D'ivers. The spice of shapeshifters. Of course.' He barked out a savage laugh that echoed in the chamber. 'The Path of Hands, Icarium. The gate – it's here.'

'More than a gate, I think,' Icarium said. 'Look upon the undamaged carvings – what do they remind you of?'

Mappo had an answer to that. He scanned the array with growing certainty, but the realization it offered held no answers, only more questions. 'I see the likeness, yet there is an . . . unlikeness, as well. Even more irritating, I can think of no possible linkage . . .'

'No such answers here,' Icarium said. 'We must go to the place we first intended to find, Mappo. We approach comprehension – I am certain of that.'

'Icarium, do you think Iskaral Pust is preparing for more visitors? Soletaken and D'ivers, the imminent opening of the gate. Is he – and by extension Shadow Realm – the very heart of this convergence?'

'I do not know. Let's ask him.'

They stepped back from the threshold.

'We approach comprehension.' Three words evoking terror within Mappo. He felt like a hare in a master archer's sights, each direction of flight so hopeless as to leave him frozen in place. He stood at the side of powers that staggered his mind, power past and powers present. *The Nameless Ones, with their charges and hints and visions, their cowled purposes and shrouded desires. Creatures of fraught antiquity, if the Trellish legends held any glimmer of truth. And Icarium, oh, dear friend, I can tell you nothing. My curse is silence to your every question, and the hand I offer as a brother will lead you only into deceit. In love's name, I do this, at my own cost . . . and such a cost.*

The bhok'arala awaited them at the stairs and followed the two men at a discreet distance up to the main level.

They found the High Priest in the vestibule he had converted into his sleeping chamber. Muttering to himself, Iskaral Pust was filling a wicker rubbish container with rotted fruit, dead bats and mangled rhizan. He threw Mappo and Icarium a scowl over one shoulder as they stood at the room's entrance.

'If those squalid apes are following you, let them 'ware my wrath,' Iskaral hissed. 'No matter which chamber I choose, they insist on using it as repository for their foul leavings. I have lost patience! They mock a High Priest of Shadow at their peril!'

'We have found the gate,' Mappo said.

Iskaral did not pause in his cleaning. 'Oh, you have, have you? Fools! Nothing is as it seems. A life given for a life taken. You have explored every corner, every cranny, have you? Idiots! Such overconfident bluster is the banner of ignorance. Wave it about and expect me to cower? Hah. I have my secrets, my plans, my schemes. Iskaral Pust's maze of genius cannot be plumbed by the likes of you. Look at you two. Both ancient wanderers of this mortal earth. Why have you not ascended like the rest of them?

I'll tell you. Longevity does not automatically bestow wisdom. Oh no, not at all. I trust you are killing every spider you spy. You had better be, for it is the path to wisdom. Oh yes indeed, the path!

'Bhok'arala have small brains. Tiny brains inside their tiny round skulls. Cunning as rats, with eyes like glittering black stones. Four hours, once, I stared into one's eyes, he into mine. Never once pulling gaze away, oh no, this was a contest and one I would not lose. Four hours, face to face, so close I could smell his foul breath and he mine. Who would win? It was in the lap of the gods.'

Mappo glanced at Icarium, then cleared his throat. 'And who, Iskaral Pust, won this . . . this battle of wits?'

Iskaral Pust fixed a pointed stare on Mappo. 'Look upon him who does not waver from his cause, no matter how insipid and ultimately irrelevant, and you shall find in him the meaning of dull-witted. The bhok'aral could have stared into my eyes for ever, for there was no intelligence behind them. Behind his eyes, I mean. It was proof of my superiority that I found distraction elsewhere.'

'Do you intend to lead the D'ivers and Soletaken to the gate below, Iskaral Pust?'

'Blunt are the Trell, determined in headlong stumbling and headlong in stumbling determination. As I said. You know nothing of the mysteries involved, the plans of Shadowthrone, the many secrets of the Grey Keep, the Shrouded House where stands the Throne of Shadow. Yet I do. I, alone among all mortals, have been shown the truth arrayed before me. My god is generous, my god is wise, as cunning as a rat. Spiders must die. The bhok'arala have stolen my broom and this quest I set before you two guests. Icarium and Mappo Trell, famed wanderers of the world, I charge you with this perilous task – find me my broom.'

* * *

Out in the hallway, Mappo sighed. 'Well, that was fruitless. What shall we do now, friend?'

Icarium looked surprised. 'It should be obvious, Mappo. We must take on this perilous quest. We must find Iskaral Pust's broom.'

'We have explored this monastery, Icarium,' the Trell said wearily. 'I noticed no broom.'

The Jhag's mouth quirked slightly. 'Explored? Every corner, every cranny? I think not. Our first task, however, is to the kitchen. We must outfit ourselves for our impending explorations.'

'You are serious.'

'I am.'

The flies were biting in the heat, as foul-tempered as everything else beneath the blistering sun. People filled Hissar's fountains until midday, crowded shoulder to shoulder in the tepid, murky waters, before retiring to the cooler shade of their homes. It was not a day for going outside, and Duiker found himself scowling as he drew on a loose, thinly woven telaba while Bult waited by the door.

'Why not under the moon,' the historian muttered. 'Cool night air, stars high overhead with every spirit looking down. Now *that* would ensure success!'

Bult's sardonic grin did not help matters. Strapping on his rope belt, Duiker turned to the grizzled commander. 'Very well, lead on, Uncle.'

The Wickan's grin widened, deepening the scar until it seemed he had two smiles instead of one.

Outside, Kulp waited with the mounts, astride his own small, sturdy-looking horse. Duiker found the cadre mage's glum expression perversely pleasing.

They rode through almost empty streets. It was marrok: early afternoon, when sane people retired indoors to wait out

177

the worst of the summer heat. The historian had grown accustomed to napping during marrok; he was feeling grumpy, all too out of sorts to attend Sormo's ritual. Warlocks were notorious for their impropriety, their deliberate discombobulating of common sense. *For the defence of decency alone, the Empress might be excused the executions.* He grimaced – clearly not an opinion to be safely voiced within hearing range of any Wickans.

They reached the city's northern end and rode out on a coastal track for half a league before swinging inland, into the wastes of the Odhan. The oasis they approached an hour later was dead, the spring long since dried up. All that remained of what had once been a lush, natural garden amidst the sands was a stand of withered, gnarled cedars rising from a carpet of tumbled palms.

Many of the trees bore strange projections that drew Duiker's curiosity as they led their horses closer.

'Are those horns in the trees?' Kulp asked.

'Bhederin, I think,' the historian replied. 'Jammed into a fork, then grown past, leaving them embedded deep in the wood. These trees were likely a thousand years old before the water vanished.'

The mage grunted. 'You'd think they'd be cut down by now, this close to Hissar.'

'The horns are warnings,' Bult said. 'Holy ground. Once, long ago. Memories remain.'

'As well they should,' Duiker muttered. 'Sormo should be avoiding hallowed sand, not seeking it out. If this place is aspected, it's likely an inimical one to a Wickan warlock.'

'I've long since learned to trust Sormo E'nath's judgement, Historian. You'd do well to learn the like.'

'It's a poor scholar who trusts anyone's judgement,' Duiker said. 'Even and perhaps especially his own.'

'"You walk shifting sands,"' Bult sighed, then gave him another grin, 'as the locals would say.'

'What would you Wickans say?' Kulp asked.

Bult's eyes glittered with mischief. 'Nothing. Wise words are like arrows flung at your forehead. What do you do? Why, you duck, of course. This truth a Wickan knows from the time he first learns to ride – long before he learns to walk.'

They found the warlock in a clearing. The drifts of sand had been swept aside, revealing a heaved and twisted brick floor – all that remained of a structure of some sort. Chips of obsidian glittered in the joins.

Kulp dismounted, eyeing Sormo who stood in the centre, hands hidden within heavy sleeves. He swatted at a fly. 'What's this, then, some lost, forgotten temple?'

The young Wickan slowly blinked. 'My assistants concluded it had been a stable. They then left without elaborating.'

Kulp scowled at Duiker. 'I despise Wickan humour,' he whispered.

Sormo gestured them closer. 'It is my intention to open myself to the sacred aspect of this kheror, which is the name Wickans give to holy places open to the skies—'

'Are you mad?' Kulp's face had gone white. 'Those spirits will rip your throat out, child. They are of the Seven—'

'They are *not*,' the warlock retorted. 'The spirits in this kheror were raised in the time before the Seven. They are the land's own and if you must liken them to a known aspect, then it must be Tellann.'

'Hood's mercy,' Duiker groaned. 'If it is indeed Tellann, then you will be dealing with T'lan Imass, Sormo. The undead warriors have turned their backs on the Empress and all that is the Empire, ever since the Emperor's assassination.'

The warlock's eyes were bright. 'And have you not wondered why?'

The historian's mouth snapped shut. He had theories in that regard, but to voice them – *to anyone* – would be treason.

Kulp's dry question to Sormo broke through Duiker's

179

thoughts. 'And has Empress Laseen tasked you with this? Are you here to seek a sense of future events or is that just a feint?'

Bult had stood a few paces from them saying nothing, but now he spat. 'We need no seer to guess that, Mage.'

The warlock raised his arms out to his sides. 'Stay close,' he said to Kulp, then his eyes slid to the historian. 'And you, see and remember all you will witness here.'

'I am already doing so, Warlock.'

Sormo nodded, closed his eyes.

His power spread like a faint, subtle ripple, sweeping over Duiker and the others to encompass the entire clearing. Daylight faded abruptly, replaced by a soft dusk, the dry air suddenly damp and smelling of marshlands.

Ringing the glade like sentinels were cypresses. Mosses hung from branches in curtains, hiding what lay beyond in impenetrable shadow.

Duiker could feel Sormo E'nath's sorcery like a warm cloak; he had never before felt a power such as this one. Calm and protective, strong yet yielding. He wondered at the Empire's loss in exterminating these warlocks. *An error she's clearly corrected, though it might well be too late. How many warlocks were lost in truth?*

Sormo loosed an ululating cry that echoed as if they stood within a vast cavern.

The next moment the air was alive with icy winds, arriving in warring gusts. Sormo staggered, his eyes now open and widening with alarm. He drew a breath, then visibly recoiled at the taste and Duiker could not blame him. Bestial stench rode the winds, growing fouler by the moment.

Taut violence filled the glade, a sure promise announced in the sudden thrashing of the moss-laden branches. The historian saw a swarming cloud approach Bult from behind and shouted a warning. The Wickan whirled, long-knives in his hands. He screamed as the first of the wasps stung.

'D'ivers!' Kulp bellowed, one hand grasping Duiker's telaba and pulling the historian back to where Sormo stood as if dazed.

Rats scampered over the soft ground, shrilly screaming as they attacked a writhing bundle of snakes.

The historian felt heat on his legs, looked down. Fire ants swarmed him up to his thighs. The heat rose to agony. He screamed.

Swearing, Kulp unleashed his warren in a pulse of power. Shrivelled ants fell from the historian's legs like dust. The attacking swarm flinched back, the D'ivers retreating.

The rats had overrun the snakes and now closed in on Sormo. The Wickan frowned at them.

Off where Bult crouched slapping futilely at the stinging wasps, liquid fire erupted in a swath, the flames tumbling over the veteran.

Tracking back to the fire's source, Duiker saw that an enormous demon had entered the clearing. Midnight-skinned and twice the height of a man, the creature voiced a roar of fury and launched a savage attack on a white-furred bear – the glade was alive with D'ivers and Soletaken, the air filled with shrieks and snarls. The demon landed on the bear, driving it to the ground with a snap and crunch of bones. Leaving the animal twitching, the black demon leapt to one side and roared a second time, and this time Duiker heard meaning within it.

'It's warning us!' he shouted at Kulp.

Like a lodestone the demon's arrival drew the D'ivers and Soletaken. They fought each other in a frenzied rush to attack the creature.

'We have to get out of here!' Duiker said. 'Pull us out, Kulp – now!'

The mage hissed in rage. 'How? This is Sormo's ritual, you damned book-grub!'

The demon vanished beneath a mob of creatures, yet clearly remained upright, as the D'ivers and Soletaken clambered up what seemed a solid pillar of stone. Black-skinned arms appeared, flinging away dead and dying creatures. But it could not last.

'Hood take you, Kulp! Think of something!'

The mage's face tightened. 'Drag Bult to Sormo. Quickly! Leave the warlock to me.' With that, Kulp bolted to Sormo, shouting in an effort to wake the youth from whatever spell held him. Duiker spun to where Bult lay huddled five paces away. His legs felt impossibly heavy beneath the prickling pain of the ant bites as he staggered to the Wickan.

The veteran had been stung scores of times, his flesh was misshapen with fiery swelling. He was unconscious, possibly dead. Duiker gripped the man's harness and dragged him to where Kulp continued accosting Sormo E'nath.

As the historian arrived, the demon gave one last shriek, then disappeared beneath the mound of attackers. The D'ivers and Soletaken then surged towards the four men.

Sormo E'nath was oblivious, his eyes glazed, unheeding of the mage's efforts to shout him into awareness.

'Wake him or we're dead,' Duiker gasped, stepping over Bult to face the charging beasts with naught but a small knife.

The weapon would little avail him as a seething cloud of hornets swiftly closed the distance.

The scene was jolted, and Duiker saw they were back in the dead oasis. The D'ivers and Soletaken were gone. The historian turned to Kulp. 'You did it! How?'

The mage glanced down at a sprawled, moaning Sormo E'nath. 'I'll pay for it,' he muttered, then met Duiker's eyes. 'I punched the lad. Damn near broke my hand doing it, too. It was *his* nightmare, wasn't it?'

The historian blinked, then shook himself and crouched down beside Bult. 'This poison will kill him long before we can get help—'

Kulp squatted, ran his good hand over the veteran's swollen face. 'Not poison. More like an infecting warren. I can deal with this, Duiker. As with your legs.' He closed his eyes in concentration.

Sormo E'nath slowly pushed himself into sitting position. He looked around, then tenderly touched his jaw, where the ridged imprint of Kulp's knuckles stood like puckered islands in a spreading flush of red.

'He had no choice,' Duiker told him.

The warlock nodded.

'Can you talk? Any loose teeth?'

'Somewhere,' he said clearly, 'a crow flaps broken-winged on the ground. There are but ten left.'

'What happened there, Warlock?'

Sormo's eyes flicked nervously. 'Something unexpected, Historian. A convergence is underway. The Path of Hands. The gate of the Soletaken and the D'ivers. An unhappy coincidence.'

Duiker scowled. 'You said Tellann—'

'And so it was,' the warlock cut in. 'Is there a blending between shapeshifting and Elder Tellann? Unknown. Perhaps the D'ivers and Soletaken are simply passing through the warren – imagining it unoccupied by T'lan Imass and therefore safer. Indeed, no T'lan Imass to take umbrage with the trespass, leaving them with only each other to battle.'

'They're welcome to annihilate each other, then,' the historian grumbled, his legs slowly giving way beneath him until like Sormo he sat on the ground.

'I shall help you in a moment,' Kulp called over.

Nodding, Duiker found himself watching a dung beetle struggle heroically to push aside a fragment of palm bark. He sensed something profound in what he watched, but was too weary to pursue it.

CHAPTER FIVE

Bhok'arala seem to have originated in the wastes of
Raraku. Before long, these social creatures spread
outward and were soon seen throughout Seven Cities.
As efficacious rat control in settlements, the bhok'arala
were not only tolerated, but often encouraged. It
was not long before a lively trade in domesticated
breeds became a major export . . .

The usage and demonic investment of this
species among mages and alchemists is a matter for
discussion within treatises more specific than this one.
Baruk's Three Hundred and Twenty-first Treatise offers
a succinct analysis for interested scholars . . .

Denizens of Raraku
Imrygyn Tallobant

With the exception of the sandstorm – which they had
waited out in Trob – and the unsettling news of a
massacre at Ladro Keep, told to them by an outrider
from a well-guarded caravan bound for Ehrlitan, the journey to
within sight of G'danisban had proved uneventful for Fiddler,
Crokus and Apsalar.

Although Fiddler knew that the risks that lay ahead, south
of the small city out in the Pan'potsun Odhan, were severe
enough to eat holes in his stomach, he had anticipated a lull in

the final approach to G'danisban. What he had not expected to find was a ragtag renegade army encamped outside the city walls.

The army's main force straddled the road but was shielded by a thin line of hills on the north side. The canal road led the three unsuspecting travellers into the camp's perimeter lines. There had been no warning.

A company of footmen commanded the rosad from flanking hills and oversaw diligent questioning of all who sought entry to the city. The company was supported by a score of Arak tribal horsewarriors who were evidently entrusted with riding down any traveller inclined to flee the approach to the makeshift barricade.

Fiddler and his charges would have to ride on through and trust to their disguises. The sapper was anything but confident, although this lent a typically Gral scowl to his narrow features which elicited a wholly proper wariness in two of the three guards who stepped forward to intercept them at the barricade.

'The city is closed,' the unimpressed guard nearest them said, punctuating his words by spitting between the hooves of Fiddler's mount.

It would later be said that even a Gral's horse knew an insult when it saw one. Before Fiddler could react, his mount's head snapped forward, stripping the reins from the sapper's hands, and bit the guardsman in the face. The horse had twisted its head so that the jaws closed round the man's cheeks and tore into cheeks, upper lip and nose. Blood gushed. The guardsman dropped like a sack of stones, a piercing, keening sound rising from him.

For lack of anything else to grip, Fiddler snagged the gelding's ears and pulled hard, backing the beast away even as it prepared to stomp on the guard's huddled form. Hiding his shock behind an even fiercer frown, the sapper unleashed a stream of Gral curses at the two remaining men, who had both backed

185

frantically clear before lowering their pikes. 'Foul snot of rabid dogs! Anal crust of dysenteried goats! Such a sight for two young newlyweds to witness! Will you curse their marriage but two weeks since the blessed day? Shall I loose the fleas on my head to rend your worthless flesh from your jellied bones?'

As Fiddler roared every Gral utterance of disgust he could recall in an effort to keep the guards unbalanced, a troop of the Arak horsewarriors rode up with savage haste.

'Gral! Ten jakatas for your horse!'

'Twelve, Gral! To me!'

'Fifteen and my youngest daughter!'

'Five jakatas for three tail hairs!'

Fiddler turned his fiercest frown on the riders. 'Not one of you is fit to smell my horse's farts!' But he grinned, unstrapping a beer-filled bladder and tossing it one-handed to the nearest Arak. 'But let us camp with your troop this night and for a sliver you may feel its heat with your palms – once only! For more you must pay!'

With wild grins, the Araks passed the skin between them, each taking deep swigs to finalize the ritual exchange. By sharing beer, Fiddler had granted them status as equals, the gesture stripping the cutting barb from the insult he had thrown their way.

Fiddler glanced back at Crokus and Apsalar. They looked properly shaken. Biting back his own nausea, the sapper winked.

The guards had recovered but before they could close in, the tribesmen drove their mounts to block them.

'Ride with us!' one of the Araks shouted to Fiddler. As one, the troop wheeled about. Regaining the reins, Fiddler spurred the gelding after them, sighing when he heard behind him the newlyweds following suit.

It was to be a race to the Arak camp, and, true to its sudden legendary status, the Gral horse was determined to burst every

186

muscle in its body to win. Fiddler had never before ridden such a game beast, and he found himself grinning in spite of himself, even as the image of the guardsman's ravaged face remained like a chill knot in the pit of his stomach.

The Arak tipis lined the edges of a nearby hill's windswept summit, each set wide apart so that no shade from a neighbour's could cast insult. Women and children came to the crest to watch the race, screaming as Fiddler's mount burst through the leading line, swerving to throw a shoulder into the fastest competitor. That horse stumbled, almost pitching its rider from his wood and felt saddle, then righted itself with a furious scream at being driven from the race.

Unimpeded, Fiddler leaned forward as his horse reached the slope and surged up its grassy side. The line of watchers parted as he reached the crest and reined in amidst the tipis.

As any plains tribe would, the Arak chose hilltops rather than valley floors for their camps. The winds kept the insects to a minimum – boulders held down the tipi edges to prevent the hide tents from blowing away – and the rising and setting of the sun could be witnessed to mark ritual thanksgiving.

The camp's layout was a familiar one to Fiddler, who had ridden with Wickan scouts over these lands during the Emperor's campaigns. Marking the centre of the ring of tipis was a stone-lined hearth. Four wooden posts off to one side, between two tipis, and joined together with a single hemp rope, provided the corral for the horses. Bundles of rolled felt lay drying nearby, along with tripods bearing stretched hides and strips of meat.

The dozen or so camp dogs surrounded the snapping gelding as Fiddler paused in the saddle to take his bearings. The scrawny, yipping mongrels might prove a problem, he realized, but he hoped that their suspicions would apply to all strangers, Gral included. If not, then his disguise was over.

The troop arrived moments later, the horsewarriors

shouting and laughing as they reined in and threw themselves from their saddles. Appearing last on the summit's crest were Crokus and Apsalar, neither of whom seemed ready to share in the good humour.

Seeing their faces reminded Fiddler of the mangled guardsman on the road below. He regained his scowl and slipped from the saddle. 'The city is closed?' he shouted. 'Another Mezla folly!'

The Arak rider who'd spoken before strode up, a fierce grin on his lean face. 'Not Mezla! G'danisban has been liberated! The southern hares have fled the Whirlwind's promise.'

'Then why was the city closed to us? Are we Mezla?'

'A cleansing, Gral! Mezla merchants and nobles infest G'danisban. They were arrested yesterday and this day they are being executed. Tomorrow morning you shall lead your blessed couple into a free city. Come, this night we celebrate!'

Fiddler squatted in Gral fashion. 'Has Sha'ik raised the Whirlwind, then?' He glanced back at Crokus and Apsalar, as if suddenly regretting having taken on the responsibility. 'Has the war begun, Arak?'

'Soon,' he said. 'We were cursed with impatience,' he added with a smirk.

Crokus and Apsalar approached. The Arak went off to assist in the preparations for the night's festivities. Coins were flung at the gelding's hooves and hands cautiously reached out to rest lightly on the animal's neck and flanks. For the moment the three travellers were alone.

'That was a sight I will never forget,' Crokus said, 'though I wish to Hood I could. Will the poor man live?'

Fiddler shrugged. 'If he chooses to.'

'We're camping here tonight?' Apsalar asked, looking around.

'Either that or insult these Arak and risk disembowelling.'

'We will not fool them for much longer,' Apsalar said.

'Crokus doesn't speak a word of this land's tongue, and mine is a Malazan's accent.'

'That soldier was my age,' the Daru thief muttered.

Frowning, the sapper said, 'Our only other choice is to ride into G'danisban, so that we may witness the Whirlwind's vengeance.'

'Another celebration of what's to come?' Crokus demanded. 'This damned Apocalypse you're always talking about? I get the feeling that this land's people do nothing but talk.'

Fiddler cleared his throat. 'Tonight's celebration in G'danisban,' he said slowly, 'will be the flaying alive of a few hundred Malazans, Crokus. If we show eagerness to witness such an event, these Arak may not be offended by our leaving early.'

Apsalar turned to watch half a dozen tribesmen approach. 'Try it, Fiddler,' she said.

The sapper came close to saluting. He hissed a curse. 'You giving me orders, Recruit?'

She blinked. 'I think I was giving orders . . . when you were still clutching the hem of your mother's dress, Fiddler. I know – the one who possessed me. It's *his* instincts that are ringing like steel on stone right now. Do as I say.'

The chance for a retort vanished as the Arak arrived. 'You are blessed, Gral!' one of them said. 'A Gral clan is on its way to join the Apocalypse! Let us hope that like you they bring their own beer!'

Fiddler made a kin gesture, then soberly shook his head. 'It cannot be,' he said, mentally holding his breath. 'I am outcast. More, these newlyweds insist we enter the city . . . to witness the executions in further blessing of their binding. I am their escort, and so must obey their commands.'

Apsalar stepped forward and bowed. 'We wish no offence,' she said.

It wasn't going well. The Arak faces arrayed before them

189

had darkened. 'Outcast? No kin to honour your trail, Gral? Perhaps we shall hold you for your brothers' vengeance, and in exchange they leave us your horse.'

With exquisite perfection, Apsalar stamped one foot to announce the rage of a pampered daughter and new wife. 'I am with child! Defy me and be cursed! We go to the city! Now!'

'Hire one of us for the rest of your journey, blessed lady! But leave the riven Gral! He is not fit to serve you!'

Trembling, Apsalar prepared to lift her veil, announcing the intention to voice her curse.

The Araks flinched back.

'You covet the gelding! This is nothing more than greed! I shall now curse you all—'

'Forgive!' 'We bow down, blessed lady!' 'Touch not your veil!' 'Ride on, then! To the city below! Ride on!'

Apsalar hesitated. For a moment Fiddler thought she would curse them anyway. Instead she spun about. 'Escort us once more, Gral,' she said.

Surrounded by worried, frightened faces, the three mounted up.

An Arak who had spoken earlier now stepped close to the sapper. 'Stay only the night, then ride on hard, Gral. Your kin will pursue you.'

'Tell them,' Fiddler said, 'I won the horse in a fair fight. Tell them that.'

The Arak frowned. 'Will they know the story?'

'Which clan?'

'Sebark.'

The sapper shook his head.

'Then they shall ride you down for the pleasure of it. But I shall tell them your words, anyway. Indeed, your horse was worth killing for.'

Fiddler thought back to the drunken Gral he'd bought the gelding from in Ehrlitan. Three jakata. The tribesmen who moved into the cities lost much. 'Drink my beer this night, Arak?'

'We shall. Before the Gral arrive. Ride on.'

As they rode onto the road and approached G'danisban's north gate, Apsalar said to him, 'We are in trouble now, aren't we?'

'Is that what your instincts tell you, lass?'

She grimaced.

'Aye,' Fiddler sighed. 'That we are. I made a mistake with that outcast story. I think now, given your performance back there, that the threat of your curse would have sufficed.'

'Probably.'

Crokus cleared his throat. 'Are we going to actually watch these executions, Fid?'

The sapper shook his head. 'Not a chance. We're riding straight through, if we can.' He glanced at Apsalar. 'Let your courage falter, lass. Another temper tantrum and the citizens will rush you out the south gate on a bed of gold.'

She acknowledged him with a wry smile.

Don't fall in love with this woman, Fid, old friend, else you loosen your guard of the lad's life, and call it an accident of fate . . .

Spilled blood stained the worn cobbles under the arched north gate and a scatter of wooden toys lay broken and crushed to either side of the causeway. From somewhere close came the screams of children dying.

'We can't do this,' Crokus said, all the colour gone from his face. He rode at Fiddler's side, Apsalar holding her mount close behind them. Looters and armed men appeared now and then farther down the street, but the way into the city seemed strangely open. A haze of smoke hung over everything, and the burnt-out shells of merchant stores and residences gaped desolation on all sides.

They rode amidst scorched furniture, shattered pottery and

ceramics, and bodies twisted in postures of violent death. The children's dying screams, off to their right, had mercifully stopped, but other, more distant screams rose eerily from G'danisban's heart.

They were startled by a figure darting across their paths, a young girl, naked and bruised. She ran as if oblivious to them, and clambered under a broken-wheeled cart not fifteen paces from Fiddler and his party. They watched her scramble under cover.

Six armed men approached from a side street. Their weapons were haphazard, and none wore armour. Blackened blood stained their ragged telaban. One spoke. 'Gral! You see a girl? We're not done with her.'

Even as he asked his question, another of them grinned and gestured to the cart. The girl's knees and feet were clearly visible.

'A Mezla?' Fiddler asked.

The group's leader shrugged. 'Well enough. Fear not, Gral, we'll share.'

The sapper heard Apsalar draw a long, slow breath. He eased back in his saddle.

The group split in passing around Fiddler, Crokus and Apsalar. The sapper casually leaned after the nearest man and thrust the point of his long-knife into the base of his skull. The Gral gelding pivoted beneath Fiddler and kicked out with both rear hooves, shattering another man's chest and propelling him backward, sprawling on the cobbles.

Regaining control of the gelding, Fiddler drove his heels into its flanks. They bolted forward, savagely riding down the group's generous leader. From under the horse's stamping hooves came the sound of snapping bones and the sickening crushing of his skull. Fiddler twisted in the saddle to find the remaining three men.

Two of them writhed in keening pain near Apsalar, who sat

calm in the saddle, a thick-bladed kethra knife in each gloved hand.

Crokus had dismounted and was now crouching over the last body, removing a throwing knife from a blood-drenched throat.

They all turned at a grinding of potsherds to see the girl claw her way clear of the cart, scramble to her feet, then race into the shadows of an alley, disappearing from view.

The sound of horsemen coming from the north gate reached them.

'Ride on!' Fiddler snapped.

Crokus leapt onto his mount's back. Apsalar sheathed her blades and gave the sapper a nod as she gathered up the reins.

'Ride through – to the south gate!'

Fiddler watched the two of them gallop on, then he slipped from the gelding's back and approached the two men Apsalar had wounded. 'Ah,' he breathed when he came close and saw their slashed-open crotches, 'that's the lass I know.'

The troop of horsemen arrived. They all wore ochre sashes diagonally across their chain-covered chests. Their commander opened his mouth to speak but Fiddler was first.

'Is no man's daughter safe in this seven-cursed city? She was no Mezla, by my ancestors! Is this your Apocalypse? Then I pray the pit of snakes awaits you in the Seven Hells!'

The commander was frowning. 'Gral, you say these men were rapists?'

'A Mezla slut gets what she deserves, but the girl was no Mezla.'

'So you killed these men. All six of them.'

'Aye.'

'Who were the other two riders with you?'

'The pilgrims I am sworn to protect.'

'And yet they ride into the city's heart . . . without you at their side.'

193

Fiddler scowled.

The commander scanned the victims. 'Two yet live.'

'May they be cursed with a hundred thousand more breaths before Hood takes them.'

The commander leaned on his saddlehorn and was silent a moment. 'Rejoin your pilgrims, Gral. They have need of your services.'

Growling, Fiddler remounted. 'Who rules G'danisban now?'

'None. The army of the Apocalypse holds but two districts. We shall have the others by the morrow.'

Fiddler pulled the horse around and kicked it into a canter. The troop did not follow. The sapper swore under his breath – the commander was right, he should not have sent Crokus and Apsalar on. He knew himself lucky in that his remaining with the rapists could so easily be construed as typically Gral – the opportunity to brag to the red-swathed riders, the chance to voice curses and display a tribesman's unassailable arrogance – but it risked offering up to contempt his vow to protect his charges. He'd seen the mild disgust in the commander's eyes. In all, he'd been *too* much of a Gral horsewarrior. If not for Apsalar's frightening talents, those two would now be in serious trouble.

He rode hard in pursuit, noting belatedly that the gelding was responding to his every touch. The horse knew he was no Gral, but it'd evidently decided he was behaving in an approved manner, well enough to accord him some respect. It was, he reflected, this day's lone victory.

G'danisban's central square was the site of past slaughter. Fiddler caught up with his companions when they had just begun walking their horses through the horrific scene. They both turned upon hearing his approach, and Fiddler could only nod at the relief in their faces when they recognized him.

Even the Gral gelding hesitated at the square's edge. The bodies covering the cobbles numbered several hundred. Old men and old women, and children, for the most part. They had all been savagely cut to pieces or, in some cases, burned alive. The stench of sun-warmed blood, bile and seared flesh hung thick in the square.

Fiddler swallowed back his revulsion, cleared his throat. 'Beyond this square,' he said, 'all pretences of control cease.'

Crokus gestured shakily. 'These are Malazan?'

'Aye, lad.'

'During the conquest, did the Malazan armies do the same to the locals here?'

'You mean, is this just reprisal?'

Apsalar spoke with an almost personal vehemence. 'The Emperor warred against armies, not civilians—'

'Except at Aren,' Fiddler sardonically interjected, recalling his words with the Tanno Spiritwalker. 'When the T'lan Imass rose in the city—'

'Not by Kellanved's command!' she retorted. 'Who ordered the T'lan Imass into Aren? I shall tell you. Surly, the commander of the Claw, the woman who took upon herself a new name—'

'Laseen.' Fiddler eyed the young woman quizzically. 'I have never before heard that assertion, Apsalar. There were no written orders – none found, in any case—'

'I should have killed her there and then,' Apsalar muttered.

Astonished, Fiddler glanced at Crokus. The Daru shook his head.

'Apsalar,' the sapper said slowly, 'you were but a child when Aren rebelled then fell to the T'lan Imass.'

'I know that,' she replied. 'Yet these memories . . . they are so clear. I was . . . sent to Aren . . . to see the slaughter. To find out what happened. I . . . I *argued* with Surly. No-one else was in the room. Just Surly and . . . and me.'

They reached the other end of the square. Fiddler reined in and regarded Apsalar for a long moment.

Crokus said, 'It was the Rope, the patron god of assassins, who possessed you. Yet your memories are—'

'Dancer's.' As soon as he said it, Fiddler knew it was true. 'The Rope has another name. Cotillion. Hood's breath, so obvious! No-one doubted that the assassinations occurred. Both Dancer and the Emperor . . . murdered by Laseen and her chosen Clawmasters. What did Laseen do with the bodies? No-one knows.'

'So Dancer lived,' Crokus said with a frown. 'And ascended. Became a patron god in the Warren of Shadow.'

Apsalar said nothing, watching and listening with a carefully controlled absence of expression on her face.

Fiddler was cursing himself for a blind idiot. 'What House appeared in the Deck of Dragons shortly afterward? Shadow. Two new Ascendants. Cotillion . . . and Shadowthrone . . .'

Crokus's eyes widened. 'Shadowthrone is Kellanved,' he said. 'They weren't assassinated – either of them. They escaped by ascending.'

'Into the Shadow Realm.' Fiddler smiled wryly. 'To nurse their thoughts of vengeance, leading eventually to Cotillion possessing a young fishergirl in Itko Kan, to begin what would be a long, devious path to Laseen. Which failed. Apsalar?'

'Your words are true,' she said without inflection.

'Then why,' the sapper demanded, 'didn't Cotillion reveal himself to us? To Whiskeyjack, to Kalam? To Dujek? Dammit, Dancer knew us all – and if that bastard understood the notion of friendship at all, then those I've just mentioned were his friends—'

Apsalar's sudden laugh rattled both men. 'I could lie and say he sought to protect you all. Do you really wish the truth, Bridgeburner?'

Fiddler felt himself flushing. 'I do,' he growled.

'Dancer trusted but two men. One was Kellanved. The other was Dassem Ultor, the First Sword. Dassem is dead. I am

196

sorry if this offends you, Fiddler. Thinking on it, I would suggest that *Cotillion* trusts no-one. Not even Shadowthrone. Emperor Kellanved . . . well enough. *Ascendant* Kellanved – Shadowthrone – ah, that is something wholly different.'

'He was a fool,' Fiddler pronounced, gathering up his reins.

Apsalar's smile was strangely wistful.

'Enough words,' Crokus said. 'Let's get out of this damned city.'

'Aye.'

The short journey from the square to the south gate was surprisingly uneventful, for all the commander's warnings. Dusk shrouded the streets and smoke from a burning tenement block spread an acrid haze that made breathing tortured. They rode through the silent aftermath of slaughter, when the rage has passed and awareness returns with shock and shame.

The moment was a single indrawn breath in what Fiddler knew would be an ever-burgeoning wildfire. If the Malazan legions had not been withdrawn from nearby Pan'potsun, there would have been the chance of crushing the life from this first spark, with a brutality to match the renegades'. When slaughter is flung back on the perpetrators, the thirst for blood is quickly quenched.

The Emperor would have acted swiftly, decisively. *Hood's breath, he would never have let it slide this far.*

Less than a tenth of a bell after leaving the square they passed beneath the smoke-blackened arch of an unguarded south gate. Beyond stretched the Pan'potsun Odhan, flanked to the west by the ridge that divided the Odhan from the Holy Desert Raraku. The night's first stars flickered alight overhead.

Fiddler broke the long silence. 'There is a village a little over two leagues to the south. With luck it won't be a carrion feast. Not yet, anyway.'

Crokus cleared his throat. 'Fiddler, if Kalam had known . . . about Dancer, I mean, Cotillion . . .'

The sapper grimaced, glanced at Apsalar. 'She'd be with him right now.'

Whatever response Crokus intended was interrupted by a squealing, flapping shape that dropped down out of the darkness to collide with the lad's back. Crokus let out a shout of alarm as the creature gripped his hair and clambered onto his head.

'It's just Moby,' Fiddler said, trying to shake off the jitters the familiar's arrival had elicited. He squinted. 'Looks like he's been in a scrap,' he observed.

Crokus pulled Moby down into his arms. 'He's bleeding everywhere!'

'Nothing serious, I'd guess,' Fiddler said.

'What makes you so sure?'

The sapper grinned. 'Ever seen bhok'arala mate?'

'Fiddler,' Apsalar's tone was tight. 'We are pursued.'

Reining in, Fiddler rose in the stirrups and twisted around. In the distant gloom was a cloud of dust. He hissed a curse. 'The Gral clan.'

'We ride weary mounts,' Apsalar said.

'Aye. Queen grant us there's fresh horses to be had in New Velar.'

At the base of three converging gorges, Kalam left the false path and carefully guided his horse through a narrow drainage channel. The old memories of the ways into Raraku felt heavy in his bones. *Everything's changed, yet nothing has changed.*

Of the countless trails that passed through the hills, all but a few led only to death. The false routes were cleverly directed away from the few waterholes and springs. Without water, Raraku's sun was a fatal companion. Kalam knew the Holy Desert, the map within his head – decades old – was seared

198

anew with every landmark he recognized. Pinnacles, tilted rocks, the wend of a flood channel – he felt as if he had never left, for all his new loyalties, his conflicting allegiances. *Once more, a child of this desert. Once more, servant to its sacred need.*

As the wind and sun did to the sand and stone, Raraku shaped all who had known it. Crossing it had etched the souls of the three companies that would come to be called the Bridgeburners. *We could imagine no other name. Raraku burned our pasts away, making all that came before a trail of ashes.*

He swung the stallion onto a scree, rocks and sand skittering and tumbling as the beast scrambled up the slope, regaining the true path along the ridge line that would run in a slow descent westward to Raraku's floor.

Stars glittered like knife-points overhead. The bleached limestone crags shone silver in the faint moonlight, as if reflecting back memories of the day just past.

The assassin led his horse between the crumbled foundations of two watchtowers. Potsherds and fractured brick crunched under the stallion's hooves. Rhizan darted from his path with a soft flit of wings. Kalam felt he had returned home.

'No farther,' a rasping voice warned.

Smiling, Kalam reined in.

'A bold announcement,' the voice continued. 'A stallion the colour of sand, red telaba . . .'

'I announce what I am,' Kalam replied casually. He had pinpointed the source of the voice, in the deep shadows of a sinkhole just beyond the left-hand watchtower. There was a crossbow trained on the assassin, but Kalam knew he could dodge the quarrel, rolling from the saddle with the stallion between him and the stranger. Two well-thrown knives into the darker shape amidst the shadows would punctuate the exchange. He felt at ease.

'Disarm him,' the voice drawled.

Two massive hands closed on his wrists from behind and

savagely pulled both his arms back, until he was dragged, cursing with rage, over the stallion's rump. As soon as he cleared the beast, the hands twisted his body around and drove him hard, face first, into the stony ground. The air knocked from his lungs, Kalam was helpless.

He heard the one who'd spoken rise up from the sinkhole and approach. The stallion snapped his teeth but was swiftly calmed at a soft word from the stranger. The assassin listened as the saddlebags were lifted away and set on the ground. Flaps opened. 'Ah, he's the one, then.'

The hands released Kalam. Groaning, the assassin managed to roll over. A giant of a man stood over him, his face tattooed like shattered glass. A long single braid hung down the left side of his chest. The man wore a cloak of bhederin hide over a vest of armour that seemed made of clam shells. The wooden handle and stone pommel of a bladed weapon of some kind jutted from just under his left arm. The broad belt over the man's loincloth was oddly decorated with what looked to Kalam like dried mushroom caps of various sizes. He was over seven foot tall, yet muscled enough to seem wide, and his flat, broad face gazed down without expression.

Regaining his breath, the assassin sat up. 'A sorcerous silence,' he muttered, mostly to himself.

The man who now held the Book of the Apocalypse heard the gruff whisper and snorted. 'You fancy no mortal could get that close to you without your hearing him. You tell yourself it must have involved magic. You are wrong. My companion is Toblakai, an escaped slave from the Laederon Plateau of Genabackis. He's seen seventeen summers and has personally killed forty-one enemies. Those are their ears on his belt.' The man rose, offering Kalam his hand. 'You are most welcome to Raraku, Deliverer. Our long vigil is ended.'

Grimacing, Kalam accepted the man's hand and felt himself pulled effortlessly to his feet. The assassin brushed the dust from his clothes. 'You are not bandits, then.'

The stranger barked a laugh. 'No, we are not. I am Leoman, Captain of Sha'ik's Bodyguard. My companion refuses his name to strangers, and we shall leave it at that. We are the two she chose.'

'I must deliver the Book into Sha'ik's hands,' Kalam said. 'Not yours, Leoman.'

The squat warrior – by his colour and clothing a child of this desert – held out the Book. 'By all means.'

Cautiously, the assassin retrieved the heavy, battered tome.

A woman spoke behind him. 'You may now give it to me, Deliverer.'

Kalam slowly closed his eyes, struggling to gather the frayed ends of his nerves. He turned.

There could be no doubting. The small, honey-skinned woman standing before him radiated power in waves, the smell of dust and sand whipped by winds, the taste of salt and blood. Her rather plain face was deeply lined, giving her an appearance of being around forty years old, though Kalam suspected she was younger – Raraku was a harsh home.

Involuntarily, Kalam dropped to one knee. He held out the Book. 'I deliver unto you, Sha'ik, the Apocalypse.' *And with it, a sea of blood – how many innocent lives shattered, to bring Laseen down? Hood take me, what have I done?*

The Book's weight left his hands as she accepted it. 'It is damaged.'

The assassin looked up, slowly rose.

Sha'ik was frowning, one finger tracing a torn corner of the leather cover. 'Well, one should not be surprised, given that it is a thousand years old. I thank you, Deliverer. Will you now join my band of soldiers? I sense great talents in you.'

Kalam bowed. 'I cannot. My destiny lies elsewhere.' *Flee, Kalam, before you test the skills of these bodyguards. Flee, before uncertainty kills you.*

Her dark eyes narrowed on his searchingly, then widened. 'I sense something of your desire, though you shield it well. Ride on, then, the way south is open to you. More, you shall have an escort—'

'I need no escort, Seer—'

'But you shall have one in any case.' She gestured and a bulky, ungainly shape appeared from the gloom.

'Holy One,' Leoman hissed warningly.

'You question me?' Sha'ik snapped.

'The Toblakai is as an army, nor are my skills lacking, Holy One, yet—'

'Since I was a child,' Sha'ik cut in, her voice brittle, 'one vision has possessed me above all others. I have seen this moment, Leoman, a thousand times. At dawn I shall open the Book, and the Whirlwind shall rise, and I shall emerge from it . . . renewed. "Blades in hands and unhanded in wisdom," such are the wind's words. Young, yet old. One life whole, another incomplete. I *have seen*, Leoman!' She paused, drew a breath. 'I see no other future but this one. We are safe.' Sha'ik faced Kalam again. 'I acquired a . . . a pet recently, which I now send with you, for I sense . . . possibilities in you, Deliverer.' She gestured again.

The huge, ungainly shape moved closer and Kalam took an involuntary step backward. His stallion voiced a soft squeal and stood trembling.

Leoman spoke. 'An aptorian, Deliverer, from the realm of Shadow. Sent into Raraku by Shadowthrone . . . to spy. It belongs to Sha'ik now.'

The beast was a nightmare, close to nine feet tall, crouching on two thin hind limbs. A lone foreleg, long and multijointed, jutted down from its strangely bifurcated chest. From a hunched, angular shoulder blade, the demon's sinuous neck rose to a flat, elongated head. Needle fangs ridged its jawline, which was swept back and naturally grinning like a dolphin's.

Head, neck and limbs were black, while its torso was a dun grey. A single, flat black eye regarded Kalam with appalling awareness.

The assassin saw barely healed scarring on the demon. 'It's been in a fight?'

Sha'ik scowled. 'A D'ivers. Desert wolves. She drove them off—'

'More like a tactical withdrawal,' Leoman added dryly. 'The beast does not eat or drink, so far as we've seen. And though the Holy One believes otherwise, it appears to be entirely brainless – that look in its eye is likely a mask hiding very little.'

'Leoman plagues me with doubts,' Sha'ik said. 'It is his chosen task and I grow increasingly weary of it.'

'Doubts are healthy,' Kalam said, then snapped his mouth shut.

The Holy One only smiled. 'I sensed you two were alike. Leave us, then. The Seven Holies know, one Leoman is enough.'

With a final glance at the young Toblakai, the assassin vaulted back into the saddle, swung the stallion to the south trail and nudged him into a trot.

The aptorian evidently preferred some distance between them; it moved parallel to Kalam at over twenty paces away, a darker stain in the night, striding awkwardly yet silently on its three bony legs.

After ten minutes of riding at a fast trot, the assassin slowed the stallion to a walk. He had delivered the Book, personally seen to the rise of the Whirlwind. Answered his blood's call, no matter how stained the motivation.

The demands of his other life lay ahead. He would kill the Empress, to save the Empire. If he succeeded, Sha'ik's rebellion was doomed. Control would be restored. *And if I fail, they will bleed each other to exhaustion, Sha'ik and Laseen, two women of the same cloth – Hood, they even looked alike.* It was not a far reach, then, for Kalam to see in his shadow a hundred thousand deaths. And he wondered if, throughout Seven Cities, readers of the Deck of Dragons now held a newly awakened Herald of Death in their trembling hands.

Queen's blessing, it's done.

Minutes before dawn, Sha'ik sat down cross-legged before the Book of the Apocalypse. Her two guards flanked her, each in the ruins of a watchtower. The Toblakai youth leaned on his two-handed ironwood sword. A battered bronze helmet missing a cheek-guard was on his head, his eyes hidden in the shadow of a slitted half-visor. His companion's arms were crossed. A cross-bow leaned against one hide-wrapped leg. Two one-handed morning stars were thrust through his broad leather belt. He wore a colourless telaba scarf over a peaked iron helm. Below it, his smooth-shaven face showed, latticed by thirty years of sun and wind. His light-blue eyes were ever restless.

The dawn's rays swept over Sha'ik. The Holy One reached down and opened the Book.

The quarrel struck her forehead an inch above her left eye. The iron head shattered the bone, plunging inward a moment before the spring-driven barbs opened like a deadly flower inside her brain. The quarrel's head then struck the inside of the back of her skull, exiting explosively.

Sha'ik toppled.

Tene Baralta bellowed and watched with satisfaction as Aralt Arpat and Lostara Yil led the twelve Red Blades in a charge towards the two hapless bodyguards.

The desert warrior had dropped and rolled a moment after Sha'ik's death. The crossbow now in his hands bucked. Aralt Arpat's chest visibly caved inward as the quarrel drove through his breastbone. The tall sergeant was knocked backward, sprawling in the dust.

The commander bellowed in fury, drew his tulwars and joined the attack.

Lostara's squad threw lances in staggered succession when but fifteen paces from the Toblakai.

Tene Baralta's eyes widened in astonishment as not one of the six lances struck home. Impossibly lithe for one of such bulk, the Toblakai seemed to simply step through them, shifting weight and dipping a shoulder before springing to close, his archaic wooden sword sweeping across in a backswing that connected with the leading Red Blade's knees. The man went down in a cloud of dust, both legs shattered.

Then the Toblakai was in the squad's midst. As Tene Baralta sprinted to reach them, he saw Lostara Yil reel back, blood spraying from her head, her helmet spinning away to bounce across the potsherd gravel. A second soldier fell, his throat crushed by a thrust from the wooden sword.

Arpat's squad attacked the desert warrior. Chains snapped as the morning stars lashed out and struck with deadly accuracy. There was no more difficult a weapon to parry than a morning star – the chain wrapped over any block, sending the iron ball unimpeded to its target. The weapon's greatest drawback was that it was slow to recover, but in the instant that Tene Baralta glanced over to gauge the battle, he saw that the desert warrior fought equally well with either hand, and was staggering his attacks, resulting in a perpetual sequence of blows that none of the soldiers facing him could penetrate. A helmed head crumpled under the impact in the momentary span of the commander's glance.

In an instant Tene Baralta's tactics shifted. Sha'ik was dead. The mission was a success – there would be no Whirlwind. It was pointless throwing lives away against these two appalling executioners – who had, after all, failed in guarding Sha'ik's life and now sought naught but vengeance. He barked out the recall, and watched as his soldiers battled to extricate themselves from the two men. The effort proved costly, as three more fell before the remaining fighters cleared a space in which to turn and run.

Two of Lostara Yil's soldiers were loyal enough to drag the dazed sergeant with them in their retreat.

Bristling at the sight of the routed Red Blades, Tene Baralta swallowed down a stream of bitter curses. Tulwars held out, he shielded the soldiers' withdrawal, his nerves on fire at the thought of either bodyguard accepting the challenge.

But the two men did not pursue, resuming their positions at the watchtowers. The desert warrior crouched to reload his crossbow.

The sight of the weapon readied was the last Tene Baralta had of the two killers, as the commander then ducked out of sight and jogged with his soldiers back to the small canyon where the horses were tethered.

In the high-walled arroyo, the Red Blades stationed their lone surviving crossbowman on the south-facing crest, then paused to staunch wounds and regain their breaths. Behind them, their horses nickered at the smell of blood. A soldier splashed water on Lostara's red-smeared face. She blinked, awareness slowly returning to her eyes.

Tene Baralta scowled down at her. 'Recover yourself, Sergeant,' he growled. 'You are to regain Kalam's trail – at a safe distance.'

She nodded, reaching up to probe the gash on her forehead. 'That sword was *wood*.'

'Yet as hard as steel, aye. Hood take the Toblakai – and the other one at that. We'll leave them be.'

A slightly wry expression coming to her face, Lostara Yil simply nodded again.

Tene reached down a gauntleted hand and pulled the sergeant to her feet. 'A fine shot, Lostara Yil. You killed the god-cursed witch and all that went with her. The Empress shall be pleased. More than pleased.'

Weaving slightly, Lostara went to her horse, pulled herself into the saddle.

'We ride to Pan'potsun,' Tene Baralta told her. 'To spread the word,' he added with a dark grin. 'Do not lose Kalam, Sergeant.'

'I've yet to fail in that,' she said.

You know I'll count these losses as yours, don't you? Too clever, lass.

He watched her ride away, then swung his glare on his remaining soldiers. 'Cowards! Lucky for you that I guarded your retreat. Mount up.'

Leoman laid out the blanket on the flat ground between the two watchtower foundations, and rolled Sha'ik's linen-wrapped body onto it. He knelt beside it a moment, motionless, then wiped grimy sweat from his brow.

The Toblakai stood nearby. 'She is dead.'

'I see that,' Leoman said dryly, reaching to collect the blood-spattered Book, which he slowly rewrapped in cloth.

'What do we do now?'

'She opened the Book. It was dawn.'

'Nothing happened, except a quarrel going through her head.'

'Damn you, I *know*!'

The Toblakai crossed his massive arms, fell silent.

'The prophecy was certain,' Leoman said after a few minutes. He rose, wincing at his battle-stiffened muscles.

'What do we do now?' the young giant asked again.

'She said she would be . . . renewed . . .' He sighed, the Book heavy in his hands. 'We wait.'

The Toblakai raised his head, sniffed. 'There's a storm coming.'

Book Two

Whirlwind

I have walked old roads
This day
That became ghosts with
Coming night
And were gone to my eyes
With dawn.
Such was my journey
Leagues across centuries
In one blink of the sun

Pardu epitaph

CHAPTER SIX

Early in Kellanved's reign, cults proliferated among
the Imperial armies, particularly among the Marines.
It should be remembered that this was also the time
of Dassem Ultor, First Sword and Supreme Commander
of the Malazan forces . . . a man sworn to Hood . . .

Malazan Campaigns, vol. II
Duiker

Beneth sat at his table in Bula's, cleaning his nails with a
dagger. They were immaculate, making the habit an
affectation. Felisin had grown familiar with his poses
and what they betrayed of his moods. The man was in a rage,
shot through with fear. Uncertainties now plagued his life; like
bloodfly larvae they crawled beneath his skin, growing as they
gnawed on his flesh.

His face, his forehead and his thick, scarred wrists all
glistened with sweat. The pewter mug of chilled Saltoan wine
sat untouched on the battered tabletop, a row of flies marching
round and round the mug's rim.

Felisin stared at the tiny black insects, memories of horror
returning to her. Hood's acolyte, who was not there. A man-
shaped swarm of Death's sprites, the buzz of wings shaping
words . . .

'There's light in your eyes again, lass,' Beneth said. 'Tells me you're realizing what you've become. An ugly light.' He pushed a small leather pouch across the table until it sat directly before her. 'Kill it.'

Her hand trembled as she reached for the bag, loosened the ties and removed a button of durhang.

He watched her crumbling the moist pollen into her pipe bowl.

Six days, and Baudin was still missing. Captain Sawark had called in Beneth more than once. Skullcup was very nearly dismantled during the search, patrols on Beetle Road up on the rim were doubled – *round and round* – and Sinker Lake was dredged. It was as if the man had simply vanished.

Beneth took it personally. His control of Skullcup was compromised. He'd called her back to his side, not out of compassion, but because he no longer trusted her. She knew something – something about Baudin – and worse, he knew she was more than she pretended to be.

Beneth and Sawark have spoken, Heboric said the day she'd left – when his ministrations had done enough to allow her to fake a well-being sufficient to justify her leaving. *Be careful, lass. Beneth is taking you back, but only to personally oversee your destruction. What was haphazard before is now precise, deliberate. He's been given guidelines.*

How do you know any of this?

True, I'm just guessing. But Baudin's escape has given Beneth leverage over Sawark, and he's likely to have used it to get the inside story on you. Sawark's granted him more control – there won't be another Baudin – neither man can afford it. Sawark has no choice but to give Beneth more control . . . more knowledge . . .

The durhang tea had given her relief from the pain of her fractured ribs and her swollen jaw, but it had not been potent enough to dull her thoughts. Minute by minute, she'd felt her mind drag her ever closer to desperation. Leaving Heboric had been a flight, her journey back to Beneth a panicked necessity.

He smiled as she set flame to the durhang.

'Baudin wasn't just a dockside thug, was he?'

She frowned at him through a haze of smoke.

Beneth set the dagger down and gave it a spin. They both watched the blade's flashing turns. When it ceased, the point faced Beneth. He scowled, spun it a second time. As the point slowed to face him again he picked up the dagger and slid it back into the sheath at his belt, then reached for the pewter mug.

The flies scattered as he raised the mug to his lips.

'I don't know anything about Baudin,' Felisin said.

His deep-set eyes studied her for a long moment. 'You haven't figured anything out about anything, have you? Which makes you either thick . . . or wilfully ignorant.'

She said nothing. A numbness was spreading through her.

'Was it me, lass? Was it so much of a surrender becoming mine? I wanted you, Felisin. You were beautiful. Sharp – I could see that in your eyes. Am I to blame for you, now?'

He saw her glance down at the pouch on the table and offered up a wry smile. 'Orders are orders. Besides, you could have said no.'

'At any time,' she said, looking away.

'Ah, not my fault, then.'

'No,' she replied, 'the faults are all mine, Beneth.'

Abruptly he rose. 'There's nothing pleasant in the air tonight. The She'gai's begun – the hot wind – all your suffering until now has just been a prelude, lass. Summer begins with the She'gai. But tonight . . .' He stared down at her but did not finish the sentence, simply taking her by the arm and pulling her upright. 'Walk with me.'

Beneth had been granted the right to form a militia, consisting of his chosen slaves, each now armed with a clout. Throughout the night they patrolled the makeshift streets of Skullcup. The curfew's restriction would now be punctuated with beating followed by execution for anyone caught out in the open after nightfall. The guards would handle the execution – Beneth's militia took their pleasure in the beating.

Beneth and Felisin joined the patrol squad, half a dozen men she knew well, as Beneth had bought their loyalty with her body. 'If it's a quiet night,' he promised them, 'we'll take time for some relaxation come the dawn.' The men grinned at that.

They walked the littered aisles of sand, watchful but seeing no-one else. Coming opposite a gambling establishment called Suruk's, they saw a crowd of Dosii guardsmen. The Dosii captain, Gunnip, was with them. Their night-hooded gazes followed the patrol as it continued on.

Beneth hesitated, as if of a mind to speak with Gunnip, then, with a loud sigh through his nostrils, resumed walking. One hand reached up to rest on the pommel of his knife.

Felisin became dully aware of something, as if the hot wind breathed a new menace into the night air. The chatter of the militiamen, she noted, had fallen away, and signs of nervousness were evident. She extracted another button of durhang and popped it into her mouth, where it rested cool and sweet between cheek and gum.

'Watching you do that,' Beneth muttered, 'reminds me of Sawark.'

She blinked. 'Sawark?'

'Aye. The worse things get, the more he shuts his eyes.'

Her words came out slurred. 'And what things are getting worse?'

As if in answer, a shout followed by harsh laughter sounded behind them, coming from the front of Suruk's. Beneth halted his men with a gesture, then walked back to the crossroads they had just passed. From there he could see Suruk's – and Gunnip's soldiers.

Like a wraith rising up and stealing through Beneth, tension slowly filled the man's posture. As she watched, vague alarms rang in Felisin's skull. She hesitated, then turned to the militiamen. 'Something's happened. Go to him.'

They were watching as well. One of them scowled, one hand sliding skittish along his belt to the clout. 'He ain't gived us no orders,' he growled. The others nodded, fidgeting as they waited in the shadows.

'He's standing alone,' she said. 'Out in the open. I think there's arrows trained on him—'

'Shut your face, girl,' the militiaman snapped. 'We ain't going out there.'

Beneth almost backed up a step, then visibly steeled himself.

'They're coming for him,' Felisin hissed.

Gunnip and his Dosii soldiers wandered into view, closing a half-circle around Beneth. Cocked crossbows resting on forearms pointed towards him.

Felisin spun to the militiamen. 'Back him up, damn you!'

'Hood take you!' one of the men spat back. The patrol was scattering, slipping back into the shadows and then into the dark alleyways beyond.

'You all alone back there, lass?' Captain Gunnip called out. His soldiers laughed. 'Come join Beneth here. We're just telling him some things, that's all. No worry, lass.'

Beneth turned to speak to her. A Dosii guardsman stepped up and struck him across the face with a gauntleted hand. Beneth staggered, swearing as he brought his hands up to his shattered nose.

Felisin stumbled backward, then twisted and ran, even as crossbows thudded. Quarrels whipped past her on either side as she plunged into an alley mouth. Laughter echoed behind her.

She ran on, the alley paralleling Rust Ramp. A hundred paces ahead waited Darkhall and the barracks. She was out of breath when she stumbled into the open area surrounding the two Malazan buildings, her heart hammering in her chest as if she was fifty years old, not fifteen. Slowly, the shock of seeing Beneth struck down spread through her.

Voices shouted from behind the barracks. Horse hooves pounded. A score of slaves appeared, running towards where Felisin stood with a half-hundred mounted Dosii soldiers behind them. Lances took some men in the back, driving them down into the dust. Unarmed, the slaves tried to flee, but the Dosii had now completed the encirclement. Belatedly, Felisin realized that escape had been denied her as well.

I saw Beneth bleed. From that thought followed another. *Now we die.*

The Dosii horses trampled men and women. Tulwars swung down. In hopeless silence, the slaves were dying. Two riders closed in on Felisin. She watched, wondering which of them would reach her first. One gripped a lance, angled down to take her in the chest. The other held his wide-bladed sword high, readied for a downward chop. In their faces she saw flushed joy and was surprised at the inhumanity of the expression.

When they were both but moments away, quarrels thudded into their chests. Reeling, both men toppled from the saddles. Felisin turned to see a troop of Malazan crossbowmen advancing in formation, the front line kneeling to reload while the second line slipped a few paces ahead, took aim, then as one loosed quarrels into the milling Dosii horsemen. Animals and men screamed in pain.

A third volley broke the Dosii, scattering them back into the darkness beyond the barracks.

A handful of slaves still lived. A sergeant barked an order and a dozen soldiers moved forward, checking the bodies littering the area, then pushing the survivors back towards the troop's position.

'Come with me,' a voice hissed beside Felisin.

She blinked, slow to recognize Pella's face. 'What?'

'We're quartering the slaves at the stables – but not you.' He gently took her arm. 'We're badly outnumbered. Defending slaves isn't a high priority, I'm afraid. Sawark wants this mutiny crushed. Tonight.'

She studied his face. 'What are you saying?'

The sergeant had pulled his troop into a more defensible position at an alley mouth. The twelve detached soldiers were pushing the slaves down the side street that led to the stables. Pella guided Felisin in the same direction. Once out of sight of the sergeant, he addressed the other soldiers. 'Three of you, with me.'

One replied, 'Has Oponn stirred your brains, Pella? I don't feel safe as it is, and you want to split the squad?'

Another growled, 'Let's just get rid of these damned slaves and get back, afore the sergeant marches to rejoin the captain.'

'This is Beneth's woman,' Pella said.

'I don't think Beneth is still alive,' Felisin said dully.

'He was not five minutes ago, lass,' Pella said, frowning. 'Bloodied a bit, nothing more. He's rallying his militia right now.' He swung to the others. 'We'll need Beneth, Reborid, never mind Sawark's bluster. Now, three of you – we're not going far.'

With a scowl, the one named Reborid gestured to two others.

A fire had been started in Skullcup's western arm – somewhere on Spit Row. Unchecked, it was spreading fast, throwing a lurid orange glow up against the underbellies of billowing smoke.

As Pella dragged Felisin along, Reborid talked unceasingly. 'Where in Hood's name is the Be'thra Garrison? You think they can't see the flames? There were Malazan squads up

217

patrolling Beetle Road – a rider would have been sent – the troop should be here by now, dammit.'

There were bodies in the streets, huddled, motionless shapes. The small party went around them without pause.

'Hood knows what Gunnip's thinking,' the soldier went on. 'Sawark will see every damn Dosii within fifty leagues of here gutted and left out under the sun.'

'This is the place,' Pella said, tugging Felisin to a halt. 'Defensive position,' he ordered the others. 'I'll be but a moment.'

They were at Heboric's house. No light leaked from the shutters. The door was locked. Snorting with disgust, Pella kicked the flimsy barrier aside. His hand against her back, he pushed her into the darkness within, then followed.

'There's no-one here,' Felisin said.

Pella did not reply, still pushing her along, until they reached the cloth divider behind which was the ex-priest's bedroom. 'Pull it aside, Felisin.'

She did, stepping into the small room. Pella followed.

Heboric sat on his cot, staring up at them in silence.

'I wasn't sure,' Pella said in a low voice, 'if you still wanted her along.'

The ex-priest grunted. 'What of you, Pella? We might manage—'

'No. Take her instead. I've got to rejoin the captain – we'll crush this mutiny – but the timing's perfect for you . . .'

Heboric sighed. 'Aye, that it is. Fener's grunt, Baudin, step out of them shadows. This lad's no risk to us.'

Pella started as a massive shape separated itself from behind the hanging. Baudin's narrow-set eyes glittered in the dimness. He said nothing.

Shaking himself, Pella stepped back to the entrance, gripping the grimy cloth with one hand. 'Fener guard you, Heboric.'

'Thank you, lad. For everything.'

Pella gave a curt nod, then was gone.

Felisin frowned at Baudin. 'You're wet.'

Heboric rose. 'Is all ready?' he asked Baudin.

The big man nodded.

'Are we escaping?' Felisin asked.

'Aye.'

'How?'

Heboric scowled. 'You'll see soon enough.'

Baudin picked up two large leather packs from behind him, and tossed one effortlessly to Heboric, who trapped it deftly between his arms. The sound the pack made when the ex-priest caught it made it obvious to Felisin that it was in fact a sealed bladder, filled with air. 'We're going to swim Sinker Lake,' she said. 'Why? There's nothing but a sheer cliff on the other side.'

'There's caves,' Heboric said. 'You can reach them when the water level's low . . . ask Baudin, since he's been hiding in one for a week.'

'We have to take Beneth,' Felisin pronounced.

'Now, lass—'

'No! You owe me – both of you! You wouldn't be alive to even do this, Heboric, if it wasn't for me. And for Beneth. I'll find him, meet you at the lakeshore—'

'No, you won't,' Baudin said. 'I'll get him.' He handed Felisin the bladder.

She watched him slip out through a back door she hadn't known was there, then slowly turned to regard Heboric. He was crouched down, examining the loose netting wrapped around the packs. 'I wasn't part of your escape plan, was I, Heboric?'

He glanced up, raised his brows. 'Until tonight, it seemed you'd made Skullcup your paradise. I didn't think you'd be interested in leaving.'

'Paradise?' For some reason the word shook her. She sat down on the cot.

Eyeing her, he shrugged. 'Beneath provided.'

She held his gaze until, after a long moment, he finally pulled away, hefting the pack as he rose with a grunt. 'We should get going,' he said gruffly.

'I'm not much in your eyes any more, am I, Heboric? Was I ever?' *Felisin, House of Paran, whose sister was Adjunct Tavore, whose brother rode with Adjunct Lorn. Nobleborn, a spoiled little girl. A whore.*

He did not reply, making his way to the gap in the back wall.

The western half of Skullcup was in flames, lighting the entire bowl a grainy, wavering red. Heboric and Felisin saw evidence of clashes as they hurried down Work Road towards the lake – downed horses, dead Malazan and Dosii guards. Bula's Inn had been barricaded, then the barriers breached. From the darkness of the doorway, as they passed, came a faint moaning.

Felisin hesitated, but Heboric hooked her arm. 'You don't want to go in there, lass,' he said. 'Gunnip's men hit that place early on, and hard.'

Beyond the town's edge, Work Road stretched empty and dark all the way to the Three Fates fork. Through the rushes on their left was the glimmer of Sinker Lake's placid surface.

The ex-priest led her down into the grasses, bade her crouch down, then did the same. 'We'll wait here,' he said, wiping sweat from his wide, tattooed forehead.

The mud under her knees was clammy, pleasantly cool. 'So we swim to the cave . . . then what?'

'It's an old mineshaft, leading up beyond the rim, well past Beetle Road. There will be supplies left for us at the other end. From there, it's out across the desert.'

'Dosin Pali?'

He shook his head. 'Straight west, to the inside coast. Nine, ten days. There's hidden springs – Baudin has memorized their locations. We'll get picked up by a boat and taken across to the mainland.'

'How? Who?'

The ex-priest grimaced. 'An old friend with more loyalty than is probably good for him. Hood knows, I'm not complaining.'

'And Pella was the contact?'

'Aye, some obscure connection to do with friends of fathers and uncles and friends of friends or something like that. He first approached you, you know, but you didn't catch on. So he found me himself.'

'I don't remember anything like that.'

'A quote, attributed to Kellanved and recorded by the man arranging our escape – Duiker.'

'A familiar name . . .'

'The Imperial Historian. He spoke on my behalf at the trial. Then, afterwards, arranged to be sent to Hissar by warren.' He fell silent, slowly shook his head. 'To save a bitter old man who more than once denounced his written histories as deliberate lies. If I live to stand face to face with Duiker, I think I owe the man an apology.'

A buzzing, frenzied sound reached them, coming from the smoky air above the town. The sound grew louder. Sinker Lake's smooth surface vanished beneath what seemed a spray of hailstones.

Felisin crouched lower in fear. 'What is it? What's happening?'

Heboric was silent a moment, then he hissed, 'Bloodflies! Drawn, then driven, by the fires. Quickly, lass, scoop up mud – cover yourself! And then me. Hurry!'

Glittering clouds of the insects swept into view, racing like gusts of fog.

Frantic, Felisin dug her fingers into the cool mud between

the reed stems, slapping handfuls against her neck, arms, face. As she worked she crawled forward on her knees until she sat in the lake water, then she turned to Heboric. 'Come closer!'

He scrambled to her side. 'They'll dive through the water, girl – you need to get out of there – cover your legs in mud!'

'Once I'm done with you,' she said.

But it was too late. All at once the air was almost unbreathable as a cloud engulfed them. Bloodflies shot down into the water like darts. Pain lanced through her thighs.

Heboric pushed her hands away, then ducked down. 'Mind yourself, lass!'

The command was unnecessary, as all thoughts of helping Heboric had vanished with the first savage bite. Felisin leapt from the water, clawed gouges of mud free and slapped them down on her blood-smeared thighs. She quickly added more down to her calves, her ankles and feet. Insects crawled through her hair. Whimpering, she clawed them away, then covered her head with mud. Bloodflies rode her drawn gasps into her mouth, biting as she gagged and spat. She found herself biting down, crunching them, and their bitter juices burned like acid. They were everywhere, blinding her as they gathered in frenzied clumps around her eyes. Screaming, she scraped them away, then reached down and found more mud. Soothing darkness, yet her screaming did not stop, would not stop. The insects were at her ears. She filled them with mud. Silence.

Handless arms wrapped tight around her, Heboric's voice reaching her as if from a great distance away. 'It's all right, lass – it's all right. You can stop screaming, Felisin. You can stop.'

She had curled into a ball amidst the reeds. The pain of the bites was passing to numbness – on her legs, around her eyes and ears, and in her mouth. Cool, soft numbness. She heard herself fall silent.

'The swarm's passing,' Heboric said. 'Fener's blessing too

fierce a touch for them. We're all right, lass. Wipe clear your eyes – see for yourself.'

She made no move. It was too easy to lie still, the numbness spreading through her.

'Wake up!' Heboric snapped. 'There's an egg in every bite, each secreting a poison that deadens, turns your flesh into something soft. And dead. Food for the larvae inside those eggs. You understanding me, lass? We need to kill those eggs – I've a tincture, in the pouch at my belt – but you'll need to apply it yourself, right? An old man without hands can't do it for you—'

She moaned.

'Wake up, damn you!'

He struck her, pushed, then kicked. Cursing, Felisin sat up. 'Stop it, I'm awake!' Her words slurred passing through her numbed mouth. 'Where is that pouch?'

'Here. Open your eyes!'

She could barely see through the puffed swelling, but a strange blue penumbra rising from Heboric's tattoos illuminated the scene. He was unbitten. *Fener's blessing too fierce a touch*.

He gestured at the pouch at his belt. 'Quickly, those eggs are about to hatch, then the larvae will start eating you – from the inside out. Open the pouch . . . there, the black bottle, the small one. Open it!'

She removed the stopper. A bitter smell made her recoil.

'One drop, on your fingertip, then push that drop right into the wound, push it hard. Then the next one and the next—'

'I – I can't feel the ones around my eyes—'

'I'll guide you, lass. Hurry.'

The horror did not end. The tincture, a foul, dark-brown juice that stained her skin yellow, did not kill the emerging larvae, but drove them out. Heboric directed her hands to the ones around her eyes and ears as each sluggishly wriggled free,

223

and she plucked them from the holes made by the bites, each larva as long as a nail clipping, limp with the soporific effect of the tincture. The bites she could see illustrated what was happening around her eyes and ears. In her mouth, the tincture's bitterness overrode the bloodfly larvae's poison, making her head spin and her heart beat alarmingly fast. The larvae fell like grains of rice onto her tongue. She spat them out.

'I'm sorry, Felisin,' Heboric said after she had done. He was examining the bites around her eyes, his expression filled with compassion.

A chill ran through her. 'What's wrong? Will I go blind? Deaf? What is it, Heboric!'

He shook his head, slowly sat back. 'Bloodfly bites . . . the deadening poison kills the flesh. You'll heal, but there will be pockmarks. I'm so sorry, lass. It's bad around your eyes. It's bad . . .'

She almost laughed, her head reeling. Another shiver rippled through her and she hugged herself. 'I've seen those. Locals. Slaves. Here and there—'

'Aye. Normally, bloodflies don't swarm. It must have been the flames. Now listen, a good enough healer – someone with High Denul – can remove the scarring. We'll find ourselves such a healer, Felisin. I swear it, by Fener's tusks, I swear it.'

'I feel sick.'

'That's the tincture. Rapid heart, chills, nausea. It's the juice of a plant native to Seven Cities. If you drank down what's left in that tiny bottle you'd be dead in minutes.'

This time she did laugh, the sound shaky and brittle. 'I might welcome Hood's Gates, Heboric.' She squinted at him. The blue glow was fading. 'Fener must be very forgiving.'

He frowned at that. 'I can make no sense of it, to be honest. I can think of more than one High Priest to Fener who'd choke at the suggestion that the boar god was . . . forgiving.' He sighed. 'But it seems you're right.'

'You might want to offer thanks. A sacrifice.'

'I might,' he growled, looking away.

'It must have been a great offence that drove you from your god, Heboric.'

He did not reply. After a moment he rose, eyes on the flame-wracked town. 'Riders coming.'

She sat up straighter, still too dizzy to stand. 'Beneth?'

He shook his head.

Moments later a troop of Malazans rode up, halting directly opposite Heboric and Felisin. At the head was Captain Sawark. A Dosii blade had laid open one cheek. His uniform was wet and dark with blood. Felisin involuntarily shrank back from his cold lizard eyes as they fixed on her.

He finally spoke, 'When you're up on the rim . . . look south.'

Heboric cursed softly in surprise. 'You're letting us go? Thank you, Captain.'

His face darkened. 'Not for you, old man. It's seditious bastards like you that are the cause of all this. I'd rather spit you on a spear right now.' He made as if to say something more, his eyes finding Felisin once again, but instead he simply reined his mount around.

The two fugitives watched the troop ride back into Skullcup. They were heading for a battle. Felisin knew this instinctively. Another sourceless certainty told her, in a whisper, that they would all die. Captain Sawark. Pella. Every Malazan. She glanced over at Heboric. The man looked thoughtful as he watched the troop reach the edge of town, then vanish into the smoke.

A moment later Baudin rose from a bed of reeds nearby.

Felisin clambered to her feet and stepped towards him. 'Where's Beneth?'

'Dead, lass.'

'You – you . . .' Her words were drowned out in a flood of

225

pain rising up within her, an anguish more thorough in shattering her than anything she'd yet suffered. She staggered back a step.

Baudin's small, flat eyes held steady on her.

Heboric cleared his throat. 'We'd best hurry. Dawn's not far off, and while I doubt our crossing the lake is likely to be noticed, there's no point in making our intentions obvious. After all, we're Malazan.' He strode down to the waiting bladders. 'The plan is to wait out the coming day at the other end of the reach, then set out after sunset. Less likely that any roving bands of Dosii will see us.'

Dully, Felisin followed the two men to the lake's edge. Baudin strapped one of the packs against Heboric's chest. Felisin realized she would have to share the other bladder with Baudin. She studied the big man as he checked the netting one last time.

Beneth's dead. So he says. He probably didn't even look for him. Beneth's alive. He must be. Nothing more than a bloodied face. Baudin's lying.

Sinker Lake's water washed the last of the mud and tincture from Felisin's skin. It was not nearly enough.

The cliff face bounced back the echoes of their harsh breaths. Chilled and feeling the water striving to pull her down, Felisin tightened her grip on the netting. 'I see no cave,' she gasped.

Baudin grunted. 'Surprised you can see anything at all,' he said.

She made no reply. The flesh around her eyes had swollen until only slits remained. Her ears felt like slabs of meat, heavy and huge, and the flesh inside her mouth had closed around her teeth. She was having difficulty breathing, constantly clearing her throat without effect. The discomforts left her feeling dislocated, as if she had no vanity left to sting, bringing an almost amused relief.

Surviving this is all that counts. Let Tavore see all the scars she's given me, the day we come face to face. I need say nothing, then, to justify my revenge.

'The opening is under the surface,' Heboric said. 'We need to puncture these bladders and swim down. Baudin will go first, with a rope tied to his waist. Hold on to that rope, lass, else you'll be pulled to the bottom.'

Baudin handed her a dagger, then laid the rope over the bobbing pack. A moment later he pushed himself towards the cliff wall and vanished beneath the lake's surface.

Felisin snatched at the rope, gripping it hard as she watched the coils play out. 'How far down?'

'Seven, eight feet,' Heboric said. 'Then about fifteen feet through the cave until you'll find your next breath. Can you manage it, lass?'

I will have to.

Faint screams drifted across the lake. The burning town's last, pitiful cries. It had happened so swiftly, almost quietly – a single night to bring Skullcup to a bloody end. It didn't seem real.

She felt a tug on the rope.

'Your turn,' Heboric said. 'Puncture the bladder, let it sink away from you, then follow the rope.'

She reversed her grip on the dagger and stabbed down. A gust of air whistled, the pack sagging. Like hands, the water pulled her down. She snatched a frantic breath before slipping under. In a moment the rope no longer led down, but up. She came up against the slick face of the cliff. The dagger fell away as she clutched the rope with both hands and pulled herself along.

The cave mouth was a deeper blackness, the water bitter cold. Already her lungs screamed for air. She felt herself blacking out, but savagely pushed the feeling away. A glimmer of reflected light showed ahead. Kicking out as her mouth filled with water, she clawed her way towards it.

Hands reached down to grip her tunic's hemmed collar and pulled her effortlessly up into air, into light. She lay on hard, cold stone, racked with coughs. An oil-wick lantern glowed beside her head. Beyond it, leaning against the wall, were two wood-framed travel packs and bladders swollen with water.

'You lost my damned knife, didn't you?'

'Hood take you, Baudin.'

He grunted his laugh, then focused his attention on reeling in the rope. Heboric's head broke the black surface moments later. Baudin pulled the ex-priest onto the rock shelf.

'Must be trouble up top,' the big man said. 'Our supplies were brought down here.'

'So I see.' Heboric sat up, gasping as he recovered his breath.

'Best you two stay here while I scout,' Baudin said.

'Aye. Off with you, then.'

As Baudin disappeared up the reach, Felisin sat up. 'What kind of trouble?'

Heboric shrugged.

'No,' she said. 'You've suspicions.'

He grimaced. 'Sawark said, "Look south."'

'So?'

'So just that, lass. Let's wait for Baudin, shall we?'

'I'm cold.'

'We spared no room for extra clothing. Food and water, a few weapons, a fire kit. There's blankets but best keep them dry.'

'They'll dry out soon enough,' she snapped, crawling over to one of the packs.

Baudin returned a few minutes later and crouched down beside Heboric. Shivering under a blanket, Felisin watched the two men. 'No, Baudin,' she said as he prepared to whisper something to the ex-priest, 'loud enough for all of us.'

The big man glanced at Heboric, who shrugged.

'Dosin Pali is thirty leagues away,' Baudin said. 'Yet you can see its glow.'

Heboric frowned. 'Even a firestorm wouldn't be visible at such a distance, Baudin.'

'True enough, and it's no firestorm. It's sorcery, old man. A mage battle.'

'Hood's breath,' Heboric muttered. 'Some battle!'

'It's come,' Baudin growled.

'What has?' Felisin asked.

'Seven Cities has risen, lass. Dryjhna. The Whirlwind's come.'

The hogg boat was all of thirteen feet in length. Duiker paused a long moment before clambering down into it. Six inches of water sloshed beneath the two flat boards that formed the craft's deck. Rags stoppered a score of minor leaks in the hull, with various degrees of efficacy. The smell of rotting fish was almost overwhelming.

Wrapped in his army-issue raincape, Kulp had not moved from where he stood on the dock. 'And what,' he asked tonelessly, 'did you pay for this . . . boat?'

The historian sighed, glancing up at the mage. 'Can you not repair it? What was your warren again, Kulp?'

'Boat repair,' the man answered.

'Very well,' Duiker said, climbing back onto the dock. 'I take your point. To cross the Strait you will need something more seaworthy than this. The man who sold me this craft seems to have exaggerated its qualities.'

'A haral's prerogative. Better had you hired a craft.'

Duiker grunted. 'Who could I trust?'

'Now what?'

The historian shrugged. 'Back to the inn. This requires a new plan.'

They made their way up the rickety dock and entered the dirt track that passed for the village's main thoroughfare. The fisher shacks on either side displayed a paucity of pride common to small communities in the shadow of a large city. Dusk had fallen, and apart from a pack of three scrawny dogs taking turns rolling on the carcass of a fish, there was no-one about. Heavy curtains blotted out most of the light coming from the shacks. The air was hot, an inland wind holding at bay the sea breeze.

The village inn stood on stilts, a sprawling, single-storey structure of bleached wood frame, burlap walls and thatched roof. Crabs scuttled in the sand beneath it. Opposite the inn was the stone blockhouse of a Malazan Coastal Guard detachment – four sailors from Cawn and two marines whose appearance betrayed nothing of their origins. For them, the old national allegiances no longer held any relevance. *The new Imperial breed*, Duiker mused as he and Kulp entered the inn and returned to the table they'd occupied earlier. The Malazan Guards were crowded around another, close to the back wall where the burlap had been pulled aside, revealing the tranquil scene of withered grasses, white sand and glittering sea. Duiker envied the soldiers the fresh air that no doubt drifted in to where they sat.

They'd yet to approach, but the historian knew it was only a matter of time. In this village travellers would be rare, and one wearing the field cape of a soldier even rarer. Thus far, however, translating curiosity into action had proved too great an effort.

Kulp gestured to the barman for a jug of ale, then leaned close to Duiker. 'There's going to be questions. Soon. That's one problem. We don't have a boat. That's another. I'm a poor excuse for a sailor, that's a third—'

'All right, all right,' the historian hissed. 'Hood's breath, let me think in peace!'

His expression sour, Kulp leaned back.

Moths danced clumsily between the sputtering lanterns in

the room. There were no villagers present, and the lone barman's attention seemed close to obsessive on the Malazan soldiers, holding his thin, dark eyes on them even as he set down the ale jug in front of Kulp.

Watching the barman leave, the mage grunted. 'This night's passing strange, Duiker.'

'Aye.' *Where is everyone?*

The scrape of a chair drew their attention to the ranking Malazan, a corporal by the sigil on his surcoat, who'd risen and now approached. Beneath the dull tin sigil was a larger stain, where the surcoat's dye was unweathered – the man had once been a sergeant.

To match his frame, the corporal's face was flat and wide, evincing north Kanese blood somewhere in his ancestry. His head was shaved, showing razor scars, some still blotted with dried blood. His gaze was fixed on Kulp.

The mage spoke first. 'Watch your tongue, lest you keep walking backwards.'

The soldier blinked. 'Backwards?'

'Sergeant, then corporal – you bucking for private now? You've been warned.'

The man seemed unaffected. 'I see no rank showing,' he growled.

'Only because you don't know what to look for. Go back to your table, Corporal, and leave our business to us.'

'You're Seventh Army.' He clearly had no intention of returning to his table. 'A deserter.'

Kulp's wiry brows rose. 'Corporal, you've just come face to face with the Seventh's entire Mage Cadre. Now back out of my face before I put gills and scales on yours.'

The corporal's eyes flicked to Duiker, then back to Kulp.

'Wrong,' the mage sighed. '*I'm* the entire cadre. This man's my guest.'

'Gills and scales, huh?' The corporal set his wide hands

231

down on the tabletop and leaned close to Kulp. 'I get even a sniff of you opening a warren, you'll find a knife in your throat. This is my guardpost, magicker, and any business you got here is my business. Now, start explaining yourselves, before I cut those big ears off your head and add 'em to my belt. Sir.'

Duiker cleared his throat. 'Before this goes any further—'

'Shut your mouth!' the corporal snapped, still glaring at Kulp.

Distant shouting interrupted them. 'Truth!' the corporal bellowed. 'Go see what's happening outside.'

A young Cawn sailor leapt to his feet, checking a newly issued short sword scabbarded at his hip as he crossed to the door.

'We are here,' Duiker told the corporal, 'to purchase a boat—'

A startled curse came from just outside, followed by a frantic scrabbling of boots on the rickety inn steps. The recruit named Truth tumbled back inside, his face white. An impressive stream of Cawn dockside curses issued from the youth's mouth, finishing with: '– got an armed mob outside, Corporal, and they ain't interested in talking. Saw them split, about ten heading to the *Ripath*.'

The other sailors were on their feet. One addressed the corporal. 'They'll torch her, Gesler, then we'll be stuck on this stinking strip of beach—'

'Arms out and form up,' Gesler growled. He rose, turning to the other marine. 'Front door, Stormy. Find out who's leading that group out there and stick a quarrel between his eyes.'

'We have to save the boat!' the sailors' spokesman said.

Gesler nodded. 'That we will, Vered.'

The marine named Stormy took position at the door, his cocked assault crossbow appearing as if from nowhere. Outside, the shouting had grown louder, closer. The mob was working itself into the courage it needed to rush the inn. The boy Truth stood in the centre of the room, the short sword twitching in his hand, his face red with rage.

'Calm yourself, lad,' Gesler said. His eyes fell to Kulp. 'I'm less likely to cut off your ears if you open a warren now, Mage.'

Duiker asked, 'You've made enemies in this village, Corporal?'

The man smiled. 'This has been coming for some time. *Ripath* is fully provisioned. We can get you to Hissar . . . maybe . . . we got to get out of this first. Can you use a crossbow?'

The historian sighed, then nodded.

'Expect some arrows through the walls,' Stormy said from the doorway.

'Found their leader yet?'

'Aye, and he's keeping his distance.'

'We can't wait – to the back door, everyone!'

The barman, who'd been crouching behind the small counter on one side of the room, now stepped forward, hunched crablike in expectation of the first flight of arrows through the burlap wall. 'The tab, Mezla – many weeks now. Seventy-two jakatas—'

'What's your life worth?' Gesler asked, gesturing for Truth to join the sailors as they slipped through the break in the rear wall.

The barman's eyes went wide, then he ducked his head. 'Seventy-two jakatas, Mezla?'

'About right,' the corporal nodded.

Cool, damp air, smelling of moss and wet stone, filled the room. Duiker looked at Kulp, who mutely shook his head. The historian rose. 'They've got a mage, Corporal—'

A roar rushed from the street outside and struck the front of the inn like a wave. The wooden frame bowed, the burlap walls bellying. Kulp loosed a warning shout, pitching from his chair and rolling across the floor. Wood split, cloth tore.

Stormy lunged away from the front, and all at once

everyone left in the room was bolting for the rear exit. The floor lifted under them as the front stilts lost their footing, pitching everyone towards the back wall. Tables and chairs toppled, joining the headlong rush. Screaming, the barman vanished under a rack of wine jugs.

Tumbling through the rent, Duiker fell through the darkness to land on a heap of dried seaweed. Kulp landed on him, all knees and elbows, driving the breath from the historian's lungs.

The inn was still rising from the front as the sorcerous wave took hold of all it touched, and *pushed.*

'Do something, Kulp!' Duiker gasped.

In answer the mage pulled the historian upright, spun him around, then gave him a hard shove. 'Run! That's what we're going to do!'

The sorcery ravaging the inn abruptly ceased. Still balanced on its rear stilts, the building pitched back down. Cross-beams snapped. The inn seemed to explode, the wood frame shattering. The ceiling collapsed straight down, hitting the floor in a cloud of sand and dust.

Stumbling beside Duiker as they hurried down to the beach, Stormy grunted, 'Hood's just paid the barman's tab, eh?' The marine gestured with the crossbow he carried. 'I'm here to take care of you. Corporal's gone ahead – we're looking at a scrap getting to *Ripath's* dock.'

'Where's Kulp?' Duiker demanded. It had all happened so fast, he was feeling overwhelmed with confusion. 'He was here beside me—'

'Gone sniffing after that spell-caster is my guess. Who can figure mages, eh? Unless'n he's run away. Hood knows he ain't showed much so far, eh?'

They reached the strand. Thirty paces to their left Gesler and the sailors were closing in on a dozen locals who'd taken up positions in front of a narrow dock. A low, sleek patrol craft with a single mast was moored there. To the right the beach stretched in a gentle curve southward, to distant Hissar . . . a city in flames. Duiker staggered to a halt, staring at the ruddy sky above Hissar.

'Togg's teats!' Stormy hissed, following the historian's gaze. 'Dryjhna's come. Guess we won't be taking you to the city after all, eh?'

'Wrong,' Duiker said. 'I need to rejoin Coltaine. My horse is in the stables – never mind the damn boat.'

'They're pinching her flanks right now, I bet. Around here, people ride camels, eat horses. Forget it.' He reached out but the historian pulled away and began running up the strand, away from *Ripath* and the scrap that had now started there.

Stormy hesitated, then, growling a curse, set off after Duiker.

A flash of sorcery ignited the air above the front street, followed by an agonized shriek.

Kulp, Duiker thought. *Delivering or dying.* He stayed on the beach, running parallel to the village, until he judged he was opposite the stables, then he turned inward, scrabbling through the weeds of the tide line. Stormy moved up beside the historian.

'I'll just see you safe on your way, eh?'

'My thanks,' Duiker whispered.

'Who are you anyway?'

'Imperial Historian. And who are you, Stormy?'

The man grunted. 'Nobody. Nobody at all.'

They slowed as they slipped between the first row of huts, keeping to the shadows. A few paces from the street the air blurred in front of them and Kulp appeared. His cape was scorched, his face red from a fireflash.

'Why in Hood's name are you two here?' he demanded in a hiss. 'There's a High Mage out prowling around – Hood knows why he's here. Problem is, he knows *I'm* here, which makes me bad company to be around – I barely squeezed the last one—'

'That scream we heard was yours?' Duiker asked.

'Ever had a spell roll onto you? My bones have been rattled damn near out of their sockets. I shat my pants, too. But I'm alive.'

'So far,' Stormy said, grinning.

'Thanks for the blessing,' Kulp muttered.

Duiker said, 'We need to—'

The night blossomed around them, a coruscating, flame-lit explosion that flung all three men to the ground. The historian's shriek of pain joined two others as the sorcery seemed to claw into his flesh, clutch icy cold around his bones, sending jolts of agony up his limbs. His scream rose higher as the relentless pain reached his brain, blotting out the world in a blood-misted haze that seemed to sizzle behind his eyes. Duiker thrashed about and rolled across the ground, but there was no escape. This sorcery was killing him, a horrifyingly personal assault, invading every corner of his being.

Then it was gone. He lay unmoving, one cheek pressed against the cool, dusty ground, his body twitching in the aftermath. He'd soiled himself. He'd pissed himself. His sweat was a bitter stink.

A hand clutched the collar of his telaba. Kulp's breath gusted hot at his ear as the mage whispered, 'I slapped back. Enough to sting. We need to get to the boat – Gesler's—'

'Go with Stormy,' Duiker gasped. 'I'm taking the horses—'

'Are you mad?'

Biting back a scream, the historian pushed himself to his feet. He staggered as memories of pain rippled through his limbs. 'Go with Stormy, damn you – go!'

Kulp stared at the man, then his eyes narrowed. 'Aye, ride as a Dosii. Might work . . .'

Stormy, his face white as death, plucked the mage's sleeve. 'Gesler won't wait for ever.'

'Aye.' With a final nod at Duiker, the mage joined the marine. They ran hard back down to the beach.

Gesler and the sailors were in trouble. Bodies lay sprawled in the churned-up sand around the dock – the first dozen locals and two of the Cawn sailors. Gesler, flanked by Truth and another sailor, were struggling to hold at bay a newly arrived score of villagers – men and women – who flung themselves forward in a spitting frenzy, using harpoons, mallets, cleavers, some with only their bare hands. The remaining two sailors – both wounded – were on *Ripath*, feebly attempting to cast off the lines.

Stormy led Kulp to within a dozen paces of the mob, then the marine crouched, took aim and fired a quarrel into the press. Someone shrieked. Stormy slung the crossbow over a shoulder and drew a short sword and gutting dagger. 'Got anything for this, Mage?' he demanded, then, without waiting for a reply, he plunged forward, striking the mob on its flank. Villagers reeled; none was killed, but many were horribly maimed as the marine waded into the press – the dead posed no burden; the wounded did.

Gesler now held the dock alone, as Truth was pulling a downed comrade back towards the boat. One of the wounded sailors on *Ripath*'s deck had stopped moving.

Kulp hesitated, knowing that whatever sorcery he unleashed would draw down on them the High Mage. The cadre mage did not think it likely that he could withstand another attack. All his joints were bleeding inside, swelling the flesh with blood. By the morning he would not be able to move. *If I survive this night*. Even so, more subtle ploys remained.

Kulp raised his arms, voicing a keening shriek. A wall of fire erupted in front of him, then rolled, tumbling and growing, rushing towards the villagers. Who broke, then ran. Kulp sent the flame up the beach in pursuit. When it reached the banked sward, it vanished.

Stormy whirled. 'If you could do that—'

'It was nothing,' Kulp said, joining the men.

'A wall of—'

'I meant *nothing*! A Hood-blinked illusion, you fool! Now, let's get out of here!'

They lost Vered twenty spans from the shore, a harpoon-head buried deep in his chest finally gushing the last of his blood onto the slick deck. Gesler unceremoniously rolled the man over the side. Remaining upright in addition to the corporal were the youth Truth, Stormy and Kulp. Another sailor was slowly losing a battle with a slashed artery in his left thigh and was but minutes from Hood's Gate.

'Everyone stay quiet,' Kulp whispered. 'Show no lights – the High Mage is on the beach.'

Breaths were held, including a pitiless hand clamped down over the dying sailor's mouth until the man's moaning ceased.

With barely a storm-sail rigged, *Ripath* slipped slowly from the shallow bay, her keel parting water with a soft susurration. Loud enough, Kulp knew. He opened his warren, threw sounds in random directions, a muted voice here, a creak of wood there. He cast a shroud of gloom over the area, holding the power of his warren back, letting it trickle forth to deceive, not challenge.

Sorcery flashed sixty spans to their left, fooled by a thrown sound. The gloom swallowed the magic's light.

The night fell silent once again. Gesler and others seemed to grasp what Kulp was doing. Their eyes held on him, hopeful, with barely checked fear. Truth held the tiller, motionless, not daring to do anything but keep the sail ahead of the soft breeze.

It seemed they merely crawled on the water. Sweat dripped from Kulp – he was soaked through with the effort of evading the High Mage's questing senses. He could feel those deadly probes, only now realizing that his opponent was a woman, not a man.

Far to the south, Hissar's harbour was a glowing wall of black-smeared flames. No effort was made to angle towards it, and Kulp understood as well as the others that there would be no succour found there. Seven Cities had risen in mutiny.

And we're at sea. Is there a safe harbour left to us? Gesler said this boat was provisioned – far enough to take us to Aren? Through hostile waters at that . . . A better option would be Falar, but that was over six hundred leagues south of Dosin Pali.

Then another thought struck him, even as the questing of the High Mage faded, then finally vanished. *Heboric Light Touch – the poor bastard's heading for the rendezvous if all's gone as planned. Crossing a desert to a lifeless coast.* 'Breathe easy now,' the mage said. 'She's abandoned the hunt.'

'Out of range?' Truth asked.

'No, just lost interest. I'd guess she has more important matters to attend to, lad. Corporal Gesler.'

'Aye?'

'We need to cross the strait. To the Otataral Coast.'

'What in Hood's name for, Mage?'

'Sorry, this time I'm pulling rank. Do as I command.'

'And what if we just push you over the side?' Gesler enquired calmly. 'There's dhenrabi out here, feeding along the edge of Sahul Shelf. You'd be a tasty morsel . . .'

Kulp sighed. 'We go to pick up a High Priest of Fener, Corporal. Feed me to a dhenrabi and no-one mourns the loss. Anger a High Priest and his foul-tempered god might well cock one red eye in your direction. Are you prepared for that risk?'

The corporal leaned back and barked a laugh. Stormy and Truth were grinning as well.

Kulp scowled. 'You find this amusing?'

Stormy leaned over the gunnel and spat into the sea. He wiped his mouth with the back of his hand, then said, 'It seems

Fener's already cocked an eye in our direction, Mage. We're Boar Company, of the disbanded First Army. Before Laseen crushed the cult, that is. Now we're just marines attached to a miserable Coastal Guard.'

'Ain't stopped us from following Fener, Mage,' Gesler said. 'Or even recruiting new followers to the warrior cult,' he added, nodding towards Truth. 'So just point the way – Otataral Coast, you said. Angle her due east, lad, and let's get this sail up and ready the spinnaker for the morning winds.'

Slowly, Kulp sat back. 'Anyone else need to wash out their leggings?' he asked.

Wrapped in his telaba, Duiker rode from the village. There were figures to either side of the coastal road, featureless in the faint moon's light. The cool desert air seemed to carry in it the residue of a sandstorm, a desiccating haze that parched the throat. Reaching the crossroads, the historian reined in. Southward the coastal road continued on, down to Hissar. A trader track led west, inland. A quarter-mile down this track was encamped an army.

There was no order evident. Thousands of tents were haphazardly pitched around a huge central corral shrouded in fire-lit clouds of dust. Tribal chants drifted across the sands. Along the track, no more than fifty long paces from Duiker's position, a hapless squad of Malazan soldiers writhed on what were locally called Sliding Beds – four tall spears each set upright, the victim set atop the jagged points, at the shoulders and upper thighs. Depending on their weight and their strength of will in staying motionless, the impaling and the slow slide down to the ground could take hours. With Hood's blessing, the morrow's sun would hasten the tortured death. The historian felt his heart grow cold with rage.

He could not help them, Duiker knew. It was challenge enough to simply stay alive in a countryside aflame with murderous lust. But there would come a time for retribution. *If the gods will it.*

Mage fires blossomed vast and – at this distance – silent over Hissar. Was Coltaine still alive? Bult? The Seventh? Had Sormo divined what was coming in time?

He tapped his heels against his mount's flanks, continued down the coastal road. The renegade army's appearance was a shock. It had emerged as if from nowhere, and for all the chaos of the encampment there were commanders there, filled with bloodthirsty intent and capable of achieving what they planned. This was no haphazard revolt. *Kulp said a High Mage. Who else is out there? Sha'ik has had years in which to build her army of the Apocalypse, despatch her agents, plan this night – and all that will follow. We knew it was happening. Laseen should have stuck Pormqual's head on a spike long ago. A capable High Fist could have crushed this.*

'Dosii kim'aral!'

Three cloaked shapes rose from the flood track on the inland side of the road. 'A night of glory!' Duiker responded, not slowing as he rode past.

'Wait, Dosii! The Apocalypse waits to embrace you!' The figure gestured towards the encampment.

'I have kin in Hissari Harbour,' the historian replied. 'I go to share in the riches of liberation!' Duiker reined in suddenly and pulled his horse around. 'Unless the Seventh has won back the city – is this the news you have for me?'

The spokesman laughed. 'They are crushed. Destroyed in their beds, Dosii! Hissar has been freed of the Mezla curse!'

'Then I ride!' Duiker kicked the horse forward again. He held his breath as he continued on, but the tribesmen did not call after him. *The Seventh gone? Does Coltaine ride a sliding bed right now?* It was hard to believe, yet it might well be true. Clearly the attack had been sudden, backed by high sorcery – *with me dragging Kulp away, on this night of all nights, Hood curse my bones.* For all the lives within him, Sormo E'nath was still a boy, his flesh hardly steeled to such a challenge. He might well have bloodied a few noses among the enemy's mages. To expect or hope for more than that was being unfair. They would have fought hard, every one of them. Hissar's price would have been high.

Nonetheless, Duiker would have to see for himself. The Imperial Historian could do no less. More, he could ride among the enemy and that was an extraordinary opportunity. *Never mind the risks.* He would gather all the information he could, anticipating an eventual return to the ranks of a Malazan punitive force, where his knowledge could be put to lethal use. *In other words, a spy. So much for objectivity, Duiker.* The image of the Malazan soldiers lining the trader track, dying slowly on the sliding beds, was enough to sear away his detachment.

Magic flared in the fishing village half a mile behind him. Duiker hesitated, then rode on. Kulp was a survivor, and by the look of that Coastal Guard, he had veterans at his side. The mage had faced powerful sorcery before – what he could not defeat, he could escape. Duiker's soldiering days were long past, his presence more of an impediment than an asset – they were better off without him.

But what would Kulp do now? If there were any survivors among the Seventh, then the cadre mage's place was with them. What, then, of Heboric's fate? *Well, I've done what I could for the old handless bastard. Fener guard you, old man.*

There were no refugees on the road. It seemed the fanatic call to arms was complete – all had proclaimed themselves soldiers of Dryjhna. Old women, fisherwives, children and pious grandfathers. Nonetheless, Duiker had been expecting to find Malazans, or at the very least signs of their passage, scenes where their efforts to escape came to a grisly end. Instead, the raised military road stretched bare, ghostly in the moon's silver light.

Against the glare of distant Hissar appeared desert cape-moths, wheeling and fluttering like flakes of ash as broad across as a splayed hand as they crossed back and forth in front of the historian. They were carrion-eaters, and they were heading in the same direction as Duiker, in growing numbers.

Within minutes the night was alive with the silent, spectral insects, whirling past the historian on all sides. Duiker struggled against the chill dread rising within him. *'The world's harbingers of death are many and varied.'* He frowned, trying to recall where he'd heard those words. *Probably from one of the countless dirges to Hood, sung by the priests during the Season of Rot in Unta.*

The first of the city's outlying slums appeared in the fading gloom ahead, a narrow cluster of shacks and huts clinging to the shelf above the beach. Smoke now rode the air, smelling of burning painted wood and scorched cloth. The smell of a city destroyed, the smell of anger and blind hatred. It was all too familiar to Duiker, and it made him feel old.

Two children raced across the road, ducking between shacks. One voiced a laugh that pealed with madness, too knowing by far to come from one so young. The historian rode past the spot, his skin crawling. He was astonished to feel the fear within him – *afraid of children? Old man, you don't belong here.*

The sky was lightening over the strait on his left. The cape-moths were plunging into the city ahead, vanishing inside the roiling clouds of smoke. Duiker reined in. The coastal road split here, the main track leading straight to become a main thoroughfare of the city. A second road, on the right, skirted the city and led to the Malazan barracks compound. The historian gazed down that road, squinting. Black columns of smoke rose half a mile away above the barracks, the columns bending high up where a desert wind caught hold and pushed them seaward.

Butchered in their beds? The possibility suddenly seemed all too real. He rode towards the barracks. On his right, as shadows appeared with the rising sun, the city of Hissar burned. Support beams were giving way, mudbrick walls tumbling, cut stone shattering explosively in the blistering heat. Smoke covered the scene with its deathly, bitter shawl. Every now and then a distant scream sounded from the city's heart. It was clear that the mutiny's destructive ferocity had turned on itself. Freedom had been won, at the cost of everything.

He reached the trampled earth where the trader encampment had once been – where he and the warlock Sormo had witnessed the divination. The camp had been hastily abandoned, possibly only hours earlier. A pack of dogs from the city now rooted through the rubbish left behind.

Opposite the grounds, and on the other side of the Faladhan road, rose the fortified wall of the Malazan compound. Duiker slowed his mount to a walk, then a halt. Streaks of black scarred the few sections of bleached stone remaining upright. The sorcery that had assailed the wall had breached it in four places that he could see, each one a sundering of stone wide enough to rush a phalanx through. Bodies crowded the breaches, sprawled amidst the tumbled blocks. None wore much in the way of armour, and the weapons Duiker saw scattered about ranged from antique pikes to butcher's cleavers.

The Seventh had fought hard, meeting their attackers at every breach; in the face of savage sorcery, they had cut down their attackers by the score. No-one had been caught asleep in his bed. The historian felt a trickle of hope seep into his thoughts.

He glanced down the road, down to where the nut trees lined the cobbled street. There had been a cavalry sortie of some kind, close to the compound's inner city gate. Two horses lay among dozens of Hissari bodies, but no lancers that he could see. Either they'd been lucky enough to lose no-one in the attack, or they'd had the time to retrieve their slain and wounded comrades. There was a hand of organization here, a strong one. *Coltaine? Bult?*

He saw no-one living down the length of the street. If battle continued, it had moved on. Duiker dismounted and approached one of the breaches in the compound wall. He clambered over the rubble, avoiding the stones slick with blood. Most of the attackers, he saw, had been killed by quarrels. Many bodies were virtually pincushioned with the stubby arrows. The range had been devastatingly short, the effect lethal. A frenzied, disorganized rush by a mob of ill-equipped Hissari stood no chance against such concentrated fire. Duiker saw no bodies beyond the ridge of tumbled stone.

The compound's training field was empty. Bulwarks had been raised here and there to establish murderous crossfire should the defence at the breaches fail – but there was no sign that that had occurred.

He stepped down from the ridge of shattered stone. The Malazan headquarters and the barracks had been torched. Duiker now wondered if the Seventh had not done it themselves. *Announcing to all that Coltaine had no intention of hiding behind walls, the Seventh and the Wickans marched out, in formation. How did they fare?*

He returned to his waiting horse. Back in the saddle he could see more smoke, billowing heavily from the Malazan Estates district. Dawn had brought a strange calm to the air. To see the city so empty of life made it all seem unreal, as if the bodies sprawled in the streets were but scarecrows left over from a harvest festival. The capemoths had found them, however, covering the forms completely, their large wings slowly fanning as they fed.

As he rode towards the Malazan Estates, he could hear the occasional shout and faint scream in the distance, barking dogs and braying mules. The roar of fires rose and fell like waves clawing a cliff face, carrying gusts of heat down the side streets hissing and rustling through the litter.

Fifty paces from the Estates Duiker found the first scene of true slaughter. The Hissari mutineers had struck the Malazan quarter with sudden ferocity, probably at the same time as the other force had hemmed in the Seventh at the compound. The merchant and noble houses had thrown their own private guards forward in frantic defence, but they were too few and, lacking cohesion, had been quickly and savagely cut down. The mob had poured into the district, battering down estate posterns, dragging out into the wide street Malazan families.

It was then, Duiker saw as his mount picked a careful path through the bodies, that madness had truly arrived. Men had been gutted, their entrails pulled out, wrapped around women – wives and mothers and aunts and sisters – who had been raped before being strangled with the intestinal ropes. The historian saw children with their skulls crushed, babies spitted on tapu skewers. However, many young daughters had been taken by the attackers as they plunged deeper into the district. If anything, their fates would be more horrific than those visited on their kin.

Duiker viewed all he saw with a growing numbness. The terrible agony that had been unleashed here seemed to remain coiled in the air, poised, ready to snatch at his sanity. In self-defence, his soul withdrew, deeper, ever deeper. His power to observe remained, however, detached completely from his feelings – the release would come later, the historian well knew: the shaking limbs, the nightmares, the slow scarification of his faith.

Expecting to see more of the same, Duiker rode towards the first square in the district. What he saw instead jarred him. The Hissari mutineers had been ambushed in the square and slaughtered by the score. Arrows had been used and then retrieved, but some shattered shafts remained. The historian dismounted to pick one up. *Wickan*. He believed he could now piece together what had occurred.

The barracks compound had been besieged. Whoever commanded the Hissari had intended to prevent Coltaine and his forces from striking out into the city, and, if the sorcery's level was any indication, had sought the complete annihilation of the Malazan army. In this the commander had clearly failed. The Wickans had sortied, broken through the encirclement, and had ridden directly to the Estates – where they well knew the planned slaughter would have already begun. Too late to prevent the first attack at the District Gates, they had altered their route, riding around the mob, and set up an ambush in the square. The Hissari, in their thirst for more blood, had plunged forward, crossing the expanse without the foresight of scouts.

The Wickans had then killed them all. There was no risk of reprisal to prevent them later retrieving their arrow shafts. The killing must have been absolute, every escape closed off, then the precise, calculated murder of every Hissari in the square.

Duiker swung about at the sound of approaching footsteps. A band of mutineers approached from the gates behind him. They were well armed, with pikes in their hands and tulwars at their hips. Chain vests glinted from beneath the red telaban they wore. On their heads were the peaked bronze helmets of the City Guard.

'Terrible slaughter!' Duiker wailed, drawing out the Dosii accent. 'It must be avenged!'

The sergeant leading the squad eyed the historian warily. 'You have the dust of the desert upon you,' he said.

'Aye, I have ridden down from the High Mage's forces to the north. A nephew, who dwelt in the harbour district. I seek to join him—'

'If he yet lives, old man, you shall find him marching with Reloe.'

'We have driven the Mezla from the city,' another soldier said. 'Outnumbered, already sorely wounded and burdened with ten thousand refugees—'

'Silence, Geburah!' the sergeant snapped. He narrowed his gaze on Duiker. 'We go to Reloe now. Come with us. All of Hissari shall be blessed in joining in the final slaughter of the Mezla.'

Conscription. No wonder there's no-one about. They're in the holy army whether they like it or not. The historian nodded. 'I shall. I have vowed to protect the life of my nephew, you see . . .'

'The vow to scourge Seven Cities of the Mezla is greater,' the sergeant growled. 'Dryjhna demands your soul, Dosii. The Apocalypse has come – armies gather all across the land and all must harken to the call.'

'Last night I joined in spilling the blood of a Mezla Coastal Guard – my soul was given to her keeping then, Hissari.' Duiker's tone held a warning to the young sergeant. *Respect your elders, child.*

The man answered the historian with an acknowledging nod.

Leading his horse by the reins, Duiker accompanied the squad as they made their way through the Estates. Kamist Reloe's army, the sergeant explained, was marshalling on the plain to the southwest of the city. Three Odhan tribes were maintaining contact with the hated Mezla, harrying the train of refugees and the too few soldiers trying to protect them. The Mezla were seeking to reach Sialk, another coastal city twenty leagues south of Hissar. What the fools did not know, the man added with a dark grin, was that Sialk had fallen as well, and even now thousands of Mezla nobles and their families were being driven up the north road. The Mezla commander

248

was about to see a doubling of citizens he was sworn to defend.

Kamist Reloe would then encircle the enemy, his forces outnumbering them seven to one, and complete the slaughter. The battle was expected to take place in three days' time.

Duiker made agreeable noises through all this, but his mind was racing. Kamist Reloe was a High Mage, one believed to have been killed in Raraku over ten years ago, in a clash with Sha'ik over who was destined to lead the Apocalypse. Instead of killing her rival, it was now apparent that Sha'ik had won his loyalty. The hint of murderous rivalry, feuds and personality clashes had served Sha'ik well in conveying to the Malazans an impression of internal weaknesses plaguing her cause. *All a lie. We were deceived, and now we are suffering the cost.*

'The Mezla army is as a great beast,' the sergeant said as they neared the city's edge, 'wounded by countless strikes, flanks streaming with blood. The beast staggers onward, blind with pain. In three days, Dosii, the beast shall fall.'

The historian nodded thoughtfully, recalling the seasonal boar hunts in the forests of northern Quon Tali. A tracker had told him that among the hunters who were killed in such hunts, most met their fate *after* the boar had taken a fatal wound. An unexpected, final lashing out, a murderous lunge that seemed to defy Hood's grip on the beast. Seeing victory only moments away stripped caution from the hunters. Duiker heard something of that overconfidence in the mutineer's words. The beast streamed with blood, but it was not yet dead.

The sun climbed the sky as they travelled south.

The chamber's floor sagged like a bowl, carpeted in thick, felt-like drifts of dust. Almost a third of a league into the hill's stone heart, the rough-cut walls had cracked like glass, fissures reaching down from the vaulted roof. In the centre of the room lay a fishing boat resting on one flank, its lone mast's unreached sail hanging like rotted webbing. The dry, hot air had driven the dowels from the joins and the planks had contracted, splaying beneath the boat's own weight.

'This is no surprise,' Mappo said from the portalway.

Icarium's lips quirked slightly, then he stepped past the Trell and approached the craft. 'Five years? Not longer – I can still smell the brine. Do you recognize the design?'

'I curse myself for having taken no interest in such things,' Mappo sighed. 'Truly I should have anticipated moments like these – what was I thinking?'

'I believe,' Icarium said slowly, resting a hand on the boat's prow, 'this is what Iskaral Pust wished us to find.'

'I thought the quest was for a broom,' the Trell muttered.

'No doubt his broom will turn up of its own accord. It was not the goal of the search we were to value, but the journey.'

Mappo's eyes narrowed suspiciously on his friend, then his canines showed in an appreciative grin. 'That is always the way, isn't it?' He followed the Jhag into the chamber. His nostrils flared. 'I smell no brine.'

'Perhaps I exaggerated.'

'I'll grant you it does not look like it's been here for centuries. What are we to make of this, Icarium? A fishing boat, found in a room deep within a cliff in a desert thirty leagues from anything bigger than a spring. The High Priest sets before us a mystery.'

'Indeed.'

'Do *you* recognize the style?'

'Alas, I am as ignorant of water craft and other things of the sea as you, Mappo. I fear we have already failed in Iskaral Pust's expectations.'

The Trell grunted, watching Icarium begin examining the boat.

'There are nets in here, deftly made. A few withered things that might have been fish once . . . ah!' The Jhag reached down. Wood clattered. He straightened, faced Mappo, in his hands the High Priest's broom.

'Do we now sweep the chamber?'

'I think our task is to return this to its rightful owner.'

'The boat or the broom?'

Icarium's brows rose. 'Now that is an interesting question, friend.'

Mappo frowned, then shrugged. If there had been anything clever in his query, it was there purely by chance. He was frustrated. Too long underground, too long inactive and at the whim of a madman's schemes. It was an effort to bend his mind to this mystery, and indeed he resented the assumption that it was worth doing at all. After a long moment, he sighed. 'Shadow swept down on this craft and its occupant, plucked them both away and delivered them here. Was this Pust's own boat? He hardly strikes me as from fisher bloodlines. I've not heard a single dockside curse pass his lips, no salty metaphors, no barbed catechisms.'

'So, not Iskaral Pust's craft.'

'No. Leaving . . .'

'Well, either the mule or Servant.'

Mappo nodded. He rubbed his bristled jaw. 'I'll grant you a mule in a boat dragging nets through shoals might be interesting enough to garner a god's curiosity, sufficient to collect the two for posterity.'

'Ah, but what would be the value without a lake or pond to complete the picture? No, I think we must eliminate the mule. This craft belongs to Servant. Recall his adept climbing skills—'

'Recall the horrid soup—'

'That was laundry, Mappo.'

'Precisely my point, Icarium. You are correct. Servant once plied waters in this boat.'

'Then we are agreed.'

'Aye. Hardly a move up in the world for the poor man.'

Icarium shook himself. He raised the broom like a standard. 'More questions for Iskaral Pust. Shall we begin the return journey, Mappo?'

Three hours later the two weary men found the High Priest of Shadow seated at the table in the library. Iskaral Pust was hunched over a Deck of Dragons. 'You're late,' he snapped, not looking up. 'The Deck keens with fierce energy. The world outside is in flux – your love of ignorance is not worthy of these precipitous times. Attend this field, travellers, or remain lost at your peril.'

Snorting his disgust, Mappo strode to where the jugs of wine waited on a shelf. It seemed even Icarium had been brought short by the High Priest's words, as he dropped the broom clattering on the floor and pulled back a chair opposite Iskaral Pust. The frustrated air about the Jhag did not make likely an afternoon of calm conversation. Mappo poured two cups of wine, then returned to the table.

The High Priest raised the Deck in both hands, closed his eyes and breathed a silent prayer to Shadowthrone. He began a spiral field, laying the centre card first.

'Obelisk!' Iskaral squealed, shifting nervously on his chair. 'I knew it! Past present future, the here, the now, the then, the when—'

'Hood's breath!' Mappo breathed.

The second card landed, its upper left corner overlapping Obelisk's lower right. 'The Rope – Shadow Patron of Assassins, hah!' Subsequent cards followed in swift succession, Iskaral Pust announcing their identities as if his audience were ignorant or blind. 'Oponn, the male Twin upright, the luck that pushes, ill luck, terrible misfortune, miscalculation, poor circumstance ... Sceptre ... Throne ... Queen of High House Life ... Spinner of High House Death ... Soldier of

High House Light . . . Knight of Life, Mason of Dark . . .' A dozen more cards followed, then the High Priest sat back, his eyes thinned to slits, his mouth hanging open. 'Renewal, a resurrection without the passage through Hood's Gates. Renewal . . .' He looked up, met Icarium's eyes. 'You must begin a journey. Soon.'

'Another quest?' the Jhag asked so quietly that Mappo's hackles rose in alarm.

'Aye! Can you not see, fool?'

'See what?' Icarium whispered.

Clearly ignorant that his life hung by a thread, Iskaral Pust rose, wildly gesturing at the field of cards. 'It's right here in front of you, idiot! As clear as my Lord of Shadow could make it! How have you survived this long?' In his frenzy, the High Priest snatched at the wispy patches of hair that remained on his head, yanking the tufts this way and that. He was fairly hopping in place. 'Obelisk! Can't you see? Mason, Spinner, Sceptre, Queens and Knights, Kings and fools!'

Icarium moved lightning fast, across the table, both hands closing around the High Priest's neck, snatching him into the air and dragging him across the tabletop. Iskaral Pust gurgled, his eyes bulging as he kicked feebly.

'My friend,' Mappo warned, fearing he would have to step in and pry Icarium's hands from his victim's neck before lasting damage was done.

The Jhag threw the man back down, shaken by his own anger. He drew a deep breath. 'Speak plainly, priest,' he said calmly.

Iskaral Pust writhed for a moment longer on the tabletop, scattering the wooden cards to the floor, then he stilled. He looked up at Icarium with wide, tear-filled eyes. 'You must venture forth,' he said in a ravaged voice. 'Into the Holy Desert.'

'Why?'

'Why? Why? Sha'ik is dead.'

* * *

'We have to assume,' Mappo said slowly, 'that the characteristic of never answering directly is bred into the man. As natural as breathing.'

They sat in the vestibule the Trell had been given as his quarters. Iskaral Pust had vanished only a few minutes after voicing his pronouncement, and of Servant there had been no sign since their return from the cavern housing the fishing boat.

Icarium was nodding. 'He spoke of a resurrection. It must be considered, for this sudden death of Sha'ik seems to defy every prophecy, unless indeed the "renewal" marks a return from Hood's Gates.'

'And Iskaral Pust expects us to attend this rebirth? How effortlessly has he ensnared us in his mad web. For myself, I am glad the witch is dead, and I hope she remains that way. Rebellion is ever bloody. If her death plucks this land back from the brink of mutiny, then to interfere would put us in great peril.'

'You fear the wrath of the gods?'

'I fear being unwittingly used by them, or their servants, Icarium. Blood and chaos is the wine and meat of the gods – most of them, anyway. Especially the ones most eager to meddle in mortal affairs. I will do nothing to achieve their desires.'

'Nor I, friend,' the Jhag said, rising from his chair with a sigh. 'Nonetheless, I would witness such a resurrection. What deceit has the power to wrest a soul from Hood's clasp? Every ritual of resurrection I have ever heard attempted inevitably resulted in a price beyond reckoning. Even as he relinquishes a soul, Hood ensures he wins in the exchange.'

Mappo closed his eyes, kneaded his broad, scarred brow. *My friend, what are we doing here? I see your desperation, seeking every path in the hopes of revelation. Could I speak openly to you,*

I would warn you from the truth. 'This is an ancient land,' he said softly. 'We cannot guess what powers have been invested in the stone, sand and earth. Generation upon generation.' He glanced up, suddenly weary. 'When we wandered the edge of Raraku, Icarium, I always felt as if I was walking the narrowest strand, in a web stretching to every horizon. The ancient world but sleeps, and I feel its restless shifting – more now than ever before.' *Do not awaken this place, friend, lest it awaken you.*

'Well,' Icarium said after a long, thoughtful moment, 'I shall venture out in any case. Will you accompany me, Mappo Trell?'

His eyes on the heaved pavestones of the floor, Mappo slowly nodded.

The wall of sand rose seamlessly into the sky's ochre dome. Somewhere in that fierce, swirling frenzy was the Holy Desert Raraku. Fiddler, Crokus and Apsalar sat on their lathered mounts at the top of a trail that led down the slope of the hills, out onto the desert wastes. A thousand paces into Raraku and the world simply disappeared.

A faint, sibilant roar reached them.

'Not,' Crokus said quietly, 'your average storm, I assume.'

His spirits had been low since awakening in the morning to find that Moby had once again disappeared. The creature was discovering its wild instincts, and Fiddler suspected they wouldn't see it again.

'When I heard mention of the Whirlwind,' the Daru thief continued after a moment, 'I assumed it was ... well ... figurative. A state of being, I suppose. So tell me, do we now look upon the *true* Whirlwind? The wrath of a goddess?'

'How can a rebellion be born in the heart of that?' Apsalar wondered. 'It would be a challenge to even open one's eyes in that storm, much less orchestrate a continent-wide uprising. Unless, of course, it's a barrier, and beyond there is calm.'

'Seems likely,' Crokus agreed.

Fiddler grunted. 'Then we've no choice. We ride through.'

Their Gral hunters were less than ten minutes behind them, driving equally exhausted horses. They numbered at least a score, and even considering Apsalar's god-given skills, and the assortment of Moranth munitions in Fiddler's pack, the option of making a stand against the warriors was not a promising prospect.

The sapper glanced at his companions. Sun and wind had burned their faces, leaving white creases at the corners of the eyes. Chapped, peeling and split lips showed as straight lines, bracketed by deeper lines. Hungry, thirsty, weaving in their saddles with exhaustion – he was in as bad a shape, he well knew. Worse, given he had not the reserves of youth to draw upon. *Mind you, Raraku marked me once before. Long ago. I know what's out there.*

The other two seemed instinctively to understand Fiddler's hesitation, waiting with something like respect, even as the sound of thundering horse hooves rolled up the trail at their backs.

Apsalar finally spoke. 'I wish to know more . . . of this desert. Its power . . .'

'You shall,' Fiddler growled. 'Wrap up your faces. We go to greet the Whirlwind.'

Like a wing sweeping them into its embrace, the storm closed around them. A savage awareness seemed to ride the spinning sand, reaching relentlessly past the folds of their teleban, a thousand abrasive fingers clawing paths across their skin. Loose cloth and rope ends spiked upward, whipping with urgent rhythm. The roar filled the air, filled their skulls.

Raraku had awakened. All that Fiddler had sensed the last time he rode these wastes, sensed as an underlying restlessness, the spectral promise of nightmares beneath the surface, was now unleashed, exultant with freedom.

Heads ducked, the horses plodded onward, buffeted by

wayward gusts of sand-filled air. The ground underneath was hard-packed clay and rubble – the once deep cloak of fine white sand had been lifted from the surface, now sang in the air, and with it were stripped away the patient, all-covering centuries.

The group dismounted, hooded their mounts' heads, then led them on.

Bones appeared underfoot. Rusting lumps of armour, chariot wheels, remnants of horse and camel tack, pieces of leather, the humped foundation stones of walls – what had been a featureless desert now showed its bones, and they crowded the floor in such profusion as to leave Fiddler in awe. He could not take a step without something crunching underfoot.

A high stone-lined bank suddenly blocked their way. It was sloped, rising to well above their heads. Fiddler paused for a long moment, then he gathered his mount's reins and led the climb. Scrambling, stumbling against the steep bank, they eventually reached the top and found themselves on a road.

The paving stones were exquisitely cut, evenly set, with the thinnest of cracks visible between them. Bemused, Fiddler crouched down, trying to hold his focus as he studied the road's surface – a task made more difficult by the streams of airborne sand racing over the stones. There was no telling its age. While he imagined that, even buried beneath the sands, there would be signs of wear, he could detect none. Moreover, the engineering showed skill beyond any masonry he'd yet seen in Seven Cities.

To his right and left the road ran spearshaft-straight as far as his squinting eyes could see. It stood like a vast breakwater that even this sorcerous storm could not breach.

Crokus leaned close. 'I thought there were no roads in Raraku!' he shouted over the storm's keening wail.

The sapper shook his head, at a loss to explain.

'Do we follow it?' Crokus asked. 'The wind's not as bad up here—'

As far as Fiddler could judge, the road angled southwest-ward, deep into the heart of Raraku. To the northeast it would reach the Pan'potsun Hills within ten leagues – in that direction they would come to the hills perhaps five leagues south of where they had left them. There seemed little value in that. He stared again down the road to his right. *The heart of Raraku. It is said an oasis lies there. Where Sha'ik and her renegades are encamped. How far to that oasis? Can water be found anywhere in between here and there?* Surely a road crossing a desert would be constructed to intersect sources of water. It was madness to think otherwise, and clearly the builders of this road were too skilled to be fools. *Tremorlor . . . If the gods will it, this track will lead us to that legendary gate. Raraku has a heart, Quick Ben said. Tremorlor, a House of the Azath.*

Fiddler mounted the Gral gelding. 'We follow the road,' he yelled to his companions, gesturing southwestward.

They voiced no complaints, turning to their mounts. They had bowed to his command, Fiddler realized, because both were lost in this land. They relied on him completely. *Hood's breath, they think I know what I'm doing. Should I now tell them that the plan to find Tremorlor rests entirely on the faith that the fabled place actually exists? And that Quick Ben's suppositions are accurate, despite his unwillingness to explain the source of his certainty? Do I tell them we're more likely to die out here than anything else – if not from wasting thirst, then at the hands of Sha'ik's fanatical followers?*

'Fid!' Crokus cried, pointing up the road. He spun around to see a handful of Gral warriors ascending the bank, less than fifty paces away. Their hunters had split up into smaller parties, as dismissive of the sorcerous storm as Fiddler's group had been. A moment later they saw their quarry and voiced faint war cries as they pulled their horses onto the flat top.

'Do we run?' Apsalar asked.

The Gral had remounted and were now unslinging their lances.

'Looks like they're not interested in conversation,' the sapper muttered. In a louder voice he said, 'Leave them to me! You two ride on!'

'What, again?' Crokus slid back down from his horse. 'What would be the point?'

Apsalar followed suit. She stepped close to Fiddler, her eyes meeting his. 'With you dead, what are our chances of surviving this desert?'

About as bad as with me leading you. He fought the temptation to give voice to his thought, simply shrugging in reply as he unlimbered his crossbow. 'I mean to make this a short engagement,' he said, loading a cusser quarrel into the weapon's slot.

The Gral had pulled their mounts into position on the road. Lances lowered, they kicked the horses into motion.

Despite himself, Fiddler's heart broke for those Gral horses, even as he aimed and fired. The quarrel struck the road three paces in front of the charging tribesmen. The detonation was deafening, the blast a bruised gout of flame that drove back the airborne sand and the wind carrying it, and flung the attackers and their mounts like a god's hand, backward onto the road and off the sides. Blood shot upward to pull sand down like hail. In a moment the wind swept the flames and smoke away, leaving nothing but twitching bodies.

A pointless pursuit, and now pointless deaths. I am not Gral. Would the crime of impersonation trigger such a relentless hunt? I wish I could have asked you, warriors.

'For all that they have twice saved us,' Crokus said, 'those Moranth munitions are horrible, Fiddler.'

Silent, the sapper loaded another quarrel, slipped a leather thong over the bone trigger to lock it, then slung the heavy weapon over a shoulder. Climbing back into the saddle, he gathered the reins in one hand and regarded his comrades. 'Stay sharp,' he said. 'We may ride into another party without warning. If we do, try to break through them.'

259

He lightly kicked the mare forward.

The wind came as laughter to his ears, the sound seemingly stained with pleasure at witnessing senseless violence. It was eager for more. *The Whirlwind awakened – this goddess is mad, riven with insanity – who is there that can stop her?* Fiddler's slitted eyes stared down the road, the featureless march of stones leading, ever leading, into an ochre, swirling maw. Into nothingness.

Fiddler growled an oath, pushing away the futility clawing at his thoughts. They would have to find Tremorlor, before the Whirlwind swallowed them whole.

The aptorian was a darker shade thirty paces on Kalam's left, striding with relentless ease through the sand-filled wind. The assassin found himself thankful for the storm – his every clear sighting of his unwanted companion scraped his nerves raw. He'd encountered demons before, on battlefields and in war-ravaged streets. Often they had been thrown into the fray by Malazan mages, and so were allies of a sort, even as they went about exacting the wills of their masters with apparent in-difference to all else. On thankfully rarer occasions, he'd come face to face with a demon unleashed by an enemy. At such times survival was his only concern, and survival meant flight. Demons were flesh and blood, to be sure – he'd seen enough of one's insides once, after it had been blown apart by one of Hedge's cusser quarrels, to retain the unwelcome intimacy of the memory – but only fools would try to face down a demon's cold rage and singularity of purpose.

Only two kinds of people die in battle, Fiddler had once said, *fools and the unlucky*. Trading blows with a demon was both unlucky and foolish.

For all that, the aptorian grated strangely on Kalam's eyes, like an iron blade trying to cut granite. Even to focus too long on the beast was to invite a wave of nausea.

There was nothing welcome in Sha'ik's gift. *Gift . . . or spy. She's unleashed the Whirlwind and now the goddess rides her, as certain as possession. That's likely to trim short the wick of gratitude. Besides, even Dryjhna would not so readily waste an aptorian demon on something so mundane as escort. So, friend Apt, I cannot trust you.*

Over the past few days he'd tried losing the beast, departing camp silently an hour before dawn, plunging into the thickest twists of spinning wind. Outracing the creature was a hopeless task – it could outpace any earthly animal in both speed and endurance, and for all his efforts Apt held on to him like a well-heeled hound – although mercifully at a distance.

The wind scoured the rock-scabbed hills with a voracious fury, carving into cracks and fissures as if hungering to spring loose every last speck of sand. The smooth, humped domes of bleached limestone lining the ridges on either side of the shallow valley he rode along seemed to age before his eyes, revealing countless wrinkles and scars.

He'd left the Pan'potsun Hills behind six days earlier, crossing the seamless border into another sawbacked ridge of hills called the Anibaj. The territory this far south of Raraku was less familiar to him. He'd come close on occasion, following the well-travelled trader tracks skirting the eastern edge of the range. The Anibaj were home to no tribes, although hidden monasteries were rumoured to exist.

The Whirlwind had rolled out of Raraku the night before, a star-blotting tidal wave of sorcery that left Kalam shaken despite his anticipating its imminent arrival. Dryjhna had awakened with a hunger fierce enough to render the assassin appalled. He feared he would come to regret his role, and every sighting of Apt only deepened that fear.

The Anibaj were lifeless to Kalam's eyes. He'd seen no sign of habitation, disguised or otherwise. The occasional stronghold ruin hinted at a more crowded past, but that was all. If ascetic monks and nuns hid in these wastelands, the blessing of their deities kept them from mortal eyes.

And yet, as he rode hunched on his saddle, the wind pummelling his back, Kalam could not shake the sense that something was trailing him. The awareness had risen within him over the past six hours. A presence was out there – human or beast – beyond the range of his sight, following, somehow clinging to his trail. He knew his and his horse's scent only preceded them, driven south on the wind, and no doubt swiftly tattered apart before it had gone ten paces. Nor did any tracks his horse left last much beyond a few seconds. Unless the hunter's vision was superior to the assassin's – which he did not think likely – so that he was able to stay just beyond Kalam's own range, the only explanation he was left with was ... *Hood-spawned sorcery. The last thing I need.*

He glared to the left again and could make out Apt's vast shape, its strangely mechanical flow as it kept pace with him. The demon showed no alarm – *mind you, how could one tell?* – but rather than drawing comfort from it he felt instead a growing unease, a suspicion that the demon's role no longer included protecting him.

Abruptly the wind fell, the roar shifting to the hiss of settling sand. Grunting in surprise, Kalam reined in and looked back over his shoulder. The storm's edge was a tumbling, stationary wall five paces behind him. Sand rained from it forming scalloped dunes along a slightly curving edge that ran to the horizon's edge both east and west. Overhead the sky had lightened to a faintly burnished copper. The sun, hanging an hour above the western horizon, was the colour of beaten gold.

The assassin walked his horse on another dozen paces, then halted a second time. Apt had not emerged from the storm. A shiver of alarm took hold and he reached for the crossbow hanging from its strap on the saddlehorn.

A jolt of sudden panic took his horse and the beast shied

sideways, head lifted and ears flattened. A strong, spicy smell filled the air. Kalam rolled from the saddle even as something passed swiftly through the air over him. Relinquishing his grip on the unloaded crossbow, the assassin unsheathed both long-knives even as his right shoulder struck the soft sand, his momentum taking him over and onto his feet in a low crouch. His attacker – a desert wolf of startling mass – had failed in clearing the sidestepping horse and was now scrambling for purchase athwart the saddle, its amber eyes fixed on Kalam.

The assassin lunged forward, thrusting with the narrow blade in his right hand. Another wolf struck him from the left, a writhing weight of thick muscle and snapping jaws, taking him to the ground. His left arm was pinned by the beast's weight. Long canines gouged into the mail links covering his shoulder. Rings popped and snapped, the teeth breaking through and pushing hard against his flesh.

Kalam reached around and drove the point of his right long-knife high into the animal's flank, the blade slipping under the spine just fore of the wolf's hip. The tightening jaws released his shoulder; jerking back, the animal kicked to pull away from him. As the assassin struggled to pull the blade free, he felt the edge bite bone. The Aren steel bent, then snapped.

Howling in pain, the wolf leapt away, back hunched, spinning as if chasing its tail in an effort to close its jaws on the jutting fragment of blade.

Spitting sand, Kalam rolled to his feet. The first wolf had been thrown from its purchase across the saddle by the horse's frenzied bucking. It had then taken a solid kick to the side of the head. The beast stood dazed half a dozen paces away, blood running from its nose.

There were others, somewhere behind the storm wall, their growls, yips and snarls muted by the wind. They battled something, it was obvious. Kalam recalled Sha'ik's mention of a D'ivers that had attacked the aptorian – *inconclusively* – some weeks earlier. It seemed the shapeshifter was trying again.

The assassin saw his horse bolt away down the trail, southward, bucking as it went. He spun back to the two wolves, only to find them gone, twin spattered paths of blood leading back to the storm. From within the Whirlwind all sounds of battle had ceased.

A moment later, Apt lumbered into view. Dark blood streamed from its flanks and dripped from its needle fangs, making the grin of its jawline all the more ghastly. It swung its elongated head and regarded Kalam with its black, knowing eye.

Kalam scowled. 'I risk enough without this damned feud of yours, Apt.'

The demon clacked its jaws, a snakelike tongue darting out to lick the blood from its teeth. He saw it was trembling – some of the puncture wounds near its neck looked deep.

Sighing, the assassin said, 'Treating you will have to await finding my horse.' He reached for the small canteen at his belt. 'But at the very least I can clean your wounds.' He stepped forward.

The demon flinched back, head ducking menacingly.

Kalam stopped. 'Perhaps not, then.' He frowned. There was something odd about the demon, standing on a low hump of bleached bedrock, its head turned as its slitted nostrils flared to test the air. The assassin's frown deepened. *Something* . . . After a long moment, he sighed, glancing down at the grip of the broken long-knife in his right hand. He'd carried the matched pair for most of his adult life, like a mirror to the twin loyalties within him. *Which of the two have I now lost?*

He brushed dust from his telaba, collected his crossbow, slinging it over a shoulder, then began the walk southward, down the trail towards the distant basin. Alongside him, and closer now, Apt followed, head sunk low, its single forelimb kicking up puffs of dust that glowed pink in the sun's failing light.

CHAPTER SEVEN

Death shall be my bridge.

Toblakai saying

Burning wagons, the bodies of horses, oxen, mules, men, women and children, pieces of furniture, clothing and other household items lay scattered on the plain south of Hissar, for as far as Duiker could see. Here and there mounds of bodies rose like earthless barrows, where warriors had made a last, desperate stand. There'd been no mercy to the killing, no prisoners taken.

The sergeant stood a few paces in front of the historian, as silent as his men as he took in the scene that was the Vin'til Basin and the battle that would become known for the village less than a league distant, Bat'rol.

Duiker leaned in his saddle and spat. 'The wounded beast had fangs,' he said sourly. *Oh, well done, Coltaine! They'll hesitate long before closing with you again.* The bodies were Hissari – even children had been flung into the fighting. Black, scorched scars crossed the battlefield as if a god's claws had swept down to join the slaughter. Pieces of burned meat clogged the scars – human or beast, there was no means of telling. Capemoths fluttered like silent madness over the scene. The air stank of sorcery, the clash of warrens had spread greasy ash over everything. The historian felt beyond horror, his heart hardened enough to feel only relief.

Somewhere to the southwest was the Seventh, remnants of loyal Hissari auxiliaries, and the Wickans. *And tens of thousands of Malazan refugees, bereft of their belongings . . . but alive.* The peril remained. Already, the army of the Apocalypse had begun regrouping – shattered survivors contracting singly and in small groups towards the Meila Oasis where awaited the Sialk reinforcements and latecoming desert tribes. When they renewed the pursuit, they would still vastly outnumber Coltaine's battered army.

One of the sergeant's men returned from his scouting to the west. 'Kamist Reloe lives,' he announced. 'Another High Mage brings a new army from the north. There will be no mistakes next time.'

The words were less reassuring to the others than they would have been a day ago. The sergeant's mouth was a thin slash as he nodded. 'We join the others at Meila, then.'

'Not I,' Duiker growled.

Eyes narrowed on him.

'Not yet,' the historian added, scanning the battlefield. 'My heart tells me I shall find the body of my nephew . . . out there.'

'Seek first among the survivors,' one soldier said.

'No. My heart does not feel fear, only certainty. Go on. I shall join you before dusk.' He swung a hard, challenging gaze to the sergeant. 'Go.'

The man gestured mutely.

Duiker watched them stride westward, knowing that should he see them again, it would be from the ranks of the Malazan army. And somehow they would be less than human then. *The game the mind must play to unleash destruction.* He'd stood amidst the ranks more than once, sensing the soldiers alongside him seeking and finding that place in the mind, cold and silent, the place where husbands, fathers, wives and mothers became killers. And practice made it easier, each time. *Until it becomes a place you never leave.*

The historian rode out into the battlefield, almost desperate to rejoin the army. It was not a time to be alone, in the heart of slaughter, where every piece of wreckage or burnt and torn flesh seemed to cry out silent outrage. Sites of battle held on to a madness, as if the blood that had soaked into the soil remembered pain and terror and held locked within it the echoes of screams and death cries.

There were no looters, naught but flies, capemoths, rhizan and wasps – Hood's myriad sprites, wings fanning and buzzing in the air around him as he rode onward. Half a mile ahead a pair of riders galloped across the south ridge, heading west, their telaban whipping twisted and wild behind them.

They had passed out of his sight by the time Duiker reached the low ridge. Before him the dusty ground was rutted and churned. The column that had departed the battlesite had done so in an orderly fashion, though its width suggested that the train was huge. *Nine, ten wagons abreast. Cattle. Spare mounts . . . Queen of Dreams! How can Coltaine hope to defend all this? Two score thousand refugees, perhaps more, all demanding a wall of soldiers protecting their precious selves – even Dassem Ultor would have balked at this.*

Far to the east the sky was smeared ruddy brown. Like Hissar, Sialk was aflame. But there had only been a small Marine garrison in that city, a stronghouse and compound down at the harbour, with its own jetty and three patrol craft. With Oponn's luck they'd made good their withdrawal, though in truth Duiker held little hope in that. More likely they would have sought to protect the Malazan citizens – *adding their bodies to the slaughter.*

It was simple enough to follow the trail Coltaine's army and the refugees had made, southwestward, inland, into the Sialk Odhan. The nearest city in which they might find succour,

Caron Tepasi, was sixty leagues distant, with the hostile clans of the Tithan occupying the steppes in between. *And Kamist Reloe's Apocalypse in pursuit.* Duiker knew he might rejoin the army only to die with them.

Nevertheless, the rebellion might well have been crushed elsewhere. There was a Fist in Caron Tepasi, another in Guran. If either or both had succeeded in extinguishing the uprising in their cities, then a feasible destination was available to Coltaine. Such a journey across the Odhan, however, would take months. While there was plenty of grazing land for the livestock, there were few sources of water, and the dry season had just begun. *No, even to contemplate such a journey is beyond desperation. It is madness.*

That left . . . counterattack. A swift, deadly thrust, retaking Hissar. Or Sialk. A destroyed city offered more opportunity for defence than did steppe land. Moreover, the Malazan fleet could then relieve them – *Pormqual might be a fool, but Admiral Nok is anything but.* The 7th Army could not be simply abandoned, for without it any hope of quickly ending the rebellion was lost.

For the moment, however, it was clear that Coltaine was leading his column to Dryj Spring, and despite the headstart, Duiker expected to rejoin him well before then. The foremost need for the Malazans now was water. Kamist Reloe would know this as well. He had Coltaine trapped into predictability, a position no commander desired. The fewer choices the Fist possessed, the more dire was the situation.

He rode on. The sun slowly angled westward as he continued following the detritus-strewn trail, its mindless regard making Duiker feel insignificant, his hopes and fears meaningless. The occasional body of a refugee or soldier who had died of wounds lay on the trackside, dumped without ceremony. The sun had swelled their corpses, turning the skin deep red and mottled black. Leaving such unburied bodies in their wake would have been a difficult thing to do. Duiker sensed something of the desperation in that beleaguered force.

An hour before dusk a dust cloud appeared a half-league inland. Tithan horsewarriors, the historian guessed, riding hard towards Dryj Spring. There would be no peace for Coltaine and his people. Lightning raids on horseback would harry the encampment's pickets; sudden drives to peel away livestock, flaming arrows sent into the refugee wagons . . . a night of unceasing terror.

He watched the Tithansi slowly pull ahead, and contemplated forcing his weary mount into a canter. The tribal riders no doubt led spare mounts, however, and the historian would have to kill his horse in the effort to reach Coltaine before them. And then he could do naught but warn of the inevitable. *Besides, Coltaine must know what's coming. He knows, because he once rode as a renegade chieftain, once harried a retreating Imperial army across the Wickan plains.*

He continued on at a steady trot, thinking about the challenge of the night ahead: the ride through enemy lines, the unheralded approach to the Seventh's nerve-frayed pickets. The more he thought on it, the less likely seemed his chances of surviving to see the dawn.

The red sky darkened with that desert suddenness, suffusing the air with the colour of drying blood. Moments before he lost the last of the light, Duiker chanced to glance behind him. He saw a grainy cloud, visibly expanding as it swept southward. It seemed to glitter with a hundred thousand pale reflections, as if a wind was flipping the underside of birch leaves at the edge of a vast forest. Capemoths, surely in their millions, leaving Hissar behind, flying to the scent of blood.

He told himself that it was a mindless hunger that drove them. He told himself that the blots, stains and smudges in that billowing, sky-filling cloud were only by chance finding the shape of a face. Hood, after all, had no need to manifest his presence. Nor was he known as a melodramatic god – the Lord of Death was reputed to be, if anything, ironically modest. Duiker's imaginings were the product of fear, the all too human need to conjure symbolic meaning from meaningless events. *Nothing more*.

Duiker kicked his horse into a canter, eyes fixed once more on the growing darkness ahead.

From the crest of the low rise, Felisin watched the seething floor of the basin. It was as if insanity's grip had swept out, from the cities, from the minds of men and women, to stain the natural world. With the approach of dusk, as she and her two companions prepared to break camp for the night's walk, the basin's sand had begun to shiver like the patter of rain on a lake. Beetles began emerging, each black and as large as Baudin's thumb, crawling in a glittering tide that soon filled the entire sweep of desert before them. In their thousands, then hundreds of thousands, yet moving as one, with a singular purpose. Heboric, ever the scholar, had gone off to determine their destination. She had watched him skirt the far edge of the insect army, then vanish beyond the next ridge.

Twenty minutes had passed since then.

Crouching beside her was Baudin, his forearms resting on the large backpack, squinting to pierce the deepening gloom. She sensed his growing unease but had decided that she would not be the one to give voice to their shared concern. There were times when she wondered at Heboric's grasp of what mattered over what didn't. She wondered if the old man was, in fact, a liability.

The swelling had ebbed, enough so that she could see and hear, but a deeper pain remained, as if the bloodfly larvae had left something behind under her flesh, a rot that did more than disfigure her appearance, but laid a stain on her soul as well. There was a poison lodged within her. Her sleep was filled with visions of blood, unceasing, a crimson river that carried her like flotsam from sunrise to sunset. Six days since their escape from Skullcup, and a part of her looked forward to the next sleep.

Baudin grunted.

Heboric reappeared, jogging steadily along the basin's edge towards their position. Squat, hunched, he was like an ogre shambling out from a child's bedtime story. Blunt knobs where his hands should be, about to be raised to reveal fang-studded mouths. *Tales to frighten children. I could write those. I need no imagination, only what I see all around me. Heboric, my boar-tattooed ogre. Baudin, red-scarred where one ear used to be, the hair growing tangled and bestial from the puckered skin. A pair to strike terror, these two.*

The old man reached them, kneeling to sling his arms through his backpack. 'Extraordinary,' he mumbled.

Baudin grunted again. 'But can we get around them? I ain't wading through, Heboric.'

'Oh, aye, easily enough. They're just migrating to the next basin.'

Felisin snorted. 'And you find that extraordinary?'

'I do,' he said, waiting as Baudin tightened the pack's straps. 'Tomorrow night they'll march to the next patch of deep sand. Understand? Like us they're heading west, and like us they'll reach the sea.'

'And then?' Baudin asked. 'Swim?'

'I have no idea. More likely they'll turn around and march east, to the other coast.'

Baudin strapped on his own pack and stood. 'Like a bug crawling the rim of a goblet,' he said.

Felisin gave him a quick glance, remembering her last evening with Beneth. The man had been sitting at his table in Bula's, watching flies circle the rim of his mug. It was one of the few memories that she could conjure up. *Beneth, my lover, the Fly King circling Skullcup. Baudin left him to rot, that's why he won't meet my eye. Thugs never lie well. He'll pay for that, one day.*

'Follow me,' Heboric said, setting off, his feet sinking into the sand so that it seemed he walked on stumps to match those at the end of his arms. He always started out fresh, displaying an energy that struck Felisin as deliberate, as if he sought to refute that he was old, that he was the weakest among them. The last third of the night he would be seven or eight hundred paces behind them, head ducked, legs dragging, weaving with the weight of the pack that nearly dwarfed him.

Baudin seemed to have a map in his head. Their source of information had been precise and accurate. Even though the desert seemed lifeless, a barrier of wasting deadliness, water could be found. Spring-fed pools in rock outcroppings, sinks of mud surrounded by the tracks of animals they never saw, where one could dig down an arm-span, sometimes less, and find the life-giving water.

They had carried enough food for twelve days, two more than was necessary for the journey to the coast. It was not a large margin but it would have to suffice. For all that, however, they were weakening. Each night, they managed less distance in the hours between the sun's setting and its rise. Months at Skullcup, working the airless reaches, had diminished some essential reserve within them.

That knowledge was plain, though unspoken. Time now stalked them, Hood's most patient servant, and with each night they fell back farther, closer to that place where the will to live surrendered to a profound peace. *There's a sweet promise to giving up, but realizing that demands a journey. One of spirit. You can't walk to Hood's Gate, you find it before you when the fog clears.*

'Your thoughts, lass?' Heboric asked. They had crossed two ridge lines, arriving on a withered pan. The stars were spikes of iron overhead, the moon yet to rise.

'We live in a cloud,' she replied. 'All our lives.'

Baudin grunted. 'That's durhang talking.'

'Never knew you were so droll,' Heboric said to the man.

Baudin fell silent. Felisin grinned to herself. The thug would say little for the rest of the night. He did not take well being mocked. *I must remember that, for when he next needs cutting down.*

'My apologies, Baudin,' Heboric said after a moment. 'I was irritated by what Felisin said and took it out on you. More, I appreciated the joke, no matter that it was unintended.'

'Give it up,' Felisin sighed. 'A mule comes out of a sulk eventually, but it's nothing you can force.'

'So,' Heboric said, 'while the swelling's left your tongue, its poison remains.'

She flinched. *If you only knew the full truth of that.*

Rhizan flitted over the cracked surface of the pan, their only company now that they'd left the mindless beetles behind. They had seen no-one since crossing Sinker Lake the night of the Dosii mutiny. Rather than loud alarms and frenetic pursuit, their escape had effected nothing. For Felisin, it made the drama of that night now seem somehow pathetic. For all their self-importance, they were but grains of sand in a storm vaster than anything they could comprehend. The thought pleased her.

Nevertheless, there was cause for worry. If the uprising had spread to the mainland, they might arrive at the coast only to die waiting for a boat that would never come.

They reached a low serrated ridge of rock outcroppings, silver in the starlight and looking like the vertebrae of an immense serpent. Beyond it stretched a wavelike expanse of sand. Something rose from the dunes fifty or so paces ahead, angled like a toppled tree or marble column, though, as they came nearer, they could see that it was blunted, crooked.

A vague wind rustled on the sands, twisting as if in the wake of a spider-bitten dancer. Gusts of sand caressed their shins as they strode on. The bent pillar, or whatever it was, was proving farther away than Felisin had first thought. As a new sense of scale formed in her mind, her breath hissed between her teeth.

'Aye,' Heboric whispered in reply.

Not fifty paces away. More like five hundred. The wind-blurred surface had deceived them. The basin was not a flat sweep of land, but a vast, gradual descent, rising again around the object – a wave of dizziness followed the realization.

The scythe of the moon had risen above the southern horizon by the time they reached the monolith. By unspoken agreement, Baudin and Heboric dropped their packs, the thug sitting down and leaning against his, already dismissive of the silent edifice towering over them.

Heboric removed the lantern and the firebox from his pack. He blew on the hoarded coals, then set alight a taper, which he used to light the lantern's thick wick. Felisin made no effort to help, watching with fascination as he managed the task with a deftness belying the apparent awkwardness of the scarred stumps of his wrists.

Slinging one forearm under the lantern's handle, he rose and approached the dark monolith.

Fifty men, hands linked, could not encircle the base. The bend occurred seven or eight man-lengths up, at about three-fifths of the total length. The stone looked both creased and polished, dark grey under the colourless light of the moon.

The glow of the lantern revealed the stone to be green, as Heboric arrived to stand before it. She watched his head tilt back as he scanned upward. Then he stepped forward and pressed a stump against the surface. A moment later he stepped back.

Water sloshed beside her as Baudin drank from a waterskin. She reached out and, after a moment, he passed it to her. Sand whispered as Heboric returned. The ex-priest squatted.

Felisin offered him the bladder. He shook his head,

his toadlike face twisted into a troubled frown.

'Is this the biggest pillar you've seen, Heboric?' Felisin asked. 'There's a column in Aren . . . or so I've heard . . . that's as high as twenty men, and carved in a spiral from top to bottom. Beneth described it to me once.'

'Seen it,' Baudin grumbled. 'Not as wide, but maybe higher. What's this one made of, Priest?'

'Jade.'

Baudin grunted phlegmatically, but Felisin saw his eyes widen slightly. 'Well, I've seen taller. I've seen wider—'

'Shut up, Baudin,' Heboric snapped, wrapping his arms around himself. He glared up at the man from under the ridge of his brows. 'That's not a column over there,' he rasped. 'It's a finger.'

Dawn stole into the sky, spreading shadows on the landscape. The details of that carved jade finger were slowly prised from the gloom. Swells and folds of skin, the whorls of the pad, all became visible. So too did a ridge in the sand directly beneath it – another finger.

Fingers, to hand. Hand to arm, arm to body . . . For all the logic of that progression, it was impossible, Felisin thought. No such thing could be fashioned, no such thing could stand or stay in one piece. A hand, but no arm, no body.

Heboric said nothing, wrapped around himself, motionless as the night's darkness faded. He held the wrist that had touched the edifice tucked under him, as if the memory of that contact brought pain. Staring at him in the growing light, Felisin was struck anew by his tattoos. They seemed to have deepened somehow, become sharper.

Baudin finally rose and began pitching the two small tents, close to the base of the finger, where the shadows would hold longest. He ignored the towering monolith as if it was nothing more than the bole of a tree, and set about driving deep into the sand the long, thin spikes through the first tent's brass-hooped corners.

An orange tint suffused the air as the sun climbed higher. Although Felisin had seen that colour of sky before on the island, it had never before been so saturated. She could almost taste it, bitter as iron.

As Baudin began on the second tent, Heboric finally roused himself, his head lifting as he sniffed the air, then squinted upward. 'Hood's breath!' he growled. 'Hasn't there been enough?'

'What is it?' Felisin demanded. 'What's wrong?'

'There's been a storm,' the ex-priest said. 'That's Otataral dust.'

At the tents, Baudin paused. He ran a hand across one shoulder, then frowned at his palm. 'It's settling,' he said. 'We'd best get under cover—'

Felisin snorted. 'As if that will do any good! We've mined the stuff, in case you've forgotten. Whatever effect it's had on us, it's happened long ago.'

'Back at Skullcup we could wash ourselves at day's end,' Heboric said, slinging an arm through the food pack's strap and dragging it towards the tents.

She saw that he still held his other stump – the one that had touched the edifice – tight against his midriff.

'And you think that made a difference?' she asked. 'If that's true, why did every mage who worked there die or go mad? You're not thinking clearly, Heboric—'

'Sit there, then,' the old man snapped, ducking under the first tent's flap and pulling the pack in after him.

Felisin glanced at Baudin. The thug shrugged, resumed readying the second tent, without evident haste.

She sighed. She was exhausted, yet not sleepy. If she took to the tent, she would in all likelihood simply lie there, eyes open and studying the weave of the canvas above her face.

'Best get inside,' Baudin said.

'I'm not sleepy.'

He stepped close, the motion fluid like a cat's. 'I don't give a damn if you're sleepy or not. Sitting out under the sun will dry you out, meaning you'll drink more water, meaning less for us, meaning get in this damned tent, lass, before I lay a hand to your backside.'

'If Beneth was here you wouldn't—'

'The bastard's dead!' he snarled. 'And Hood take his rotten soul to the deepest pit!'

She sneered. 'Brave *now* – you wouldn't have dared stand up against him.'

He studied her as he would a bloodfly caught in a web. 'Maybe I did,' he said, a sly grin showing a moment before he turned away.

Suddenly cold, Felisin watched the thug stride over to the other tent, crouch down and crawl inside. *I'm not fooled, Baudin. You were a mongrel skulking in alleys, and all that's changed is that you've left the alleys behind. You'd squirm in the sand at Beneth's feet, if he were here.* She waited another minute in defiance before entering her own tent.

Unfurling her bedroll, she lay down. Her eagerness to sleep was preventing her from doing so. She stared up at the dark imperfections in the canvas weave, wishing she had some durhang or a jug of wine. The crimson river of her dreams had become an embrace, protective and welcoming. She conjured from memory an echo of the image, and all the feelings that went with it. The river flowed with purpose, ordered and inexorable; when in its warm currents, she felt close to understanding that purpose. She knew she would discover it soon, and with that knowledge her world would change, become so much more than it was now. Not just a girl, plump and out of shape and used up, the vision of her future reduced to days when it should be measured in decades

277

– a girl who could call herself young only with sneering irony.

For all that the dream promised her, there was a value in self-contempt, a counterpoint between her waking and sleeping hours, what was and what could be. A tension between what was real and what was imagined, or so Heboric would put it from his acid-pocked critical eye. The scholar of human nature held it in low opinion. He would deride her notions of destiny, and her belief that the dream offered something palpable would give him cause to voice his contempt. *Not that he's needed cause. I hate myself, but he hates everyone else. Which of us has lost the most?*

She awoke groggy, her mouth parched and tasting of rust. The air was grainy, a dim grey light seeping through the canvas. She heard sounds of packing outside, a short murmur from Heboric, Baudin's answering grunt. Felisin closed her eyes, trying to recapture the steady, flowing river that had carried her through her sleep, but it was gone.

She sat up, wincing as every joint protested. The others experienced the same, she knew. A nutritional deficiency, Heboric guessed, though he did not know what it might be. They had dried fruit, strips of smoked mule and some kind of Dosii bread, brick-hard and dark.

Muscles aching, she crawled from the tent into the chill morning air. The two men sat eating, the packets of rations laid out before them. There was little left, with the exception of the bread, which was salty and tended to make them desperately thirsty. Heboric had tried to insist that they eat the bread first – over the first few days – while they were still strong, not yet dehydrated, but neither she nor Baudin had listened, and for some reason he abandoned the idea with the next meal. Felisin had mocked him for that, she recalled. *Unwilling to follow your own advice, eh, old man?* Yet the advice had been good. They would reach the salt-laden, deathly coast with naught but even saltier bread to eat, and little water to assuage their thirst.

Maybe we didn't listen because none of us believed we would ever reach the coast. Maybe Heboric decided the same after that first meal. Only I wasn't thinking that far ahead, was I? No wise acceptance of the futility of all this. I mocked and ignored the advice out of spite, nothing more. As for Baudin, well, rare was the criminal with brains, and he wasn't at all rare.

She joined the breakfast, ignoring their looks as she took an extra mouthful of lukewarm water from the bladder when washing down the smoked meat.

When she was done, Baudin repacked the food.

Heboric sighed. 'What a threesome we are!' he said.

'You mean our dislike of each other?' Felisin asked, raising a brow. 'You shouldn't be surprised, old man,' she continued. 'In case you haven't noticed, we're all broken in some way. Aren't we? The gods know you've pointed out my fall from grace often enough. And Baudin's nothing more than a murderer – he's dispensed with all notions of brotherhood, and is a bully besides, meaning he's a coward at heart . . .' She glanced over to see him crouched at the packs, flatly eyeing her. Felisin gave him a sweet smile. 'Right, Baudin?'

The man said nothing, the hint of a frown in his expression as he studied her.

Felisin returned her attention to Heboric. 'Your flaws are obvious enough – hardly worth mentioning—'

'Save your breath, lass,' the ex-priest muttered. 'I don't need no fifteen-year-old girl telling me my failings.'

'Why *did* you leave the priesthood, Heboric? Skimmed the coffers, I suppose. So they cut your hands off, then tossed you onto the rubbish heap behind the temple. That's certainly enough to make anyone take up writing history as a profession.'

'Time to go,' Baudin said.

'But he hasn't answered my question—'

'I'd say he has, girl. Now shut up. Today you carry the other pack, not the old man.'

'A reasonable suggestion, but no thanks.'

Face darkening, Baudin rose.

'Leave it be,' Heboric said, moving to sling the straps through his arms. In the gloom Felisin saw the stump that had touched the jade finger for the first time. It was swollen and red, the puckered skin stretched. Tattoos crowded the end of the wrist, turning it nearly solid dark. She realized then that the etchings had deepened everywhere on him, grown riotous like vines.

'What's happened to you?'

He glanced over. 'I wish I knew.'

'You burned your wrist on that statue.'

'Not burned,' the old man said. 'Hurts like Hood's own kiss, though. Can magic thrive buried in Otataral sand? Can Otataral give birth to magic? I've no answers, lass, for any of this.'

'Well,' she muttered, 'it was a stupid thing to do – touching the damned thing. Serves you right.'

Baudin started off without comment. Ignoring Heboric, Felisin fell in behind the thug. 'Is there a waterhole ahead this night?' she asked.

The big man grunted. 'Should've asked that before you took more than your ration.'

'Well, I didn't. So, is there?'

'We lost half a night yesterday.'

'Meaning?'

'Meaning no water until tomorrow night.' He looked back at her as he walked. 'You'll wish you'd saved that mouthful.'

She made no reply. She had no intention of being honourable when the time came for her next drink. *Honour's for fools. Honour's a fatal flaw. I'm not going to die on a point of honour, Baudin. Heboric's probably dying anyway. It'd be wasted on him.*

The ex-priest trudged in her wake, the sound of his footfalls dimming as he fell farther back as the hours passed. In the end, she concluded, it would be she and Baudin, just the two of them, standing facing the sea at the western edge of this Queen-forsaken island. The weak always fall to the wayside. It was the first law of Skullcup; indeed, it was the first lesson she'd learned – in the streets of Unta on the march to the slaveships.

Back then, in her naivety, she'd looked upon Baudin's murder of Lady Gaesen as an act of reprehensible horror. If he were to do the same today – *putting Heboric out of his misery –* she would not even blink. *A long journey, this one. Where will it end?* She thought of the river of blood, and the thought warmed her.

True to Baudin's prediction, there was no waterhole to mark the end of the night's journey. The man selected as a campsite a sandy bed surrounded by wind-sculpted projections of limestone. Bleached human bones littered the bed, but Baudin simply tossed them aside when laying out the tents.

Felisin sat down with her back to rock and watched for Heboric's eventual appearance at the far end of the flat plain they had just crossed. He had never lagged behind this distance before – the plain was over a third of a league across – and as the dawn's blush lightened the skyline before her, she began to wonder if his lifeless body wasn't lying out there somewhere.

Baudin crouched beside her. 'I told you to carry the food pack,' he said, squinting eastward.

Not out of sympathy for the old man, then. 'You'll just have to go find it, won't you?'

Baudin straightened. Flies buzzed around him in the still-cool air as he stared eastward for a long moment.

She watched him set off, softly gasping as he loped into a steady jog once clear of the rocks. For the first time she became truly frightened of Baudin. *He's been hoarding food – he has a hidden skin of water – there's no other way he could still have such reserves.* She scrambled to her feet and rushed over to the other pack.

The tents had been raised, the bedrolls set out within them. The pack sat in a deflated heap close by. Left in it was a wrapped pouch that she recognized as containing their first-aid supplies, a battered flint and tinder box that she'd not seen before – *Baudin's own* – and, beneath a flap sewn along one edge at the bottom of the pack, a small, flat packet of deer hide.

No skin of water, no hidden pockets of food. Unaccountably, her fear of the man deepened.

Felisin sat down in the soft sand beside the pack. After a moment she reached to the hide packet, loosened its drawstrings and unfolded it to reveal a set of fine thief's tools – an assortment of picks, minute saws and files, knobs of wax, a small sack of finely ground flour, and two dismantled stilettos, the needlelike blades deeply blued and exuding a bitter, caustic smell, the bone hafts polished and dark-stained, the small hilts in pieces that hinged together to form an X-shaped guard, and holed and weighted pommels of iron wrapped around lead cores. *Throwing weapons. An assassin's weapons.* The last item in the packet was tucked into a leather loop: the talon of some large cat, amber-coloured and smooth. She wondered if it held poison, painted invisibly on its surface. The item was ominous in its mystery.

Felisin rewrapped the packet, returning it and everything else to the pack. She heard heavy footsteps approach from the east and straightened.

Baudin appeared from between the limestone projections, the pack on his shoulders and Heboric in his arms.

The thug was not even out of breath.

'He needs water,' Baudin said as he strode into the camp and laid the unconscious man down on the soft sand. 'In this pack, lass, quickly—'

Felisin did not move. 'Why? We need it more, Baudin.'

The man paused for a heartbeat, then slipped his arms free of the pack and dragged it around. 'Would you want him saying the same, if you were the one lying here? Soon as we get off this island, we can go our separate ways. But for now, we need each other, girl.'

'He's dying. Admit it.'

'We're all dying.' He unstoppered the bladder and eased it between Heboric's cracked lips. 'Drink, old man. Swallow it down.'

'Those are your rations you're giving him,' Felisin said. 'Not mine.'

'Well,' he said with a cold grin, 'no-one would think you anything but nobleborn. Mind you, opening your legs for anyone and everyone back in Skullcup was proof enough, I suppose.'

'It kept us all alive, you bastard.'

'Kept you plump and lazy, you mean. Most of what me and Heboric ate came from the favours I did for the Dosii guards. Beneth gave us dregs to keep you sweet. He knew we wouldn't tell you about it. He used to laugh at your noble cause.'

'You're lying.'

'As you say,' he said, still grinning.

Heboric coughed, his eyes opening. He blinked in the dawn's light.

'You should see yourself,' Baudin said to him. 'From five feet away you're one solid tattoo – as dark as a Dal Honese warlock. Up this close and I can see every line – every hair of the Boar's fur. It's covered your stump, too, not the one that's swollen but the other one. Here, drink some more—'

'Bastard!' Felisin snapped. She watched as the last of their water trickled into the old man's mouth. *He left Beneth to die.*

283

Now he's trying to poison the memory of him, too. It won't work. I did what I did to keep them both alive, and they hate that fact – both of them. It eats them inside, the guilt for the price I paid. And that's what Baudin's now trying to deny. He's cutting his conscience loose, so when he slips one of those knives into me he won't feel a thing. Just another dead nobleborn. Another Lady Gaesen.

She spoke loudly, meeting Heboric's eyes. 'I dream a river of blood every night. I ride it. And you're both there, at first, but only at first, because you both drown in that river. Believe anything you like. I'm the one who's going to live through this. Me. Just me.'

She left the two men to stare at her back as she walked to her tent.

The next night, they found the spring an hour before the moon rose. It revealed itself at the base of a stone depression, fed from below by some unseen fissure. The surface appeared to be grey mud. Baudin went down to its edge, but made no move to scoop out a hole and drink the water that would seep into it. After a moment, her head spinning with weakness, Felisin dropped the food pack from her shoulders and stumbled down to kneel beside him.

The grey was faintly phosphorescent and consisted of drowned capemoths, their wings spread out and overlapping to cover the entire surface. Felisin reached to push the floating carpet aside but Baudin's hand snapped out, closing on her wrist.

'It's fouled,' he said. 'Full of capemoth larvae, feeding off the bodies of their parents.'

Hood's breath, not more larvae. 'Strain the water through a cloth,' Felisin said.

He shook his head. 'The larvae piss poison, fill the water with it. Eliminates any competition. It'll be a month before the water's drinkable.'

'We need it, Baudin.'

'It'll kill you.'

She stared down at the grey sludge, her desire desperate, an agonized fire in her throat, in her mind. *This can't be. We'll die without this.*

Baudin turned away. Heboric had arrived, weaving as he staggered down the bedrock slope. His skin was black as the night, yet shimmering silver as the etched highlights of the boar hair reflected the stars overhead. Whatever infection had seized the stump of his right wrist had begun to fade, leaving a suppurating, crackled network of split skin. It exuded a strange smell of powdered stone.

He was an apparition, and in answer to his nightmarish appearance Felisin laughed, on the edge of hysteria. 'Remember the Round, Heboric? In Unta? Hood's acolyte, the priest covered in flies . . . who was naught but flies. He had a message for you. And now, what do I see? Staggering into view, a man aswarm – not in flies but in tattoos. Different gods, but the same message, that's what I see. Let Fener speak through those peeling lips, old man. Will your god's words echo Hood's? Is the world truly a collection of balances, the infinite tottering to and fro of fates and destinies? Boar of Summer, Tusked Sower of War, what do you say?'

The old man stared at her. His mouth opened, but no words came forth.

'What was that?' Felisin cupped an ear. 'The buzzing of wings? Surely not!'

'Fool,' Baudin muttered. 'Let's find a place to camp. Not here.'

'Ill omens, murderer? I never knew they meant anything to you.'

'Save your breath, girl,' Baudin said, facing the stone slope.

'Makes no difference,' she replied. 'Not now. We're still dancing in the corner of a god's eye, but it's only for show.

We're dead, for all our twitching about. What's Hood's symbol in Seven Cities? They call him the Hooded One here, don't they? Out with it, Baudin, what's carved on the Lord of Death's temple in Aren?'

'I'd guess you already know,' Baudin said.

'Capemoths, the harbingers, the eaters of rotting flesh. It's the nectar of decay for them, the rose bloating under the sun. Hood delivered us a promise in the Round at Unta, and it's just been fulfilled.'

Baudin climbed to the rim of the depression, her words following him up. Orange-tinged by the rising sun, he turned and looked down on her. 'So much for your river of blood,' he said in a low, amused voice.

Dizziness washed through her. Her legs buckled and she abruptly sat down, jarring her tailbone on the hard bedrock. She glanced over to see Heboric lying huddled an arm-span away. The soles of his moccasins had worn through, revealing ravaged, glistening flesh. Was he already dead? *As good as.* 'Do something, Baudin.'

He said nothing.

'How far to the coast?' she asked.

'Doubt it would matter,' he replied after a moment. 'The boat was to have patrolled for three or so nights, no longer. We're at least four days from the coast and getting weaker by the hour.'

'And the next water?'

'About seven hours' walk. More like fourteen, the shape we're in.'

'You seemed spry enough last night!' she snapped. 'Running off to collect Heboric. You don't seem as parched as us, either—'

'I drink my own piss.'

'You what?'

He grunted. 'You heard me.'

286

'Not a good enough answer,' she decided after thinking a moment. 'And don't tell me you're eating your own shit, too. It still wouldn't explain things. Have you made a pact with some god, Baudin?'

'You think doing something like that's a simple task? Hey, Queen of Dreams, save me and I'll serve you. Tell me, how many of *your* prayers have been answered? Besides, I ain't got faith in anything but me.'

'So you haven't given up yet?'

She thought he wouldn't answer, but after a long minute in which she'd begun to sink into herself, he startled her awake with a blunt 'No.'

He removed his pack, then skidded back down the slope. Something in the able economy of his movements filled her with sudden dread. *Calls me plump, eyes me like a piece of flesh – not to use like Beneth did, but more as if he's eyeing his next meal.* Heart hammering, she watched for the first move, a hungry flash in his small, bestial eyes.

Instead he crouched down beside Heboric, pulling the unconscious man onto his back. He leaned close to listen for breath, then sat back, sighing.

'He's dead?' Felisin asked. 'You do the skinning – I won't eat tattooed skin no matter how hungry I am.'

Baudin glanced at her momentarily, but said nothing, returning to his examination of the ex-priest.

'Tell me what you're doing,' she finally said.

'He lives, and that alone may save us.' He paused. 'How far you fall, girl, matters nothing to me. Just keep your thoughts to yourself.'

She watched him peel Heboric's rotting clothing away, revealing the astonishing weave of tattooing beneath. Baudin then moved to keep his own shadow behind him before bending close to study the dark patterning on the ex-priest's chest. He was looking for something.

'A raised nape,' she said dully, 'the ends pulled down and almost touching, almost a circle. It surrounds a pair of tusks.'

He stared, eyes narrowing.

'Fener's own mark, the one that's sacred,' she said. 'It's what you're looking for, isn't it? He's excommunicated, yet Fener remains within him. That much is obvious by those living tattoos.'

'And the mark?' he asked coolly. 'How did you come to know such things?'

'A lie I spun for Beneth,' she explained as the man resumed his examination of the ex-priest's crowded flesh. 'I needed Heboric to support it. I needed details of the cult. He told me. You mean to call on the god.'

'Found it,' he said.

'Now what? How do you reach another man's god, Baudin? There's no keyhole in that mark, no sacred lock you can pick.'

He jerked at that, his eyes glittering as they bore into her own.

She didn't blink, revealed nothing.

'How do you think he lost his hands?' Felisin asked innocently.

'He was a thief, once.'

'He was. But it was the excommunication that took them. There *was* a key, you see. The High Priest's warren to his god. Tattooed on the palm of his right hand. Held to the sacred mark – hand to chest, basically – as simple as a salute. I spent days healing from Beneth's beating, and Heboric talked. Told me so many things – I should have forgotten all of it, you know. Drinking durhang tea by the gallon, but that brew just dissolved the surface, that filter that says what's important, what isn't. His words poured in unobstructed, and stayed. You can't do it, Baudin.'

He raised Heboric's right forearm, studied the glistening, flushed stump in the growing light.

'You can never go back,' she said. 'The priesthood made sure of that. He isn't what he was, and that's that.'

With a silent snarl Baudin pulled the forearm around to push the stump against the sacred mark.

The air screamed. The sound battered them, flung them both down to scrabble, claw, mindlessly dig into the rock – *away . . . away from the pain. Away!* There was such agony in that shriek, it descended like fire, darkening the sky overhead, spreading hairline fissures through the bedrock, the cracks spreading outward from under Heboric's motionless body.

Blood streaming from her ears, Felisin tried to crawl away, up the trembling slope. The fissures – Heboric's tattoos had blossomed out from his body, leapt the unfathomable distance from skin to stone – swept under her, turning the rock into something slick and greasy under her palms.

Everything had begun to shake. Even the sky seemed to twist, yanked down into itself as if a score of invisible hands had reached through unseen portals, grasping the fabric of the world with cold, destructive rage.

The scream was unending. Rage and unbearable pain meshed together like twin strands in an ever-tightening rope. Closing in a noose around her neck, the sound blocked the outside world – its air, its light.

Something struck the ground, the bedrock under her shuddering, throwing her upward. She came back down hard on one elbow. The bones of her arm shivered like the blade of a sword. The glare of the sun dimmed as Felisin fought for air. Her wide eyes caught a glimpse of something beyond the basin, lifting ponderously from the plain in a heaving cloud of dust. Two-toed, a fur-snarled hoof, too large for her to fully grasp, rising up, pulled skyward into a midnight gloom.

The tattoo had leapt from stone to the air itself, a woad-stained web growing in crazed, jerking blots, snapping outward in all directions.

She could not breathe. Her lungs burned. She was dying, sucked airless into the void that was a god's scream.

Sudden silence, out beyond the ringing echoes in her skull. Air flooded her, cold and bitter, yet sweeter than anything she had known. Coughing, spitting bile, Felisin pushed herself onto her hands and knees, shakily raised her head.

The hoof was gone. The tattoo hung like an after-image across the entire sky, slowly fading as she watched. Movement pulled her gaze down, to Baudin. He'd been on his knees, hands cupping the sides of his head. He now slowly straightened, tears of blood filling the lines of his face.

The ground under her feeling strangely fluid, Felisin tottered to her feet. She looked down, blinking dumbly at the mosaic of limestone. The swirling furred patterns of the tattoo still trembled, rippling outward from her moccasins as she struggled for balance. *The cracks, the tattoos . . . they go down, and down, all the way down. As if I'm standing atop a bed of league-deep nails, each nail kept upright only by the others surrounding it. Have you come from the Abyss, Fener? It's said your sacred warren borders Chaos itself. Fener? Are you among us now?* She turned to meet Baudin's eyes. They were dull with shock, though she could detect the first glimmers of fear burning through.

'We wanted the god's attention,' she said. 'Not the god himself.' A trembling seized her. She wrapped her arms around herself, forcing more words forth. 'And he *didn't want to come!*'

His flinch was momentary, then he rolled his shoulders in something that might have been a shrug. 'He's gone now, ain't he?'

'Are you sure of that?'

He shook off the need to answer, looking instead at Heboric. After a moment's study, he said, 'He breathes steadier now. Nor so wrinkled and parched. Something's happened to him.'

She sneered. 'The reward for missing getting stomped on by a hair's breadth.'

Baudin grunted, his attention suddenly elsewhere.

She followed his gaze. The pool of water was gone, drained away until only a carpet of capemoth corpses remained. Felisin barked a laugh. 'Some salvation we've had here.'

Heboric slowly curled himself into a ball. 'He's here,' he whispered.

'We know,' Baudin said.

'In the mortal realm . . .' the ex-priest continued after a moment. 'Vulnerable.'

'You're looking at it the wrong way,' Felisin said. 'The god you no longer worship took your hands. So now you pulled him down. Don't mess with mortals.'

Either her cold tone or brutal words in some way steeled through Heboric. He uncurled, raised his head, then sat up. His gaze found Felisin. 'Out of the mouth of babes,' he said with a grin that knew nothing of humour.

'So he's here,' Baudin said, looking around. 'How can a god hide?'

Heboric rose to his feet. 'I'd give what's left of an arm to study a field of the Deck right now. Imagine the maelstrom among the Ascendants. This is not a fly-specked visitation, not a pluck and strum on the strands of power.' He lifted his arms, frowning down at the stumps. 'It's been years, but the ghosts are back.'

Watching Baudin's confusion was a struggle in itself. 'Ghosts?'

'The hands that aren't there,' Heboric explained. 'Echoes. Enough to drive a man mad.' He shook himself, squinted sunward. 'I feel better.'

'You look it,' Baudin said.

The heat was building. In an hour it would soar.

Felisin scowled. 'Healed by the god he rejected. It doesn't

matter. If we stay in our tents today we'll be too weak to do anything come dusk. We have to walk now. To the next water-hole. If we don't we're dead.' *But I'll outlive you, Baudin. Enough to drive the dagger home.*

Baudin shouldered his pack. Grinning, Heboric slung his arms through the straps of the pack she'd been carrying. He rose easily, though taking a step to catch his balance once he straightened.

Baudin led the way. Felisin fell in behind him. *A god stalks the mortal realm, yet is afraid. He has power unimaginable, yet he hides.* And somehow Heboric had found the strength to with-stand all that had happened. *And the fact that he's responsible. This should have broken him, shattered his soul. Instead, he bends.* Could his wall of cynicism withstand such a siege for long? What *did* he do to lose his hands?

She had her own inner turmoil to manage. Her thoughts plundered every chamber in her mind. She still envisaged murder, yet felt a vaguely mocking wave of comradeship for her two companions. She wanted to run from them, sensing that their presence was a vortex tugging her into madness and death, yet she knew that she was also dependent on them.

Heboric spoke behind her. 'We'll make it to the coast. I smell water. Close. To the coast, and when we get there, Felisin, you will find that nothing has changed. Nothing at all. Do you grasp my meaning?'

She sensed a thousand meanings to his words, yet under-stood none of them.

Up ahead, Baudin gave a shout of surprise.

Mappo Trell's thoughts travelled westward almost eight hundred leagues, to a dusk not unlike this one but two centuries past. He saw himself crossing a plain of chest-high grass, but the grass had been plastered down, laden with what looked like grease, and as he walked the very earth beneath his

292

hide boots shifted and shied. He'd known centuries already, wedded to war in what had become an ever-repeating cycle of raids, feuding and bloody sacrifices before the god of honour. Youth's game, and he'd long grown weary of it. Yet he'd stayed, nailed to a single tree but only because he'd grown used to the scenery around it. It was amazing what could be endured when in the grip of inertia. He had reached a point where anything strange, unfamiliar, was cause for fear. But unlike his brothers and sisters, Mappo could not ride that fear across the full span of his life. For all that, it had taken the horror he now approached to prise him from the tree.

He had been young when he walked out of the trader town that was his home. He was caught – like so many of his age back then – in a fevered backlash, rejecting the rotting immobility of the Trell towns and the elder warriors who'd become merchants trading in bhederin, goats and sheep, and now relived their fighting paths in the countless taverns and bars. He embraced the wandering ways of old, willingly suffered initiation into one of the back-land clans that had retained the traditional lifestyle.

The chains of his convictions held for hundreds of years, snapped at last in a way he could never have foreseen.

His memories remained sharp, and in his mind he once again strode across the plain. The ruins of the trader town where he'd been born were now visible. A month had passed since its destruction. The bodies of the fifteen thousand slain – those that had not burned in the raging fires – had long since been picked clean by the plain's scavengers. He was returning home to bleached bone, fragments of cloth and heat-shattered brick.

The ancient shoulder-women of his adopted clan had divined the tale from the flat bones they burned, as the Nameless Ones had predicted months earlier. While the Trell of the towns had become strangers to them all, they were kin.

The task that remained was not, however, one of vengeance. This pronouncement silenced the many companions who, like Mappo, had been born in the destroyed town. No, all notions of vengeance must be purged in the one chosen for the task ahead. Thus were the words of the Nameless Ones, who foresaw this moment.

Mappo still did not understand why he had been chosen. He was no different from his fellow warriors, he believed. Vengeance was sustenance. More than meat and water, the very reason to eat and drink. The ritual that would purge him would destroy all that he was. *You will be an unpainted hide, Mappo. The future will offer its own script, writing and shaping your history anew. What was done to the town of our kin must never happen again. You will ensure that. Do you understand?*

Expressions of dreadful necessity. Yet, without the horrific destruction of the town of his birth Mappo would have defied them all. He'd walked the overgrown main street, with its riotous carpet of weeds and roots, and had seen the glimmer of sun-bleached bones at his feet.

Near the market round, he discovered a Nameless One awaiting him, standing in the clearing's centre, grey-faded robes flickering in the prairie wind, hood drawn back to reveal a stern woman's visage. Pale eyes met his as he approached. The staff she held in one hand seemed to writhe in her grip.

'We do not see in years,' she hissed.

'But in centuries,' Mappo replied.

'It is well. Now, warrior, you must learn to do the same. Your elders shall decree it so.'

The Trell slowly gazed around, squinting at the ruins. 'It has more the feel of a raider's army – it's said that such forces exist south of Nemil—'

Her sneer surprised him with its unveiled contempt. 'One day he shall return to his home, as you've done here and now. Until that time, you must attend—'

'Why me, damn you!'

Her answer was a faint shrug.

'And if I defy you?'

'Even that, warrior, will demand patience.' She raised the staff then, the gesture drawing his eye. The twisting, buckling wood seemed to reach hungrily for the Trell, growing, filling his world until he was lost in its tortured maze.

'Strange how a land untravelled can look so familiar.'

Mappo blinked, the memories scattered by the sound of that familiar soft voice. He glanced up at Icarium. 'Stranger still how the mind's eye can travel so far and so fast, yet return in an instant.'

The Jhag smiled. 'With that eye you might explore the entire world.'

'With that eye you might escape it.'

Icarium's gaze narrowed as he scanned the rubble-strewn sweep of desert below. They'd climbed a tel the better to see the way ahead. 'Your memories always fascinate me, since I seem to have so few of my own, and more so since you have always been so reluctant to share them.'

'I was recalling my clan,' Mappo said, shrugging. 'It is astonishing the trivial things one comes to miss. Birthing season for the herds, the way we winnowed the weak in unspoken agreement with the plains' wolves.' He smiled. 'The glory I earned when I'd snuck into a raiding party's camp and broken the tips of every warrior's knife, then sneaked back out with no-one awakening.' He sighed. 'I carried those points in a bag for years, tied to my war belt.'

'What happened to them?'

'Stolen back by a cleverer raider.' Mappo's smile broadened. 'Imagine *her* glory!'

'Was that all she stole?'

'Ah, leave me some secrets, friend.' The Trell rose, brushing sand and dust from his leather leggings. 'If anything,' he said after a pause, 'that sandstorm has grown a third in size since we stopped.'

Hands on his hips, Icarium studied the dark wall bisecting the plain. 'I believe it has marched closer, as well,' he said. 'Born of sorcery, perhaps the very breath of a goddess, its strength still grows. I can feel it reaching out to us.'

'Aye.' Mappo nodded, repressing a shiver. 'Surprising, assuming that Sha'ik is indeed dead.'

'Her death may have been necessary,' Icarium said. 'After all, can mortal flesh command this power? Can a living being stay alive being the gateway between Dryjhna and this realm?'

'You're thinking she's become Ascendant? And in doing so left her flesh and bones behind?'

'It's possible.'

Mappo fell silent. The possibilities multiplied each time they discussed Sha'ik, the Whirlwind and the prophecies. Together, he and Icarium were sowing their own confusion. *And whom might that serve?* Iskaral Pust's grinning face appeared in his mind. Breath hissed through his teeth. 'We're being manipulated,' he growled. 'I can feel it. Smell it.'

'I've noted your raised hackles,' Icarium said with a grim smile. 'For myself, I've become numb to such notions – I have felt manipulated all my life.'

The Trell shook himself to disguise his flinch. 'And,' he asked softly, 'who would be doing that?'

The Jhag shrugged, glanced down with a raised eyebrow. 'I stopped asking that question long ago, friend. Shall we eat? The lesson needed here is that mutton stew is a taste superior to that of sweet curiosity.'

Mappo studied Icarium's back as the warrior strode down into camp. *But what of sweet vengeance, friend?*

They rode down the ancient road, harried by banshee gusts of sand-filled wind. Even the Gral gelding was stumbling with exhaustion, but Fiddler had run out of options. He had no answer to what was happening.

Somewhere in the impenetrable sweeps of sand to their right a running battle was under way. It was close – it *sounded* close, but of the combatants they could see no sign, nor was Fiddler of a mind to ride to investigate. In his fear and exhaustion, he'd arrived at a fevered, panicky conviction that staying on the road was all that kept them alive. If they left it they would be torn apart.

The battle sounds were not clashing steel, nor the death cries of men. The sounds were of beasts – roars, snaps, snarls, keening songs of terror and pain and savage fury. Nothing human. There might have been wolves in the unseen struggle, but other, wholly different throats voiced their own frantic participation. The nasal groans of bears, the hiss of large cats, and other sounds – reptilian, avian, simian. *And demons. Mustn't forget those demonic barks – Hood's own nightmares couldn't be worse.*

He rode without reins. Both hands gripped the sand-pitted stock of his crossbow. It was cocked, a flamer quarrel nocked in place, and had been since the scrap began, *ten hours ago*. The gut-wound cord was weary by now, he well knew. The wider than usual spread of the steel ribs told him as much. The quarrel would not fly far, and its flight would be soft. But he needed neither accuracy nor range for the flamer to be effective. The knowledge that to drop the weapon would result in their being engulfed – he and his horse both – in raging fire, kept reminding him of that efficacy each time his aching, sweat-slick hands let the weapon slip slightly in his grip.

He could not go on much longer. A single glance back over his shoulder showed Apsalar and Crokus still with him, their horses past the point of recovery and now running until life fled their bodies. Not long now.

The Gral gelding screamed and slewed sideways. Fiddler was suddenly awash in hot liquid. Blinking and cursing, he shook the fluid from his eyes. *Blood. A Fener-born Hood-damned gushing fountain of blood.* It had shot out from the impenetrable air-borne sand. *Something got close. Something else stopped it from getting any closer. Queen's blessing, what in the Abyss is going on?*

Crokus shouted. Fiddler looked back in time to see him leap clear of his collapsing mount. The animal's front legs folded under it. He watched the horse's chin strike hard on the cobbles, leaving a smear of blood and froth. It jerked its head clear in one last effort to recover, then rolled, legs kicking in the air a moment before sagging and falling still.

The sapper pried a hand loose from the crossbow, gathered the reins and drew his gelding to a halt. He swung the stumbling beast around. 'Dump the tents!' he shouted to Crokus, who had regained his feet. 'That's the freshest of the spare mounts. Quickly, damn you!'

Slumped in her saddle, Apsalar rode close. 'It's no use,' she said through cracked lips. 'We have to stop.'

Snarling, Fiddler glared out into the biting sheets of sand. The battle was getting closer. Whatever was holding them back was giving ground. He saw a massive shape loom into view, then vanish again as quickly. It seemed to have leopards riding its shoulders. Off to one side four hulking shapes appeared, low to the ground and rolling forward black and silent.

Fiddler swung the crossbow around and fired. The bolt struck the ground a half-dozen paces from the four beasts. Sheets of flame washed over them. The creatures shrieked.

He spared no time to watch, pulling at random another quarrel from the hardened case strapped to the saddle. He'd only a dozen quarrel-mounted Moranth munitions to start with. He was now down to nine, and of those only one more cusser. He spared a glance as he loaded the quarrel – another flamer – then resumed scanning the wall of heaving sand, leaving his hands to work by memory.

Shapes were showing, flashing like grainy ghosts. A dozen dog-sized winged reptiles shuddered into view twenty feet up, rising on a column of air. *Esanthan'el – Hood's breath, these are D'ivers and Soletaken!* A huge cape-shape swept over the esanthan'el, engulfing them.

Crokus was frantically rummaging in a pack for the short sword he'd purchased in Ehrlitan. Apsalar crouched beside him, daggers glinting in her hands as she faced down the road.

Fiddler was about to shout that the enemy was to her left, when he saw what she'd seen. Three Gral hunters rode shoulder to shoulder in full charge, less than a dozen horse-strides from their position. Their lances lowered.

The range was too close for a safe shot. The sapper could only watch as the warriors closed in. Time seemed to slow down as Fiddler stared, helpless to intervene. A massive bear bolted up from the side of the road, colliding with the Gral rider on the left. The Soletaken was as big as the horse it pulled down. Its jaws closed sideways around the warrior's waist, between ribs and hips, the canines sinking in almost past the far side. The jaws squeezed seemingly without effort. Bile and blood sprayed from the warrior's mouth.

Apsalar sprang at the other two men, flashing beneath the lanceheads, both knives thrusting up and out as she slipped between the horses. Neither Gral had time to parry. As if in mirror reflection, each blade vanished up and under the ribcage, the one on the left finding a heart, the one on the right rupturing a lung.

Then she was past, leaving both weapons behind. A dive and a shoulder roll avoided the lance of a fourth rider Fiddler hadn't seen earlier. In a single, fluid motion, Apsalar regained her feet and sprang in an astonishing surge of strength, and was suddenly sitting behind the Gral, her right arm closing around his throat, her left reaching down over the man's head, two fingers sinking deep into each eye, then yanking back in time for the small knife that suddenly appeared in her right hand to slide back across the warrior's exposed throat.

Fiddler's rapt attention was violently broken by something large and scaled whipping across his face, knocking him from the saddle, sending his crossbow flying from his hands. He struck the road surface in an explosion of pain. Ribs snapped, the shattered ends grinding and tearing as he rolled onto his stomach. Any thoughts of trying to rise were quickly killed as a vicious battle burst into life directly above him. Hands behind his head, Fiddler curled himself tight, willed himself smaller. Bony hooves battered him, clawed feet scored his chain armour, ravaged his thighs. One sudden push crushed his left ankle, then pivoted on what was left before lifting away.

He heard his horse screaming, not in pain, but in terror and rage. The sound of the gelding's hooves connecting with something solid was a momentary flash of satisfaction amidst the pain flooding Fiddler's mind.

A huge body thumped to the ground beside the sapper, rolling to press a scaled flank against him. He felt the muscles twitching, sending sympathetic shivers through his own pummelled body.

The sounds of battle had ceased. Only the moaning wind and hissing sand was left. He tried to sit up but found he could barely lift his head. The scene was one of carnage. Immediately in front of him, within an arm's reach, stood the four trembling legs of his gelding. Off to one side lay his crossbow, flamer gone – the weapon must have discharged when it struck the ground, catapulting the deadly quarrel into the storm. Just ahead the lung-stabbed Gral lay coughing blood. Standing over him speculatively was Apsalar, the assassin's throat-slitter held loosely in one hand. A dozen paces past her, the hulking brown back of the Soletaken bear was visible, rippling as it tore at the meat of the horse it had brought down. Crokus stepped into view – he'd found his short sword but had yet to unsheathe it.

300

Fiddler felt a wave of compassion at the expression on the lad's face.

The sapper reached one arm behind him, groaning with the effort. His hand found and rested against scaled hide. The twitches had ceased.

The bear roared in sudden alarm. Fiddler twisted around in time to see the beast bolt away. *Oh, Hood, if he's fleeing . . .*

The trembling of the mare's legs increased, making them almost blurry to Fiddler's eyes, but the animal did not run, stepping only to interpose herself between the sapper and whatever was coming. The gesture rent the man's heart. 'Dammit, beast,' he rasped. 'Get out of here!'

Apsalar was backing towards him. Crokus stood motionless, the sword falling unheeded from his hands.

He finally saw the newcomer. *Newcomers.* Like a seething, lumpy black carpet, the D'ivers rolled over the cobbles. *Rats, hundreds. Yet one. Hundreds? Thousands. Oh, Hood, I know of this one.* 'Apsalar!'

She glanced at him, expressionless.

'In my saddlebag,' the sapper said. 'A cusser—'

'Not enough,' she said coolly. 'Too late anyway.'

'Not them. Us.'

Her reaction was a slow blink, then she stepped up to the gelding.

A stranger's voice rose above the wailing wind. 'Gryllen!'

Yes, that's the D'ivers's name. Gryllen, otherwise known as the Tide of Madness. Flushed out of Y'ghatan in the fire. Oh, it comes around, don't it just!

'Gryllen!' the voice bellowed again. 'Leave here, D'ivers!'

Hide-bound legs stepped into view. Fiddler looked up, saw an extraordinarily tall man, lean, wearing a faded Tano telaba. His skin was somewhere between grey and green, and he held in his long-fingered hands a recurved bow and a rune-wrapped arrow nocked and ready. His long, grey hair showed remnants of black dye, making his mane appear spotted. The sapper saw the ragged tips of tusks bulging the line of his thin lower lip. *A Jhag. Didn't know they travelled this far east. Why in Hood's name that should matter, I don't know.*

The Jhag took another step towards the heaving mass of rats that now covered what was left of the bear-killed horse and rider, and laid a hand on the shoulder of the mare. The trembling stilled. Apsalar stepped back, warily studying the stranger.

Gryllen was hesitating – Fiddler could not believe his eyes. He glanced again at the Jhag. Another figure had appeared beside the tall bowman. Short and wide as a siege engine, his skin a deep, warm brown, his black hair braided and studded with fetishes. If anything, his canines were bigger than his companion's, and looking much sharper. *A Trell. A Jhag and a Trell. That rings a towerful of bells, if only I could get through the pain to spare it another thought.*

'Your quarry has fled,' the Jhag said to Gryllen. 'These people here do not pursue the Trail of Hands. Moreover, I now protect them.'

The rats hissed and twittered in a deafening roar, and surged higher on the road. Dust-grey eyes glittered in a seething storm.

'Do not,' the Jhag said slowly, 'try my patience.'

A thousand bodies flinched. The tide withdrew, a wave of greasy fur. A moment later they were gone.

The Trell squatted beside Fiddler. 'You will live, soldier?'

'Seems I'll have to,' the sapper replied, 'if only to make some sense of what just happened. I should know you two, shouldn't I?'

The Trell shrugged. 'Can you stand?'

'Let's see.' He pulled an arm under him, pushed himself up an inch, then remembered nothing more.

CHAPTER EIGHT

It is said that on the night of Kellanved and Dancer's
Return, Malaz City was a maelstrom of sorcery
and dire visitations. It is not a far reach to find
one sustained in the belief that the assassinations
were a messy, confused affair, and that success
and failure are judgements dependent on one's
perspective . . .

Conspiracies in the Imperium
Heboric

Coltaine had surprised them all. Leaving the footsoldiers
of the Seventh to guard the taking-on of water at Dryj
Spring, he had led his Wickans out onto the Odhan.
Two hours after sunset, the Tithansi tribesmen, resting their
horses by walking with lead reins over a league from the oasis,
suddenly found themselves the centre of a closing-horseshoe
charge. Few had time to so much as remount, much less wheel
in formation to meet the attack. Though they outnumbered
the Wickans seven to one, they broke, and died a hundred for
every one of Coltaine's clan warriors who fell. Within two
hours the slaughter was complete.

Riding the south road towards the oasis, Duiker had seen
the glow from the Tithansi's burning wagons way off on his
right. It was a long moment before he grasped what he was

seeing. There was no question of riding into that conflagration. The Wickans rode the blood of butchery – they would not pause to think before taking him down. Instead he swung his mount northwest and rode at a canter until he ran into the first of the fleeing Tithansi, from whom he gleaned the story.

The Wickans were demons. They breathed fire. Their arrows magically multiplied in mid-air. Their horses fought with uncanny intelligence. A Mezla Ascendant had been conjured and sent to Seven Cities, and now faced the Whirlwind goddess. The Wickans could not be killed. There would never come another dawn.

Duiker left the man to whatever fate awaited him and rode back to the road, resuming his journey to the oasis. He had lost two hours, but had gleaned invaluable information amidst the Tithansi deserter's terror-spawned ravings.

This, the historian realized as he rode on, was more than the simple lashing-out of a wounded, tormented beast. Coltaine clearly did not view the situation in that way. Perhaps he never did. The Fist was conducting a campaign. Engaged in a war, not a panicked flight. *The leaders of the Apocalypse had better reorder their thoughts, if they're to hold any hope of wresting the fangs from this serpent. More, they'd better kill the notion evidently already rampant that the Wickans were more than just human, and that's easier said than done.*

Kamist Reloe still retained superior numbers, but the quality of the troops was beginning to tell – Coltaine's Wickans were disciplined in their mayhem, and the Seventh was a veteran force that the new Fist had taken pains in preparing for this kind of war. There was still the likelihood that the Malazan forces would be destroyed eventually – if things were as bad elsewhere, there'd be little hope for the stranded army and the thousands of refugees that clung to it. *All these minor victories cannot win the war – Reloe's potential recruits number in the hundreds of thousands – assuming Sha'ik recognizes the threat*

Coltaine poses and sends them in pursuit of the High Fist.

When he came within sight of the small oasis surrounding Dryj Spring, he was shocked to see that almost every palm tree had been cut down. The stands were gone, leaving only stumps and low plants. Smoke drifted over the area, ghostly under the paling sky. Duiker rose in his stirrups, scanning for campfires, pickets, the tents of the encampment. *Nothing . . . perhaps on the other side of the spring . . .*

The smoke thickened as he rode into the oasis, his mount picking its way around the hacked stumps. There were signs everywhere – first the pits dug into the sand by the outlying picket stations, then the deep ruts where wagons had been positioned in a defensive line. In the hearth-places only smouldering ashes remained.

Dumbfounded and suddenly exhausted, Duiker let his horse wander through the abandoned camp. The deep sinkhole beyond was the spring – it had been virtually emptied and was only now beginning to refill: a small brownish pool surrounded by the mud-coated husks of palm bark and rotting fronds. Even the fish had been taken.

While the Wickan horsewarriors had set off to ambush the Tithansi, the Seventh and the refugees had already left the oasis. The historian struggled to comprehend that fact. He envisioned the scene of departure, the stumbling, red-eyed refugees, children piled onto wagons, the stricken gazes of the veteran soldiers guarding the exodus. Coltaine gave them no rest, no pause to assimilate the shock, to come to terms with all that had happened, *was* happening. They'd arrived, stripped the oasis of water and everything else that might prove useful, then they'd left.

Where?

Duiker nudged his mount forward. He came to the oasis's southwestern edge, his eyes tracking the wide swath left behind by the wagons, cattle and horses. Off to the southeast rose the weathered range of the Lador Hills. Westward stretched the Tithansi Steppes. *Nothing in that direction until the Sekala River – too far for Coltaine to contemplate. If northwest, then the village of Manot, and beyond that, Caron Tepasi, on the coast of the Karas Sea. Almost as far as Sekala River.* The trail led due west, into the steppes. *Hood's breath, there's nothing there!*

There seemed little point in trying to anticipate the Wickan Fist. The historian wheeled back to the spring and stiffly dismounted, wincing at the ache in his hips and thighs, the dull throb in his lower back. He could go no farther, nor could his horse. They needed to rest – and they needed the soupy water at the bottom of the lakebed.

He removed his bedroll from the saddle, tossing it onto the leaf-strewn sand. Unhitching the mare's girth strap, he slid the ornate saddle from its sweat-covered back. Taking the reins, he led the animal down to the water.

The spring had been plugged with rocks, which explained its slowed trickle. Duiker removed his scarf and strained the water through the fabric into his helmet. He let the horse drink first, then repeated the filtering process before quenching his own thirst and refilling his canteen.

He fed the mare from the bag of grain strapped to the saddle, then rubbed the beast down before turning his attention to setting up his own makeshift camp. He wondered whether he would ever rejoin Coltaine and the army; whether, perhaps, he was trapped in some nightmarish pursuit of ghosts. *Maybe they are demons, after all.* His weariness was getting the better of him.

Duiker laid out the bedroll, then rigged over it a sunshade using his telaba. Without the trees the sun would scorch this oasis – it would be years in recovering, if it ever did. Before sleep took him, he thought long on the war to come. Cities meant less than did sources of water. Armies would have to occupy oases, which would become as important as islands in a vast sea. Coltaine would ever be at a disadvantage – his every destination known, his every approach prepared for ... *provided Kamist Reloe can get to them first, and how can he fail in that? He doesn't have thousands of refugees to escort.* For all the Fist's surprises, Coltaine was tactically constrained.

The question the historian asked himself before falling asleep held a blunt finality: how long could Coltaine delay the inevitable?

He awoke at dusk, and twenty minutes later was on the trail, a solitary rider beneath a vast cloak of capemoths so thick as to blot out the stars.

Breakers rolled over a reef a quarter of a mile out, a phosphorescent ribbon beneath a cloud-filled sky. The sun's rise was an hour away. Felisin stood on a grassy shelf overlooking a vast beach of white sand, light-headed and weaving slightly as the minutes passed.

There was no boat in sight, no sign that anyone had ever set foot on this stretch of coast. Driftwood and heaps of dead seaweed marked the tide line. Sand crabs crawled everywhere she looked.

'Well,' Heboric said beside her, 'at least we can eat. Assuming those are edible, that is, and there's only one way to find out.'

She watched as he removed a sackcloth from the pack, then made his way down onto the sand. 'Watch those claws,' she said to him. 'Wouldn't want to lose a finger, would we?'

The ex-priest laughed, continuing on. She could see him only because of his clothes. His skin was now completely black, the traceries barely detectable even up close and in daylight. The visible changes were matched by other, more subtle ones.

'You can't hurt him any more,' Baudin said from where he crouched over the other backpack. 'No matter what you say.'

'Then I've no reason to stay quiet,' she replied.

They had water to last another day, maybe two. The clouds over the straits promised rain, but Felisin knew every promise was a lie – salvation was for others. She looked around again. *This is where our bones will rest, humps and ripples in the sand. Then, one day, even those signs will be gone. We've reached the shore, where Hood awaits and no-one else. A journey of the spirit as much as of the flesh. I welcome the end to both.*

Baudin had pitched the tents and was now collecting wood for a fire. Heboric returned with the sackcloth gripped between his stumps. The tips of claws showed through the bag's loose weave. 'These will either kill us or make us very thirsty – I'm not sure which will be worse.'

The last fresh water was eleven hours behind them, a damp patch in a shallow basin. They'd had to dig down an arm-span to find it, and it had proved brackish, tasting of iron and difficult to keep down. 'Do you truly believe Duiker's still out there, sailing back and forth for – what, five days now?'

Heboric squatted, setting the sack down. 'He's not published anything in years – what else would he have to do with all his time?'

'Do you think frivolity is the proper way to meet Hood?'

'I didn't know there was a proper way, lass. Even if I was certain death was coming – which I'm not, at least in the immediate future – well, each of us has to answer it in our own way. After all, even the priests of Hood argue over the preferred manner in which to finally face their god.'

'If I'd known a lecture was coming, I'd have kept my mouth shut.'

'Coming to terms with life as an adolescent, are you?'

Her scowl made him laugh in delight.

Heboric's favourite jokes are the unintended ones. Mockery is just hate's patina, and every laugh is vicious. She didn't have the strength to continue riposting. *The last laugh won't be yours, Heboric. You'll discover that soon enough. You and Baudin both.*

308

They cooked the crabs in a bed of coals, needing sticks to push the creatures back into the searing heat until their struggles ceased. The white flesh was delicious, but salty. A bounteous feast and an endless supply that could prove fatal.

Baudin then collected more driftwood, intending to build a beacon fire for the night to come. In the meantime, as the sun broke the eastern skyline, he piled damp seaweed on the fire and studied with a satisfied expression the column of smoke that rose into the air.

'You planning to do that all day?' Felisin asked. *What about sleep? I need you sleeping, Baudin.*

'Every now and then,' he replied.

'Don't see the point if those clouds roll in.'

'They ain't rolled in yet, have they? If anything, they're rolling out – back to the mainland.'

She watched him working the fire. He'd lost the economy of his movements, she realized; there was now a sloppiness there that betrayed the extremity of his exhaustion, a weakness that probably came with finally reaching the coast. They'd lost any control over their fates. *Baudin believed in Baudin and no-one else. Now just like us he's depending on someone else. And maybe it was all for nothing. Maybe we should've taken our chances going to Dosin Pali.*

The crab meat began taking its toll. Waves of desperate thirst assailed Felisin, followed by sharp cramps as her stomach rebelled at being full.

Heboric disappeared inside his tent, clearly suffering the same symptoms.

Felisin did little over the next twenty minutes, simply clawing through the pain and watching Baudin, willing on him the same affliction. If he was similarly assailed he showed no sign. Her fear of him deepened.

The cramps faded, although the thirst remained. The clouds over the straits retreated, the sun's heat rose.

Baudin dumped a last pile of seaweed on the fire, then made ready to retire to the tent.

'Take mine,' Felisin said.

His head jerked around, his eyes narrowing.

'I'll join you in a moment.'

He still stared.

'Why not?' she snapped. 'What other escape is there? Unless you've taken vows—'

He flinched almost imperceptibly.

Felisin went on, '– sworn to some sex-hating Ascendant. Who would that be? Hood? Wouldn't that be a surprise! But there's always a little death in lovemaking—'

'That what you call it?' Baudin muttered. 'Lovemaking?'

She shrugged.

'I'm sworn to no god.'

'So you've said before. Yet you've never made use of me, Baudin. Do you prefer men? Boys? Throw me on my stomach and you won't know the difference.'

He straightened, still staring, his expression unreadable. Then he walked to the tent. Felisin's tent.

She smiled to herself, waited a hundred heartbeats, then joined him.

His hands moved over her clumsily, as if he was trying to be gentle but did not know how. The rags of their clothing had taken but moments to remove. Baudin guided her down until she lay on her back, looking up at his blunt, bearded face, his eyes still cold and unfathomable as his large hands gathered her breasts and pushed them together.

As soon as he was inside her, his restraint fell away. He became something other than human, reduced to an animal. He was rough, but not as rough as Beneth had been, nor a good number of Beneth's followers.

He was quickly done, settling his considerable weight on her, his breath harsh and heavy in her ear. She did not move him; her every sense was attuned to his breathing, to the twitching of muscles as sleep stole up on him. She had not expected him to surrender so easily, she had not anticipated his helplessness.

Felisin's hand stole into the sands beside the pallet and probed until it found the grip of the dagger. She willed calm into her own breathing, though she could do nothing to slow her hammering heart. He was asleep. He did not stir.

She slipped the blade free, shifting her grasp to angle the point inward. She drew a deep breath, held it.

His hand caught her wrist the instant she began her thrust. He rose fluidly, wrenching her arm around and twisting her until she rolled onto her stomach beneath him. His weight pinned her down.

Baudin squeezed her wrist until the dagger fell free. 'You think I don't check my gear, lass?' he whispered. 'You think you're a mystery to me? Who else would steal one of my throat-stickers?'

'You left Beneth to die.' She couldn't see his face, and was almost glad for that when he replied.

'No, lass. I killed the bastard myself. Snapped his neck like a reed. He deserved more pain, something slower, but there wasn't any time for that. He didn't deserve the mercy, but he got it.'

'Who *are* you?'

'Never done a man or a boy. But I'll pretend. I'm good at pretending.'

'I'll scream—'

'Heboric's sleep isn't the kind you can shake him out of. He dreams. He thrashes about. I've slapped him and he didn't stir. So scream away. What are screams anyway? Voicing your outrage – didn't think you were capable of outrage any more, Felisin.'

She felt the hopelessness flood through her body. *It's just more of the same. I can survive it, I can even enjoy it. If I try.*

Baudin rose from her. She writhed onto her back, stared at him. He'd collected the dagger and had backed to the entrance. He smiled. 'Sorry if I disappointed you, but I wasn't in the mood.'

'Then why—'

'To see if you're still what you were.' He did not need to voice his conclusion. 'Get some sleep, lass.'

Alone, Felisin curled up on the pallet, numbness filling her. *To see if you're still . . . yes, you still are. Baudin knew that already. He just wanted to show you to yourself, girl. You thought you were using him but he was using you. He knew what you planned. Think on that. Think on it long and hard.*

Hood came striding out of the waves, the reaper of carved-out souls. He'd waited long enough, his amusement at their suffering losing its flavour. Time had come for the Gates.

Feeling bleached and withered as the dead driftwood around her, Felisin sat facing the straits. Clouds flickered over the water, lightning danced to the rumbling beat of thunder. Spume rose fierce along the line of the reef, launching blue-white explosions into the darkness.

An hour earlier Heboric and Baudin had come back from their walk up the beach, dragging between them the prow of a shattered boat. It was old, but they'd talked about building a raft. The discussion had the sound of pointless musing – no-one had the strength for such a task. They would start dying by dawn, and they all knew it.

Felisin realized that Baudin would be the last to die. Unless Heboric's god returned to scoop up his wayward child. Felisin finally began to believe she would be the first. No vengeance achieved. Not Baudin, not sister Tavore, not the entire Hood-warped Malazan Empire.

A strange wave of lightning leapt up beyond the breakers

hammering the reef. It played out tumbling and pitching as if wrapped around an invisible log leagues long and thirty paces thick. The crackling spears struck the sheets of spume with a searing hiss. Thunder slapped the beach hard enough to shiver the sand. The lightning rolled on, straight towards them.

Heboric was suddenly at her side, his froglike face split wide in a grimace of fear. 'That's sorcery, lass! Run!'

Her laugh was a harsh bark. She made no move. 'It'll be quick, old man!'

Wind howled.

Heboric spun to face the approaching wave. He snarled a curse that was flung away by the growing roar, then interposed himself between Felisin and the sorcery. Baudin crouched down beside her, his face lit in a blue glow that intensified as the lightning reached the shore, then rolled up to them.

It shattered around Heboric as if he was a spire of rock. The old man staggered, his tattoos a tracery of fire that flared bright, then vanished.

The sorcery was gone. For all its threat, it swiftly died up and down the beach.

Heboric sagged, settling on his knees in the sand. 'Not me,' he said in the sudden silence. 'Otataral. Of course. Nothing to fear. Nothing at all.'

'There!' Baudin shouted.

A boat had somehow cleared the reef and now raced towards them, its lone sail aflame. Sorcery stabbed at the craft from all sides like vipers, then fell away as the boat neared shore. A moment later it scraped bottom and slid to a halt, canting to one side as it settled. Two figures were at the ratlines in an instant, cutting away the burning sail. The cloth swept down like a wing of flame, instantly doused as it struck the water. Two other men leapt down and waded onto shore.

'Which one's Duiker?' Felisin asked.

Heboric shook his head. 'Neither, but the one on the left is a mage.'

'How can you tell?'

He made no reply.

The two men swiftly approached, both staggering in exhaustion. The mage, a small, red-faced man wearing a singed cape, was the first to speak – in Malazan. 'Thank the gods! We need your help.'

Somewhere beyond the reef waited an unknown mage – a man unconnected to the rebellion, a stranger trapped within his own nightmare. As the vortex of a savage storm, he had risen from the deep on the second day out. Kulp had never before felt such unrestrained power. Its very wildness was all that saved them, as the madness that gripped the sorcerer tore and flayed his warren. There was no control, the warren's wounds gushed, the winds howled with the mage's own shrieks.

The *Ripath* was flung about like a piece of bark in a cascading mountain stream. At first Kulp countered with illusions – believing he and his companions were the object of the mage's wrath – but it quickly became apparent that the insane wielder was oblivious to them, fighting an altogether different war. Kulp contracted his own warren into a protective shell around *Ripath*, then, as Gesler and his crewmen struggled to keep the craft upright, he crouched down to withstand the onslaught.

The unleashed sorcery instinctively hunted them and no illusion could deceive something so thoroughly mindless. They became its lodestone, the attacks endless and wildly fluctuating in strength, battering Kulp relentlessly for two days and nights.

They were driven westward, towards the Otataral shores. The mage's power assailed that coastline, with little effect, and Kulp finally began to make sense of it – the mage's mind must have been destroyed by Otataral. Likely an escaped miner, a prisoner of war who had scaled the walls only to find he took his prison with him. Losing control of his warren, it had then taken control of him. It surged with power far beyond anything the mage himself had ever wielded.

The realization left Kulp horrified. The storm threatened to fling them onto that shore. Was the same fate awaiting him?

Gesler and his crew's skill was all that kept the *Ripath* from striking the reef. For eleven hours they managed to sail parallel to the razor-sharp rocks beneath the breakers.

On the third night Kulp sensed a change. The coastline on their right – which he had felt as an impenetrable wall of negation, the bloodless presence of Otataral – suddenly . . . *softened*. A power resided there, bruising the will of the magic-deadening ore, pushing it back on all sides.

There was a cut in the reef. It gave them, Kulp decided, their only chance. Rising from where he crouched amidships, he shouted to Gesler. The corporal grasped his meaning instantly, with desperate relief. They had been losing the struggle to exhaustion, to the overwhelming stress of watching sorcery speed towards them, only to wash over Kulp's protective magic – a protection they could see weakening with every pass.

Another attack came, even as they swept between the jagged breakers, sundering Kulp's resistance. Flame lit the storm-jib, the lines, the sail. Had any of the men been dry they would have become beacons of fire. As it was, the sorcery swept over them in a wave of hissing steam, then was gone, striking the shore and rolling up the beach until it fizzled out.

Kulp had half expected that the strangely blunted effect on this part of shore was in some way connected to the man he was sent to find, and so was not surprised to see three figures emerge from the gloom beyond the beach. Weary as he was, something about the way the three stood in relation to each other jangled alarms in his head. Circumstances had forced

315

them together, and expedience cared little for the bonds of friendship. Yet it was more than that.

The motionless ground beneath his feet was making him dizzy. When Kulp's weary gaze fell on the handless priest, a wave of relief washed through him, and there was nothing ironic in his call for help.

The ex-priest answered it with a dried-out laugh.

'Get them water,' the mage said to Gesler. The corporal pulled his eyes from Heboric with difficulty, then nodded and spun about. Truth had swung down to inspect *Ripath*'s hull for damage, while Stormy sat perched on the prow, his crossbow cradled in his arms. The corporal shouted for one of the water casks. Truth clambered back into the boat to retrieve it.

'Where's Duiker?' Heboric asked.

Kulp frowned. 'Not sure. We went our separate ways in a village north of Hissar. The Apocalypse—'

'We know. Dosin Pali was ablaze the night we escaped the pit.'

'Yeah, well.' Kulp studied the other two. The big man lacking an ear met his eyes coolly. Despite the ravages of deprivation evident in his bearing, there was a measure of self-control to him that made the mage uneasy. He was clearly more than the scarred dockyard thug he first took him for.

The young girl was no less disturbing, though in a way Kulp could not define. He sighed. *Worry about it later. Worry about everything later.*

Truth arrived with the water cask, Gesler a step behind him.

The three escapees converged on the young marine as he breached the cask, then held the tin cup that was tied to it and splashed it full of water.

'Go slow on that,' Kulp said. 'Sips, not gulps.'

As he watched them drink, the mage sought out his warren. It felt slippery, elusive, yet he was able to take hold, stealing power to bolster his senses. When he looked again upon

Heboric he almost shouted in surprise. The ex-priest's tattoos swarmed with a life of their own: flickering waves of power raced across his body and spun a handlike projection beyond the stump of his left wrist. That ghost-hand reached into a warren, was clenched as if gripping a tether. A wholly different power pulsed around his right stump, shot through with veins of green and Otataral red, as if two snakes writhed in mortal combat. The blunting effect arose exclusively from the green bands, radiating outward with what felt like conscious will. That it was strong enough to push back the effects of the Otataral was astonishing.

Denul healers often described diseases as waging war, with the flesh as the battleground, which their warren gave them sight to see. Kulp wondered if he wasn't seeing something similar. *But not a disease. A battle of warrens – Fener's own, linked by one ghostly hand, the other ensnared by Otataral, yet waxing nonetheless – a warren I can't recognize, a force alien to every sense I possess.* He blinked. Heboric was staring at him, a faint smile on his broad mouth.

'What in Hood's name has happened to you?' Kulp demanded.

The ex-priest shrugged. 'I wish I knew.'

The three marines now approached Heboric. 'I'm Gesler,' the corporal said in gruff deference. 'We're all that's left of the Boar Cult.'

The old man's smile faded. 'That would make three too many.' He turned away and strode off to retrieve a pair of backpacks.

Gesler stared after him, expressionless.

That man recovers damned quick. The boy Truth had gasped at the harsh words of a man he took to be his god's priest. Kulp saw something crumbling into ruins behind the lad's light-blue eyes. Stormy revealed the dark clouds that likely gave reason to his name, but he laid a hand on

317

Truth's shoulder a moment before facing the one-eared man.

'Your hands keep hovering over those hidden blades and I'm gonna get nervous,' he said in a low growl, shifting grip on his crossbow.

'That's Baudin,' the young woman said. 'He murders people. Old women, rivals. You name them, he's got their blood on his hands. Isn't that right, Baudin?' Without awaiting a reply she went on, 'I'm Felisin, House of Paran. Last in the line. But don't let any of that fool you.'

She did not elaborate.

Heboric returned with a pack slung over each forearm. He set them down, then moved close to Kulp. 'We're in no shape to help you, but after crossing this damned desert the thought of death by drowning is oddly appealing.' He stared out over the thrashing waves. 'What's out there?'

'Imagine a child holding a leash and at the other end is a Hound of Shadow. The child's the mage, the Hound's his warren. Too long in the mines before making his escape, is my guess. We need to rest before trying to run his storm again.'

'How bad are things on the mainland?'

Kulp shrugged. 'I don't know. We saw Hissar in flames. Duiker went to rejoin Coltaine and the Seventh – that old man's got a streak of optimism that'll get him stuck on a sliding bed. I'd say the Seventh's history, and so's Coltaine and his Wickans.'

'Ah, *that* Coltaine. When I was chained at the base of the crevasse behind Laseen's Palace I half expected to meet the man as a neighbour. Hood knows there was worthy enough company down there.' After a moment he shook his head. 'Coltaine's alive, Mage. You don't kill men like that easily.'

'If that's true, then I'm bound to rejoin him.'

Heboric nodded.

'He was excommunicated,' Felisin said loudly.

Both men turned to see Gesler facing the girl. She continued, 'More than that, he's the bane of his own god. Of

318

yours, I gather. Beware scorned priests. You'll have to lead your own prayers to Fener, lads, and I'd advise you to pray. A lot.'

The ex-priest swung back to Kulp with a sigh. 'You opened your warren to look upon me. What did you see?'

Kulp scowled. 'I saw,' he said after a moment, 'a child dragging a Hound as big as a Hood-damned mountain. In one hand.'

Heboric's expression tightened. 'And in the other?'

'Sorry,' Kulp replied, 'no easy answer there.'

'I'd let go . . .'

'If you could.'

Heboric nodded.

Kulp lowered his voice. 'If Gesler realized . . .'

'He'd cut me loose.'

'Messily.'

'I take it we're understood,' Heboric said with a faint smile.

'Not really, but I'll let it lie for now.'

The ex-priest acknowledged him with a nod.

'Did you choose your company here, Heboric?' Kulp asked, eyes on Baudin and Felisin.

'Aye, I did. More or less. Hard to believe, isn't it?'

'Walk up the beach with me,' the mage said, heading off. The tattooed man followed. 'Tell me about them,' Kulp said after they'd gone a distance.

Heboric shrugged. 'You have to compromise to stay alive in the mines,' he said. 'And that which one person thinks of value, another is the first to sell. Cheap. Well, that's what they are now. What they were before . . .' He shrugged again.

'Do you trust them?'

Heboric's wide face split in a grin. 'Do you trust *me*, Kulp? I know, it's too soon to answer that. Yours is not an easy question. I trust Baudin to work with us so long as it's in his interest to do so.'

'And the girl?'

The old man was a long time in answering. 'No.'

Not what I'd expected. This should have been the easy part. 'All right,' he said.

'And what of your companions? Those foolish men and their foolish cult?'

'Harsh words for a priest of Fener—'

'An excommunicated priest. The girl spoke the truth. My soul is my own, not Fener's. I took it back.'

'Didn't know that was possible.'

'Maybe it isn't. Please, I can walk no farther, Mage. Our journey has been . . . difficult.'

You're not the only one, old man.

They shared no more words on the way back to the others. For all the chaos of the crossing, Kulp had expected this part of the plan to be relatively straightforward. They would come to the coast. They would find Duiker's friend waiting . . . or not. He'd fought down his misgivings when the historian first came to him, asking for help. *Idiot.* Well, he would take them off this damned island, deposit them on the mainland, and that would be that. It was all he'd been asked to do.

The sun was rising, the sorcerous storm over the sea withdrawing from shore to boil black and bruised over the middle of the straits.

Food had been brought from *Ripath*. Heboric joined his two companions in a silent, tense meal. Kulp strode to where Gesler sat watch over his two sleeping soldiers, the three of them beneath a square of sailcloth rigged on four poles.

The corporal's scarred face twisted into an ironic grin. 'Fener's joke, this one,' he said.

Kulp squatted down beside the corporal. 'Glad you're enjoying it.'

'The boar god's humour ain't the laughing kind, Mage. Strange, though, I could've sworn the Lord of Summer was . . . *here*. Like a crow on that priest's shoulder.'

'You've felt Fener's touch before, Gesler?'

The man shook his head. 'Gifts don't come my way. Never did. It was just a feeling, that's all.'

'Still have it?'

'I don't think so. Don't know. Doesn't matter.'

'How's Truth?'

'Took it hard, finding a priest of Fener who then turns around and denies us all. He'll be all right – me and Stormy, we look out for him. Now it's your turn to answer some questions. How're we getting back to the mainland? That damned wizard's still out there, ain't he?'

'The priest will see us through.'

'How's that?'

'That'd be a long explanation, Corporal, and all I can think of right now is sleep. I'll take next watch.' He rose and went off to find some shade of his own.

Wide awake, arms wrapped around herself, Felisin watched the mage rig a sunshade, then slip beneath it to sleep. She glanced over at the marines, feeling a wave of gleeful disdain. *Followers of Fener, that's a laugh. The boar god with nothing between his ears. Hey, you fools, Fener's here, somewhere, cowering in the mortal realm. Ripe for any hunter with a sharp spear. We saw his hoof. You can thank that old man for that. Thank him any way you care to.*

Baudin had gone down to the water to wash himself. He now returned, his beard dripping.

'Scared yet, Baudin?' Felisin asked. 'Look at that soldier over there, the one that's awake. Too tough for you by far. And that one with the crossbow – didn't take him long to figure you out, did it? Hard men – harder than you—'

Baudin drawled, 'What, you bedded them already?'

'You used me—'

'What of it, girl? You've made being used a way of life.'

'Hood take you, bastard!'

Standing over her, he grunted a laugh. 'You won't pull me down – we're getting off this island. We've survived it. Nothing you can say's going to change my mood, girl. Nothing.'

'What's the talon signify, Baudin?'

His face became an expressionless mask.

'You know, the one you've got hidden away, along with all your thieving tools.'

The man's flat gaze flicked past her. She turned to find Heboric standing a few paces away. The ex-priest's eyes were fixed on Baudin as he said, 'Did I hear that right?'

The one-eared man said nothing.

She watched what had to be comprehension sweep across Heboric's face, watched as he glanced down at her, then back to Baudin. After a moment, he smiled. 'Well done,' he said. 'So far.'

'You really think so?' Baudin asked, then turned away.

'What's going on, Heboric?' Felisin demanded.

'You should have paid better attention to your history tutors, lass.'

'Explain.'

'Like Hood I will.' He shambled off.

Felisin wrapped herself tighter in her own arms, pivoting to face the straits. *We're alive. I can be patient again. I can bide my time.* The mainland burned with rebellion against the Malazan Empire. A pleasing thought. Maybe it would pull it all down – the Empire, the Empress . . . the Adjunct. And without the Malazan Empire, peace would once again come. *An end to repression, an end to the threat of restraint as I set about exacting revenge. The day you lose your bodyguards, sister Tavore, I will appear. I swear it, by every god and every demon lord that ever existed.* In the meantime, she would have to make use of these people around her, she would have to get them on her side. Not Baudin or Heboric – it was too late for them. But the others. The mage, the soldiers . . .

Felisin rose.

The corporal watched her approach with sleepy eyes.

'When did you last lie with a woman?' Felisin asked him.

It was not Gesler who answered, however. The cross-bowman's – Stormy's – voice drifted out from the shadow beneath the sailcloth: 'That would be a year and a day, the night I dressed up as a Kanese harlot – had Gesler fooled for hours. Mind you, he was pretty drunk. Mind you, so was I.'

The corporal grunted. 'That's a soldier's life for you. Too thick to know the difference . . .'

'Too drunk to care,' the crossbowman finished.

'You got it, Stormy.' Gesler's heavy eyes slid up to Felisin. 'Play your games elsewhere, lass. No offence, but we've done enough rutting to know when an offer's got hidden chains. You can't buy what ain't for sale, anyhow.'

'I told you about Heboric,' she said. 'I didn't have to.'

'Hear that, Stormy? The girl took pity on us.'

'He'll betray you. He despises you already.'

The boy named Truth sat up at that.

'Go away,' Gesler told her. 'My men are trying to get some sleep.'

Felisin met Truth's startling blue eyes, saw nothing but innocence in them. She threw him a pouty kiss, smiled as colour flooded his face. 'Careful or those ears will catch fire,' she said.

'Hood's breath,' Stormy muttered. 'Go on, lad. She wants it that bad. Give her a taste.'

'Not a chance,' she said, turning away. 'I only sleep with men.'

'Fools, you mean,' Gesler corrected, an edge to his tone.

Felisin strode down to the beach, walked out until the waves lapped her knees. She studied the *Ripath*. Flashburns painted the hull black in thick, random streaks. The front railing of the forecastle glittered as if the wood had been studded with a hail of quartz. The lines were frayed, unravelled where knives had cut.

The sun's reflection off the water was blinding. She closed her eyes, let her mind fall away until there was nothing but the feel of the warm water slipping around her legs. She felt an exhaustion that was beyond physical. She could not stop herself lashing out, and every face she made turn her way became a mirror. *There has to be a way to reflect something other than hate and contempt.*

No, not a way.

A reason.

'My hope is that the Otataral entwined in you is enough to drive away that insane mage,' Kulp said. 'Otherwise, we're in for a rough voyage.' Truth had lit a lantern and now crouched in the triangular forecastle, waiting for them to set out for the reef. The yellow light caught reflective glimmers in Heboric's tattoos as he grimaced in response to Kulp's words.

Gesler sat leaning over the steering oar. Like everyone else, he was waiting for the ex-priest. Waiting for a small measure of hope.

The sorcerous storm raged beyond the reef, its manic flashes lighting up the night, revealing tumbling black clouds over a frothing sea.

'If you say so,' Heboric eventually said.

'Not good enough—'

'Best I can do,' the old man snapped. He raised one stump, jabbed it in front of Kulp. 'You see what I can't even feel, Mage!'

The mage swung to Gesler. 'Well, Corporal?'

The soldier shrugged. 'We got a choice?'

'It's not that simple,' Kulp said, fighting to stay calm. 'With Heboric aboard I don't even know if I can open my warren – he's got taints to him I wouldn't want spreading.

324

Without my warren I can't deflect that sorcery. Meaning—'

'We get roasted crisp,' Gesler said, nodding. 'Look alive up there, Truth. We're heading out!'

'Yours is a misplaced faith, Corporal,' Heboric said.

'Knew you'd say that. Now everyone stay low – me and Stormy and the lad got work to do.'

Although he sat within arm's reach of the tattooed old man, Kulp could sense his own warren. It felt ready – almost eager – for release. The mage was frightened. Meanas was a remote warren, and every fellow practitioner Kulp had met characterized it the same way: cool, detached, amused intelligence. The game of illusions was played with light, dark, texture and shadows, crowing victory when it succeeded in deceiving an eye, but even that triumph felt emotionless, the satisfaction clinical. Accessing the warren always had the feel of interrupting a power busy with other things. As if shaping a small fraction of that power was a distraction barely worth acknowledging.

Kulp did not trust his warren's uncharacteristic attentiveness. It wanted to join the game. He knew he was falling into the trap of thinking of Meanas as an entity, a faceless god, where access was worship, success a reward of faith. Warrens were not like that. A mage was not a priest and magic was not divine intervention. Sorcery could be the ladder to Ascendancy – a means to an end, but there was no point to worshipping the means.

Stormy had rigged a small, square sail, enough to give control but not so large that it would risk the weakened mast. The *Ripath* slipped forward in front of a mild shore breeze. Truth lay on the bowsprit, scanning the breakers ahead. The cut they'd come in through was proving hard to find. Gesler barked out commands and swung the craft to run parallel to the reef.

Kulp glanced at Heboric. The ex-priest sat with his left

shoulder against the mast, squinting out into the darkness. The mage was desperate to open his warren – to look upon the old man's ghost-hands, to gauge the serpent of Otataral – but he held back, suspicious of his own curiosity.

'There!' Truth shouted, pointing.

'I see it!' Gesler bellowed. 'Move it, Stormy!'

The *Ripath* swung around, bow wheeling to face the breakers ... and a gap that Kulp could barely make out. The wind picked up, the sail stretching taut.

Beyond it, the billowing clouds twisted, creating an inverted funnel. Lightning leapt up from the waves to frame it. The *Ripath* slipped through the reef and plunged directly into the spinning vortex.

Kulp did not even have time to scream. His warren opened, locking in instant battle with a power demonic in its fury. Spears of water slanted down from overhead, shredding the sail in moments. They struck the deck like quarrels, punching through the planks. Kulp saw one shaft pierce Stormy's thigh, pinning him shrieking to the deck. Others shattered against Heboric's hunched back – he had thrown himself over the girl, Felisin, shielding her as the spears rained down. His tattoos raged with fire the colour of mud-smeared gold.

Baudin had hurled himself onto the forecastle, one arm reaching down and out of sight. Truth was nowhere to be seen.

The spears vanished. Pitching as if on a single surging wave, the *Ripath* lurched forward, stern lifting. Overhead the sky raged, bruised and flushing with blooms of power. Kulp's eyes widened as he stared up – a tiny figure rode the storm above, limbs flailing, the fragments of a cloak whipping about like a tattered wing. Sorcery flung the figure around as if it was no more than a straw-stuffed doll. Blood exploded outward as a coruscating wave engulfed the hapless creature. When the wave swept past, the figure rolled and tumbled after it, webs of blood spreading out like a fisherman's net behind it.

Then it was falling.

Gesler pushed past Kulp. 'Take the oar!' he yelled above the roaring wind.

The mage scrambled aft. *Steer? Steer through what?* He was certain it was not water carrying them. They'd plunged into a madman's warren. Closing his hands around the oar's handle, he felt his own warren flow down into the wood and take hold. The pitching steadied. Kulp grunted. There was no time to wonder – being appalled demanded all his attention.

Gesler clambered forward, grasping Baudin's ankles just as the big man started to slip over the bow. Pulling him back revealed that Baudin held, with one hand, onto Truth, his fingers wrapped in the lad's belt. Blood streamed from that hand, and Baudin's face was white with pain.

The unseen wave beneath them slumped. The *Ripath* charged forward into dead calm. Silence.

Heboric scrambled to Stormy. The marine lay motionless on the deck, blood gushing in horrifying amounts from his punctured thigh. The flow lost its fierceness even as Kulp watched.

Heboric did the only thing he could, or so Kulp would remember it in retrospect. At that instant, however, the mage screamed a warning – but too late – as Heboric plunged a ghostly, loam-smeared hand directly into the wound.

Stormy spasmed, giving a bark of pain. The tattoos flowed out from Heboric's wrist to spread a glowing pattern on the soldier's thigh.

When the old man pulled his arm away, the wound closed, the tattoos knitting together like sutures. Heboric scrambled back, eyes wide with shock.

A hissing sigh escaped Stormy's grimacing lips. Trembling and bone white, he sat up. Kulp blinked. He'd seen something more than just healing pass from Heboric's arm into Stormy. Whatever it had been, it was virulent and tinged with madness. *Worry about it later – the man's alive, isn't he?* The mage's attention swung to where Gesler and Baudin knelt on either side of a prone, motionless Truth. The corporal had turned the lad onto his stomach and was rhythmically pushing down with both hands to expel the water that filled Truth's lungs. After a moment the boy coughed.

The *Ripath* sat heavily, listing to one side. The uniform grey sky hung close and faintly luminous over them. They were becalmed, the only sound coming from water pouring into the hold somewhere below.

Gesler helped Truth sit up. Baudin, still on his knees, clutched his right hand in his lap. Kulp saw that all the fingers had been pulled from their joints, skin split and streaming blood.

'Heboric,' the mage whispered.

The old man's head jerked around. He was drawing breath in rapid gasps.

'Tend to Baudin with that healing touch,' Kulp said quietly. *We won't think about what comes with it.* 'If you can . . .'

'No,' Baudin growled, studying Heboric intently. 'Don't want your god's touch on me, old man.'

'Those joints need resetting,' Kulp said.

'Gesler can do it. The hard way.'

The corporal looked up, then nodded and moved over.

Felisin spoke. 'Where are we?'

Kulp shrugged. 'Not sure. But we're sinking.'

'She's stove through,' Stormy said. 'Four, five places.' The soldier stared down at the tattoos covering his thigh and frowned.

The young woman struggled to her feet, one hand reaching out to grip the charred mast. The slant of the deck had sharpened.

'She might capsize,' Stormy said, still studying the tattoos. 'Any time now.'

Kulp's warren subsided. He slumped in sudden exhaustion. He wouldn't last long in the water, he knew.

Baudin grunted as Gesler set the first finger of his right hand. The corporal spoke as he moved on to the next one. 'Rig up some casks, Stormy. If you can walk, that is. Divide up the fresh water among them. Felisin, get the emergency food stores – that's the chest on this side of the forecastle. Take the whole thing.' Baudin moaned as he set the next finger. 'Truth, you up to getting some bandages?'

His dry heaves having stopped a few moments earlier, the boy slowly pushed himself to his hands and knees and starting crawling aft.

Kulp glanced at Felisin. She had not moved in response to Gesler's orders and seemed to be debating a few choice words. 'Come on, lass,' Kulp said, rising, 'I'll give you a hand.'

Stormy's fears of capsizing were not realized: as the *Ripath* settled, the cant slowly diminished. Water had filled the hold and now lapped the hatch, thick as soup and pale blue in colour.

'Hood's breath,' Stormy said, 'we're sinking in goat's milk.'

'With a seasoning of brine,' Gesler added. He finished working on Baudin's hand. Truth joined them with a medic's kit.

'We won't have to go far,' Felisin said, her gaze off to starboard. Joining her, Kulp saw what she was looking at. A large ship sat motionless in the thick water less then fifty arm-spans away. It had twin banks of oars, hanging down listlessly. A single rudder was visible. There were three masts, the main and fore both rigged with tattered square sails, the mizzen mast with the shredded remnants of a lateen. There was no sign of life.

Baudin, his right hand now a blunt bandaged lump, joined them, the corporal a step behind. The one-eared man grunted. 'That's a Quon dromon. Pre-Imperial.'

'You know your ships,' Gesler said, giving the man a sharp glance.

Baudin shrugged. 'I worked in a prison gang, scuttling the republic's fleet in Quon Harbour. That was twenty years ago – Dassem had been using them to train his Marines—'

'I know,' Gesler said, his tone revealing first-hand knowledge.

'Young to be in a prison gang,' Stormy said from where he squatted amidst the water casks. 'You were what, ten? Fifteen?'

'Something like that,' Baudin said. 'And what got me there ain't your business, soldier.'

There was a long silence, then Gesler shook himself. 'You done, Stormy?'

'Aye, all rigged up.'

'All right, let's swim over before our lady makes her rush to the bottom. No gain if we end up all getting pulled down in her wake.'

'I ain't happy,' Stormy said as he eyed the dromon. 'That's right out of a tavern tale told at midnight. Could be Hood's Herald, could be cursed, plague-ridden—'

'Could be the only dry underfoot we'll find,' Gesler said. 'As for the rest, think of the tale you'll spin in the next tavern, Stormy. You'll have them pissing their pants and rushing off to the nearest temple for a blessing. You could set it up to take a cut from the avatars.'

'Well, maybe you ain't got enough brains to be scared of anything . . .'

The corporal grinned. 'Let's get wet, everyone. I hear noble-women pay in gold for a bath like the one we're about to take. That right, lass?'

Felisin did not answer.

Kulp shook his head. 'You're just happy to be alive,' he said to Gesler.

'Damn right.'

The water was cool, strangely slick and not easy to swim through. The *Ripath* settled behind them, its decks awash.

330

Then the mast leaned to one side, pausing a moment before sweeping down to the water. Within seconds it had slipped beneath the surface.

Half an hour later they reached the dromon, gasping with exhaustion. Truth proved the only one capable of climbing up the steering oar. He clambered over the high sterncastle railing. A few moments later a thick-twined hemp ladder tumbled down to the others.

It was a struggle, but eventually everyone was aboard, Gesler and Stormy pulling up the food chest and water casks last.

From the sterncastle, Kulp looked down the length of the ship's deck. The abandonment had been a hasty thing. Coiled ropes and bundles of supplies wrapped in sealskin lay scattered about, along with discarded body armour, swords and belts. A thick, pale, greasy dust clung to everything.

The others joined him in silent study.

'Anybody see a name on the hull?' Gesler asked eventually. 'I looked, but . . .'

'*Silanda*,' Baudin said.

Stormy growled, 'Togg's teats, man, there wasn't no—'

'Don't need one to know this ship,' Baudin said. 'That cargo lying about down there, that's from Drift Avalii. *Silanda* was the only craft sanctioned to trade with the Tiste Andii. She was on her way to the island when the Emperor's forces overran Quon. She never returned.'

Silence followed his words.

It was broken by a soft laugh from Felisin. 'Baudin the thug. Did your prison gangs work in libraries as well?'

'Anybody else notice the waterline?' Gesler asked. 'This ship hasn't moved in years.' He shot one last, piercing glare at Baudin, then descended to the main deck. 'Might as well be a pile of rock knee-deep in guano,' he said, stopping at one of the sealskin bundles. He crouched down to unwrap it. A moment later he hissed a curse and lurched back. The bundle's flaps fell away, releasing its contents: a severed head. It rolled crazily across the deck, thumping up against the lip of the hold's hatchway.

Kulp pushed past a motionless Heboric, scrambled down to the main deck and approached the head. He raised his warren. Stopped.

'What do you see?' the ex-priest asked.

'Nothing I like,' the mage replied. He stepped closer, crouched. 'Tiste Andii.' He glanced over at Gesler. 'What I'm about to suggest is not pleasant, but . . .'

The corporal, his face white, nodded. 'Stormy,' he said as he turned to the next bundle. 'Give me a hand.'

'Doing what?'

'Counting heads.'

'Fener save me! Gesler—'

'You gotta be cold to spin a tale like this one. Takes practice. Get down here and get your hands dirty, soldier.'

There were dozens of bundles. Each contained a head, cleanly severed. Most were Tiste Andii, but some were human. Gesler began stacking them into a grisly pyramid around the main mast. The corporal's recovery from his initial shock had been swift – clearly, the man had seen his share of horrors as a Marine of the Empire. Stormy was almost as quick in casting aside his revulsion, although a superstitious terror seemed to replace it – he worked frantically fast, and before too long every head had joined the ghastly pyramid.

Kulp turned his attention to the hatch leading down into the oar pit. A faint aura of sorcery rose from it, visible to his warren-touched senses as waves rippling the still air. He hesitated long before approaching it.

Apart from the mage and Gesler and Stormy, the others remained in the sterncastle, watching the proceedings with something like numb shock.

The corporal joined Kulp. 'Ready to check below?'

'Absolutely not.'

'Lead on, then,' Gesler said with a tight grin. He unsheathed his sword.

Kulp glanced down at it.

The corporal shrugged. 'Yeah, I know.'

Muttering under his breath, Kulp headed for the hatch. The lack of light below did nothing to hide what he saw. Sorcery lined everything, sickly yellow and faintly pulsing. Both hands on the railing, the mage descended the encrusted steps, Gesler close behind him.

'Can you see anything?' the corporal asked.

'Oh yes.'

'What's that smell?'

'If patience has a smell,' Kulp said, 'you're smelling it.' He cast a wave of light down the length of the centre walkway between the bench rows, spun it sideways and left it there.

'Well,' Gesler said, dry and rasping, 'there's a certain logic, isn't there?'

The oars were manned by headless corpses, three to a bench. Other sealskin bundles crowded every available space. Another headless figure sat behind a skin drum, both hands gripping strange, gourdlike batons. The figure was massively muscled. There was no evidence of decay on any of the bodies. White bone and red flesh glistened at the necks.

Neither man spoke for a long time, then Gesler cleared his throat, to little effect as he squeezed out gravel words. 'Did you say patience, Kulp?'

'Aye.'

'I ain't misheard, then.'

Kulp shook his head. 'Someone took the ship, beheaded everyone aboard . . . then put them to work.'

'In that order.'

'In that order.'

'How long ago?'

'Years. Decades. We're in a warren, Corporal. No telling how time works here.'

Gesler grunted. 'What say we check the captain's cabin? There might be a log.'

'And a "take to the oars" whistle.'

'Yeah. You know, if we hide that drum-beater, I could send Stormy down here to beat the time.'

'You've a wicked sense of humour, Gesler.'

'Aye. Thing is, Stormy tells the world's most boring sea tales. It'd do a favour to anyone he meets from now on to spice things up a little.'

'Don't tell me you're serious.'

The corporal sighed. 'No,' he said after a moment. 'I won't invite madness on anyone, Mage.'

They returned to the main deck. The others stared at them. Gesler shrugged. 'What you'd expect,' he said, 'if you was completely insane, that is.'

'Well,' Felisin replied, 'you're talking to the right crowd.'

Kulp strode towards the cabin hatch. The corporal sheathed his sword and then followed. The hatch descended two steps, then opened out into a galley. A large wooden table commanded the centre. Opposite them was a second hatch, leading to a narrow walkway with berths on either side. At the far end was the door to the captain's cabin.

No-one occupied the berths, but there was gear aplenty, all waiting for owners who no longer needed it.

The cabin door opened with a loud squeal.

Even with all they had seen thus far, the interior was a scene of horror. Four bodies were immediately visible, three of them twisted grotesquely in postures of sudden death. There was no evidence of decay, but no blood was visible. Whatever had killed them had crushed them thoroughly without once breaking skin. The exception sat in the captain's chair at the end of a map table, as if presiding over

Hood's own stage. A spear jutted from his chest, and had been pushed through to the chair, then beyond. Blood glistened down the front of the figure's body, pooled in his lap. It had stopped flowing, yet looked still wet.

'Tiste Andii?' Gesler asked in a whisper.

'They have that look,' Kulp replied softly, 'but not quite.' He stepped into the cabin. 'Their skins are grey, not black. Nor do they look very . . . refined.'

'The Tiste Andii of Drift Avalii were said to be pretty barbaric – not that anyone living has visited the isle.'

'None returned, in any case,' Kulp conceded. 'But these are wearing skins – barely cured. And look at their jewellery . . .' The four bodies were adorned in bone fetishes, claws, the canines of beasts, and polished seashells. There was none of the fine Tiste Andii craftwork that Kulp had had occasion to see in the past. Moreover, all four were brown-haired, the hair hanging loose and uncombed, stringy with grease. Tiste Andii hair was either silver-white or midnight black.

'What in Hood's name are we seeing?' Gesler asked.

'The killers of the Quon sailors and the Tiste Andii, is my guess,' Kulp said. 'They then sailed into this warren, maybe by choice, maybe not. And ran into something nastier than them.'

'You think the rest of the crew escaped?'

Kulp shrugged. 'If you've got the sorcery to command headless corpses, who needs a bigger crew than the one we're looking at right here?'

'They still look like Tiste Andii,' the corporal said, peering closely at the man in the chair.

'We should get Heboric in here,' Kulp said. 'Maybe he's read something somewhere that'll bring light to all this.'

'Wait here,' Gesler said.

The ship was creaking now as the rest of the group began moving around on the main deck. Kulp listened to the corporal's footsteps recede up the walkway. The mage leaned both hands on the table, scanning the charts splayed out on its surface. There was a map there, showing a land he could not recognize: a ragged coastline of fjords studded with cursory sketches of pine trees. Inland was a faint whitewash, as of ice or snow. A course had been plotted, striking east from the jagged shoreline, then southward across a vast ocean. The Malazan Empire purported to have world maps, but they showed nothing like the land he saw here. The Empire's claim to dominance suddenly seemed pathetic.

Heboric stepped into the cabin behind him. Kulp did not turn from his study of the chart. 'Give them a close look,' the mage said.

The old man moved past Kulp, crouching down to frown at the captain's face. The high cheekbones and angular eye sockets looked Tiste Andii, as did the man's evident height. Heboric reached out tentatively—

'Wait,' Kulp growled. 'Be careful what you touch. And which arm you use.'

Heboric hissed in exasperation and dropped his arm. After a moment, he straightened. 'I can only think of one thing. Tiste Edur.'

'Who?'

'*Gothos's Folly*. There's mention of three Tiste peoples arriving from another realm. Of course the only one that's known to us is the Tiste Andii, and Gothos only names one of the other groups – Tiste Edur. Grey-skinned, not black. Children of the unwelcome union of Mother Dark with the Light.'

'Unwelcome?'

Heboric grimaced. 'The Tiste Andii considered it a degradation of pure Dark, and the source of all their subsequent ills. Anyway, *Gothos's Folly* is the only tome where you'll find mention of them. It also happens to be the oldest.'

'Gothos was Jaghut, correct?'

336

'Aye, and as sour-tempered a writer as I've ever had the displeasure of reading. Tell me, Kulp, what does your warren reveal?'

'Nothing.'

Heboric glanced over in surprise. 'Nothing at all?'

'No.'

'But they look to be in stasis – this blood's still wet.'

'I know.'

Heboric gestured at something around the captain's neck. 'There's your whistle, assuming we're going to make use of what's below decks.'

'Either that or we sit here and starve.' Kulp stepped closer to the captain's corpse. A long bone whistle hung from a leather thong, resting alongside the spear's shaft. 'I sense nothing from that bone tube either. It may not even work.'

Heboric shrugged. 'I'm going back up for what passes for fresh air. That spear's Barghast, by the way.'

'It's too damned big,' Kulp countered.

'I know, but that's what it looks like to me.'

'It's too big.'

Heboric made no reply, disappearing up the walkway. Kulp glared at the spear. *It's too big.* After a moment he reached out and gingerly removed the whistle from around the corpse's neck.

Emerging onto the main deck, the mage glanced again at the whistle. He grunted. It was alive with sorcery now. *The breath of Otataral's in that cabin. No wonder their sorcery couldn't defend them.* He looked around. Stormy had positioned himself at the prow, his ever-present crossbow strapped to his back. Baudin stood near him, cradling his bandaged hand. Felisin leaned against the railing near the main mast, arms crossed, appallingly cool with a pyramid of severed heads almost at her feet. Heboric was nowhere to be seen.

Gesler approached. 'Truth is heading up to the crow's nest,' he said. 'You got the whistle?'

Kulp tossed it over. 'Chosen a course yet?'

'Truth will see what he sees, then we'll decide.'

The mage craned his head, eyes narrowing on the lad as he lithely scrambled up the rigging. Five breaths later Truth clambered into the crow's nest and vanished from sight.

'Fener's hoof!' The curse drifted down, snared everyone's attention.

'Truth!'

'Three pegs to port! Storm sails!'

Gesler and Kulp rushed to the starboard railing. A smudge marred the formless horizon, flickering with lightning. Kulp hissed. 'That Hood-damned wizard's followed us!'

The corporal spun around. 'Stormy! Check what's left of these sails.' Without pause he put the whistle to his lips and blew. The sound was a chorus of voices, keening tonelessly. It chilled the air, the wail of souls twisted past torture, transforming pain into sound, fading with reluctance as Gesler pulled the whistle away.

Wood thumped on either side as oars were readied. Heboric stumbled from the hold hatch, his tattoos glowing like phosphor, his eyes wide as he swung to Gesler. 'You've got your crew, Corporal.'

'Awake,' Felisin muttered, stepping away from the main mast.

Kulp saw what she had seen. The severed heads had opened their eyes, swiveling to fix on Gesler as if driven by a single ghastly mechanism.

The corporal seemed to flinch, then he shook it off. 'Could've used one of these when I was a drill sergeant,' he said with a tight grin.

'Your drummer's ready down below,' Heboric said from where he stood peering down into the rowers' pit.

'Forget the sails,' Stormy said. 'Rotted through.'

'Man the steering oar,' Gesler ordered him. 'Three pegs to

port – we can't do nothing but run.' He raised the whistle again and blew a rapid sequence. The drum started booming in time. The oars swung, blades flipping from horizontal to vertical, then dipped down into the sluggish water and pulled.

The ship groaned, crunching through the meniscus of crust that had clung to the hull. The *Silanda* lurched into motion and slowly eased round until the rapidly approaching storm cloud was directly astern. The oars pushed slimy water with relentless precision.

Gesler looped the whistle's thong around his neck. 'Wouldn't the old Emperor have loved this old lady, Kulp, eh?'

'Your excitement's nauseating, Corporal.'

The man barked a laugh.

The twin banks of oars lifted the *Silanda* into a ramming pace and stayed there. The cadence of the drum was a too swift heartbeat. It reverberated in Kulp's bones with a resonance that etched his nerves with pain. He did not need to descend into the pit to affirm his vision of that thick-muscled, headless corpse pounding the gourds against the skin, the relentless heave and pull of the rowers, the searing play of Hood-bound sorcery in the stifling atmosphere. His eyes went in search of Gesler, and found him standing at the sterncastle alongside Stormy. These were hard men, harder than he could fathom. They'd taken the grim black humour of the soldier further than he'd thought possible, cold as the sunless core of a glacier. *Bloody-minded confidence . . . or fatalism? Never knew Fener's bristles could be so black.*

The mad sorcerer's storm still gained on them, slower than before, yet an undeniable threat nonetheless. The mage strode to Heboric's side.

'Is this your god's warren?'

The old man scowled. 'Not my god. Not his warren. Hood knows where in the Abyss we are, and it seems there's no easy wakening from this nightmare.'

'You drove the god-touched hand into Stormy's wound.'

'Aye. Nothing but chance. Could have as easily been the other one.'

'What did you feel?'

Heboric shrugged. 'Something passing through. You'd guessed as much, didn't you?'

Kulp nodded.

'Was it Fener himself?'

'I don't know. I don't think so. I'm not an expert in matters religious. Doesn't seem to have affected Stormy . . . apart from the healing. I didn't know Fener granted such boons.'

'He doesn't,' the ex-priest muttered, eyes clouding as he looked back at the two marines. 'Not without a price, anyway.'

Felisin sat apart from the others, her closest company the pyramid of staring heads. They didn't bother her much, since their attention remained on Gesler, on the man with the siren whistle of bone dangling on his chest. She thought back to the round in Unta, to the priest of flies. That had been the first time sorcery had been visited upon her. For all the stories of magic and wild wizards, of sorcerous conflagrations engulfing cities in wars at the very edges of the Empire, Felisin had never before witnessed such forces. It was never as common as the tales purported it to be. And the witnessing of magic left scars, a feeling of overwhelming vulnerability in the face of something beyond one's control. It made the world suddenly fey, deadly, frightening and bleak. That day in Unta had shifted her place in the world, or at least her sense of it. And she'd felt off-balance ever since.

But maybe it wasn't that. Not that at all. Maybe it was what I lived through on the march to the galleys, maybe it was that sea of faces, the storm of hate and mindless fury, of the freedom and hunger to deliver pain writ so plain in all those so very normal faces. Maybe it was the people that sent me reeling.

She looked over at the severed heads. The eyes did not blink. They were drying, crackling like egg white splashed on hot cobblestones. *Like mine. Too much has been seen. Far too much.* If demons rose out of the waters around them right now she would feel no shock, only a wonder that they had taken so long to appear *and could you be swift in ending it all, now? Please.*

Like a long-limbed ape, Truth came scrambling down from the rigging, landing lightly on the deck and pausing close to her as he brushed dusty rope fibres from his clothes. He had a couple of years on her, yet looked much younger to her eyes. *Unpocked, smooth skin. The wisps of beard, all too clear eyes. No gallons of wine, no clouds of durhang smoke, no weighty bodies taking turns to push inside, into a place that had started out vulnerable yet was soon walled off from anything real, anything that mattered. I only gave them the illusion of getting inside me, a dead-end pocket. Can you grasp what I'm talking about, Truth?*

He noted her attention, gave her a shy smile. 'He's in the clouds,' he said, his voice hoarse with adolescence.

'Who is?'

'The sorcerer. Like an untethered kite, this way and that, trailing streamers of blood.'

'How poetic, Truth. Go back to being a marine.'

He reddened, turned away.

Baudin spoke behind her. 'The lad's too good for you and that's what makes you mean.'

'What would you know?' she sneered without turning.

'I can't scry you much, lass,' he admitted. 'But I can scry you some.'

'So you'd like to believe. Let me know when that hand starts rotting – I want to be there when it's cut off.'

The oars clacked in counterpoint to the thundering drum. The wind arrived like a gasping exhalation, and the sorcerer's storm was upon them.

* * *

Something ragged across his brow awoke Fiddler. He opened his eyes to a mass of bristle ends that suddenly lifted clear to reveal a wizened black face peering critically down. The face concluded its examination with an expression of distaste.

'Spiders in your beard . . . or worse. Can't see them, but I know they're there.'

The sapper drew a deep breath and winced at the throbbing protest from his broken ribs. 'Get away from me!' he growled. Stinging pain wrapped his thighs, reminders of the gouging claws that had raked them. His left ankle was heavily bandaged – the numbness from his foot was worrying.

'Can't,' the old man replied. 'No escape is possible. Bargains were sealed, arrangements made. The Deck speaks plain in this. A life given for a life taken, and more besides.'

'You're Dal Honese,' Fiddler said. 'Where am I?'

The face split into a wide grin. 'In Shadow. Hee hee.'

A new voice spoke from behind the strange old man. 'He wakens and you torment him, High Priest. Move aside, the soldier needs air, not airs.'

'It's a matter of justice,' the High Priest retorted, though he pulled back. 'Your tempered companion kneels before that altar, does he not? These details are vital to understanding.' He took another step back as the massive form of the other speaker moved into view.

'Ah,' Fiddler sighed. 'The Trell. Memory returns. And your companion . . . the Jhag?'

'He entertains your companions,' the Trell said. 'Feebly, I admit. For all his years, Icarium has never mastered the social grace necessary to put others at ease.'

'Icarium, the Jhag by that name. The maker of machines, the chaser of time—'

The Trell showed his canines in a wide, wry smile. 'Aye, lord of the sand grains – though that poetic allusion's lost on most and awkward besides.'

342

'Mappo.'

'Aye again. And your friends name you Fiddler, relieving you of the guise of a Gral horsewarrior.'

'Hardly matters that I awoke out of character, then,' Fiddler said.

'There's no punishment awaiting the lapse, soldier. Thirsty? Hungry?'

'Good, yes and yes. But first, where are we?'

'In a temple carved into a cliff. Out of the Whirlwind. Guests of a High Priest of Shadow – whom you've met. Iskaral Pust.'

'Pust?'

'Even so.'

The Dal Honese High Priest pushed into view again, scowling. 'You mock my name, soldier?'

'Not I, High Priest.'

The old man grunted, adjusted his grip on the broom, then scampered from the room.

Fiddler sat up gingerly, moving like an ancient. He was tempted to ask Mappo for an assessment of the damage, especially his ankle, but decided to hold off hearing the likely bad news a while longer. 'What's that man's story?'

'I doubt even he knows.'

'I awoke when he was sweeping my head.'

'Not surprising.'

There was an ease to the Trell's presence that relaxed Fiddler. Until he recalled the warrior's name. *Mappo, a name ever chained to another's. And enough rumours to fill a tome. If any were true . . .* 'Icarium scared off the D'ivers.'

'His reputation carries weight.'

'Is it earned, Mappo?' Even as he asked, Fiddler knew he should have bitten back the question.

The Trell winced, withdrew slightly. 'I shall get you food and drink, then.'

343

Mappo left the small room, moving silently despite his considerable bulk, the combination raising an echo that brought Kalam to mind. *Did you outrun the storm, old friend?*

Iskaral Pust eased back into the chamber. 'Why are you here?' he whispered. 'Do you know why? You don't, but I'll tell you. You and no-one else.' He leaned close, plucking at his spiral wisps of hair with both hands. '*Tremorlor!*'

Laughing at Fiddler's expression, he spun about in wild, capering steps before settling once more in front of the sapper, their faces inches apart. 'The rumour of a path, a way home. A small wriggling worm of a rumour, even less, a grub, smaller than a nail clipping, the compacted and knotted mess wrapped around something that might be a truth. Or not. Hee hee!'

Fiddler had had enough. Grimacing through the pain, he grabbed the man's collar and shook. Spittle struck his face, the High Priest's eyes rolled about like marbles in a cup.

'What, again?' Iskaral Pust managed to say.

Fiddler pushed him away.

The old man staggered, righted himself and made a show of reassembling his dignity. 'A concurrence of reactions. Too long out of social engagements and the like. Must examine my manners, and more, my personality.' He cocked his head. 'Honest. Forthright. Amusing. Gentle and impressive integrity. Well! Where's the problem, then? Soldiers are crude. Callow and thick. Distempered. Do you know the Chain of Dogs?'

Fiddler started, blinked as if shaken from a trance. 'What?'

'It's begun, though not yet known. Anabar Thy'lend. Chain of Dogs in the Malazan tongue. Soldiers have no imaginations, meaning they're capable of vast surprises. There are some things even the Whirlwind cannot sweep aside.'

Mappo Trell returned, bearing a tray. 'Harassing our guest again, Iskaral Pust?'

'Shadow-borne prophecies,' the High Priest muttered, eyeing Fiddler with cool appraisal. 'The gutter under the flood,

344

raising ripples on the plunging surface. A river of blood, the flow of words from a hidden heart. All things sundered. Spiders in every crook and corner.' He whirled about, stamped out of the room.

Mappo stared after him.

'Pay him no heed, right?'

The Trell swung around, his heavy brows lifting. 'Hood, no, pay that man every heed, Fiddler.'

'I was afraid you'd say that. He mentioned Tremorlor. He knows.'

'He knows what even your companions don't,' Mappo said, carrying the tray to the sapper. 'You seek the fabled Azath House, out in the desert. Somewhere.'

Aye, and the gate Quick Ben swears it holds . . . 'And you?' Fiddler asked. 'What has brought you to Raraku?'

'I follow Icarium,' the Trell replied. 'A search without end.'

'And you've devoted your life to helping him in his search?'

'No,' Mappo sighed, then whispered without meeting Fiddler's gaze, 'I seek to keep it endless. Here, break your fast. You've been unconscious for two days. Your friends are restless with questions, eager to speak with you.'

'I suppose I've no choice – I'd better answer those questions.'

'Aye, and once you've mended some, we can begin our journey . . .' He smiled cautiously. 'To find Tremorlor.'

Fiddler frowned. 'Mended, you said. My ankle was crushed – I can barely feel a thing beyond my knee. Seems likely you'll have to cut that foot off.'

'I've some experience in healing,' Mappo said. 'This temple once specialized in such alchemies, and the nuns left much behind. And, oddly enough, Iskaral Pust seems to show some talent as well, though one has to keep an eye on him. His wits scatter sometimes and he confuses elixirs with poisons.'

'He's an avatar of Shadowthrone,' the sapper said, eyes

narrowing. 'Or the Rope, Cotillion, the Patron of Assassins – there's little difference between the two.'

The Trell shrugged. 'The art of assassination requires a complementary knowledge of healing. Two sides to the same alchemical coin. In any case, he actually did surgery on your ankle – fear not, I observed. And, I admit, learned much. Essentially, the High Priest rebuilt your ankle. Using an unguent, he sealed the fragments – I've never before seen the like. Thus, you will heal, and quickly.'

'A pair of hands devoted to Shadow poked around under my skin? Hood's breath!'

'It was that or lose your foot. You had a punctured lung as well – beyond my skills, that, but the High Priest contrived to drain your lung of blood, then made you breathe a healing vapour. You owe Iskaral Pust your life.'

'Precisely my point,' Fiddler muttered.

There were voices outside, then Apsalar appeared in the doorway, Crokus behind her. The two days out of the desiccating storm had done much to revive both of them. They entered, Crokus rushing past to crouch beside Fiddler's bed.

'We have to get out of here!' he hissed.

The sapper glanced at Mappo, noted his wry smile as he slowly backed away. 'Calm down, lad. What is the problem?'

'The High Priest – he's of the Shadow Cult, Fiddler. Don't you see – Apsalar . . .'

Something cold slithered along the sapper's bones. 'Oh, damn,' he whispered. 'I see your point.' He looked up as the young woman stepped to the foot of the bed, and spoke in a low tone. 'Your mind still your own, lass?'

'The little man treats me well,' she said, shrugging.

'Well?' Crokus spluttered. 'Like the prodigal returned, you mean! What's to stop Cotillion from possessing you all over again?'

'You need only ask his servant,' a new voice said from the

346

doorway. Icarium stood leaning, arms crossed, against the frame. His slitted grey eyes were fixed on the room's far corner.

From the gloom of the shadows there a figure took shape. Iskaral Pust, seated on a strangely wrought chair, squirmed and flung a glare at the Jhag. 'I was to remain unseen, fool! What gift shadows when you so clearly divine what they hide? Pah! I am undone!'

Icarium's thin lips quirked slightly. 'Why not give them answer, Iskaral Pust? Put them at ease.'

'Put them at ease?' The High Priest seemed to find the words awkward. 'What value that? I must think. At ease. Relaxed. Unmindful of restraint. Careless. Yes, of course! Excellent idea.' He paused, swung his head to Fiddler.

The sapper watched a smile slide aboard the wizened man's face, oiled and smooth and pathetically insincere.

'Everything's fine, my friends,' he purred. 'Be calm. Cotillion is done with possessing the lass. The bane of Anomander Rake's threat remains. Who wants that crude conveyor of uncivilized mayhem crashing through the temple door? Not Shadowthrone. Not the Patron of Assassins. She is protected still. Besides which, Cotillion finds no further value in using her, and indeed the residue of his talents still within her gives cause for secret concern—' His face twisted on itself. 'No, better keep that thought unspoken!' He smiled again. 'Cultured conversation has been rediscovered and used with guile and grace. Look upon them, Iskaral Pust, they are won over one and all.'

There was a long silence.

Mappo cleared his throat. 'The High Priest rarely has company,' he said.

Fiddler sighed, suddenly exhausted. He leaned back, closed his eyes. 'My horse? Did it live?'

'Yes,' Crokus said. 'It's been taken care of, as have the others – those that Mappo had time to tend to, that is. And there's a servant here, somewhere. We haven't seen him, but he does good work.'

Apsalar spoke. 'Fiddler, tell us about Tremorlor.'

A new tension filled the air. The sapper sensed it even as sleep pulled at him, alluring with its promise of temporary escape. After a moment he pushed it away with another sigh and opened his eyes. 'Quick Ben's knowledge of the Holy Desert is, uh, vast. When we last rode the Holy Desert – as we rode out, in fact – he spoke of the Vanished Roads. Like the one we found, an ancient road that sleeps beneath the sands and appears only occasionally – if the winds are right, that is. Well, one of those roads leads to Tremorlor—'

Crokus cut in, 'Which is?'

'A House of the Azath.'

'Like the one that arose in Darujhistan?'

'Aye. Such buildings exist – or are rumoured to exist – on virtually every continent. No-one knows their purpose, though it does seem that they are a lodestone to power. There's the old story that the Emperor and Dancer . . .' *Oh, Hood, Kellanved and Dancer, Ammanas and Cotillion, the possible linkage with Shadow . . . this temple . . .* Fiddler shot Iskaral Pust a sharp look. The High Priest sported an avid grin, his eyes glittering. 'Uh, the legend goes that Kellanved and Dancer once occupied one such House, in Malaz City—'

'Deadhouse,' Icarium said from the doorway. 'The legend is true.'

'Aye,' Fiddler muttered, then shook himself. 'Well enough. In any case, it's Quick Ben's belief that such Houses are all linked to one another, via gates of some sort. And that travel between them is possible – virtually instantaneous travel—'

'Excuse me,' Icarium said, stepping into the room with an air of sudden attentiveness. 'I have not heard the name Quick Ben. Who is this man purporting to possess such arcane knowledge of the Azath?'

The sapper fidgeted under the Jhag's intent gaze, then scowled at himself and straightened slightly. 'A squad mage,' he answered, making it clear he did not intend to elaborate.

Icarium's eyes went oddly heavy. 'You put much weight on a squad mage's opinions.'

'Aye, I do.'

Crokus spoke. 'You mean to find Tremorlor to use the gate to take us to Malaz City. To this Deadhouse. Which would leave us—'

'A half-day's sail from the Itko Kanese coast,' Fiddler said, meeting Apsalar's eyes. 'And home to your father.'

'Father?' Mappo asked, frowning. 'You now confuse me.'

'We're delivering Apsalar back home,' Crokus explained. 'To her family. She was possessed by Cotillion, stolen away from her father, her life—'

'Her life as what?' Mappo asked.

'A fishergirl.'

The Trell fell silent, but Fiddler thought he knew Mappo's unspoken thoughts. *After what she's been through, she's going to settle for a life dragging nets?*

Apsalar herself said nothing.

'A life given for a life taken!' Iskaral Pust shouted, leaping from his chair and spinning in place, both hands clenched in his tufts of hair. 'Such patience is enough to drive one mad! But not me! Anchored to the currents of weathered stone, the trickling away of sand under the sun's glare! Time stretched, stretching, immortal players in a timeless game. There is poetry in the pull of elements, you know. The Jhag understands. The Jhag seeks the secrets – he is stone and the stone forgets, the stone is ever now, and in this lies the truth of the Azath – but wait! I've rambled on with such hidden thoughts and heard nothing of what is being said!' He fell abruptly silent and subsided back into the chair.

Icarium's study of the High Priest could well have been

something carved from charged stone. Fiddler's attention was being pulled every which way. Thoughts of sleep had long since vanished. 'I'm not certain of these details,' he said slowly, drawing everyone's attention, 'but I have the distinct feeling of being a marionette joining a vast and intricate dance. What's the pattern? Who clutches the strings?'

All eyes swung to Iskaral Pust. The High Priest retained his fixed attentiveness a moment longer, then blinked. 'A question asked of modest me? Excuses and apologies admittedly insincere. Vast and intricate mind wanders on occasion. Your query?' He ducked his head, smiled into the shadows. 'Are they deceived? Subtle truths, vague hints, a chance choice of words in unmindful echo? They know not. Bask in their awe with all wide-eyed innocence, oh, this is exquisite!'

'You've answered us eloquently,' Mappo said to the High Priest.

'I have? This is unwell. Rather, how kind of me. You're welcome. I shall command Servant to ready your party, then. A journey to fabled Tremorlor, where all truths shall converge with the clarity of unsheathed blades and unveiled fangs, where Icarium shall find his lost past, the once possessed fisher-girl shall find what she does not yet know she seeks, where the lad shall find the price of becoming a man, or perhaps not, where the hapless Trell shall do whatever he must, and where a weary sapper shall at least receive his Emperor's blessing, oh yes. Unless, of course,' he added, one finger to his lips, 'Tremorlor is naught but a myth and these quests nothing but hollow artifice.'

The High Priest – finger still against his lips – settled back in the strange chair. Shadows closed around him. A moment later he and the chair vanished.

Fiddler found himself starting out of a vague, floating trance. He shook his head, rubbed his face and glanced at the others, only to see they were reacting in similar ways – as if they had one and all been pulled into a subtle, seductive sorcery. Fiddler released a shaky breath. 'Can there be magic in mere words?' he asked to no-one in particular.

Icarium answered. 'Magic powerful enough to drive gods to their knees, soldier.'

'We have to get out of here,' Crokus muttered.

This time everyone nodded agreement.

CHAPTER NINE

The Malazan engineers are a unique breed.
Cantankerous, foul-mouthed, derisive of
authority, secretive and thick-headed. They
are the heartstone of the Malazan Army . . .

The Imperial Military
Senjalle

As he descended into the Orbala Odhan, Kalam came upon the first signs of the uprising. A train of Malazan refugees had been ambushed while travelling along a dried stream bed. The attackers had come from the high grass lining both banks, first with arrow fire, then a rush to close with the hapless Malazans.

Three wagons had been set aflame. The assassin sat motionless on his horse, studying the smoke-hazed heaps of charred wood, ash and bone. A small bundle of child's clothing was all that remained of the victims' possessions, a small knot of colour ten paces from the smouldering remains of wagons.

After one last glance around in search of Apt – the demon was nowhere to be seen, though he knew it was close – Kalam dismounted. Tracks revealed that the train's livestock had been led away by the ambushers. The only bodies were those that had been burned in the wagons. His search revealed that there had been survivors, a small group abandoning the scene

352

and fleeing south, out across the Odhan. It did not appear that they had been pursued, but Kalam well knew that there was little chance of salvation out on the plain. The town of Orbal was five, perhaps six days away on foot, and it was likely that it was in rebel hands in any case, since the Malazan detachment there had always been undermanned.

He wondered where the refugees had come from. There was little to be found for leagues in any direction.

Making a sound on the sand like the beat of a skin drum, Apt ambled into view from downstream. The beast's wounds had healed, more or less, leaving puckered scars on its black hide. Five days had passed since the D'ivers attack. There had been no sign that the shapeshifter still pursued them, and Kalam hoped that it had taken enough damage to be discouraged from persisting in the hunt.

Nevertheless, they were being trailed by . . . *someone*. The assassin felt it in his bones. He was tempted to lay an ambush of his own, but he was one man alone and his pursuers might be many. Moreover, he was uncertain whether Apt would assist his efforts – he suspected not. His only advantage was the swiftness of his travel. He'd found his horse after the battle without much trouble, and the animal seemed impervious to the rigours of the journey. He'd begun to suspect that an issue of pride had arisen between the stallion and the demon – his mount's bolting from the fight must have stung, and it was as if the horse was determined to recover whatever delusions of dominance he possessed.

Kalam climbed back into the saddle. Apt had found the trail left by the fleeing survivors and was sniffing the air, swinging its long, blunt head from side to side.

'Not our problem,' Kalam told it, loosening the lone surviving long-knife at his belt. 'We've enough troubles of our own, Apt.' He nudged his mount and set off in a direction that would take him well around the trail.

In deepening dusk he rode across the plain. Despite its size, the demon seemed to vanish within the gloom. *A demon born in the Shadow Realm, I shouldn't be surprised.*

The grassland dipped ahead – another ancient river track. As he approached, figures rose from cover along the nearest bank. Cursing under his breath, Kalam slowed his mount, raising both hands, palms forward.

'Mekral, Obarii,' Kalam said. 'I ride the Whirlwind!'

'Closer then,' a voice replied.

Hands still raised, Kalam guided his horse forward with his heels and knees.

'Mekral,' the same voice acknowledged. A man stepped clear of the high grasses, a tulwar in one hand. 'Come join us in our feast, rider. You have news of the north?'

Relaxing, Kalam dismounted. 'Months old, Obarii. I've not spoken aloud in weeks – what stories can you tell me?'

The spokesman was simply another bandit who now marauded behind the rebellion's noble mask. He showed the assassin a gap-toothed smile. 'Vengeance against the Mezla, Mekral. Sweet as spring water, such vengeance.'

'The Whirlwind has seen no defeat, then? Have the Mezla armies done nothing?'

Leading his horse, Kalam strode with the raiders down into the encampment. It had been carelessly laid out, revealing a sloppy mind in command. A large pile of wood was about to be set alight, promising a cooking fire that would be visible across half the Odhan. A small herd of oxen had been paddocked inside a makeshift kraal just downwind of the camp.

'The Mezla armies have done nothing but die,' the leader said, grinning. 'We have heard that but one remains, far to the southeast. Led by a Wickan with a heart of black, bloodless stone.'

Kalam grunted. A man passed him a wineskin and, nodding his thanks, he drank deep. Saltoan, booty from the Mezla –

probably the wagons I saw earlier. Same for the oxen. 'Southeast? One of the coastal cities?'

'Aye, Hissar. But Hissar is now in Kamist Reloe's hands. As are all the cities but Aren, and Aren has the Jhistal within. The Wickan flees overland, chained with refugees by the thousand – they beg his protection even as they lap his blood.'

'Not black-hearted enough, then,' Kalam muttered.

'True. He should leave them to Reloe's armies, but he fears the wrath of the coddled fools commanding in Aren, not that they'll breathe much longer.'

'What is this Wickan's name?'

'Coltaine. It's said he is winged like a crow, and finds much to laugh about amidst slaughter. A long, slow death awaits him, this much Kamist Reloe has promised.'

'May the Whirlwind reap every reward it's earned,' the assassin said, drinking again.

'A beautiful horse you have, Mekral.'

'And loyal. Beware the stranger seeking to ride him.' Kalam hoped the warning was not too subtle for the man.

The bandit leader shrugged. 'All things can be tamed.'

The assassin sighed, set down the wineskin. 'Are you betrayers of the Whirlwind?' he asked.

All motion around him ceased. Off to his left the fire's bone-dry wood crackled in a rising flame.

The leader spread his hands, an offended expression on his face. 'A simple compliment, Mekral! How have we earned such suspicion? We are not thieves or murderers, friend. We are believers! Your fine horse is yours, of course, though I have gold—'

'Not for sale, Obarii.'

'You have not heard my offer!'

'All Seven Holy Treasures will not sway me,' Kalam growled.

'Then no more shall be said of such matters.' The man retrieved the wineskin and offered it to Kalam.

He accepted but did no more than wet his lips.

'These are sad times,' the bandit leader continued, 'when trust is a rare thing among fellow soldiers. We all ride in Sha'ik's name, after all. We share a single, hated enemy. Nights such as these, granted peace under the stars amidst this holy war, are cause for celebration and brotherhood, friend.'

'Your words have captured the beauty of our crusade,' Kalam said. *Words can so easily glide over mayhem and terror and horror, it's a wonder trust exists at all.*

'You will now give me your horse and that fine weapon at your belt.'

The assassin's laugh was a soft rumble. 'I count seven of you, four before me, three hovering behind.' He paused, smiling as he met the bandit leader's fire-lit eyes. 'It will be a close thing, but I will be certain to kill you first, *friend*.'

The man hesitated, then answered with his own smile. 'You've no sense of humour. Perhaps it is due to travelling so long without company that you have forgotten the games soldiers play. Have you eaten? We came upon a party of Mezla only this morning, and they were all too generous with their food and possessions. We shall visit them again, at dawn. There are women among them.'

Kalam scowled. 'And this is your war against the Mezla? You are armed, you are mounted – why have you not joined the armies of the Apocalypse? Kamist Reloe needs warriors like you. I ride south to join in the siege of Aren, which must surely come.'

'As do we – to walk through Aren's yawning gates!' the man replied fervently. 'And more, we bring livestock with us, to help feed our brothers in the army! Do you suggest we ignore the rich Mezla we come upon?'

'The Odhan will kill them without our help,' the assassin

said. 'You have their oxen.' *Aren's yawning gates . . . the Jhistal within. What does that mean? Jhistal, not a familiar word, not Seven Cities. Falari?*

The man's expression had cooled in response to Kalam's words. 'We attack them at dawn. Do you ride with us, Mekral?'

'They are south of here?'

'They are. Less than an hour's ride.'

'Then it is the direction I am already travelling, so I shall join you.'

'Excellent!'

'But there is nothing holy in rape,' Kalam growled.

'No, not holy.' The man grinned. 'But just.'

They rode in the night, beneath a vast scatter of stars. One of the bandits had stayed behind with the oxen and other booty, leaving Kalam riding with a party of six. All carried short recurved bows, though their supply of arrows was low – not a single quiver held more than three, and all with ragged fletching. The weapons would be effective at close range only.

Bordu, the bandit leader, told the assassin that the Malazan refugees consisted of one man – a Malazan soldier – two women and two young boys. He was certain that the soldier had been wounded in the first ambush. Bordu did not expect much of a fight. They would take down the men first. 'Then we can play with the women and boys – perhaps you will change your mind, Mekral.'

Kalam's only response was a grunt. He knew men such as these. Their courage held so long as they outnumbered their victims, the hollow glory they thirsted for came with overpowering and terrorizing the helpless. Such creatures were common in the world, and a land locked in war left them to run free, the brutal truths behind every just cause. They were given a name in the Ehrlii tongue: e'ptarh le'gebran, the vultures of violence.

The withered skin of the prairie broke up ahead. Hump-shouldered knobs of granite were visible above the grasses, studding the slopes of a series of low hills. Faint firelight blushed the air behind one such large outcropping. Kalam shook his head. Far too careless in a hostile land – the soldier with them should have known better.

Bordu raised a hand, slowing them to a halt about fifty paces from the monolithic outcrop. 'Keep your eyes from the hearth,' he whispered to the others. 'Let those fools be cursed with blindness, not us. Now, spread out. The Mekral and I will ride around to the other side. Give us fifty breaths, then attack.'

Kalam's eyes narrowed on the bandit leader. Coming at the camp from the opposite side, he would run an obvious risk of taking an arrow or three from these attackers in the melee. *More soldier's humour, I take it.* But he said nothing, pulling away when Bordu did and riding side by side on a route that would circumvent the refugees' camp.

'Your men are skilled with their bows?' the assassin asked a few minutes later.

'Like vipers, Mekral.'

'With about the same range,' Kalam muttered.

'They'll not miss.'

'No doubt.'

'You are afraid, Mekral? You, such a large, dangerous-looking man. A warrior, without doubt. I am surprised.'

'I've a bigger surprise,' Kalam said, reaching over and sliding a blade across Bordu's throat.

Blood sprayed. Gurgling, the bandit leader reeled back in his saddle, his head flopping horribly.

The assassin sheathed his knife. He rode closer in time to prop the man back up in his saddle and hold him balanced there, one hand to Bordu's back. 'Ride with me a while longer,' Kalam said, 'and may the Seven Holies flay your treacherous soul.' *As they will mine, when the time comes.*

The glimmering firelight lay ahead. Distant shouts announced the bandits' charge. Horse hooves thumped the hard ground. Kalam tapped his mount into a canter. Bordu's horse matched the pace, the bandit leader's body weaving, his head now lolling almost on its side, ear against one shoulder.

They reached the hill's slope, which was gentler on this side and mostly unobstructed. The attackers were visible now, riding into the shell of firelight, arrows zinging to thud into the blanket-wrapped figures around the hearth.

From the sound those arrows made Kalam knew instantly that there were no bodies beneath those blankets. The soldier had proved his worth, had laid a trap. The assassin grinned. He pushed Bordu down over the saddlehorn and gave the bandit leader's horse a slap on the rump. It charged into the light.

The assassin quickly checked his own mount's canter, slipped to the ground still in the darkness beyond the firelight, and padded forward noiselessly.

The crisp snap of a crossbow sounded. One of the bandits pitched back in his saddle and tumbled to the ground. The four others had pulled up, clearly confused. Something like a small bag flew into the hearth, landing with a spray of sparks. A moment later the night was lit up in a cascading flame, and the four bandits were clearly outlined. The crossbow loosed again. A bandit shrieked, arching to reach for a quarrel embedded in his back. A moment later he groaned, sagging as his horse stepped in a confused circle.

Kalam had escaped exposure in the burst of light, but his night vision was gone. Swearing under his breath, he edged forward, long-knife in his right hand, double-edged dagger in his left.

He heard another rider coming in hard from one side. Both bandits wheeled their mounts to meet the charge. The horse appeared, slowing from what had been a bolt. There was no-one in the saddle.

The flare-up from the hearth was ebbing.

His nerves suddenly tingling, Kalam stopped and crouched down. He watched as the riderless horse trotted aimlessly to the right of the bandits, the animal moving closer to come alongside one of the attackers. In a fluid, graceful motion, the rider swung up into view – a woman, who had been crouching down out of sight over one stirrup – twisting to chop down at the nearest bandit with a butcher's cleaver. The huge blade connected with the man's neck and cut through to lodge in his vertebra.

Then the woman had both feet on the saddle. Even as the bandit toppled she stepped onto his horse, taking the lance from the saddle holster and jabbing it like a spear at the second bandit.

Cursing, the man reacted with a warrior's training. Instead of leaning back in what would have been a hopeless effort to avoid the lancehead flashing at his chest, he drove both heels into his horse, twisting to let the lance slip past. His mount rammed the other horse, chest to flank. With a startled yelp the woman lost her balance and fell heavily to the ground.

The bandit leapt from the saddle, unsheathing his tulwar.

Kalam's dagger took him in the throat three paces from the dazed woman. Spitting in fury, hands clutching his neck, the bandit fell to his knees. Kalam approached to deliver a killing thrust.

'Stand still,' a voice snapped behind him. 'Got a quarrel trained on you. Drop that lizard-sticker. Now!'

Shrugging, the assassin let the weapon fall from his hand. 'I'm Second Army,' he said. 'Onearm's Host—'

'Are fifteen hundred leagues away.'

The woman had regained the breath that had been driven from her lungs. She rose to her hands and knees, long black hair hanging down over her face.

The last bandit finished dying with a faint, wet gurgle.

'You're Seven Cities,' the voice behind Kalam said.

'Aye, yet a soldier of the Empire. Listen, work it out. I rode up from the other side, with the bandits' leader. He was dead before his horse carried him into your camp.'

'So why does a soldier wear a telaba and no colours and ride alone? Desertion, and that's a death sentence.'

Kalam hissed in exasperation. 'And clearly you chose to protect your family instead of whatever company you're attached to. By Imperial Military Law *that* counts as desertion, soldier.' As he spoke the Malazan stepped around, his crossbow still trained on the assassin.

Kalam saw a man half dead on his feet. Short and wide, he wore the tattered remnants of an Outpost detachment uniform, light-grey leather jerkin, dark-grey surcoat. His face was covered in a network of scratches, as were his hands and forearms. A deep wound marred his bristly chin, and the helm shadowing his eyes was dented. The clasp of his surcoat ranked him a captain.

The assassin's eyes widened upon seeing that. 'Though a captain deserting is a rare thing . . .'

'He didn't desert,' the woman said, now fully recovered and sorting through the weapons of the dead bandits. She found a lightweight tulwar and tested its balance with a few swings. In the firelight Kalam could see she was attractive, medium-boned, her hair streaked with iron. Her eyes were a startling light grey. She collected a belted sword-hoop and strapped it on.

'We rode out of Orbal,' the captain said, pain evident in his voice. 'A whole company escorting out refugees – our families. Ran smack into a Hood-damned army on the march south.'

'We're all that's left,' the woman said, turning to gesture into the darkness. Another woman – a younger, thinner version of the other one – and two children stepped cautiously into the light, then rushed to the captain's side.

The man continued to aim an unsteady crossbow at Kalam. 'Selv, my wife,' he said, gesturing to the woman now at his side. 'Our children, there. And Selv's sister Minala. That's us. Now, let's hear your story.'

'Corporal Kalam, Ninth Squad . . . Bridgeburners. Now you know why I'm out of uniform, sir.'

The man grinned. 'You've been outlawed. So why aren't you marching with Dujek? Unless you've returned to your homeland to join the Whirlwind.'

'Is that your horse?' Minala asked.

The assassin turned to see his mount step casually into the camp. 'Aye.'

'You know your horses,' she said.

'It cost me a virgin's ransom. I figure if something's expensive it's probably good, and that's how much I know horses.'

'You still haven't explained why you're here,' the captain muttered, but Kalam could see he was relaxing his guard.

'Smelled the uprising in the wind,' the assassin said. 'The Empire brought peace to Seven Cities. Sha'ik wants a return to the old days – tyrants, border wars and slaughter. I ride for Aren. That's where the punitive force will land – and if I'm lucky I can slip myself in, maybe as a guide.'

'You'll ride with us, then, Corporal,' the captain said. 'If you're truly a Bridgeburner you'll know how to soldier, and if that's what you show me on the way to Aren, I'll see you rejoin the Imperial ranks without fuss.'

Kalam nodded. 'Can I retrieve my weapons now, Captain?'

'Go ahead.'

The assassin crouched down, reached for his long-knife, paused. 'Oh, one thing, Captain . . .'

The man had sagged against his wife. He swung bleary eyes on Kalam. 'What?'

'Better my name should change . . . I mean, officially. I wouldn't welcome the gallows if I'm marked in Aren. Granted,

Kalam is common enough, but there's always the chance I'd be recognized—'

'You're *that* Kalam? You said the Ninth, didn't you? Hood's breath!' If the captain had planned to say more it was lost as the man's knees buckled. With a soft whimper his wife eased him down to the ground, looked up at her sister with frightened eyes, then over at Kalam.

'Relax, lass,' the assassin said, straightening. He grinned. 'I'm back in the army now.'

The two boys, one about seven and the other four, moved with exaggerated caution towards the unconscious man and his wife. She saw them and opened her arms. They rushed to her embrace.

'He was trampled,' Minala said. 'One of the bandits dragged him behind his horse. Sixty paces before he cut himself free.'

Women who lived with garrisons were either harlots or wives – there was little doubt which one Minala had been. 'Your husband was in the company as well?'

'He commanded it, but he's dead.'

It could have been a statement about the weather for all the emotion expressed, and Kalam sensed the rigid control that held the woman. 'And the captain's your brother-in-law?'

'His name is Keneb. You've met my sister Selv. The older boy is Kesen, the younger Vaneb.'

'You're from Quon?'

'Long ago.'

Not the talkative type. The assassin glanced over at Keneb. 'Will he live?'

'I don't know. He has dizzy spells. Blackouts.'

'Sagging face, slurred words?'

'No.'

Kalam went to his horse and gathered up the reins.

'Where are you going?' Minala demanded.

'There's one bandit standing guard over food, water and horses. We need all three.'

'Then we all go.'

Kalam started to argue but Minala raised a hand. 'Think, Corporal. We have the bandits' horses. We can ride, all of us. The boys sat in saddles before they could walk. And who guards us when you're gone? What happens if you get wounded fighting that last bandit?' She spun to her sister. 'We'll get Keneb over a saddle, Selv. Agreed?'

She nodded.

The assassin sighed. 'But leave the guard to me.'

'We will. It seems you've a reputation, by Keneb's reaction.'

'Fame, or notoriety?'

'I expect he'll say more when he comes around.'

I hope not. The less they know about me the better.

The sun was still an hour from rising when Kalam raised a hand to bring the party to a halt. 'That old river bed,' he hissed, gesturing a thousand paces ahead. 'All of you wait here. I won't be long.'

Kalam removed the best of the bandits' recurved bows from its saddle sheath and selected two of the least tattered arrows. 'Load that crossbow,' he said to Minala. 'In case something goes wrong.'

'How will I know?'

The assassin shrugged. 'In your gut.' He glanced at Keneb. The captain was laid over a saddle, still unconscious. That wasn't good. Head injuries were always unpredictable.

'He's still breathing,' Minala said quietly.

Kalam grunted, then set off at a dogtrot across the plain.

He saw the glow of the campfire well before he reached the high grass lining the bank. Still careless. A good sign. The voices he could hear weren't. He dropped down and slid forward through the dew-wet grass on his stomach.

Another party of raiders had arrived. Bearing gifts. Kalam saw the motionless, sprawled bodies of five women flung down around the camp. All had been raped, then murdered. In addition to Bordu's guard there were seven others, all sitting around the fire. All well armed and armoured in boiled leather.

Bordu's guard was speaking a dozen words for every breath. '—won't tire the horses. So the prisoners will walk. Two women. Two boys. Like I said. Bordu plans these things. And a horse worthy of a prince. You'll see soon enough—'

'Bordu will gift the horse,' one of the newcomers growled. Not a question.

'Of course he will. And a boy too. Bordu is a generous commander, sir. Very generous . . .'

Sir. True soldiers of the Whirlwind, then.

Kalam edged back, then hesitated. A moment later, his eyes coming to rest again on the murdered women, he breathed a silent curse.

A soft clack sounded almost at his shoulder. The assassin went rigid, then slowly turned his head. Apt crouched beside him, head ducked low, a long thread of drool hanging from its jaws. It blinked knowingly.

'This time, then?' Kalam whispered. 'Or come to watch?'

The demon gave nothing away. Naturally.

The assassin nocked the better of the two arrows, licked his fingers and ran them along the feather guides. There was little gain in elaborate planning. He had eight men to kill.

Still concealed by the high grass, he rose into a crouch, drawing the bowstring as he took a deep breath. He held both for a long moment.

It was the shot he needed. The arrow entered the troop commander's left eye and went straight through to the back of the skull, the iron point making a solid crunching sound as it drove into the bone. The man's head snapped back, skullcap helmet flying from his head.

Kalam was drawing for his second shot even as the body rocked, falling forward from the waist. He chose the man fastest to react, a big warrior with his back to the assassin.

The arrow went high – betrayed by a warped shaft. Sinking into the warrior's right shoulder, it was deflected off the blade and up under the rim of the helmet. Kalam's luck held as the man pitched forward onto the fire, instantly dead. Sparks rose as the body swallowed up the flames. Darkness swept down like a cloak.

The assassin dropped the bow and closed swiftly on the shouting, frightened men. A brace of knives in his right hand, Kalam selected his targets. His left hand was a blur as he threw the first knife. A warrior screamed. Another caught sight of the assassin.

Kalam unsheathed his long-knife and close-work dagger. A tulwar flashed at his head. He ducked, stepped close and stabbed the man under the chin. With no solid bone to bite down on the dagger blade, he was instantly able to withdraw it, in time to parry a lance thrust, take another step and stab the long-knife's point into a man's throat.

A tulwar skidded across his shoulders, the blow too wild to penetrate the chain under Kalam's telaba. He spun, a back-hand slice opening the attacker's cheek and nose. The man reeled.

The assassin kicked him away. The three warriors still prepared to fight, and Bordu's guard, all backed off to regroup. Their reaction made it clear that they imagined that a whole squad had attacked them. Kalam took advantage of their frantic searching of the shadows to finish off the man whose face he'd cut.

'Spread out!' one of the warriors hissed. 'Jelem, Hanor, get the crossbows—'

Waiting for that was suicide. Kalam attacked, rushing the man who'd taken command. He backed off desperately, the tulwar in his hand twitching in every direction as he tried to follow the assassin's intricate feints, hoping to catch the one feint that was in fact the genuine attack. Then instinct made the man abandon the effort and lash out in a counterattack.

Which the assassin had been waiting for. He intercepted the downward swing at the man's wrist – with the point of his dagger. Spitting his arm on the blade, the warrior screamed in pain, weapon flying from a spasming hand.

Kalam thrust the long-knife into the man's chest, ducked and spun to evade a rushing attack from Bordu's guard. The move was a surprise, since the assassin had not expected to find much courage in the man. He came very close to dying then. Straightening inside the guard's reach was all that saved him. Kalam drove his dagger low, stabbing just under the man's belt buckle. Hot fluid gushed over the assassin's forearm. The guard shrieked, doubling over, trapping both knife and the hand gripping it.

The assassin surrendered the weapon and stepped around the guard.

The remaining two warriors crouched twenty feet away, loading their crossbows. The weapons were Malazan, assault-issue, and both men revealed a fatal lack of familiarity with the loading mechanisms. Kalam himself could ready such a crossbow in four seconds.

He did not grant the warriors even that, closing with them in a flash. One still tried to lock the crank, his frantic terror undoing his efforts as the quarrel jumped from its slot and fell to the ground. The other man tossed his crossbow down with a snarl and retrieved his tulwar in time to meet Kalam's charge. He had advantage in both the reach and weight of his weapon, yet neither availed him when a sudden loss of courage froze him in his tracks.

'Please—'

The word rode his last breath as Kalam batted the tulwar

aside and cross-swung his long-knife's razor-sharp edge, opening the warrior's throat. The swing continued, spinning to transform into a sideways thrust that pierced the other man's chest, through boiled leather, skin, between ribs and into the lung. Choking, the warrior crumpled. The assassin finished him with another thrust.

Behind the moans of Bordu's guard lay silence. From a copse of low trees thirty paces down the river bed came the first peeps of birds awakening to dawn. Kalam dropped to one knee, sucking in lungfuls of sweet, cool air.

He heard a horse descend the south bank and turned to see Minala. The crossbow in her hands pointed from one corpse to the next as she checked the clearing, then she visibly relaxed, fixing Kalam with wide eyes. 'I count eight.'

Still struggling for breath, the assassin nodded. He reached out and cleaned his long-knife's blade and hilt on his last victim's telaba, then checked the weapon's edge before sheathing it at his side.

Bordu's guard finally fell silent.

'Eight.'

'How's the captain?'

'Awake. Groggy, maybe fevered.'

'There's another clearing about forty paces east of here,' Kalam said. 'I suggest we camp there for the day. I need some sleep.'

'Yes.'

'We need to strip this camp . . . the bodies . . .'

'Leave that to Selv and me. We don't shock easily. Any more . . .'

With a grunt the assassin straightened and went to retrieve his other weapons. Minala watched him.

'There were two others,' she said.

Kalam paused over a body, looked up. 'What?'

'Guarding the horses. They look . . .' She hesitated, then

368

continued grimly, 'They were torn to pieces. Big chunks . . . missing. Bite marks.'

The assassin voiced a second grunt, rose slowly. 'I hadn't had much to eat lately,' he muttered.

'Maybe a plains bear, the big brown kind. Took advantage of the ruckus to ambush the two guards. Did you hear the horses screaming?'

'Maybe.' He studied her face, wondering what was going on behind those almost silver eyes.

'I didn't, but there were plenty of screams and sound does jump around in river beds like these. Anyway, it'll do as an explanation, don't you think?'

'Just might.'

'Good. I'll ride back for the others now. I won't be long.'

She swung her mount around without using the reins, since she still held the crossbow in her hands. Kalam wasn't sure how she managed it. He recalled her crouch over one stirrup hours earlier, her dance across the saddles. *This woman can sit a horse.*

As she rode back up the bank, the assassin surveyed the grisly camp. 'Hood,' he breathed, 'I need a rest.'

'Kalam, who rode with Whiskeyjack across Raraku . . .' Captain Keneb shook his head and poked again at the fire.

It was dusk. The assassin had just awakened from a long, deep sleep. His first hour was never a pleasant one. Aching joints, old wounds – his years always caught up with him while he slept. Selv had brewed a strong tea. She poured Kalam a cup. He stared into the dying flames.

Minala said, 'I would never have believed that one man could kill eight, all within minutes.'

'Kalam was recruited into the Claw,' Keneb said. 'That's rare. They usually take children, train them—'

'Train?' the assassin grunted. 'Indoctrination.' He looked up

369

at Minala. 'Attacking a group of warriors isn't as impossible as you think. For the lone attacker, there's no-one else to make the first move. Eight – ten men ... well, they figure they should just all close in and hack me down. Only, who goes first? They all pause, they all look for an opening. It's my job to keep moving, make sure every opening is closed before they can react. Mind you, a good veteran squad knows how to work together . . .'

'Then you were lucky they didn't.'

'I was lucky.'

The older boy, Kesen, spoke up. 'Can you teach me how to fight like that, sir?'

Kalam grunted. 'I expect your father has a better life in mind for you, lad. Fighting is for people who fail at everything else.'

'But fighting isn't the same as soldiering,' Keneb said.

'That's a fact,' the assassin agreed, sensing that he'd somehow stung the captain's pride. 'Soldiers are worth respect, and it's true that sometimes fighting's required. Soldiering means standing firm when that time comes. So, lad, if you still want to learn how to fight, learn how to soldier first.'

'In other words, listen to your father,' Minala said, giving Kalam a quick, wry smile.

Following some gesture or look the assassin did not catch, Selv rose and led the boys off to finish breaking camp. As soon as they were out of earshot Keneb said, 'Aren's what, three months away? Hood's breath, there has to be a Malazan-held city or fortification that's closer than that, Corporal.'

'All the news I've heard has been bad,' Kalam said. 'Everything south of here is tribal lands, all the way to the River Vathar. Ubaryd's close to the river, but I'd guess it's been taken by Sha'ik's Apocalypse – too valuable a port to leave unsecured. Secondly, I would think most of the tribes between here and Aren have set off to join Kamist Reloe.'

Keneb looked startled. 'Reloe?'

Kalam frowned. 'The bandits spoke of him as being south-east of here . . .'

'More east than south. Reloe is chasing Fist Coltaine and the Seventh Army. He's probably wiped them out by now, but even so his forces are east of the Sekala River and that's the territory he's been charged to hold.'

'You know much more of this than I,' the assassin said.

'We had Tithansi servants,' Minala explained. 'Loyal.'

'They paid for that with their lives,' the captain added.

'Then is there an army of the Apocalypse south of here?'

Keneb nodded. 'Aye, preparing to march on Aren.'

The assassin frowned. 'Tell me, Captain . . . you ever heard the word "Jhistal"?'

'No, not Seven Cities. Why?'

'The bandits spoke of "a jhistal inside" Aren. As if it was a shaved knuckle.' He fell silent for a moment, then sighed. 'Who commands this army?'

'That bastard Korbolo Dom.'

Kalam's eyes narrowed. 'But he's a Fist—'

'Was, till he married a local woman who just happened to be the daughter of Halaf's last Holy Protector. He's turned renegade, had to execute half his own legion who refused to step across with him. The other half divested the Imperial uniform, proclaimed themselves a mercenary company, and took on Korbolo's contract. It was that company that hit us in Orbal. Call themselves the Whirlwind Legion or something like that.' Keneb rose and kicked at the fire, scattering the last embers. 'They rode in like allies. We didn't suspect a thing.'

There was more to this tale, the assassin sensed. 'I remember Korbolo,' Kalam muttered.

'Thought you might. He was Whiskeyjack's replacement, wasn't he?'

'For a time. After Raraku. A superb tactician, but a little too bloodthirsty for my tastes. For Laseen, too, which was why she holed him in Halaf.'

'And promoted Dujek instead.' The captain laughed. 'Who's now been outlawed.'

'Now there's an injustice I'll tell you about some day,' Kalam said, rising. 'We should get going. Those raiders may have friends nearby.'

He felt Minala's eyes on him as he readied his horse and was not a little disturbed. Husband dead only twenty-four hours ago. An anchor cut away. Kalam was a stranger who'd as much as taken charge despite being outranked by her brother-in-law. She must have thought for the first time in a long time that they stood a chance of surviving with him along. It was not a responsibility he welcomed. *Still, I've always appreciated capable women. Only an interest this soon after her husband's death is like a flower on a dead stalk. Attractive but not for long.* She was capable, but if he let her, her own needs would end up undermining that capability. *Not good for her. And besides, if I led this one on, she'd stop being what attracted me to her in the first place. Best to leave well alone. Best to stay remote.*

'Corporal Kalam,' Minala said behind him.

He swung about. 'What?'

'Those women. I think we should bury them.'

The assassin hesitated, then resumed checking his horse's girth strap. 'No time,' he grunted. 'Worry about the living, not the dead.'

Her voice hardened. 'I am. There are two young boys who need to be reminded about respect.'

'Not now.' He faced her again. 'Respect won't help them if they're dead, or worse. See that everyone else is ready to ride, then get to your horse.'

'Captain gives the orders,' she said, paling.

'He's got a busted head and keeps thinking this is a picnic.

Watch the times he comes round – his eyes fill with fear. And here you go wanting to add yet another burden on the man. Even the slightest nudge might make him retreat into his head for good, and then what use is he? To anyone?'

'Fine,' she snapped, whirling away.

He watched her stalk off. Selv and Keneb stood by their horses, too far away to have heard anything but close enough to know that dark waters had been stirred between Minala and the assassin. A moment later the children rode into view on a single horse, the seven-year-old in front and sitting tall with his younger brother's arms wrapped around him. Both looked older than their years.

Respect for life. Sure. The other lesson is just how cheap that life can become. Maybe the former comes from the latter, in which case they're well on their way as it is.

'Ready,' Minala said in a cold voice.

Kalam swung into the saddle. He scanned the growing darkness. *Stay close, Apt. Only not too close.*

They rode out of the river bed and onto the grassy Odhan, Kalam in the lead. Luckily, the demon was shy.

The rogue wave took them from the port side, a thick, sludgy wall that seemed to leap over the railing, crashing down on the deck like a landslide of mud. The water drained from the silts within seconds, leaving Felisin and the others on the main deck knee-deep in the foul-smelling muck. The pyramid of heads was a shapeless mound.

Crawling, Heboric reached her, his face smeared a dull ochre. 'This silt!' he gasped, pausing to spit some from his mouth. 'Look at what's in it!'

Almost too miserable to respond, she nevertheless reached down and scooped up a handful. 'It's full of seeds,' she said. 'And rotting plants—'

'Aye! Grass seeds and rotting grasses – don't you understand,

373

lass? That's not sea bottom down there. It's prairie. Inundated. This warren's flooded. Recently.'

She grunted, unwilling to share in his excitement. 'That's a surprise? Can't sail a ship on prairie, can you?'

His eyes narrowed. 'You got something there, Felisin.'

The silt around her shins felt strange, crawling, restless. Ignoring the ex-priest, she clambered her way towards the stern-castle. The wave had not gone that high. Gesler and Stormy were both at the steering oar, all four hands needed to maintain a course. Kulp was near them, waiting to relieve the first man whose strength gave out. And he'd been waiting long enough for it to be obvious that Gesler and Stormy were locked in a battle of pride, neither one wanting to surrender before the other. Their bared grins confirmed it for Felisin. *Idiots! They'll both collapse at once, leaving the mage to handle the steering oar by himself.*

The sky continued to convulse over them, lashing lightning in all directions. The surface of the sea resisted the shrieking wind, the silt-heavy water lifting in turgid swells that seemed reluctant to go anywhere. The headless oarsmen continued their ceaseless rowing, though a dozen oars had snapped, the splintered shafts keeping time with those still pushing water. The drum beat on, answering the thunder overhead with its measured, impervious patience.

She reached the steps and climbed clear of the mud, then stopped in surprise. The silt fled her skin as if alive, poured down from her legs to rejoin the quaking pool that covered the main deck.

Crouched near the main mast, Heboric yelled in sudden alarm, eyes on the mud surrounding him as its shivering increased. 'There's something in it!'

'Come this way!' Truth shouted from the forecastle steps, reaching out with one hand. Baudin anchored him with a single-handed grip on the lad's other arm. 'Quick! Something's coming out!'

Felisin climbed another step higher.

The mud was transmogrifying, coalescing into the shapes of figures. Flint blades appeared, some grey, some the deep red of chalcedony. Bedraggled fur slowly sprouted, riding broad, bony shoulders. Bone helmets gleamed polished gold and brown – the skulls of beasts that Felisin could not imagine existing anywhere. Long ropes of filthy hair were now visible, mostly black or brown. The mud did not so much fall away as *change*. These creatures were one with the clay.

'T'lan Imass!' Kulp shouted from where he stood clinging to the mizzen mast. *Silanda* was rocking with a wild energy. 'Logros T'lan!'

They numbered six. All wore furs except one, who was smaller than the others and last to appear. It was bedecked in the oily, ragged feathers of colourful birds, and its long hair was iron grey streaked with red. Shell, antler and bone jewellery hung from its rotting hide shirt, but it appeared to carry no weapons.

Their faces were withered, the bones underneath close to the surface and robust. The sockets of their eyes were black pits. The wiry remnants of beards remained, except on the silver-haired one, who now straightened and faced Kulp.

'Stand aside, Servant of the Chained One, we have come for our kin, and for the Tiste Edur.' The voice was a woman's, the language Malazan.

Another T'lan Imass turned to the silver-haired one. It was by far the biggest of the group. The fur humped over its shoulders came from some kind of bear, the hairs were silver-tipped. 'Mortal worshippers are a bane themselves,' it said in a bored tone. 'We should kill them as well.'

'We shall,' the other one said. 'But our quarry comes first.'

'There are no kin of yours here,' Kulp said shakily. 'And the Tiste Edur are dead. Go see for yourself. In the captain's cabin.'

The female T'lan Imass cocked her head. Two of her

companions strode towards the hatch. She then swung about and stared at Heboric, who stood by the forecastle railing. 'Call down the mage linked to you. He is a wound. And he spreads. This must be stopped. More, tell your god that such games place him in great peril. We shall not brook such damage to the warrens.'

Felisin laughed, the sound tinged with hysteria.

As one, the T'lan Imass looked at her.

She flinched from those lifeless gazes, then drew a breath to steady herself. 'You may be immortal and powerful enough to threaten the boar god,' she said, 'but you haven't got one thing right yet.'

'Explain,' the female said.

'Ask someone who cares,' she said, meeting that depthless gaze, surprised that she neither flinched nor broke away.

'I am no longer a priest of Fener,' Heboric said, raising both stumps. 'If the boar god is here, among us, then I am not aware of it, nor do I much care. The sorcerer riding this storm pursues us, seeking to destroy us. I know not why.'

'He is the madness of Otataral,' the female said.

The two Imass sent to the cabin now returned. Though no words were spoken aloud, the female nodded. 'They are dead, then. And our kin have departed. We must continue the hunt.' She swung her gaze back to Heboric. 'I would lay hands upon you.'

Felisin barked another laugh. 'That'll make him complete.'

'Shut up, girl,' Kulp growled, pushing past to descend to the main deck. 'We're not Servants of the Chained One,' he said. 'Hood's breath, what *is* the Chained One? Never mind, I don't even want to know. We're on this ship by accident, not design—'

'We did not anticipate this warren would be flooded,' the female said.

'It's said you can cross oceans,' the mage muttered, frowning.

Felisin could see he was having trouble following the T'lan Imass's statements. So was she.

'We can cross bodies of water,' the female acknowledged. 'But we can only find our shapes on land.'

'So, like us, you came to this ship to get your feet dry—'

'And complete our task. We pursue renegade kin.'

'If they were here, they've since left,' Kulp said. 'Before we arrived. You are a Bonecaster.'

The female inclined her head. 'Hentos Ilm, of Logros T'lann Imass.'

'And the Logros no longer serve the Malazan Empire. Glad to see you're staying busy.'

'Why?'

'Never mind.' Kulp looked skyward. 'He's eased up some.'

'He senses us,' Hentos Ilm said. She faced Heboric again. 'Your left hand is in balance, it is true. Otataral and a power unknown to me. If the mage in the storm continues to grow in power, the Otataral shall prevail, and you too shall know its madness.'

'I want it gone from me,' Heboric growled. 'Please.'

Hentos Ilm shrugged, and approached the ex-priest. 'We must destroy the one in the skies. Then we must seal the warren's wound.'

'In other words,' Felisin said, 'you're probably not worth the trouble, old man.'

'Bonecaster,' Kulp said. 'What warren is this?'

Hentos Ilm paused, attention still on Heboric. 'Elder. Kurald Emurlahn.'

'I've heard of Kurald Galain – the Tiste Andii warren.'

'This is Tiste Edur. You surprise me, Mage. You are Meanas Rashan, which is the branch of Kurald Emurlahn accessible to mortal humans. The warren you use is the child of this place.'

Kulp was scowling at the Bonecaster's back. 'This makes no

sense. Meanas Rashan is the warren of Shadow. Of Ammanas and Cotillion, and the Hounds.'

'Before Shadowthrone and Cotillion,' Hentos Ilm said, 'there were Tiste Edur.' The Bonecaster reached towards Heboric. 'I would touch you.'

'Be my guest,' he said.

Felisin watched her place the palm of one withered hand against the old man's chest. After a moment she stepped back and turned away as if dismissing him. She addressed the bear-furred T'lan Imass who'd spoken earlier. 'You are clanless, Legana Breed.'

'I am clanless,' he agreed.

She pointed at Kulp. 'Mage. Do nothing.'

'Wait!' Heboric said. 'What did you sense in me?'

'You are shorn from your god, though he continues to make use of you. I see no other purpose in your existence.'

Felisin bit back a nasty comment. *Not this one.* She could see Heboric's shoulders slowly sag, as if some vital essence had been pulled, pulped and dripping blood, from his chest. He'd clung hard to something, and the Bonecaster had just pronounced it dead. *I'm running out of things to wound in him. Maybe that'll keep me from trying.*

Hentos Ilm tilted her head back, then began dissolving, the dust of her being spinning in place. A moment later it spiralled upward, swiftly vanishing in the low clouds boiling overhead.

Lightning cracked, a rap of pain in Felisin's ears. Crying out, she fell to her knees. The others suffered in like manner, with the exception of the remaining T'lan Imass, who stood in motionless indifference. The *Silanda* bucked. The mud-smeared pyramid of severed heads around the main mast collapsed. Heads tumbled and bounced heavily on the deck.

The T'lan Imass spun at that, weapons suddenly out.

Thunder bellowed in the roiling stormclouds. The air shivered again.

The one named Legana Breed reached down and lifted one head by its long, black hair. It was Tiste Andii, a woman. 'She still lives,' the undead warrior said, revealing a muted hint of surprise. 'Kurald Emurlahn, the sorcery has locked their souls to their flesh.'

A faint shriek bounced down through the clouds, a sound filled with despair and – jarringly – release. The clouds spilled out in every direction, tearing into thin wisps. A pale amber sky burned through. The storm was gone, and so too was the mad sorcerer.

Felisin ducked as something winged past her, leaving in its wake a musty, dead smell. When she looked up Hentos Ilm stood once again on the main deck, facing Legana Breed. Neither moved, suggesting a silent conversation was underway.

'Hood's breath,' Kulp breathed beside Felisin. She glanced over. He was staring into the sky, his face pale. She followed his gaze.

A vast, black lesion, rimmed in fiery red and as large as a full moon, marred the amber sky. Whatever leaked from it seemed to steal into Felisin through her eyes, as if the act of simply seeing it was capable of transmitting an infection, a disease that would spread through her flesh. *Like the poison of a bloodfly.* A small whimper escaped her throat, then she desperately pulled her eyes away.

Kulp still stared, his face getting whiter, his mouth hanging listlessly. Felisin nudged him. 'Kulp!' He did not respond. She struck him.

Gesler was suddenly beside them, wrapping an arm around Kulp's eyes. 'Dammit, Mage, snap out of it!'

Kulp struggled, then relaxed. She saw him nod. 'Let him go now,' she said to the corporal.

As soon as Gesler relinquished his hold, the mage rounded on Hentos Ilm. His voice was a shaken rasp. 'That's the wound you mentioned, isn't it? It's spreading – I can feel it, like a cancer—'

'A soul must bridge it,' the Bonecaster said.

Legana Breed was on the move. All eyes followed him as he strode to the sterncastle steps, ascended and stood before Stormy. The scarred veteran did not recoil.

'Well,' the marine muttered, 'this is as close as I've ever been.' His grin was sickly. 'Once is enough.'

The T'lan Imass raised his grey flint sword.

'Hold it,' Gesler growled. 'If you need a soul to stopper that wound . . . use mine.'

Legana Breed's head pivoted.

Gesler's jaw clenched. He nodded.

'Insufficient,' Hentos Ilm pronounced.

Legana Breed faced Stormy again. 'I am the last of my clan,' he rumbled. 'L'echae Shayn shall end. This weapon is our memory. Carry it, mortal. Learn its weight. Stone ever thirsts for blood.' He offered the marine the four-foot-long sword.

Face blank, Stormy accepted it. Felisin saw the muscles of his forearms stiffen as they took the weight and held it.

'Now,' Hentos Ilm said.

Legana Breed stepped back and collapsed in a column of dust. The column twisted, spinning in on itself. The air on all sides stirred, then swept inward, pulled to the whirling emanation. A moment later the wind fell away and Legana Breed was gone. The remaining T'lan Imass turned and lifted their gazes skyward.

Felisin was never certain whether she only imagined seeing the T'lan Imass reassume his form upon striking the heart of that wound, a tiny, seemingly insignificant splayed figure that was quickly swallowed in the inky darkness. A moment later the wound's edges seemed to flinch, faint waves rippling outward. Then the lesion began folding in on itself.

Hentos Ilm continued staring upward. Finally she nodded. 'Sufficient. The wound is bridged.'

Stormy slowly lowered the flint sword's point until it rested on the deck.

A beat-up old veteran, knocked down cynical, just another of the Empire's cast-offs. He was clearly overwhelmed. *Insufficient, she said. Indeed.*

'We shall go now,' Hentos Ilm said.

Stormy shook himself. 'Bonecaster!'

There was obvious disdain in her tone as she said, 'Legana Breed claimed his right.'

The marine did not relent. 'This "bridging" . . . tell me, is it a thing of pain?'

Hentos Ilm's shrug was an audible grate of bones, her only answer.

'Stormy—' Gesler warned, but his companion shook his head, descended to the main deck. As he approached the Bonecaster, another T'lan Imass stepped forward to block him.

'Soldier!' Gesler snapped. 'Stand off!'

But Stormy only moved back to clear space as he raised the flint sword.

The T'lan Imass facing him closed again, the motion a blur, one arm shooting out, the hand closing on Stormy's neck.

Cursing, Gesler pushed past Felisin, his own hand finding the sword's grip at his side. The corporal slowed when it became obvious that the T'lan Imass was simply holding Stormy. And the marine himself had gone perfectly still. Quiet words slipped between them. Then the undead warrior released his grip and stepped back. Stormy's anger had vanished. Something in the set of his shoulders reminded Felisin of Heboric.

All five T'lan Imass began to dissolve.

'Wait!' the mage shouted, rushing forward. 'How in Hood's name do we get out of here?'

It was too late. The creatures were gone.

Gesler rounded on Stormy. 'What did that bastard tell you?' he demanded.

The soldier's eyes were wet – shocking Felisin – as he turned to his corporal.

Gesler whispered, 'Stormy . . .'

'He said there was great pain,' the man muttered. 'I asked *How long?* He said *For ever*. The wound heals around him, you see. She couldn't command, you see. Not for something like that. He volunteered—' The man's throat closed up, then. He spun away, bolted through the gangway and out of sight.

'Clanless,' Heboric said from the forecastle. 'As good as useless. Existence without meaning . . .'

Gesler kicked one of the severed heads across the deck. Its uneven thumping was loud in the still air. 'Who still wants to live for ever?' he growled, then spat.

Truth spoke, his voice quavering. 'Didn't anybody else see?' he asked. 'The Bonecaster didn't – I'm sure of it, she didn't . . .'

'What're you going on about, lad?' Gesler demanded.

'That T'lan Imass. He tied it to his belt. By the hair. His bear cloak hid it.'

'What?'

'He took one of the heads. Didn't anybody else see?'

Heboric was the first to react. With a wild grin he leapt down to the main deck, making for the galley. Even as he plunged through the doorway Kulp was clambering down to the first oar deck. He disappeared from view.

Minutes passed.

Gesler, still frowning, went to join Stormy and the ex-priest.

Kulp returned. 'One of them's dead as a post,' he said.

Felisin thought to ask him what it all meant, but a sudden exhaustion swept the impulse away. She looked around until she saw Baudin. He was at the prow, his back to everything . . . to everyone. She wondered at his indifference. Lack of imagination, she concluded after a moment, the thought bringing a sneer to her lips. She made her way to him.

'All too much for you, eh, Baudin?' she asked, leaning beside him on the arching rail.

'T'lan Imass were never nothing but trouble,' he said. 'Always two sides to whatever they did, maybe more than two. Maybe hundreds.'

'A thug with opinions.'

'You set your every notion in stone, lass. No wonder people always surprise you.'

'Surprise? I'm way past surprise, thug. We're in something, every one of us. There's more to come, so you can forget about thinking of a way out. There isn't one.'

He grunted. 'Wise words for a change.'

'Don't soften up on me,' Felisin said. 'I'm just too tired to be cruel. Give me a few hours' sleep and I'll be back to my old self.'

'Planning ways to murder me, you mean.'

'Keeps me amused.'

He was silent a long moment, eyes on the meaningless horizon ahead, then he turned to her. 'You ever think that maybe what you are is what's trapping you inside whatever it is you're trapped inside?'

She blinked. There was a glint of sardonic judgement in his small, beastlike eyes. 'I'm not following you, Baudin.'

He smiled. 'Oh yes, you are, lass.'

CHAPTER TEN

It is one thing to lead by example with half a dozen
soldiers at your back. It is wholly another with
ten thousand.

Life of Dassem Ultor
Duiker

I t had been a week since Duiker came upon the trail left by
the refugees from Caron Tepasi. They had obviously been
driven south to place further strain on Coltaine's stumbling
city in motion, the historian thought. There was nothing else
in this ceaseless wasted land. The dry season had taken hold,
the sun in the barren sky scorching the grasses until they
looked and felt like brittle wire.

Day after day had rolled by, yet Duiker still could not catch
up with the Fist and his train. The few times he had come
within sight of the massive dust cloud, Reloe's Tithansi outriders had prevented the historian from getting any closer.

Somehow, Coltaine kept his forces moving, endlessly
moving, driving for the Sekala River. *And from there? Does he
make a stand, his back to the ancient ford?*

So Duiker rode in the train's wake. The detritus from the
refugees diminished, yet grew more poignant. Tiny graves
humped the old encampments; the short-bones of horses and
cattle lay scattered about; an oft-repaired but finally

384

abandoned wagon axle marked one departure point, the rest of the wagon dismantled and taken for spares. The latrine trenches reeked beneath clouds of flies.

Places where skirmishing had occurred revealed another story. Amidst the naked, unrecovered bodies of Tithansi horse-warriors were shattered Wickan lances, the heads removed. Everything that could be reused had been stripped from the Tithansi bodies: leather thongs and straps, leggings and belts, weapons, even braids of hair. Dead horses were dragged away entire, leaving swathes of blood-matted grass in their wake.

Duiker was well past astonishment at anything he saw. Like the Tithansi tribesmen he'd occasionally exchanged words with, he'd begun to believe that Coltaine was something other than human, that he had carved his soldiers and every refugee into unyielding avatars of the impossible. Yet for all that, there was no hope for victory. Kamist Reloe's Apocalypse consisted of the armies of four cities and a dozen towns, countless tribes and a peasant horde as vast as an inland sea. And it was closing in, content for the moment simply to escort Coltaine to the Sekala River. Every current was drawing to that place. A battle was taking shape, an annihilation.

Duiker rode through the day, parched, hungry, wind-burned, his clothes reduced to rags. A straggler from the peasant army, an old man determined to join the last struggle. Tithansi riders knew him on sight and paid him little heed apart from a distant wave. Every two or three days a troop would join him, pass him bundles of food, water and feed for the horse. In some ways, he had become their icon, his journey symbolic, burdened with unasked-for significance. The historian felt pangs of guilt at that, yet accepted the gifts with genuine gratitude – they kept him and his horse alive.

Nonetheless, his faithful mount was wearing down. More and more each day Duiker led the animal by the reins.

Dusk approached. The distant dust cloud continued to

march on, until the historian was certain that Coltaine's vanguard had reached the river. The Fist would insist that the entire train drive on through the night to the encampment that the vanguard was even now preparing. If Duiker was to have any chance of rejoining them, it would have to be this night.

He knew of the ford only from maps, and his recollection was frustratingly vague. The Sekala River averaged five hundred paces in width, flowing north to the Karas Sea. A small village squatted in the crook of two hills a few hundred paces south of the ford itself. He seemed to remember something about an old oxbow, as well.

The dying day spread shadows across the land. The brightest of the night's stars glittered in the sky's deepening blue. Wings of capemoths rose with the heat that fled the parched ground, like black flakes of ash.

Duiker climbed back into the saddle. A small band of Tithansi outriders rode a ridge half a mile to the north. Duiker judged that he was at least a league from the river. The patrols of horsewarriors would increase the closer he approached. He had no plan for dealing with them.

The historian had walked his mount for most of the day, preparing for a hard ride into the night. He would need all that the beast could give him, and was afraid that it would not be enough. He nudged the mare into a trot.

The distant Tithansi paid him no attention, and soon rode out of sight. Heart thumping, Duiker urged his horse into a canter.

A wind brushed his face. The historian hissed a blessing to whatever god was responsible. The hanging dust cloud ahead began to edge his way.

The sky darkened.

A voice shouted a few hundred paces to his left. A dozen horsemen, strips of fur trailing from their lances. Tithansi. Duiker saluted them with a raised fist.

'With the dawn, old man!' one of them bellowed. 'It is suicide to attack now!'

'Ride to Reloe's camp!' another yelled. 'Northwest, old man – you are heading for the enemy lines!'

Duiker waved their words away, gesturing like a madman. He rose slightly in the saddle, whispered into the mare's ear, squeezed gently with his knees. The animal's head ducked forward, the strides lengthened.

Reaching the crest of a low hill, the historian finally saw what was arrayed before him. The encampment of the Tithansi lancers lay ahead and to his right, a thousand or more hide tents, the gleam of cooking fires. Mounted patrols moved in a restless line beyond the tents, protecting the camp from the enemy forces dug in at the ford. To the left of the Tithansi camp spread a score thousand makeshift tents – the peasant army. Smoke hung like an ash-stained cloak over the sprawling tattered shanty town. Meals were being cooked. Outlying pickets consisted of entrenchments, again facing the river. Between the two encampments there was a corridor, no more than two wagons wide, running down the sloping floodplain to meet Coltaine's earthen defences.

Duiker angled his horse down the corridor, riding at full gallop. The Tithansi outriders behind him had not pursued, though the warriors patrolling the encampment now watched him, converging but without obvious concern . . . yet.

As he cleared the inside edge of the tribe's camp on his right, then the peasants' sea of tents on his left, he saw raised earthworks, orderly rows of tents, solidly manned pickets – the horde had additional protection. The historian saw two banners, Sialk and Hissar – regular infantry. Helmed heads had turned, eyes drawn to the sound of his horse's hooves and now the alarmed shouts of the Tithansi riders.

The mare was straining. Coltaine's pickets were five hundred paces ahead, seeming to get no nearer. He heard horses in pursuit, gaining. Figures appeared on the Malazan bulwarks, readying bows. The historian prayed for quick-witted minds among the soldiers he rode towards. He cursed as he saw the bows raised, then drawn back.

'Not me, you bastards!' he bellowed in Malazan.

The bows loosed. Arrows sped unseen in the night.

Horses screamed behind him. His pursuers were drawing rein. More arrows flew. Duiker risked one backward glance and saw the Tithansi scrambling to withdraw out of arrow range. Thrashing horses and bodies lay on the ground.

He slowed the mare to a canter, then a trot as he approached the earthworks. She was lathered, her limbs far too loose, her head sagging.

Duiker rode into the midst of blue-skinned Wickans – Weasel Clan – who stared at him in silence. As he glanced around, the historian felt himself in well-suited company – the plains warriors from northeast Quon Tali had the look of spectres, their faces drawn with an exhaustion to match his own.

Beyond the Weasel Clan's encampment were military-issue tents and two banners – the Hissari Guard who had remained loyal, and a company whose standard Duiker did not recognize, apart from a central stylized crossbow signifying Malazan Marines.

Hands reached up to help him from the saddle. Wickan youths and elders gathered around, a soothing murmur of voices rising. Their concern was for the mare. An old man gripped the historian's arm. 'We will tend to this brave horse, stranger.'

'I think she's finished,' Duiker said, a wave of sorrow flooding him. *Gods, I'm tired.* The setting sun broke through the clouds on the horizon, bathing everything in a golden glow.

The old man shook his head. 'Our horsewives are skilled in such things. She shall run again. Now, an officer comes – go.'

A captain from the unknown company of Marines approached. He was Falari, his beard and long, wavy hair a fiery red. 'You rode in your saddle like a Malazan,' he said, 'yet dress like a damned Dosii. Explain yourself and be quick about it.'

'Duiker, Imperial Historian. I've been trying to rejoin this train since it left Hissar.'

The captain's eyes widened. 'A hundred and sixty leagues – you expect me to believe that? Coltaine left Hissar almost three months ago.'

'I know. Where's Bult? Has Kulp rejoined the Seventh? And who in Hood's name are you?'

'Lull, Captain of the Sialk Marines, Cartheron Wing, Sahul Fleet. Coltaine's called a briefing – you'd better come along, Historian.'

They began making their way through the encampment. Duiker was appalled at what he saw. Beyond the ragged entrenchments of the Marines was a broad, sloping field, a single roped road running through it. On the right were wagons in their hundreds, their beds crowded with wounded. The wagon wheels were sunk deep in blood-soaked mud. Birds filled the torchlit air, voicing a frenzied chorus – it seemed they had acquired a taste for blood. On the left the churned field was a solid mass of cattle, shoulder to shoulder, shifting in a seething tide beneath a hovering haze of rhizan – the winged lizards feasting on the swarms of flies.

Ahead, the field dropped away to a strip of marsh bridged by wooden slats. The swampy pools of water gleamed red. Beyond it was a broad humped-back oxbow island on which, in crowded mayhem, were encamped the refugees – in their tens of thousands.

'Hood's breath,' the historian muttered, 'are we going to have to walk through that?'

The captain shook his head and gestured towards a large

farmhouse on the cattle side of the ford road. 'There. Coltaine's own Crow Clan are guarding the south side, along the hills, making sure none of the livestock strays or gets plucked by the locals – there's a village over on the other side.'

'Did you say Sahul Fleet? Why aren't you with Admiral Nok in Aren, Captain?'

The red-haired soldier grimaced. 'Wish we were. We left the fleet and pulled up in Sialk for repairs – our transport was seventy years old, started shipping water two hours out from Hissar. The mutiny happened the same night, so we left the ship, gathered up what was left of the local Marine company, then escorted the exodus out of Sialk.'

The farmhouse they approached was a sturdy, imposing structure, its inhabitants having just fled the arrival of Coltaine's train. Its foundation was of cut stone, and the walls were split logs chinked with sun-fired clay. A soldier of the Seventh stood guard in front of a solid oak door. He nodded to Captain Lull, then narrowed his eyes on Duiker.

'Ignore the tribal garb,' Lull told him, 'this one's ours. Who's here?'

'Everybody but the Fist, the Warlocks and the captain of the sappers, sir.'

'Forget the captain,' Lull said. 'He ain't bothered showing for one of these yet.'

'Yes sir.' The soldier thumped a gauntleted fist on the door, then pushed it open.

Woodsmoke drifted out. Duiker and the captain stepped inside. Bult and two officers of the Seventh were crouched at the massive stone fireplace at the room's far end, arguing over what was obviously a blocked chimney.

Lull unclipped his sword belt and hung the weapon on a hook by the door. 'What in Hood's name are you building a fire for?' he demanded. 'Ain't it hot and stinking enough in here?' He waved at the smoke.

One of the Seventh's officers turned and Duiker recognized him as the soldier who'd stood at his side when Coltaine and his Wickans first landed in Hissar. Their eyes met.

'Togg's feet, it's the historian!'

Bult straightened and swung around. Scar and mouth both shifted into twin grins. 'Sormo was right – he'd sniffed you on our trail weeks back. Welcome, Duiker!'

His legs threatening to give way under him, Duiker sat down in one of the chairs pushed against a wall. 'Good to see you, Uncle,' he said, leaning back and wincing at his aching muscles.

'We were going to brew some herbal tea,' the Wickan said, his eyes red and watering. The old veteran had lost weight, his pallor grey with exhaustion.

'For the love of clear lungs give it up,' Lull said. 'What's keeping the Fist anyway? I can't wait to hear what mad scheme he's concocted to get us out of this one.'

'He's pulled it off this far,' Duiker said.

'Against one army, sure,' Lull said, 'but we're facing two now—'

The historian lifted his head. 'Two?'

'The liberators of Guran,' the captain known to Duiker said. 'Can't recall if we were ever introduced. I'm Chenned. That's Captain Sulmar.'

'You're it for the Seventh's ranking officers?'

Chenned grinned. 'Afraid so.'

Captain Sulmar grunted. 'Not quite. There's the man in charge of the Seventh's sappers.'

'The one who never shows at these briefings.'

'Aye.' Sulmar looked dour, but Duiker already suspected that the expression was the captain's favourite. He was dark, short, appearing to have Kanese and Dal Honese blood in his ancestry. His shoulders sloped as if carrying a lifetime of burdens. 'Though why the bastard thinks he's above the rest of us I don't know. Damned sappers've been doing nothing but repairing wagons and collecting big chunks of stone and getting in the cutters' way.'

'Bult commands us in the field,' Captain Chenned said.

'I am the Fist's will,' the Wickan veteran rumbled.

There was the sound of horses pulling up outside, the jangle of tack and armour, then the door thumped once and a moment later swung open.

Coltaine looked unchanged to Duiker's eyes, as straight as a spear, his lean face wind-burned to the colour and consistency of leather, his black feather cape bellying in his wake as he strode into the centre of the large room. Behind him came Sormo E'nath and half a dozen Wickan youths who spread out to array themselves haphazardly against walls and pieces of furniture. They reminded the historian of a pack of dock rats in Malaz City, lords over the small patch they held.

Sormo walked up to Duiker and held out both hands to grip his wrists. Their eyes met. 'Our patience is rewarded. Well done, Duiker!'

The boy looked infinitely older, lifetimes closing in around his hooded eyes.

'Rest later, Historian,' Coltaine said, fixing each person in the room with a slow, gauging study. 'I made my command clear,' he said, turning at last to Bult. 'Where is this captain of the Engineers?'

Bult shrugged. 'Word was sent. He's a hard man to find.'

Coltaine scowled. 'Captain Chenned, your report.'

'Third and Fifth companies are across the ford, digging in. The crossing's about four hundred and twenty paces, not counting the shallows on both sides, which add another twenty or so. Average depth is one and a half arm-spans. Width is between four and five most of the way, a few places narrower, a few wider. The bottom's about two fingers of muck over a solid spine of rocks.'

'The Foolish Dog Clan will join your companies on the other side,' Coltaine said. 'If the Guran forces try to take that side of the ford during the crossing, you will stop them.' The Fist wheeled to Captain Lull. 'You and the Weasel Clan shall guard this side while the wounded and the refugees cross. I will maintain position to the south, blocking the village road, until the way is clear.'

Captain Sulmar cleared his throat. 'About the order of crossing, Fist. The Council of Nobles will scream—'

'I care not. The wagons cross first, with the wounded. Then the livestock, then the refugees.'

'Perhaps if we split it up more,' Sulmar persisted, sweat glistening on his flat brow, 'a hundred cattle, then a hundred nobles—'

'Nobles?' Bult asked. 'You meant refugees, surely.'

'Of course—'

Captain Lull sneered at Sulmar. 'Trying to buy favours on both sides, are you? And here I thought you were a soldier of the Seventh.'

Sulmar's face darkened.

'Splitting the crossing would be suicide,' Chenned said.

'Aye,' Bult growled, eyeing Sulmar as if he was a piece of rancid meat.

'We've a responsibility—' the captain snapped before Coltaine cut him off with a snarled curse.

It was enough. There was silence in the room. From outside came the creak of wagon wheels.

Bult grunted. 'Mouthpiece ain't enough.'

The door opened a moment later and two men entered. The one in the lead wore a spotless light-blue brocaded coat. Whatever muscle he'd carried in youth had given way to fat, and that fat had withered with three months of desperate flight. With a face like a wrinkled leather bag, he nonetheless projected a coddled air that was now tinged with indignant hurt. The man a step behind him also wore fine clothes – although reduced by dust and sweat to little more than shapeless sacks hanging from his lean frame. He was bald, the skin of his scalp patchy with old sunburn. He squinted at the others with watery eyes, blinking rapidly.

The first nobleman spoke. 'Word of this gathering reached the Council belatedly—'

'Unofficially, too,' Bult muttered dryly.

The nobleman continued with the barest of pauses. 'Events such as these are admittedly concerned with military discussions for the most part, and Heavens forbid the Council involve itself with such matters. However, as representatives of the nearly thirty thousand refugees now gathered here, we have assembled a list of . . . issues . . . that we would like to present to you.'

'You represent a few thousand nobles,' Captain Lull said, 'and as such your own Hood-damned interests and no-one else's, Nethpara. Save the piety for the latrines.'

Nethpara did not deign to acknowledge the captain's comments. His gaze held on Coltaine, awaiting a reply.

The Fist gave no sign that he was prepared to provide one. 'Find the sappers, Uncle,' he said to Bult. 'The wagons begin crossing in an hour.'

The veteran Wickan slowly nodded.

'We were expecting a night of rest,' Sulmar said, frowning. 'Everyone's dead on their feet—'

'An hour,' Coltaine growled. 'The wagons with the wounded first. I want at least four hundred across by dawn.'

Nethpara spoke, 'Please, Fist, reconsider this order of crossing. While my heart breaks for those wounded soldiers, your responsibility is to protect the refugees. More, it will be viewed by many in the Council as a grievous insult that the livestock should cross before unarmed civilians of the Empire.'

'And if we lose the cattle?' Lull asked the nobleman.

'I suppose you could spit the orphaned children over a fire.'

Nethpara smiled resignedly. 'Ah, yes, the matter of the reduced rations numbers in our list of concerns. We have it on good account that such reductions have not been applied to the soldiers of the Seventh. Perhaps a more balanced method of distribution could be considered? It is so very difficult to see the children wither away.'

'Less meat on their bones, eh?' Lull's face was flushed with barely restrained rage. 'Without well-fed soldiers between you and the Tithansi, your stomachs will be flopping around your knees in no time.'

'Get them out of here,' Coltaine said.

The other nobleman cleared his throat. 'While Nethpara speaks for the majority of the Council, his views are not unanimously held.' Ignoring the dark glare his companion threw him, the old man continued. 'I am here out of curiosity, nothing more. For example, these wagons filled with wounded – it seems there are many more wounded than I had imagined: the wagons are veritably crowded, yet there are close to three hundred and fifty of them. Two days ago we were carrying seven hundred soldiers, using perhaps a hundred and seventy-five wagons. Two small skirmishes have occurred since then, yet we now have twice as many wagons being used to transport the wounded. More, the sappers have been crawling all over them, keeping everyone away even to the point of discouraging the efforts of the cutters. What, precisely, is being planned here?'

There was silence. Duiker saw the two captains of the Seventh exchange puzzled looks. Sulmar's baffled expression was almost comical as his mind stumbled back over the details presented by the old man. Only the Wickans seemed unaffected.

'We have spread the wounded out,' Bult said. 'Strengthened the side walls—'

'Ah, yes,' the nobleman said, pausing to dab his watering eyes with a grey handkerchief. 'So I first concluded. Yet why do those wagons now ride so heavy in the mud?'

'Is this really necessary, Tumlit?' Nethpara asked in exasperation. 'Technical nuances may be your fascination, but Hood knows, no-one else's. We were discussing the Council's position on certain vital issues. No permission shall be accorded such digressions—'

'Uncle,' Coltaine said.

Grinning, Bult grasped both noblemen by their arms and guided them firmly to the door. 'We've a crossing to plan,' he said. 'Digressions unwelcome.'

'Yet what of the stonecutters and the renderers—' Tumlit attempted.

'Out, the both of you!' Bult pushed them forward. Nethpara was wise enough to open the door just in time as the commander gave them a final shove. The two noblemen stumbled outside.

At a nod from Bult, the guard reached in and pulled the door shut.

Lull rolled his shoulders beneath the weight of his chain shirt. 'Anything we should know, Fist?'

'I'm concerned,' said Chenned after it was clear that Coltaine would not respond to Lull's question, 'about the depth of this ford. The crossing's likely to be damned slow – not that there's much of a current, but with the mud underfoot and four and a half feet of water ain't nobody going to cross fast. Even on a horse.' He glanced at Lull. 'A fighting withdrawal won't be pretty.'

'You all know your positions and tasks,' Coltaine said. He swung to Sormo, eyes narrowing as he studied the warlock, then the children arrayed behind him. 'You'll each have a warlock,' he said to his officers. 'All communication will be through them. Dismissed.'

Duiker watched the officers and the children leave, until only Bult, Sormo and Coltaine remained.

The warlock conjured a jug seemingly from nowhere and passed it to his Fist. Coltaine drank down a mouthful, then passed it to Duiker. The Fist's eyes glittered. 'Historian, you've a story to tell us. You were with the Seventh's mage, Kulp. Rode out with him only hours before the uprising. Sormo cannot find the man . . . anywhere. Dead?'

'I don't know,' Duiker said truthfully. 'We were split up.' He downed a mouthful from the jug, then stared at it in surprise. *Chilled ale, where did Sormo get this from?* He glanced at the warlock. 'You've searched for Kulp through your warren?'

The young man crossed his arms. 'A few times,' he replied. 'Not lately. The warrens have become . . . difficult.'

'Lucky us,' Bult said.

'I don't understand.'

Sormo sighed. 'Recall our one ritual, Historian? The plague of D'ivers and Soletaken? They infest every warren now – at least on this continent. All are seeking the fabled Path of Hands. I have been forced to turn my efforts to the old ways, the sorceries of the land, of life spirits and totem beasts. Our enemy, the High Mage Kamist Reloe, does not possess such Elder knowledge. So he dares not unleash his magery against us. Not for weeks now.'

'Without it,' Coltaine said, 'Reloe is but a competent commander. Not a genius. His tactics are simplistic. He looks upon his massive army and lets his confidence undervalue the strength and will of his opponents.'

'He don't learn from his defeats, either,' Bult said.

Duiker held his gaze on Coltaine. 'Where do you lead this train, Fist?'

'Ubaryd.'

The historian blinked. *Two months away, at least.* 'We still hold that city, then?'

Silence stretched.

'You don't know,' Duiker said.

'No,' Bult said, retrieving the jug from the historian's hand and taking a mouthful.

'Now, Duiker,' Coltaine said, 'tell us of your journey.'

The historian had no intention of explaining his efforts regarding Heboric Light Touch. He sketched a tale that ran close enough to the truth, however, to sound convincing. He and Kulp had ridden to a coastal town to meet some old friends in a Marine detachment. Ill luck that it was the night of the Mutiny. Seeing an opportunity to pass through the enemy ranks in disguise, gathering information as he went, Duiker elected to ride. Kulp had joined the marines in an effort to sail south to Hissar's harbour. As he spoke, the muted sounds of wagons lurching into motion on the oxbow island reached the men.

It was loud enough for Kamist Reloe's soldiers to hear, and rightly guess that the crossing had begun. Duiker wondered how the Whirlwind commander would respond.

As the historian began elaborating on what he had observed of the enemy, Coltaine cut him off with a raised hand. 'If all your narratives are as dull, it's a wonder anyone reads them,' he muttered.

Smiling, Duiker leaned back and closed his eyes. 'Ah, Fist, it's the curse of history that those who should read them, never do. Besides, I am tired.'

'Uncle, find this old man a tent and a bedroll,' Coltaine said. 'Give him two hours. I want him up to witness as much of the crossing as possible. Let the events of the next day be written, lest history's lesson be lost to all who follow.'

'Two hours?' Duiker mumbled. 'I can't guarantee I won't have a blurry recollection, assuming I survive to record the tale.'

* * *

A hand shook his shoulder. The historian opened his eyes. He had fallen asleep in the chair. A blanket had been thrown across him, the Wickan wool foul-smelling and dubiously stained. A young corporal stood over him.

'Sir? You are to rise now.'

Every bone ached. Duiker scowled. 'What's your name, Corporal?'

'List, sir. Fifth Company, sir.'

Oh. Yes, the one who died and died in the mock engagements.

Only now did the composite roar from outside reach the historian's senses. He sat up. 'Hood's breath! Is that a battle out there?'

Corporal List shrugged. 'Not yet. Just the drovers and the livestock. They're crossing. There's been some clashes on the other side – the Guran army's arrived. But we're holding.'

Duiker flung the blanket aside and stood up. List handed him a battered tin cup.

'Careful, sir, it's hot.'

The historian stared down at the dark-brown liquid. 'What is it?'

'Don't know, sir. Something Wickan.'

He took a sip, wincing at the scalding, bitter taste. 'Where is Coltaine? Something I forgot to tell him last night.'

'He rides with his Crow Clan.'

'What time is it?'

'Almost dawn.'

Almost dawn, and the cattle are only starting to cross? He felt himself becoming alert, glanced down again at the drink and took another sip. 'This one of Sormo's brews? It's got my nerves jumping.'

'Some old woman handed it to me, sir. Are you ready?'

'You've been assigned to me, List?'

'Yes, sir.'

'Your first task then, Corporal, is to direct me to the latrine.'

They stepped outside to mayhem. Cattle covered the oxbow island, a mass of humped backs slowly edging forward to the shouts of drovers. The other side of the Sekala was obscured in clouds of dust that had begun drifting over the river.

'This way, sir.' List gestured towards a trench behind the farmhouse.

'Dispense with the "sirs",' Duiker said as they headed towards the latrine. 'And find me a rider. Those soldiers on the other side have some serious trouble heading their way.'

'Sir?'

Duiker stood at the edge of the trench. He hitched back his telaba, then paused. 'There's blood in this trench.'

'Yes, sir. What was that about the other side of the river, sir?'

'Heard from some Tithansi outriders,' the historian said as he relieved his bladder. 'The Semk have come south. They'll be on the Guran side, I'd guess. That tribe has sorcerers, and their warriors put the fear in the Tithansi, so you can expect they're a nasty bunch. I'd planned on mentioning it last night but forgot.'

A troop of horsewarriors was passing in front of the house at that moment. Corporal List raced back to intercept them.

Duiker finished and rejoined his aide. He slowed. The troop's standard was instantly recognizable. List was breathlessly conveying the message to the commander. The historian shook off his hesitation and approached.

'Baria Setral.'

The Red Blade commander's eyes flicked to Duiker, went cold. Beside him his brother Mesker growled wordlessly.

'Seems your luck's held,' the historian said.

'And yours,' Baria rumbled. 'But not that white-haired mage. Too bad. I was looking forward to hanging his hide from our banner. This word of the Semk – from you?'

'From the Tithansi.'

400

Mesker barked a laugh and grinned. 'Shared their tents on the way, did you?' He faced his brother. 'It's a lie.'

Duiker sighed. 'What would be the point of that?'

'We ride to support the Seventh's advance picket,' Baria said. 'We shall pass on your warning.'

'It's a trap—'

'Shut up, brother,' Baria said, his eyes still on Duiker. 'A warning is just that. Not a lie, not a trap. If Semk show, we will be ready. If not, then the tale was false. Nothing surrendered.'

'Thank you, Commander,' Duiker said. 'We're on the same side, after all.'

'Better late than never,' Baria growled. A hint of a smile showed in his oiled beard. 'Historian.' He raised a gauntleted fist, opened it. At the gesture the troop of Red Blades resumed their canter to the ford, Mesker alone flinging a dark glare Duiker's way as he rode past.

The pale light of dawn edged its way into the valley. Above the Sekala an impenetrable cloud of dust eased crossways to the faint breeze, descending on the ford itself, then staying there. The entire crossing was obscured. Duiker grunted. 'Nice touch, that.'

'Sormo,' Corporal List said. 'It's said he's awakened the spirits of the land and the air. From a sleep of centuries, for even the tribes have left those ways behind. Sometimes you can . . . smell them.'

The historian glanced at the young man. 'Smell?'

'Like when you flip a big rock over. The scent that comes up. Cool, musty.' He shrugged. 'Like that.'

An image of List as a boy – only a few years younger than he was now – flashed into Duiker's mind. Flipping rocks. A world to explore, the cocoon of peace. He smiled. 'I know that smell, List. Tell me, these spirits – how strong are they?'

'Sormo says they're pleased. Eager to play.'

'A spirit's game is a man's nightmare. Well, let's hope they take their play seriously.'

The mass of refugees – Duiker saw as he resumed his study of the situation – had been pushed off the oxbow island, across the ford road, to the south slope and swampy bed of the old oxbow channel. There were too many for the space provided, and he saw the far edge of the crowd creeping onto the hills beyond. A few had taken to the river, south of the ford, and were moving slowly out into the current.

'Who is in charge of the refugees?'

'Elements of the Crow Clan. Coltaine has his Wickans oversee them – the refugees are as scared of them as they are of the Apocalypse.'

And the Wickans won't be bought, either.

'There, sir!' List pointed to the east.

The enemy positions that Duiker had ridden between the night before had begun moving. The Sialk and Hissar infantry were on the right, Hissari lancers on the left and Tithansi horsewarriors down the centre. The two mounted forces surged forward towards the Weasel Clan's defences. Mounted Wickan bowmen accompanied by lancers rode out to meet them. But the thrust was a feint, the Hissari and Tithansi wheeling west before locking antlers. Their commanders had called it too fine, however, as the Wickan bowmen had edged into range. Arrows flew. Riders and horses fell.

Then it was the turn of the Wickan lancers to bolt forward in a sudden charge and their enemy quickly withdrew back to their original positions. Duiker watched in surprise as the lancers pulled up, a number of them dismounting as their bowmen kin covered them. Wounded enemy were summarily despatched, scalps and equipment taken. Ropes appeared. Minutes later the Wickans rode back to their defences, dragging the horse carcasses with them, along with a handful of wounded mounts they had managed to round up.

'The Wickans feed themselves,' List said. 'They'll use the hides, too. And the bones, and the tails and mane, and the teeth, and the—'

'Got it,' Duiker cut in.

The enemy infantry continued their slow march. The Hissari and Tithansi horsewarriors had recovered and now made a slower, more cautious approach.

'There's an old wall on the island,' List said. 'We could climb it and get a better view of all sides. If you don't mind walking on the backs of cattle to get there, that is. It's not as hard as it sounds – you just have to keep moving.'

Duiker raised an eyebrow.

'Honest, sir.'

'All right, Corporal. Lead the way.'

They took the roped road westward towards the ford. The old channel of the oxbow was bridged by wooden slats, bolstered with new supports placed by the Seventh's sappers. This avenue was maintained to allow for the movement back and forth of mounted messengers, but, as everywhere else, chaos reigned. Duiker held close in List's wake as the corporal weaved and danced his way down to the bridge. Beyond it rose the hump of the island and thousands of cattle.

'Where did this herd come from?' the historian asked as they reached the slatted crossing.

'Purchased, for the most part,' List replied. 'Coltaine and his clans laid claim to land outside Hissar, then started buying up cattle, horses, oxen, mules, goats – just about anything on four legs.'

'When did all this happen?'

'About the same day they arrived,' the corporal said. 'When the uprising came, most of the Foolish Dog Clan was with the herds – the Tithansi tribes thought to snatch the livestock and got their noses bloodied instead.'

As they neared the trailing end of the herd the noise rose to a roar with shouting drovers, the bark of cattle-dogs – solidly muscled, half-wild beasts born and bred on the Wickan Plains – the lowing of the cattle and the ceaseless rumbling thunder of their hooves. The dust cloud engulfing the river was impenetrable.

Duiker's eyes narrowed on the seething mass ahead. 'Not sure about your idea, Corporal – these beasts look jumpy. We're likely to get crushed in seconds flat.'

A shout from behind caught their attention. A young Wickan girl was riding towards them.

'Nether,' List said.

Something in his tone pulled Duiker around. The lad was pale under his helmet.

The girl, no more than nine or ten, halted her horse before them. She was dark, her eyes like black liquid, her hair cut bristly short. The historian recalled seeing her among Sormo's charges the night before. 'You seek the wall as vantage,' she said. 'I will clear you a path.'

List nodded.

'There is aspected magic on the other side,' she said, eyes on Duiker. 'A lone god's warren, no D'ivers, no Soletaken. A tribe's god.'

'Semk,' the historian said. 'The Red Blades are carrying word.' He fell silent as he realized the import of her words, the significance of her presence at the meeting last night. *One of the warlocks reborn. Sormo leads a clan of children empowered by lifetimes.*

'I go to face them. The spirit of the land is older than any god.' She guided her horse around the two men, then loosed a piercing cry. A clear avenue began to take shape, animals pushing away to either side and moaning in fear.

Nether rode down that aisle. After a moment List and Duiker followed, jogging to keep up. As soon as they trod on the path they could feel the earth shivering beneath their boots – not the deep reverberations of countless hooves, but something more intense, muscular. *As if we stride the spine of an enormous serpent . . . the land awakened, the land eager to show its power.*

Fifty paces ahead the ridge of a weathered, vine-cloaked wall appeared. Squat and thick, it was evidently the remnant of an ancient fortification, rising over a man's height and clear of the cattle. The path that Nether had created brushed one edge of it, then continued on down to the river.

The girl rode on without glancing back. Moments later List and Duiker reached the stone edifice and clambered up on its ragged but wide top.

'Look south,' List said, pointing.

Dust rose in a gold haze from the line of hills beyond the heaving mass of refugees.

'Coltaine and his Crows are in a fight,' List said.

Duiker nodded. 'There's a village on the other side of those hills, right?'

'Yes, sir. L'enbarl, it's called. The scrap looks to be on the road linking it to the ford. We haven't seen the Sialk cavalry, so it's likely Reloe sent them around to try and take our flank. Like Coltaine always says, the man's predictable.'

Duiker faced north. The other side of the island consisted of marsh grasses filling the old oxbow channel. The far side was a narrow stand of dead leadwood trees, then a broad slope leading to a steep-sided hill. The regularity of that hill suggested that it was a tel. Commanding its flat plateau was an army, weapons and armour glinting in the morning light. Heavy infantry. Dark banners rose amidst large tents behind two front-line legions of Tithansi archers. The archers had begun moving down the slope.

'That's Kamist Reloe and his hand-picked elites,' List said. 'He's yet to use them.'

To the east the feints and probes between the Weasel Clan's

horsewarriors and their Tithansi and Hissari counterparts continued, while the Sialk and Hissar infantry steadily closed the distance to the Wickan defences. Behind these legions, the peasant army swirled in restless motion.

'If that horde decides to charge,' Duiker said, 'our lines won't hold.'

'They'll charge,' List affirmed grimly. 'If we're lucky, they'll wait too long and give us room to fall back.'

'That's the kind of risk Hood loves,' the historian muttered.

'The ground under them whispers fear. They won't be moving for a while.'

'Do I see control on all sides, or the illusion of control?'

List's face twisted slightly. 'Sometimes the two are one and the same. In terms of their effect, I mean. The only difference – or so Coltaine says – is that when you bloody the real thing, it absorbs the damage, while the other shatters.'

Duiker shook his head. 'Who would have imagined a Wickan warleader to think of war in such . . . alchemical terms? And you, Corporal, has he made you his protégé?'

The young man looked dour. 'I kept dying in the war games. Gave me lots of time to stand around and eavesdrop.'

The cattle were moving more quickly now, plunging into the stationary clouds of dust masking the ford. If anything, to Duiker's eyes the heaving flow was too quick. 'Four and a half feet deep, over four hundred paces . . . those animals should be crossing at a crawl. More, how to hold the herds to the shallows? Those dogs will have to swim, the drovers will get pushed off to the deeps, and with all that dust, who can see a damned thing down there?'

List said nothing.

Thunder sounded on the other side of the ford, followed by rapid percussive sounds. Columns of smoke pillared upward and the air was suddenly febrile. *Sorcery. The Semk wizard-priests. A lone child to oppose them.* 'This is all taking too long,'

Duiker snapped. 'Why in Hood's name did it take all night just to get the wagons across? It will be dark before the refugees even move.'

'They're closing,' List said. His face was covered in dust-smeared sweat.

To the east the Sialk and Hissar infantry had made contact with the outer defences. Arrows swarmed the air. Weasel Clan horsewarriors battled on two sides – against Tithansi lancers at the front, and pike-wielding infantry on their right flank. They were struggling to withdraw. Holding the earthen defences were Captain Lull's marines, Wickan archers and a scattering of auxiliary units. They were yielding the first breastworks to the hardened infantry. The horde had begun to boil on the slopes beyond.

To the north the two legions of Tithansi archers were rushing forward for the cover of the leadwoods. From there they would start killing cattle. There was no-one to challenge them.

'And so it shatters,' Duiker said.

'You're as bad as Reloe. Sir.'

'What do you mean?'

'Too quick to count us out. This isn't our first engagement.'

Faint shrieks drifted across from the leadwoods. Duiker squinted through the dust. The Tithansi archers were screaming, thrashing about, vanishing from sight in the high marsh grasses beneath the skeletal trees. 'What in Hood's name is happening to those men?'

'An old, thirsty spirit, sir. Sormo promised it a day of warm blood. One last day. Before it dies or ceases or whatever it is spirits do when they go.'

The archers had routed, their panicked flight taking them back to the slope beneath the tel.

'There go the last of them,' List said.

For a moment Duiker thought the corporal referred to the Tithansi archers, then he realized, with a start, that the cattle were gone. He wheeled to face the ford, cursing at the tumbling clouds of dust. 'Too fast,' he muttered.

The refugees had begun moving, streamers of humanity flowing across the old oxbow channel and onto the island. There was no semblance of order, no way to control almost thirty thousand exhausted and terrified people. And they were about to sweep over the wall where Duiker and the corporal stood.

'We should move,' List said.

The historian nodded. 'Where?'

'Uh, east?'

To where the Weasel Clan now covered the marines and other footmen as they relinquished one earthen rampart after another, the soldiers falling back so quickly that they would be at the slatted bridge in minutes. *And then? Up against this mob of shrieking refugees. Oh, Hood! What now?*

List seemed to read his mind. 'They'll hold at the bridge,' he asserted. 'They have to. Come on!'

Their flight took them across the front of the leading edge of the refugees. The awakened land trembled beneath them, steam rising with a reek like muddy sweat. Here and there along the east edge of the island, the ground bulged and split open. Duiker's headlong sprint faltered. Shapes were clambering from the broken earth, skeletal beneath arcane, pitted and encrusted bronze armour, battered helms with antlers on their heads and long red-stained hair hanging in matted tufts down past their shoulders. The sound that came from them chilled Duiker's soul. *Laughter. Joyous laughter. Hood, are you twisting in affronted rage right now?*

'Nil,' List gasped. 'Nether's twin – that boy over there. Sormo said that this place has seen battle before – said this oxbow island wasn't natural ... oh, Queen of Dreams, yet another Wickan nightmare!'

The ancient warriors, voicing blood-curdling glee, were now

breaking free of the earth all along the eastern end of the island. On Duiker's right and behind him, refugees screamed with terror, their headlong flight staggering to a halt as the horrific creatures rose among them.

The Weasel Clan and the footmen had contracted to a solid line this side of the bridge and channel. That line twitched and shuffled as the raised warriors pushed through their ranks, single-edged swords rising – the weapons almost shapeless beneath mineral accretions – as they marched into the milling mass of the Hissar and Sialk infantry. The laughter had become singing, a guttural battle chant.

Duiker and List found themselves in a cleared area pocked with smouldering, broken earth, the refugees behind them withdrawing as they pushed towards the ford, the rearguard before them finally able to draw breath as the undead warriors waded into their foe.

The boy Nil, Nether's twin, rode a huge roan horse, wheeling back and forth along the line, in one hand a feather-bedecked, knobbed club of some sort which he waved over his head. The undead warriors that passed near him bellowed and shook their weapons in salute – or gratitude. Like them, the boy was laughing.

Reloe's veteran infantry broke before the onslaught and fell back to collide with the horde that had now checked its own advance.

'How can this be?' Duiker asked. 'Hood's Warren – this is necromantic, not—'

'Maybe they're not true undead,' List suggested. 'Maybe the island's spirit simply uses them—'

The historian shook his head. 'Not entirely. Hear that laughter – that song – do you hear the language? These warriors have had their souls awakened. Those souls must have remained, held by the spirit, never released to Hood. We'll pay for this, Corporal. Every one of us.'

Other figures were emerging from the ground on all sides: women, children, dogs. Many of the dogs still wore leather harnesses, still dragged the remnants of travois. The women held their children to their bosoms, gripping the bone hafts of wide-bladed bronze knives they had plunged into those children. An ancient, final tragedy in frozen tableau, as a whole tribe faced slaughter at the hands of some unknown foe – *how many thousands of years ago did this happen, how long have these trapped souls held on to this horrifying, heart-rending moment? And now? Are they doomed to repeat that eternal anguish?* 'Hood bless these,' Duiker whispered, 'please. Take them. Take them now.'

The women were locked into that fatal pattern. He watched them thrusting daggers home, watched the children jerk and writhe, listened to their short-lived wails. He watched as the women then fell, heads crumpling to unseen weapons – to memories only they could see . . . and feel. The remorseless executions went on, and on.

Nil had ceased his frenzied ride and now guided his roan at a walk towards the ghastly scene. The boy was sickly pale beneath his tanned skin. Something whispered in Duiker's mind that the young warlock was seeing more than anyone else – rather, anyone else who was alive. The boy's head moved, tracking ghost-killers. He flinched at every death-dealing blow.

The historian, his legs as awkward as wooden crutches beneath him, stumbled towards the boy. He reached up and took the reins from the warlock's motionless hands. 'Nil,' he said quietly. 'What do you see?'

The boy blinked, then slowly looked down to meet Duiker's gaze. 'What?'

'You can see. Who kills them?'

'Who?' He ran a trembling hand across his brow. 'Kin. The clan split, two rivals for the Antlered Chair. Kin, Historian. Cousins, brothers, uncles . . .'

Duiker felt something breaking inside him at Nil's words. Half-formed expectations, held by desperate need, had insisted that the killers were ... Jaghut, Forkrul Assail, K'Chain Che'Malle ... *someone* ... *someone other*. 'No,' he said.

Nil's eyes, young yet ancient, held his as the warlock nodded. 'Kin. This has been mirrored. Among the Wick. A generation ago. Mirrored.'

'But no longer.' *Please*.

'No longer.' Nil managed a small wry smile. 'The Emperor, as our enemy, united us. By laughing at our small battles, our pointless feuds. Laughing and more: sneering. He shamed us with contempt, Historian. When he met with Coltaine, our alliance was already breaking apart. Kellanved mocked. He said he need only sit back and watch to see the end of our rebellion. With his words he branded our souls. With his words and his offer of unity he bestowed on us wisdom. With his words we knelt before him in true gratitude, accepted what he offered us and gave him our loyalty. You once wondered how the Emperor won our hearts. Now you know.'

The enemy resolve stiffened as the corroded weapons of the ancient warriors shattered and snapped against modern iron. Skeletal, desiccated bodies proved as unequal to the task. Pieces flew, figures stumbled, then fell, too broken to rise again.

'Must they live through their defeat a second time?' Duiker asked.

Nil shrugged. 'They purchased us a spell to breathe, to steady ourselves. Remember, Historian, had these warriors won the first time, they would have done to their victims what was done to their own families.' The child warlock slowly shook his head. 'There is little good in people. Little good.'

The sentiment jarred coming from one so young. *Some old man's voice comes from the boy, remember that.* 'Yet it can be found,' Duiker countered. 'All the more precious for its rarity.'

Nil reclaimed the reins. 'You'll find none here, Historian,' he said, his voice as hard as the words. 'We are known by our madness – this, the island's ancient spirit shows us. The memories that survive are all horror, our deeds so dark as to sear the land itself. Keep your eyes open,' he added, spinning his mount around to face the battle that had resumed at the slatted bridge, 'we're not finished yet.'

Duiker said nothing, watching the child warlock ride towards the line.

Impossibly to the historian's mind, the path before the refugees suddenly cleared, and they began crossing. He looked into the sky. The sun edged towards noon. Somehow, it had felt much later. He glared back at the dust-shrouded river – the crossing would be a terrible thing, the deep water perilous on both sides, the screaming of children, the old men and women, too weak to manage, slipping away in the current, vanishing beneath the surface. Dust and horror, the swirling water absorbing every echo.

Crow Clan horsewarriors rode around the edges of the milling, fearful thousands, as if tending a vast herd of mindless beasts. With long blunted poles, they kept the crowds from spreading and spilling outward, swinging them down to crack shins and knees, stabbing at faces. The refugees flinched back en masse wherever they rode.

'Historian,' List said at his side. 'We should find horses.'

Duiker shook his head. 'Not yet. This rearguard defence is now the heart of the battle – I'm not leaving. I have to witness it—'

'Understood, sir. But when they do withdraw, they'll be collected by the Wickans, an extra soldier for each rider. Coltaine and the rest of his clan should be joining them soon. They'll hold this side of the ford to allow the rearguard to cross. If we don't want our heads on spears, sir, we'd better find some horses.'

412

After a moment Duiker nodded. 'Do it, then.'

'Yes, sir.' The young soldier headed off.

The defensive line along the old channel writhed like a serpent. The enemy's regular infantry, having destroyed the last of the skeletal warriors, now pushed hard. Bolstered by the steady nerves and efficient brutality of the marines among them, the auxiliaries continued to drive the regulars back. The Weasel Clan horsewarriors had split into smaller troops, mixed bowmen and lancers. Wherever the line seemed about to buckle, they rode to support.

The warlock Nil commanded them, his shouted orders piercing through the clash and roar of battle. He seemed able to sense weakening elements before such faltering was physically reflected. His magically enhanced sense of timing was all that kept the line from collapsing.

To the north Kamist Reloe had finally begun moving with his elite force. Archers to the fore, the heavy infantry marched in ranks behind the Tithansi screen. They would not challenge the leadwoods and marsh, however, slowly wheeling eastward to skirt its deadly edge.

The peasant army now pushed behind the Sialk and Hissar infantry, the weight of tens of thousands building to an unstoppable tide.

Duiker looked anxiously to the south. Where was Coltaine? Dust and now smoke rose from the hills. The village of L'enbarl was burning, and the battle still raged – if Coltaine and the bulk of his Crow Clan could not disengage soon, they would be trapped on this side of the river. The historian noted he was not alone in his trepid attention. Nil's head jerked in that direction again and again. Then Duiker finally realized that the young warlock was in communication with his fellow warlocks – the ones in Coltaine's company. *Control . . . and the illusion of control.*

List rode up, leading Duiker's own mare. The corporal did

not dismount as he passed the reins over. The historian swung himself into the familiar worn saddle, whispering a word of gratitude to the Wickan elders who had so lovingly attended to his horse. The animal was fit and full of life. *Now if they could manage the same with me.*

The rearguard began yielding ground once again, relinquishing the old channel as the enemy pushed relentlessly. Kamist Reloe's heavy infantry was perhaps five minutes from striking the north flank.

'This isn't looking good,' Duiker said.

Corporal List adjusted his helmet strap and said nothing, but the historian saw the tremble in the lad's hands.

Weasel Clan riders were streaming from the line now, burdened with wounded soldiers. They rode past Duiker's position, blood- and dust-streaked wraiths, their tattooed faces and bodies making them look demonic. The historian's gaze followed them as they headed towards the seething refugees. The mass of civilians on this side of the river had shrunk considerably since he last looked. *Too fast. They must have panicked at the ford. Thousands drowning in the deeps. A disaster.*

'We should withdraw now, sir,' List said.

The rearguard was crumbling, the stream of wounded growing, the horses thundering past were each carrying two, sometimes three fighters. The line contracted, the flanking edges drawing in towards the centre. In minutes they would be encircled. *Then slaughtered.* He saw Captain Lull bellowing commands to form a square. Soldiers still on their feet were pitifully few.

In one of those mysterious vagaries of battle, the Sialk and Hissar infantry paused, there on the threshold of complete victory. Off to one side the heavy infantry arrived, two rectangular blocks fifty soldiers across and twenty deep, bands of archers now in between those blocks and to either side. For a moment, stillness and silence rose like a barrier in the open space between the two forces.

The Weasel Clan continued plucking footmen. Lull's square was disintegrating from this side, becoming a three-sided, hollow ring.

'The last of the refugees are in the water,' Lull said, his breath coming faster than before, his hands twitching as they gripped the reins. 'We have to ride—'

'Where in Hood's name is Coltaine?' Duiker demanded.

From a dozen paces away Nil reined in amidst a rolling cloud of dust. 'We wait no longer! Thus the Fist commands! Ride, Historian!'

Horsemen gathered the last of Lull's troops even as, with an air-trembling roar, the enemy ranks rushed in. Avenues opened between the infantry, releasing at last the frenzied rage of the peasant horde.

'Sir!' List's cry was a frantic plea.

Cursing, Duiker wheeled his mount and drove his heels into the mare's flanks. They bolted after the Wickan horsewarriors.

Now unleashed, the horde poured in pursuit, eager to claim this side of the ford. The Sialk and Hissar infantry and Kamist's heavy infantry let them go unescorted, maintaining their discipline.

Wickan riders were plunging into the dust clouds ahead at full gallop. At that speed they would clash with the rear elements of the refugees who were still in the midst of crossing. Then, when the peasant army hit, the river would run red. Duiker reined in, shouting to List. The corporal glanced back, his expression one of shock. He sawed the reins, his horse skidding and slipping on the muddy slope.

'Historian!'

'We ride south, along the bank!' Duiker yelled. 'We swim the horses – ahead lies chaos and death!'

List was fiercely shaking his head in denial.

Without awaiting a reply, the historian swung his mount to the left. If they rode hard, they would clear the island before the horde reached the ford's bank. He drove his heels into the mare's flanks. The animal lunged forward.

'Historian!'

'Ride or die, damn you!'

A hundred paces along the shore was the sunken mouth of the old oxbow, a thick, verdant swath of cattails miraculously untouched by the day's events. Beyond it rose the hills shielding L'enbarl. *If Coltaine extricates himself, he'll do the smart thing – straight into the river. Even if the current carries them down to the ford itself, they'll have a head start. A few hundred drowned is a damned sight better than three thousand slaughtered trying to retake this side of the ford.*

As if to defy his every thought, Wickan horsewarriors appeared, sweeping down the opposite slope. Coltaine rode at the head, his black feather cape a single splayed wing behind him. Lances were lowered, flanking bowmen nocking arrows on the fly. The charge was coming directly for Duiker.

The historian, half disbelieving, dragged the mare around into a staggering about-face. 'Oh Hood, might as well join this doomed charge!' He saw List doing the same, the lad's face white as death beneath his dusty helm.

They would strike the peasant army's flank like a knife blade plunging into the side of a whale. *And about as effective. Suicide! Even if we make the ford, we'll flounder. Horses will fall, men will drown, and the peasants will descend to reap slaughter.* Still they rode on. Moments before contact, he saw Weasel Clan horsewarriors reappear from the dust cloud. *Counterattack. More madness!*

Crow riders swept to either side of the historian, the momentum of their charge at its peak. Duiker turned his head at Coltaine's fierce, joyous shout.

Arrows whizzed past. The flank of the peasant army contracted, flinched back. When the Wickans struck, it was into a solidly packed mass of humanity. Yet, at the last moment, the

Crow Clan riders wheeled towards the river and rode alongside the flank. *Not a knife plunge. A sabre slash.*

Peasants died. Others fell in their frantic retreat and were trampled by the frenzied horses. The entire flank bloomed red as the savage Wickan blades travelled its length.

The peasants holding the ford's landing were crumpling beneath the Weasel Clan's counterattack. Then the lead riders of the Crow Clan struck the north edge.

The peasant line seemed to melt away before Duiker's eyes. He now rode with the Crow Clan, horse shoulders hammering his legs to either side. Blood rained from raised weapons, spattering his face and hands. Ahead, the Weasel Clan's riders parted, covering their kin's wild charge straight into the clouds of dust.

Now the mayhem truly begins. For all the glory of Coltaine's charge, ahead lay the river. Wounded soldiers, refugees and Hood knew what else.

The historian snatched what he felt would be his last breath a moment before plunging into the sunlit dust.

His mare splashed water, yet barely slowed. The way before him stretched clear, a swirling, strangely choppy sweep of muddy water. Other riders were barely visible farther ahead, their horses at full gallop. Duiker could feel the unyielding, solid impact his mare's hooves made as they rode on. There was not four and a half feet of river beneath them, but half that. And the hooves struck stone, not mud. He did not understand.

Corporal List appeared alongside the historian, as well as a straggling squad of Crow horsewarriors. One of the Wickans grinned. 'Coltaine's road – his warriors fly like ghosts across the river!'

Various comments the night before returned to Duiker. *Tumlit – that nobleman's observations. Reinforced wagons apparently overloaded with wounded. Stone cutters and Engineers. The wagons crossing first and taking most of the night to do so. The wounded were laid atop the stone blocks. The damned Engineers had built a road!*

It still seemed impossible, yet the evidence was there beneath him as he rode. Poles had been raised to either side, strung with rope made from Tithansi hair to mark the edges. A little over ten feet wide – what was surrendered in width was made up for with the relative swiftness of crossing the more than four hundred paces to the other side. The ford's depth was no more than two and a third feet now, and had clearly proved manageable for both livestock and refugees.

The dust thinned ahead and the historian realized they were approaching the river's west side. The thunder of sorcery reached him. *This battle's far from over. We've temporarily outrun one army, only to charge headlong into another. All this, just to get crushed between two rocks?*

They reached the shallows and a moment later rode upslope twenty strides, emerging from the last drifting shrouds of dust.

Duiker shouted in alarm, he and his companions frantically sawing their reins. Directly in front of them was a squad of soldiers – Engineers – who had been running at full speed towards the ford's landing. The sappers now scattered with foul curses, ducking and dodging around the stumbling, skidding horses. One, a solid, mountainous man with a sun-burnished, smooth-shaven, flat face, flung his battered helm off, revealing a bald pate, and threw the iron skullcap at the nearest Wickan rider – missing the warrior's head by scant inches. 'Clear out, you flyblown piles of gizzards! We got work to do!'

'Yeah!' another growled, limping in circles after a hoof had landed full on a foot. 'Go fight or something! We got a plug to pull!'

Ignoring their demands, Duiker spun the mare around to face the ford. Whatever sorcery had held the dust over the water was now gone. The clouds had already drifted fifty paces downstream. And Coltaine's Road was a mass of armed, screaming peasants.

The second sapper who'd spoken now scrambled to a shallow pit overlooking the muddy landing.

'Hold off there, Cuttle!' the big man commanded, his eyes on the surging thousands – the lead elements now in the middle of the crossing. The man anchored his huge hands on his hips, glowering and seemingly unaware of the rapt attention his squad held on him, as well as that from Duiker, List and the half-dozen Wickan horsemen. 'Got to maximize,' the man rumbled. 'Bastard Wickans ain't the only ones who know about timing.'

The horde's vanguard, glittering with weapons, looking like the iron-fanged maw of a giant snake, was three-quarters across. The historian could make out individual faces, the expressions of fear and murderous intent that make up the faces of battle. A glance behind him showed rising columns of smoke and the flash of sorcery, concentrated on the right flank of the Seventh's defensive positions. The faint screeching Semk war cry drifted from that flank, a sound like claws scraping taut skin. A fierce melee was underway at the first earthworks.

'All right, Cuttle,' the big man drawled. 'Yank the hair.'

Duiker swung back to see the sapper in the pit raise both hands, gripping a long, black cord that trailed down into the water. Cuttle's dirt-smeared face twisted into a fierce grimace, his eyes squeezing shut. Then he pulled. The cord went slack.

Nothing happened.

The historian chanced to look the big man's way. He had a finger stuck in each ear, though his eyes remained open and fixed on the river. Realization struck Duiker even as List cried, 'Sir!'

The ground seemed to drop an inch under them. The water on the ford rose up, humped, blurred, the hump seeming to roll with lightning swiftness down the submerged road's length. The peasants on the river simply vanished. Then reappeared a heart-beat later – even as the concussion struck everyone on shore with a wind like a god's fist – in blossoms of red and pink and yellow, fragments of flesh and bone, limbs, hair, tufts of cloth, all lifting higher and higher as the water exploded up and out in a muddy, ghastly mist.

Duiker's mare backstepped, head tossing. The sound had been deafening. The world shivered on all sides. A Wickan rider had tumbled from his saddle and now writhed on the ground, hands held to his ears.

The river began to fall back, horridly churned with bodies and pieces of bodies, steam twisting away on sudden gusts of wind. The giant snake's head was gone. Obliterated. As was another third of its length – all who had been in the water were gone.

Though he now stood close by, the big man's words sounded faint and distant to Duiker's ringing ears as he said, 'Fifty-five cussers – what the Seventh's been hoarding for years. That ford's now a trench. Ha.' Then his satisfied expression drained away. 'Hood's toes, we're back to digging with shovels.'

A hand plucked the historian's sleeve. List leaned close and whispered, 'Where to now, sir?'

The historian looked downstream at the twisting eddies, red-stained and full of human flotsam. For a moment he could not comprehend the corporal's question. *Where to? Nowhere that's good, no place where giving pause to slaughter will yield something other than despair.*

'Sir?'

'To the melee, Corporal. We see this through.'

The swift arrival of Coltaine and his Crow horsewarriors to strike at the west flank of the Tithansi lancers on this side of the river had turned the tide of battle. As they rode towards the engagement at the earthworks, Duiker and List could see the Tithansi crumbling, exposing the Semk footmen to the mounted Wickan bowmen. Arrows raked through the wild-haired Semk fighters.

At the centre stood the bulk of the Seventh's infantry, holding at bay the frenzied efforts of the Semk, while a hundred paces to the north, the Guran heavy infantry still waited to close with the hated Malazans. Their commander was evidently having second thoughts. Kamist Reloe and his army were trapped – for this battle at least – on the other side of the river. Apart from the battered rearguard marines and the Weasel Clan, Coltaine's force was relatively intact.

Five hundred paces farther west, out on a broad, stony plain, the Weasel Clan pursued remnants of Guran cavalry.

Duiker saw a knot of colour amidst the Seventh, gold and red – Baria Setral and his Red Blades, in the heart of the fighting. The Semk seemed eager to close on the Malazan lapdogs, and were paying in blood for their desire. Nonetheless, Setral's troop looked at no more than half strength – less than twenty men.

'I want to get closer,' Duiker announced.

'Yes, sir,' List said. He pointed. 'That rise there – it'll put us in bow range though, sir.'

'I'll take that risk.'

They rode towards the Seventh. The company standard stood solitary and dust-streaked on a low hill just behind the line. Three grey-haired veterans guarded it – Semk bodies strewn on the slope indicated that the hill had been hotly contested earlier in the day. The veterans had been in the fight, and all bore minor wounds.

As the historian and the corporal rode to their position, Duiker saw that the three men crouched around a fallen comrade. Tears had clawed crooked trails down their dusty cheeks. Arriving, the historian slowly dismounted.

'You've a story here, soldiers,' he said, pitching his voice low to reach through the clangour and shouts of the struggle thirty paces north of them.

One of the veterans glanced up, squinting. 'The old Emperor's historian, by Hood's grin! Saw you in Falar, or maybe the Wickan Plains—'

'Both. The standard was challenged, I see. You lost a friend in defending it.'

The man blinked, then glanced around until he focused on the Seventh's standard. The pikeshaft leaned to one side, its tattered banner bleached into ghost colours by the sun. 'Hood's breath,' the man growled. 'Think we'd fight to save a piece of cloth on a pole?' He gestured at the body his friends knelt around. 'Nordo took two arrows. We held off a squad of Semk so he could die in his own time. Those bastard tribesmen snatch wounded enemies and keep 'em alive so's they can torture 'em. Nordo wasn't gettin' none of that.'

Duiker was silent for a long moment. 'Is that how you want the tale told, soldier?'

The man squinted some more, then he nodded. 'Just like that, Historian. We ain't just a Malazan army any more. We're Coltaine's.'

'But he's a Fist.'

'He's a cold-blooded lizard.' The man then grinned. 'But he's all ours.'

Smiling, Duiker twisted in his saddle and studied the battle at the line. Some threshold of spirit had been crossed. The Semk were broken. Dying by the score with three legions of supposed allies sitting motionless on the slopes behind them, they had carved out the last of zeal in the holy cause – at least for this engagement. There would be curses and hot accusations in the enemy camps this coming night, Duiker knew. *Good, let them crack apart of their own accord.*

Once again, it was not to be the Whirlwind's day.

* * *

Coltaine did not let his victorious army rest as the afternoon's light sank in the earth. New fortifications were raised, others reinforced. Trenches were dug, pickets established. The refugees were led out onto the stony plain west of the ford, their tents arranged in blocks with wide avenues in between. Wagons loaded with wounded soldiers were moved into those avenues, and the cutters and healers set to work.

The livestock were driven south, to the grassy slopes of the Barl Hills – a weathered, humped range of bleached rock and twisted jackpine. Drovers supported by riders of the Foolish Dog Clan guarded the herds.

In the Fist's command tent, as the sun dropped beneath the horizon, Coltaine held a debriefing.

Duiker, with the now ever-present Corporal List standing at his shoulder, sat wearily in a camp chair, listening to the commanders make their reports with a dismay that slowly numbed. Lull had lost fully half his marines, and the auxiliaries that had supported him had fared even worse. The Weasel Clan had been mauled during the withdrawal – a shortage of horses was now their main concern. From the Seventh, captains Chenned and Sulmar recounted a seemingly endless litany of wounded and dead. It seemed that their officers and squad sergeants, in particular, had taken heavy losses. The pressure against the defensive line had been enormous, especially early in the day – before support had arrived in the form of the Red Blades and the Foolish Dog Clan. The tale of Baria Setral and his company's fall rode many a breath. They had fought with demonic ferocity, holding the front ranks, purchasing with their lives a crucial period in which the infantry was able to regroup. The Red Blades had shown valour, enough to earn comment from Coltaine himself.

Sormo had lost two of his warlock children in the struggle against the Semk wizard-priests, although both Nil and Nether survived. 'We were lucky,' he said after reporting the deaths in a cool, dispassionate tone. 'The Semk god is a vicious Ascendant. It uses the wizards to channel its rage, without regard for their mortal flesh. Those unable to withstand their god's power simply disintegrated.'

'That'll cut their numbers down,' Lull said with a grunt.

'The god simply chooses more,' Sormo said. More and more he had begun to look like an old man, even in his gestures. Duiker watched the youth close his eyes and press his knuckles against them. 'More extreme measures must be taken.'

The others were silent, until Chenned gave voice to everyone's uncertainty. 'What does that mean, Warlock?'

Bult said, 'Words carried on breath can be heard ... by a vengeful, paranoid god. If no alternative exists, Sormo, then proceed.'

The warlock slowly nodded.

After a moment Bult sighed loudly, pausing to drink from a bladder before speaking. 'Kamist Reloe is heading north. He'll cross at the river mouth – Sekala town has a stone bridge. But to do so means he loses ten, maybe eleven days.'

'The Guran infantry will stay with us,' Sulmar said. 'As will the Semk. They need not stand toe to toe to do us damage. Exhaustion will claim us before much longer.'

Bult's wide mouth pressed into a straight line. 'Coltaine has proclaimed tomorrow a day of rest. Cattle will be slaughtered, the enemy's dead horses butchered and cooked. Weapons and armour repaired.'

Duiker lifted his head. 'Do we still march for Ubaryd?'

No-one answered.

The historian studied the commanders. He saw nothing hopeful in their faces. 'The city has fallen.'

'So claimed a Tithansi warleader,' Lull said. 'He had nothing to lose in telling us since he was dying anyway. Nether said he spoke truth. The Malazan fleet has fled Ubaryd. Even now tens of thousands of refugees are being driven northeast.'

'More squalling nobles to perch on Coltaine's lap,' Chenned said with a sneer.

'This is impossible,' Duiker said. 'If we cannot go to Ubaryd, what other city lies open to us?'

'There is but one,' Bult said. 'Aren.'

Duiker sat straight. 'Madness! Two hundred leagues!'

'And another third, to be precise,' Lull said, baring his teeth.

'Is Pormqual counterattacking? Is he marching north to meet us halfway? Is he even aware that we exist?'

Bult's gaze held steady on the historian. 'Aware? I would think so, Historian. Will he march out from Aren? Counterattack?' The veteran shrugged.

'I saw a company of Engineers on my way here,' Lull said. 'They were weeping, one and all.'

Chenned asked, 'Why? Is their invisible commander lying on the bottom of the Sekala with a mouthful of mud?'

Lull shook his head. 'They're out of cussers now. Just a crate or two of sharpers and burners. You'd think every one of their mothers had just croaked.'

Coltaine finally spoke. 'They did well.'

Bult nodded. 'Aye. Wish I'd been there to see the road go up.'

'We were,' Duiker said. 'Victory tastes sweetest in the absence of haunting memories, Bult. Savour it.'

In his tent, Duiker awoke to a soft, small hand on his shoulder. He opened his eyes to darkness.

'Historian,' a voice said.

'Nether? What hour is this? How long have I slept?'

'Perhaps two,' she answered. 'Coltaine commands you to come with me. Now.'

Duiker sat up. He'd been too tired to do more than simply lay his bedroll down on the floor. The blankets were sodden with sweat and condensation. He shivered with chill. 'What has happened?' he asked.

'Nothing, yet. You are to witness. Quickly now, Historian. We have little time.'

He stepped outside to a camp quietly moaning in the deepest hour of darkness before the arrival of false dawn. Thousands of voices made the dreadful, gelid sound. Wounds troubling exhausted sleep, the soft cries of soldiers beyond the arts of the healers and cutters, the lowing of livestock, shifting hooves underscoring the chorus in a restless, rumbling beat. Somewhere out on the plain north of them rose faint wailing, wives and mothers grieving the dead.

As he followed Nether's spry, wool-cloaked form down the twisting lanes of the Wickan encampment, the historian was drawn into sorrow-laden thoughts. The dead were gone through Hood's Gate. The living were left with the pain of their passage. Duiker had seen many peoples as Imperial Historian, yet among them not one in his recollection did not possess a ritual of grief. *For all our personal gods, Hood alone embraces us all, in a thousand guises. When the breath from his gates brushes close, we ever give voice to drive back that eternal silence. Tonight, we hear the Semk. And the Tithansi. Uncluttered rituals. Who needs temples and priests to chain and guide the expression of loss and dismay – when all is sacred?*

'Nether, why do the Wickans not grieve this night?'

She half turned as she continued walking. 'Coltaine forbids it.'

'Why?'

'For that answer you must ask him. We have not mourned our losses since this journey began.'

Duiker was silent for a long moment, then he said, 'And how do you and the others in the three clans feel about that, Nether?'

'Coltaine commands. We obey.'

They came to the edge of the Wickan encampment. Beyond the last tent stretched a flat killing strip, perhaps twenty paces wide, then the freshly raised wicker walls of the pickets, with their long bamboo spikes thrust through them, the points outward and at the height of a horse's chest. Mounted warriors of the Weasel Clan patrolled along them, eyes on the dark, stone-studded plain beyond.

In the killing strip stood two figures, one tall, the other short, both lean as spectres. Nether led Duiker up to them Sormo. Nil. 'Are you,' the historian asked the tall warlock, 'all that remain? You told Coltaine you lost but two yesterday.'

Sormo E'nath nodded. 'The others rest their young flesh. A dozen horsewives tend to the mounts and a handful of healers tend to wounded soldiers. We three are the strongest, thus we are here.' The warlock stepped forward. There was a febrile air about him, and in his voice was a tone that asked for something more than the historian could give. 'Duiker, whose eyes met mine across the Whirlwind ghosts in the trader camp, listen to my words. You will hear the fear – every solemn chime. You are no stranger to that dark chorus. Know, then, that this night I had doubts.'

'Warlock,' Duiker said quietly, as Nether stepped forward to take position on Sormo's right – turning so that all three now faced the historian – 'what is happening here?'

In answer Sormo E'nath raised his hands.

The scene shifted around them. He saw moraines and scree slopes rising behind the three warlocks, the dark sky seeming to throb its blackness overhead. The ground was wet and cold beneath Duiker's moccasins. He looked down to see glittering sheets of brittle ice covering puddles of muddy water. The crazed patterns in the ice reflected myriad colours from a sourceless light.

A breath of cold wind made him turn around. A guttural bark of surprise was loosed from his throat. The historian stepped back, his being filling with horror. Rotten, blood-smeared ice formed a shattered cliff before him, the tumbled, jagged blocks at its foot less than ten paces away. The cliff rose, sloping back until the streaked face vanished within mists.

The ice was full of bodies, human-shaped figures, twisted and flesh-torn. Organs and entrails were spilled out at the base as if from a giant abattoir. Slowly melting chunks of blood-soaked ice created a lake from which the body parts jutted or rose in islands humped and slick.

Exposed flesh had begun to putrefy into misshapen gelatinous mounds, through which bones could faintly be seen.

Sormo spoke behind him. 'He is within it, but close.'

'Who?'

'The Semk god. An Ascendant from long ago. Unable to challenge the sorcery, he was devoured with the others. Yet he did not die. Can you feel his anger, Historian?'

'I think I'm beyond feeling. What sorcery did this?'

'Jaghut. To stem the tides of invading humans, they raised ice. Sometimes swiftly, sometimes slowly, as their strategy dictated. In places it swallowed entire continents, obliterating all that once stood upon them. Forkrul Assail civilizations, the vast mechanisms and edifices of the K'Chain Che'Malle, and of course the squalid huts of those who would one day inherit the world. The highest of Omtose Phellack, these rituals never die, Historian. They rise, subside, and rise yet again. Even now, one is born anew on a distant land, and those rivers of ice fill my dreams, for they are destined to create vast upheaval, and death in numbers unimaginable.'

Sormo's words held a timbre of antiquity, the remorseless cold of ages folding over one another, again and again, until it seemed to Duiker that every rock, every cliff, every mountain moved in eternal motion, like mindless leviathans. Shivers raced the blood in his veins until he trembled uncontrollably.

'Think of all such ice holds,' Sormo went on. 'Looters

of tombs find riches, but wise hunters of power seek . . . ice.'

Nether spoke. 'They have begun assembling.'

Duiker finally turned away from the ravaged, flesh-marred ice. Shapeless swirls and pulses of energy now surrounded the three warlocks. Some waxed bright and energetic, while others blossomed faintly in fitful rhythm.

'The spirits of the land,' Sormo said.

Nil fidgeted in his robes, as if barely restraining the desire to dance. A dark smile showed on his child-face. 'The flesh of an Ascendant holds much power. They all hunger for a piece. With this gift we bring them, further service is bound.'

'Historian.' Sormo stepped closer, reaching out one thin hand until it rested on Duiker's shoulder. 'How thin is this slice of mercy? All that anger . . . brought to an end. Torn apart, each fragment consumed. Not death, but a kind of dissipation—'

'And what of the Semk wizard-priests?'

The warlock winced. 'Knowledge, and with it great pain. We must carve the heart from the Semk. Yet that heart is worse than stone. How it uses the mortal flesh . . .' He shook his head. 'Coltaine commands.'

'You obey.'

Sormo nodded.

Duiker said nothing for a dozen heartbeats, then he sighed. 'I have heard your doubts, Warlock.'

Sormo's expression showed an almost fierce relief. 'Cover your eyes, then, Historian. This will be . . . messy.'

Behind Duiker, the ice erupted with an explosive roar. Cold crimson rain struck the historian in a rolling wall, staggering him.

A savage shriek sounded behind him.

The spirits of the land bolted forward, spinning and tumbling past Duiker. He whirled in time to see a figure – flesh rotted black, arms long as an ape's – clawing its way out of the dirty, steaming slush.

The spirits reached it, swarming over the figure. It managed a single, piercing shriek before it was torn to pieces.

The eastern horizon was a streak of red when they returned to the killing strip. The camp was already awakening, the demands of existence pressing once more upon ragged, weary souls. Wagon-mounted forges were being stoked, fresh hides scraped, leather stretched and punched or boiled in huge blackened pots. Despite a lifetime spent in cities, the Malazan refugees were learning to carry their city with them – or at least those meagre remnants vital to survival.

Duiker and the three warlocks were sodden with old blood and clinging fragments of flesh. Their reappearance on the plain was enough to announce their success and the Wickans raised a wail that ran through each clan's encampment, the sound as much sorrowful as triumphant, a fitting dirge to announce the fall of a god.

From the distant Semk camps to the north, the rituals of mourning had fallen off, leaving naught but ominous silence.

Dew steamed from the earth, and the historian could feel – as he crossed the killing strip back towards the Wickan encampment – a darker reverberation to the power of the spirits of the land. The three warlocks parted from him as they approached the camp's edge.

The reverberating power found a voice only moments later, as every dog in the vast camp began howling. The cries were strangely lifeless and cold as iron, filling the air like a promise.

Duiker slowed his walk. *A promise. An age of devouring ice—*

'Historian!'

He looked up to see three men approach. He recognized two of them, Nethpara and Tumlit. The fellow nobleman accompanying them was short and round, burdened beneath a gold-brocaded cloak that would have looked imposing on a man twice his height and half his girth. As it was, the effect held more pathos than anything else.

Nethpara was breathless as he hurried up, his slack folds of flesh quivering and mud-spattered. 'Imperial Historian Duiker, we wish to speak with you.'

Lack of sleep – and a host of other things – had drawn Duiker's tolerance short, but he managed to keep his tone calm. 'I suggest another time—'

'Quite impossible!' snapped the third nobleman. 'The Council is not to be brushed off yet again. Coltaine holds the sword and so may keep us at bay with his barbaric indifference, but we will have our petition delivered one way or the other!'

Duiker blinked at the man.

Tumlit cleared his throat apologetically and dabbed his watering eyes. 'Historian, permit me to introduce the Highborn Lenestro, recent resident of Sialk—'

'No mere resident!' Lenestro squealed. 'Sole representative of the Kanese family of the same name, in all Seven Cities. Factor in the largest trade enterprise exporting the finest tanned camel hide. I am chief within the Guild, granted the honour of First Potency in Sialk. More than one Fist has bowed before me, yet here I stand, reduced to demanding audience with a foul-bespattered scholar—'

'Lenestro, please!' Tumlit said in exasperation. 'You do your cause little good!'

'Slapped across the face by a lard-smeared savage the Empress should have had spiked on a wall years ago! I warrant she will regret her mercy when news of this horror reaches her!'

'Which horror would that be, Lenestro?' Duiker quietly asked.

The question made Lenestro gape and sputter, his face reddening.

Nethpara elected to answer. 'Historian, Coltaine

conscripted our servants. It was not even a request. His Wickan dogs simply collected them – indeed, when one of our honoured colleagues protested, he was struck upon his person and knocked to the ground. Have our servants been returned? They have not. Are they even alive? What horrible suicide stand was left to them? We have no answers, Historian.'

'Your concern is for the welfare of your servants?' Duiker asked.

'Who shall prepare our meals?' Lenestro demanded. 'Mend our clothes and raise our tents and heat the water for our baths? This is an outrage!'

'Their welfare is uppermost in *my* mind,' Tumlit said, offering a sad smile.

Duiker believed the man. 'I shall enquire on your behalf, then.'

'Of course you shall!' Lenestro snapped. 'Immediately.'

'When you can,' Tumlit said.

Duiker nodded, turned away.

'We are not yet done with you!' Lenestro shouted.

'We are,' Duiker heard Tumlit say.

'Someone must silence these dogs! Their howling has no end!'

Better howling than snapping at the heel. He walked on. His desire to wash himself was becoming desperate. The residue of blood and flesh had begun to dry on his clothes and on his skin. He was attracting attention as he shuffled down the aisle between the tents. Warding gestures were being made as he passed. Duiker feared he had inadvertently become a harbinger, and the fate he promised was as chilling as the soulless howls of the camp dogs.

Ahead, the morning's light bled across the sky.

Book Three

Chain of Dogs

When the sands
Danced blind,
She emerged from the face
Of a raging goddess

Sha'ik
Bidithal

CHAPTER ELEVEN

If you seek the crumbled bones
of the T'lan Imass,
gather into one hand
the sands of Raraku

The Holy Desert
Anonymous

Kulp felt like a rat in a vast chamber crowded with ogres, caged in by shadows and but moments away from being crushed underfoot. Never before when entering the Meanas Warren had it felt so . . . *fraught*.

There were strangers here, intruders, forces so inimical to the realm that the very atmosphere bridled. The essence of himself that had slipped through the fabric was reduced to a crouching, cowering creature. And yet, all he could feel was a series of fell passages, the spun wakes that marked the paths the unwelcome had taken. His senses shouted at him that – for the moment at least – he was alone, the dun sprawled-out landscape devoid of all life.

Still he trembled with terror.

Within his mind he reached back a ghostly hand, finding the tactile reassurance of the place where his body existed, the heave and slush of blood in his veins, the solid weight of flesh and bone. He sat cross-legged in the captain's cabin of the *Silanda*, watched over by a wary, restless Heboric, while the others waited on the deck, ever scanning the unbroken, remorselessly flat horizon on all sides.

They needed a way out. The entire Elder Warren they'd found themselves in was flooded, a soupy, shallow sea. The oarsmen could propel *Silanda* onward for a thousand years, until the wood rotted in their dead hands, the shafts snapping, until the ship began to disintegrate around them, still the drum would beat and the backs would bend. *And we'd be long dead by then, nothing but mouldering dust*. To escape, they must find a means of shifting warrens.

Kulp cursed his own limitations. Had he been a practitioner of Serc, or Denul or D'riss or indeed virtually any of the other warrens accessible to humans, he would find what they needed. *But not Meanas. No seas, no rivers, not even a Hood-damned puddle*. From within his warren, Kulp was seeking to effect a passage through to the mortal world . . . and it was proving problematic.

They were bound by peculiar laws, by rules of nature that seemed to play games with the principles of cause and effect. Had they been riding a wagon, the passage through the warrens would unerringly have taken them on a dry path. The primordial elements asserted an intractable consistency across all warrens. Land to land, air to air, water to water.

Kulp had heard of High Mages who – it was rumoured – had found ways to cheat those illimitable laws, and perhaps the gods and other Ascendants possessed such knowledge as well. But they were as beyond a lowly cadre mage as the tools of an ogre's smithy to a cowering rat.

His other concern was the vastness of the task itself. Pulling a handful of companions through his warren was difficult, but manageable. *But an entire ship!* He'd hoped he would find in-spiration once within the Meanas Warren, some thunderbolt delivering a simple, elegant solution. *With all the grace of poetry. Was it not Fisher Kel'Tath himself who once said poetry and sorcery were the twin edges to the knife in every man's heart? Where then are my magic cants?*

Kulp sourly admitted that he felt as stupid within Meanas as he did sitting in the captain's cabin. *The art of illusion is grace itself. There must be a way to . . . to trick our way through. What's real versus what isn't is the synergy within a mortal's mind. And greater forces? Can reality itself be fooled into asserting an unreality?*

His shouting senses changed pitch. Kulp was no longer alone. The thick, turgid air of the Meanas Warren – where shadows were textured like ground glass and to slip through them was to feel a shivering ecstasy – had begun to bulge, then bow, as if something huge approached, pushing the air before it. And whatever it was, it was coming fast.

A sudden thought flooded the mage's mind. And moreover, it possessed . . . *elegance. Togg's toes, can I do this? Building pressure, then vacuous wake, a certain current, a certain flow. Hood, it ain't water, but close enough.*

I hope.

He saw Heboric jump back in alarm, striking his head on a low crossbeam in the cabin. Kulp slipped back into his body and loosed a rasping gasp. 'We're about to go, Heboric. Get everyone ready!'

The old man was rubbing a stump against the back of his head. 'Ready for what, Mage?'

'Anything.'

Kulp slid back out, mentally clambering back over his anchor within Meanas.

The Unwelcome was coming, a force of such power as to make the febrile atmosphere shiver. The mage saw nearby shadows vibrate into dissolution. He felt outrage building in the air, in the loamy earth underfoot. Whatever was passing

437

through this warren had drawn the attention of . . . *of whatever – Shadowthrone, the Hounds – or perhaps warrens truly are alive.* In any case, on it came, in arrogant disregard.

Kulp suddenly thought back to Sormo's ritual that had drawn them into the T'lan Imass warren outside Hissar. *Oh, Hood, Soletaken or D'ivers . . . but such power! Who in the Abyss has such power?* He could think of but two: Anomander Rake, the Son of Darkness, and Osric. Both Soletaken, both supremely arrogant. *If there were others, the tales of their activities would have reached him, he was certain. Warriors talk about heroes. Mages talk about Ascendants.* He would have heard.

Rake was on Genabackis, and Osric was reputed to have journeyed to a continent far to the south a century or so back. *Well, maybe the cold-eyed bastard's back.* Either way, he was about to find out.

The presence arrived. His spiritual belly flat on the soft ground, Kulp craned his head skyward.

The dragon came low to the earth. It defied every image of a draconian being Kulp had ever seen. *Not Rake, not Osric.* Hugely boned, with skin like dry shark hide, its wing-span dwarfed even that of the Son of Darkness – *who has within him the blood of the draconian goddess* – and the wings had nothing of the smooth, curving grace; the bones were multi-jointed in a crazed pattern, like that of a crushed bat wing, each knobbed joint prominent beneath taut, cracked skin. The dragon's head was as wide as it was long, like a viper's, the eyes high on its skull. There was no ridged forehead, instead the skull sloped back to a basal serration almost buried in neck and jaw muscles.

A dragon roughly cast, a creature exhaling an aura of primordial antiquity. And, Kulp realized with a breathless start as his senses devoured all that the creature projected, it was *undead.*

438

The mage felt it become aware of him as it sailed in a whisper twenty arm-spans overhead. A sudden sharpening of intensity that quickly passed into indifference.

As the dragon's wake arrived with a piercing wind, Kulp rolled onto his back and hissed the few words of High Meanas he possessed. The warren's fabric parted, a tear barely large enough to allow the passage of a horse. But it opened onto a vacuum, and the shrieking wind became a roar.

Still hovering between realms, Kulp watched in awe as *Silanda*'s mud-crusted, battered prow filled the rent. The fabric split wider, then yet wider. Suddenly, the ship's beam seemed appallingly broad. The mage's awe turned to fear, then terror. *Oh no, I've really done it now.*

Milky, foaming water gushed in around the ship's hull. The portalway was tearing wider on all sides, uncontrolled, as the weight of a sea began to rush through.

A wall of water descended on Kulp and a moment later it struck, destroying his anchor, his spiritual presence. He was back in the pitching, groaning captain's cabin. Heboric was half in and half out of the cabin doorway, scrambling to find purchase as *Silanda* rode the wave.

The ex-priest shot Kulp a glare when he saw the mage clamber upright. 'Tell me you planned this! Tell me you've got it all under control, Mage!'

'Of course, you idiot! Can't you tell?' He climbed his way round the bolted-down furniture to the passage, stepping over Heboric as he went. 'Hold the fort, old man, we're counting on you!'

Heboric snarled a few choice words after him as Kulp made his way to the main deck.

If the Unwelcome's passage was to be bitterly tolerated and not directly opposed by the powers within Meanas, the rending of the warren obliterated the option of restraint. This was damage on a cosmic scale, a wounding quite possibly beyond repair.

I may just have destroyed my own warren. If reality can't be fooled. Of course it can be fooled – I do it all the time!

Kulp scrambled onto the main deck and hurried to the sterncastle. Gesler and Stormy were at the steering oar, both men grinning like demented fools as they struggled to stay the course. Gesler pointed forward and Kulp turned to see the vague, ghostlike apparition of the dragon, its narrow, bony tail waving in side-to-side rhythm like a snake crossing sand. As he watched, the creature's wedge-shaped head appeared as it twisted to cast its dead, black eye sockets in their direction.

Gesler waved.

Shaking himself, Kulp forced his way into the wind, coming to the stern rail which he gripped with both hands. The rent was already far away – *yet still visible, meaning it must be . . . oh, Hood!* Water gushed in a tumbling torrent within the wake left by the Soletaken dragon. That it did not spread out to all sides was due entirely to the mass of shadows Kulp saw assailing its edges – and being destroyed in the effort. Yet still more arrived. The task of healing the breach was so overwhelming as to deny any opportunity of approaching the rent, of sealing the wound itself.

Shadowthrone! And every other hoary Ascendant bastard within hearing! Maybe I've got no faith in any of you, but you'd better acquire a faith in me. And fast! Illusion's my gift, here and now. Believe! Eyes on the rent, Kulp braced his legs wide, then released the stern rail and raised high both arms.

It shall close . . . it shall heal! The scene before him wavered, the tear sealing, stitching together the edges. The water slowed. He pushed harder, willing the illusion to become real. His limbs shook. Sweat sprang out on his skin, soaked his clothing.

Reality pushed back. The illusion blurred. Kulp's knees buckled. He gripped the railing to keep himself upright. He was failing. *No strength left. Failing. Dying . . .*

The force that struck him from behind was like a physical blow to the back of his head. Stars spasmed across his vision. An alien power swept through him, flinging his body back upright. Spread-eagled, he felt his feet leave the tilted deck. The power held him, hovering in place, a will as cold as ice flooding his flesh.

The power was undead. The will that gripped him was a dragon's. Tinged with irritation, reluctant to act, it nevertheless grasped the illogic of Kulp's sorcerous effort . . . and gave it all the force it needed. Then more.

He screamed, pain lancing through him with glacial fire.

Undead cared nothing for the limits of mortal flesh, a lesson now burning in his bones.

The distant rent closed. All at once other powers were channelling through the mage. Ascendants, grasping Kulp's outrageous intent, swept in to join the game with dark glee. *Always a game. Damn you bastards one and all! I take back my prayers! Hear me? Hood take you all!*

He realized the pain was gone, the Soletaken dragon withdrawing its attention as soon as other forces arrived to take its place. He remained hovering a few feet above the deck, however, his limbs twitching as the powers using him playfully plucked at his mortality. Not the indifference of an undead, but malice. Kulp began to yearn for the former.

He fell suddenly, cracking both knees on the dirt-smeared deck. *Tool done with, now discarded . . .*

Stormy was at his side, waving a wineskin before the mage's face. Kulp grasped it and poured until his mouth was full of the tart liquid.

'We ride the dragon's wake,' the soldier said. 'Though not on water any more. That gush has closed up tight as a sapper's arse. Whatever you did, Mage, it worked.'

'Not over yet,' Kulp muttered, trying to still his trembling limbs. He swallowed more wine.

'Watch yourself with that, then,' Stormy said with a grin. 'It packs a punch, right to the back of the head—'

'I won't notice the difference – my skull's already full of pulp.'

'You lit up with blue fire, Mage. Never seen anything like it. Make a damned good tavern tale.'

'Ah, I've achieved immortality at last. Take that, Hood!'

'Well enough to stand?'

Kulp was not too proud to accept the soldier's arm as he tottered to his feet. 'Give me a few moments,' he said, 'then I'll try to slip us from the warren . . . back to our realm.'

'Will the ride be as rough, Mage?'

'I hope not.'

Felisin stood on the forecastle deck, watching the mage and Stormy passing the wineskin between them. She had felt the presence of the Ascendants, the cold, bloodless attention plucking and prodding at the ship and all who were upon it. The dragon was the worst of them all, gelid and remote. *Like fleas on its hide, that's all we were to it.*

She swung about. Baudin was studying the massive winged apparition cleaving the path ahead, his bandaged hand resting lightly on the carved rail. Whatever they rode rolled beneath them in a whispering surge. The oars still plied with remorseless patience, though it was clear that *Silanda* was moving more swiftly than anything muscle and bone could achieve – even when those muscles and bones were undead.

Look at us. A handful of destinies. We command nothing, not even our next step in this mad, fraught journey. The mage has his sorcery, the old soldier his stone sword and the other two their faith in the Tusked God. Heboric . . . Heboric has nothing. And as for me, I have pocks and scars. So much for our possessions.

'The beast prepares . . .'

She glanced over at Baudin. *Oh yes, I forgot the thug. He has*

442

his secrets, for what that's worth, like as not scant little. 'Prepares what? Are you an expert in dragons as well?'

'Something's opening ahead – there's a change in the sky. See it?'

She did. The unrelieved grey pall had acquired a stain ahead, a smudge of brass that deepened, grew larger. *A word to the mage, I think—*

But even as she turned, the stain blossomed, filling half the sky. From somewhere far behind them came a howl of curdled outrage. Shadows sped across their path, tumbled to the sides as *Silanda*'s prow clove through them. The dragon crooked its wings, vanishing into a blazing inferno of bronze fire.

Spinning, Baudin wrapped Felisin in his huge arms and ducked down around her as the fire swept over the ship. She heard his hiss as the flames engulfed them.

The dragon's found a warren . . . to sear the fleas from its hide!

She flinched as the flames licked around Baudin's protective mass. She could smell him burning – the leather shirt, the skin of his back, his hair. Her gasps drew agony into her lungs.

Then Baudin was running, carrying her effortlessly in his arms, leaping down the companionway to the main deck. Voices were shouting. Felisin caught a glimpse of Heboric – his tattoos wreathed in black smoke – staggering, striking the port rail, then plummeting over the ship's side.

Silanda burned.

Still running, Baudin plunged past the mainmast. Kulp lunged into view and grasped the thug's arms as he tried to scream something the roaring fires swept away. But Baudin had become a thing mindless in its pain. His arm flung outward, and the mage was hurled back through the flames.

Bellowing, Baudin lurched on, a blind, hopeless flight to the sterncastle. The marines had vanished – either incinerated or dying somewhere below decks. Felisin did not struggle. Seeing that no escape was possible, she almost welcomed the bites of fire that now came with increasing frequency.

She simply watched as Baudin carried her over the stern rail.

They fell.

The breath was knocked from her lungs as they struck hard-packed sand. Still clutched in an embrace, they rolled down a steep slope and came to rest amidst a pile of water-smoothed cobbles. The bronze fire was gone.

Dust settling around them, Felisin stared up at bright sunlight. Somewhere near her head flies buzzed, the sound so natural that she trembled – as if desperately held defensive walls were crumbling within her. *We've returned. Home.* She knew it with instinctive certainty.

Baudin groaned. Slowly he pushed himself away, the cobbles sliding and grating beneath him.

She looked at him. The hair was gone from his head, leaving a flash-burned pate the colour of mottled bronze. His leather shirt was nothing but stitched strips hanging down his broad back like fragments of charred webbing. If anything, the skin of his back was darker and more mottled than that of his head. The bandages on his hand were gone as well, revealing swollen fingers and bruised joints. Incredibly, his skin was not cracked, not split open; instead, he had the appearance of having been gilded. *Tempered.*

Baudin rose, slowly, each move aching with precision. She saw him blink, draw a deep breath. His eyes widened as he looked down at himself.

Not what you were expecting. The pain fades – I see it in your face – now only a memory. You've survived, but somehow . . . it all feels different. It feels. You feel.

Can nothing kill you, Baudin?

He glanced at her, then frowned.

'We're alive,' she said.

She followed suit when he clambered upright. They stood in

444

a narrow arroyo, a gorge where flash floods had swept through with such force as to pack the bends of the channel with skull-sized rocks. The cut was less than five paces wide, the sides twice the height of a man and banded in variously coloured layers of sand.

The heat was fierce. Sweat ran in runnels down her back. 'Can you see anywhere we can climb out?' she asked.

'Can you smell Otataral?' Baudin muttered.

A chill wrapped her bones. *We're back on the island—* 'No. Can you?'

He shook his head. 'Can't smell a damned thing. Just a thought.'

'Not a nice one,' she snapped. 'Let's find a way out.' *You expect me to thank you for saving my life, don't you? You're waiting for even a single word, or maybe something as small as a look, a meeting of the eyes. You can wait for ever, thug.*

They worked their way along the choked channel, surrounded by a whirring cloud of flies and their own echoes.

'I'm . . . heavier,' Baudin said after a few minutes.

She paused, glanced back at him. 'What?'

He shrugged. 'Heavier.' He kneaded his own arm with his uninjured hand. 'More solid. I don't know. Something's changed.'

Something's changed. She stared at him, the emotions within her twisting around unvoiced fears.

'I could've sworn I was burning away to bones,' he said, his frown deepening.

'I haven't changed,' she said, turning and continuing on. She heard him follow a moment later.

They found a side channel, a cleft where torrents of water had rushed down to join the main channel's course, cutting through the layers of sandstone. This track quickly lost its depth, opening out after twenty or so paces. They emerged onto the edge of a range of blunt hills overlooking a broad valley of cracked earth. More hills, sharper and ragged, rose on the other side, blurry behind waves of heat.

Five hundred paces out on the pan stood a figure. At its feet lay a humped shape.

'Heboric,' Baudin said, squinting. 'The one standing.'

And the other one? Dead or alive? And who?

They walked side by side towards the ex-priest, who now watched them. His clothing too had burned away to little more than charred rags. Yet his flesh, beneath that skein of tattooing, was unmarred.

As they neared, Heboric gestured towards his own bald pate. 'Suits you, Baudin,' he said with a wry grin.

'What?' Felisin's tone was caustic. 'Are you two a brotherhood now?'

The figure at the old man's feet was the mage, Kulp. Her gaze fell to him. 'Dead.'

'Not quite,' Heboric said. 'He'll live, but he hit something going over the side.'

'Awaken him, then,' Felisin said. 'I don't plan on waiting in this heat just so he can get some beauty sleep. We're in a desert again, old man, in case you hadn't noticed. And desert means thirst, not to mention the fact that we're without food or anything like supplies. And finally, we've no idea where we are—'

'On the mainland,' Heboric said. 'Seven Cities.'

'How do you know that?'

The ex-priest shrugged. 'I know.'

Kulp groaned, then sat upright. One hand gingerly probing a lump above his left eye, the mage looked around. His expression soured.

'The Seventh Army's camped just over yonder,' Felisin said.

For a moment he looked credulous, then he gave a weary smile. 'Funny, lass.' He climbed to his feet and scanned the horizon on all sides before tilting his head back and sniffing the air. 'Mainland,' he pronounced.

'Why didn't all that white hair burn off?' Felisin asked. 'You're not even singed.'

'That dragon's warren,' Heboric said, 'what was it?'

'Damned if I know,' Kulp admitted, running a hand through the white shock on his head as if to confirm that it still existed. 'Chaos, maybe – a storm of it between warrens – I don't know. Never seen anything like it before, though that don't mean much – I'm no Ascendant, after all—'

'I'll say,' Felisin muttered.

The mage squinted at her. 'Those pocks on your face are fading.'

This time it was she who was startled.

Baudin grunted.

She whirled on him. 'What's so funny?'

'I saw that, only it don't make you any prettier.'

'Enough of this,' Heboric said. 'It's midday, meaning it'll get hotter before it gets cooler. We need somewhere to shelter.'

'Any sign of the marines?' Kulp asked.

'They're dead,' Felisin said. 'They went below decks, only the ship was on fire. Dead. Fewer mouths to feed.'

No-one replied to that.

Kulp took the lead, evidently choosing as their destination the far ridge of hills. The others followed without comment.

Twenty minutes later Kulp paused. 'We'd better pick up our pace. I smell a storm coming.'

Felisin snorted. 'All I smell is rank sweat – you're standing too close, Baudin, go away.'

'I'm sure he would if he could,' Heboric muttered, not unsympathetically. A moment later he looked up in surprise, as if he had not intended to voice aloud that thought. His toadlike face twisted in dismay.

Felisin waited to regain control of her breathing, then she swung to face the thug.

Baudin's small eyes were like dull coins, revealing nothing.

'Bodyguard,' Kulp said, with a slow nod. His voice was cold as he addressed Heboric. 'Out with it. I want to know who our companion is, and where his loyalties lie. I let it slide before, because Gesler and his soldiers were on hand. But not now. This girl has a bodyguard – why? Right now, I can't see anyone caring a whit for a cruel-hearted creature like this one, meaning this loyalty's been bought. Who is she, Heboric?'

The ex-priest grimaced. 'Tavore's sister, Mage.'

Kulp blinked. 'Tavore? The Adjunct? Then what in Hood's name was she doing in a mining pit?'

'She sent me there,' Felisin said. 'You're right – no loyalty involved. I was just one more in Unta's cull.'

Clearly shaken, the mage spun to Baudin. 'You're a Claw, aren't you?' The air around Kulp seemed to glitter – Felisin realized he'd opened his warren. The mage bared his teeth. 'The Adjunct's remorse, in the flesh.'

'Not a Claw,' Heboric said.

'Then what?'

'That'll take a history lesson to explain—'

'Start talking.'

'An old rivalry,' the ex-priest said. 'Dancer and Surly. Dancer created a covert arm for military campaigns. In keeping with the Imperial symbol of the demon hand gripping a sphere, he called them his Talons. Surly used that model in creating the Claw. The Talons were external – outside the Empire – but the Claw were internal, a secret police, a network of spies and assassins.'

'But the Claw are used in covert military operations,' Kulp said.

'They are now. When Surly became Regent in the absence of Kellanved and Dancer, she sent her Claws after the Talons. The betrayal started subtly – a string of disastrous botched missions – but someone got careless and gave the game away. The two locked daggers and fought it out to the bitter end.'

'And the Claw won.'

Heboric nodded. 'Surly becomes Laseen, Laseen becomes Empress. The Claws sit atop the pile of skulls like well-fed crows. The Talons went the way of Dancer. Dead and gone . . . or, as a few mused now and then, so far underground as to *seem* extinct.' The ex-priest grinned. 'Like Dancer himself, maybe.'

Felisin studied Baudin. *Talon. What's my sister got to do with some secret sect of revivalists still clinging to the memory of the Emperor and Dancer? Why not use a Claw? Unless she needed to work outside anyone else's knowledge.*

'It was too bitter to contemplate from the very start,' Heboric was saying. 'Throwing her younger sister into shackles like any other common victim. An example proclaiming her loyalty to the Empress—'

'Not just hers,' Felisin said. 'House Paran. Our brother's a renegade with Onearm on Genabackis. It made us . . . vulnerable.'

'It all went wrong,' Heboric said, staring at Baudin. 'She wasn't meant to stay long in Skullcup, was she?'

Baudin shook his head. 'Can't pull out a person who don't want to go.' He shrugged, as if those words were enough and he would say nothing more on that subject.

'So the Talons remain,' Heboric said. 'Then who commands you?'

'No-one,' Baudin answered. 'I was born into it. There's a handful left, kicking around here and there, either old or drooling or both. A few first sons inherited . . . the secret. Dancer's not dead. He ascended, alongside Kellanved – my father was there to see it, in Malaz City, the night of the Shadow Moon.'

Kulp snorted but Heboric was slowly nodding.

'I got close in my suppositions,' the ex-priest said. 'Too close for Laseen, as it turned out. She suspects or knows outright, doesn't she?'

Baudin shrugged. 'I'll ask next time we chat.'

'My need for a bodyguard is ended,' Felisin said. 'Get out of my sight, Baudin. Take my *sister's* concern through Hood's gates.'

'Lass—'

'Shut up, Heboric. I will try to kill you, Baudin. Every chance I get. You'll have to kill me to save your own skin. Go away. Now.'

The big man surprised her again. He made no appeal to the others, but simply turned away, taking a route at right angles to the one they had been travelling.

That's it. He's leaving. Out of my life, without a single word. She stared after him, wondering at the twisting in her heart.

'Damn you, Felisin,' the ex-priest snarled. 'We need him more than he needs us.'

Kulp spoke. 'I've a mind to join him and drag you with me, Heboric. Leave this foul witch to herself and Hood take her with my blessings.'

'Go ahead,' Felisin challenged.

The mage ignored her. 'I took on the responsibility of saving your skin, Heboric, and I'll stick to it because Duiker asked me. It's your call, now.'

The old man hugged himself. 'I owe her my life—'

'Thought you'd forgotten that,' Felisin sneered.

He shook his head.

Kulp sighed. 'All right. I suspect Baudin will do better without us, in any case. Let's get going before I melt, and maybe you can explain to me your comment about Dancer still being alive, Heboric? That's a very intriguing idea . . .'

Felisin shut their words away as she walked. *This changes nothing, dear sister. Your cherished agent murdered my lover, the only person in Skullcup who gave a damn about me. I was Baudin's assignment, nothing more, and worse, he was incompetent, a bumbling, thick-skulled fool. Carrying around his father's secret sigil*

– how pathetic! I will find you, Tavore. There, in my river of blood. That I promise—

'—sorcery.'

The word jarred her into awareness. She looked over at Kulp. The mage had quickened his step, his face pale.

'What did you say?' she asked.

'I said that storm rolling up behind us isn't natural, that's what I said.'

She glanced back. A bruised wall of sand cut the valley down its length – the hills she and Baudin had left earlier had vanished. The wall rolled towards them like a leviathan.

'Time to run, I think,' Heboric gasped at her side. 'If we can reach the hills—'

'I know where we are!' Kulp shouted. 'Raraku! That's the Whirlwind!'

Ahead, two hundred or more paces away, rose the ragged, rock-strewn slopes of the hills. Deep defiles cut between each hump, like the imprint of vast ribs.

The three of them ran, knowing that they would not make it in time. The wind that struck their back howled like a thing demented. A moment later, the sand engulfed them.

'The truth of it was, we were out hunting Sha'ik's corpse.'

Fiddler frowned at the Trell sitting opposite him. 'Corpse? She's dead? How? When?' *Was this your doing, Kalam? I can't believe it—*

'Iskaral Pust claims she was murdered by a troop of Red Blades from Ehrlitan. Or so the Deck whispered to him.'

'I had no idea the Deck of Dragons could be so precise.'

'As far as I know, it cannot.'

They were sitting on stone benches within a burial chamber at least two levels below the Shadow priest's favoured haunts. The benches were attached alongside a rough-hewn wall that had once held painted tiles, and the indents in the limestone beneath them made it clear that the benches were actually pedestals, meant to hold the dead.

Fiddler flexed his leg, reached down and kneaded his knuckles in the still-swollen flesh around the mended bone. *Elixirs, unguents . . . forced healing still hurts.* His emotions were dark – had been for days now as the High Priest of Shadow found one excuse after another for delaying their departure, the latest being the need for more supplies. In a strange way Iskaral Pust reminded the sapper of Quick Ben, the squad's mage. An endless succession of plans within plans. He imagined peeling through them one by one, right down to thumbprint schemes all awhirl in devious patterns. *It's quite possible that his very existence is nothing more than a collection of if-this and then-that suppositions. Hood's Abyss, maybe that's all we all are!*

The High Priest made his head spin. *As bad as Quick Ben and this Togg's thorn called Tremorlor. An Azath House, like the Deadhouse in Malaz City. But what are they, precisely? Does anyone know? Anyone at all?* There were nothing but rumours, obscure warnings, and few of those at that. Most people did their best to ignore such Houses – the denizens of Malaz City seemed to nurture an almost deliberate ignorance. *'Just an abandoned house,'* they say. *'Nothing special, except maybe a few spooks in the yard.' But there's a skittish look in the eyes of some of them.*

Tremorlor, a House of the Azath. *Sane people don't go looking for places like that.*

'Something on your mind, soldier?' Mappo Runt quietly asked. 'I've been watching such a progression of expressions on your face as to fill a wall in Dessembrae's temple.'

Dessembrae. The Cult of Dassem.

'It appears I've just said something unwelcome to your ears,' Mappo continued.

'Eventually a man reaches a point where every memory is

unwelcome,' Fiddler said, gritting his teeth. 'I think I've reached that point, Trell. I'm feeling old, used up. Pust has something in mind – we're part of some colossal scheme that'll likely see us dead before too long. Used to be I'd get a sniff or two of stuff like that. Had a nose for trouble, you might say. But I can't work it out – not this time. He's baffled me, plain and simple.'

'I think it's to do with Apsalar,' Mappo said after a time.

'Aye. And that worries me. A lot. She don't deserve any more grief.'

'Icarium pursues the question,' the Trell said, squinting down at the cracked, worn pavestones. The lantern's oil was getting low, deepening the chamber's gloom. 'I admit I have been wondering if the High Priest is intending to force Apsalar into a role she seems made for . . .'

'A role? Like what?'

'Sha'ik's prophecy speaks of a rebirth . . .'

The sapper paled, then vehemently shook his head. 'No. She wouldn't do it. This land's not hers, the goddess of the Whirlwind means nothing to her. Pust can try and force it all he wants, the lass will turn her back – mark my words.' Suddenly restless, Fiddler stood up and began pacing. His footfalls whispered with faint echoes in the chamber. 'If Sha'ik's dead, she's dead. Hood take any obscure prophecies! The Apocalypse will fizzle out, the Whirlwind sink back into the ground to sleep another thousand years or however long it is until the next Year of Dryjhna comes around . . .'

'Yet Pust seems to place much significance on this uprising,' Mappo said. 'It's far from over – or so he seems to believe.'

'How many gods and Ascendants are playing in this game, Trell?' Fiddler paused, eyeing the ancient warrior. 'Does she physically resemble Sha'ik?'

Mappo shrugged his massive shoulders. 'I saw the Whirlwind Seer but once, and that at a distance. Light-skinned for a Seven

Cities native. Dark eyes, not especially tall or imposing. It's said the power is – was – within her eyes. Dark and cruel.' He shrugged a second time. 'Older than Apsalar. Perhaps twice her years. Same black hair, though. Details are irrelevant in matters of faith and attendant prophecies, Fiddler. Perhaps only the role need be reborn.'

'The lass ain't interested in vengeance against the Malazan Empire,' the sapper growled, resuming his pacing.

'And what of the shadowy god who once possessed her?'

'Gone,' he snapped. 'Nothing but memories and blissfully few of those.'

'Yet daily she discovers more. True?'

Fiddler said nothing. If Crokus had been present, the walls would have been resounding with his anger – the lad had a fierce temper when it came to Apsalar. Crokus was young, not by nature cruel, but the sapper felt certain that the lad would kill Iskaral Pust without hesitation at the mere possibility of the High Priest seeking to use Apsalar. *And trying to kill Pust would probably prove suicidal.* Bearding a priest in his den was never a wise move.

The lass was finding her memories, it was true. And they weren't shocking her as much as Fiddler would have expected – *or hoped.* Another disturbing sign. Although he told Mappo that Apsalar would refuse such a role, the sapper had to admit – to himself at least – that he couldn't be so certain.

With memories came the remembrance of power. *And let's face it, there are few – in this world or any other – who'd turn their back on the promise of power.* Iskaral Pust would know that, and that knowledge would shape any offer he made. *Take on this role, lass, and you can topple an empire ...*

'Of course,' Mappo said, leaning back against the wall and sighing; 'we may be on entirely the wrong ...' He slowly sat forward again, brows knitting. '... trail.'

Fiddler's eyes narrowed on the Trell. 'What do you mean?'

'The Path of Hands. The convergence of Soletaken and D'ivers – Pust is involved.'

'Explain.'

Mappo pointed a blunt finger at the paving stones beneath them. 'At the lowest levels of this temple there lies a chamber. Its floor – flagstones – displays a series of carvings. Inscribing something like a Deck of Dragons. Neither Icarium nor I have seen anything like it before. If it is indeed a Deck, it's an Elder version. Not Houses, but Holds, the forces more elemental, more raw and primitive.'

'How does that relate to shapeshifting?'

'You can view the past as something like a mouldy old book. The closer you get to the beginning, the more fragmented are the pages. They veritably fall apart in your hands, and you're left with but a handful of words – most of them in a language you can't even understand.' Mappo closed his eyes for a long moment, then he looked up and said, 'Somewhere among those scattered words is recounted the creation of shapeshifters – the forces that are Soletaken and D'ivers are that old, Fiddler. They were old even in Elder times. No one species can claim propriety, and that includes the four Founding Races: Jaghut, Forkrul Assail, Imass and K'Chain Che'Malle.

'No shapeshifter can abide another – under normal circumstances, that is. There are exceptions but I need not go into them here. Yet, within them all, there is a hunger as deep in the bone as the bestial fever itself. The lure to *dominance*. To command all other shapeshifters, to fashion an army of such creatures – all slaved to your desire. From an army, an Empire. An Empire of ferocity unlike anything that has been seen before—'

Fiddler grunted. 'Are you implying that an Empire born of Soletaken and D'ivers would be inherently worse – more evil – than any other? I'm surprised, Trell. Nastiness grows like a cancer in any and every organization – human or otherwise, as you well know. And nastiness gets nastier. Whatever evil you let ride becomes commonplace, eventually. Problem is, it's easier to get used to it than carve it out.'

Mappo's answering smile was broken-hearted. 'Well said, Fiddler. When I said ferocity I meant a miasma of chaos. But I will grant you that terror thrives equally well in order.' He rolled his shoulders a third time, sat straighter to work out kinks in his back. 'The shapeshifters are gathering to the promise of a gate through which they can attain such Ascendancy. To become a god of the Soletaken and D'ivers – each shapeshifter seeks nothing less, and will abide no obstacle. Fiddler, we think the gate lies below, and we think that Iskaral Pust will do all he can to prevent the shapeshifters from finding it – even to painting false trails in the desert, to mimic the trail of handprints that all lead to the place of the gate.'

'And Pust has a role in mind for you and Icarium?'

'Likely,' Mappo conceded. His face was suddenly ashen. 'I believe he knows about us – about Icarium, that is. He *knows* . . .'

Knows what? Fiddler was tempted to ask, though he realized that the Trell would not willingly explain. The name Icarium was known – not widely, but known nonetheless. A Jaghut-blood wanderer around whom swirled, like the blackest wake, rumours of devastation, appalling murders, genocide. The sapper mentally shook his head. The Icarium he was coming to know made those rumours seem ludicrous. The Jhag was generous, compassionate. If horrors still trailed in his wake they must be ancient – youth was the time of excess, after all. This Icarium was too wise, too scarred, to tumble into power's river of blood. What did Pust hope would be unleashed by these two?

'Perhaps,' Fiddler said, 'you and Icarium are Pust's last line of defence. Should the Path converge here.' *Aye, preventing the shapeshifters from reaching the gate's a good thing, but the effort may prove fatal . . . or, it seems, something worse.*

'Possibly,' Mappo admitted glumly.

'Well, you could leave.'

The Trell looked up, smiled wryly. 'Icarium has his own quest, I'm afraid. Thus, we shall remain.'

Fiddler's eyes narrowed. 'You two would seek to prevent the gate from being used, wouldn't you? That's what Iskaral Pust knows, that's what he relies upon, isn't it? He's used your sense of duty and honour against you.'

'A powerful ploy. And given its efficacy, he might well use it again – with the three of you.'

Fiddler scowled. 'He'd be hard-pressed to find me that loyal about anything. While being a soldier relies on such things as duty and honour, it's also something that beats Hood out of both of them. As for Crokus, his loyalty is to Apsalar. And as for her . . .' He fell silent.

'Aye.' Mappo reached out and settled a hand on the sapper's shoulder. 'And so I can see the cause of your distress, Fiddler. And empathize.'

'You say you'll escort us to Tremorlor.'

'We shall. The journey will be fraught. Icarium has decided to guide you.'

'Then it truly exists.'

'I certainly hope so.'

'I think it's time we rejoined the others.'

'And recount for them our thoughts?'

'Hood's breath, no!'

The Trell nodded, pushing himself to his feet.

Fiddler hissed.

'What is it?' Mappo asked.

'The lantern's out. Has been for some time. We're in the dark, Trell.'

* * *

457

The temple was oppressive to Fiddler's mind. The squat, cyclopean walls leaned and sagged in the lower levels, as if buckling under the weight of the stone overhead. Dust sifted like water from the ceiling joins in places, leaving pyramids on the paving stones. He limped in Mappo's wake as they made their way to the spiral stairs that would take them back up to the others.

Half a dozen bhok'arala shadowed them on the way, each gripping leafy branches that they used to sweep and swat the stones as they scampered along. The sapper would have been more amused if the creatures had not achieved such perfection in their mimicry of Iskaral Pust and his obsession with spiders – right down to the fierce concentration on their round, wrinkled black faces.

Mappo had explained that the creatures worshipped the High Priest. Not like a dog its master, but like acolytes their god. Offerings, obscure symbols and fitful icons crowded their awkward rituals. Many of those rituals seemed to involve bodily wastes. *When you can't produce holy books, produce what you can, I suppose.* The creatures drove Iskaral Pust to distraction. He cursed them, and had taken to carrying rocks in a sack. He flung the missiles at the bhok'arala at every opportunity.

The winged creatures gathered those god-sent objects and clearly revered them – the High Priest had found the sack carefully refilled when he awoke this morning. Pust had flown into a spitting rage at the discovery.

Mappo nearly stumbled over a cache of torches on the way. Darkness was anathema to shadows. Pust wanted to encourage an escort of his god's minions. They lit one each, sardonically aware of their ulterior value. While Mappo could see well enough without their aid, Fiddler had been left groping, one hand clutching the Trell's chest harness.

They reached the staircase and paused. The bhok'arala held

back a dozen paces down the aisle, twittering among themselves in some obscure but vehement argument.

'Icarium has passed this way recently,' Mappo said.

'Does sorcery heighten your sensitivity?' Fiddler asked.

'Not precisely. More like centuries of companionship—'

'That which links you to him, you mean.'

The Trell grunted. 'Not one chain but a thousand, soldier.'

'Is your friendship such a burden, then?'

'Some burdens are willingly embraced.'

Fiddler was silent for a few breaths. 'It's said Icarium is obsessed with time, true?'

'Aye.'

'He builds bizarre constructs to measure it, places those constructs in locations all over the world.'

'His temporal maps, yes.'

'He feels he is nearing his goal, doesn't he? He's about to find his answer – the one you would do anything to prevent. Is that your vow, Mappo? To keep the Jhag ignorant?'

'Ignorant of the past, yes. His past.'

'That notion frightens me, Mappo. Without history there's no growth—'

'Aye.'

The sapper fell silent again. He'd run out of things he dared to say. *There's such pain in this giant warrior. Such sadness. Has Icarium never wondered? Never questioned this centuries-long partnership? And what is friendship to the Jhag? Without memory it's an illusion, an agreement taken on faith and faith alone. How on earth is Icarium's generosity born from that?*

They resumed their journey, climbing the saddle-backed stone steps. After a short pause, punctuated by what Fiddler was convinced was heated whispering, the bhok'arala fell silent and slipped into their wake once again.

Emerging onto the main level, Mappo and Fiddler were accosted with the harsh echo of a shouting voice, bouncing down the hallway from the altar chamber. The sapper grimaced. 'That would be Crokus.'

'Not in prayer, I take it.'

They found the young Daru thief at the extreme edge of his patience. He held Iskaral Pust by the front of his robe, pushed up against the wall behind the dusty altarstone. Pust's feet dangled ten inches above the flagstones, kicking feebly. Off to one side stood Apsalar, arms crossed, watching the scene without expression.

Fiddler stepped forward and laid a hand on the lad's shoulder. 'You're choking the life out of him, Crokus—'

'Precisely what he deserves, Fiddler!'

'I won't argue that, but in case you haven't noticed, there's shadows gathering.'

'He's right,' Apsalar said. 'Like I said before, Crokus. You're moments from Hood's Gates yourself.'

The Daru hesitated; then, with a snarl, he flung Pust away. The High Priest skidded along the wall, gasping, then straightened and began adjusting his robe. He spoke in a rasp. 'Precipitous youth! I am reminded of my own melodramatic gestures when I but toddled about in Aunt Tulla's yard. Bullying the chickens when they objected to the straw hats I had spent hours weaving. Incapable of appreciating the intricate plaits I devised. I was deeply offended.' He cocked his head, grinned up at Crokus. 'She'll look good in my new and improved straw hat—'

Fiddler intercepted Crokus's lunge and grappled with the lad. With Mappo's help he pulled him back as the High Priest scampered away, giggling.

The giggle broke into a fit of coughing that had Pust staggering about as if suddenly blinded. One groping hand found a wall, which he sagged against like a drunkard. The cough ended with a last hack, then he wiped his eyes and looked up.

Crokus growled, 'He wants Apsalar to—'

'We know,' Fiddler said. 'We worked that much out, lad. The point is, it's up to her, isn't it?'

Mappo glanced at him in surprise. The sapper shrugged. *Late in this wisdom, but I got there eventually.*

'I have been used by an Ascendant once,' Apsalar said. 'I'll not willingly be used again.'

'You are not to be used,' Iskaral Pust hissed, beginning a strange dance, 'you lead! You command! You impose your will! Dictate terms! Free to express every tantrum, enforce every whim, act like a spoiled child and be worshipped for it!' He ducked down suddenly, paused, then said in a whisper, 'Such lures as to entice! Self-examination is dispensed with at the beck and at the call of privileges unfettered! She wavers, she leans – see it in her eyes!'

'I do not,' Apsalar said coolly.

'She does! Such percipience in the lass as to sense my every thought – as if she could hear them aloud! The Rope's shadow remains within her, a linkage not to be denied! Gods, I am brilliant!'

With a disgusted snort Apsalar strode from the chamber.

Iskaral Pust scurried after her.

Fiddler held back the Daru's attempt to pursue. 'She can handle him, Crokus,' the sapper said. 'That should be plain – even to you.'

'There are more mysteries here than you imagine,' Mappo said, frowning after the High Priest.

They heard voices in the hall, then Icarium appeared at the entrance, wearing his deer-hide cloak with the dust of the desert on his dusky green skin. He saw the question in Mappo's eyes and shrugged. 'He's left the temple – I trailed him as far as the storm's edge.'

Fiddler asked, 'Who are you talking about?'

'Servant,' Mappo answered, his frown deepening. He

glanced at Crokus. 'We think he's Apsalar's father.'

The lad's eyes widened. 'Is he one-armed?'

'No,' Icarium replied. 'Iskaral Pust's servant is a fisherman, however. Indeed, his barque can be found in a lower chamber of this temple. He speaks Malazan—'

'Her father lost an arm at the siege of Li Heng,' Crokus said, shaking his head. 'He was among the rebels who held the walls, and had his arm burned off when the Imperial Army retook the city.'

'When a god intervenes . . .' Mappo said, then shrugged. 'One of his arms looks . . . young . . . younger than the other, Crokus. Servant was sent into hiding when we brought you back here. Pust was hiding him from you. Why?'

Icarium spoke. 'Was it not Shadowthrone who arranged the possession? When Cotillion took her, Shadowthrone may well have taken *him*. There is little point in trying to guess at motivations – the Lord of the Shadow Realm is notoriously obscure. Nonetheless, I see a certain logic in the possibility.'

Crokus had gone pale. His gaze snapped to the vacant entranceway. 'Leverage,' he whispered.

Fiddler instantly grasped the Daru's meaning. He turned to Icarium. 'You said Servant's trail led into the Whirlwind storm. Is there a particular place where Sha'ik is expected to be reborn?'

'The High Priest says her body has not been moved from where it fell at the hands of the Red Blades.'

'Within the storm?'

The Jhag nodded.

'He's telling her right now,' Crokus growled, his hands balling into fists, the knuckles whitening. ' "*Be reborn, and you shall be reunited with your father.*" '

' "A life given for a life taken," ' Mappo muttered. The Trell eyed the sapper. 'Are you mended well enough for a pursuit?'

Fiddler nodded. 'I can ride, walk . . . or crawl if it comes to that.'

'I shall prepare for our departure, then.'

In the small storage room where the gear and travel packs had been assembled, Mappo crouched down over his own sack. He rummaged amidst the bedrolls and canvas tent until his hands found the hard, hide-wrapped object he sought. The Trell pulled it forth and slipped the waxed elk hide away, revealing a solid long-bone half again the length of his forearm. The shaft was golden in lustre, polished by age. Leather cord was wrapped around the grip, enough for two hands. The distal end was ringed in similarly polished spike-shaped teeth – each the size of his thumb – set in an iron collar.

A hint of sage reached Mappo's nostrils. The sorcery within the weapon was still potent. The efforts of seven Trell witches was not a thing to fade with time. The long-bone had been found in a mountain stream. The mineral-rich water had made it hard as iron, and just as heavy. Other parts of the strange, unknown beast's skeleton had been recovered as well, though those had remained with the Clan as revered objects, each invested with power.

Only once had Mappo seen all the fragments laid out together, hinting at a beast twice the mass of a plains bear, the upper and lower jaws both sporting a row of fangs that roughly interlocked. The thigh bone – which he now held in his hands – had the shape of a bird's, yet impossibly huge and twice as thick as the hollow shaft it surrounded. Ridges appeared here and there along the shaft, where what must have been massive muscles were attached.

His hands trembled beneath the burden of the weapon.

Icarium spoke behind him. 'I do not recall you ever using that, friend.'

Unwilling as yet to turn to the Jhag, Mappo closed his eyes. 'No.' *You do not.*

'I am continually astonished,' Icarium went on, 'at just how much you manage to fit into that tattered sack.'

Another trick of the Clan witches – this small, private warren beyond the drawstrings. Should never have lasted this long. They said a month, maybe two. Not centuries. His gaze fell again to the weapon in his hands. *There was power in these bones to start with – the witches simply did some enhancements, spells of binding to keep the parts together and such. Perhaps the bone feeds the warren in the sack somehow . . . or the handful of irritating people I've stuffed inside in my own fits of ill temper. Wonder where they all went . . .* He sighed and rewrapped the weapon, returned it to the sack and cinched tight the drawstrings. Then he straightened, turning to offer Icarium a smile.

The Jhag had collected his own weapons. 'It seems our journey to find Tremorlor shall have to wait a while longer,' he said, shrugging. 'Apsalar has set off in pursuit of her father.'

'And thus will be led to the place where Sha'ik's body awaits.'

'We are to go after her,' Icarium said. 'Perhaps we can circumvent Iskaral Pust's intentions.'

'Not just Pust, it seems, but the Whirlwind goddess – who may well have shaped this from the very start.'

The Jhag frowned.

Mappo sighed again. 'Think on it, friend. Sha'ik was anointed as the Seeress of the Apocalypse almost as soon as she was born. Forty or more years in Raraku, preparing for this year . . . Raraku is not a kind place, and four decades will wear down even a chosen one. Perhaps preparation was all the Seeress was meant to achieve – the war itself requires new blood.'

'Yet did not the soldier say that Cotillion's relinquishing of the lass was forced upon him by the threat of Anomander Rake? The possession was meant to last much longer, taking the lass ever closer to the Empress herself . . .'

'So everyone assumes,' Mappo said. 'Iskaral Pust is a High Priest of Shadow. I think it best to assume that no matter how devious Pust is, Shadowthrone and Cotillion are more devious. By far. A truly possessed Apsalar would never get close to Laseen – the Claws would sniff it out, not to mention the Adjunct and her Otataral sword. But an Apsalar no longer possessed . . . well . . . and Cotillion's made sure she's not just a simple fishergirl any more, hasn't he?'

'A scheme within a scheme. Have you discussed this with Fiddler?'

Mappo shook his head. 'I may be wrong. It may be that the Rulers of Shadow simply saw an opportunity here, a means to take advantage of the convergence – the dagger is honed, then slipped in amidst the tumult. I have been wondering why Apsalar's memories are returning so swiftly . . . and so painlessly.'

'And we have no role in this?'

'That I do not know.'

'Apsalar becomes Sha'ik. Sha'ik defeats the Malazan armies, liberates the Seven Cities. Laseen, forced to take charge herself, arrives with an army to reconquer the unruly citizens of this land.'

'Armed with Cotillion's skill and knowledge, Sha'ik kills Laseen. End of Empire—'

'End?' Icarium's brows rose. 'More likely a new Emperor or Empress with Shadow the patron gods . . .'

Mappo grunted. 'A worrying thought.'

'Why?'

The Trell scowled. 'I had a sudden vision of Emperor Iskaral Pust . . .' He shook himself, lifted the sack and swung it over a shoulder. 'For the moment, I think it best we keep this conversation to ourselves, friend.'

Icarium nodded. He hesitated, then said, 'I have one question, Mappo.'

'Aye?'

'I feel closer to discovering . . . who I am . . . than ever before. Tremorlor is said to be time-aspected—'

'Aye, so it's said, though what that means is anyone's guess.'

'Answers, I believe. For me. For my life.'

'What do you ask, Icarium?'

'Should I discover my past, Mappo, how will that change me?'

'You are asking me? Why?'

Icarium's gaze was half-lidded as he smiled at Mappo. 'Because, friend, within you reside my memories – none of which you are prepared to reveal.'

And so we come to this point . . . again. 'Who you are, Icarium, is not dependent on me, nor on my memories. What value would it be to seek to become my version of you? I accompany you, friend, in your quest. If the truth – if *your* truth – is to be found, then you shall find it.'

Icarium was nodding, past echoes of this conversation returning to him – *but little else, by the Ancients, little else, please* – 'Yet something tells me that you, Mappo, are a part of that hidden truth.'

Ice filled the Trell's heart. *He's not taken it that far before – is Tremorlor's proximity nudging open the locked gate?* 'Then, when the time comes, you shall face a decision.'

'I think I shall.'

They studied each other, their eyes searching the altered reflection before them, one set plagued with innocent questing, the other disguising devastating knowledge. *And between us, hanging in the balance, a friendship neither understands.*

Icarium reached out and clasped Mappo's shoulder. 'We should join the others.'

Fiddler sat astride the Gral gelding as they waited at the base of the cliff. Bhok'arala scampered along the temple face, squealing and barking as they struggled with the lowering of the mule packs and assorted supplies. One had got its tail snagged in the rope and screamed pitifully as it slowly descended with the gear. Iskaral Pust hung half out of the tower window, throwing rocks at the hapless creature – none of which came close.

The sapper eyed Mappo and Icarium, sensing a new tension between them, though they continued to work together with familiar ease. The tension was in the words unspoken between the two, Fiddler suspected. *Changes are coming to us all, it seems.* He glanced over at Crokus, who sat rigid with barely restrained impatience on the spare mount he had inherited. He'd caught the lad running through a gamut of close-in knife-fighting moves a short while earlier. The few times the sapper had seen him use the knives before there'd been a kind of desperation marring his technique. Crokus had some skill but he lacked maturity – he was too conscious of himself behind the blades. That had changed, Fiddler realized as he watched the lad go through his routine. Taking cuts was essential to delivering killing thrusts. Knife-fighting was a messy business. Cold determination backed Crokus now – he would do more than just hold his own from now on, the sapper knew. Nor would he be so quick to throw his knives, unless he had plenty of spares tucked within easy reach in the folds of his telaba. *Now more likely, I'd hazard.*

The late-afternoon sky was hazy ochre, filled with the suspended residue of the Whirlwind, which still raged in the heart of Raraku no more than ten leagues distant. The heat was made even more oppressive by that suffocating cloak.

Mappo freed the snared bhok'aral, earning a nasty bite on the wrist for his kindness. The creature half scampered, half flew back up the cliff face, voicing an abusive torrent as it went.

Fiddler called out to the Trell. 'Set us a pace, then!'

Mappo nodded and he and Icarium set off down the trail.

The sapper was glad he was the only one to glance back to see a score of bhok'arala on the cliff face waving farewell, with Iskaral Pust almost falling from the window in his efforts to sweep the nearest creatures from the tower's stone wall with his broom.

The renegade Korbolo Dom's army of the Apocalypse was spread over the rumpled carpet of grassy hills that marked the south edge of the plain. On each hilltop stood command tents and the raised banners of various tribes and self-proclaimed battalions. Between small towns of tents and wagons roamed vast herds of cattle and horses.

The encampment's pickets were marked by three ragged rows of crucified prisoners. Kites and rhizan and capemoths swarmed around each victim.

The outermost line rose above the earthworks and trench less than fifty paces away from Kalam's position. He lay flat in the high yellow grasses, the heat of the parched ground rising up around him with a smell of dust and sage. Insects crawled over him, their prickling feet tracking aimless paths across his hands and forearms. The assassin ignored them, his eyes on the nearest of the crucified victims.

A young Malazan lad of no more than twelve or thirteen. Capemoths rode his arms from shoulder to wrist, making them look like wings. Rhizan gathered in writhing clumps at his hands and feet, where the spikes had been driven through bones and flesh. The boy had no eyes, no nose – his face was a ravaged wound – yet he still lived.

The image was etching itself into Kalam's heart like acid into bronze. His limbs felt cold, as if his own claim to life was withdrawing, pooling in his gut. *I cannot save him. I cannot even kill him in swift mercy. Not this lad, not a single one of these hundreds of Malazans surrounding this army. I can do nothing.*

The knowledge was a whisper of madness. The assassin feared but one thing that left him skeined with terror: *helplessness*. But not the helplessness of being a prisoner, or of undergoing torture – he'd been victim to both, and he well knew that torture could break anyone – anyone at all. *But this . . .* Kalam feared insignificance, he feared the inability to produce an effect, to force a change upon the world beyond his flesh.

It was this knowledge that the scene before him was searing into his soul. *I can do nothing. Nothing.* He stared across the intervening fifty paces into the young man's sightless sockets, the distance between diminishing with every breath, until he felt close enough to brush his lips against the boy's sun-cracked forehead. To whisper lies – *your death won't be forgotten, the truth of your precious life which you still refuse to surrender because it's all you have. You are not alone, child* – lies. The lad was alone. Alone with his withering, collapsing life. And when the body became a corpse, when it rotted and fell away to join all those others ringing a place that had once held an army, he would be forgotten. Another faceless victim. One in a number that beggared comprehension.

The Empire would exact revenge – if it was able – and the numbers would grow. The Imperial threat was ever thus: *The destruction you wreak upon us and our kind, we deliver back to you tenfold.* If Kalam succeeded in killing Laseen, then perhaps he would also succeed in guiding to the throne someone with spine enough to avoid ruling from a position of crisis. The assassin and Quick Ben had someone in mind for that. *If all goes as planned.* But for these, it was too late.

He let out a slow breath, only now realizing he was lying on an ants' nest and its inhabitants were telling him to leave in no uncertain terms. *I lie with the weight of a god on their world, and these ants don't like it. We're so much more alike than most would think.*

Kalam edged back through the grasses. *Not the first scene of horror I've witnessed, after all. A soldier learns to wear every kind of armour, and so long as he stays in the trade, it works well enough. Gods, I don't think my sanity would survive peace!*

With that chilling thought seeping like weakness into his limbs, Kalam reached the back slope, out of the victims' line of sight. He scanned the area, seeking sign of Apt's presence, but the demon seemed to have vanished. After a moment he rose into a crouch and padded back to the aspen grove where the others waited.

Minala rose from cover as he approached the low brush encircling the silver-leafed trees, crossbow in her hands.

Kalam shook his head. In silence they both slipped between the spindly boles and rejoined the group.

Keneb had succumbed to yet another bout of fever. His wife, Selv, hovered over him in tight-lipped fear that seemed on the edge of panic, holding a water-soaked cloth to Keneb's forehead and murmuring in an effort to still his thrashing and twitching. The children, Vaneb and Kesen, stood nearby, studiously attending to their horses.

'How bad is it?' Minala asked, carefully uncocking the crossbow.

Kalam was preoccupied with plucking and brushing ants from his body for a moment, then he sighed. 'We'll not get around them. I saw standards from the west tribes – those camps are still growing, meaning the Odhan to the west won't be empty. Eastward we'd run into villages and towns, all liberated and occupied by garrisons. That whole horizon is nothing but smoke.'

'If it was just you you'd get through,' Minala said, reaching up to brush her black hair from her face. Her light-grey eyes held hard on him. 'Just another soldier of the Apocalypse, it would be a simple task to take picket duty on the south edge, then slip away one night.'

Kalam grunted. 'Not as easy as you think. There're mages in

that encampment.' *And I've held the Book in my hands – not likely I'd stay anonymous—*

'What difference would that make?' Minala asked. 'Maybe you've got a reputation, but you're no Ascendant.'

The assassin shrugged. He straightened, retrieved his pack, set it down and began rummaging through its contents.

'You haven't answered me, Corporal,' Minala continued, watching him. 'Why all this self-importance? You're not the type to delude yourself, so you must be holding something back from us. Some other . . . *significant* detail about yourself.'

'Sorcery,' Kalam muttered, pulling free a small object from the pack. 'Not mine. Quick Ben's.' He held up the object and quirked a wry grin.

'A rock.'

'Aye. Granted, it'd be more dramatic if it was a faceted gem or a torc of gold. But there's not a mage in this world stupid enough to invest power in a valuable object. After all, who'd steal a rock?'

'I've heard legends otherwise—'

'Oh, you'll find magic embedded in jewels and such – sorcerers make up dozens of them, all cursed in some way or other. Most of them are a kind of magical spying device – the sorcerer can track them, sometimes even see through them. Claws use that intelligence-gathering method all the time.' He tossed the rock in the air, caught it, then suddenly sobered. 'This was intended to be used as a last resort . . .' *In the palace at Unta, actually.*

'What does it do?'

The assassin grimaced. *I haven't a clue. Quick Ben's not the expansive type, the bastard.* 'It's your shaved knuckle in the hole, Kalam. With this you can stride right into the throne room. I guarantee it.' He glanced around, saw a low, flat rock nearby. 'Get everyone ready to move.'

The assassin crouched down before the flat rock, set the

stone on it, then found a fist-sized cobble. He hefted it thoughtfully before bringing it crashing down on the stone.

He was shocked as it splattered like wet clay.

Darkness swept over them. Kalam looked up, slowly straightened. *Damn, I should've guessed.*

'Where are we?' Selv demanded in a high, taut voice. 'Mother!'

The assassin turned to see Kesen and Vaneb stumbling in knee-deep ash. Ash that was filled with charred bones. The horses were shying, tossing their heads as grey dust rose like smoke.

Hood's breath, we're in the Imperial Warren! Kalam found himself standing on a broad, raised disc of grey basalt. Sky merged with land in a formless, colourless haze. *I could wring your neck, Quick Ben!* The assassin had heard rumours that such a warren had been created and the description matched, but the tales he'd picked up on Genabackis suggested that it was barely nascent, extending no more than a few hundred leagues – *if leagues mean much here* – in a ring around Unta. *Instead, it reaches all the way into Seven Cities. And Genabackis? Why not? Quick Ben, there could be a Claw riding your shoulder right now . . .*

The children had settled their horses and were now in the saddles, well away from the grisly scorched mound. Kalam glanced over to see Minala and Selv tying Keneb onto his saddle.

The assassin approached his own stallion. The beast snorted disdainfully as he swung himself up and gathered the reins.

'We're in a warren, aren't we?' Minala asked. 'I'd always believed all those tales of other realms were nothing but elaborate inventions wizards and priests used to prop up all the fumbling around they did.'

Kalam grunted. He'd been run through enough warrens and plunged into enough chaotic maelstroms of sorcery to take it for granted. Minala had just reminded him that for most people such a reality was remote, viewed with scepticism if acknowl-edged at all. *Is such ignorance a comfort or a source of blind fear?*

'I take it we're safe from Korbolo Dom here?'

'I certainly hope so,' the assassin muttered.

'How do we select a direction? There're no landmarks, no trail . . .'

'Quick Ben says you travel with an intention in mind and the warren will take you there.'

'And the destination you have in mind?'

Kalam scowled, was silent for a long moment. Then he sighed. 'Aren.'

'How safe are we?'

Safe? We've stepped into a hornets' nest. 'We'll see.'

'Oh, that's a comfort!' Minala snapped.

The image of the crucified Malazan boy rose once again in the assassin's thoughts. He glanced over at Keneb's children. 'Better this risk than a . . . different certainty,' he muttered.

'Are you going to explain that comment?'

Kalam shook his head. 'Enough talk. I've a city to visualize . . .'

Lostara Yil walked her mount up to the gaping hole, under-standing at once that, although she had never seen one before, this was a portalway into another warren. Its edges had begun fading, like a wound closing.

She hesitated. The assassin had chosen a short-cut, a means of slipping past the traitor's army between him and Aren. The Red Blade knew she had no choice but to follow, for the trail would prove far too cold should she manage the long way to Aren. Even getting through Korbolo Dom's forces would likely prove impossible – as a Red Blade she was bound to be recog-nized, even wearing unmarked armour as she did now.

Still, Lostara Yil hesitated.

Her horse reared back squealing as a figure staggered from

the portalway. A man, grey-clothed, grey-skinned – even his hair was grey – straightened before her, glanced around with strangely luminous eyes, then smiled.

'Not a hole I expected to fall through,' he said in lilting Malazan. 'My apologies if I startled you.' He sketched a bow, the gesture resulting in clouds of dust cascading from him. The grey was ash, Lostara realized. Dark skin revealed itself in patches on the man's lean face.

He eyed her knowingly. 'You carry an aspected sigil. Hidden.'

'What?' Her hand drifted towards her sword hilt.

The man caught the motion, his smile broadening. 'You are a Red Blade, an officer in fact. Which makes us allies.'

Her eyes narrowed. 'Who are you?'

'Call me Pearl. Now, it seems you were about to enter the Imperial Warren. I suggest we do so before continuing our conversation – before the portalway closes.'

'Can you not keep it open, Pearl? After all, you were travelling it . . .'

The man's exaggerated frown was mocking. 'Alas, this is a door where no door should be possible. Granted, north of here even the Imperial Warren is fraught with . . . unwelcome intruders . . . but their means of entry is far more . . . primitive, shall we say . . . in nature. So, since this portalway is clearly not of your making, I suggest we take immediate advantage of its presence.'

'Not until I know who you are, Pearl. Rather, *what* you are.'

'I am a Claw, of course. Who else is granted the privilege of travelling the Imperial Warren?'

She nodded at the portalway. 'Someone's just granted that privilege to himself.'

Pearl's eyes sparkled. 'And this is what you shall tell me about, Red Blade.'

She sat in silence, thinking, then nodded. 'Yes. Ideal. I shall accompany you.'

Pearl took a step backward and beckoned with one gloved hand.

Lostara Yil tapped heels to her mount's flanks.

Quick Ben's shaved knuckle in the hole was slower in closing than anyone had anticipated. Seven hours after the Red Blade and the Claw had vanished within the Imperial Warren, stars glittered in the moonless sky overhead, and still the portalway gaped, its red-lined edges fading to dull magenta.

Sounds drifted into the glade, echoes of panic and alarm in Korbolo Dom's encampment. Parties of riders set out in all directions, bearing torches. Mages risked their warrens, seeking trails through the now perilous pathways of sorcery.

Thirteen hundred Malazan children had vanished, the liberation unseen by the pickets or the mounted patrols. The X-shaped wooden crosses were bare, with only stains of blood, urine and excrement to show that living beings had once hung from them in agony.

In the darkness the plain was strangely alive with shadows, flowing sourcelessly over the motionless grasses.

Apt strode silently into the glade, her daggerlike fangs gleaming their natural grin. Sweat glistened on her black hide, the thick spiny bristles of her hair wet with dew. She stood erect, her single forelimb clutching the limp body of a young boy. Blood dripped from his hands and feet, and his face had been horribly chewed and pecked, leaving him eyeless and with a gaping red hole where his nose had been. Faint breaths from fevered, shallow lungs showed in misty plumes that drifted forlornly in the clearing.

The demon squatted down on her haunches and waited.

Shadows gathered, pouring like liquid between the trees to hover before the portalway.

Apt cocked her head and spread wide her mouth in something like a canine yawn.

A vague shape took form within the shadows. The glowing eyes of guardian Hounds appeared to flank the figure.

'I thought I had lost you,' Shadowthrone whispered to the demon. 'Snared so long by Sha'ik and her doomed goddess. Yet this night you return, not alone – oh no, not alone, aptorian. You've grown ambitious since you were but a Demon Lord's concubine. Tell me, my dear, what am I to do with over a thousand dying mortals?'

The Hounds were eyeing Apt as if the demon was a potential meal.

'Am I a cutter? A healer?' Shadowthrone's voice was rising, octave by octave. 'Is Cotillion a kindly uncle? Are my Hounds farmyard skulkers and orphans' puppies?' The shadow that was the god flared wildly. 'Have you gone entirely insane?'

Apt spoke in a rapid, rasping series of clicks and hisses.

'Of course Kalam wanted to save them!' Shadowthrone shrieked. 'But *he* knew it was impossible! Only *vengeance* was possible! But now! Now I must exhaust my powers healing a thousand maimed children! And for what?'

Apt spoke again.

'Servants? And precisely how *big* do you think Shadow Keep is, you one-armed imbecile!'

The demon said nothing, her slate-grey multifaceted eye glimmering in the starlight.

Shadowthrone hunched suddenly, his gauzelike cloak wrapping close as he hugged himself. 'An army of servants,' he whispered. '*Servants*. Abandoned by the Empire, left to their fates at the hand of Sha'ik's bloodlusted bandits. There will be . . . ambivalence . . . in their scarred, malleable souls . . .' The god glanced up at the demon. 'I see long-term benefits in your precipitous act, demon. Lucky for you!'

Apt hissed and clicked.

'You wish to claim for your own the one in your clutches? And – if indeed you are to resume your guardianship of the

Bridgeburner assassin – how precisely will you co-ordinate such conflicting responsibilities?'

The demon replied.

Shadowthrone spluttered. 'Such nerve, you coddled bitch! No wonder you fell from the Aptorian Lord's favour!' He fell silent, then, after a moment, flowed forward. 'Forced healing demands a price,' Shadowthrone murmured. 'The flesh recovers while the mind writhes with the memory of pain, that bludgeon of helplessness.' He raised a sleeve-shrouded hand to the boy's forehead. 'This child who shall ride you shall be . . . unpredictable.' He hissed a laugh as the wounds began closing, as new flesh formed on the boy's ravaged face. 'What manner of eyes do you wish him to have, my dear?'

Apt answered.

Shadowthrone seemed to flinch, then he laughed again, harsh and cold this time. ' "The eyes are love's prism," are they now? Will you go hand in hand to the fishmonger's on Market Day, my dear?'

The boy's head jerked back, bones altering shape, the twin gaping orbits merging to form a single larger one above a nose bridge that branched to either side, then ran up the outer edge of the socket in a thin, raised ridge. An eye to match the demon's blurred into existence.

Shadowthrone stepped back to examine his handiwork. 'Aai,' he whispered. 'Who then is it who now looks upon me through such a prism? Abyss Below, answer not!' The god spun abruptly to stare at the portalway. 'Cunning Quick Ben – I know his handiwork. He could have gone far under my patronage . . .'

The Malazan boy clambered to sit behind Apt's narrow, jutting shoulder blade. His frail body shook with the trauma of forced healing, and an eternity nailed to a cross, but his ghastly face showed a slightly ironic smile in a line that perfectly matched the demon's.

Apt approached the portalway.

Shadowthrone gestured. 'Go on then, trail the ones trailing the Bridgeburner. Whiskeyjack's soldiers were ever loyal, I seem to recall. Kalam does not intend to kiss Laseen's cheeks when he finds her, of that I'm certain.'

Apt hesitated, then spoke one last time.

A grimace entered the god's tone as he replied. 'That High Priest of mine alarms even me. If he cannot deceive the hunters on the Path of Hands, my precious realm – which has seen more than its share of intruders of late – will become very crowded indeed . . .' Shadowthrone wagged his head. 'It was a simple task, after all.' He began to drift away, his Hounds following suit. 'Can anyone find reliable, competent help these days, I wonder . . .'

A moment later Apt was alone, the shadows slipping away.

The portalway had begun to weaken, slowly closing the wound between the realms. The demon rasped words of comfort. The boy nodded.

They slid into the Imperial Warren.

CHAPTER TWELVE

> Ages unveiled the Holy Desert.
> Raraku was once an ochre sea.
> She stood in the wind
> on the pride of a spire
> and saw ancient fleets –
> ships of bone, sails of bleached
> hair, charging the crest
> to where the waters slipped
> beneath the sands
> of the desert to come.
>
> *The Holy Desert*
> Anonymous

A line of feral white goats stood on the crest of the tel known as Samon, silhouetted against a startlingly blue sky. Like bestial gods carved from marble, they watched as the vast train wound through the valley swathed in a massive cloud of dust. That they numbered seven was an omen not lost on Duiker as he rode with the south flanking patrol of Foolish Dog Wickans.

Nine hundred paces behind the historian marched five companies of the Seventh, slightly under a thousand soldiers, while the same distance behind them rode another patrol of two hundred and fifty Wickans. The three units comprised the

479

south-facing guard for the now close to fifty thousand refugees, as well as livestock, that made up the main column, and were mirrored with similar forces on the north side. An inner ring of loyal Hissari Infantry and Marines were spread out along the column's edges – walking alongside the hapless civilians.

A rearguard of a thousand Wickans from each of the clans rode in the train's dust over two-thirds of a league east of Duiker's position. Though split and riding in troops of a dozen or less, their task was impossible. Tithansi raiders nipped at the battered tail of the refugee column, snaring the Wickans in an eternal running skirmish. The back end of Coltaine's train was a bleeding wound never allowed to heal.

The vanguard to the refugees consisted of the surviving elements of the Seventh's attachment of medium-equipped cavalry – slightly more than two hundred riders in all. Before them rode the Malazan nobles in their carriages and wagons, flanked on either side by ten companies of the 7th Infantry. Close to a thousand additional soldiers of the Seventh – the walking wounded – provided the nobles with their own vanguard, while ahead of them rolled the wagons bearing the cutters and their more seriously injured charges. Coltaine and a thousand riders of his Crow Clan spearheaded the entire column.

But there were too many refugees and too few able combatants, and for all the Malazan efforts, Kamist Reloe's raiding parties struck like vipers in brilliantly co-ordinated mayhem. A new commander had come to Reloe's army of the Apocalypse, a nameless Tithansi warleader charged with harrying the train day and night as it crawled painfully westward – a bloodied and battered serpent that refused to die – and this warrior now posed the most serious threat to Coltaine.

A slow, calculated slaughter. We're being toyed with. The endless dust had scratched the historian's throat raw, making every swallow agony. They were running perilously low on water, the

W H O ARE YOU?

(We'd like to know)

Tell us about yourself and you could win a free limited edition Steven Erikson T-shirt

I am: male ☐   female ☐

under 18 ☐   18-24 ☐   25-34 ☐
35-44 ☐   45-54 ☐   55+ ☐

My other favourite writers are: ....
....

My favourite newspapers are: ....

My favourite magazines are: ....

My favourite websites are: ....
....

I buy most of my books at: ....

What made you buy this book? Please tick any that apply:

Recommended by a friend ☐   Received as a present ☐
Saw an advertisement ☐   Read a review ☐
Already a Steven Erikson fan ☐   Impulse purchase ☐
Other (please specify) .... ☐

Thanks for taking the time to fill in this card.

The first 15 people to respond will receive a free limited edition
Steven Erikson T-shirt – high quality, collectors' items for the future!

Name: ....
Address: ....
....
.... Postcode: ....
Email: ....

If you do not want to receive further information from the Bertelsmann Group, please tick here ☐
(Your details will not be forwarded to any other companies)

STEVEN ERIKSON READER RESPONSE

FREEPOST PAM 2876

TRANSWORLD PUBLISHERS

61-63 UXBRIDGE ROAD

LONDON W5 5BR

memories of Sekala River now a parched yearning. The nightly slaughter of cattle, sheep, pigs and goats had intensified, as animals were released from suffering, then butchered to flavour the vast cauldrons of blood-stew, marrow and oats that had become everyone's main sustenance. Each night the encampment became an abattoir of screaming beasts, the air alive with rhizan and capemoths drawn to the killing stations. The cacophonous uproar and chaos each dusk had scraped Duiker's nerves raw – and he was not alone in that. Madness haunted their days, stalking them as relentlessly as Kamist Reloe and his vast army.

Corporal List rode alongside the historian in numbed silence, his head dropped low on his chest, his shoulders slumped. He seemed to be ageing before Duiker's eyes.

Their world had dwindled. *We totter on edges seen and unseen. We are reduced, yet defiant. We've lost the meaning of time. Endless motion broken only by its dulled absence – the shock of rest, of those horns sounding an end to the day's plodding. For that moment, as the dust swirls on, no-one moves. Standing in disbelief that another day has passed, and yet still we live.*

He'd walked the refugee camp at night, wandering between the ragged rows of tents, lean-tos and canopied wagons, his eyes taking in all that he saw with perverse detachment. *The historian, now witness, stumbling in the illusion that he will survive. Long enough to set the details down on parchment in the frail belief that truth is a worthwhile cause. That the tale will become a lesson heeded. Frail belief? Outright lie, a delusion of the worst sort. The lesson of history is that no-one learns.*

Children were dying. He'd crouched, one hand on a mother's shoulder, and watched with her as life ebbed from the baby in her arms. *Like the light of an oil lamp, dimming, dimming, winking out. The moment when the struggle's already lost, surrendered, and the tiny heart slows in its own realization, then stops in mute wonder. And never stirs again.* It was then that pain filled the vast caverns within the living, destroying all it touched with its rage at inequity.

No match for the mother's tears, he'd moved on. Wandering, smeared in dirt, sweat and blood, he was becoming a spectral presence, a self-proclaimed pariah. He'd stopped attending Coltaine's nightly sessions, despite direct orders to the contrary. Accompanied only by List, he rode with the Wickans, to the flanks and to the rear, he marched with the Seventh, with the Hissari Loyals, the Marines, the sappers, the nobles and the mud-bloods – as the lowborn refugees had taken to calling themselves.

Through it all he said little, his presence becoming commonplace enough to permit a relaxation among the people around him. No matter what the depredations, there always seemed energy enough to expend in opinions.

Coltaine's a demon in truth, Laseen's dark joke on us all. He's in league with Kamist Reloe and Sha'ik – this uprising is naught but an elaborate charade since Hood's come to embrace the realm of humans. We've bowed to our skull-faced patron, and in return for all this spilled blood Coltaine, Sha'ik and Laseen will all ascend to stand alongside the Shrouded One.

Hood reveals himself in the flight of these capemoths – he shows his face again and again, greeting each dusk with a hungry grin in the dimming sky.

The Wickans have made a pact with the earth spirits. We're here to make fertile soil—

You've taken the wrong path with that, friend. We're sport for the Whirlwind goddess, nothing more. We are a lesson drawn long in the telling.

The Council of Nobles are eating children.

Where did you hear that?

Someone stumbled onto a grisly feast last night. The Council's petitioned dark Elder gods in order to stay fat—

To what?

482

Fat, I said. Truth. And now bestial spirits wander the camp at night, collecting children dead or near enough to dead to make no difference, except those ones are juicier.

You've gone mad—

He may have something there, friend! I myself saw picked and gnawed bones this morning, all in a heap – no skulls but the bones looked human enough, only very small. Wouldn't you do for a roasted baby right now, eh? Instead of the half-cup of brown sludge we're getting these days?

I heard Aren's army is only days away, led by Pormqual himself. He's got a legion of demons with him, too—

Sha'ik's dead – you heard the Semk wailing into the night, didn't you? And now they wear greased ash like a second skin. Someone in the Seventh told me he came face to face with one at last night's ambush – the scrap at the dried-up waterhole. Said the Semk's eyes were black pits, dull as dusty stones, they were. Even when the soldier spitted the bastard on his sword, nothing showed in those eyes. I tell you, Sha'ik's dead.

Ubaryd's been liberated. We're going to swing south any day now – you'll see – it's the only thing that makes sense. There's nothing west of here. Nothing at all—

Nothing at all . . .

'Historian!'

That harsh Falari-accented shout came from the dust-covered rider angling his mount alongside Duiker. Captain Lull, Cartheron Wing, his long, red hair hanging in greasy strands from under his helmet. The historian blinked at him.

The grizzled soldier grinned. 'Word is, you've lost your way, old man.'

Duiker shook his head. 'I follow the train,' he said woodenly, wiping at the grit that stung his eyes.

'We've got a Tithansi warleader out there needs to be found, hunted down,' Lull said, eyes narrow on the historian. 'Sormo and Bult have volunteered some names for the task.'

'I shall dutifully record them in my List of the Fallen.'

The breath hissed between the captain's teeth. 'Abyss Below, old man, they ain't dead yet – we ain't dead yet, dammit! Anyway, I'm here to inform you that you've volunteered. We head out tonight, tenth bell. Gathering at Nil's hearth by the ninth.'

'I decline the offer,' Duiker said.

Lull's grin returned. 'Request denied, and I'm to stay at your side so you don't slip away as you're wont to do.'

'Hood take you, bastard!'

'Aye, soon enough.'

Nine days to the River P'atha. We stretch to meet each minor goal, there's a genius in this. Coltaine offers the marginally possible to fool us into achieving the impossible. All the way to Aren. But for all his ambition, we shall fail. Fail in the flesh and the bone. 'We kill the warleader, another will step into his place,' Duiker said after a time.

'Probably not as talented nor as brave as the task demands. A part of him will know: if his efforts are mediocre, we're likely to let him live. If he shows us brilliance, we'll kill him.'

Ah, that rings of Coltaine. His well-aimed arrows of fear and uncertainty. He's yet to miss the mark. So long as he does not fail, he cannot fail. The day he slips up, shows imperfection, is the day our heads will roll. Nine days to fresh water. Kill the Tithansi warleader and we'll get there. Make them reel with every victory, let them draw breath with every loss – Coltaine trains them as he would beasts, and they don't even realize it.

Captain Lull leaned over the saddlehorn. 'Corporal List, you awake?'

The young man's head swung up and turned from side to side.

'Damn you, Historian,' Lull growled. 'The lad's fevered from lack of water.'

Looking at the corporal, Duiker saw the high colour beneath the dust streaks on List's drawn cheeks, his all too bright eyes. 'He wasn't like that this morning—'

'Eleven hours ago!'

Eleven?

The captain twisted his horse away, his shouts for a healer breaking through the incessant rumble of hooves, wagon wheels and countless footfalls which made up the train's unceasing roar.

Eleven?

Animals shifted position in the clouds of dust. Lull returned, alongside him Nether, the girl looking tiny atop the huge, muscular roan she rode. The captain collected the reins of List's horse and passed them over to Nether. Duiker watched the Wickan child lead the corporal away.

'I'm tempted to have her attend to you afterward,' Lull said. 'Hood's breath, man – when did you last take a sip of water?'

'What water?'

'We've casks left for the soldiers. You take a skin every morning, Historian, up where the wagons carrying the wounded are positioned. Each dusk you bring the skin back.'

'There's water in the stew, isn't there?'

'Milk and blood.'

'If there are casks left for the soldiers, what of everyone else?'

'Whatever they managed to carry with them from the Sekala River,' Lull said. 'We'll protect them, aye, but we'll not mother them. Water's become the currency, I hear, and the trading's fierce.'

'Children are dying.'

Lull nodded. 'That's a succinct summary of humankind, I'd say. Who needs tomes and volumes of history? Children are dying. The injustices of the world hide in those three words. Quote me, Duiker, and your work's done.'

*The bastard's right. Economics, ethics, the games of the gods –
all within that single, tragic statement. I'll quote you, soldier. Be
assured of that. An old sword, pitted and blunt and nicked, that cuts
clean to the heart.* 'You humble me, Captain.'

Lull grunted, passing over a waterskin. 'A couple of mouth-
fuls. Don't push it or you'll choke.'

Duiker's smile was wry.

'I trust,' the captain continued, 'you've kept up on that List
of the Fallen you mentioned.'

'No, I've . . . stumbled of late, I'm afraid.'

Lull jerked a tight nod.

'How do we fare, Captain?'

'We're getting mauled. Badly. Close to twenty killed a day,
twice that wounded. Vipers in the dust – they suddenly appear,
arrows fly, a soldier dies. We send out a troop of Wickans in
pursuit, they ride into an ambush. We send out another, we got
a major tangle on our hands, leaving flanks open to either side.
Refugees get cut down, drovers get skewered and we lose a few
more animals – unless those Wickan dogs are around, that is,
those are nasty beasts. Mind you, their numbers are dropping
as well.'

'In other words, this can't go on much longer.'

Lull bared his teeth, a white gleam amidst his grey-shot red
beard. 'That's why we're going for the warleader's head. When
we reach the River P'atha, there'll be another full-scale battle.
He ain't invited.'

'Another disputed crossing?'

'No, the river's ankle-deep and getting shallower as the
season drags on. More likely on the other side – the trail winds
through some rough country – we'll find trouble there. In any
case, we either carve ourselves some breathing space then, or
we're purple meat under the sun and it don't matter.'

The Wickan horns sounded.

'Ah,' Lull said, 'we're done. Get some rest, old man – we'll find us a spot in the Foolish Dog camp. I'll wake you with a meal in a few hours.'

'Lead on, Captain.'

Scrapping over something unrecognizable in the tall grasses, the pack of Wickan cattle-dogs paused to watch Duiker and Lull stride past at a distance of twenty or so paces. The historian frowned at the wiry, mottled beasts.

'Best not look them in the eye,' Lull said. 'You ain't Wickan and they know it.'

'I was just wondering what they're eating.'

'Not something you want to find out.'

'There's been a rumour about dug-up child graves . . .'

'Like I said, you don't want to know, Historian.'

'Well, some of the tougher mud-bloods have been hiring themselves out to stand guard over those graves—'

'If they ain't got Wickan blood in that mud they'll regret it.'

The dogs resumed their snapping and bickering once the two men had moved past.

Hearthfires flickered in the camp ahead. A last line of defenders patrolled the perimeter of the round hide tents, old folk and youths, who revealed a silent, vaguely ominous watchfulness that matched that of the cattle-dogs as the two men strode into the Wickan enclave.

'I get a sense,' Duiker muttered, 'that the cause of protecting the refugees is cooling among these people . . .'

The captain grimaced but said nothing.

They continued on, winding between the tent rows. Smoke hung heavy in the air, as did the smell of horse urine and boiled bones, the latter acrid yet strangely sweet. Duiker paused as they passed close to an old woman tending one such iron pot of bones. Whatever boiled in the pot wasn't entirely water. The woman was using a flat blade of wood to collect the thick bone fat and marrow that congealed on the surface, scraping it into an intestine to be later twisted and tied off into sausages.

The old woman noticed the historian and held up the wooden blade – as she would if offering it to a toddler to lick clean. Flecks of sage were visible in the fat – a herb Duiker had once loved but had come to despise, since it was one of the few native to the Odhan. He smiled and shook his head.

As he caught up with Lull, the captain said, 'You're known, old man. They say you walk in the spirit world. That old horsewife wouldn't offer food to just anybody – not me, that's for certain.'

The spirit world. Yes, I walked there. Once. Never again. 'See an old man in crusty rags . . .'

'And he's gods-touched, aye. Don't mock out loud – it might save your skin one day.'

Nil's hearth was unique among the others in sight in that it held no cooking pot, nor was it framed in drying racks bedecked with curing strips of meat. The burning dung within the small ring of stones was almost smokeless, revealing a naked, blue-tinged flame. The young warlock sat to one side of the hearth, his hands deftly pleating strips of leather into something like a whip.

Four of Lull's marines squatted nearby, each running through a last check of their weapons and armour. Their assault crossbows had been freshly blackened, then smeared in greasy dust to remove the gleam.

One glance told Duiker that these were hard soldiers, veterans, their movements economical, their preparations professional. Neither the man nor the three women were under thirty, and none spoke or looked up as their captain joined them.

Nil nodded to Duiker as the historian crouched down opposite him. 'It promises to be a cold night,' the boy said.

'Have you found the location of this warleader?'

'Not precisely. A general area. He may possess some minor wards against detection – once we get closer they will not avail him.'

'How do you hunt down someone distinguished only by his or her competence, Nil?'

The young warlock shrugged. 'He's left . . . other signs. We shall find him, that is certain. And then it is up to them—' He jerked his head towards the marines. 'I have come to a realization, Historian, over these past months on this plain.'

'And that is?'

'The Malazan professional soldier is the deadliest weapon I know. Had Coltaine three armies instead of only three-fifths of one, he would end this rebellion before year's end. And with such finality that Seven Cities would never rise again. We could shatter Kamist Reloe now – if not for the refugees whom we are sworn to protect.'

Duiker nodded. There was truth enough in that.

The sounds of the camp were a muffled illusion of normality, an embrace from all sides that the historian found unsettling. He was losing the ability to relax, he bleakly realized. He picked up a small twig and tossed it towards the fire.

Nil's hand snapped it out of the air. 'Not this one,' he said.

Another young warlock arrived, his thin, bony arms ridged in hatch-marked scars from wrist to shoulder. He squatted down beside Nil and spat once into the fire.

There was no answering sizzle.

Nil straightened, tossing aside the cord of leather, and glanced over at Lull and his soldiers. They stood ready.

'Time?' Duiker asked.

'Yes.'

Nil and his fellow warlock led the group through the camp. Few of their clan kin looked their way, and it was a few minutes before Duiker realized that their seemingly casual indifference was deliberate, possibly some kind of culturally prescribed display of respect. *Or something else entirely.* *To look is to ghost-touch, after all.*

They reached the encampment's north edge. Fog wafted on

the plain beyond the wicker barriers. Duiker frowned. 'They'll know it isn't natural,' he muttered.

Lull grunted. 'We've a diversion planned, of course. Three squads of sappers are out there right now with sacks full of fun—'

He was interrupted by a detonation off to the northeast, followed by a pause in which faint screams wailed in the shrouded darkness. Then a rapid succession of explosions shattered the night air.

The fog swallowed the flashes, but Duiker recognized the distinctive crack of sharpers and thumping whoosh of flamers. More screams, then the swift thudding of horse hooves converging to the northeast.

'Now we let things settle,' Lull said.

Minutes passed, the distant screams fading. 'Has Bult finally managed to track down that captain of the sappers?' the historian eventually asked.

'Ain't seen his face at any of the jaw sessions, if that's what you mean. But he's around. Somewhere. Coltaine's finally accepted that the man's shy.'

'Shy?'

Lull shrugged. 'A joke, Historian. Remember those?'

Nil finally turned to face them.

'That's it,' the captain said. 'No more talking.'

Half a dozen Wickan guards pulled up the spikes anchoring one of the wicker barriers, then quietly lowered it flat. A thick hide was unrolled over it to mask the inevitable creaking of the party's passage.

The mist beyond was dissipating into patches. One such cloud drifted over, then settled around the group, keeping pace as they struck out onto the plain.

Duiker wished he'd asked more questions earlier. How far to the enemy camp's pickets? What was the plan for getting through them undiscovered? What was the fallback should things go awry? He laid a hand on the grip of the short sword at his hip, and was alarmed at how strange it felt – it had been a long time since he'd last used a weapon. *Being pulled from the front lines had been the Emperor's reward all those years ago. That and the various alchemies that keep me tottering on well past my prime. Gods, even the scars from that last horror have faded away!*

'No-one who's grown up amidst scrolls and books can write of the world,' Kellanved had told him once, 'which is why I'm appointing you Imperial Historian, soldier.'

'Emperor, I cannot read or write.'

'An unsullied mind. Good. Toc the Elder will be teaching you over the next six months – he's another soldier with a brain. Six months, mind. No more than that.'

'Emperor, it seems to me that he would be better suited than I—'

'I've something else in store for him. Do as I say or I'll have you spiked on the city wall.'

Kellanved's sense of humour had been strange even at the best of times. Duiker recalled those learning sessions: he a soldier of thirty-odd years who'd been campaigning for over half that, seated alongside Toc's own son, a runt of a boy who always seemed to be suffering from a cold – the sleeves of his shirt were crusty with dried snot. It had taken longer than six months, but by then it was Toc the Younger doing the teaching.

The Emperor loved lessons in humility. So long as it was never thrown back at him. What happened to Toc the Elder, I wonder? Vanishing after the assassinations – I'd always imagined it as Laseen's doing . . . and Toc the Younger – he'd rejected a life amidst scrolls and books . . . now lost in the Genabackan campaign—

A gauntleted hand gripped the historian's shoulder and squeezed hard. Duiker focused on Lull's battered face, nodded. *Sorry. Mind wandering still, it seems.*

They had stopped. Ahead, vague through the mists, rose a spike-bristling ridge of packed earth. The glow of fires painted the fog orange beyond the earthwork perimeter.

Now what?

The two warlocks knelt in the grass five paces in front. Both had gone perfectly still.

They waited. Duiker heard muffled voices from the other side of the ridge, slowly passing from left to right, then fading as the Tithansi patrol continued on. Nil twisted around and gestured.

Crossbows cocked, the marines slipped forward. After a moment the historian followed.

A tunnel mouth had opened in the earth before the two warlocks. The soil steamed, the rocks and gravel popping with heat. It looked to have been clawed open by huge taloned hands – from below.

Duiker scowled. He hated tunnels. No, they *terrified* him. There was nothing rational in it – *wrong again. Tunnels collapse. People get buried alive. All perfectly reasonable, possible, probable, inevitable.*

Nil led the way, slithering down and out of sight. The other warlock quickly followed. Lull turned to the historian and gestured him forward.

Duiker shook his head.

The captain pointed at him, then pointed to the hole and mouthed *Now*.

Hissing a curse, the historian edged forward. As soon as he was within reach Lull's hand snapped out, gathering a handful of dusty telaba, and dragged Duiker to the tunnel mouth.

It took all his will not to shriek as the captain unceremoniously stuffed him down into the tunnel. He scrambled, clawed wildly. He felt his kicking heel connect with something in the air behind him. *Lull's jaw, I bet. Serves you right, bastard!* The rush of satisfaction helped. He scrabbled past the old flood silts and found himself cocooned in warm bedrock. Collapse was unlikely, he told himself, the thought almost a gibber. The tunnel continued to angle downward, the warm rock turning

492

slippery, then wet. Nightmare visions of drowning replaced collapsing.

He hesitated until a sword point was pressed against the worn sole of his moccasin, then punched through to jab his flesh. Whimpering, Duiker pulled himself foward.

The tunnel levelled out. It was filling with water, the rock bleeding from fissures on all sides. The historian sloshed through a cool stream as he slithered along. He paused, took a tentative sip, tasted iron and grit. *But drinkable*.

The level stretch went on and on. The stream deepened with alarming swiftness. Soaked and increasingly weighed down by his clothing, Duiker struggled on, exhausted, his muscles failing him. The sound of coughing and spitting behind him was all that kept him moving. *They're drowning back there, and I'm next!*

He reached the upward slope, clawed his way along through mud and sifting earth. A rough sphere of grey fog appeared ahead – he'd reached the mouth.

Hands gripped him and pulled him clear, rolling him to one side until he came to rest in a bed of sharp-bladed grasses. He lay quietly gasping, staring up at the mist's low ceiling above him. He was vaguely aware of the marines clambering out of the tunnel and forming a defensive cordon, breaths hissing, their weapons dripping muddy water. *Those crossbow cords will stretch, unless they've been soaked in oil and waxed. Of course they have – those soldiers aren't idiots. Plan for any eventuality, even swimming beneath a dusty plain. I once saw a fellow soldier find use for a fishing kit in a desert. What makes a Malazan soldier so dangerous? They're allowed to think.*

Duiker sat up.

Lull was communicating with his marines with elaborate hand gestures. They responded in kind, then edged out into the mists. Nil and the other warlock began snaking forward through the grass, towards the glow of a hearthfire that showed dull red through the fog.

Voices surrounded them, the harsh Tithan tongue spoken in low murmurs that cavorted alarmingly until Duiker was certain a squad stood but a pace behind him, calmly discussing where in his back to drive their spears. Whatever games the fog played with sound, the historian suspected that Nil and his comrade had magically amplified the effect and they would soon be gambling their lives on that aural confusion.

Lull tapped Duiker's shoulder, waved him forward to where the warlocks had vanished. The fog pocket was impenetrable – he could see no farther than the stretch of an arm. Scowling, the historian dropped to his belly, sliding his sword scabbard around to the back of his hip and then began to worm his way forward to where Nil waited.

The hearthfire was big, the flames lurid through the veil of mist. Six Tithansi warriors stood or sat within sight, all seemingly bundled in furs. Their breaths plumed.

Peering at the scene beside Nil, Duiker could now see a thin patina of frost covering the ground. Chill air wafted over them with a wayward turn of the faint night wind.

The historian nudged the warlock, nodded at the frost and raised his brows questioningly.

Nil's response was the faintest of shrugs.

The warriors were waiting, red-painted hands stretched out towards the flames in an effort to stay warm. The scene was unchanged for another twenty breaths, then those seated or squatting all rose and with the others faced in one direction – to Duiker's left.

Two figures emerged into the firelight. The man in the lead was built like a bear, the comparison strengthened by the fur of that animal riding his broad shoulders. A single-bladed throwing axe jutted from each hip. His leather shirt was unlaced from the breastbone up, revealing solid muscles and thick, matted hair. The crimson slashes of paint on his cheeks announced him as a warleader, each slash denoting a recent

494

victory. The multitude of freshly painted bands made plain the Malazans' ill fortune at his hands.

Behind this formidable creature was a Semk.

That's one assumption obliterated. Evidently the Semk tribe's avowed hatred of all who were not Semk had been set aside in obeisance to the Whirlwind goddess. *Or, more accurately, to the destruction of Coltaine.*

The Semk was a squatter, more pugnacious-looking version of the Tithan warleader, hairy enough to dispense with the need for a bear fur. His only clothing was a hide loincloth and a brace of belts cinched tight over his stomach. The man was covered in greasy ash, his shaggy black hair hanging in thick threads, his beard knotted with finger-bone fetishes. The contemptuous sneer twisting his face had a permanence about it.

The last detail that revealed itself as the Semk stepped closer to the fire was the gut-stitching closing his mouth. *Hood's breath, the Semk take their vows of silence seriously!*

The air grew icy. Faint alarm whispered at the back of Duiker's mind and he reached out to nudge Nil yet again.

Before he could make contact with the warlock, crossbows snapped. Two quarrels jutted from the Tithan warleader's chest, while two other Tithan warriors grunted before pitching to the ground. A fifth quarrel sank deep in the Semk's shoulder.

The earth beneath the hearth erupted, flinging coals and burning wood skyward. A multilimbed, tar-skinned beast clambered free, loosing a bone-shivering scream. It plunged in among the remaining Tithansi, claws ripping through armour and flesh.

The warleader fell to his knees, staring dumbly down at the leather-finned quarrels buried in his chest. Blood sprayed as he coughed, convulsed, then toppled face down on the dusty ground.

A mistake – the wrong—

The Semk had torn the quarrel from his shoulder as if it was a carpenter's nail. The air around him swirled white. Dark eyes fixing on the earth spirit, he leapt to meet it.

Nil was motionless at the historian's side. Duiker twisted to shake him, and found the young warlock unconscious.

The other Wickan youth was on his feet, reeling back under an invisible sorcerous onslaught. Strips of flesh and blood flew from the warlock – in moments there was only bone and cartilage where his face had been. The sight of the boy's eyes bursting had Duiker spinning away.

Tithansi were converging from all sides. As he dragged Nil back, the historian saw Lull and one of his marines releasing quarrels at almost point-blank range into the Semk's back. A lance flew out of the darkness and skidded from the marine's chain-armoured back. Both soldiers wheeled, flinging away their crossbows and unsheathing long-knives to meet the first warriors to arrive.

The earth spirit was shrieking now, three of its limbs torn off its body and lying twitching on the ground. The Semk was silent mayhem, ignoring the quarrels in his back, closing again and again to batter the earth spirit. Cold poured in waves from the Semk – a cold Duiker recognized: *The Semk god – a piece of him survived, a piece of him commands one of his chosen warriors*—

Detonations erupted to the south. Sharpers. Screams filled the night. Malazan sappers were blasting a hole through the Tithansi lines. *And here I'd concluded this was a suicide mission.*

Duiker continued dragging Nil southward, towards the explosions, praying that the sappers wouldn't mistake him for an enemy.

Horses thundered nearby. Iron rang.

One of the marines was suddenly at his side. Blood sheathed one side of her face, but she flung away her sword and pulled the warlock from the historian's hands, hoisting the lad effortlessly over one shoulder. 'Pull out that damned sword and cover me!' she snarled, bolting forward.

Without a shield? Hood take us, you can't use a short sword without a shield! But the weapon was in his hand as if it had leapt free of its scabbard and into his palm of its own will. The tin-pitted iron blade looked pitifully short as he backed away in the marine's wake, the weapon held out before him.

His heels struck something soft and with a curse he stumbled and fell.

The marine glanced back. 'On your feet, dammit! Someone's after us!'

Duiker had tripped over a body, a Tithansi lancer who'd been dragged by his horse before the mangled mess of his left hand finally released the reins. A throwing star was buried deep in his neck. The historian blinked at that – *a Claw's weapon, that star* – as he scrambled to his feet. *More unseen back-up?* Sounds of battle echoed through the mists, as if a full-scale engagement was underway.

Duiker resumed covering the marine as she continued on, Nil's limp body hanging like a sack of turnips over one shoulder.

A moment later three Tithansi warriors plunged out of the fog, tulwars swinging.

Decades-old training saved the historian from their initial onslaught. He ducked low and closed with the warrior on his right, grunting as the man's leather-wrapped forearm cracked down on his left shoulder, then gasping as the tulwar it held whipped down – the Tithansi bending his wrist – and chopped deep into Duiker's left buttock. Even as the pain jolted through him, he'd driven his short sword up and under the warrior's ribcage, piercing his heart.

Tearing the blade free, the historian jumped right. There was a falling body between him and the two remaining warriors, both of whom had the added disadvantage of being right-handed. The slashing tulwars missed Duiker by an arm's length.

The nearest weapon had been swung with enough force to drive it into the ground. The historian stamped a boot down hard on the flat of the blade, springing the tulwar from the Tithan's hand. Duiker followed up with a savage chop between the man's shoulder and neck, snapping through the collarbone.

He launched himself behind the reeling warrior's back to challenge the third Tithan, only to see the man face down on the ground, a silver-pommelled throwing knife jutting from between his shoulder blades. *A Claw's sticker – I'd recognize it anywhere!*

The historian paused, glared around, but could see no-one. The mists swirled thick, smelling of ash. A hiss from the marine brought him around. She crouched at the inside edge of the picket trench, gesturing him forward.

Suddenly soaked with sweat and shivering, Duiker quickly joined her.

The woman grinned. 'That was damned impressive swordplay, old man, though I couldn't make out how you done the last one.'

'You saw no-one else?'

'Huh?'

Struggling to draw breath, Duiker only shook his head. He glanced down to where Nil lay motionless on the earthen bank. 'What's wrong with him?'

The marine shrugged. Her pale-blue eyes were still appraising the historian. 'We could use you in the ranks,' she said.

'What I've lost in speed I've made up in experience, and experience tells me not to get into messes like this one. Not an old man's game, soldier.'

She grimaced, but with good humour, 'Nor an old woman's. Come on, the scrap's swung east – we shouldn't have any

498

trouble crossing the trench.' She lifted Nil back onto her shoulder with ease.

'You nailed the wrong man, you know . . .'

'Aye, we'd guessed as much. That Semk was possessed, wasn't he?'

They reached the slope and picked their way carefully through the spikes studding the earth. Tents were burning in the Tithansi camp, adding smoke to the fog. Screams and the clash of weapons still echoed in the distance.

Duiker asked, 'Did you see anyone else get out?'

She shook her head.

They came upon a score of bodies, a Tithansi patrol who'd been hit with a sharper. The grenado's slivers of iron had ripped through them with horrific efficiency. Blood trails indicated the recent departure of survivors.

The fog quickly thinned as they approached the Wickan lines. A troop of Foolish Dog lancers who had been patrolling the wicker barriers spotted them and rode up.

Their eyes fixed on Nil.

The marine said, 'He lives, but you'd better find Sormo.'

Two riders peeled off, cantered back to the camp.

'Any news of the other marines?' Duiker asked the nearest horsewarrior.

The Wickan nodded. 'The captain and one other made it.'

A squad of sappers emerged from the mists in a desultory dog-trot that slowed to a walk as soon as they saw the group. 'Two sharpers,' one was saying, disbelief souring his voice, 'and the bastard just got back up.'

Duiker stepped forward. 'Who, soldier?'

'That hairy Semk—'

'Ain't hairy no more,' another sapper threw in.

'We were the mop-up mission,' the first man said, showing a red-stained grin. 'Coltaine's axe – you were the edge, we were the wedge. We hammered that ogre but it done no good—'

'Sarge took an arrow,' said the other sapper. 'His lung's bleeding—'

'Just one of them and it's a pinprick,' the sergeant corrected, pausing to spit. 'The other one's fine.'

'Can't breathe blood, Sarge—'

'I shared a tent with you, lad – I've breathed worse.'

The squad continued on, arguing over whether or not the sergeant should go find a healer. The marine stared after them, shaking her head. Then she turned to the historian. 'I'll leave you to talk with Sormo, sir, if that's all right.'

Duiker nodded. 'Two of your friends didn't make it back—'

'But one did. Next time for sword practice, I'll come looking for you, sir.'

'My joints are already seizing, soldier. You'll have to prop me up.'

She gently lowered Nil to the grass, then moved off.

Ten years younger, I'd have the nerve to ask her . . . well, never mind. Imagine the arguments at the cooking fire . . .

The two Wickan riders returned, flanking a travois harnessed to a brutal-looking cattle-dog. A hoof had connected with its head some time in its past, and the bones had healed lopsided, giving the animal a manic half-snarl that seemed well suited to the vicious gleam in its eyes.

The riders dismounted and carefully laid Nil on the travois. Disdaining its escort, the dog moved off, back towards the Wickan encampment.

'That was one ugly beast,' Captain Lull said behind the historian.

Duiker grunted. 'Proof that their skulls are all bone and no brain.'

'Still lost, old man?'

The historian scowled. 'Why didn't you tell me we had hidden help, Captain? Who were they, Pormqual's?'

'What in Hood's name are you talking about?'

500

He turned. 'The Claw. *Someone* was covering our retreat. Using stars and stickers and moving unseen like a Hood-damned breath on my back!'

Lull's eyes widened.

'How many more *details* is Coltaine keeping to himself?'

'There's no way Coltaine knows anything about this, Duiker,' Lull said, shaking his head. 'If you're certain of what you saw – and I believe you – then the Fist will want to know. Now.'

For the first time that Duiker could recall, Coltaine looked rattled. He stood perfectly still, as if suddenly unsure that no-one hovered behind him, invisible blades but moments from their killing thrust.

Bult growled low in his throat. 'The heat's got you addled, Historian.'

'I know what I saw, Uncle. More, I know what I *felt*.'

There was a long silence, the air in the tent stifling and still.

Sormo entered, stopping just inside the entrance as Coltaine pinned him with a glare. The warlock's shoulders were slumped, as if no longer able to bear the weight they had carried all these months. Shadows pouched his eyes with fatigue.

'Coltaine has some questions for you,' Bult said to him.

'Later.'

The young man shrugged. 'Nil has awakened. I have answers.'

'Different questions,' the scarred veteran said with a dark, humourless grin.

Coltaine spoke. 'Explain what happened, Warlock.'

'The Semk god isn't dead,' Duiker said.

'I'd second that opinion,' Lull muttered from where he sat on a camp saddle-chair, his unbuckled vambraces in his lap, his legs stretched out. He met the historian's eyes and winked.

'Not precisely,' Sormo corrected. He hesitated, drew a deep breath, then continued. 'The Semk god was indeed destroyed. Torn to pieces and devoured. Sometimes, a piece of flesh can contain such malevolence that it corrupts the devourer—'

Duiker sat forward, wincing at the pain from the force-healed wound in his backside. 'An earth spirit—'

'A spirit of the land, aye. Hidden ambition and sudden power. The other spirits . . . suspected naught.'

Bult's face twisted in disgust. 'We lost seventeen soldiers tonight just to kill a handful of Tithan warchiefs and unmask a rogue spirit?'

The historian flinched. It was the first time he'd heard the full count of losses. *Coltaine's first failure. If Oponn smiles on us, the enemy won't realize it.*

'With such knowledge,' Sormo explained quietly, 'future lives will be saved. The spirits are greatly distressed – they were perplexed at being unable to detect the raids and ambushes, and now they know why. They did not think to look among their own kin. Now they will deliver their own justice, in their own time—'

'Meaning the raids continue?' The veteran looked ready to spit. 'Will your spirit allies be able to warn us now – as they once did so effectively?'

'The rogue's efforts will be blunted.'

'Sormo,' Duiker said, 'why was the Semk's mouth sewn shut?'

The warlock half smiled. 'That creature is sewn shut *everywhere*, Historian. Lest that which was devoured escapes.'

Duiker shook his head. 'Strange magic, this.'

Sormo nodded. 'Ancient,' he said. 'Sorcery of guts and bone. We struggle with knowledge we once possessed instinctively.' He sighed. 'From a time before warrens, when magic was found *within*.'

A year ago Duiker would have been galvanized with

curiosity and excitement at such comments, and would have relentlessly interrogated the warlock without surcease. Now, Sormo's words were a dull echo lost in the vast cavern of the historian's exhaustion. He wanted nothing but sleep, and knew it would be denied him for another twelve hours – the camp outside was already stirring, even though another hour of darkness remained.

'If that's the case,' Lull drawled, 'why didn't that Semk burst apart like a bloated bladder when we pricked him?'

'What was devoured hides deep. Tell me, was this possessed Semk's stomach shielded?'

Duiker grunted. 'Belts, thick leather.'

'Just so.'

'What happened to Nil?'

'Caught unawares, he made use of that very knowledge we struggle to recall. As the sorcerous attack came, he retreated within himself. The attack pursued but he remained elusive, until the malevolent power spent itself. We learn.'

Into Duiker's mind arose the image of the other warlock's horrific death. 'At a cost.'

Sormo said nothing, but pain revealed itself for a moment in his eyes.

'We increase our pace,' Coltaine announced. 'One less mouthful of water for each soldier each day—'

Duiker straightened. 'But we have water.'

All eyes turned to him. The historian smiled wryly at Sormo. 'I understand Nil's report was rather . . . dry. The spirits made for us a tunnel through the bedrock. As the Captain can confirm, the rock weeps.'

Lull grinned. 'Hood's breath, the old man's right!'

Sormo was staring at the historian with wide eyes. 'For lack of asking the right questions, we have suffered long – and needlessly.'

A new energy infused Coltaine, culminating in a taut baring

of his teeth. 'You have one hour,' the Fist told the warlock, 'to ease a hundred thousand throats.'

From bedrock that split the prairie soil in weathered out-croppings, sweet tears seeped forth. Vast pits had been excavated. The air was alive with joyous songs and the blessed silence of beasts no longer crying their distress. And beneath it all was a warm, startling undercurrent. For once, the spirits of the land were delivering a gift untouched by death. Their pleasure was palpable to Duiker's senses as he stood close to the north edge of the encampment, watching, listening.

Corporal List was at his side, his fever abated. 'The seepage is deliberately slow but not slow enough – stomachs will rebel – the reckless ones could end up killing themselves . . .'

'Aye. A few might.'

Duiker raised his head, scanning the valley's north ridge. A row of Tithansi horsewarriors lined its length, watching in what the historian imagined was fearful wonder. He had no doubt that Kamist Reloe's army was suffering, even though they had the advantage of seizing and holding every known waterhole on the Odhan.

As he studied them, his eyes caught a flash of white that flowed down the valleyside, then vanished beyond Duiker's line of sight. He grunted.

'Did you see something, sir?'

'Just some wild goats,' the historian said. 'Switching sides . . .'

The blowing sand had bored holes into the mesa's sides, an onslaught that began by sculpting hollows, then caves, then tunnels, finally passages that might well exit out of the other side. Like voracious worms ravaging old wood, the wind devoured the cliff face, hole after hole appearing, the walls between them thinning, some collapsing, the tunnels

504

widening. The mantle of the plateau remained, however, a vast cap of stone perched on ever-dwindling foundations.

Kulp had never seen anything like it. *As if the Whirlwind's deliberately attacked it. Why lay siege to a rock?*

The tunnels shrieked with the wind, each one with its own febrile pitch, creating a fierce chorus. The sand was fine as dust where it spun and swirled on updraughts at the base of the cliff. Kulp glanced back to where Heboric and Felisin waited – two vague shapes huddled against the ceaseless fury of the storm.

The Whirlwind had denied them all shelter for three days now, ever since it had first descended upon them. The wind assailed them from every direction – *as if the mad goddess has singled us out.* The possibility was not as unlikely as it first seemed. The malevolent will was palpable. *We're intruders, after all. The Whirlwind's focus of hate has always been on those who do not belong. Poor Malazan Empire, to have stepped into such a ready-made mythos of rebellion . . .*

The mage scrambled back to the others. He had to lean close to be heard above the endless roar. 'There's caves! Only the wind's plunging down their throats – I suspect it's cut right through the hill!'

Heboric was shivering, beset since morning by a fever born of exhaustion. He was weakening fast. *We all are.* It was almost dusk – the unrelieved ochre dimming over their heads – and the mage estimated they had travelled little more than a league in the past twelve hours.

They had no water, no food. Hood stalked their heels.

Felisin clutched Kulp's tattered cloak, pulling him closer. Her lips were split, sand gumming the corners of her mouth. 'We try anyway!' she said.

'I don't know. That whole hill could come down—'

'The caves! We go into the caves!'

Die out here, or die in there. At least the caves offer us a tomb for our corpses. He gave a sharp nod.

They half dragged Heboric between them. The cliff offered them a score of options with its ragged, honeycombed visage. They made no effort to select one, simply plunging into the first cave mouth they came to, a wide, strangely flattened tunnel that seemed to run level – at least for the first few paces.

The wind was a hand at their backs, dismissive of hesitation in its unceasing pressure. Darkness swept around them as they staggered on, within a cauldron of screams.

The floor had been sculpted into ridges, making walking difficult. Fifteen paces on, they stumbled into an outcropping of quartzite or some other crystalline mineral that resisted the erosive wind. They worked their way around it and found in its lee the first surcease from the Whirlwind's battering force in over seventy hours.

Heboric sagged in their arms. They set him down in the ankle-deep dust at the base of the outcropping. 'I'd like to scout ahead,' Kulp told Felisin, yelling to be heard.

She nodded, lowering herself to her knees.

Another thirty paces took the mage to a larger cavern. More quartzite filled the space, reflecting a faint luminescence from what appeared to be a ceiling of crushed glass fifteen feet above him. The quartzite rose in vertical veins, the gleaming pillars creating a gallery effect of startling beauty, despite the racing wind's dust-filled stream. Kulp strode forward. The piercing shriek dimmed, losing itself in the vastness of the cavern.

Closer to the centre of the cavern rose a heap of tumbled stones, their shapes too regular to be natural. The glittering substance of the ceiling covered them in places – a single side of their vaguely rectangular forms, the mage realized after a moment's examination. Crouching, he ran a hand along one such side, then bent still lower. *Hood's breath, it's glass in truth! Multicoloured, crushed and compacted . . .*

He looked up. A large hole gaped in the ceiling, its edges glowing with that odd, cool light. Kulp hesitated, then opened his warren. He grunted. *Nothing. Queen's blessing, no sorcery – it's mundane.*

Hunching low against the wind, the mage made his way back to the others. He found them both asleep or unconscious. Kulp studied them, feeling a chill at the composed finality he saw in their dehydrated features.

Might be more merciful not to awaken them.

As if sensing his presence, Felisin opened her eyes. They filled with instant awareness. 'You'll never have it that easy,' she said.

'This hill's a buried city, and we're under what's buried.'

'So?'

'The wind's got into one chamber at least, emptied it of sand.'

'Our tomb.'

'Maybe.'

'All right, let's go.'

'One problem,' Kulp said, not moving. 'The way in is about fifteen feet over our heads. There's a pillar of quartzite, but it wouldn't be an easy climb, especially not in our condition.'

'Do your warren trick.'

'What?'

'Open a gate.'

He stared at her. 'It's not that simple.'

'Dying's simple.'

He blinked. 'Let's get the old man on his feet, then.'

Heboric's eyes were blistered shut, weeping grit-filled tears. Slow to awaken, he clearly had no idea where he was. His wide mouth split into a ghastly smile. 'They tried it here, didn't they?' he asked, tilting his head as they helped him forward. 'Tried it and paid for it, oh, the memories of water, all those wasted lives . . .'

They arrived at the place of the breached ceiling. Felisin laid a hand on the quartzite column nearest the hole. 'I'd have to climb this like a Dosii does a coconut palm.'

'And how's that done?' Kulp asked.

'Reluctantly,' Heboric muttered, cocking his head as if hearing voices.

Felisin glanced at the mage. 'I'll need those straps from your belt.'

With a grunt, Kulp began removing the leather band at his waist. 'Damned strange time to be wanting to see me without my breeches, lass.'

'We can all do with the laugh,' she replied.

He handed her the belt, and watched as she affixed the binding strips at each end to her ankles. He winced at how savagely she tightened the knots.

'Now, what's left of your raincloak, please.'

'What's wrong with your tunic?'

'No-one gets to ogle my breasts – not for free, anyway. Besides, that cloak's a tougher weave.'

'There was retribution,' Heboric said. 'A methodical, dispassionate cleaning-up of the mess.'

As he pulled off his sand-scoured cloak, Kulp scowled down at the ex-priest. 'What are you going on about, Heboric?'

'First Empire, the city above. They came and put things aright. Immortal custodians. Such a debacle! Even with my eyes closed I can see my hands – they're groping blind, so blind now. So empty.' He sank down, suddenly racked with shuddering grief.

'Never mind him,' Felisin said, stepping up as if to embrace the jagged pillar. 'The old toad's lost his god and it's broken his mind.'

Kulp said nothing.

Felisin reached around the column and linked her hands on the other side by gripping two ends of the cloak and twisting them taut. The belt between her feet hugged this side of the pillar.

'Ah,' Kulp said. 'I see. Clever Dosii.'

She hitched the cloak as high as she could on the opposite side, then leaned back and, in a jerking motion, jumped a short distance upward – knees drawn up, the belt snapping against the pillar. He saw the pain rip through her as the bindings dug into her ankles.

'I'm surprised the Dosii have feet,' Kulp said.

Gasping, she said, 'Guess I got some minor detail wrong.'

In all truth, the mage did not think she would make it. Before she had gone two arm-spans – a full body's length from the ceiling – her ankles streamed blood. She trembled all over, using unimagined but quickly waning reserves of energy. Yet she did not stop. *This is a hard, hard creature. She surpasses us all, again and again.* The thought led him to Baudin – banished, likely to be somewhere out there, suffering the storm. *Another hard one, stubborn and stolid. How fare you, Talon?*

Felisin finally came to within reach of the hole's ragged edge. And there she hesitated.

Aye, now what?

'Kulp!' Her voice bounced in an eerie echo that was quickly swept away by the wind.

'Yes?'

'How close are my feet to you?'

'Maybe three arm-spans. Why?'

'Prop Heboric beside the pillar. Climb onto his shoulders—'

'In Hood's name what for?'

'You've got to reach my ankles, then climb over me – I can't let go – nothing left!'

Gods, I'm not as hard as you, lass. 'I think—'

'Do it! We have no choice, damn you!'

Hissing, Kulp swung to Heboric. 'Old man, can you understand me? Heboric!'

The ex-priest straightened, grinned. 'Remember the hand of stone? The finger? The past is an alien world. Powers unimagined. To touch is to recall someone else's memories,

509

someone so unlike you in thought and senses that they beckon you into madness.'

Hand of stone? The bastard's raving. 'I need to climb onto your shoulders, Heboric. You need to stand firm – once we get up we'll rig a harness to pull you up, OK?'

'On my shoulders. A mountain of stone, each one carved and shaped by a life long since lost to Hood. How many yearnings, desires, secrets? Where does it all go? The unseen energy of life's thoughts is food for the gods, did you know that? This is why they must – they *must* – be fickle!'

'Mage!' Felisin wailed. 'Now!'

Kulp stepped behind the ex-priest and set his hands on Heboric's shoulders. 'Stand steady now—'

Instead, the old man turned to face him. He brought both wrists together, leaving a space between them where hands should be. 'Step. I'll launch you straight to her.'

'Heboric – you've no hands to hold my foot—'

The man's grin broadened. 'Humour me.'

Something pushed Kulp beyond wonder as his moccasined foot settled into the firm stirrup of interlaced fingers he could not see. He placed his hands on the ex-priest's shoulders once again.

'Straight up you'll go,' Heboric said. 'I'm blind. Position me, Mage.'

'Back a step, a little more. There.'

'Ready?'

'Aye.'

But he wasn't prepared for the immense surge of strength that lifted him, flung him effortlessly straight up. Kulp made an instinctive grab for Felisin, missed – luckily, as he was then past her, through the ceiling's hole. He almost fell straight back down. A panicked twisting of his upper body, however, landed him painfully on an edge. It groaned, sagged.

His fingers clawing unseen flagstones, the mage clambered onto the floor.

Felisin's voice keened from below. 'Mage! Where are you?'

Feeling a slightly hysterical grin frozen on his face, Kulp said, 'Up here. I'll have you in a moment, lass.'

Heboric used his invisible hands to swiftly climb the makeshift rope of leather and cloth that Kulp sent snaking down ten minutes later. Seated nearby in the small, gloomy chamber, Felisin silently watched with fear racing unchecked within her.

Her body tortured her with pain, the feeling returning to her feet with silent outrage. Fine white dust coated the blood on her ankles and where the pillar's crystalline edges had scored her wrists. She shook uncontrollably. *That old man looked dead on his feet. Dead. He was burning up, yet his ravings were not just empty words. There was knowing in them, impossible knowing. And now his ghost-hands have become real.*

She glanced over at Kulp. The mage was frowning at the torn shambles of the raincloak in his hands. Then he sighed and swung his gaze to a silent study of Heboric, who seemed to be sinking back into his fevered stupor.

Kulp had conjured a faint glow to the chamber, revealing bare stone walls. Saddled steps rose along one wall to a solid-looking door. At the base of the wall opposite, round indentations ran in a row on the floor, each of a size to fit a cask or keg. Rust-pitted hooks depended on chains from the ceiling at the room's far end. Everything seemed blunted to Felisin's eyes; either it was strangely worn down or the effect was a product of the mage's sorcerous light.

She shook her head, wrapping her arms around herself to fight the trembling.

'That was some climb you managed, lass,' Kulp said.

She grunted. 'And pointless, as it turns out.' *And now it's likely to kill me. There was more to making that climb than just muscle and bone. I feel . . . emptied, with nothing left in me to rebuild.* She laughed.

511

'What?'

'We've found a cellar for a tomb.'

'I ain't ready to die yet.'

'Lucky you.'

She watched him totter to his feet. He looked around. 'This room was flooded once. With water that flowed.'

'From where to where?'

He shrugged and approached the stairs in a slow, laboured shuffle.

He looks a century old. As old as I feel. Together, we can't make up even one Heboric. I'm learning to appreciate irony, at least.

After some minutes Kulp finally reached the door. He laid a hand against it. 'Bronze sheeting – I can feel the hammer strokes that flattened it.' He rapped a knuckle on the dark metal. The sound that came was a rustling, sifting whisper. 'Wood's rotted behind it.'

The latch broke in his hand. The mage muttered a curse, then set his weight against the door and pushed.

The bronze cracked, crumpled inward. A moment later the door fell back, taking Kulp with it in a cloud of dust.

'Barriers are never as solid as one thinks,' Heboric said as the echoes of that crash faded. He stood holding his stubbed arms out before him. 'I understand this now. To a blind man his entire body is a ghost. Felt but not seen. Thus, I raise invisible arms, move invisible legs, my invisible chest rising and falling to unseen air. So now I stretch fingers, then make fists. I am everywhere solid – and always have been – if not for the deceit perpetrated by my own eyes.'

Felisin looked away from the ex-priest. 'Maybe if I go deaf you'll disappear.'

Heboric laughed.

At the landing, Kulp was making moaning sounds, his breath oddly harsh and laboured. She pushed herself upright, stumbling as pain closed iron bands around her ankles. Gritting her teeth, she hobbled to the stairs.

The eleven steps left her reeling with exhaustion. She fell to her knees beside the mage and waited a long minute before her breathing steadied. 'You all right?'

Kulp lifted his head. 'Broke my damned nose, I think.'

'From that new accent I'd say you were right. I take it you'll live, then.'

'Loudly.' He rose to his hands and knees, thick blood hanging in dusty threads from his face. 'See what's ahead? Ain't had a chance to look, yet.'

'It's dark. The air smells.'

'Like what?'

She shrugged. 'Not sure. Lime? As in limestone, that is.'

'Not bitter fruit? I'm surprised.'

Shuffling steps on the stairs indicated Heboric's approach.

A glow rose ahead, raising vague highlights that slowly etched a scene. Felisin stared.

'Your breath's quickened, lass,' Kulp said, still unwilling or unable to lift his head. 'Tell me what you're seeing.'

Heboric's voice echoed from halfway up the stairs: 'Remnants of a ritual gone awry is what she's seeing. Frozen memories of ancient pathos.'

'Sculptures,' Felisin said. 'Sprawled all over the floor – it's a big room. Very big – the light doesn't reach the far end—'

'Wait, you said sculptures? What kind?'

'People. Carved as if lying around – at first I thought they were real—'

'And why don't you think that any more?'

'Well . . .' Felisin crawled forward. The nearest one was a dozen paces away, a nude woman of advanced years, lying on her side as if dead or sleeping. The stone she had been fashioned from was dull white, limned and mottled with mould. Every wrinkle of her withered body had been artfully

513

rendered, no detail left out. She looked down on the peaceful, aged face. *Lady Gaesen – this woman could be her sister.* She reached out.

'Don't touch anything, mind,' Kulp said. 'I'm still seeing stars, but I've got raised hackles that says there's sorcery in that chamber.'

Felisin withdrew her hand, sat back. 'They're just statues—'

'On pedestals?'

'Well, no, just on the floor.'

The light suddenly brightened, filling the chamber. Felisin looked back to see Kulp on his feet, leaning against the crumbled door frame. The mage was blinking myopically as he took in the scene. 'Sculptures, lass?' he growled. 'Not a chance. A warren's ripped through here.'

'Some gates should never be opened,' Heboric said, blithely stepping past the mage. He walked unerringly to Felisin's side, where he stopped, cocking his head and smiling. 'Her daughter chose the Path of the Soletaken, a fraught journey, that. She was hardly unique, the twisted route was a popular alternative to Ascension. More . . . earthly, they claimed. And older, and that which was old was in high favour in the last days of the First Empire.' The ex-priest paused, sudden sorrow crumpling his features. 'It was understandable that Elders of the day sought to ease their children's chosen path. Sought to create a new version of the old, risk-laden one – for that had crumbled, weakened, was cancerous. Too many of the Empire's young were being lost – and never mind the wars to the west—'

Kulp had laid a hand on Heboric's shoulder. It was as if the touch closed a valve. The ex-priest raised a ghost-hand to his face, then sighed. 'Too easy to become lost . . .'

'We need water,' the mage said. 'Does her memory hold such knowledge?'

'This was a city of springs, fountains, baths and canals.'

'Probably filled with sand one and all,' Felisin said.

'Maybe not,' Kulp said, glancing around with bloodshot eyes. The break in his nose was a bad one, the swelling cracking the too dry skin on either side. 'This one's been emptied out recently – feel how the air still stirs.'

Felisin eyed the woman at her feet. 'She was once real, then. Flesh.'

'Aye, they all were.'

'Alchemies that slowed ageing,' Heboric said. 'Six, seven centuries for each citizen. The ritual killed them, yet the alchemies remained potent—'

'Then water deluged the city,' Kulp said. 'Mineral-rich.'

'Turning not just bone to stone, but flesh as well.' Heboric shrugged. 'The flood was born of distant events – the immortal custodians had already come and gone.'

'What immortal custodians, old man?'

'There may yet be a spring,' the ex-priest said. 'Not far.'

'Lead on, blind man,' Felisin said.

'I've got more questions,' Kulp said.

Heboric smiled. 'Later. Our immediate journey shall explain much.'

The chamber's mineralized occupants were all elderly, and numbered in the hundreds. Their deaths appeared to be, one and all, peaceful ones, which had a vaguely disquieting effect on Felisin. *Not all ends are tortured. Hood's indifferent to the means. So the priests claim, anyway. Yet his greatest harvests come from war, disease and famine. Those countless ages of deliverance must surely have marked the High King of Death. Disorder crowds his Gates and there's a flavour to that. Quiet genocide must ring very different bells.*

She felt Hood was with her now, in these hours and those since their return to this world. She found herself musing on him as if he was her lover, driven deep inside her with a claim that felt permanent and oddly reassuring.

And now, I fear only Heboric and Kulp. It's said gods fear mortals more than they do each other. Is that the source of my terror? Have I captured an echo of Hood within me? The god of death must surely dream rivers of blood. Perhaps I have been his all this time.

Thus I am blessed.

Heboric turned suddenly, seeming to regard her with his sunburned, swollen-shut eyes.

Can you now read my mind, old man?

Heboric's broad mouth twisted wryly. After a moment he swung back, continued on.

The chamber ended in a portalway that funnelled their path into a low-ceilinged tunnel. Past torrents of water had smoothed and polished the heavy stones on every side. Kulp maintained the diffuse, sourceless light as they stumbled onward.

We shamble like animated corpses, cursed in a journey without end. Felisin smiled. *Hood's own.*

They came to what had once been a street, narrow and crooked, its cobbles heaved and buckled. Low residential buildings crowded the sides beneath a roof of crusted, compacted glass. Along all the walls in sight ran narrow bands of similar substance, as if marking water levels or layers in the sand that had once filled every space.

In the street lay more bodies, but there was no peace to be found in their twisted, malformed shapes. Heboric paused, cocking his head. 'Ah, now we come upon altogether different memories.'

Kulp crouched down beside a figure. 'Soletaken, caught in the act of veering. Into something . . . reptilian.'

'Soletaken and D'ivers,' the ex-priest said. 'The ritual unleashed powers that ran wild. Like a plague, shapeshifting claimed thousands, unwelcomed, no initiation – many went mad. Death filled the city, every street, every house. Families were torn apart by their own.' He shook himself. 'All within but a handful of hours,' he whispered.

Kulp's eyes fixed on another figure, almost lost in the midst of a pile of mineralized corpses. 'Not just Soletaken and D'ivers . . .'

Heboric sighed. 'No.'

Felisin approached the subject of the mage's rapt attention. She saw thick, nut-brown limbs – an arm and a leg, still attached to an otherwise dismembered torso. Withered skin wrapped the thick bones. *I've seen this before. On the* Silanda. *T'lan Imass.*

'Your immortal custodians,' Kulp said.

'Aye.'

'They took losses here.'

'Oh, that they did,' Heboric said. 'Appalling losses. There is a bond between the T'lan Imass and Soletaken and D'ivers, a mysterious kinship that was unsuspected by the dwellers of this city – though they claimed for themselves the proud title of First Empire. That would have irritated the T'lan Imass – assuming such creatures can feel irritation – to have so boldly assumed a title that rightly belonged to them. Yet what drew them here was the ritual, and the need to set things right.'

Kulp was frowning behind the battered mask of his features. 'Our brushes with Soletaken . . . and the Imass. What's beginning again, Heboric?'

'I don't know, Mage. A return to that ancient gate? Another unleashing?'

'That Soletaken dragon we followed . . . it was undead.'

'It was T'lan Imass,' the ex-priest elaborated. 'A Bonecaster. Perhaps it is the old gate's custodian, drawn once again in answer to an impending calamity. Shall we move on? I can smell water – the spring we seek lives yet.'

* * *

The pool lay in the centre of a garden. Pale undergrowth carpeted the cracked flagstones on the footpath, white and pink leaves like shreds of flesh, colourless globes of some kind of fruit depending from vines wrapping stone columns and fossilized tree trunks. A garden thriving in darkness.

Eyeless white fish darted in the pool, seeking shadows as the sorcerous light pulsed bright.

Felisin fell to her knees, reached trembling hands down, slipped them into the cool water. The sensation rushed through her with ecstasy.

'Residue of alchemies,' Heboric said behind her.

She glanced back. 'What do you mean?'

'There will be . . . benefits . . . in drinking this nectar.'

'Is this fruit edible?' Kulp asked, hefting one of the pale globes.

'It was when it was bright red, nine thousand years ago.'

The thick ash hung motionless in their wake for as far as Kalam could see, though distance in the Imperial Warren was not a thing easily gauged. Their trail had the appearance of being as straight as a spear shaft. His frown deepened.

'We *are* lost,' Minala said, leaning back in her saddle.

'Better than dead,' Keneb muttered, offering the assassin at least that much sympathy.

Kalam felt Minala's hard grey eyes on him. 'Get us out of this Hood-cursed warren, Corporal! We're hungry, we're thirsty, we don't know where we are. Get us out!'

I've visualized Aren, I've picked the place – an unobtrusive niche at the end of the final twist of No Help Alley . . . in the heart of Dregs, that Malazan expatriate hovel close to the riverfront. Right down to the cobbles underfoot. So why can't we get there? What's blocking us? 'Not yet,' Kalam said. 'Even by warren, Aren is a long journey.' *That makes sense, doesn't it? So why all this unease?*

'Something's wrong,' Minala persisted. 'I can see it in your face. We should have arrived by now.'

The taste of ash, its smell, its feel, had become a part of him, and he knew it was the same for the others. The lifeless grit seemed to stain his very thoughts. Kalam had suspicions of what that ash had once been – the heap of bones they had stumbled onto when arriving had not proved unique – yet he found himself instinctively shying from acknowledging those suspicions. The possibility was too ghastly, too overwhelming, to contemplate.

Keneb grunted, then sighed. 'Well, Corporal, shall we continue on?'

Kalam glanced at the captain. The fever from his head wound was gone, though a barely perceptible slowness to his movements and expressions betrayed a healing yet incomplete. The assassin knew he could not count on the man in a fight. And with the apparent loss of Apt, he felt his back exposed. Minala's inability to trust him diminished the reliance he placed in her: she would do what was necessary to protect her sister and the children – that and nothing more.

Better were I alone. He nudged the stallion forward. After a moment the others followed.

The Imperial Warren was a realm with neither day nor night, just a perpetual dusk, its faint light sourceless – a place without shadows. They measured the passage of time by the cyclical demands imposed by their bodies. The need to eat and drink, the need to sleep. Yet, when gnawing hunger and thirst grew constant and unappeased, when exhaustion pulled at every step, the notion of time sank into meaninglessness; indeed, it revealed itself as something born of faith, not fact.

'Time makes of us believers. Timelessness makes of us unbelievers.' Another Saying of the Fool, another sly quote voiced by the sages of my homeland. Used most often when dismissing precedent, a derisive scoff at the lessons of history. The central assertion of sages was to believe nothing. More, that assertion was a central tenet of those who would become assassins.

'Assassination proves the lie of constancy. Even as the upraised dagger is itself a constant, your freedom to choose who, to choose when, is the constant's darker lie. An assassin is chaos unleashed, students. But remember, the upraised dagger can quench firestorms as easily as light them . . .'

And there, plainly carved in his thoughts as if with a dagger-point, stretched the thin, straight track that would lead him to Laseen. Every justification he needed rode unerring within that fissure. *Yet, while the track cuts through Aren, it seems all unknowing something's nudged me from it, left me wandering this plain of ash.*

'I see clouds ahead,' Minala said, now riding beside him.

Ridges of low-hanging dust crisscrossed the area before them. Kalam's eyes narrowed. 'As good as footprints in mud,' he muttered.

'What?'

'Look behind us – we leave the selfsame trail. We've company in the Imperial Warren.'

'And any company's unwelcome,' she said.

'Aye.'

Arriving at the first of the ragged ruts only deepened Kalam's unease. *More than one. Bestial. No servants sworn to the Empress left these . . .*

'Look,' Minala said, pointing.

Thirty paces ahead was what appeared to be a sinkhole or dark stain on the ground. Suspended ash rimmed the pit in a motionless, semi-translucent curtain.

'Is it just me,' Keneb growled behind them, 'or is there a new smell to this Hood-rotted air?'

'Like wood spice,' Minala agreed.

Hackles rising, Kalam freed his crossbow from its binding on the saddle, cranked the claw back until it locked, then slid a quarrel into the slot. He felt Minala's eyes on him throughout and was not surprised when she spoke.

'That particular smell's one you're familiar with, isn't it? And not from rifling some merchant's bolt-chest, either. What should we be on the lookout for, Corporal?'

'Anything,' he said, kicking his horse into a walk.

The pit was at least a hundred paces across, the edges heaped in places with excavated fill. Burned bone jutted from those mounds.

Kalam's stallion stopped a few yards from the edge. Still gripping the crossbow, the assassin lifted one leg over the saddlehorn, then slipped down, landing in a puff of grey cloud. 'Best stay here,' he told the others. 'No telling how firm the sides are.'

'Then why approach at all?' Minala demanded.

Not answering, Kalam edged forward. He came to within two paces of the rim, close enough to see what lay at the bottom of the pit, although at first it was the far side that held his attention. *Now I know what we're walking on and refusing to think on it didn't help at all. Hood's breath!* The ash formed compacted layers, revealing past variations in the temperature and ferocity of the fires that had incinerated this land – and everything on it. The layers varied in thickness as well. One of the thickest was an arm's length in depth and looked solid with compacted, shattered bone. Immediately below it was a thinner, reddish layer of what looked like brick dust. Other layers revealed only charred bones, mottled with black patches rimmed in white. Those few that he could identify looked human in size – perhaps slightly longer of limb. The banded wall opposite him was at least six arm-spans deep. *We stride ancient death, the remains of . . . millions.*

His gaze slowly descended to the pit's floor. It was crowded with rusted, corroded mechanisms, all alike though strewn about. Each was the size of a trader's wagon, and indeed huge spoked iron wheels were visible.

Kalam studied them a long time, then he swung about and

returned to the others, uncocking the crossbow as he did so.

'Well?'

The assassin shrugged, pulling himself back into the saddle. 'Old ruins at the bottom. Odd ones – the only time I've seen anything like them was in Darujhistan, within the temple that housed Icarium's Circle of Seasons, which was said to measure the passage of time.'

Keneb grunted.

Kalam glanced at the man. 'Something, Captain?'

'A rumour, nothing more. Months old.'

'What rumour?'

'Oh, that Icarium was seen.' The man suddenly frowned. 'What do you know of the Deck of Dragons, Corporal?'

'Enough to stay away from it.'

Keneb nodded. 'We had a Seer pass through around that time – some of my squads chipped in for a reading, ended up getting their money back since the Seer couldn't take the field past the first card – the Seer wasn't surprised, I recall. Said that'd been the case for weeks, and not just for him, but for every other reader as well.'

Alas, that wasn't my luck the last time I saw a Deck. 'Which card?'

'One of the Unaligned I think it was. Which are those?'

'Orb, Throne, Sceptre, Obelisk—'

'Obelisk! That's the one. The Seer claimed it was Icarium's doing, that he'd been seen with his Trell companion in Pan'potsun.'

'Does any of this matter?' Minala demanded.

Obelisk . . . past, present, future. Time, and time has no allies . . . 'Probably not,' the assassin replied.

They rode on, skirting the pit at a safe distance. More dust trails crossed their route, with only a few suggesting the passage of a human. Athough it was hard to be certain, they seemed to be heading in the opposite direction to the one Kalam had chosen. *If indeed we're travelling south, then the Soletaken and D'ivers are all travelling north. That might be reassuring, except that if there're more shapeshifters on the way, we'll run right into them.*

A thousand paces later, they came to a sunken road. Like the mechanisms in the pit, it was six arm-spans down. While dust filled the air above the cobbles, making them blurry, the steeply banked sides had not slumped. Kalam dismounted, tied a long, thin rope to his stallion's saddlehorn, then, gripping the rope's other end, began making his way down. To his surprise he did not sink into the bank. His boots crunched. The slope had been solidified somehow. Nor was it too steep for the horses.

The assassin glanced up at the others. 'This can lead us in the direction we've been travelling along, more or less. I suggest we take it – we'll make much better time.'

'Going nowhere faster,' Minala said.

Kalam grinned.

When everyone had led their mounts down, the captain spoke. 'Why not camp here for a while? We're not visible and the air's a bit cleaner.'

'And cooler,' Selv added, her arms around her all too quiet children.

'All right,' the assassin agreed.

The bladders of water for the horses were getting ominously light – the animals could last a few days on feed alone, Kalam knew, though they would suffer terribly. *We're running out of time.* As he unsaddled, fed and watered the horses, Minala and Keneb laid out the bedrolls, then assembled the meagre supplies that would make up their own meal. The preparations were conducted in silence.

'Can't say I'm encouraged by this place,' Keneb said as they ate.

Kalam grunted, appreciating the gradual emergence of the captain's sense of humour. 'Could do with a good sweeping,' he agreed.

'Aye. Mind you, I've seen bonfires get out of control before . . .'

Minala took a last sip of water, set the bladder down. 'I'm done,' she announced, rising. 'You two can discuss the weather in peace.'

They watched her stride to her bedroll. Selv repacked the remaining food, then led her children away as well.

'It's my watch,' Kalam reminded the captain.

'I'm not tired—'

The assassin barked a laugh.

'All right, I'm tired. We all are. Thing is, this dust has us all snoring so loud we'd drown out stags in heat. I end up just lying there, staring up at what should be sky but looks more like a shroud. Throat on fire, lungs aching like they were full of sludge, eyes drier than a forgotten luckstone. We won't get any decent sleep until we've cleared this place out of our bodies—'

'We have to get out of here first.'

Keneb nodded. He glanced over to where the snores had already begun and lowered his voice. 'Any predictions on when that will be, Corporal?'

'No.'

The captain was silent a long time, then he sighed. 'You've somehow crossed blades with Minala. That's an unwelcome tension to our little family, wouldn't you say?'

Kalam said nothing.

After a moment, Keneb continued. 'Colonel Tras wanted a quiet, obedient wife, a wife to perch on his arm and make pretty sounds—'

'Not very observant, was he?'

'More like stubborn. Any horse can be broken, was his philosophy. And that's what he set about doing.'

'Was the colonel a subtle man?'

'Not even a clever one.'

'Yet Minala is both – what in Hood's name was she thinking?'

Keneb's eyes narrowed on the assassin's, as if he'd suddenly grasped something. Then he shrugged. 'She loves her sister.'

Kalam looked away with a humourless grin. 'Isn't the officer corps a wonderful life.'

'Tras wasn't long for that backwater garrison post. He used his messengers to weave a broad net. He was maybe a week away from catching a new commission right at the heart of things.'

'Aren.'

'Aye.'

'You'd get the garrison command, then.'

'And ten more Imperials a month. Enough to hire good tutors for Kesen and Vaneb, instead of that wine-addled old toad with the fiddling hands attached to the garrison staff.'

'Minala doesn't look broken,' Kalam said.

'Oh, she's broken all right. Forced healing was the colonel's mainstay. It's one thing to beat a person senseless, then have to wait a month or more for her to mend before you can do it again. With a squad healer with gambling debts at your side, you can break bones before breakfast and have her ready for more come the next sunrise.'

'With you smartly saluting through it all—'

Keneb winced, glanced away. 'Can't object to what you don't know, Corporal. If I'd had as much as a suspicion . . .' He shook his head. 'Closed doors. It was Selv who found out, through a launderer we shared with the colonel's household. Blood on the sheets and all that. When she told me I went to call him out to the compound.' He grimaced. 'The rebellion interrupted me – I walked into an ambush well under way, and then my only concern was in keeping us all alive.'

'How did the good colonel die?'

'You've just come to a closed door, Corporal.'

Kalam smiled. 'That's all right. Times like these I can see through them well enough.'

'Then I needn't say any more.'

'Looking at Minala, none of this makes sense,' the assassin said.

'There's different kinds of strength, I guess. And defences. She used to be close with Selv, with the children. Now she wraps herself around them like armour, just as cold and just as hard. What she's having trouble with is you, Kalam. You've wrapped yourself in the same way but around her – and the rest of us.'

And she's feeling redundant? Maybe that's how it would look to Keneb. 'Her trouble with me is that she doesn't trust me, Captain.'

'Why in Hood's name not?'

Because I'm holding daggers unseen. And she knows it. Kalam shrugged. 'From what you've told me, I'd expect trust to be something she wouldn't easily grant to anyone, Captain.'

Keneb mused on this, then he sighed and rose. 'Well, enough of that. I've a shroud to stare up at and snores to count.'

Kalam watched the captain move away and settle down beside Selv. The assassin drew a deep, slow breath. *I expect your death was a quick one, Colonel Tras. Be fickle, dear Hood, and spit the bastard back out. I'll kill him again, and Queen turn away, I'll not be quick.*

On his belly, Fiddler wormed his way down the rock-tumbled slope, heedlessly scraping his knuckles as he held out his cocked crossbow before him. *That bastard Servant's dissolving in a dozen stomachs by now. Either that or his head's riding a pike minus the ears now dangling from someone's hip.*

526

All of Icarium's and Mappo's skills had been stretched to the limit with the simple effort of keeping everyone alive. The Whirlwind, for all its violence, was no longer an empty storm scouring a dead land. Servant's trail had led the group into a more focused mayhem.

Another lance flew out from the swirling ochre curtain to his left and landed with a clatter ten paces from where the sapper lay. *Your goddess's wrath leaves you as blind as us, fool!*

They were in hills crawling with Sha'ik's desert warriors. There was both coincidence and something else in this fell convergence. *Convergence indeed. The followers seek the woman they're sworn to follow. Too bad that the other path happens to be here as well.*

Distant screams rose above the wind's more guttural howl. *Lo, the hills are alive with beasts. Foul-tempered ones at that.* Three times in the past hour Icarium had led them around a Soletaken or a D'ivers. There was some kind of mutually agreed avoidance going on – the shapeshifters wanted nothing to do with the Jhag. *But Sha'ik's fanatics . . . ah, now they're fair game. Lucky for us.*

Still, the likelihood that Servant still lived seemed, to Fiddler's mind, very small indeed. He worried for Apsalar as well, and found himself – ironically – praying that a god's skills would prove equal to the task.

Two desert warriors wearing leather armour appeared ahead and below, scampering with panicked haste down towards the base of the gorge.

Fiddler hissed a curse. He was the group's flank on this side – if they got past him . . .

The sapper raised his crossbow.

Black cloaks swept over the two figures. They shrieked. The cloaks swarmed, crawled. Spiders, big enough to make out each one even at this distance. Fiddler's skin prickled. *You should have brought brooms, friends.*

He pushed himself up from the crevasse he had wedged himself into, angled right as he scrambled along the slope. *And if I don't get back into Icarium's influence soon, I'll be wishing I had as well.*

The screams of the desert warriors ceased, either with the distance the sapper put between him and them, or blissful release – he hoped the latter. Directly ahead rose the side of the ridge that had – thus far – marked Apsalar and her father's trail.

The wind tugged at him as he clambered his way to the top. Almost immediately he stumbled onto the spine and caught sight of the others, no more than ten paces ahead. The three were crouched over a motionless figure.

Fiddler went cold. *Oh, Hood, make it a stranger . . .*

It was. A young man, naked, his skin too pale to make him one of Sha'ik's desert tribesmen. His throat had been cut, the wound gaping down to the vertebra's flattened inner side. There was no blood.

As Fiddler slowly crouched down, Mappo looked over at the sapper. 'A Soletaken, we think,' he said.

'That's Apsalar's work,' Fiddler said. 'See how the head was pushed forward and down, chin tucked to anchor the blade – I've seen it before . . .'

'Then she's alive,' Crokus said.

'As I said,' Icarium rumbled. 'As is her father.'

So far so good. Fiddler straightened. 'There's no blood,' he said. 'Any idea how long ago he was killed?'

'No more than an hour,' Mappo said. 'As for the lack of blood . . .' He shrugged. 'The Whirlwind is a thirsty goddess.'

The sapper nodded. 'I think I'll stick closer from now on, if you don't mind – I don't think we'll have any more trouble from Sha'ik's warriors – call it a gut feeling.'

Mappo nodded. 'For the moment, we ourselves walk the Path of Hands.'

And why is that, I wonder?

They resumed their journey. Fiddler mused on the half-dozen times he'd seen desert warriors in the past twelve hours. Desperate men and women in truth. Raraku was the centre of the Apocalypse, yet the rebellion was headless and had been for some time. What was going on beyond the Holy Desert's ring of crags?

Anarchy, I'd wager. Slaughter and frenzy. Hearts of ice and the mercy of cold steel. Even if the illusion of Sha'ik is being maintained – her ranking followers now issuing commands – she's not led her army out to make it the rebellion's lodestone. Doesn't sit well proclaiming an uprising, then not showing up to lead it . . .

Apsalar would have her hands full, should she accept the role. An assassin's skills might keep her alive, but they offered nothing of the intangible magnetism necessary to lead armies. *Commanding* armies was easy enough – the traditional structures ensured that, as the barely competent Fists of the Malazan Empire clearly showed – but *leading* was another thing entirely.

Fiddler could think of only a handful of people possessing that magnetic quality. Dassem Ultor, Prince K'azz D'Avore of the Crimson Guard, Caladan Brood and Dujek Onearm. *Tattersail if she'd had the ambition. Likely Sha'ik herself. And Whiskeyjack.*

As alluring as Apsalar was, the sapper had seen nothing of such force of personality. Competence, without a doubt. Quiet confidence as well. But she clearly preferred observing over participating – *at least until the time came to draw the sticker. Assassins don't bother honing their powers to persuade – why bother? She'll need the right people around her . . .*

Fiddler scowled to himself. He'd already taken it as given that the lass would assume the guise, twined to the central thread of this goddess-woven tapestry. *And here we are, racing through the Whirlwind . . . to arrive in time to witness the prophetic rebirth.*

Eyes narrowed against the blowing grit, the sapper glanced at Crokus. The lad strode half a dozen paces ahead, a step behind Icarium. Even leaning as he did into the biting wind, he betrayed something fraught and fragile in his posture. *She'd said nothing to him before leaving – she'd dismissed him and his concerns as easily as she did the rest of us. Pust offered her father to seal the pact. But sent him out here first. That suggested the old man was a willing player in the scheme, a co-conspirator. If I was that lass, I'd have some hard questions for ol' Dadda . . .*

On all sides, the Whirlwind seemed to howl with laughter.

The bruise was vaguely door-shaped and twice a man's height. Pearl paced before it, muttering to himself, while Lostara Yil watched in weary patience.

Finally he turned, as if suddenly recalling her presence. 'Complications, my dear. I am . . . torn.'

The Red Blade eyed the portal. 'Has the assassin left the warren, then? This does not look the same as the other one . . .'

The Claw wiped ash from his brow, leaving a dusky streak. 'Ah, no. This represents a . . . a detour. I'm the last surviving operative, after all. The Empress so despises idle hands . . .' He gave her a wry smile, then shrugged. 'This is not my only concern, alas. We are being tracked.'

She felt a chill at those words. 'We should double back, then. Prepare an ambush—'

Pearl grinned, waved an arm. 'Choose us a likely place, then. Please.'

She glanced around. Flat horizons in all directions. 'What of those raised humps we passed a while back?'

'Never mind those,' the Claw said. 'Safe distance the first time and no closer now.'

'Then that pit . . .'

'Mechanisms to measure futility. I think not, my dear. For the moment, I fear, we must ignore that which stalks us—'

'What if it's Kalam?'

'It isn't. Thanks to you, we're keeping our eyes on him. Our assassin's mind wanders, and so therefore does his path. An embarrassing lack of discipline for one so weighty. I admit I am disappointed in the man.' He swung to face the portal. 'In any case, we have digressed a rather vast distance here. A small measure of assistance is required – not lengthy, I assure you. The Empress agrees that Kalam's journey suggests . . . personal risks to her person, and so must take ultimate precedence. Nonetheless . . .'

The Claw removed his half-cloak, carefully folding it before setting it down. Across his chest was a belt containing throwing stars. A brace of knives jutted pommel-forward under his left arm. Pearl went through a ritual of checking every weapon.

'Do I wait here?'

'As you like. While I cannot guarantee your safety if you accompany me, I am for a skirmish.'

'The enemy?'

'Followers of the Whirlwind.'

Lostara Yil unsheathed her tulwar.

Pearl grinned, as if well aware of the effect his words would have. 'When we appear, it shall be night. Thick mists, as well. Our foes are Semk and Tithansi, and our allies—'

'Allies? This is a skirmish already underway?'

'Oh, indeed. Wickans and marines of the Seventh.'

Lostara bared her teeth. 'Coltaine.'

His grin broadening, Pearl drew on a pair of thin leather gloves. 'Ideally,' he continued, 'we should remain unseen.'

'Why?'

'If help appears once, the expectation is it will appear again. The risk is dulling Coltaine's edge, and by the Hidden Ones, the Wickan will need that edge in the weeks to come.'

'I am ready.'

'One thing,' the Claw drawled. 'There's a Semk demon. Stay

531

away from it, for while we know virtually nothing of its powers, what we do know suggests an appalling . . . temper.'

'I shall be right behind you,' Lostara said.

'Hmm, in that case, once we're through, pull left. I'll go right. Not an auspicious entry my getting trampled, after all.'

The portal flared. In a blur Pearl slid forward and vanished. Lostara jabbed her heels into her mount's flanks. The horse bolted through the portal—

—her hooves thumping hard soil. Fog twisted wildly around her, through a darkness that was alive with screams and detonations. She'd already lost Pearl, but that concern was quickly flung aside as four Tithansi warriors on foot stumbled into view.

A sharper had chewed them up, and none was prepared as Lostara charged them, her tulwar flashing. They scattered, but their wounds made them fatally slow. Two fell to her blade with the first pass. She spun her horse to ready a return charge.

The other two warriors were nowhere to be seen, the mists closing in like slowly tumbling blankets. A flurry of sound to her left brought her wheeling her horse around, in time to see Pearl sprint into view. He spun in midstride and sent a star flashing behind him.

The huge, bestial man that lumbered into sight had his head rocked back as the iron star embedded itself in his forehead. It barely slowed him.

Lostara snarled, quickly dropping the tulwar to swing wildly from the loop around her wrist as she brought her crossbow around.

Her shot went low, the quarrel sinking in just below the Semk's sternum and above the odd thick leather belts protecting his midriff. It proved far more efficacious than Pearl's star. As the man grunted and buckled, she saw with shock that his mouth and nostrils had been sewn shut. *He draws no breath! Here's our demon!*

The Semk straightened, flinging his arms forward. The power that erupted from them was unseen, but both Pearl and Lostara were thrown, tumbling through the air. The horse screamed in mortal agony amidst a rapid crunching and cracking of bones.

The Red Blade landed on her right hip, feeling the bone resound within her like a fractured bell. Then waves of pain closed taloned hands around her leg. Her bladder went, flooding her underclothes in a hot bloom.

Moccasined feet landed beside her. A knife grip was thrust into her hand. 'Take yourself once I'm done! Here it comes!'

Teeth clenched, Lostara Yil twisted around.

The Semk demon was ten paces away, huge and unstoppable. Pearl crouched between them, holding knives that dripped red fire. Lostara knew he considered himself already dead.

The thing that suddenly closed from the demon's left was a nightmare. Black, three-limbed, a jutting shoulder blade like a cowl behind a long-necked head, a grinning jaw crowded with fangs, and a single, flat black eye that glistened wetly.

Even more terrifying was the humanoid figure that sat behind that shoulder blade, its face a mocking mimicry of the beast it rode, the lips peeled back to reveal daggerlike fangs as long as a toddler's fingers, its lone eye flashing.

The apparition struck the Semk demon like a runaway armoured wagon. The single forelimb snapped forward to plunge deep into the demon's belly, then pulled back in an explosion of spurting fluids. Clenched in that forelimb's grip was something that radiated fury in palpable waves. The air went icy.

Pearl backed away until his heels struck Lostara, then he reached down one hand, eyes still on the scene, and gripped her weapon harness.

The Semk's body seemed to fold in on itself as it staggered

back. The apparition reared, still clutching the fleshy, dripping object.

Its rider made a grab for it, but the creature hissed, twisting to keep it out of his reach. Instead it flung the object away into the mists.

The Semk stumbled after it.

The apparition's long head swung to face Lostara and Pearl with that ghastly grin.

'Thank you,' Pearl whispered.

A portal blossomed around them.

Lostara blinked up at a dull, ash-laden sky. There was no sound but their breathing. *Safe*. A moment later unconsciousness slipped over her like a shroud.

CHAPTER THIRTEEN

> An exquisite match of dog to master, the Wickan
> cattle-dog is a vicious, unpredictable breed, compact
> yet powerful, though by far its most notable
> characteristic is its stubborn will.
>
> *Lives of the Conquered*
> Ilem Trauth

As Duiker strode between the large, spacious tents, a
chorus of shouts erupted ahead. A moment later one of
the Wickan dogs appeared, head low, a surging rush
of muscle, heading straight for the historian.

Duiker fumbled for his sword, already knowing it was far too
late. At the last instant the huge animal dodged lithely around
him, and the historian saw that it held in its mouth a lapdog,
its eyes dark pools of terror.

The cattle-dog ran on, slipping between two tents and disappearing from sight.

Ahead of the historian, a number of figures appeared, armed
with large rocks and – bizarrely – Kanese parasols. One and all,
they were dressed as if about to attend a royal function,
although in their expressions Duiker saw raw fury.

'You there!' one yelled imperiously. 'Old man! Did you see a
mad hound just now?'

'I saw a running cattle-dog, aye,' the historian quietly replied.

535

'With a rare Hengese roach dog in its mouth?'

A dog that eats cockroaches? 'Rare? I assumed it was raw.'

The nobles grew quiet as gazes focused on Duiker.

'A foolish time for humour, old man,' the spokesman growled. He was younger than the others, his honey-coloured skin and large eyes denoting his Quon Talian lineage. He was lean, with the physical assurance of a duellist – the identification confirmed by the basket-hilted rapier at his belt. Moreover, there was something in the man's eyes that suggested to Duiker that here was someone who enjoyed killing.

The man approached, his walk becoming a swagger. 'An apology, peasant – though I'll grant it won't save you from a beating, at least you'll stay breathing . . .'

A horseman approached from behind at a canter.

Duiker saw the duellist's eyes dart over the historian's shoulder.

Corporal List reined in, ignoring the nobleman. 'My apologies, sir,' he said. 'I was delayed at the smithy. Where is your horse?'

'With the main herd,' Duiker replied. 'A day off for the poor beast – long overdue.'

For a young man of low rank, List managed an impressive expression of cold regard as he finally looked down at the nobleman. 'If we arrive late, sir,' he said to Duiker, 'Coltaine will demand an explanation.'

The historian addressed the nobleman. 'Are we done here?'

The man gave a curt nod. 'For now,' he said.

Escorted by the corporal, Duiker resumed his journey through the nobles' camp. When they had gone a dozen paces, List leaned over his saddle. 'Alar looked ready to call you out, Historian.'

'He's known, then? Alar.'

'Pullyk Alar—'

'How unfortunate for him.'

List grinned.

They came to a central clearing in the encampment and discovered a whipping underway. The short, wide man with the leather cat-tail in one heat-bloated hand was familiar. The victim was a servant. Three other servants stood off to one side, their eyes averted. A few other nobleborn stood nearby, gathered around a weeping woman and voicing murmurs of consolation.

Lenestro's gold-brocaded cloak had lost some of its brilliant sheen, and in his red-faced frenzy as he swung the cat-tail he looked like a frothing ape performing the traditional King's Mirror farce at a village fair.

'I see the nobles are pleased by the return of their servant-folk,' List said dryly.

'I suspect this has more to do with a snatched lapdog,' the historian muttered. 'In any case, this stops now.'

The corporal glanced over. 'He'll simply resume it later, sir.'

Duiker said nothing.

'Who would steal a lapdog?' List wondered, staying alongside the historian as he approached Lenestro.

'Who wouldn't? We've water but we're still hungry. In any case, one of the Wickan cattle-dogs thought it up before the rest of us – to our collective embarrassment.'

'I blame preoccupation, sir.'

Lenestro noted their approach and paused his whipping, his breath loud as a bellows.

Ignoring the nobleman, Duiker went to the servant. The man was old, down on his elbows and knees, hands held protectively behind his head. Red welts rode his knuckles, his neck and down the length of his bony back. Beneath the ruin were the tracks of older scars. A jewel-studded leash with a broken collar lay in the dust beside him.

'Not your business, Historian,' Lenestro snapped.

'These servants stood a Tithansi charge at Sekala,' Duiker said. 'That defence helped to keep your head on your shoulders, Lenestro.'

'Coltaine stole property!' the nobleman squealed. 'The Council so judged him, the fine has been issued!'

'Issued,' List said, 'and duly pissed on.'

Lenestro wheeled on the corporal, raised his whip.

'A warning,' Duiker said, straightening. 'Striking a soldier of the Seventh – or, for that matter, his horse – will see you hung.'

Lenestro visibly struggled with his temper, his arm still raised, the whip quivering.

Others were gathering, their sympathy clearly united with Lenestro. Even so, the historian did not anticipate violence. The nobles might well possess unrealistic notions, but they were anything but suicidal.

Duiker spoke, 'Corporal, we'll take this man to the Seventh's healers.'

'Yes, sir,' List replied, briskly dismounting.

The servant had passed out. Together they carried him to the horse and laid him belly-down across the saddle.

'He shall be returned to me once healed,' Lenestro said.

'So you can do it all over again? Wrong, he'll not be returned to you.' *And if you and your comrades are outraged, wait till an hour from now.*

'All such acts contrary to Malazan law are being noted,' the nobleman said shrilly. 'There shall be recompense, with interest.'

Duiker had heard enough. He suddenly closed the distance to grasp Lenestro's cloak collar with both hands, and gave the man a teeth-rattling shake. The whip fell to the ground. The nobleman's eyes were wide with terror – reminding the historian of the lapdog's as it rode the hound's mouth.

'You probably think,' Duiker whispered, 'that I'm about to tell you about the situation we're all in. But it's already quite evident that there'd be little point. You are a small-brained thug, Lenestro. Push me again, and I'll have you eating pigshit and liking it.' He shook the pathetic creature again, then dropped him.

Lenestro collapsed.

Duiker frowned down at the man.

'He's fainted, sir,' List said.

'So he has.' *Old man scared you, did he?*

'Was that really necessary?' a voice asked plaintively. Nethpara emerged from the crowd. 'As if our ongoing petition is not crowded enough, now we have personal bullying to add to our grievances. Shame on you, Historian—'

'Excuse me, sir,' List said, 'but you might wish to know – before you resume berating the historian – that scholarship came late to this man. You will find his name among the Noted on the First Army's Column at Unta, and had you not just come late to this scene, you would have witnessed an old soldier's temper. Indeed, it was admirable restraint that the historian elected to use both hands to grip Lenestro's cloak, lest he use one to unsheathe that well-worn sword at his hip and drive it through the toad's heart.'

Nethpara blinked sweat from his eyes.

Duiker slowly swung to face List.

The corporal noted the dismay in the historian's face and answered it with a wink. 'We'd best move on, sir,' he said.

They left behind a gathering in the clearing that broke its silence only after they'd entered the opposite aisle.

List walked alongside the historian, leading his horse by the reins. 'It still astonishes me that they persist in the notion that we will survive this journey.'

Duiker glanced over in surprise. 'Are you lacking such faith, then, Corporal?'

'We'll never reach Aren, Historian. Yet the fools compile

their petitions, their grievances – against the very people keeping them alive.'

'There's great need to maintain the illusion of order, List. In us all.'

The young man's expression turned wry. 'I missed your moment of sympathy back there, sir.'

'Obviously.'

They left the nobles' encampment and entered the mayhem of the wagons bearing wounded. Voices moaned a constant chorus of pain. A chill crept over Duiker. Even wheeled hospitals carried with them that pervasive atmosphere of fear, the sounds of defiance and the silence of surrender. Mortality's many comforting layers had been stripped away, revealing wracked bones, a sudden comprehension of death that throbbed like an exposed nerve.

Awareness and revelations thickened the prairie air in a manner priests could only dream of for their temples. *To fear the gods is to fear death. In places where men and women are dying, the gods no longer stand in the spaces in between. The soothing intercession is gone. They've stepped back, back through the gates, and watch from the other side. Watch and wait.*

'We should've gone around,' List muttered.

'Even without that man in need on your horse,' Duiker said, 'I would have insisted we pass through this place, Corporal.'

'I've learned this lesson already,' List replied, a tautness in his tone.

'From your earlier words, I would suggest that the lesson you have learned is different from mine, lad.'

'This place encourages you, Historian?'

'Strengthens, Corporal, though in a cold way, I admit. Never mind the games of Ascendants. This is what we are. The endless struggle laid bare. Gone is the idyllic, the deceit of self-import as well as the false humility of insignificance. Even as we battle wholly personal battles, we are unified. This is the place of level earth, Corporal. That is its lesson, and I wonder if it is an accident that that deluded mob in gold threads must walk in the wake of these wagons.'

'Either way, few revelations have bled back to stain noble sentiments.'

'No? I smelled desperation back there, Corporal.'

List spied a healer and they delivered the servant into the woman's blood-smeared hands.

The sun was low on the horizon directly ahead by the time they reached the Seventh's main camp. The faint smoke from the dung fires hung like gilded gauze over the ordered rows of tents. Off to one side two squads of infantry had set to in a contest of belt-grip, using a leather-strapped skullcap for a ball. A ring of cheering, jeering onlookers had gathered. Laughter rang in the air.

Duiker remembered the words of an old marine from his soldiering days. *Some times you just have to grin and spit in Hood's face*. The contesting squads were doing just that, running themselves ragged to sneer at their own exhaustion besides, and well aware that Tithansi eyes watched from a distance.

They were a day away from the River P'atha, and the impending battle was a promise that thickened the dusk.

Two of the Seventh's marines flanked Coltaine's command tent, and the historian recognized one of them.

She nodded. 'Historian.'

There was a look in her pale eyes that seemed to lay an invisible hand against his chest, and Duiker was stilled to silence, though he managed a smile.

As they passed between the drawn flaps, List murmured, 'Well now, Historian.'

'Enough of that, Corporal.' But he did not glance over to nail the young man's grin, as he was tempted to do. *A man gets to an age where he's wise not to banter on desire with a comrade half his age. Too pathetic by far, that illusion of competition. Besides, that look of hers was likely more pitying than anything else, no matter what my heart whispered. Put an end to your foolish thoughts, old man.*

Coltaine stood near the centre pole, his expression dark. Duiker and List's arrival had interrupted a conversation. Bult and Captain Lull sat on saddle-chairs, looking glum. Sormo stood wrapped in an antelope hide, his back to the tent's far wall, his eyes hooded in shadow. The air was sweltering and tense.

Bult cleared his throat. 'Sormo was explaining about the Semk godling,' he said. 'The spirits say something damaged it. Badly. The night of the raid – a demon walked the land. Lightly, I gather, leaving a spoor not easily sniffed out. In any case, it appeared, mauled the Semk, then left. It seems, Historian, that the Claw had company.'

'An Imperial demon?'

Bult shrugged and swung his flat gaze to Sormo.

The warlock, looking like a black vulture perched on a fence pole, stirred slightly. 'There is precedent,' he admitted. 'Yet Nil believes otherwise.'

'Why?' Duiker asked.

There was a long pause before Sormo answered. 'When Nil fled into himself that night . . . no, that is, he *believed* that it was his own mind that sheltered him from the Semk's sorcerous attack . . .' It was clear that the warlock was in difficulty with his words. 'The Tano Spiritwalkers of this land are said to be able to quest through a hidden world – not a true warren, but a realm where souls are freed of flesh and bone. It seems that Nil stumbled into such a place, and there he came face to face with . . . someone else. At first he thought it but an aspect of himself, a monstrous reflection—'

'Monstrous?' Duiker asked.

'A boy of Nil's own age, yet with a demonic face. Nil believes it was bonded with the apparition that attacked

542

the Semk. Imperial demons rarely possess human familiars.'

'Then who sent it?'

'Perhaps no-one.'

No wonder Coltaine's had his black feathers ruffled.

After a few minutes Bult sighed loudly, stretching out his gnarled, bandy legs. 'Kamist Reloe has prepared a welcome for us the other side of the River P'atha. We cannot afford to go around him. Therefore we shall go through him.'

'You ride with the marines,' Coltaine told Duiker.

The historian glanced at Captain Lull.

The red-bearded man grinned. 'Seems you've earned a place with the best, old man.'

'Hood's breath! I'll not last five minutes in a line of battle. My heart nearly gave out after a skirmish lasting all of three breaths the other night—'

'We won't be front line,' Lull said. 'There ain't enough of us left for that. If all goes as planned we won't even get our swords nicked.'

'Oh, very well.' Duiker turned to Coltaine. 'Returning the servants to the nobles was a mistake,' he said. 'It seems the nobleborn have concluded that you'll not take them away again if they're not fit to stand.'

Bult said, 'They showed spine, those servants, at Sekala Crossing. Just holding shields, mind, but hold is what they did.'

'Uncle, do you still have that scroll demanding compensation?' Coltaine asked.

'Aye.'

'And that compensation was calculated based on the worth of each servant, in coin?'

Bult nodded.

'Collect the servants and pay for them in full, in gold jakatas.'

'Aye, though all that gold will burden the nobles sorely.'

'Better them than us.'

Lull cleared his throat. 'That coin's the soldiers' pay, ain't it?'

'The Empire honours its debts,' Coltaine growled.

It was a statement that promised to grow in resonance in the time to come, and the momentary silence in the tent told Duiker that he was not alone in that recognition.

Capemoths swarmed across the face of the moon. Duiker sat beside the flaked embers of a cooking fire. A nervous energy had driven the historian from his bedroll. On all sides the camp slept, a city exhausted. Even the animals had fallen silent.

Rhizan swept through the warm air above the hearth, plucking hovering insects on the wing. The soft crunch of exoskeletons was a constant crackle.

A dark shape appeared at Duiker's side, lowered itself into a squat, held silent.

After a while, Duiker said, 'A Fist needs his rest.'

Coltaine grunted. 'And a historian?'

'Never rests.'

'We are denied in our needs,' the Wickan said.

'It was ever thus.'

'Historian, you joke like a Wickan.'

'I've made a study of Bult's lack of humour.'

'That much is patently clear.'

There was silence between them for a time. Duiker could make no claim to know the man at his side. If the Fist was plagued by doubts he did not show it, nor, of course, would he. A commander could not reveal his flaws. With Coltaine, however, it was more than his rank dictating his recalcitrance. Even Bult had occasion to mutter that his nephew was a man who isolated himself to levels far beyond the natural Wickan stoicism.

Coltaine never made speeches to his troops, and while he

was often seen by his soldiers, he did not make a point of it as many commanders did. Yet those soldiers belonged to him now, as if the Fist could fill every silent space with a physical assurance as solid as a gripping of forearms.

What happens the day that faith is shattered? What if we are but hours from that day?

'The enemy hunts our scouts,' Coltaine said. 'We cannot see what has been prepared for us in the valley ahead.'

'Sormo's allies?'

'The spirits are preoccupied.'

Ah, the Semk godling.

'Can'eld, Debrahl, Tithan, Semk, Tepasi, Halafan, Ubari, Hissari, Sialk and Guran.'

Four tribes now. Six city legions. Am I hearing doubt?

The Fist spat into the embers. 'The army that awaits us is one of two holding the south.'

How in Hood's name does he know this? 'Has Sha'ik marched out of Raraku, then?'

'She has not. A mistake.'

'What holds her back? Has the rebellion been crushed in the north?'

'Crushed? No, it commands all. As for Sha'ik . . .' Coltaine paused to adjust his crow-feather cape. 'Perhaps her visions have taken her into the future. Perhaps she knows the Whirlwind shall fail, that even now the Adjunct to the Empress assembles her legions – Unta's harbour is solid with transports. The Whirlwind's successes will prove but momentary, a first blood-rush that succeeded only because of Imperial weakness. Sha'ik knows . . . the dragon has been stirred awake, and moves ponderously still, yet when the full fury comes, it shall scour this land from shore to shore.'

'This other army, here in the south . . . how far away?'

Coltaine straightened. 'I intend to arrive at Vathar two days before it.'

545

Word must have reached him that Ubaryd has fallen, along with Devral and Asmar. Vathar – the third and last river. If we make Vathar, it's a straight run south to Aren – through the most forbidding wasteland on this Hood-cursed continent. 'Fist, the River Vathar is still months away. What of tomorrow?'

Coltaine pulled his gaze from the embers and blinked at the historian. 'Tomorrow we crush Kamist Reloe's army, of course. One must think far ahead to succeed, Historian. You should understand that.'

The Fist strolled away.

Duiker stared at the dying fire, a sour taste in his mouth. *That taste is fear, old man. You've not got Coltaine's impenetrable armour. You cannot see past a few hours from now, and you await the dawn in the belief that it shall be your last, and therefore you must witness it. Coltaine expects the impossible, he expects us to share in his implacable confidence. To share in his madness.*

A rhizan landed on his boot, delicate wings folding as it settled. A young capemoth was in the winged lizard's mouth, its struggles continuing even as the rhizan methodically devoured it.

Duiker waited until the creature had finished its meal before a twitch of his foot sent it winging away. The historian straightened. The sounds of activity had risen in the Wickan encampments. He made his way towards the nearest one.

The horsewarriors of the Foolish Dog Clan had gathered to ready their equipment beneath the glare of torch poles. Duiker strode closer. Ornate boiled leather armour had appeared, dyed in deep and muddy shades of red and green. The thick, padded gear was in a style the historian had never seen before. Wickan runes had been burned into it. The armour looked ancient, yet never used.

Duiker approached the nearest warrior, a peach-faced youth busy rubbing grease into a horse's brow-guard. 'Heavy armour for a Wickan,' the historian said. 'And for a Wickan horse as well.'

The young man nodded soberly, said nothing.

'You're turning yourselves into heavy cavalry.'

The lad shrugged.

An older warrior nearby spoke up. 'The warleader devised these during the rebellion . . . then agreed peace with the Emperor before they could be used.'

'And you have been carrying them around with you all this time?'

'Aye.'

'Why didn't you use this armour at Sekala Crossing?'

'Didn't need to.'

'And now?'

Grinning, the veteran raised an iron helm with new bridge and cheek-guards attached. 'Reloe's horde hasn't faced heavy cavalry yet, has it?'

Thick armour doesn't make heavy cavalry. Have you fools ever trained for this? Can you gallop in an even line? Can you wheel? How soon before your horses are winded beneath all that extra weight? 'You'll look intimidating enough,' the historian said.

The Wickan caught the scepticism and his grin broadened.

The youth set down the brow-guard and began strapping on a sword belt. He slid the blade from the scabbard, revealing four feet of blackened iron, its tip rounded and blunt. The weapon looked heavy, oversized in the lad's hands.

Hood's breath, one swing'll yank him from his saddle.

The veteran grunted. 'Limber up there, Temul,' he said in Malazan.

Temul immediately launched into a complex choreography, the blade blurring in his hand.

'Do you intend to dismount once you reach the enemy?'

'Sleep would have done much for your mind's cast, old man.'

Point taken, bastard.

Duiker wandered away. He'd always hated the hours before a battle. None of the rituals of preparation had ever worked for

547

him. A check of weapons and gear rarely took an experienced soldier more than twenty heartbeats. The historian had never been able to repeat that check mindlessly, again and again, as did so many soldiers. Keeping the hands busy while the mind slowly slid into a sharp-edged world of saturated colours, painful clarity and a kind of lustful hunger that seized body and soul.

Some warriors ready themselves to live, some ready themselves to die, and in these hours before the fate unfolds, it's damned hard to tell one from the other. The lad Temul's dance a moment ago might be his last. That damned sword may never again leap from its sheath and sing on the end of his hand.

The sky was lightening in the east, the cool wind beginning to warm. The vast dome overhead was cloudless. A formation of birds flew high to the north, the pattern of specks almost motionless.

The Wickan camp behind him, Duiker entered the regimental rows of tents that marked the Seventh. The various elements maintained their cohesion in the encampment's layout, and each was clearly identifiable to the historian. The medium infantry, who formed the bulk of the army, were arranged by company, each company consisting of cohorts that were in turn made up of squads. They would go into battle with full-body shields of bronze, pikes and short swords. They wore bronze scale hauberks, greaves and gauntlets, and bronze helmets reinforced with iron bars wrapped in a cage around the skullcap. Chain camails protected their necks and shoulders. The other footmen consisted of marines and sappers, the former a combination of heavy infantry and shock troops – the old Emperor's invention and still unique to the Empire. They were armed with crossbows and short swords as well as long swords. They wore blackened chain beneath grey leathers. Every third soldier carried a large, round shield of thick, soft wood that would be soaked for an hour before battle. These shields were used to catch and hold enemy weapons ranging from swords to flails. They would be discarded after the first few minutes of a fight, usually studded with an appalling array of edged and spiked iron. This peculiar tactic of the Seventh had proved effective against the Semk and their undisciplined, two-handed fighting methods. The marines called it *pulling teeth*.

The sappers' encampment was set somewhat apart from the others – as far away as possible when they carried Moranth munitions. Though he looked, Duiker could not see its location, but he knew well what he'd find. *Look for the most disordered collection of tents and foul-smelling vapours aswarm with mosquitoes and gnats and you'll have found Malazan Engineers. And in that quarter you'll find soldiers shaking like leaves, with splash-burn pockmarks, singed hair and a dark, manic gleam in their eyes.*

Corporal List stood with Captain Lull at one end of the Marine encampment, close to the attachment of loyal Hissari Guards – whose soldiers were readying their tulwars and round shields in grim silence. Coltaine held them in absolute trust, and the Seven Cities natives had proved themselves again and again with fanatic ferocity – as if they had assumed a burden of shame and guilt and could only relieve it by slaughtering every one of their traitorous kin.

Captain Lull smiled as the historian joined them. 'Got a cloth for your face? We'll be eating dust today, old man, in plenty.'

'We will be the back end of the wedge, sir,' List said, looking none too pleased.

'I'd rather swallow dust than a yard of cold iron,' Duiker said. 'Do we know what we're facing yet, Lull?'

'That's "Captain" to you.'

'As soon as you stop calling me "old man", I'll start calling you by your rank.'

'I was jesting, Duiker,' Lull said. 'Call me what you like, and that includes pig-headed bastard if it pleases you.'

'It just might.'

Lull's face twisted sourly. 'Didn't get any sleep, did you?' He swung to List. 'If the old codger starts nodding off, you've my permission to give him a clout on that bashed-up helmet of his, Corporal.'

'If I can stay awake myself, sir. This good cheer is wearing me out.'

Lull grimaced at Duiker. 'The lad's showing spark these days.'

'Isn't he just.'

The sun was burning clear of the horizon. Pale-winged birds flitted over the humped hills to the north. Duiker glanced down at his boots. The morning dew had seeped through the worn leather. Strands of snagged spiderwebs made a stretched, glittering pattern over the toes. He found it unaccountably beautiful. *Gossamer webs . . . intricate traps. Yet it was my thoughtless passage that left the night's work undone. Will the spiders go hungry this day because of it?*

'Shouldn't dwell on what's to come,' Lull said.

Duiker smiled, looked up at the sky. 'What's the order?'

'The Seventh's marines are the spear's point. Crow riders to either side are the flanking barbs. Foolish Dog – now a Togg-thundering heavy cavalry – are the weight behind the marines. Then come the wounded, protected on all sides by the Seventh's infantry. Taking up the tail are the Hissari Loyals and the Seventh's cavalry.'

Duiker was slow to react, then he blinked and faced the captain.

Lull nodded. 'The refugees and herds are being held back, this side of the valley but slightly south, on a low shelf of land the maps call the Shallows, with a ridge of hills south of that. The Weasel Clan guards them. It's the safest thing to do – that clan's turned dark and nasty since Sekala. Their horse-warriors have all filed their teeth, if you can believe that.'

'We go to this battle unencumbered,' the historian said.

'Excepting the wounded, aye.'

Captains Sulmar and Chenned emerged from the infantry encampment. Sulmar's posture and expression radiated outrage, Chenned's was mocking if slightly bemused.

'Blood and guts!' Sulmar hissed, his greased moustache bristling. 'Those damned sappers and their Hood-spawned captain have done it this time!'

Chenned met Duiker's gaze and shook his head. 'Coltaine went white at the news.'

'What news?'

'The sappers lit out last night!' Sulmar snarled. 'Hood rot the cowards one and all! Poliel bless them with pestilence, pox their illegitimate brood with her pus-soaked kiss! Togg trample that captain's ba—'

Chenned was laughing in disbelief. 'Captain Sulmar! What would your friends in the Council say to such foul-mouthed cursing?'

'Burn take you, too, Chenned! I'm a soldier first, damn you. A trickle to a flood, that's what we're facing—'

'There won't be any desertions,' Lull said, his battered fingers slowly raking through his beard. 'The sappers ain't run away. They're up to something, I'd hazard. It's not easy reining in that unwashed, motley company when you can't even track down its captain – but I don't imagine Coltaine will make the same mistake again.'

'He'll not have the chance,' Sulmar muttered. 'The first worms will crawl into our ears before the day's done. It's the oblivious feast for us all, mark my words.'

Lull raised his brows. 'If that's as encouraging as you can manage, Sulmar, I pity your soldiers.'

'Pity's for the victors, Lull.'

A lone horn wailed its mournful note.

'Waiting's over,' Chenned said with obvious relief. 'Save

me a patch of grass when you go down, gentlemen.'

Duiker watched the two Seventh captains depart. He'd not heard that particular send-off in a long time.

'Chenned's father was in Dassem's First Sword,' Lull said. 'Or so goes the rumour – even when names are swept from official histories, the past shows its face, eh, old man?'

Duiker was in no mood to rise to either jibe. 'Think I'll check my gear,' he said, turning away.

It was noon before the final positioning was completed. There had been a near riot when the refugees finally understood that the main army was to make the crossing without them. Coltaine's selection of the Weasel Clan as their escort – the horsewarriors presented a truly terrifying visage with their threaded skin, black tattooing and filed teeth – proved his cunning yet again, although the Weasel riders almost took it too far with their bloodthirsty taunts flung at the very people they were sworn to protect. Desultory calm was established, despite the frenzied, fear-stricken efforts of the nobleborn's Council and their seemingly inexhaustible capacity to deliver protests and writs.

With the main force finally assembled, Coltaine issued the command to move forward.

The day was blisteringly hot, the parched ground rising in clouds of dust as soon as the brittle grass was worn away by hooves and tramping boots. Lull's prediction of eating dust proved depressingly accurate, as Duiker once more raised his tin belt-flask to his lips, letting water seep into his mouth and down the dry gully of his throat.

Marching on his left was Corporal List, his face caked white, helmet sliding down over his sweat-sheened forehead. On the historian's right strode the veteran marine – he did not know her name, nor would he ask. Duiker's fear of what was to come had spread through him like an infection. His thoughts felt fevered, spinning around an irrational terror of ... of knowledge. Of the details that remind one of humanity. Names to faces are like twinned serpents threatening the most painful bite of all. I'll never return to the List of the Fallen, because I see now that the unnamed soldier is a gift. The named soldier – dead, melted wax – demands a response among the living ... a response no-one can make. Names are no comfort, they're a call to answer the unanswerable. Why did she die, not him? Why do the survivors remain anonymous – as if cursed – while the dead are revered? Why do we cling to what we lose while we ignore what we still hold?

Name none of the fallen, for they stood in our place, and stand there still in each moment of our lives. Let my death hold no glory, and let me die forgotten and unknown. Let it not be said that I was one among the dead to accuse the living.

The River P'atha bisected a dry lake bed two thousand paces east to west and over four thousand north to south. As the vanguard reached the eastern ridge and proceeded down into the basin, Duiker was presented with a panoramic view of what would become the field of battle.

Kamist Reloe and his army awaited them, the glitter of iron vast and bright in the morning glare, city standards and tribal pennons hanging dull and listless above the sea of peaked helms. The arrayed soldiers rustled and rippled as if tugged by unseen currents. Their numbers were staggering.

The river was a thin, narrow strip six hundred paces ahead, studded with boulders and lined in thorny brush on both sides. A trader track marked the traditional place of crossing, then wound westward to what had once been a gentle slope to the opposite ridge – but Reloe's sappers had been busy: a ramp of sandy earth had been constructed, the natural slope to either side carved away to create a steep, high cliff. To the south of the lake bed was a knotted jumble of arroyos, basoliths, screes and jagged outcroppings; to the north rose a serrated ridge of hills bone white under the sun. Kamist Reloe had made sure there was only one point of exit westward, and at the summit waited his elite forces.

'Hood's breath!' muttered Corporal List. 'The bastard's rebuilt Gelor Ridge, and look to the south, sir, that column of smoke – that was the garrison at Melm.'

Squinting that way, Duiker saw another feature closer at hand. Set atop a pinnacle looming over the southeast end of the lake bed was a fortress. 'Who did that belong to?' he wondered aloud.

'A monastery,' List said. 'According to the only map that showed it.'

'Which Ascendant?'

List shrugged. 'Probably one of the Seven Holies.'

'If there's anyone still in there, they'll get quite a view of what's to come.'

Kamist Reloe had positioned forces down and to either side of his elite companies, blocking the north and south ends of the basin. Standards of the Sialk, Halafan, Debrahl and Tithansi contingents rose from the southern element; Ubari the northern. Each of the three forces outnumbered Coltaine's by a large margin. A roar began building from the army of the Apocalypse, along with a rhythmic clash of weapons on shields.

The marines marched towards the crossing in silence. Voices and clangour rolled over them like a wave. The Seventh did not falter.

Gods below, what will come of this?

The River P'atha was an ankle-deep trickle of warm water, less than a dozen paces across. Algae covered the pebbles and stones of the bottom. The larger boulders were splashed white with guano. Insects buzzed and danced in the air. The river's cool breath vanished as soon as Duiker stepped onto the opposite bank, the basin's baked heat sweeping over him like a cloak.

Sweat soaked the quilted undergarment beneath his chain

hauberk; it ran down in dirty runnels beneath gauntlets and into the historian's palms. He tightened his grip on the shield strap, his other hand resting on the pommel of his short sword. His mouth was suddenly bone dry, though he resisted the urge to drink from his flask. The air stank of the soldiers he followed, a miasma of sweat and fear. There was a sense of something else, as well, a strange melancholy that seemed to accompany the relentless forward motion of the company.

Duiker had known that sense before, decades ago. It was not defeat, nor desperation. The sadness arose from whatever lay beyond such visceral reactions, and it felt measured and all too aware.

We go to partake of death. And it is in these moments, before the blades are unsheathed, before blood wets the ground and screams fill the air, that the futility descends upon us all. Without our armour, we would all weep, I think. How else to answer the impending promise of incalculable loss?

'Our swords will be well notched this day,' List said beside him, his voice dry and breaking. 'In your experience, sir, what's worse – dust or mud?'

Duiker grunted. 'Dust chokes. Dust blinds. But mud slips the world from under your feet.' *And we'll have mud soon enough, when enough blood and bile and piss have soaked the ground. An equal measure of both curses, lad.* 'Your first battle, then?'

List grimaced. 'Attached to you, sir, I've not been in the thick of things yet.'

'You sound resentful.'

The corporal said nothing, but Duiker understood well enough. The soldier's companions had all gone through their first blooding, and that was a threshold both feared and anticipated. Imagination whispered untruths that only experience could shatter.

Nevertheless, the historian would have preferred a more remote vantage point. Marching with the ranks, he could see nothing beyond the press of humanity around him. *Why did Coltaine put me here? He's taken from me my eyes, damn him.*

They were a hundred paces from the ramp. Horsewarriors galloped across the front of the flanking enemy forces, ensuring that all held position. The drumming shields and screams of rage promised blood and would not be held in check for much longer. *Then we will be assailed from three sides, and an effort will be made to cut us away from the Seventh's infantry while they struggle to defend the wounded. They'll behead the serpent, if they can.*

The Crow horsewarriors were readying bows and lances to either side, heads turned and fixed on the enemy positions. A horn announced the command to ready shields, the front line locking while the centre and rear lofted theirs overhead. Archers were visible, scrambling into position at the top of the ramp.

There was no wind, the motionless air heavy.

It may have been disbelief that held the flanking forces back. Coltaine had displayed no reaction to the enemy's positions and strength; indeed the Seventh simply marched on and, reaching the ramp, began the ascent without pause.

The slope was soft, boulders and sand, deliberately treacherous underfoot. Soldiers stumbled.

Suddenly arrows filled the sky, sweeping down like rain. Horrendous clattering racketed over Duiker's head as shafts snapped, skidded across the upraised shields, some slipping through to strike armour and helms, some piercing flesh. Voices grunted beneath the turtle's back. Cobbles pitched underfoot. Yet the carapaced wedge climbed on without pause.

The historian's elbows buckled as an arrow struck his shield a solid blow. Three more rapped down in quick succession, all glancing impacts that then skittered away across other shields.

The air beneath the shields grew sour and turgid – sweat, urine and a growing anger. An attack that could not be answered was a soldier's nightmare. The determination to reach the crest, where waited howling Semk and Guran heavy infantry, burned like a fever. Duiker knew that the marines were being driven towards a threshold. The first contact would be explosive.

The ramp was banked on either side closer to the ridge, steep and high, its top flattened and broad across. Warriors from a tribe Duiker could not identify – Can'eld? – began assembling on the banks and readying short horn bows. *They'll fire down on us from both sides once we lock with the Semk and Guran. An enfilade.*

Bult rode with the flanking Crow horsewarriors, and the historian clearly heard the veteran's bellowing command. In a flash of dust and iron, riders wheeled and swept towards the banks. Arrows flew. The Can'eld – caught by the swiftness of the Wickan response – scattered. Bodies fell, tumbling down to the ramp. The Crow warriors rode along the ditch, raking the high bank with murderous missile fire. Within moments the flat top was clear of standing tribesmen.

A second shout reined in the horsewarriors, their lead riders less than a dozen paces from the bristling line of Semk and Guran. The sudden halt drew the wild Semk forward. Throwing axes flew end over end through the intervening space. Arrows darted in return fire.

The forward tip of the wedge surged as the marines saw the disorder in the enemy front line. Crow riders spun their horses, rising high in their saddles as they careered to avoid being pinned between the closing footsoldiers and inadvertently breaking up the marines' momentum. They pulled clear with moments to spare.

The wedge struck.

Through the shield Duiker felt the impact's thunder, a resounding roll that jarred his bones. He could see little from his position apart from a small patch of blue sky directly above the heads of the soldiers, and into that air spun a snapped pike-shaft and a helm that might have still held in its strap a bearded jaw, before dust rose up in an impenetrable shroud.

'Sir!' A hand tugged at his shield arm. 'You're to turn now!'

Turn? Duiker glared at List.

The corporal pulled him round. 'So you can see, sir—'

They were standing in the next to last line of the wedge. A space of ten paces yawned between the marines and the mounted, arcanely armoured Foolish Dog horsewarriors, who stood motionless, heavy swords bared and resting crossways across their saddles. Beyond them, the basin stretched – the historian's position high on the earthen ramp afforded him a view of the rest of the battle.

To the south were closed ranks of Tithansi archers supported by Debrahl cavalry. Legions of Halafan infantry marched east of them – to their right – and in their midst a company of Sialk heavy infantry. Further east were more cavalry and archers. *One jaw, and to the north, the other. Now inexorably snapping shut.*

He looked to the north. The Ubari legions – at least three – along with Sialk and Tepasi cavalry, were less than fifty paces from contacting the Seventh's infantry. Among the standards jutting from the Ubari, Duiker saw a flash of grey and black colours. *Marine-trained locals, now there's irony for you.*

East of the river a huge battle was underway, if the vast pall of drifting dust was any indication. The Weasel Clan had found their fight after all. The historian wondered which of Kamist Reloe's forces had managed to circle round. *A strike for the herds, and the gift of slaughter among the refugees. Hold fast, Weasels, you'll get no relief from the rest of us.*

Jostling from the soldiers around him brought Duiker's attention back to his immediate surroundings. The clash of weapons and screams from the ridge was growing as the wedge slowly flattened out against an anvil of stiff, disciplined resistance. The first reeling knock-back rippled through the press.

Togg's three masks of war. Before the day's done we'll each of us wear them all. Terror, rage and pain. We won't take the ridge—

A deeper roar sounded in the basin behind them. The historian twisted around. The jaws had closed. The Seventh's hollow box around the wagons of the wounded was crumpling, writhing, like a worm beset by ants. Duiker stared, a wave of dread rising within him, expecting to see that box disintegrate, torn apart by the ferocity assailing it.

The Seventh resisted, impossible though it seemed to the historian's mind. On all sides the enemy reared back as if those jaws had closed on poisonous thorns and the instinct was to flinch away. There was a pause, a visceral chill that kept the two sides apart – the space between them carpeted with the dead and dying – then the Seventh did the unexpected. In a silence that raised the hair on the historian's nape, they rushed forward, the box bulging, distorting into an oval, pikes levelled.

Enemy ranks crumbled, melted, suddenly broke.

Stop! Too far! Too thin! Stop!

The oval stretched, paused, then drew back with a measured precision that was almost sinister – as if the Seventh had become some kind of mechanism. *And they'll do it again. Little surprise the next time, but likely just as deadly. Like a lung drawing breath, a rhythm of calm sleep, again and again.*

His attention was snared by movement among the Foolish Dog. Nil and Nether had emerged from the front line, on foot, the latter leading a Wickan mare. The animal's head was high, ears pricked forward. Sweat glistened on its ruddy flanks.

The two warlocks halted to either side of the mare, Nether leaving the reins to dangle, and laid hands on the beast.

A moment later Duiker was stumbling, as the rear lines of the wedge were pulled forward, up the ramp, as if carried on an indrawn breath.

'Ready close weapons!' a sergeant shouted nearby.

Oh, Hood's wet dream—

'This is it,' List said beside him, his voice as taut as a bowstring.

There was no time for a reply, no time for thought itself, for suddenly they were among the enemy. Duiker caught a flash of the scene before him. A soldier stumbling and cursing, his helm slipped down over his eyes. A sword flying through the air. A shrieking Semk warrior being pulled backward by his braid, his scream cut to a wet gurgle as the point of a short sword burst from under his chest amidst a coiled mass of intestines. A woman marine wheeling from an attack, her own urine splattering the tops of her boots. And everywhere ... Togg's three masks and a cacophony of noise, throats making sounds they were never meant to make, blood gushing, people dying – *everywhere, people dying.*

'Ware your right!'

Duiker recognized the voice – his nameless marine companion – and pivoted in time to parry a spear blade, his short sword skittering along the tin-sheathed shaft. He stepped in past the thrust and drove his sword point into a Semk woman's face. She sank down in red ruin, but it was the historian's cry of pain that ripped the air, a savage piercing of his soul. He stumbled back and would have fallen if not for a solid shield thudding against his back. The unnamed woman's voice was close by his ear. 'Tonight I'll ride you till you beg, old man!'

In that baffling twist that was the human mind, Duiker mentally wrapped himself around those words, not in lust, but as a drowning man clings to a mooring pole. He drew a sobbing breath, straightened away from the shield's support, stepped forward.

Ahead battled the front line of marines, horribly thinned, yielding step after step as the Guran heavy infantry pushed down the slope. The wedge was about to shatter.

Semk warriors ranged in the midst of the marines in wild, frenzied mayhem, and it was these ash-stained warriors that the rear ranks had been driven forward to deal with.

The task was quickly done, brutal discipline more than a match for individual warriors who held no line, offered no support weapon-side, and heard no voice except their own manic battle cries.

For all that sudden deliverance, the marines began to buckle.

Three horns sounded in quick, braying succession: the Imperial call to split. Duiker gaped, spun round to look for List – but the corporal was nowhere in sight. He saw his marine companion and staggered over to her. 'Four's the withdraw, were there four blasts? I heard—'

She bared her teeth. 'Three, old man. Split! Now!'

She pulled away. Baffled, Duiker followed. The slope was treacherous, blood- and bile-soaked mud over shifting cobbles. They stumbled with the others this side of the divide – the south – towards the high bank, and descended into the narrow ditch, finding themselves ankle-deep in a stream of blood.

The Guran heavy infantry had paused, sensing a trap – no matter how improbable events had made that possibility – as they shuffled to close ranks four strides down from the crest. A ram's horn bleated, pulling the formation back to the summit in ragged back-step.

Duiker turned in time to see, seventy paces farther down the ramp, the Foolish Dog heavy cavalry edging forward, parting around Nil and Nether, who still stood on either side of the stationary mare, their hands pressed against the animal.

'Lord's push,' cursed the woman at his side.

They mean to charge up this ramp, with its bodies and wreckage and mud and stones. A slope steep enough to force the riders onto their mounts' necks – and all that weight onto their forelegs. Coltaine means them to charge. Into the face of heavy infantry—

'No!' the historian whispered.

561

Rocks and sand pattered down the bank. Around Duiker helmed heads turned in sudden alarm – someone was on the bank's top. More dirt slewed down on them.

A stream of Malazan curses sounded from above, then a helmed head peered over the edge.

'It's a Hood-damned sapper!' one of the marines grunted.

. The dirt-smeared face above them grinned. 'Guess what turtles do in the winter?' he shouted down, then pulled back and out of sight.

Duiker glanced back at the Foolish Dog horsewarriors. Their forward motion had ceased, as if suddenly uncertain. The Wickans had their heads raised, gazes fixed on the tops of the banks to either side.

The Guran heavy infantry and surviving Semk stared as well.

Through the dust rolling down the ramp from the crest, Duiker squinted towards the north bank. Activity swarmed along it – sappers, wearing shields on their backs, had begun moving forward, dropping down onto the ramp in the body-piled space below the crest.

Another horn sounded, and the Foolish Dog horsewarriors rolled forward again, pushing their mounts into a trot, then a clambering canter. But now a company of sappers blocked their path to the ridge.

A turtle burrows come winter. The bastards snuck onto the banks last night – under the very noses of Reloe – and buried themselves. What in Hood's name for?

The sappers, still wearing their shields on their backs, milled about, preparing weapons and other gear. One stepped free to wave the Foolish Dog riders forward.

The ramp trembled.

The armour-clad horses surged up the steep slope in an explosion of muscle, swifter than the historian thought possible. Broadswords lifted skyward. In their arcane, bizarre armour, the Wickans sat their saddles like demonic con-jurations above equally nightmarish mounts.

The sappers rushed the Guran line. Grenados flew, followed by the rap of explosions and dreadful screams.

Every munition left to the sappers arced a path into the press of heavy infantry. Sharpers, burners, flamers. The solid line of Reloe's elite soldiers disintegrated.

The Foolish Dog's galloping charge reached the sappers, who went down beneath the hooves in resounding clangs that beat a dreadful rhythm as horse after horse surged over them.

Into the gutted, chaotic maelstrom that had moments before been a solid line of heavy infantry, the Wickan horse-warriors cleared the crest and plunged, broadswords swinging down in fearful slaughter.

Another signal wailed above the din.

The woman at Duiker's side rapped a gauntleted hand against his chest. 'Forward, old man!'

He took a step, then hesitated. *Aye, time for the soldier to go forward. But I'm a historian – I have to see, I have to witness, and to Hood with arrow-fire!* 'Not this time,' Duiker said, turning to scramble his way up the embankment.

'See you tonight!' she shouted after him, before joining the rest of the marines as they marched forward.

Duiker pulled himself to the top, gaining a mouthful of sandy earth in the bargain. Coughing and gagging, he pushed himself to his feet, then looked around.

The bank's flat surface was honeycombed with angled shafts. Cocoons of tent cloth lay half in, half out of some of the man-sized holes. The historian stared at them a moment longer in disbelief, then swung his attention to the ramp.

The marines' forward momentum had been stalled by the retrieval of the trampled sappers. There were broken bones aplenty, Duiker could see, but the shields – now battered into so much scrap – and their dented helms had for the most part protected the crazed soldiers.

Beyond the crest, on the flatland to the west, the Foolish Dog horsewarriors pursued the routed remnants of Kamist Reloe's vaunted elites. The commander's own tent, situated on a low hill a hundred paces from the crest, was sinking beneath flames and smoke. Duiker suspected that the rebel High Mage had set that fire himself, destroying anything of potential use to Coltaine before fleeing through whatever paths his warren offered him.

Duiker turned to survey the basin.

The battle down there still raged. The Seventh's ring of defence around the wagons of the wounded remained, though distorted by a concerted, relentless push from the Ubari heavy infantry on the northern side. The wagons themselves were rolling southward. Tepasi and Sialk cavalry harried the rear guard, where the Hissari Loyals stood fast . . . and died by the score.

We could lose this one yet.

A double blast of horns from the crest commanded the Foolish Dog's recall. Duiker could see Coltaine, his black feather cape grey with dust, sitting astride his charger on the crest. The historian saw him gesture to his staff and the recall horns sounded again, in quicker succession. *We need you now!*

But those mounts will be spent. They did the impossible. They charged uphill, with a speed that grew and grew, with a speed like nothing I have ever seen before. The historian frowned, then spun around.

Nil and Nether still stood to either side of the lone mare. A light wind was ruffling the beast's mane and tail, but it did not otherwise move. A ripple of unease chilled Duiker. *What have they done?*

Distant howling caught the historian's attention. A large mounted force was crossing the river, their standards too distant to discern their identity. Then Duiker spied small tawny shapes streaming out ahead of the riders. *Wickan cattle-dogs. That's the Weasel Clan.*

The horsewarriors broke into a canter as they cleared the river bed.

The Tepasi and Sialk cavalry were caught completely unawares, first by a wave of ill-tempered dogs that ignored horses to fling themselves at riders, sixty snarling pounds of teeth and muscle dragging soldiers from their saddles, then by the Wickans themselves, who announced their arrival by launching severed heads through the air before them and raising an eerie, blood-freezing cry a moment before striking the cavalry's flank.

Within a score of heartbeats the Tepasi and Sialk riders were gone – dead or dying or in full flight. The Weasel horsewarriors barely paused in re-forming before wheeling at a canter to close with the Ubari, the mottle-coated cattle-dogs loping alongside them.

The enemy broke on both sides, flinching away with a timing that, although instinctive, was precise.

Foolish Dog riders poured back down the ramp, parting around the warlocks and their motionless horse, then wheeling to the south in pursuit of the fleeing Halafan and Sialk infantry and the Tithansi archers.

Duiker sank to his knees, suddenly overwhelmed, his emotions a cauldron of grief, anger and horror. *Speak not of victory this day. No, do not speak at all.*

Somone stumbled onto the bank, breath ragged. Footsteps dragged closer, then a gauntleted hand fell heavily on the historian's shoulder. A voice that Duiker struggled to identify spoke. 'They mock our nobleborn, did you know that, old man? They've a name for us in Dhebral. You know what it translates into? The Chain of Dogs. Coltaine's Chain of Dogs. He leads, yet is led, he strains forward, yet is held back, he bares his fangs, yet what nips at his heels if not those he is sworn to protect? Ah, there's profundity in such names, don't you think?'

The voice was Lull's, yet altered. Duiker raised his head and stared into the face of the man crouched beside him. A single blue eye glittered from a ravaged mass of torn flesh. A mace had caught him a solid blow, driving the cheek guard into his face, shattering cheek, bursting one eye and tearing away the captain's nose. The horrifying ruin that was Lull's face twisted into something like a grin. 'I'm a lucky man, Historian. Look, not a single tooth knocked out – not even a wobble.'

The count of losses was a numbing litany to war's futility. To the historian's mind, only Hood himself could smile in triumph.

The Weasel Clan had awaited the Tithansi lancers and the godling commander who led them. An ambush by earth spirits had taken the Semk warleader down, tearing his flesh to pieces in their hunger to rip apart and devour the Semk god's remnant. Then the Weasel Clan had sprung their own trap, and it had held its own horror, for the refugees had been the bait, and hundreds had been killed or wounded in the trap's clinical, cold-blooded execution.

The Weasel Clan's warleaders could claim that they had been outnumbered four to one, that some among those they were sworn to protect had been sacrificed to save the rest. All true, and providing a defensible justification for what they did. Yet the warleaders said nothing, and though that silence was met with outrage by the refugees and especially by the Council of Nobles, Duiker saw it in a different light. The Wickan tribe held voiced reasons and excuses in contempt – they accepted none from others and were derisive of those who tried. And in turn, they offered none, because, Duiker suspected, they held those who were sacrificed – and their kin – in a respect that could not survive something so base and self-serving as its utterance.

It was unfortunate for them that the refugees understood none of this, that for them the Wickans' silence was in itself an expression of contempt, a disdain for the lives lost.

The Weasel Clan had, however, offered yet another salute to those refugees who had died. With the slaughter of the Tithansi archers in the basin added to the Weasel Clan's actions, an entire plains tribe had effectively ceased to exist. The Wickans' retribution had been absolute. Nor had they stopped there, for they had found Kamist's peasant army, arriving late to the battle from the east. The slaughter exacted there was a graphic revelation of the fate the Tithansi sought to inflict on the Malazans. This lesson, too, was lost on the refugees.

For all that scholars tried, Duiker knew there was no explanation possible for the dark currents of human thought that roiled in the wake of bloodshed. He need only look upon his own reaction, when stumbling down to where Nil and Nether stood, their hands gummed with congealing sweat and blood on the flanks of a mare standing dead. Life forces were powerful, almost beyond comprehension, and the sacrifice of one animal to gift close to five thousand others with appalling strength and force of will was on the face of it worthy and noble.

If not for a dumb beast's incomprehension at its own destruction beneath the loving hands of two heartbroken children.

The Imperial Warren's horizon was a grey shroud on all sides. Details were blurred behind the gauze of the still, thick air. No wind stirred, yet echoes of death and destruction remained, suspended as if trapped outside time itself.

Kalam settled back in his saddle, eyes on the scene before him.

567

Ashes and dust shrouded the tiled dome. It had collapsed in one place, revealing the raw edges of the bronze plates that covered it. A grey haze lay over the gaping hole. From the dome's curvature, it was clear that less than a third of it was above the surface.

The assassin dismounted. He paused to pluck at the cloth wrapped over his nose and mouth to loosen the caked grit, glanced back at the others, then approached the structure.

Somewhere beneath their feet stood a palace or a temple. Reaching the dome, the assassin leaned forward and brushed the ash from one of the bronze tiles. A deeply carved symbol revealed itself.

A breath of cold recognition swept through him. He had last seen that stylized crown on another continent, in an unexpected war against resistance that had been purchased by desperate enemies. *Caladan Brood and Anomander Rake, and the Rhivi and the Crimson Guard. A gathering of disparate foes to challenge the Malazan Empire's plans for conquest. The Free Cities of Genabackis were a squabbling, back-stabbing lot. Gold-hungry rulers and thieving factors squealed loudest at the threat to their freedom . . .*

His mind over a thousand leagues away, Kalam lightly touched the engraved sigil. *Blackdog . . . we were warring against mosquitoes and leeches, poisonous snakes and blood-sucking lizards. Supply lines cut, the Moranth pulling back when we needed them the most . . . and this sigil I remember, there on a ragged standard, rising above a select company of Brood's forces.*

What did that bastard call himself? The High King? Kallor . . . the High King without a kingdom. Thousands of years old, if legends speak true, perhaps tens of thousands. He claimed to have once commanded empires, each one making the Malazan Empire no larger than a province. He then claimed to have destroyed them by his own hand, destroyed them utterly. Kallor boasted he had made worlds lifeless . . .

And this man now stands as Caladan Brood's second in command. And when I left, Dujek, the Bridgeburners and the reformed Fifth Army were about to seek an alliance with Brood.

Whiskeyjack . . . Quick Ben . . . keep your heads low, friends. There's a madman in your midst . . .

'If you're done daydreaming . . .'

'The thing I hate most about this place,' Kalam said, 'is how the ground swallows footfalls.'

Minala's startling grey eyes were narrow above the scarf covering the lower half of her face as she studied the assassin. 'You look frightened.'

Kalam scowled, turning back to the others. He raised his voice. 'We're leaving this warren now.'

'What?' Minala scoffed. 'I see no gate!'

No, but it feels right. We've covered enough distance, and I've suddenly realized that the power of deliberation is not as much in the travelling as in the arriving. He closed his eyes, shutting Minala and everyone else out as he forced his mind into stillness. One final thought escaped: *I hope I'm right.*

A moment later a portal formed, making a tearing sound as it spread wider.

'You thick-headed bastard,' Minala snapped with sharp comprehension. 'A little discussion might have led us to this a little sooner – unless you were deliberately delaying our progress. Hood knows what you're about, Corporal.'

Interesting choice of words, woman. I imagine he does.

Kalam opened his eyes. The gate was an impenetrable black stain a dozen paces away. He grimaced. *As simple as that. Kalam, you are a thick-headed bastard. Mind you, fear can focus even the most insipid of creatures.*

'Follow closely,' the assassin said, loosening the long-knife in its sheath before striding towards the portal and plunging through.

His moccasins slid on sandy cobbles. It was night, stars

bright overhead through the narrow slit between two high brick buildings. The alley wound on ahead in a tortuous path that Kalam knew well. There was no-one in sight.

The assassin moved to the wall on his left. Minala appeared, leading her own horse and Kalam's. She blinked, head turning. 'Kalam? Where—'

'Right here,' the assassin replied.

She started, then hissed in frustration. 'Three breaths in a city and you're already skulking.'

'Habit.'

'No doubt.' She led the horses farther on. A moment later Keneb and Selv appeared, followed by the two children.

The captain glared around until he spotted Kalam. 'Aren?'

'Aye.'

'Damned quiet.'

'We're in an alley that winds through a necropolis.'

'How pleasant,' Minala remarked. She gestured at the buildings flanking them. 'But these look like tenements.'

'They are . . . for the dead. The poor stay poor in Aren.'

Keneb asked, 'How close are we to the garrison?'

'Three thousand paces,' Kalam replied, unwinding the scarf from his face.

'We need to wash,' Minala said.

'I'm thirsty,' Vaneb said, still astride his horse.

'Hungry,' added Kesen.

Kalam sighed, then nodded.

'I hope,' added Minala, 'a walk through dead streets isn't an omen.'

'The necropolis is ringed by mourners' taverns,' the assassin muttered. 'We won't have much of a walk.'

Squall Inn claimed to have seen better days, but Kalam suspected it never had. The floor of the main room sagged like an enormous bowl, tilting every wall inward until angled wooden posts were needed to keep them upright. Rotting food and dead rats had with inert patience migrated to the floor's centre, creating a mouldering, redolent heap like an offering to some dissolute god.

Chairs and tables stood on creatively sawed legs in a ring around the pit, only one still occupied by a denizen not yet drunk into senselessness. A back room no less disreputable provided the more privileged customers with some privacy, and it was there that Kalam had deposited his group to eat while a washtub was being prepared in the tangled garden. The assassin had then made his way to the main room and sat himself down opposite the solitary conscious customer.

'It's the food, isn't it?' the grizzled Napan said as soon as the assassin took his seat.

'Best in the city.'

'Or so voted the council of cockroaches.'

Kalam watched the blue-skinned man raise the mug to his lips, watched his large Adam's apple bob. 'Looks like you'll have another one.'

'Easily.'

The assassin twisted slightly in his chair, caught the drooped gaze of the old woman leaning against a support post beside the ale keg, raised two fingers. She sighed, pushed herself upright, paused to adjust the rat-cleaver tucked through her apron belt, then went off in search of two tankards.

'She'll break your arm if you paw,' the stranger said.

Kalam leaned back and regarded the man. He could have been anywhere between thirty and sixty, depending on his life's toll. Deeply weathered skin was visible beneath the iron-streaked snarl of beard. The dark eyes roved restlessly and had yet to fix on the assassin. The man was dressed in baggy, thread-bare rags. 'You force the question,' the assassin said. 'Who are you and what's your story?'

571

The man straightened up. 'You think I tell that to just anyone?'

Kalam waited.

'Well,' the man continued. 'Not everyone. Some people get rude and stop listening.'

An unconscious patron at a nearby table toppled from his chair, his head crunching as it struck the flagstones. Kalam, the stranger and the serving woman – who had just reappeared with two tin mugs – all watched as the drunk slid down on grease and vomit to join the central heap.

It turned out one of the rats had been just playing at being dead, and it popped free and clambered onto the patron's body, nose twitching.

The stranger opposite the assassin grunted. 'Everyone's a philosopher.'

The serving woman delivered the drinks, her peculiar shuffle to their table displaying long familiarity with the pitched floor. Eyeing Kalam, she spoke in Dhebral. 'Your friends in the back have asked for soap.'

'Aye, I imagine they have.'

'We got no soap.'

'I have just realized that.'

She wandered away.

'Newly arrived, I take it,' the stranger said. 'North gate?'

'Aye.'

'That's quite a climb, with horses yet.'

'Meaning the north gate's locked.'

'Sealed, along with all the others. Maybe you arrived by the harbourside.'

'Maybe.'

'Harbour's closed.'

'How do you close Aren Harbour?'

'All right, it's not closed.'

Kalam took a mouthful of ale, swallowed it down and went perfectly still.

'Gets even worse after a few,' the stranger said.

The assassin set the tankard back down on the table. He struggled a moment to find his voice. 'Tell me some news.'

'Why should I?'

'I've bought you a drink.'

'And I should be grateful? Hood's breath, man, you've tasted it!'

'I'm not usually this patient.'

'Oh, very well, why didn't you say so?' He finished the first tankard, picked up the new one. 'Some ales grow on you. Some grow *in* you. To your health, sir.' He quaffed the ale down.

'I have slit uglier throats than yours,' the assassin said.

The man paused, his eyes flicking for the briefest of moments to skitter over Kalam, then he set his tankard down. 'Kornobol's wives locked him out last night – the poor bastard was left wandering the streets till one of the High Fist's patrols picked him up for breaking curfew. It's becoming common practice. Wives all over the city are having revelations. What else? Can't get a decent fillet without paying an arm and a leg for it – there's more maimed beggars than ever crowding the streets where the markets used to be. Can't buy a reading without Hood's Herald poking up on the field – tell me, do you think it's even possible that the High Fist is casting someone else's shadow like they say? Of course, who can cast a shadow hiding in the palace wardrobe? Fish ain't the only slippery things in this city, let me tell you. Why, I've been arrested four times in the last two days, had to identify myself and show my Imperial charter, if you can believe it. Turned out lucky, though, since I found my crew in one of those gaols. With Oponn's smile I'll have them out come tomorrow – got a deck to scrub and believe you me, those drunken louts will be scrubbing till the Abyss swallows the world. What's worse is the way some people step right around that charter, make demands of a person so he's left with an aching head delivering messages beneath common words, as if life's not

573

complicated enough – any idea how a hold groans when it's full of gold? And now you're going to say, "Well, Captain, it just so happens that I'm looking to buy passage back to Unta," and I'll say, "The gods are smiling upon you, sir! It just so happens that I'm sailing in two days' time, with twenty marines, the High Fist's treasurer and half of Aren's riches on board – but we've room, sir, oh, yes indeed. Welcome aboard!"'

Kalam was silent for a dozen heartbeats, then he said, 'The gods are smiling indeed.'

The captain's head bobbed. 'Smooth and beguiling, them smiles.'

'Who do I thank for this arrangement?'

'Says he's a friend of yours, though you've never met – though you will aboard my ship, *Ragstopper*, in two days.'

'His name?'

'Salk Elan, he called himself. Says he's been waiting for you.'

'And how did he know I would come to this inn? I did not know of its existence an hour ago.'

'A guess, but an informed one. Something about this being the first one you come to down from the gate in the necropolis. Too bad you weren't here last night, friend, it was even quieter, at least until the wench fished a drowned rat out of that keg over yonder. Too bad you and your friends missed this morning's breakfast.'

Kalam slammed the rickety door behind him, pausing to regain control. *Quick Ben's arrangements? Not likely. Impossible, in fact—*

'What's wrong?' Minala was sitting at the table, a wedge of melon in one hand. Voices from the garden indicated parents bathing reluctant children.

The assassin closed his eyes for a long moment, then opened them with a sigh. 'You've been delivered to Aren – and now we must go our separate ways. Tell Keneb to go out until he finds

574

a patrol or one finds him, and then make his report to the City Guard's commander – leaving me entirely out of that report—'

'And how does he explain us getting into the city?'

'A fisherman brought you in. Keep it simple.'

'And that's it? You won't even say goodbye to Keneb, or Selv, or the children? You won't even let them show their gratitude for saving their lives?'

'If you can, Minala, get yourself and your kin out of Aren – go back to Quon Tali.'

'Don't do it like this, Kalam.'

'It's the safest way.' The assassin hesitated, then said, 'I wish it could have been . . . different.'

The wedge of melon caught him flush on one cheek. He spent a moment wiping his face, then picked up his saddlebags and threw them over one shoulder. 'The stallion's yours, Minala.'

In the main room, Kalam made his way to the captain's table. 'All right, I'm ready.'

Something like disappointment flickered in the man's eyes, then he sighed and tottered upright. 'So you say. It's a middling long walk to where *Ragstopper*'s moored – with luck I'll only have to show my charter a dozen or so times. Hood knows, what else do you do with an army camped in a city, eh?'

'That rag of a shirt you're wearing won't help matters, Captain. I imagine you're looking forward to ditching the disguise.'

'What disguise? This is my lucky shirt.'

Lostara Yil leaned back against the wall of the small room, her arms crossed as she watched Pearl pacing back and forth near the window.

'Details,' he muttered, 'it's all in the details. Don't blink or you might miss something.'

'I must report to the Red Blade commander,' Lostara said. 'Then I shall return here.'

'Will Orto Setral give you leave, lass?'

'I am not relinquishing this pursuit ... unless you forbid me.'

'Gods forbid! I enjoy your company.'

'You are being facetious.'

'Only slightly. Granted, you've displayed little ease of humour. However, we have shared quite an adventure thus far, have we not? Why end it now?'

Lostara examined her uniform. Its weight was a comfort – the armour she had worn when disguised was a shattered mess and she had happily discarded it after the Claw's healing of her wounds.

Pearl had offered nothing to relieve the mystery of the demon that had appeared during the night engagement out on the plain, but it was clear to the Red Blade that the incident still troubled the man. *As it does me, but that is past now. We have made it to Aren, still on the assassin's trail. All is as it should be.*

'Will you wait here for me?' she asked.

Pearl's smile broadened. 'Until the end of time, my dear.'

'Dawn will suffice.'

He bowed. 'I shall count the heartbeats until then.'

She left the room, shutting the door behind her. The inn's hallway led to a wooden staircase that took her into the crowded main room. The curfew made for a captive clientele, although the mood was anything but festive.

Lostara ducked under the staircase and passed through the kitchen. The eyes of the cook and her helpers followed her as she walked to the back door, which had been left ajar to provide a draught. It was a reaction she was used to. The Red Blades were much feared.

She pushed open the door and stepped out into the alley.

The river's breath, mingled with the salt of the bay, was cool against her face. *I pray I never travel the Imperial Warren again.*

She walked to the main street, her boots loud on the cobbles.

A dozen soldiers of the High Fist's army accosted her as she reached the first intersection on her way to the garrison compound. The sergeant commanding them stared at her with disbelief.

'Good evening, Red Blade,' he said.

She nodded. 'I understand that the High Fist has imposed a curfew. Tell me, do the Red Blades patrol the streets as well?'

'Not at all,' the sergeant replied.

There was an expectancy among the soldiers that Lostara found vaguely disturbing.

'They are tasked with other responsibilities, then?'

The sergeant slowly nodded. 'I imagine they are. From your words and from . . . other things, I gather you are newly arrived.'

She nodded.

'How?'

'By warren. I had an . . . an escort.'

'The makings of an interesting story, no doubt,' the sergeant said. 'I will have your weapons now.'

'Excuse me?'

'You wish to join your fellow Red Blades, yes? Speak with Commander Orto Setral?'

'Yes.'

'By the High Fist's order, issued four days ago, the Red Blades are under detention.'

'What?'

'And await trial for treason against the Malazan Empire. Your weapons, please.'

Stunned, Lostara Yil made no resistance as the soldiers

disarmed her. She stared at the sergeant. 'Our loyalty has been
. . . challenged?'

There was no malice in his eyes as he nodded. 'I am sure
your commander will have more to say on the situation.'

'He's gone.'

Keneb's jaw dropped. 'Oh,' he managed after a moment.
Frowning, he watched Minala packing her gear. 'What are you
doing?'

She whirled on him. 'Do you think he gets away leaving it
like that?'

'Minala—'

'Be quiet, Keneb! You'll wake the children.'

'I wasn't shouting.'

'Tell your commander everything, you understand me?
Everything – except about Kalam.'

'I am not stupid, no matter what you may think.'

Her glare softened. 'I know. Forgive me.'

'You'd better ask that of your sister, I think. And Kesen and
Vaneb.'

'I will.'

'Tell me, how will you pursue a man who does not want to
be pursued?'

A hard grin flashed on her dark features. 'You ask that of a
woman?'

'Oh, Minala . . .'

She reached up to brush his cheek with one hand. 'No need
for tears, Keneb.'

'I blame my sentimental streak,' he said with a weary smile.
'But know this, I shall remain hopeful. Now, go and say goodbye to your sister and the children.'

CHAPTER FOURTEEN

The Goddess drew breath,
and all was still . .

The Apocalypse
Herulahn

'We can't stay here.'

Felisin's eyes narrowed on the mage. 'Why not? That storm outside will kill us. There's no sheltering from it – except here, where there's water . . . food—'

'Because we're being hunted,' Kulp snapped, wrapping his arms around himself.

From where he sat against a wall, Heboric laughed. He raised his invisible hands. 'Show me a mortal who is not pursued, and I'll show you a corpse. Every hunter is hunted, every mind that knows itself has stalkers. We drive and are driven. The unknown pursues the ignorant, the truth assails every scholar wise enough to know his own ignorance, for that is the meaning of unknowable truths.'

Kulp looked up from where he sat on the low wall encircling the fountain, the lids of his eyes heavy as he studied the ex-priest. 'I was speaking literally,' he said. 'There are living shapeshifters in this city – their scent rides every wind and it's getting stronger.'

'Why don't we just give up?' Felisin said.

The mage sneered.

'I am not being flippant. We're in Raraku, the home of the Whirlwind. There won't be a friendly face within a hundred leagues of here, not that there's a chance of making it that far in any case.'

'And the faces closer at hand aren't even human,' Heboric added. 'Every mask unveiled, and you know, the presence of D'ivers and Soletaken is most likely *not* at the Whirlwind's beckoning. All a tragic coincidence, this Year of Dryjhna and the unholy convergence—'

'You're a fool if you think that,' Kulp said. 'The timing is anything but accidental. I've a hunch that someone *started* those shapeshifters on that convergence, and that someone acted precisely because of the uprising. Or it went the other way around – the Whirlwind goddess guided the prophecy to ensure that the Year of Dryjhna was now, when the convergence was under way, in the interest of creating chaos within the warrens.'

'Interesting notions, Mage,' Heboric said, slowly nodding. 'Natural, of course, coming from a practitioner of Meanas, where deceit breeds like runaway weeds and inevitability defines the rules of the game . . . but only when useful.'

Felisin stayed silent, watching the two men. *One conversation, here on the surface, yet another beneath. The priest and the mage are playing games, the entwining of suspicion with knowledge. Heboric sees a pattern, his plundering of ghostly lives gave him what he needed, and I think he's telling Kulp that the mage himself is closer to that pattern than he might imagine. 'Here, wielder of Meanas, take my invisible hand . . .'*

Felisin decided she had had enough. 'What do you know, Heboric?'

The blind man shrugged.

'Why does it matter to you, lass?' Kulp growled. 'You're suggesting surrender: let the shapeshifters take us – we're dead anyway.'

'I asked, why do we struggle on? Why leave here? We haven't got a chance out in the desert.'

'Stay, then!' Kulp snapped, rising. 'Hood knows you've nothing useful to offer.'

'I've heard all it takes is a bite.'

He went still and slowly turned to her. 'You heard wrong. It's common enough ignorance, I suppose. A bite can poison you, a cyclical fever of madness, but you do not become a shapeshifter.'

'Really, then how *are* they created?'

'They aren't. They're born.'

Heboric clambered to his feet. 'If we're to walk through this dead city, let us do so now. The voices have stilled, and I am clear of mind.'

'What difference does that make?' Felisin demanded.

'I can guide us on the swiftest route, lass. Else we wander lost until the ones who hunt us finally arrive.'

They drank one last time from the pool, then gathered as many of the pale fruits as they could carry. Felisin had to admit to herself that she felt healthier – more *mended* – than she had in a long time, as if memories no longer bled and she was left with naught but scars. Yet the cast of her mind remained fraught. She had run out of hope.

Heboric led them swiftly down tortuous streets and alleys, through houses and buildings, and everywhere they went, they trod over and around bodies, human, shapeshifter and T'lan Imass, ancient scenes of fierce battle. Heboric's plundered knowledge was lodged in Felisin's mind, a trembling of ancient horror that made every new scene of death they stumbled upon resonate within her. She felt she was close to grasping a profound truth, around which orbited all human endeavour since the very beginning of existence. *We do naught but scratch the world, frail and fraught. Every vast drama of civilizations, of peoples with their certainties and gestures, means nothing, affects nothing. Life crawls on, ever on.* She wondered if the gift of revelation – of discovering the meaning underlying humanity – offered nothing more than a devastating sense of futility. *It's the ignorant who find a cause and cling to it, for within that is the illusion of significance. Faith, a king, queen or Emperor, or vengeance . . . all the bastion of fools.*

The wind moaned at their backs, raising small gusts of dust at their feet, rasping like tongues against their skin. It carried in it a faint scent of spice.

Felisin judged an hour had passed before Heboric paused. They stood before the grand entrance to a temple of some kind, where the columns, squat and broad, had been carved into a semblance of tree trunks. A frieze ran beneath the cracked, sagging plinth, each panel a framed image which Kulp's warren-cast light eerily lit from beneath.

The mage was staring up at the images. *Hood's breath!* he mouthed.

The ex-priest was smiling.

'It's a Deck,' Kulp said.

Yet another pathetic assertion of order.

'The Elder Deck, aye,' Heboric nodded. 'Not Houses but Holds. Realms. Can you discern Death and Life? And Dark and Light? Do you see the Hold of the Beast? Who sits upon that antlered throne, Kulp?'

'It's empty, assuming I'm looking at the one you mean – the frame displays various creatures. The throne is flanked by T'lan Imass.'

'Aye, that is the one. No-one on the throne, you say? Curious.'

'Why?'

'Because every echo of memory tells me there *used* to be.'

Kulp grunted. 'Well, it's not been defaced – you can see the back of the throne, and it looks as weathered as everywhere else.'

582

'There should be the Unaligned – can you detect those?'

'No. Perhaps around the sides and back?'

'Possibly. Among them you'll find Shapeshifter.'

'All very fascinating,' Felisin drawled. 'I take it we're to enter this place – since that's where the wind is going.'

Heboric smiled. 'Aye. The far end shall provide our exit.'

The interior of the temple was nothing more than a tunnel, its walls, floor and ceiling hidden behind packed layers of sand. The wind raised its voice the farther in they went. Forty paces later they could discern pale ochre light ahead.

The tunnel narrowed, the howling wind making it difficult to resist being pushed forward headlong, and they were forced to duck into a shambling crouch near the exit point.

Heboric held back just before the threshold to let Kulp pass, then Felisin. The mage was the first to step outside; Felisin followed.

They stood on a ledge, the mouth of a cave high on a cliff face. The wind tore at them as if seeking to cast them out, flinging them into the air – and a fatal drop to jagged rocks two hundred or more arm-spans below. Felisin moved to grip one crumbling edge of the cave mouth. The vista had taken her breath away, weakened her knees.

The Whirlwind raged, not before them but beneath them, filling the vast basin that was the Holy Desert. A fine haze of suspended dust drifted above a floor of seething yellow and orange clouds. The sun was an edgeless ball of red fire to the west, deepening its hue as they watched.

After a long moment Felisin barked a laugh. 'All we need now is wings.'

'I become useful once again,' Heboric said, grinning as he stepped out to stand beside her.

Kulp's head whipped around. 'What do you mean?'

'Tie yourselves to my back – both of you. This man's got a

pair of hands and he can use them, and for once my blindness will prove a salvation.'

Kulp peered down the cliff face. 'Climb down this? It's rotten rock, old man—'

'Not the handholds I'll find, Mage. Besides, what choice do you have?'

'Oh, I simply can't wait,' Felisin said.

'All right, but I'll have my warren open,' Kulp said. 'We'll fall just as far, but the landing will be softer – not that it'll make much difference, I suppose, but at least it gives us a chance.'

'You have no faith!' Heboric shouted, his face twisting as he fought back peals of laughter.

'Thanks for that,' Felisin said. *How far do we have to be pushed? We're not slipping into madness, we're being nudged, tugged and pulled into it.*

A hot, solid pressure closed on her shoulder. She turned. Heboric had laid an invisible hand on her – she could see nothing, yet the thin weave of her shirt's fabric was compressed, slowly darkening with sweat. She could feel its weight. He leaned close. 'Raraku reshapes all who come to it. This is one truth you can cling to. What you were falls away, what you become is something different.' His smile broadened at her snort of disdain. 'Raraku's gifts are harsh, it's true,' he said in a tone of sympathy.

Kulp was readying harnesses. 'These straps are rotting,' he said.

Heboric swung to him. 'Then you must hold tight.'

'This is madness.'

Those were my words.

'Would you rather await the D'ivers and Soletaken?'

The mage scowled.

Heboric's body felt like gnarled tree roots. Felisin clung with trembling muscles, not trusting the straining leather straps.

584

Her gaze remained fixed on the ex-priest's wrists – the unseen hands themselves were plunged into the rock face – while below she heard his feet scrambling for purchase again and again. The old man was carrying the weight of the three of them with his hands and arms alone.

The battered cliff was bathed in the setting sun's red glare. *As if we're descending into a cauldron of fire, into some demonic realm. And this is a one-way trip – Raraku will claim us, devour us. The sands will bury every dream of vengeance, every desire, every hope. We will all of us drown, here in this desert.*

Wind slapped them against the cliff face, then yanked them outward in a biting swirl of airborne sand. They had entered the Whirlwind once again. Kulp shouted something lost in the battering roar. Felisin felt herself being pulled away, raised up horizontal by the frantic, hungry wind. She hooked one arm around Heboric's right shoulder.

Her muscles began shuddering with the strain, her joints burning like fanned coals. She felt the harness straps around her tightening as they slowly, inevitably, assumed the strain. *Hopeless. The gods mock us at every turn.*

Heboric continued the climb downward, into the heart of the maelstrom.

From inches away, Felisin watched as the blowing sand began abrading the skin stretched over her elbow joint. The sensation was nothing more than that of a cat's tongue, yet the skin was peeling back, vanishing.

Her legs and body rode the wind, and from everywhere she felt that dreadful rasp of the storm's tongue. *I will be nothing but bones and sinew when we reach bottom, tottering fleshless with a rictus grin. Felisin unveiled in all her glory . . .*

Heboric stepped away from the cliff face. The three of them fell in a heap onto a ragged floor of rocks. Felisin screamed as the stones and sand pressed hard against the ravaged skin of her back. She found herself staring back up the cliff, revealed in patches where the gusting sand momentarily thinned. She thought she saw a figure, fifty arm-spans above them, then it was swallowed once more by the storm.

Kulp tugged at the straps with frantic haste. Felisin rolled clear, pushing herself onto her hands and knees. *There's something . . . even I can feel it—*

'On your feet, lass!' the mage shouted. 'Quickly!'

Whimpering, Felisin struggled upright. The wind slapped her back down in a lash of pain. Warm hands closed on her, lifted her up into the crook of rope-muscled arms.

'Life's like that,' Heboric said. 'Hold tight.'

They were running, leaning into the raging wind. She squeezed shut her eyes, the agony of her flayed skin flashing like lightning behind her eyelids. *Hood take this! All of it!*

They stumbled into sudden calm. Kulp hissed his surprise.

Felisin opened her eyes on a motionless mist of dust, describing a sphere in the midst of the Whirlwind. A large, vague shape was tottering towards them through the haze. The air was redolent with citrus perfume. She struggled until Heboric set her down.

Four pale men in rags were carrying a palanquin on which sat, beneath an umbrella, a vast, corpulent figure wearing voluminous silks in a splash of discordant colours. Slitted eyes peered out from sweat-beaded folds of flesh. The man raised one bloated hand and the bearers halted.

'Perilous!' he squealed. 'Join me, strangers, and take leave of yon dangers – a desert filled with beasts of most unpleasant disposition. I offer humble sanctuary through artful sorcery invested into this chair at great personal expense. Do you hunger? Do you thirst? Ahh, but look at the wounds upon the frail lass! I possess healing unguents, I would see such a delectable morsel with skin smoothed once again into youthful perfection. Tell me, is she perchance a slave? Might I make an offer?'

'I am *not* a slave,' Felisin said. *And I am no longer for sale.*

'The reek of lemon is making my blind eyes water,' Heboric whispered. 'I sense greed but no ill will . . .'

'Nor I,' Kulp said beside them. 'Only . . . his porters are undead, not to mention strangely . . . *chewed*.'

'I see you hesitate and I applaud caution at all times. Aye, my servants have seen better days, but they are harmless, I assure you.'

'How is it,' Kulp called out, 'you oppose the Whirlwind?'

'Not oppose, sir! I am a true believer and most humble. The goddess grants me ease of passage, for which I make constant propitiation! I am naught but a merchant, my trade is select merchandise – of the magical kind, that is. I am making my return journey to Pan'potsun, you see, after a lucrative venture to Sha'ik's rebel camp.' The man smiled. 'Aye, I know you as Malazans and no doubt enemies of the great cause. But cruel retribution finds no root in my soil, I assure you. And truth to tell, I would enjoy your company, for these dread servants are obsessed with their own deaths and there is no end to their complaints.'

At a gesture, the four bearers set the sedan chair down. Two of them immediately began removing camp gear from the storage rack behind the seat, their movements careless and loose, while the other pair set to levering their master onto his feet.

'There is a most potent salve,' the man wheezed. 'In yon wooden chest – there! The one called Nub carries it. Nub! Set that down, you gnawed grub! Nub the grub, hee! Leave off fumbling with the catch – such nimble escapades will melt your rotting brain. Aai! You've no hands!' The man's eyes had found Heboric, as if for the first time. 'A crime, to have done such a thing! Alas, none of my healing unguents could manage such complex regeneration.'

'Please,' Heboric said, 'do not feel distressed at what I lack,

587

or even at what you lack. I've need for nothing, although this shelter from the wind is most welcome.'

'Yours is assuredly a tragic tale of abandonment, once-priest of Fener, and I shall not pry. And you –' the man swung to Kulp – 'forgive me, the warren of Meanas, perchance?'

'You do more than sell sorcerous trinkets,' Kulp growled, his face darkening.

'Long proximity, kind sir,' the man said, bowing his head. 'Nothing more, I assure you. I have devoted my life to magery, yet I do not practise it. The years have granted me a certain . . . sensitivity, that is all. My apologies if I gave offence.' He reached out and cuffed one of his servants. 'You, what name did I give you?'

Felisin stared in fascination as the corpse's gnawed lips peeled back in a twisted grin. 'Clam, though I once knew myself as Iryn Thalar—'

'Oh, shut up with what you once knew! You are Clam now.'

'I had a horrid death—'

'Shut up!' his master shrieked, his face suddenly darkening. The undead servant fell silent.

'Now,' the man gasped, 'find us that Falari wine – let us celebrate with the Empire's most civil gifts.'

The servant stumbled off. Its nearest companion's head swivelled to follow with desiccated eyes. 'Yours was not as horrid as mine—'

'The Seven Holies preserve us!' the merchant hissed. 'I beg of you, Mage, a spell of silence about these ill-chosen animations! I shall pay in jakata imperials, and pay well!'

'Beyond my abilities,' Kulp muttered.

Felisin's eyes narrowed on the cadre mage. *That has to be a lie.*

'Ah, well,' the man sighed. 'Gods below, I have not yet introduced myself! I am Nawahl Ebur, humble merchant of the Holy City Pan'potsun. And what names do you three wish to be known by?'

Oddly put.

'I'm Kulp.'

'Heboric.'

Felisin said nothing.

'While the lass is shy,' Nawahl said, his lips curving into an indulgent smile as he looked upon her.

Kulp crouched down at the wooden chest, released the catch and lifted the lid.

'The white clay bowl with the wax seal,' the merchant said.

The wind was a distant moan, the ochre dust of the calm slowly settling around them. Heboric, still gifted with an awareness that dispensed with the need for sight, sat down on a weathered boulder. A faint frown wrinkled his broad forehead, and his tattoos were dull beneath a veil of dust.

Kulp strode to Felisin, the bowl in one hand. 'It's a healing salve,' he affirmed. 'And potent indeed.'

'Why didn't the wind tear your skin, Mage? You've not got Heboric's protection—'

'I don't know, lass. I had my warren open – perhaps that was enough.'

'Why didn't you extend its influence over me?'

He glanced away. 'I thought I had,' he muttered.

The salve was cool and seemed to absorb the pain. Beneath its colourless patina, she saw her skin grow anew. Kulp applied it where she could not reach, and half a bowl later, the last flare of agony was healed. Suddenly exhausted, Felisin sat down on the sand.

A broken-stemmed glass of wine appeared before her face. Nawahl smiled down on her. 'This shall restore you, gentle lass. A pliant current will take the mind past suffering, into life's most peaceful stream. Here, drink, my dear. I care for your well-being most deeply.'

She accepted the glass. 'Why?' she demanded. 'Why do you care most deeply?'

'A man of my wealth can offer you much, child. All that you grant of your free will is my reward. And know, I am most gentle.'

She downed a mouthful of the tart, cool wine. 'Are you now?'

His nod was solemn, his eyes glittering between the folds of dimpled flesh. 'This I promise.'

Hood knows I could do worse. Riches and comfort, ease and indulgences. Durhang and wine. Pillows to lie on . . .

'I sense wisdom in you, my dear,' Nawahl said, 'so I shall not press. Let you, rather, yourself ascend to the proper course.'

Bedrolls had been laid out. One of the undead servants had fanned to life a camp stove, the remnants of one sleeve catching light and smouldering in the process, a detail none commented on.

Darkness swiftly closed in around them. Nawahl commanded the lighting of lanterns and their positioning on poles situated in a circle around the camp. One of the corpses stood beside Felisin and refilled her glass after every mouthful. The creature's flesh looked gnawed. Gaping bloodless wounds lined his pallid arms. All his teeth had fallen out.

Felisin glanced up at him, willing herself against recoiling. 'And how did you die?' she asked sardonically.

'Terribly.'

'But how?'

'I am forbidden to say more. I died terribly, a death to match one of Hood's own nightmares. It was long, yet swift, an eternity that passed in an instant. I was surprised, yet knowing. Small pain, yet great pain, the flood of darkness, yet blinding—'

'All right. I see your master's point.'

'So you shall.'

'Go easy on that, lass,' Kulp said from near the camp stove. 'Best have your wits about you.'

'Why? It's not availed me yet, has it?' In defiance, she drained the glass and held it up to be refilled. Her head was swimming, her limbs seeming to float. The servant splashed wine over her hand.

Nawahl had returned to his wide, padded chair, watching the three of them with a contented smile on his lips. 'Mortal company, such a difference!' he wheezed. 'I am so much delighted, I need only bask in the mundane. Tell me, where do you seek to go? Whatever launched you on such a perilous journey? The rebellion? Is it truly as bloody as I have heard rumoured? Such injustice is ever repaid in full, alas. This lesson is lost, I am afraid.'

'We're going nowhere,' Felisin said.

'Might I convince you to revise your chosen destination, then?'

'And you offer protection?' she asked. 'How reliable? What happens if we run into bandits, or worse?'

'No harm shall come to you, my dear. A man who deals in sorcery has many resorts in defence of selves. Not once in all my travels have I been beset by nefarious fools. Accosted on occasion, yes, but all have turned away when I gifted them wisdom. My dear, you are positively breathtaking – your smooth, sun-honeyed skin is a balm to my eyes.'

'What would your wife say?' Felisin murmured.

'Alas, I am a widower. My dearest passed through the Hooded One's Gates almost a year ago to this day. Hers was a full, happy life, I am pleased to say – and that gives me great comfort. Ah, would that her spirit could arise and set you at ease with reassurances, my dear.'

Tapu skewers sizzled on the camp stove.

'Mage,' Nawahl said, 'you have opened your warren. Tell me, what do you see? Have I given you cause for mistrust?'

'No, merchant,' Kulp said. 'And I see nothing untoward –

yet the spells surrounding us are High castings ... I am impressed.'

'Only the best in protection of oneself, of course.'

The ground trembled suddenly and something huge pushed a brown-furred shoulder into the sphere opposite Felisin. The beast's shoulder was almost three arm-lengths high. After a moment the creature growled and withdrew.

'Beasts! They plague this desert! But fear not, none shall defeat my wards. I urge calm.'

Calm, I am very calm. We're finally safe. Nothing can reach us—

Finger-long claws tore a swath down the sphere's blurry wall, a bellow of rage ripping forth to shiver the air.

Nawahl surged upright with surprising speed. 'Back, damned one! Away! One thing at a time!'

She blinked. *One thing at a time?*

The sphere glowed as the jagged tears closed. The apparition beyond bellowed again, this time in what was clearly frustration. Claws scored another path, which healed even as it appeared. A body thundered against the barrier, withdrew, then tried again.

'We are safe!' Nawahl cried, his face dark with fury. 'It shall not succeed, no matter how stubborn! But still, how shall we sleep in such racket!'

Kulp strode up to the merchant, who unaccountably backed away a step. The mage then turned to face the determined intruder. 'That's a Soletaken,' he said. 'Very strong—'

From where Felisin sat, all that followed appeared in a seamless flow, with something close to grace. As soon as Kulp swung his back to the merchant, Nawahl seemed to blur beneath his silks, his skin deepening into glistening black fur. Sharp spice overpowered the citrus perfume in a hot gust. Rats poured forth, a growing flood.

Heboric screamed a warning, but it was already too late.

The rats flowed over Kulp and swallowed him entirely in a seething cloak, not by the score but in the hundreds.

The mage's shriek was a dull muffle. A moment later the mound of creatures seemed to buckle, their weight crushing Kulp down.

The four bearers stood off to one side, watching.

Heboric plunged into the mass of rats, his ghost-hands now glowing gauntlets of fire, one jade green, the other rust-red. Rats flinched away. Each one he grasped burned into black, mangled flesh and bone. Yet the swarm spread outward, more and more of the silent creatures, clambering over one another, heaving in waves over the ground.

They dissipated from the place where Kulp had lain. Felisin saw the flash of wet bones, a ragged raincape. She could not comprehend its significance.

The Soletaken beyond the wards was attacking the barrier in a frenzy. The torn wounds were slower in closing. A bear's paw and forearm, as wide around as Felisin's waist, plunged through a rent.

The rats rose in a writhing crest to sweep down on Heboric. Still screaming, the ex-priest staggered back.

A hand clutched Felisin's collar from behind and yanked her upright. 'Grab him and run, lass.'

Head spinning, she twisted around, to find herself staring up into Baudin's weathered face. He held in his other hand four of the lanterns. 'Get moving, damn you!' He pushed her hard towards the ex-priest, who was still stumbling back, the tide seething in pursuit. Behind Heboric, two tons of bear was pushing through the barrier.

Baudin leapt past Heboric, smashing one of the lanterns against the ground. Lamp oil sprayed in gushing streaks of flame.

A furious scream erupted from the rats.

The four servants broke into hacking laughter.

The crest crashed over Baudin, but they could not drag him down as they had Kulp. He swung the lanterns, shattering them. Fire leapt around him. A moment later he and hundreds of rats were engulfed in flames.

Felisin reached Heboric. The old man was sheathed in blood from countless small wounds. His sightless eyes seemed focused on an inner horror that matched the scene before them. Grasping an arm, she pulled him to one side.

The merchant's voice filled her mind. *Do not fear for yourself, my dear. Wealth and peace, every indulgence to sate your desires, and I am gentle – to those I choose, oh so gentle . . .*

She hesitated.

Leave to me this hard-skinned stranger and the old man, then I shall deal with Messremb, that foul, most rude Soletaken who so dislikes me . . .

Yet she heard pain in his words, an edge of desperation. The Soletaken was sundering the barrier, its hungry roar deafening in its reverberations.

Baudin would not fall. He killed rat after rat, all within a shroud of flame, yet they surged over him in ever-growing numbers, the sheer mass of bodies smothering the burning oil.

Felisin glanced at the Soletaken, gauging its awesome power, its fearless rage. She shook her head. 'No. You're in trouble, D'ivers.' She took hold of Heboric once again and dragged him to the dying barrier.

My dear! Wait! Oh, you stubborn mortal, why won't you die!

Felisin could not help but grin. *That won't work – I should know.*

The Whirlwind had begun its own assault against the sphere. Wind-whipped sand rasped against her face.

'Wait!' Heboric gasped. 'Kulp—'

Cold gripped Felisin. *He's dead, oh, gods, he's dead! Devoured. And I watched, drunk and uncaring, noticing nothing – 'one thing at a time.' Kulp's dead.* She bit back a sob, pushed the ex-priest into, then through, the barrier, even as it finally collapsed. The Soletaken's roar of triumph announced its surging charge into the midst of the rats. Felisin did not turn to watch the attack, did not turn to discover Baudin's fate. Dragging Heboric, she ran into the dusk-darkened storm.

They did not get far. The sandstorm's fury battered them, pushed them, finally drove them into the frail shelter offered by an overhanging spur of rock. They collapsed at its base, huddling together, awaiting death.

The alcohol in Felisin pulled her down into sleep. She thought to resist it, then surrendered, telling herself that the horror would soon find them, and to witness her own death offered no comfort. *I should tell Heboric the true worth of knowledge now. Yet he will learn that himself. Not long. Not long at all . . .*

She awoke to silence, but no, not silence. Someone nearby was weeping. Felisin opened her eyes. The Whirlwind's storm had ceased. The sky overhead was a golden shroud of suspended dust. It was so thick on all sides that she could see no more than half a dozen paces. Yet the air was still. *Gods, the D'ivers is back* – but no, the calm was everywhere.

Head aching and mouth painfully dry, she sat up.

Heboric knelt a few paces away, vague behind a refulgent haze. Invisible hands were pressed against his face, pulling the skin into bizarre folds, as if he was wearing a grotesque mask. His whole body heaved with grief and he rocked back and forth with dull, senseless repetition.

Memory flooded Felisin. *Kulp.* She felt her own face twisting. 'He should have sensed something,' she croaked.

Heboric's head shot up, his sightless eyes red and hooded as they fixed on her. 'What?'

'The mage,' she snapped, wrapping herself in a frail hug. 'The bastard was a D'ivers. *He should have known!*'

'Gods, girl, would that I had your armour!'

And should I bleed within it, you see nothing, old man. No-one shall see. No-one shall know.

'If I had,' Heboric continued after a moment, 'I would be able to stay at your side, to offer what protection I could – though wondering why I bothered, granted. Yet I would.'

'What are you babbling about?'

'I am fevered. The D'ivers has poisoned me, lass. And it wars with the other strangers in my soul – I do not know if I shall survive this, Felisin.'

She barely heard him. Her attention had been pulled away by a scuffing sound. Someone was approaching, haltingly, a stagger and a scrape of pebbles. Felisin pushed herself to her feet to face the sound.

Heboric fell silent, his head cocked.

The figure that emerged from the ochre mist sank talons into her sanity. She heard a whimper from her own throat.

Baudin was burned, gnawed, parts completely eaten away. He had been charred down to the bone in places, and the heat had swelled the gases in his belly, bloating him until he looked with child, the skin and flesh cracked open. There was nothing left of his features except ragged holes where his eyes, nose and mouth should have been. Yet Felisin knew it was him.

He staggered another step closer, then slowly sank down to the ground.

'What is it?' Heboric demanded in a hiss. 'This time I am truly blind – who has come?'

'No-one,' Felisin said after a long moment. She walked slowly to the thing that had once been Baudin. She sank down into the warm sand, reached out and lifted his head, cradled it on her thighs.

He was aware of her, reaching up an encrusted, fused hand to hover a moment near her elbow before falling back. He spoke, each word like rope on rock. 'I thought . . . the fire . . . immune.'

'You were wrong,' she whispered, an image of armour within her suddenly cracking, fissures spreading. And beneath it, behind it, something was building.

'My vow.'

'Your vow.'

'Your sister . . .'

'Tavore.'

'She—'

'Don't. No, Baudin. Say nothing of her.'

He drew a ragged breath. 'You . . .'

Felisin waited, hoping the life would flee this husk, flee it now, before—

'You . . . were . . . not what I expected . . .'

Armour can hide anything until the moment it falls away. Even a child. Especially a child.

There was nothing to distinguish sky from earth. Gold stillness had embraced the world. Stones pattered down the trail as Fiddler pulled himself onto the crest, the clatter appallingly loud to his ears. *She's drawn breath. And waits.*

He wiped sweaty dust from his brow. *Hood's breath, this bodes ill.*

Mappo emerged from the haze ahead. The huge Trell's exhaustion made his walk more of a shamble than usual. His eyes were red-rimmed, the lines that bracketed his prominent canines were deeply etched into his weathered skin. 'The trail winds ever onward,' he said, crouching beside the sapper. 'I believe she's with her father now – they walk together. Fiddler . . .' He hesitated.

'Aye. The Whirlwind goddess . . .'

'There is . . . expectancy . . . in the air.'

Fiddler grunted at the understatement.

'Well,' Mappo sighed after a moment, 'let us join the others.'

Icarium had found a flat stretch of rock surrounded by large boulders. Crokus sat with his back against stone, watching the Jhag laying out foodstuffs in the centre. The expression the young Daru swung to the sapper when he arrived belonged to a much older man. 'She's not turning back,' Crokus said.

Fiddler said nothing, unslinging his crossbow and setting it down.

Icarium cleared his throat. 'Come and eat, lad,' he said. 'The realms are overlapping, and all is possible ... including the unexpected. Distress over what has not yet happened avails you nothing. In the meantime, the body demands sustenance, and it will do none of us good if you've no reserves of energy when comes the time to act.'

'It's already too late,' Crokus muttered, but he clambered to his feet nonetheless.

'There is too much mystery in this path to be certain of anything,' Icarium replied. 'Twice we have travelled warrens – their aspects I cannot say. They felt ancient and fragmented, woven into the very rock of Raraku. At one point I smelled the sea ...'

'As did I,' Mappo said, shrugging his broad shoulders.

'More and more,' Crokus said, 'her journey takes a tack where such things as rebirth become more probable. I am right in that, aren't I?'

'Perhaps,' Icarium conceded. 'Yet, this pensive air hints at uncertainty as well, Crokus. Be mindful of that.'

'Apsalar is not seeking to flee us,' Mappo said. 'She is leading us. What significance should we place in that? With her godly gifts she could easily mask her trail – that shadow-wrought residue that, to Icarium and to myself, is as plain and undisguised as an Imperial road.'

'There might be something else besides,' Fiddler muttered. Faces swung his way. He drew a deep breath, let it out slowly. 'The lass knows our intent, Crokus – what Kalam and I had planned and what is still – as far as I know – being followed.

598

She could well have taken the notion that by assuming the guise of Sha'ik, she can . . . indirectly . . . support our efforts. In a manner wholly her own rather than that of the god who once possessed her.'

Mappo smiled wryly. 'There is much you've held from myself and Icarium, soldier.'

'An Imperial matter,' the sapper said, not meeting the Trell's eyes.

'Yet one that sees advantage in this land's rebellion.'

'Only in the short run, Mappo.'

'In becoming Sha'ik reborn, Apsalar will not simply be engaging in a change of costume, Fiddler. The cause of the goddess will take hold of Apsalar's mind, her soul. Such visions and visitations will *change* her.'

'She may not realize that particular possibility, I'm afraid.'

'She's not a fool,' Crokus snapped.

'I'm not saying she is,' Fiddler replied. 'Like it or not, Apsalar possesses something of a god's arrogance – I was witness to the full force of that back on Genabackis, and I can see that its stain still resides within her. Consider her present decision to leave Iskaral's temple, alone, in pursuit of her father.'

'In other words,' Mappo said, 'you think she might believe she can withstand the influence of the goddess, even as she assumes the role of prophetess and warleader.'

Crokus scowled. 'My mind's tumbling from one thing to the next. What if the patron god of assassins has reclaimed her? What will it mean if the rebellion is suddenly led by Cotillion – and, by extension, Ammanas? The dead Emperor returns to wreak vengeance.'

There was silence. Fiddler had been gnawing on that possibility like an obsessed hound since it had occurred to him days earlier. The notion of a murdered Emperor turned Ascendant suddenly reaching out from the shadows to reclaim the

Imperial throne was anything but a pleasant prospect. It was one thing seeking to assassinate Laseen – that was, in the end, a mortal affair. Gods ruling a mortal Empire, on the other hand, would draw other Ascendants, and in such a contest entire civilizations would be destroyed.

They finished their meal without another word spoken.

The dust filling the air refused to settle; it simply hung motionless, hot and lifeless. Icarium repacked the supplies. Fiddler strode over to Crokus.

'No value in fretting, lad. She's found her father, after all these years – there's something to be said for that, don't you think?'

The Daru's smile was wry. 'Oh, I've thought on that, Fid. And yes, I am happy for her, yet mistrustful. What should have been a wondrous reunion has been compromised. By Iskaral Pust. By Shadow's manipulation. It's soured everything—'

'However you may have envisioned it, Crokus, it belongs to Apsalar.'

The lad was silent for a long minute, then he nodded.

Fiddler retrieved his crossbow and slung it over one shoulder. 'At the very least, we've had a respite from Sha'ik's soldiers and the D'ivers and Soletaken.'

'Where is she leading us, Fid?'

The sapper shrugged. 'I suspect we'll find that out soon enough.'

The weathered man stood on the hump of rock, facing Raraku. The shroud of silence was absolute; he could hear his own heart, a steady, mindless rhythm in his chest. It had begun to haunt him.

Rocks skittered at his back, and a moment later the Toblakai appeared, dropping a brace of arm-long lizards onto the bleached bedrock. 'Everything's come out for a look around,' the giant youth rumbled. 'For once, a meal worth eating.'

The Toblakai was gaunt. His rages of impatience were gone, and Leoman was thankful for that, though he well knew that a withering of strength was the cause. *We wait until Hood comes to take us*, the huge barbarian had whispered a few days back, when the Whirlwind had burgeoned in renewed frenzy.

Leoman had had no answer to that. His faith was in tatters. Sha'ik's wrapped corpse still lay between the wind-sculpted stone gateposts. It had shrunk. The tent-cloth shroud had frayed in the ceaseless, clawing wind. The dry knobs of her joints protruded through the worn weave. Her hair, which had continued to grow for weeks, had been pulled free and whipped endlessly in the storm.

Yet now a change had come. The Whirlwind held its immortal breath. The desert, which had been lifted entire from its bones of rock, filling the air, refused to settle.

The Toblakai saw this as the Whirlwind's death. Sha'ik's murder had triggered a prolonged tantrum, a defeated goddess rampaging in frustration and fury. Even as the rebellion spread its bloody cloak over Seven Cities, its heart was dead. The armies of the Apocalypse were the still-twitching limbs on a corpse.

Leoman, plagued with hunger-born visions and fevers, had begun a slow stumbling towards the same belief.

Yet . . .

'This meal,' the Toblakai said, 'will give us the strength needed, Leoman.'

For leaving. And where do we go? To the oasis in the centre of Raraku, where a dead woman's army still waits? Are we the chosen deliverers of the news of tragic failure? Or do we abandon them? Set off for Pan'potsun, then on to Ehrlitan, a flight into anonymity?

The warrior turned. His gaze travelled over the ground and came to rest on the Book of Dryjhna where it waited, unmarred by the Whirlwind, immune even to the dust that found its way into everything. *The power abides. Unquenched. When I look upon that tome, I know I cannot let go . . .*

'*Blades in hand and unhanded in wisdom. Young, yet old, one life whole, another incomplete – she shall emerge renewed . . .*' Did still-hidden truths remain within those words? Had his imagination – his wilful yearning – betrayed him?

The Toblakai squatted before the dead lizards, flipped the first one onto its back and set a knifeblade to its belly. 'I would go west,' he said. 'Into the Jhag Odhan . . .'

Leoman glanced over. *The Jhag Odhan, there to come face to face with other giants. The Jhag themselves. The Trell. More savages. The lad will feel right at home in that wasteland.* 'This is not over,' the warrior said.

The Toblakai bared his teeth, a hand plunging through the slit in the lizard's belly to re-emerge with slick entrails. 'This one's female. It's said the roe is good for fevers, isn't it?'

'I am not fevered.'

The giant said nothing, but Leoman saw a new set to his shoulders. The Toblakai had made a decision.

'Take what's left of your kill,' the warrior said. 'You'll need it more than I.'

'You jest, Leoman. You do not see yourself as I see you. You are skin on bones. You have devoured your own muscles. I see the skull behind the face when I look at you.'

'I am clear of mind nonetheless.'

The Toblakai grunted. 'A hale man would not say so with such certainty. Is that not the secret revelation of Raraku? "Madness is simply a state of mind."'

'The Sayings of the Fool are aptly named,' Leoman muttered, his voice falling away. A charge was filling the hot, motionless air. The warrior felt his heart beat faster, harder.

The Toblakai straightened, his huge hands smeared with blood.

The two men slowly turned to face the ancient gate. The black hair emerging from the bundled corpse stirred, the strands gently lifting. The suspended dust had begun to swirl beyond the pillars. Sparks winked in its midst, like jewels set in an ochre cloak.

'What?' the Toblakai asked.

Leoman glanced over at the Holy Book. Its hide cover glistened as if with sweat. The warrior took a step towards the gate.

Something was emerging from the dust cloud. Two figures, side by side, their arms locked around one another, staggering, heading straight towards the pillars – and the corpse lying between the bleached gateposts.

'Blades in hand and unhanded in wisdom . . .'

One was an old man, the other a young woman. Heart hammering in his chest, Leoman let his gaze fix on her. *So alike. Dark threat pours from her. Pain, and from pain, rage.*

There was a thump and a grate of stones beside the warrior. He turned to see the Toblakai on his knees, head bowed before the approaching apparitions.

Raising her head, the woman found first Sha'ik's wrapped corpse, then lifted her eyes higher to fix on Leoman and the kneeling giant. She halted, almost standing over the body, her long black hair rising as if with a static charge.

Younger. Yet the fire within . . . it's the same. Ah, my faith . . .

Leoman lowered himself to one knee. 'You are reborn,' he said.

The woman's low laugh was triumphant. 'So I am,' she said.

She shifted her grip on the old man, whose head hung down, his clothes nothing but rags. 'Help me with him,' she commanded. 'But beware his hands . . .'

BOOK FOUR

DEADHOUSE GATES

Coltaine rattles slow
across the burning land.
The wind howls through the bones
of his hate-ridden command.
Coltaine leads a chain of dogs
ever snapping at his hand.

Coltaine's fist bleeds the journey home
along rivers of red-soaked sand.
His train howls through his bones
in spiteful reprimand.
Coltaine leads a chain of dogs
ever snapping at his hand.

Coltaine
A marching song of the Bonehunters

CHAPTER FIFTEEN

A god walking mortal earth trails blood.

Sayings of the Fool
Thenys Bule

'The chain of dogs,' the sailor growled, his voice as dark and heavy as the air of the hold. 'Now there's a curse no man would wish upon his worst enemy. What, thirty thousand starving refugees? Forty? Sweat-jowled noble-born among 'em, too, bleating this and that. Coltaine's hourglass is about run out, I'd wager.'

Kalam shrugged in the gloom, his hands still running along the damp hull. *Name a ship* Ragstopper *and worry starts before you weigh anchor.* 'He's survived this long,' he muttered.

The sailor paused in his stacking of bales. 'Look at this, will ya? Three-fifths' stowage gone before e'en the food and water comes 'board. Korbolo Dom's collected Reloe and his army – added up with his own and making what? Fifty thousand swords in all? Sixty? The traitor will catch hold o' that chain at Vathar. Then with the tribes massing to the south, aye, Beru fend, that Wickan mongrel's all but done for.' The man grunted as he heaved another canvas-wrapped bale. 'Heavy as gold . . . and that ain't no empty rumour, I'd say. That blob of whale grease calling himself High Fist has his nose up in the wind – look here, his seal's on everything. The rotten worm's

607

turning tail with his loot. Why else is the Imperial Treasurer comin' 'board, hey? And twenty marines besides . . .'

'You may have a point,' the assassin said, distracted. He'd yet to find a dry plank.

'You the caulker's man, then, eh? Got a woman here in Aren? Bet you wish you was comin' wi' us, hey? Mind you, we'll be cramped enough what with the Treasurer and two perfumed elects.'

'Perfumed elects?'

'Aye, saw one of 'em come 'board not ten minutes ago. Smooth as rat-spit, that one, all airs and dainty but no amount of flower juice could hide the spunk, if you know what I mean.'

Kalam grinned in the darkness. *Not precisely, you old swab, but I can guess.* 'What of the other one?' he asked.

'I'd hazard the same, only I ain't seen him yet. Came 'board with the captain, I heard. Seven Cities blood, if you can believe that. That was before the captain sprung us from the harbour hole – not that we deserved to be arrested in the first place – Hood's breath, when a squad of soldiers comes on ya demanding this and that, it's only natural to put a fist in their mawks, hey? We wasn't ten paces from the gangplank – so much for shore leave!'

'Your last port of call?'

'Falar. Big red-haired women all gruff and muscle just like I like 'em. Ah, that was a time!'

'Your haul?'

'Weapons, in advance of Tavore's fleet. Rode the waves like a sow, let me tell you – like we're gonna do this one, too, all the way to Unta. Bulge the belly like that and your master's got wet hands and feet, hey? Good coin, though, I wager.'

Kalam straightened. 'There won't be time for a full refit,' he said.

'Never is, but Beru bless you – do what you can.'

The assassin cleared his throat. 'Sorry to say, you've

608

got me as the wrong man. I'm not one of the caulker's men.'

The sailor paused over a bale. 'Hey?'

Kalam dried his hands on his cloak. 'I'm the other perfumed elect.'

There was silence from the other side of the hold, then a soft muttering, followed by, 'Beg your pardon, sir.'

'No need for that,' the assassin said. 'What's the likelihood of finding one of the captain's guests down here pressing the planks? I'm a cautious man and, alas, my nerves haven't been eased.'

'She ships, to be true,' the sailor said, 'but captain's got three dedicated hands on the pumps, workin' through every flip o' the glass, sir. And she'll ride any blow and that she has, more than once. Captain's got a lucky shirt, y'see.'

'I've seen it,' Kalam said, stepping over a row of chests each bearing the High Fist's seal. He made his way to the hatch, laid a hand on the ladder rail, then paused. 'What's the rebel activity out in the Sahul?'

'Gettin' hotter, sir. Bless them Marines, 'cause we won't be outrunnin' a scow on this run.'

'No escort?'

'Pormqual's commanded Nok's fleet to hold this harbour. We'll have cover crossing Aren Bay out to the edge of Dojal Hading Sea, at least.'

Kalam grimaced at that, but said nothing. He climbed the ladder to the main deck.

Ragstopper wallowed heavily at the Imperial berth. Stevedores and crewmen were busy with their tasks, making it difficult for the assassin to find a place out of anyone's path. He finally found a spot on the sterncastle near the wheel, from which he could observe. A huge Malazan transport, high in the water, sat on the opposite side of the broad stone dock. The horses it had brought from Quon had been unloaded an hour earlier, with only a dozen dockhands left behind with the task of removing the butchered remains of the animals that had not survived the lengthy journey. It was common practice to salt the meat from such losses, provided the ship's cutter pronounced it edible. The hides found innumerable uses on board. The dockhands were left with heads and bones and no shortage of eager buyers crowding the harbour front on the other side of the Imperial barrier.

Kalam had not seen the captain since the morning they had boarded, two days past. The assassin had been shown to the small stateroom Salk Elan had purchased for Kalam's passage, then promptly left to his own devices while the captain went off to manage the release of his gaoled crew.

Salk Elan . . . I weary of waiting to make your acquaintance . . .

Voices barked from the gangplank and Kalam glanced over to see the captain arrive on deck. Accompanying him was a tall, stooped man of middle years, his hatchet face painfully thin, his gaunt cheeks powdered light blue in some recent court fashion, and wearing oversized Napan sea gear. This man was flanked by a pair of bodyguards, both huge, their red faces buried in black, snarled beards and rudely plaited moustaches. They wore pot helms with bridge-guards, full shirts of mail, and broad-bladed tulwars at their hips. Kalam was unable to guess at their cultural origins. Neither the bodyguards nor their master stood comfortably on the mildly rocking deck.

'Ah,' said a soft voice behind the assassin, 'that would be Pormqual's treasurer.'

Startled, Kalam turned to find the speaker leaning against the stern rail. *A knife's thrust away.*

The man smiled. 'You were well described indeed.'

The assassin studied the stranger. He was lean, young, dressed in a loose, sickly green silk shirt. His face was handsome enough, though a touch too sharp-featured to be called friendly. Rings glittered on his long fingers. 'By whom?' Kalam snapped, disconcerted by the man's sudden appearance.

'Our mutual friend in Ehrlitan. I am Salk Elan.'

'I have no friends in Ehrlitan.'

'Poor choice of word, then. One who was indebted to you, and to whom I was in turn indebted, with the result that I was tasked with arranging your departure from Aren, which I have now done, thus freeing me of further obligations – which has proved timely, I might add.'

Kalam could see no obvious weapons on the man, which told him plenty. He sneered. 'Games.'

Salk Elan sighed. 'Mebra, who entrusted you with the Book, which was duly delivered to Sha'ik. You were bound for Aren, or so Mebra concluded. He further suspected that, with your, uh, talents, you were determined to take the Holy Cause into the heart of the Empire. Or rather, *through* one heart in particular. Among other preparations, I arranged for a tripwire of sorts to be set at the Imperial Warren's gate, which when activated would immediately trigger various prearranged events.' The man swung his head, scanning the sprawling rooftops of the city. His smile broadened. 'Now, as it turned out, my activities in Aren have been curtailed somewhat of late, making such arrangements difficult to maintain. Even more disconcerting, a bounty has been placed on my head – all a dreadful misunderstanding, I assure you, yet I've little faith in Imperial justice, especially when the High Fist's own Guard are involved. Hence, I booked not one berth but two – the cabin opposite yours, in fact.'

'The captain does not strike me as a man with cheap loyalties,' Kalam said, struggling to conceal his alarm – *If Mebra worked out I was planning to kill the Empress, who else might have? And this Salk Elan, whoever he is, clearly doesn't know when to shut up . . . unless, of course, he's fishing for a reaction. Besides, there's a classic tactic that might be at work here. No time to test veracity when you're reeling . . .*

The treasurer's high-pitched voice wheedled up from the

main deck behind him, in varied complaints flung at the captain – who if he made reply did so under his breath.

'No, not cheap,' Salk Elan agreed. 'Nonexistent would be more accurate.'

Kalam grunted, both disappointed at the failed feint and pleased that he'd heard confirmation of his assessment of the captain's character. *Hood's breath, Imperial charters aren't worth the oilskin they're written on these days . . .*

'Yet another source of consternation,' Elan continued, 'the man's far above average in wits, and seems to find his only intellectual stimulus in gestures of subterfuge and obfuscation. No doubt he went overboard – as it were – in his mysterious meeting with you at the inn.'

Kalam grinned in spite of himself. 'No wonder I took an instant liking to him.'

Elan's laugh was soft, yet appreciative. 'And it should be no surprise that I so look forward to our meals at his table each night of this pending voyage.'

Kalam held his smile as he said, 'I'll not make the mistake of leaving my back open to you again, Salk Elan.'

'You were distracted, of course,' the man said, unperturbed. 'I do not expect such a potential opportunity to recur.'

'I'm glad we're understood, because your explanation thus far has more leaks than this ship.'

'Glad? Such understatement, Kalam Mekhar! I am *delighted* we're so clearly understood!'

Kalam stepped to one side and glanced back down at the main deck. The treasurer was continuing his tirade against the captain. The crew was motionless, all eyes on the scene.

Salk Elan tsked. 'An appalling breach of etiquette, wouldn't you say?'

'Ship's command is the captain's,' the assassin said. 'If he'd the mind to, he'd have put a halt to things by now. Looks to me like the captain's letting this squall run out.'

'Nonetheless, I suggest you and I join the proceedings.'

Kalam shook his head. 'Not our business and there's no value in making it so. Mind you, don't let my opinion stop you.'

'Ah, but it is our business, Kalam. Would you have *all* the passengers tarred by the crew? Unless you enjoy the cook's spit in your gruel, that is.'

The bastard has a point.

He watched Salk Elan step casually down to the main deck, and, after a moment, followed suit.

'Noble sir!' Elan called out.

The treasurer and his two bodyguards all turned.

'I trust you are fully appreciative of the captain's patience,' Elan continued, still approaching. 'On most ships you and your effete servants would be over the side by now, and at least two of you would have sunk like ballast stones – a most pleasing image.'

One of the bodyguards growled and edged forward, a large, hairy hand closing on the grip of his tulwar.

The treasurer was strangely pale beneath the sealskin hood, his face showing not a drop of sweat despite the heat and the heavy swaths of the Napan raincloak covering his thin frame. 'You insolent excuse for a crab's anus!' he squealed. 'Roll back into your hole, blood-smeared turd, before I call on the harbour magistrate to throw you in chains!' The man raised one pallid, long-fingered hand. 'Megara, beat this man senseless!'

The bodyguard with his hand on his weapon stepped forward.

'Belay that!' the captain bellowed. Half a dozen sailors closed in, moving between the moustached bodyguard and Salk Elan. Pins and knives waved about menacingly. The bodyguard hesitated, then backed away.

The captain smiled, anchoring his hands on his hips. 'Now,' he said in a quiet, reasonable tone, 'me and the coin-stacker will resume our discussion in my cabin. In the meantime, my crew will help these two servants out of their Hood-damned chain and stow it somewhere safe. Said servants will then bathe and ship's cutter will examine them for vermin – which I don't tolerate 'board *Ragstopper* – and when the delousing's done they can help load the last of their master's provisions, minus the leadwood bench which we'll donate to the customs officer to ease our departure. Finally, any further cursing on this ship – no matter how inventive – comes from me and no-one else. That, gentlemen, will be all.'

If the treasurer intended a challenge, it was pre-empted by his sudden collapse onto the deck. The two bodyguards spun about at the loud thump, then stood stock still, staring down at their unconscious master.

After a moment, the captain said, 'Well, not all, it seems. Get the coin-stacker below and get him out of those sealskins. Ship's cutter has more work to do, and we ain't even cast off yet.' He swung to Salk Elan and Kalam. 'Now, you two gentlemen can join me in my cabin.'

The room was not much larger than the assassin's own, and almost empty of possessions. It was a few minutes before the captain managed to find three tankards into which he poured local sour ale from a clay jug. Without offering a toast, the man drained half his tankard's contents, then wiped his mouth with the back of one hand. His eyes roved restlessly, not once settling on the two men before him. 'The rules,' he said, grimacing. 'Simple. Stay out of the treasurer's way. The situation is . . . confused. With the Admiral under arrest—'

Kalam choked on the ale, then managed to rasp, 'What? By whose command?'

The captain was frowning down at Elan's shoes. 'That would be the High Fist's, of course. No other means, you see, of keeping the fleet in the bay.'

'The Empress—'

'Probably doesn't know. There's been no Claw in the city for months – no-one knows why.'

'And their absence,' Elan said, 'gives implicit authority to Pormqual's decisions, I take it.'

'More or less,' the captain conceded, his eyes now fixed on a crossbeam. He finished his ale, poured more. 'In any case, the High Fist's personal treasurer has arrived with a writ granting him commander status for this voyage, meaning he has the privilege of overriding me if he so chooses. Now, while I hold an Imperial charter, neither me nor my ship and crew are actually in the Imperial Navy, which leaves things, like I said earlier, confused.'

Kalam set his tankard down on the room's lone table. 'Right opposite us is an Imperial transport ship, getting ready to leave as much as we are. Why in Hood's name hasn't Pormqual sent his treasurer and his loot there? It's bigger and better defended, after all—'

'So it is. And it has indeed been commandeered by the High Fist, and will depart for Unta shortly after we do, loaded with Pormqual's household and his precious breeding stallions, meaning it will be very crowded, and rank to boot.' He shrugged as if his shoulders had been tugged upwards by invisible hands. He glanced nervously towards the door before returning his somewhat desperate gaze to the cross-beam overhead. '*Ragstopper*'s fast when she has to be. Now, that's all. Drink up. The marines will board any moment now, and I mean for us to cast off within the hour.'

In the companionway outside the captain's cabin, Salk Elan shook his head and muttered, 'He couldn't have been serious.'

The assassin eyed the man. 'What do you mean?'

'The ale was atrocious. "Drink up" indeed.'

Kalam scowled. 'No Claw in the city – now why would that be?'

The man's shrug was loose. 'Aren's not its old self, alas. Filled with monks and priests and soldiers, the gaols crowded with innocents while Sha'ik's fanatics – only the most cunning left alive, of course – spread murder and mayhem. It's also said the warrens aren't what they used to be, either, though I gather you know more about that than I.' Elan smiled.

'Was that an answer to my question?'

'And am I an expert on the activities of the Claw? Not only have I never run into one of those horrid throat-slitters, I make it policy that my curiosity about them is thoroughly curtailed.' He brightened suddenly. 'Perhaps the treasurer will not survive his heat prostration! Now there's a pleasing thought!'

Kalam swung about and made his way to his cabin. He heard Salk Elan sigh, then head in the opposite direction, ascending the companionway ladder to the main deck.

The assassin closed the door behind him and leaned against it. *Better to walk into a trap that you can see than one you can't.* Yet the thought gave him scant comfort. He wasn't even sure if there *was* a trap. Mebra's web was vast – Kalam had always known that, and had himself plucked those strands more than once. Nor, it seemed, had the Ehrlitan spy betrayed him when it came to delivering the Book of Dryjhna – Kalam had placed it into Sha'ik's hands, after all.

Salk Elan was likely a mage, and he also had the look of a man capable of handling himself in a fight. He had not so much as flinched when the treasurer's bodyguard had closed on him.

None of which puts me at ease.

The assassin sighed. *And the man knows bad ale when he tastes it . . .*

When the High Fist's breeding stallions were led through the gate into the Imperial yard, chaos ensued. Stamping, nervous horses jostled with stablers, dockhands, soldiers and various officials. The Master of the Horse shrieked and ran about in an effort to impose some order, fomenting even more confusion in the seething press.

The woman holding the reins of one magnificent stallion was notable only for her watchful calm, and when the Master finally managed to arrange the loading, she was among the first to lead her charge up the broad gangplank onto the Imperial transport. And though the Master knew every one of his workers and every one of the breeders in his care, his attention was so tugged and strained in multiple directions that he did not register that both woman and horse were unknown to him.

Minala had watched *Ragstopper* cast off two hours earlier, following the boarding of two squads of marines and their gear. The trader was towed clear of the inside harbour before being allowed to stretch sails, flanked by Imperial galleys that would provide escort crossing Aren Bay. Four similar warships awaited the Imperial transport a quarter-league out.

The complement of Marines aboard the Imperial transport was substantial, at least seven squads. Clearly, the Dojal Hading Sea was not secure.

Kalam's stallion tossed his head as he stepped down onto the main deck. The massive hatch that led down into the hold was in fact an elevator, raised and lowered by winches. The first four horses had been led onto the platform.

An old, grizzled stabler standing near Minala eyed her and the stallion. 'The latest in the High Fist's purchases?' he asked.

She nodded.

'Magnificent animal,' the man said. 'He's a good eye, has the High Fist.'

And not much else worth mentioning. The bastard's making a show of his imminent flight, and when he finally leaves, he'll have an entire fleet of warships for escort, no doubt. Ah, Keneb, is this what we've delivered you to?

Get out of Aren, Kalam had said. She'd urged the same to Selv before saying goodbye, but Keneb was among the army's ranks now. Attached to Blistig's City Garrison. They were going nowhere.

Minala suspected she would never see any of them again.

All to chase a man I don't understand. A man I'm not even sure I like. Oh, woman, you're old enough to know better . . .

The southern horizon ran in a thin, grey-green vein that wavered in the streams of heat rising from the road. The land that stretched before it was barren, studded with stones except along the path of the potsherd-strewn trader track that branched out from the Imperial Road.

The vanguard sat their horses at the crossroads. To the east and southeast lay the coast, with its clustering of villages and towns and the Holy City of Ubaryd. The skyline in that direction was bruised with smoke.

Slumped in his saddle, Duiker listened with the others as Captain Sulmar spoke.

'—and the consensus on this is absolute, Fist. We've no choice but to hear Nethpara and Pullyk out. It is, after all, the refugees who will suffer the most.'

Captain Lull grunted his contempt.

Sulmar's face paled beneath the dust, but he went on, 'Their rations are at starvation level as it is – oh, there'll be water at Vathar, but what of the wasteland beyond?'

Bult raked fingers through his beard. 'Our warlocks say they sense nothing, but we are still distant – a forest and a wide river between us and the drylands. It may be that the spirits of the land down there are simply buried deep – Sormo has said as much.'

Duiker glanced at the warlock, who offered nothing and who sat wrapped in an Elder's cloak atop his horse, his face hidden beneath the hood's shadow. The historian could see the now constant tremble in Sormo's long-fingered hands where they rested on the saddlehorn. Nil and Nether were still recovering from their ordeal at Gelor Ridge, not once emerging from the covered wagon that carried them, and Duiker had begun to wonder whether they still lived at all. *Our last three mages, and two of them are either dead or too weak to walk, while the third has aged ten years for every week of this Hood-cursed journey.*

'The tactical advantages must be clear to you, Fist,' Sulmar said after a moment. 'No matter how sundered Ubaryd's walls may be, they'll provide a better defence than a land devoid even of hills—'

'Captain!' Bult barked.

Sulmar subsided, lips pressing into a thin, bloodless line.

Duiker shivered in response to a chill that had nothing to do with the dying day's slow cooling. *Such a vast concession, Sulmar, according to a Wickan war chief the rules of courtesy expected from one of lower rank. What skin is this that's wearing so thin on you, Captain? No doubt quickly cast off when you sup wine with Nethpara and Pullyk Alar . . .*

Coltaine did not take Sulmar to task. He never did. He met every jibe and dig of nobleborn presumption and arrogance in the same manner that he dealt with everything else: cold indifference. It may well have worked for the Wickan, but Duiker could see how bold it was making Sulmar and others like him.

And the captain was not finished. 'This is not just a military concern, Fist. The civil element of the situation—'

'Promote me, Commander Bult,' Lull said, 'so that I may whip this dog until his hide's just a memory.' He bared his teeth at his fellow captain. 'Otherwise, a word with you somewhere private, Sulmar . . .'

The man replied with a silent sneer.

Coltaine spoke. 'There is no civil element. Ubaryd will

prove a fatal trap should we retake it. Assailed from the land and the sea, we would never hold. Explain that to Nethpara, Captain, as your last task.'

'My last task, sir?'

The Fist said nothing.

'Last,' Bult rumbled. 'Means just that. You've been stripped of rank, drummed out.'

'Begging the Fist's pardon, but you cannot do that.'

Coltaine's head turned and Duiker wondered if the captain had finally got to the Fist.

Sulmar shrugged. 'My Imperial commission was granted by a High Fist, sir. Based on that, it is within my right to ask for adjudication. Fist Coltaine, it has always been the strength of the Malazan Army that a tenet of our discipline insists that we speak our mind. Regardless of your commands – which I will obey fully – I have the right to have my position duly recorded, as stated. If you wish, I can recite the relevant Articles to remind you of these rights, sir.'

There was silence, then Bult swung in his saddle to Duiker. 'Historian, did you understand any of that?'

'As well as you, Uncle.'

'Will his position be duly recorded?'

'Aye.'

'And presumably adjudication requires the presence of advocates, not to mention a High Fist.'

Duiker nodded.

'Where is the nearest High Fist?'

'Aren.'

Bult nodded thoughtfully. 'Then, to resolve this matter of the captain's commission, we must make all haste to Aren.' He faced Sulmar. 'Unless, of course, the views of the Council of Nobles are to take precedence over the issue of the fate of your career, Captain.'

'Retaking Ubaryd will allow relief from Admiral Nok's

fleet,' Sulmar said. 'Through this avenue, a swift and safe journey to Aren can be effected.'

'Admiral Nok's fleet is in Aren,' Bult pointed out.

'Yes, sir. However, once news reaches them that we are in Ubaryd, the obvious course will be clear.'

'You mean they will hasten to relieve us?' Bult's frown was exaggerated. 'Now I am confused, Captain. The High Fist holds his army in Aren. More, he holds the entire Seven Cities fleet as well. Neither has moved in months. He has had countless opportunities to despatch either force to our aid. Tell me, Captain, in your family's hunting estates, have you ever seen a deer caught in lantern light? How it stands, frozen, unable to do anything. The High Fist Pormqual is that deer. Coltaine could deliver this train to a place three miles up the coast from Aren and Pormqual would not set forth to deliver us. Do you truly believe that an even greater plight, such as you envisage for us in Ubaryd, will shame the High Fist into action?'

'I was speaking more of Admiral Nok—'

'Who is dead, sick or in a dungeon, Captain. Else he would have sailed long ere now. One man rules Aren, and one man alone. Will you place your life in his hands, Captain?'

Sulmar's expression had soured. 'It seems I have in either case, Commander.' He drew on his riding gloves. 'And it also seems that I am no longer permitted to venture my views—'

'You are,' Coltaine said. 'But you are also a soldier of the Seventh.'

The captain's head bobbed. 'I apologize, Fist, for my presumption. These are strained times indeed.'

'I wasn't aware of that,' Bult said, grinning.

Sulmar swung to Duiker suddenly. 'Historian, what are your views on all this?'

As an objective observer . . . 'My views on what, Captain?'

The man's mouth twitched into a smile. 'Ubaryd, or the River Vathar and the forest and wastes southward? As a civilian who knows well the plight of the refugees, do you truly believe they will survive such a fraught journey?'

The historian said nothing for a long minute, then he cleared his throat and shrugged. 'As ever, the greater of the threats has been the renegade army. The victory at Gelor Ridge has purchased for us time to lick our wounds—'

'Hardly,' Sulmar interjected. 'If anything, we have been pushed even harder since then.'

'Aye, we have, and for good reason. It is Korbolo Dom who now pursues us. The man was a Fist in his own right, and is a very able commander and tactician. Kamist Reloe is a mage, not a leader of soldiers – he wasted his army, thinking to rely upon numbers and numbers alone. Korbolo will not be so foolish. If our enemy arrives at the River Vathar before we do, we are finished—'

'Precisely why we should surprise him and recapture Ubaryd instead!'

'A short-lived triumph,' Duiker replied. 'We'd be left with two days at the most to prepare the city's defences before Korbolo's arrival. As you said, I am a civilian, not a tactician. Yet even I can see that retaking Ubaryd would prove suicidal, Captain.'

Bult shifted in his saddle, making a show of looking around. 'Let us find a cattle-dog, so that we may have yet another opinion. Sormo, where's that ugly beast that's adopted you? The one the marines call Bent?'

The warlock's head lifted slightly. 'Do you really wish to know?' His voice was a rasp.

Bult frowned. 'Aye, why not?'

'Hiding in the grass seven paces from you, Commander.'

It was inevitable that everyone began looking, including Coltaine. Finally, Lull pointed and, after peering for a moment longer, Duiker could make out a tawny body amidst the high prairie spikegrass. *Hood's breath!*

'I am afraid,' Sormo said, 'that he will offer little in the way of opinion, Uncle. Where you lead, Bent follows.'

'A true soldier, then,' Bult said, nodding.

Duiker guided his horse around on the crossroads, then looked back over the vast column stretching its length northward. The Imperial Road was designed for the swift travel of armies. It was wide and level, the cobbles displaying geometric precision. It could manage a troop of fifteen horsewarriors riding abreast. Coltaine's Chain of Dogs was over an Imperial league long, even with the three Wickan clans riding the grasslands to either side of the road.

'Discussion is ended,' Coltaine announced.

Bult said, 'Report to your companies, captains.' It was not necessary to add, *We march for the River Vathar.* The command meeting had revealed positions, in particular Sulmar's conflicting loyalties, and beyond the mundane discussion of troop placement, supply issues and so on, nothing else was open to debate.

Duiker felt a wave of pity for Sulmar, realizing the level of pressure the man must be under from Nethpara and Pullyk Alar. The captain was nobleborn, after all, and the threat of displeasure visited upon his kin made Sulmar's position untenable.

'*The Malazan Army shall know but one set of rules,*' Emperor Kellanved had proclaimed, during the first 'cleansing' and 'restructuring' of the military early in his reign. '*One set of rules, and one ruler . . .*' His and Dassem Ultor's imposition of merit as the sole means of advancement had triggered a struggle for control within the hierarchies of the Army and Navy commands. *Blood was spilled on the palace steps, and Laseen's Claw was the instrument of that surgery. She should have learned from that episode. We had our second cull, but it came far too late.*

Captain Lull interrupted Duiker's thoughts. 'Ride back with me, old man. There's something you should see.'

'Now what?'

Lull's grin was ghastly in his raw, ravaged face. 'Patience, please.'

'Ah, well, I've acquired that with plenty to spare, Captain.' *Waiting to die, and such a long wait it's been.*

Lull clearly understood Duiker's comment. He squinted his lone eye out across the plain, northwest, to where Korbolo Dom's army was, less than three days away and closing fast. 'It's an official request, Historian.'

'Very well. Ride on, then.'

Coltaine, Bult and Sormo had ridden down to the trader track. Voices shouted from the Seventh's advance elements as preparations began to leave the Imperial Road. Duiker saw the cattle-dog Bent loping ahead of the three Wickans. *And so we follow. We are indeed well named.*

'How fares the corporal?' Lull asked as they rode down the corridor towards Lull's company.

Duiker frowned. List had taken a vicious wound at Gelor Ridge. 'Mending. We face difficulties with the healers – they're wearing down, Captain.'

'Aye.'

'They've drawn so much on their warrens that it's begun to damage their own bodies – I saw one healer's arm snap like a twig when he lifted a pot from a hearth. That frightened me more than anything else I've yet to witness, Captain.'

The man tugged at the patch covering his ruined eye. 'You're not alone in that, old man.'

Duiker fell silent. Lull had nearly succumbed to a septic infection. He had become gaunt beneath his armour, and the scars on his face had set his features into a tortured expression that made strangers flinch. *Hood's breath, not just strangers. If the Chain of Dogs has a face, it is Lull's.*

They rode between columns of soldiers, smiled at the shouts and grim jests thrown their way, though for Duiker the smile was strained. It was well that spirits were high, the strange melancholy that came with victory drifting away, but the spectre of what lay ahead nevertheless loomed with monstrous certainty. The historian had felt his own spirits deepening to sorrow, for he'd long since lost the ability to will himself into blind faith.

The captain spoke again. 'This forest beyond the river, what do you know of it?'

'Cedar,' Duiker replied. 'Source of Ubaryd's fame in ship-building. It once covered both sides of the River Vathar, but now only the south side remains, and even that has dwindled close to the bay.'

'The fools never bothered replanting?'

'A few efforts, when the threat was finally recognized, but herders had already claimed the land. Goats, Captain. Goats can turn a paradise into a desert in no time at all. They eat shoots, they strip bark entirely around the boles of trees, killing them as surely as a wildfire. However, there's plenty of forest left upriver – we'll be a week or more travelling through it.'

'So I'd heard. Well, I'll welcome the shade . . .'

A week or more, indeed. More like eternity – how does Coltaine defend his vast winding train amidst a forest, where ambushes will come from every direction, where troops cannot wheel and respond with anything like swiftness and order? Sulmar's concerns about the dry lands beyond the forest are moot, as far as I'm concerned. And I wonder if I'm alone in thinking that?

They rode between wagons loaded with wounded soldiers. The air was foul here with flesh rotting where forced healing had failed to stem the advance of infection. Soldiers in fever raved and rambled, delirium prying open the doors of their minds to countless other realms – *from this nightmare world into countless others. Only Hood's gift offers surcease . . .*

Off to their left on the flat grassland, the train's dwindling herds of cattle and goats moved amidst turgid clouds of dust.

625

Wickan cattle-dogs patrolled the edges, accompanied by Weasel Clan riders. The entire herd would be slaughtered at the River Vathar, for the lands beyond the forest would not sustain them. *For there are no spirits of the land there.*

The historian found himself musing as he eyed the herd. The animals had matched them step for step on this soul-destroying journey. Month after month of suffering. *That is one curse we all share – the will to live.* Their fates had been decided, though thankfully they knew nothing of that. *Yet even that will change in the last moments. The dumbest of beasts seems capable of sensing its own impending death. Hood grants every living thing awareness at the very end. What mercy is that?*

'The horse's blood had burned black in its veins,' Lull said suddenly.

Duiker nodded, not needing to ask which horse the captain meant. *She carried them all, such a raging claim on her life force, it seared her from within.* Such thoughts took him past words, into a place of raw pain.

'It's said,' Lull went on, 'that their hands are stained black now. They are marked for ever more.'

As am I. He thought of Nil and Nether, two children curled foetally beneath the hood of the wagon, there in the midst of their silent kin. *The Wickans know that the gift of power is never free. They know enough not to envy the chosen among them, for power is never a game, nor are glittering standards raised to glory and wealth. They disguise nothing in trappings, and so we all see what we'd rather not, that power is cruel, hard as iron and bone, and it thrives on destruction.*

'I am falling into your silences, old man,' Lull said softly.

Duiker could only nod again.

'I find myself impatient for Korbolo Dom. For an end to this. I can no longer see what Coltaine sees, Historian.'

'Can you not?' Duiker asked, meeting the man's eye. 'Are you certain that what he sees is different from what you see, Lull?'

Dismay slowly settled on his twisted features.

'I fear,' Duiker continued, 'that the Fist's silences no longer speak of victory.'

'A match to your own growing silence, then.'

The historian shrugged. *An entire continent pursues us. We should not have lived this long. And I can take my thoughts no further than that, and am diminished by that truth. All those histories I've read . . . each an intellectual obsession with war, the endless redrawing of maps. Heroic charges and crushing defeats. We are all naught but twists of suffering in a river of pain. Hood's breath, old man, your words weary even yourself – why inflict them on others?*

'We need to stop thinking,' Lull said. 'We're well past that point. Now we simply exist. Look at those beasts over there. We're the same, you and I, the same as them. Struggling beneath the sun, pushed and ever pushed to our place of slaughter.'

Duiker shook his head. 'It is our curse that we cannot know the bliss of being mindless, Captain. You'll find no salvation where you're looking, I'm afraid.'

'Not interested in salvation,' Lull growled. 'Just a way to keep going.'

They approached the captain's company. In the midst of the Seventh's infantry stood a knot of haphazardly armed and armoured men and women, perhaps fifty in all. Faces were turned expectantly towards Lull and Duiker.

'Time to be a captain,' Lull muttered under his breath, his tone so dispirited that it stung the historian's heart.

A waiting sergeant barked out a command to stand at attention and the motley gathering made a ragged but determined effort to comply. Lull eyed them for a moment longer, then dismounted and approached.

'Six months ago you knelt before purebloods,' the captain addressed them. 'You shied away your eyes and had the taste of

627

dusty floors on your tongues. You exposed your backs to the whips and your world was high walls and foul hovels where you slept, where you loved, and gave birth to children who would face no better future. Six months ago I wouldn't have wasted a tin jakata on the lot of you.' He paused, nodding to his sergeant.

Soldiers of the Seventh came forward, each carrying folded uniforms. Those uniforms were faded, stained and restitched where weapons had pierced the cloth. Resting atop each pressed bundle was an iron sigil. Duiker leaned forward on his saddle to examine one more closely. The medallion was perhaps four inches in diameter, a circlet of chain affixed to a replica Wickan dog-collar, and in the centre was a cattle-dog's head – not snarling, simply staring outward with hooded eyes.

Something twisted inside the historian so that he barely managed to contain it.

'Last night,' Captain Lull said, 'a representative of the Council of Nobles came to Coltaine. They were burdened with a chest of gold and silver jakatas. It seems the nobles have grown weary of cooking their own food, mending their own clothes . . . wiping their own asses—'

At another time such a comment would have triggered dark looks and low grumbling – just one more spit in the face to join a lifetime of others. Instead, the former servants laughed. *The antics of when they were children. Children no more.*

Lull waited for the laughter to fall away. 'The Fist said nothing. The Fist turned his back on them. The Fist knows how to gauge value . . .' The captain paused, a slow frown descending on his scarred features. 'There comes a time when a life can't be bought by coin, and once that line's crossed, there's no going back. You are soldiers now. Soldiers of the Seventh. Each of you will join regular squads in my infantry, to stand alongside your fellow soldiers – and not one of them gives a damn what you were before.' He swung to the sergeant. 'Assign these soldiers, Sergeant.'

Duiker watched the ritual in silence, each issuing of uniform as a man or woman's name was called out, the squads coming forward to collect their new member. Nothing was overplayed, nothing was forced. The perfunctory professionalism of the act carried its own weight, and a deep silence enveloped the scene. The historian saw inductees in their forties, but none was unfit. Decades of hard labour and the culling of two battles had ensured a collection of stubborn survivors.

They will stand, and stand well.

The captain appeared at his side. 'As servants,' Lull softly rumbled, 'they might have survived, been sold on to other noble families. Now, with swords in their hands, they will die. Can you hear this silence, Duiker? Do you know what it signifies? I imagine you do, all too well.'

With all that we do, Hood smiles.

'Write of this, old man.'

Duiker glanced at the captain and saw a broken man.

At Gelor Ridge, Corporal List had leapt down into the ditch beside the earthen ramp to avoid a swarm of arrows. His right foot had landed on a javelin head thrust up through the dirt. The iron point had driven through the sole of his boot, then the flesh between his big toe and the next one along.

A small wound, naught but mischance, yet punctures were the most feared of all battle wounds. They carried a fever that seized joints, including those of the jaw, that could make the mouth impossible to open, closing the throat to all sustenance and bringing agonizing death.

The Wickan horsewives had experience of treating such injuries, yet their supply of powders and herbs had long since dwindled, leaving them with but one treatment – burning the wound, and the burning had to be thorough. The hours after the battle of Gelor Ridge, the air was foul with the stench of burned hair and the macabre, sweetly enticing smell of cooked meat.

Duiker found List hobbling in a circle with a determined expression on his thin, sweat-beaded face. The corporal glanced up as the historian approached. 'I can ride as well, sir, though for only an hour at a time. The foot goes numb and it's then that infection could return – or so I'm told.'

Four days ago the historian had walked alongside the travois that carried List, looking down on a young man that he was certain was dying. A harried Wickan horsewife had quickly checked on the corporal during the march. Duiker had seen a grim expression settle into her lined features as she probed with her fingers the swollen glands beneath List's sparsely bearded chin. Then she had glanced up at the historian.

Duiker recognized her then, and she him. *The woman who once offered me food.*

'It's not good,' he'd said.

She hesitated, then reached under the folds of her hide cloak to withdraw a knuckle-sized, misshapen object that looked to Duiker like nothing more than a knob of mouldy bread. 'A jest of the spirits, no doubt,' she said in Malazan. Then she bent down, grasped List's injured foot – which had been left unbandaged and open to the hot, dry air – and pressed the knob against the puncture wound, binding it in place with a strip of hide.

A jest to make Hood frown.

'You should be ready to rejoin the ranks soon, then,' Duiker now said.

List nodded, approached. 'I must tell you something, sir,' he said quietly. 'My fever showed me visions of what's ahead—'

'That happens sometimes.'

'A god's hand reached out from the darkness, grasped my soul and dragged it forward, through days, weeks. Historian—' List paused to wipe the sweat from his brow – 'the land south of Vathar . . . we're going to a place of old truths.'

Duiker's gaze narrowed. 'Old truths? What does that mean, List?'

'Something terrible happened there, sir. Long ago. The earth – it's lifeless—'

That is something only Sormo and the High Command know. 'This god's hand, Corporal, did you see it?'

'No, but I felt it. The fingers were long, too long, with more joints than there should be. Sometimes that grip comes back, like a ghost's, and I start shivering in its icy clutch.'

'Do you recall that ancient slaughter at Sekala Crossing? Did your visions echo those, Corporal?'

List frowned, then shook his head. 'No, what lies ahead of us now is much older, Historian.'

Shouts arose as the train readied to lurch into motion again, down off the Imperial Road and onto the trader track.

Duiker looked out over the studded plain to the south. 'I will walk alongside your travois, Corporal,' he said, 'while you describe for me in detail these visions of yours.'

'They might be naught but fevered delusions, Historian—'

'But you don't believe so . . . and neither do I.' His eyes remained on the plain. *A many-jointed hand. Not a god's hand, Corporal, though one of such power that you might well have thought so. You've been chosen, lad, for whatever reason, to witness an Elder vision. Out from the darkness comes the cold hand of a Jaghut.*

Felisin sat on a block of masonry that had fallen from the ancient gate, her arms wrapped around herself, her eyes on the ground before her, steadily rocking in a slow cadence. The motion brought peace to her mind, as if she was nothing more than a vessel filled with water.

Heboric and the giant warrior were arguing. About her, about prophecies and ill chance, about the desperation of fanatics. Mutual contempt swirled and bubbled between the two men, seemingly born in the instant they met, and growing darker with every moment that passed.

The other warrior, Leoman, crouched nearby, matching her silence. He had before him the Holy Book of Dryjhna, guarding the tome in her stead, awaiting what he seemed to see as her inevitable acceptance that she was indeed Sha'ik reborn.

Reborn. Renewed. Heart of the Apocalypse. Delivered by the unhanded in the suspended breath of the goddess. Who waits still. Waits as Leoman waits. Felisin, hinge of the world.

A smile cracked her features.

She rocked to distant cries, the ancient echoes of sudden, soul-jarring deaths – they seemed so far away now. Kulp, devoured beneath a seething mound of rats. Gnawed bones and a shock of white hair streaked red. Baudin, burned in a fire of his own making – *oh, the irony of that, he lived by his own rule and died with that same godless claim. Even as he gave up his life for someone else. Still, he'd say he made his vow freely.*

These are the things that bring stillness.

Deaths that had already withdrawn, far down the endless, dusty track, too distant to make their demands heard or felt. *Grief rapes the mind, and I know all about rape. It's a question of acquiescence. So I shall feel nothing. No rape, no grief.*

Stones grated beside her. Heboric. She knew the feeling of his presence and had no need to look up. The one-time priest of Fener was muttering under his breath. Then he fell silent, as if steeling himself to reach into her silence. *Rape.* A moment later he spoke, 'They want to get moving, lass. They're both far gone. The oasis – Sha'ik's encampment – is a long walk. There's water to be found on the way, but little in the way of food. The Toblakai will hunt, but game's gone very scarce – the Soletaken and D'ivers, I gather. In any case, whether you open the Book or not, we have to move.'

She said nothing, continued rocking.

Heboric cleared his throat. 'For all I rage against their mad, fevered notions, and counsel most strongly against your accepting them ... we need these two, and the oasis. They know Raraku – better than anyone else. If we're to have any chance of surviving ...'

Surviving.

'I'll grant you,' Heboric went on after a moment, 'I've acquired ... senses ... that make my blindness less of a liability. And these hands of mine, reborn ... Nonetheless, Felisin, I'm not enough to guard you. And besides, there is no guarantee that these two will let us walk away from them, if you understand my meaning.'

Surviving.

'Wake up, lass! You've got some decisions to make.'

'Sha'ik drew her blade against the Empire,' she said, eyes still on the dusty ground.

'A foolish gesture—'

'Sha'ik would face the Empress, would send the Imperial armies into a blood-filled Abyss.'

'History recounts similar rebellions, lass, and the tale is an endless echo. Glorious ideals lend a vigour of health to Hood's bleached grin, but it's naught but a glamour, and righteousness—'

'Who cares about what's righteous, old man? The Empress must needs answer Sha'ik's challenge.'

'Aye.'

'And shall despatch an army from Quon Tali.'

'Likely already on the way.'

'And,' Felisin continued, feeling a cold breath touch her flesh, 'who commands this army?'

She heard him draw a sharp breath of his own and felt him flinch back.

'Lass—'

She snapped out a hand as if batting away a wasp, and rose to her feet. She turned to find Leoman staring at her, his sun-scoured face striking her suddenly as Raraku's own. *Harder than Beneth's, without any of the affectations. Sharper than Baudin, oh, there's wit there, in those cold, dark eyes.* 'To Sha'ik's encampment,' she said.

He glanced down at the Book, then back to her.

Felisin raised an eyebrow. 'Would you rather walk through a storm? Let the goddess wait a little longer before renewing her fury, Leoman.'

She saw him reappraise her, a glimmer of uncertainty newly arriving in his eyes, and was pleased. After a moment, he bowed his head.

'Felisin,' Heboric hissed, 'have you any idea—'

'Better than you, old man. Now keep quiet.'

'Perhaps we should part ways now—'

She swung to him. 'No. I think I shall have need for you, Heboric.'

He gave her a bitter smile. 'As your conscience, lass? I'm a poor choice.'

Yes, you are, and all the better for that.

The ancient path showed signs of having once been a road, running the length of a ridge that twisted like a crooked spine towards a distant mesa. Cobbles showed like bone where the wind had scoured away the sandy soil. The path was littered with red-glazed potsherds that crunched underfoot.

The Toblakai scouted five hundred paces ahead, unseen in the ochre haze, while Leoman led Felisin and Heboric at a measured pace, rarely speaking. The man was frighteningly gaunt and moved so silently over the ground that Felisin had begun to imagine him no more than a spectre. Nor did Heboric stumble in his blindness as he walked behind her.

Glancing back, she saw him smiling. 'Something amusing you?'

'This road is crowded, lass.'

'The same ghosts as in the buried city?'

He shook his head. 'Not as old. These are memories of an age that followed the First Empire.'

Leoman stopped and turned at that.

Heboric's broad mouth extended into a grin. 'Oh aye, Raraku is showing me her secrets.'

'Why?'

The ex-priest shrugged.

Felisin eyed the desert warrior. 'Does that make you nervous, Leoman?' *Because it should.*

He glanced at her, his eyes dark and appraising. 'What is this man to you?'

I don't know. 'My companion. My historian. Of great value since I am to make Raraku my home.'

'The Holy Desert's secrets are not his to possess. He plunders them as would any foreign raider. If you desire Raraku's truths, look within yourself.'

She almost gave a laugh at that, but knew its bitterness would frighten even her.

They continued on, the morning's heat rising, the sky turning into gold fire. The ridge narrowed, revealing the ancient road's foundation stones, ten or more feet down on either side, the slope beyond falling away a further fifty or sixty feet. The Toblakai awaited them at a place where the road bed had collapsed to create large, dark holes in the ground. From one of them issued the soft trickle of water.

'An aqueduct beneath the road,' Heboric said. 'It used to flow in a torrent.'

Felisin saw the Toblakai scowl.

Leoman gathered the waterskins and proceeded to crawl down into the hole.

Heboric sat down to rest. After a moment, he cocked his head. 'Sorry you had to wait for us, Toblakai-with-the-secret-name, though I imagine you'd have trouble getting your head through that cave mouth in any case.'

The giant savage sneered, revealing filed teeth. 'I collect tokens of the people I kill. Tied here on my belt. One day I will have yours.'

'He means your ears, Heboric,' Felisin said.

'Oh, I know, lass,' the ex-priest said. 'Tortured spirits writhe in this bastard's shadow – every man, woman and child that he's killed. Tell me, Toblakai, did those children beg to live? Did they weep, cry out for their mothers?'

'No more than grown men did,' the giant said, yet Felisin saw that he had paled, though she sensed that it was not his killing of children that bothered him. No, there was something else in what Heboric had said.

Tortured spirits. He's haunted by the ghosts of those he's slain. Forgive me, Toblakai, if I spare you no pity.

'This land is not home to Toblakai,' Heboric said. 'Has the Rebellion's lure of slaughter called you here? From where did you crawl, bastard?'

'I have said to you all that I shall say. When I speak to you next it will be when I kill you.'

Leoman emerged from the hole, cobwebs snagged in his bound hair, the waterskins bulging at his back. 'You will kill no-one until I say so,' he growled to the Toblakai, then swung a glare on Heboric. 'And I've not yet said so.'

There was something in the giant's expression that spoke of immense patience coupled with unwavering certainty. He rose to his full height, accepted a waterskin from Leoman, then set off down the trail.

Heboric stared sightlessly after him. 'The wood of that weapon is soaked in pain. I cannot imagine he sleeps well at night.'

'He barely sleeps at all,' Leoman muttered. 'You shall cease baiting him.'

The ex-priest grimaced. 'You've not seen the ghosts of

children tied to his heels, Leoman. But I shall make the effort to keep my mouth shut.'

'His tribe made few distinctions,' Leoman said. 'There was kin, and those who were not kin were the enemy. Now, enough talk.'

A hundred paces on, the road suddenly widened, opening out onto the flat of the mesa. To either side ran row upon row of oblong humps of fired, reddish clay, each hump seven feet long and three wide. Despite the foreshortened horizons created by the suspended dust, Felisin could see that the rows, scores deep, encircled the entire plateau – entirely surrounding the ruined city that lay before them.

The cobbles were fully exposed now, revealing a broad causeway that ran in a straight line towards what had once been a grand gate, worn down by centuries of wind to knee-high stumps of bleached stone – as was the entire city beyond.

'A slow death,' Heboric whispered.

The Toblakai was already striding through the distant gates.

'We must cross through to the other side, down to the harbour,' Leoman said. 'Where we shall find a hidden camp. And a cache . . . unless it has been pillaged.'

The city's main street was a dusty mosaic of shattered pottery: red-glazed body sherds, grey, black and brown rims. 'I will think of this,' Felisin said, 'when I next carelessly break a pot.'

Heboric grunted. 'I know of scholars who claim they can map entire extinct cultures through the study of such detritus.'

'Now there's a lifetime of excitement,' Felisin drawled.

'Would that I could trade places with one of them!'

'You are not serious, Heboric.'

'I am not? Fener's tusk, lass, I am not the adventurous type—'

'Perhaps not at first, but then you were broken. Shattered. Like these pots here.'

'I appreciate the observation, Felisin.'

'You cannot be remade unless you are first broken.'

'You have become very philosophic in your advanced years, I see.'

More than you realize. 'Tell me you've learned no truths, Heboric.'

He snorted. 'Aye, I've learned one. There are no truths. You'll understand that yourself, years from now, when Hood's shadow stretches your way.'

'There are truths,' Leoman said ahead of them, not turning as he continued. 'Raraku. Dryjhna. The Whirlwind and the Apocalypse. The weapon in the hand, the flow of blood.'

'You've not made our journey, Leoman,' Heboric growled.

'Your journey was rebirth – as she has said – and so there was pain. Only fools would expect otherwise.'

The old man made no reply to that.

They walked on in the city's sepulchral silence. The foundation stones and the low ridges of inner walls mapped the floor plans of the buildings to either side. A precise geometric plan was evident in the layout of streets and alleys, a half-circle of concentric rings, with the flat side the harbour itself. The remains of a large, palatial structure were visible ahead; the massive stones at the centre had been more successful in withstanding the centuries of erosion.

Felisin glanced back at Heboric. 'Still plagued by ghosts?'

'Not plagued, lass. There was no great unleashing of brutality here. Only sadness, and even that was naught but a subcurrent. Cities die. Cities mimic the cycle of every living thing: birth, vigorous youth, maturity, old age, then finally ... dust and potsherds. In the last century of this place, the sea was already receding, even as a new influence arrived, something foreign. There was a brief renaissance – we'll see evidence of that ahead, at the harbour – but it was short-lived.' He was silent for a dozen or so paces. 'You know, Felisin, I begin to understand something of the lives of the Ascendants. To live for hundreds, then thousands of years. To witness this flowering in all its futile glory, ah, is it any wonder that their hearts grow hard and cold?'

'This journey has brought you closer to your god, Heboric.'

The comment stung him to silence.

She saw what Heboric had hinted at when they reached the city's harbour. What had once been the bay had silted in, yet four cyclopean channels had been constructed, reaching out to vanish in the haze. Each was as wide as three city streets and almost as deep.

'The last ships sailed out from these canals,' Heboric said at her side. 'The heaviest transports scraped bottom at the far mouths, and could only make way with the tide at peak. A few thousand denizens remained, until the aqueducts dried up. This is one story of Raraku, but alas, not the only one, and the others were far more violent, far more bloody. Yet I wonder, which was the more tragic?'

'You waste your thoughts on the past—' Leoman began, but was interrupted by a shout from the Toblakai. The giant had appeared near one of the canal heads. Falling silent, the desert warrior set off towards his companion.

As Felisin moved to follow, Heboric grasped her arm, the unseen hand a cool, tingling contact. He waited until Leoman was beyond earshot, then said, 'I have fears, lass—'

'I'm not surprised,' she cut in. 'That Toblakai means to kill you.'

'Not that fool. I mean Leoman.'

'He was Sha'ik's bodyguard. If I am to become her I'll not need to mistrust his loyalty, Heboric. My only concern is that he and the Toblakai did such a poor job of protecting Sha'ik the first time around.'

'Leoman is no fanatic,' the ex-priest said. 'Oh, he might well make appropriate noises to lead you to believe otherwise, but there is an ambivalence in him. I don't for a moment believe he thinks you are truly Sha'ik reborn. The simple fact is the rebellion needs a figurehead – a young, strong one, not the worn-down old woman that the original Sha'ik must have been. Hood's breath, she was a force in this desert twenty-five years ago. You might want to consider the possibility that these two bodyguards didn't break a sweat in their efforts to defend her.'

She looked at him. The tattoos made an almost solid whirling pattern on his weathered, toadlike face. His eyes were red and rimmed in dried mucus and a thin, grey patina dulled his pupils. 'Then I can also assume they will have greater cause this time around.'

'Provided you play their game. Leoman's game, to be more precise. He will be the one to speak for you to the army at the encampment – if he has cause he will hint at doubts, and they will tear you apart—'

'I have no fear of Leoman,' Felisin said. 'I understand men like him, Heboric.'

His lips closed to a thin line.

She drew her arm away from that unnatural grip and began walking.

'Beneth was less than a child to this Leoman,' the ex-priest hissed behind her. 'He was a thug, a bully, a tyrant to a handful of the downtrodden. Any man can preen with great ambitions, no matter how pathetic his station, Felisin. You are doing worse than clinging to the memory of Beneth – you are clinging to the airs he projected, and they were naught but delusions—'

She whirled. 'You know nothing!' she hissed, trembling with fury. 'You think I fear what a man can do? Any man? You think you know me? That you can know my thoughts, know what I feel? You presumptuous bastard, Heboric—'

His laughter struck her like a blow, shocking her into silence. 'Dear lass,' he said. 'You would keep me at your side.

As what? An ornament? A macabre curiosity? Would you burn out my tongue to balance my blindness? I am here to keep you amused, then, even as you accuse me of presumption. Oh, that is sweet indeed—'

'Stop talking, Heboric,' Felisin said quietly, suddenly weary. 'If one day we do come to understand each other, it will be without words. Who needs swords when we have our tongues, you and I? Let us sheathe them and have done with it.'

He cocked his head. 'One last question, then. Why would you have me stay, Felisin?'

She hesitated before answering him, wondering at how he would take this particular truth. *Well, that is something. Not long ago I would not have cared.* 'Because it means survival, Heboric. I offer . . . for Baudin.'

Head still cocked, the ex-priest slowly wiped one forearm across his dusty brow. 'Perhaps,' he said, 'we'll yet come to understand each other.'

The canal mouth was marked by a broad series of stone steps, over a hundred in all. At the base, on what had once been the seabed, a more recent stone wall had been constructed, providing attachment points for a canvas shelter. A ring of stones surrounded an ash-stained firepit nearby, and the old cobbles that had once covered the cache were now tumbled about, a gutted cairn.

The subject of the Toblakai's outcry were the seven half-eaten corpses scattered about the camp, each a mass of flies. The blood in the fine, white sand was only a few hours old, still gummy to the touch. The stench of loosened bowels soured the hazy air.

Leoman crouched by the stairs, studying the bestial prints that marked a bloodstained ascent back up into the city. After a long moment, he glanced over at the Toblakai. 'If you want this one, you'll go on your own,' he said.

The giant bared his teeth. 'I will have no-one else crowding me,' he replied, unslinging his waterskin and bedroll and letting them drop to the ground. He unsheathed his wooden sword, holding it as if it was no more than a twig.

Heboric snorted from where he leaned against the stone wall. 'You plan to hunt down this Soletaken? I take it that in your tribe you are nearing the end of the average expected lifespan, assuming your kin are as stupid as you. Well, I for one will not grieve your death.'

The Toblakai maintained his vow, refusing to address Heboric, though his grin broadened. He swung to Leoman. 'I am Raraku's vengeance against such intruders.'

'If you are, then avenge my kin,' the desert warrior replied.

The Toblakai set off, taking the steps three at a time and not slowing until he reached the top, where he paused to study tracks. A moment later he slipped beyond their line of sight.

'The Soletaken will kill him,' Heboric said.

Leoman shrugged. 'Perhaps. Sha'ik saw far into his future, however . . .'

'And what did she see?' Felisin asked.

'She would not say. Yet it . . . appalled her.'

'The Seer of the Apocalypse was *appalled*?' Felisin looked at Heboric. The ex-priest's expression was drawn taut, as if he'd just heard confirmation of some glimmer of the future he had himself sensed. 'Tell me, Leoman,' she said, 'of her other visions.'

The man had begun dragging the bodies of his kin to one side. He paused at her question, glanced over. 'When you open the Holy Book, they shall be visited upon you. This is Dryjhna's gift . . . among others.'

'You expect me to go through with this ritual before we reach the encampment.'

'You must. The ritual is the proof that you are truly Sha'ik reborn.'

Heboric grunted. 'And what does that mean, precisely?'

'If she is false, the ritual shall destroy her.'

The ancient island rose in a flat-topped hump above the cracked clay plain. Grey, weathered stumps marked mooring poles and more substantial piers just beyond what had once been the shoreline, along with remnants of the usual garbage that had once been dumped over the sides of ships. Sinkholes in what had been the bay's muddy bottom glittered with compacted layers of glittering fish-scale.

Crouching beside Fiddler, Mappo watched as Icarium made his way up the crumbled remains of a sea wall. Crokus stood just behind the Trell, near the hobbled horses. The lad had fallen strangely silent since their last meal stop, a certain economy coming to his movements, as if he had chained himself to his own vow of patience. And seemingly unconsciously, the Daru had begun to emulate Icarium in his speech and mannerisms. Mappo was neither amused nor displeased when he noticed. The Jhag had always been an overwhelming presence, all the more so because he made no affectation or pretence.

Still, better for Crokus had he looked to Fiddler. This soldier's a wonder in his own right.

'Icarium climbs like he knows where he's going,' the sapper observed.

Mappo winced. 'I had come to the same observation,' he ruefully admitted.

'Have you two been here before?'

'I have not, Fiddler. But Icarium . . . well, he's wandered this land before.'

'But in returning to a place he'd been to before, how would he know?'

The Trell shook his head. *He shouldn't. He never has before. Are those blessed barriers breaking down? Queen of Dreams, return Icarium to the bliss of not knowing. I beg you . . .*

'Let us join him,' Fiddler said, slowly straightening.

'I'd rather—'

'As you wish,' the soldier replied, setting off after the Jhag, who had vanished into the thorn-choked city ruins beyond the sea wall. After a moment, Crokus strode past Mappo as well.

The Trell grimaced. *I must be getting old, to let being distraught cow me so.* He sighed, rising from his crouch and lumbering after the others.

The slope of detritus at the base of the sea wall was a treacherous scree of splintered wood, slabs of plaster, brick and potsherds. Halfway up, Fiddler grunted and paused, reaching down to pull free a shaft of grey wood. 'I've some rethinking to do,' he said, glancing back down. 'All this wood's turned to stone.'

'Petrified,' Crokus said. 'My uncle described the process to me once. The wood soaks up minerals. But that's supposed to take tens of thousands of years.'

'Well, a High Mage of the D'riss Warren could manage the same in the blink of an eye, lad.'

Mappo pulled free a fragment of pottery. Not much thicker than an eggshell, the shard was sky blue in colour and very hard. It revealed the torso of a figure painted on the surface, black with a green outline. The image was stiff, stylized, but without doubt human. He let the sherd drop.

'This city was dead long before the sea dried up,' Fiddler said, resuming his climb.

Crokus called up after him, 'How do you know?'

'Because everything's water-worn, lad. Waves crumbled this sea wall. Century after century of waves. I grew up in a port city, remember. I've seen what water can do. The Emperor had Malaz Bay dredged before the Imperial piers were built – revealed old sea walls and the like.' Reaching the top, he paused to catch his breath. 'Showed everyone that Malaz City's older than anybody'd realized.'

'And that the sea levels have risen since,' Mappo observed.

'Aye.'

At the top of the sea wall the city stretched out before them. While the remains were weathered, it was clear that the city had been deliberately destroyed. Every building had been reduced to rubble, revealing a cataclysmic use of force and fury. Scrub brush filled every open space that remained and low, gnarled trees clung to foundation stones and surmounted the mounds of wreckage.

Statuary had been a primary feature of the architecture, lining the broad colonnades and set in niches on every building wall. Marble body parts lay everywhere, each displaying the rigid style that Mappo had seen on the potsherd. The Trell began to sense a familiarity with the assortment of human figures portrayed.

A legend, told on the Jhag Odhan . . . a tale told by the elders in my tribe . . .

Icarium was nowhere to be seen.

'Now where?' Fiddler asked.

A frail keening rising in his head, bringing sweat to his dark skin, Mappo stepped forward.

'Caught a scent of something, have you?'

He barely heard the sapper's question.

The city's pattern was hard to distinguish from what remained, yet Mappo followed his own mental map, born of his memory of the legend, its cadence, its precise metering when recounted in the harsh, clashing dialect of archaic Trell. People who possessed no written language carried the use of speech to astonishing extremes. Words were numbers were codes were formulae. Words held secret maps, the measuring of paces, the patterns of mortal minds, of histories, of cities, of continents and warrens.

The tribe Mappo had adopted all those centuries ago had chosen to return to the old ways, rejecting the changes that were afflicting the Trell. The elders had shown Mappo and the others all that was in danger of being lost, the power that resided in the telling of tales, the ritual unscrolling of memory.

Mappo knew where Icarium had gone. He knew what the Jhag would find. His heart thundering savagely in his chest, his pace increased as he scrambled over the rubble, pushing through thickets of thorn which lacerated even his tough hide.

Seven main avenues within each city of the First Empire. The Sky Spirits look down upon the holy number, seven scorpion tails, seven stings facing the circle of sand. To all who would make offerings to the Seven Holies, look to the circle of sand.

Fiddler called out somewhere behind him, but the Trell did not respond. He'd found one of the curving avenues and was making for the centre.

The seven scorpion-sting thrones had once towered over the enclosure, each seventy-seven arm-spans high. Each had been shattered . . . *by sword blows, by an unbreakable weapon in hands powered by a rage almost impossible to comprehend.*

Little remained of the offerings and tributes that had once crowded the circle of sand, with one exception, before which Icarium now stood. The Jhag was motionless, his head tilted upwards to take in the immense construction that rose before him.

Its iron gears showed no rust, no corrosion, and would still be moving in a measure that could not be seen by mortal eyes. The enormous disc that dominated the structure stood at an angle, its marble face smothered with etched symbols. It faced the sun, though that fiery orb was barely visible through the sky's golden haze.

Mappo slowly walked towards Icarium and stopped two paces behind him.

His presence was sensed, for Icarium spoke. 'How can this be, friend?'

It was the voice of a lost child, and it twisted like a barbed shaft in the Trell's heart.

'This is mine, you see,' the Jhag continued. 'My . . . *gift*. Or so I can read, in this ancient Omtose script. More, I have marked – with knowing – its season, its year of construction. And see how the disc has turned, so that I may see the Omtose correspondence for this year . . . allowing me to calculate . . .'

His voice fell away.

Mappo hugged himself, unable to speak, unable even to think. Anguish and fear filled him until he too felt like a child, come face to face with a nightmare.

'Tell me, Mappo,' Icarium continued after a long moment, 'why did the destroyers of this city not destroy this as well? True, sorcery invested it, made it immune to time's own ravages . . . but so too were these seven thrones . . . so too were many other gifts in this circle. All things made can be broken, after all. Why, Mappo?'

The Trell prayed his friend would not turn around, would not reveal his face, his eyes. *The child's worst fears, the nightmare's face – a mother, a father, all love stripped away, replaced by cold intent, or blind disregard, the simple lack of caring . . . and so the child wakens shrieking . . .*

Do not turn, Icarium, I cannot bear to see your face.

'Perhaps I made an error,' Icarium said, still in that quiet, innocent tone. Mappo heard Fiddler and Crokus arrive on the sand behind him. Something in the air held them to silence, stalled their approach. 'A mistake in the measurement, a slip of the script. It's an old language, Omtose, faint in my memory – perhaps as faint back then, when I first built this. The knowledge I seem to retain feels . . . precise, yet I am not perfect, am I? My certainty could be a self-delusion.'

No, Icarium, you are not perfect.

'I calculate that ninety-four thousand years have passed since I last stood here, Mappo. Ninety-four thousand. There must be some error in that. No city ruin could survive that long, could it?'

Mappo found himself shrugging. *How could we know one way or the other?*

'The investiture of sorcery, perhaps . . .'

Perhaps.

'Who destroyed this city, I wonder?'

You did, Icarium, yet even in your rage a part of you recognized what you yourself had built, and left it intact.

'They had great power, whoever they were,' the Jhag continued. 'T'lan Imass arrived here, sought to drive the enemy back – an old alliance between the denizens of this city and the Silent Host. Their shattered bones lie buried in the sand beneath us. In their thousands. What force was there that could do such a thing, Mappo? Not Jaghut, even in their pre-eminence a thousand millennia past. And the K'Chain Che'Malle have been extinct for even longer. I do not understand this, friend . . .'

A callused hand fell on Mappo's shoulder, offered a solid grip briefly, then withdrew as Fiddler stepped past the Trell.

'The answer seems clear enough to me, Icarium,' the soldier said, halting at the Jhag's side. 'An Ascendant power. The fury of a god or goddess unleashed this devastation. How many tales have you heard of ancient empires reaching too high in their pride? Who were the Seven Holies to begin with? Whoever they were, they were honoured here, in this city and no doubt its sister cities throughout Raraku. Seven thrones, look at the rage that assailed each of them. Looks . . . personal, to me. A god's or a goddess's hand slapped down here, Icarium – but whoever it was has since drifted away from mortal minds, for I, at least, cannot think of any known Ascendant able to unleash such power on the mortal plain as we see here—'

'Oh, they could,' Icarium said, a hint of renewed vigour in his voice, 'but they have since learned the greater value of subtlety when interfering in the activities of mortals – the old way was too dangerous in every respect. I suspect you have answered my question, Fiddler . . .'

The sapper shrugged.

Mappo found his heart slowing. *Just do not again think of that lone, surviving artefact, Icarium.* Sweat dripping in an uneven patter on the sand, he shivered, drew a deep breath. He glanced back at Crokus. The lad's attention was elsewhere in such a studied pose of casual indifference that the Trell was left wondering at his state of mind.

'Ninety-four thousand years – that must be an error,' Icarium said. He turned from the structure, offering the Trell a weak smile.

The scene blurred in Mappo's eyes. He nodded and looked away to fight back a renewed surge of sorrow.

'Well,' Fiddler said, 'shall we resume our pursuit of Apsalar and her father?'

Icarium shook himself, then murmured, 'Aye. We are close . . . to many things, it seems.'

A perilous journey indeed.

The night of his leavetaking all those centuries ago, in the hours when the last of his old loyalties was ritually shriven from him, Mappo had knelt before the tribe's eldest shoulder-woman in the smoky confines of her yurt. 'I must know more,' he'd whispered. 'More of these Nameless Ones, who would so demand this of me. Are they sworn to a god?'

'Once, but no more,' the old woman had replied, unable or unwilling to meet his eye. 'Cast out, cast down. In the time of the First Empire which was not, in truth, the first – for the T'lan Imass claimed that title long before. They were the left hand, another sect the right hand – both guiding, meant to be clasped. Instead, those who would come to be Unnamed, in their journeys into mysteries—' She chopped with one hand, a gesture Mappo had not seen before among the tribe's elders. A gesture, he realized with a start, of a Jhag. 'Mysteries of another led them astray. They bowed to a new master. That is all there is to say.'

'Who was this new master?'

The woman shook her head, turned away.

'Whose power resides in those staves they carry?'

She would not answer.

In the passage of time, Mappo believed he had found the answer to that question, but it was a knowledge devoid of comfort.

They left the ancient island behind and struck out across the clay plain as the day's light slowly faded from the sky. The horses were suffering, needing water that even Icarium and Mappo's desert craft could not find. The Trell had no idea how Apsalar and her father fared, yet they'd managed to stay ahead, day after day.

This trail and its goal has naught to do with Sha'ik. We have been led far from the places of such activity, far from where Sha'ik was killed, far from the oasis. Fiddler knows our destination. He has divined the knowledge from whatever secrets he holds within him. Indeed, we all suspect, though we speak nothing of it – perhaps Crokus alone remains ignorant, but I may well be underestimating the young man. He's grown within himself . . . Mappo glanced across to Fiddler. *We go to the place you sought all along, soldier.*

Dusk closed in on the barren landscape, but enough light remained to reveal a chilling convergence of tracks. Soletaken and D'ivers by the score, the number frightening to contemplate, closing to join the twin footsteps of Apsalar and her father.

Crokus fell back a dozen paces as they walked their horses. Mappo took little note of the detail until, a short while later, he whirled at a shout from the Daru. Crokus was on the

650

ground, grappling with a man in the dusty gloom. Shadows flitted across the cracked clay. The lad managed to pin the man down, gripping his wrists.

'I knew you were lurking about, you weasel!' Crokus snarled. 'For hours and hours, since before the island! All I had to do was wait and now I've got you!'

The others backtracked to where Crokus straddled Iskaral Pust. The High Priest had ceased his writhing efforts to escape. 'Another thousand paces!' he hissed. 'And the deceit is complete! Have you seen the signs of my glorious success? Any of you? Are you all dimwits? Oh, so unkind in my nefarious thoughts! But see me respond to their accusations with manly silence, hah!'

'You might let him up,' Icarium said to Crokus. 'He'll not run now.'

'Let him up? How about stringing him up?'

'The next tree we come to, lad,' Fiddler said, grinning, 'and that's a promise.'

The Daru released the High Priest. Iskaral scrambled to his feet, crouching like a rat deciding which way to dart. 'Deadly proliferation! Do I dare accompany them? Do I risk the glory of witnessing with my own eyes the fullest yield of my brilliant efforts? Well disguised, this uncertainty, they know nothing!'

'You're coming with us,' Crokus growled, hands on the two daggers jutting from his belt. 'No matter what happens.'

'Why, of course, lad!' Iskaral spun to face the Daru, his head bobbing. 'I was but hastening to catch up!' He ducked his head. 'He believes me, I can see it in his face. The soft-brained dolt! Who is a match for Iskaral Pust? No-one! I must remain quietly triumphant, so very quietly. The key to understanding lies in the unknown nature of warrens. Can they be torn into fragments? Oh yes, oh, yes indeed. And that is the secret of Raraku! They wander more than one world, all unknowing . . . and before us, ah, the slumbering giant that is the heart! The true heart, not Sha'ik's grubby oasis, oh, such fools abound!' He paused, looked up at the others. 'Why do you stare so? We should be walking. A thousand paces, no more, to your heart's desire, hee hee!' He broke into a dance, knees jerking high as he jumped in place.

'Oh, for Hood's sake!' Crokus grasped the High Priest's collar, flung him stumbling forward. 'Let's go.'

'The cajoling good-humoured jostling of youth,' Iskaral murmured. 'Such warm comradely gestures, oh, I am softened, am I not?'

Mappo glanced at Icarium and found the Jhag staring at him. Their gazes locked. *A fragmented warren. What on earth has happened to this land?* The question was shared in silence, though in the Trell's mind a further thought ensued. *The legends claim that Icarium emerged from this place, strode out from Raraku. A warren torn to pieces – Raraku changes all who stride its broken soil – gods, have we indeed come to the place where Icarium's living nightmare was born?*

They continued on. Overhead, the sky's faded bronze deepened to impenetrable black, a starless void that seemed to be slowly sinking, lowering itself around them. Iskaral Pust's muttering dwindled as if swallowed up by the night. Mappo could see that both Fiddler and Crokus were having difficulty, though both continued walking, hands held out like blind men.

A dozen strides in front of the others, Icarium halted, turned.

Mappo tilted his head, acknowledging that he too had spied the two figures standing fifty paces further on. Apsalar and Servant – *the only name by which I know that old man, a simple but ominous title.*

The Jhag strode over to take one of Crokus's outstretched hands. 'We have found them,' he said in a low tone that nevertheless carried, bringing everyone to a stop. 'They await us, it seems,' Icarium continued, 'before a threshold.'

'Threshold?' Fiddler snapped. 'Quick Ben never mentioned anything like that. Threshold to what?'

'*A knotted, torn piece of warren!*' Iskaral Pust hissed. 'Oh, see how the Path of Hands has led into it – the fools followed, one and all! The High Priest of Shadow was tasked to set a false trail, and look, oh, look how he has done so!'

Crokus turned to the sound of Iskaral Pust's voice. 'But why did her father lead us here? So that we may all be set upon and slaughtered by a horde of Soletaken and D'ivers?'

'Servant journeys home, you withered mole carcass!' The High Priest danced in place again. 'If the convergence does not kill him first, of course! Hee hee! And takes her, and the sapper, too – and you, lad. You! Ask the Jhag what waits within the warren! Waits like a clenched hand holding down this fragment of realm!'

Apsalar and her father approached side by side.

Mappo had wondered at this reunion, but no expectations he'd envisioned would match the reality. Crokus had yet to notice them, and was instead drawing his daggers and preparing to close in on the sound of the High Priest's voice. Icarium stood behind the Daru, a moment from disarming him. The scene was almost comic, for Crokus could see nothing, and Iskaral Pust began throwing his voice so that it emerged from a dozen places at once, while he continued his capering dance.

Fiddler, cursing under his breath, had removed a battered lantern from his pack and was now hunting for a flint.

'Do you dare tread the path?' Iskaral Pust sang out. 'Do you dare? Do you dare?'

Apsalar halted before Mappo. 'I knew you would win through,' she said. She swung her head. 'Crokus! I am here—'

He whirled, sheathed his daggers and closed.

Sparks flashed and bounced from where Fiddler crouched.

The Trell watched as the Daru's reaching arms were captured by Apsalar and guided around her in a tight embrace.

Oh, lad, you do not know how poignant your blindness is . . .

An aura that was an echo of a god clung to her, yet it had become wholly her own. The Trell's sense of it did not leave him at ease.

Icarium came close to Mappo. 'Tremorlor,' he said.

'Aye.'

'There are some who claim the Azath are in truth benign, a force to keep power in check, that they arise where and when there is need. My friend, I am beginning to see much truth in those claims.'

The Trell nodded. *This torn warren possesses such pain. If it could wander, drift, it would deliver horror and chaos. Tremorlor holds it here – Iskaral Pust speaks the truth – but even so, how Raraku has twisted on all sides . . .*

'I sense Soletaken and D'ivers within,' Icarium said. 'Closing, seeking to find the House—'

'Believing it to be a gate.'

The lantern glowed into light, a lurid yellow that reached no more than a few paces in any direction. Fiddler rose from his crouch, eyes on Mappo. 'There *is* a gate there, just not the one the shapeshifters seek. Nor will they get to it – the grounds of the Azath will take them.'

'As it might all of us,' spoke a new voice.

They turned to see Apsalar's father standing nearby. 'Now,' he grated, 'I'd be obliged if you could bend your efforts into talkin' my daughter out of going any farther – we can't try the gate, 'cause it's inside the House . . .'

'Yet you led her here,' Fiddler said. 'Granted, we were looking for Tremorlor in any case, but whatever reasons you have are Iskaral Pust's, aren't they?'

Mappo spoke, 'Do you have a name, Servant?'

The old man grimaced. 'Rellock.' Glancing back to Fiddler, he shook his head. 'I can't guess the High Priest's motives. I only did what I was told. A final task for the High Priest, one to clear the debt and I always clears my debt, even to gods.'

'They gave you back the arm you'd lost,' the sapper said.

'And spared me and the life of my daughter, the day the Hounds came. No-one else survived, you know . . .'

Fiddler grunted. 'It was *their* Hounds, Rellock.'

'Even so, even so. It's the false trail, you see, the one that leads the shapeshifters astray, leads them—'

'Away from the true gate,' Icarium said, nodding. 'The one beneath Pust's temple.'

Rellock nodded. 'We had to finish the false trail, is all, me and my daughter. Plantin' signs, leaving trails and the like. Now that's done. We hid in shadow while the shapeshifters rushed in. If I'm fated to die in bed in my village in Itko Kan, then it don't matter how long's the walk.'

'Rellock wants to go back to fishing, hee hee!' Iskaral Pust sang. 'But the place you left is not what you return to, oh no. From one day to the next, never mind years. Rellock's done work guided by the hands of gods, yet he dreams of dragging nets, with the sun on his face and lines between his toes! He is the heart of the Empire – Laseen should take note! Take note!'

Fiddler returned to his horse, drew out the crossbow and set the crank, then locked it. 'The rest of you can choose as you like; I've got to go in.' He paused, glancing back at the horses. 'And we should let the beasts go.' He walked over to his mount and began loosening the girth straps. He sighed, patting the Gral gelding on the neck. 'You've done me proud, but you'll do better out here – lead the others, friend, to Sha'ik's camp . . .'

After a moment, the others strode to their own mounts.

Icarium turned to the Trell. 'I too must go.'

Mappo closed his eyes, willing a stillness to his inner turmoil. *Gods, I am a coward. In all ways imaginable, a coward.*

'Friend?'

The Trell nodded.

'Oh, you will all go!' the High Priest of Shadow crooned, still dancing. 'Seeking answers and yet more answers! But in my silent thoughts I snigger and warn you all with words that you will not hear – *beware sleight of hand. Compared to the Azath, my immortal lords are but fumbling children!*'

CHAPTER SIXTEEN

Tremorlor, the Throne of Sand
is said to lie within Raraku.
A House of the Azath, it
stands alone on uprooted soil
where all tracks are ghosts
and every ghost leads to
Tremorlor's door.

Patterns in the Azath
The Nameless Ones

For as far as Duiker could see, stretching west and east, the cedar forest was filled with butterflies. The dusty green of the trees was barely visible through a restless canopy of pale yellow. Along Vathar's gutted verge, bracken rose amidst skeletal branches, forming a solid barrier but for the trader track that carved its way towards the river.

The historian had ridden out from the column and halted his horse on a low hilltop that rose from the studded plain. The Chain of Dogs was stretched, exhaustion straining its links. Dust rode the air above it like a ghostly cape, grasped by the wind and pulled northward.

Duiker drew his eyes from the distant scenes and scanned the hilltop beneath him. Large, angular boulders had been placed in roughly concentric rings: the summit's crown. He

657

had seen such formations before, but could not recall where. A pervasive unease hung in the air over the hilltop.

A rider approached at a trot from the train, showing obvious discomfort with each rise in the stirrups. Duiker scowled. Corporal List was anything but hale. The young man was risking a permanent limp with all this premature activity, but there was no swaying him.

'Historian,' List said as he reined in.

'Corporal, you're a fool.'

'Yes, sir. Word's come from the rearguard's western flank. Korbolo Dom's lead elements have been sighted.'

'West? He plans to reach the river before us then, as Coltaine predicted.'

List nodded, wiping sweat from his brow. 'Aye. Cavalry, at least thirty companies.'

'If we have to push through thirty companies of soldiers to gain the ford, we'll be held up—'

'And Korbolo's main force will close jaws on our tail, aye. That's why the Fist is sending the Foolish Dog ahead. He asks that you join them. It'll be a hard ride, sir, but your mare's fit – fitter than most, anyway.'

Two notches up on her girth straps, the bones of her shoulders hard against my knees, yet fitter than most. 'Six leagues?'

'Closer to seven, sir.'

An easy afternoon's ride, under normal circumstances. 'We might well arrive only to wheel mounts and meet a charge.'

'They'll be as weary as we will, sir.'

Not by half, Corporal, and we both know it. Worse, we'll be outnumbered by more than three to one. 'Likely to be a memorable ride, then.'

List nodded, his attention drawn to the forest. 'I've never seen so many butterflies in one place.'

'They migrate, like birds.'

'It's said the river is very low.'

'Good.'

'But the crossing's narrow in any case. Most of the river cuts through a gorge.'

'Do you ride in the same fashion, Corporal? Tug one way, tug the other.'

'Just weighing things out, sir.'

'What do your visions reveal of that river?'

List's expression tightened. 'It is a border, sir. Beyond it lies the past.'

'And the rings of stones here on this hill?'

The man started, looking down. 'Hood's breath,' he muttered, then met the historian's eyes.

Duiker crooked a grin, gathered up his reins. 'I see the Foolish Dog's on its way forward. It wouldn't do to have them wait for us.'

A loud yapping bit the air at the vanguard, and as the historian trotted to join the gathered officers he was startled to see, among the cattle-dogs, a small, long-haired lapdog, its once perfectly groomed coat a snarl of tangles and burrs.

'I'd supposed that rat had long since gone through one of the dogs,' Duiker said.

'I'm already wishing it had,' List said. 'That bark hurts the ears. Look at it, prancing around like it rules the pack.'

'Perhaps it does. Attitude, Corporal, has a certain efficacy that should never be underestimated.'

Coltaine swung his horse around at their approach. 'Historian. I have called yet again for the captain of the company of Engineers. I begin to believe the man does not exist – tell me, have you ever seen him?'

Duiker shook his head. 'I am afraid not, although I have been assured that he still lives, Fist.'

'By whom?'

The historian frowned. 'I . . . I can't actually recall.'

'Precisely. It occurs to me that the sappers have no captain, and they'd rather not acquire one.'

'That would be a rather complicated deceit to carry off, Fist.'

'You feel they are incapable?'

'Oh no, sir, not at all.'

Coltaine waited, but the historian had nothing further to say on the matter, and after a moment the Fist sighed. 'You would ride with the Foolish Dog?'

'Yes, Fist. However, I ask that Corporal List remain here, with the main column—'

'But sir—'

'Not another word from you, Corporal,' Duiker said. 'Fist, he's anything but healed.'

Coltaine nodded.

Bult's horse surged between the Fist and the historian. The veteran's lance darted from his hand, speeding in a blur into the high grasses lining the trail. The yapping lapdog shrieked in alarm and raced off, bounding like a ragged ball of mud and straw. 'Hood's curse!' Bult snarled. 'Again!'

'It's little wonder it won't quieten,' Coltaine commented, 'with you trying to kill it daily.'

'You've been shouted down by a lapdog, Uncle?' Duiker asked, brows rising.

'Careful, old man,' the scarred Wickan growled.

'Time for you to ride,' Coltaine told Duiker, his eyes lighting on a new arrival. The historian turned to see Nether. She was pale, looking drawn into herself. Raw pain still showed in her dark eyes, but she sat straight in her saddle. Her hands were black, including the flesh under her fingernails, as if dipped in pitch.

Sorrow flooded the historian and he had to look away.

The butterflies rose from the track in a swirling cloud as they reached the forest edge. Horses reared, a few stumbling when struck from behind by those that followed, and what had been a scene of unearthly beauty a moment before now threatened chaos and injury. Then, with the mounts skidding and staggering, jostling, heads tossing, a score of cattle-dogs bolted forward, taking the lead. They plunged into the swarms ahead, the insects rising, parting over the road.

Duiker, spitting out ragged wings that tasted of chalk, caught a momentary glimpse of one of the dogs that made him blink and shake his head in disbelief. *No, I didn't see what I thought I saw. Absurd.* The animal was the one known as Bent and it seemed to be carrying a four-limbed snag of fur in its mouth.

Order was restored, the dogs managing to clear the path, and the canter resumed. Before long, Duiker found himself settling into the steady cadence. There was nothing of the usual shouting, jests or Wickan riding songs to accompany the thunder of hooves and the eerie whisper of hundreds of thousands of butterfly wings caressing the air above them.

The journey assumed a surreal quality, sliding into a rhythm that seemed timeless, as if beneath and above the noise they rode a river of silence. To either side the bracken and dead trees gave way to stands of young cedars, too few on this side of the river to be called a forest. Of mature trees only stumps remained. The stands became a backdrop against which pale yellow swirled in endless motion, the fluttering filling Duiker's peripheral vision until his head ached.

They rode at the pace of the cattle-dogs, and those animals proved tireless, far fitter than the horses and riders that followed in their wake. Each hour was marked by a rest spell, the mounts slowed to a walk, the last reserves of water offered in wax-sealed hide bags. The dogs waited impatiently.

The trader track provided the Clan's best chance of reaching the crossing first. Korbolo Dom's cavalry would be riding through the thinned cedar stands, though what might slow them more than anything else was the butterflies.

When they had travelled slightly over four leagues, a new sound reached them from the west, a strange susurration that Duiker barely registered at first, until its unnatural irregularity brushed him aware. He nudged his mount forward to gain Nether's side.

Her glance of acknowledgement was furtive. 'A mage rides with them, clearing the way.'

'Then the warrens are no longer contested.'

'Not for three days now, Historian.'

'How is this mage destroying the butterflies? Fire? Wind?'

'No, he simply opens his warren and they vanish within. Note, the time is longer between each effort – the man tires.'

'Well, that's good.'

She nodded.

'Will we reach the crossing before them?'

'I believe so.'

A short while later they came to a second cleared verge. Beyond it, rock pushed up from the earth to the east and west, creating a ragged line against the insect-filled sky. Directly ahead, the track began a downward slope along the path of a pebble-filled moraine, and at its base was a broad clearing, beyond which was revealed a flattened yellow carpet of butterflies that moved in a mass eastward.

The River Vathar. The funeral procession of drowned insects, down to the sea.

The crossing itself was marked by twin lines of wooden poles spanning the river, each pole bearing tied rags, like the faded standards of a drowned army. On the eastern downstream side, just beyond the poles, a large ship rested at anchor, bow into the current.

The breath hissed from Nether upon seeing it, and Duiker felt his own tremble of disquiet.

The ship had been burned, scorched in fire from one end to the other, making it entirely black, and not a single butterfly had alighted on it. The sweeps of oars – many snapped – jutted in disarray from the craft's flanks; those with blades were dipped into the current and dead insects adhered to them in lumps.

The Clan rode down towards the open flat that marked this side of the crossing. A sailcloth awning stood on poles near a small hearth which smouldered with foul smoke. Beneath the makeshift tent sat three men.

The cattle-dogs ringed them at a wary distance.

Duiker winced at a sudden yapping bark. *Gods below, I didn't imagine it!*

The historian and Nether rode up to halt near the restlessly circling dogs. One of the men beneath the awning, his face and forearms a strangely burnished bronze hue, rose from the coil of rope he'd been sitting on and stepped out.

The lapdog rushed him, then skidded to a halt, its barks ceasing. A ratty tail managed a fitful wag.

The man crouched down, picked up the dog and scratched it behind its mangy ears. He eyed the Wickans. 'So who else claims to be in charge of this scary herd?' he asked in Malazan.

'I am,' said Nether.

The man scowled. 'It figures,' he muttered.

Duiker frowned. There was something very familiar about these men. 'What does that mean?'

'Let's just say I've had my fill of imperious little girls. I'm Corporal Gesler and that's our ship, the *Silanda.*'

'Few would choose that name these days, Corporal,' the historian said.

'We ain't inviting a curse. This *is* the *Silanda.* We come on her . . . somewhere far from here. So, are you what's left of them Wickans as landed in Hissar?'

Nether spoke. 'How did you come to be awaiting us, Corporal?'

'We didn't, lass. We was just outside Ubaryd Bay, only the city had already fallen and we saw more than one unfriendly sail about, so we holed up here, planning to make passage tonight. We decided to make for Aren—'

'Hood's breath!' Duiker exclaimed. 'You're the marines from the village! The night of the uprising . . .'

Gesler scowled at the historian. 'You were the one with Kulp, weren't you—'

'Aye, it's him,' Stormy said, rising from his stool and approaching. 'Fener's hoof, never thought to see you again.'

'I imagine,' Duiker managed, 'you've a tale to tell.'

The veteran grinned. 'You got that right.'

Nether spoke, her eyes on the *Silanda*. 'Corporal Gesler, what's your complement?'

'Three.'

'The ship's crew?'

'Dead.'

Had he not been so weary, the historian would have noted a certain dryness to that reply.

The eight hundred horsewarriors of the Foolish Dog Clan set up three corrals in the centre of the clearing, then began establishing perimeter defences. Scouts struck out through the stands to the west, returning almost immediately with the news that Korbolo Dom's advance outriders had arrived. Weapons were readied among an outer line of defenders, while the rest of the warriors continued the entrenchments.

Duiker dismounted near the awning, as did Nether. As Truth joined Stormy and Gesler outside the awning, Duiker saw that they all shared the same bronze cast to their skin. All three were beardless and their pates sported the short stubble of recent growth.

Despite the chorus of questions crowding his thoughts, the historian's eyes were drawn to the *Silanda*. 'You've no sails left, Corporal. Are you suggesting that the three of you man oars and rudder?'

Gesler turned to Stormy. 'Ready weapons – these Wickans are already worn down to the bone. Truth, to the dory – we may need to yank our arses out of here fast.' He swung back to study the historian. '*Silanda* goes on her own, y'might say – I doubt we got time to explain, though. This ragtag mess of Wickans are face to face with a last stand, from the looks of it – we might be able to take a hundred or so, if you ain't fussy about the company you'd be in—'

'Corporal,' Duiker snapped. 'This "ragtag mess" is part of the Seventh. You are Marines—'

'Coastal. Remember? We ain't officially in the Seventh and I don't care if you was Kulp's long-lost brother, if you're of a mind to use that tone on me, you'd better start telling me about the tragic loss of your uniform and maybe I'll buy the song and start callin' you "sir" or maybe I won't and you'll get your nose busted flat.'

Duiker blinked – *I seem to recall we've gone through something like this once before* – then continued slowly, 'You are Marines and Fist Coltaine might well be interested in your story, and as Imperial Historian so am I. The Coastal detachments were headquartered in Sialk, meaning Captain Lull is your commander. No doubt he too will want to hear your report. Finally, the rest of the Seventh and two additional Wickan clans are on their way here, along with close to forty-five thousand refugees. Gentlemen, wherever you came from to get here, here you are, meaning you are back in the Imperial Army.'

Stormy stepped forward to squint at Duiker. 'Kulp had a lot to say about you, Historian, though I can't quite recall if any of it was good.' He hesitated, then cradled his crossbow in one arm and held out a thick, hairless hand. 'Even so, I've dreamed of meeting the bastard to blame for all we've been through, though I wish we still had a certain grumpy old man with us so I could wrap him in ribbons and stuff him down your throat.'

'That was said in great affection,' Gesler drawled.

Duiker ignored the proffered hand, and after a moment the soldier withdrew it with a shrug. 'I need to know,' the historian said in a low voice, 'what happened to Kulp.'

'We wouldn't mind knowing that, too,' Stormy said.

Two of the Clan's warleaders came down to speak with Nether. She frowned at their words.

Duiker pulled his attention away from the marines. 'What is happening, Nether?'

She gestured and the warleaders withdrew. 'The cavalry are establishing a camp upriver, less than three hundred paces away. They are making no preparations to attack. They've begun felling trees.'

'Trees? Both banks are high cliffs up there.'

She nodded.

Unless they're simply building a palisade, not a floating bridge, which would be pointless in any case – they can't hope to span the gorge, can they?

Gesler spoke behind them. 'We could take the dory upstream for a closer look.'

Nether turned, her eyes hard as they fixed on the corporal. 'What is wrong with your ship?' she demanded in a febrile tone.

Gesler shrugged. 'Got a little singed, but she's still seaworthy.'

She said nothing, her gaze unwavering.

The corporal grimaced, reached under his burnt jerkin and withdrew a bone whistle that hung by a cord around his neck. 'The crew's dead but that don't slow 'em any.'

'Had their heads chopped off, too,' Stormy said, startling the historian with a bright grin. 'Just can't hold good sailors down, I always say.'

'Mostly Tiste Andii,' Gesler added, 'only a handful of humans. And some others, in the cabin . . . Stormy, what did Heboric call 'em?'

'Tiste Edur, sir.'

Gesler nodded, his attention now on the historian. 'Aye, us and Kulp plucked Heboric from the island, just like you wanted. Him and two others. The bad news is we lost them in a squall—'

'Overboard?' Duiker asked in a croak, his thoughts a maelstrom. 'Dead?'

'Well,' said Stormy, 'we can't be sure of that. Don't know if they hit water when they jumped over the side – we was on fire, you see and it might have been wet waves we was riding, then again it might not.'

A part of the historian wanted to throttle both men, cursing the soldiers' glorious and excruciating love of understatement. The other part, the rocking shock of what he was hearing, dropped him with a jarring thud to the muddy, butterfly-carpeted ground.

'Historian, accompany these marines in the dory,' Nether said, 'but be sure to keep well out from shore. Their mage is exhausted, so you need not worry about him. I must understand what is happening.'

Oh, we are agreed in that, lass.

Gesler reached down and gently lifted Duiker upright. 'Come along now, sir, and Stormy will spin the tale while we're about it. It's not that we're coy, you see, we're just stupid.'

Stormy grunted. 'Then when I'm done, you could tell us how Coltaine and all the rest managed to live this long. Now that'll surely be a story worth hearing.'

'It's the butterflies, you see,' Stormy grunted as he pulled on the oars. 'A solid foot of 'em, moving slower than the current underneath. Without that, we'd be making no gain at all.'

'We've paddled worse,' Gesler added.

'So I gather,' Duiker said. They'd been sitting in the small rowboat for over an hour, during which time Stormy and Truth had managed to pull them a little over a hundred and fifty paces upriver through the thick sludge of drowned butterflies. The north bank had quickly risen to a steep cliff, festooned with creepers, vines covering its pitted face. They were approaching a sharp bend in the gorge created by a recent collapse on that side.

Stormy had spun his tale, allowing for his poor narrative skills, and it was his painfully obvious lack of imagination that lent it the greatest credence. Duiker was left with the bleak task of attempting to comprehend the significance of the events these soldiers had witnessed. That the warren of fire they had survived had changed the three men was obvious, and went beyond the strange hue of their skin. Stormy and Truth were tireless at the oars, and pulled with a strength to match twice their number. Duiker both longed to board the *Silanda* and dreaded it. Even without Nether's mage-heightened sensitivity, the aura of horror emanating from that craft preyed on the historian's senses.

'Will you look at that, sir,' Gesler said.

They had edged into the river's awkward crook. The collapsed cliffside had narrowed the channel, creating a churning, white-frothed torrent through the gap. A dozen taut ropes spanned the banks at a height of over ten arm-spans. A dozen Ubari archers in harnesses were making their way across the gulf.

'Easy pickings,' Gesler said from the tiller, 'and Stormy's the man for the task. Can you hold us in place, Truth?'

'I can try,' the young man said.

'Wait,' Duiker said. 'This is one hornet's nest we're better off not stirring up, Corporal. Our advance force is seriously outnumbered. Besides, look to the other side – at least a hundred soldiers have already gone over.' He fell silent, thinking.

'If they was chopping down trees, it wasn't to build a bridge,' the corporal muttered, squinting at the north cliff edge, where figures appeared every now and then. 'Someone in charge's just come for a look at us, sir.'

Duiker's gaze narrowed on the figure. 'Likely the mage. Well, if we won't bite, hopefully neither will he.'

'Makes a nice target, though,' Gesler mused.

The historian shook his head. 'Let's head back, Corporal.'

'Aye, sir. Ease up there, lads.'

The mass of Korbolo Dom's forces had arrived, taking position to either side of the ford. The sparse forest was fast disappearing as every tree in sight was felled, the branches stripped and the trunks carried deeper into the encampment. A no-man's zone of less than seventy paces separated the two forces. The trader track had been left open.

Duiker found Nether seated cross-legged beneath the awning, her eyes closed. The historian waited, suspecting that she was in sorcerous communication with Sormo. After a few minutes she sighed. 'What news?' she asked, eyes still shut.

'They've strung lines across the gorge and are sending archers to the other side. What is happening, Nether? Why hasn't Korbolo Dom attacked? He could crush us and not break into a sweat.'

'Coltaine is less than two hours away. It seems the enemy commander would wait.'

'He should have heeded the lesson of Kamist Reloe's arrogance.'

'A new Fist and a renegade Fist – does it surprise you that Korbolo Dom would choose to make this contest personal?'

'No, but it certainly justifies Empress Laseen's dismissal of Dom.'

'Fist Coltaine was chosen over him. Indeed, the Empress had made it clear that Korbolo would never advance further in the Imperial Command. The renegade feels he has something to prove. With Kamist Reloe, we faced battles of brute strength. But now, we shall see battles of wits.'

'If Coltaine comes to us, he will be stepping into the jaws of a dragon, and that's hardly disguised.'

'He comes.'

'Then perhaps arrogance has cursed both commands.'

Nether opened her eyes. 'Where is the corporal?'

Duiker shrugged. 'Somewhere. Not far.'

'The *Silanda* shall take as many wounded soldiers as it can carry – those who will eventually mend, that is. To Aren. Coltaine enquires if you wish to accompany them, Historian.'

Not arrogance at all, then, but fatal acceptance. He knew he should have hesitated, given the suggestion sober thought, but heard his own voice reply, 'No.'

She nodded. 'He knew you would answer thus, and say it quickly as well.' Frowning, she searched Duiker's face. 'How does Coltaine know such things?'

Duiker was startled. 'You are asking me? Hood's breath, lass, the man's a Wickan!'

'And no less a cipher to us, Historian. The clans do as he commands and say nothing. It is not shared certainty or mutual understanding that breeds our silence. It is awe.'

Duiker could say nothing to that. He found himself turning away, eyes caught and gathered into the sky's sweeping blurs of pale yellow. *They migrate. Creatures of instinct. A mindless plunge into fatal currents. A beautiful, horrifying dance to Hood, every step mapped out. Every step . . .*

The Fist arrived in darkness, the warriors of the Crow slipping forward to establish a corridor down which the vanguard rode, followed by the wagons burdened with those wounded that had been selected for the *Silanda*.

Coltaine, his face gaunt and lined with exhaustion, strode down to where Duiker, Nether and Gesler waited near the awning. Behind the Fist came Bult, captains Lull and Sulmar, Corporal List and the warlocks Sormo and Nil.

Lull strode up to Gesler.

The marine corporal scowled. 'You ain't as pretty as I remembered, sir.'

'I know you by reputation, Gesler. Once a captain, then a sergeant, now a corporal. You've got your boots to the sky on the ladder—'

'And head in the horseshit, aye, sir.'

'Two left in your squad?'

'Well, one officially, sir. The lad's sort of a recruit, though not properly inducted, like. So, just me and Stormy, sir.'

'Stormy? Not Cartheron Fist's Adjutant Stormy—'

'Once upon a time.'

'Hood's breath!' Lull swung to Coltaine. 'Fist, we've got two of the Emperor's Old Guard here . . . as Coastal Marines.'

'It was a quiet posting, sir, until the uprising, anyway.'

Lull loosed his helm strap, pulled the helm from his head and ran a hand through sparse, sweat-plastered hair. He faced Gesler again. 'Call your lad forward, Corporal.'

Gesler beckoned and Truth stepped into view.

Lull scowled. 'You're now officially in the Marines, lad.'

Truth saluted, thumb pulled in and pinning the little finger.

Bult snorted. Captain Lull's scowl deepened. 'Where – oh, don't bother.' He addressed Gesler again. 'As for you and Stormy—'

'If you promote us, sir, I will punch you in what's left of your face. And Stormy will likely kick you while you're down. Sir.' Gesler then smiled.

Bult pushed past Lull and stood face to face with the corporal, their noses almost touching. 'And, Corporal,' the commander hissed, 'would you punch me as well?'

Gesler's smile did not waver. 'Yes, sir. And Hood take me, I'll give the Fist's crack-thong a yank too, if you ask sweetly.'

671

There was a moment of dead silence.

Coltaine burst out laughing. The shock of it brought Duiker and the others around to stare at the Wickan.

Muttering his disbelief, Bult stepped back from Gesler, met the historian's eyes and simply shook his head.

Coltaine's laughter set the dogs to wild howling, the animals suddenly close and swarming about like pallid ghosts.

Animated for the first time and still laughing, Coltaine spun to the corporal. 'And what would Cartheron Crust have said to that, soldier?'

'He'd have punched me in the—'

Gesler got no further as Coltaine's fist lashed out and caught the corporal flush on the nose. The marine's head snapped back, his feet leaving the ground. He fell on his back with a heavy thud. Coltaine wheeled around, clutching his hand as if he'd just connected with a stone wall.

Sormo stepped forward and grasped the Fist's wrist to examine the hand. 'Spirits below, it's shattered!'

All eyes swung to the supine corporal, who now sat up, blood gushing from his nose.

Both Nil and Nether hissed, lurching back from the man. Duiker grasped Nether's shoulder and pulled her around. 'What is it, lass? What's wrong—'

Nil answered, his voice a whisper. '*That blood – that man has almost ascended!*'

Gesler did not hear the comment. His gaze was on Coltaine. 'I guess I'll take that promotion now, Fist,' he said through split lips.

'—*almost ascended. Yet the Fist . . .*' Both warlocks now stared at Coltaine, and for the first time Duiker could clearly see the awe in their expressions.

Coltaine cracked open Gesler's face. Gesler, a man on the edge of Ascendancy . . . and into what? The historian thought back to Stormy and Truth manning the dory's sweeps . . . their extraordinary strength, and the tale of the burning warren. *Abyss below, all three of them . . . And . . . Coltaine?*

There was such confusion among the group that none heard the slow approach of horses, until Corporal List grunted, 'Commander Bult, we have visitors.'

They turned, with the exception of Coltaine and Sormo, to see half a dozen Crow horsewarriors surrounding an Ubari officer wearing silver inlaid scale armour. The stranger's dark face was shrouded in beard and moustache, the curls dyed black. He was unarmed, and now held out both hands to the sides, palms forward.

'I bring greetings from Korbolo Dom, Humblest Servant of Sha'ik, Commander of the South Army of the Apocalypse, to Fist Coltaine and the officers of the Seventh Army.'

Bult stepped forward, but it was Coltaine, now standing straight, his broken hand behind his back, who spoke. 'Our thanks for that. What does he want?'

A new handful of figures rushed into the gathering, and Duiker scowled as he recognized Nethpara and Pullyk Alar at their head.

'Korbolo Dom wishes only peace, Fist Coltaine, and as proof of his honour he spared your Wickan riders who came here to this crossing earlier today – when he could have destroyed them utterly. The Malazan Empire has been driven from six of the Seven Holy Cities. All lands north of here are now free. We would see an end to the slaughter, Fist. Aren's independence can be negotiated, to the gain of Empress Laseen's treasury.'

Coltaine said nothing.

The emissary hesitated, then continued. 'As yet further proof of our peaceful intentions, the crossing of the refugees to the south bank will not be contested – after all, Korbolo Dom well knows that it is those elements that provide the greatest difficulty to you and your forces. Your soldiers can well defend themselves – this we all have seen, to your glory. Indeed, our own warriors sing to honour your prowess. You are truly an army worthy of challenging our goddess.' He paused, twisting in his saddle to look at the gathered nobles. 'But these worthy citizens, ah, this war is not theirs.' He faced Coltaine again. 'Your journey across the wastelands beyond the forest shall be difficult enough – we shall not pursue to add to your tribulations, Fist. Go in peace. Send the refugees across the Vathar tomorrow, and you will see for yourselves – and without risk to your own soldiers – Korbolo Dom's mercy.'

Pullyk Alar stepped forward. 'The Council trusts in Korbolo Dom's word on this,' he announced. 'Give us leave to cross tomorrow, Fist.'

Duiker frowned. *There has been communication.*

The Fist ignored the nobleman. 'Take words back to Korbolo Dom, Emissary. The offer is rejected. I am done speaking.'

'But Fist—'

Coltaine turned his back, his ragged feather cape glistening like bronze scales in the firelight.

The Crow horsewarriors closed around the emissary and forced the man's mount around.

Pullyk Alar and Nethpara rushed towards the officers. 'He must reconsider!'

'Out of our sight,' Bult growled, 'or I shall have your hides for a new tent. Out!'

The pair of noblemen retreated.

Bult glared about until he found Gesler. 'Ready your ship, Captain.'

'Aye, sir.'

Stormy muttered beside the historian, 'None of this smells right, sir.'

Duiker slowly nodded.

* * *

Leoman led them unerringly across the clay plain, through impenetrable darkness, to another cache of supplies, this one stored beneath a lone slab of limestone. As he unwrapped the hardbread, dried meat and fruits, Felisin sat down on the cool ground and wrapped her arms around herself in an effort to stop shivering.

Heboric sat beside her. 'Still no sign of the Toblakai. With Oponn's luck bits of him are souring that Soletaken's stomach.'

'He fights like no other,' Leoman said, sharing out the food. 'And that is why Sha'ik chose him—'

'An obvious miscalculation,' the ex-priest said. 'The woman's dead.'

'Her third guardian would have prevented that, but Sha'ik relinquished its binding. I sought to change her mind, but failed. All foreseen, each of us trapped within our roles.'

'Convenient, that. Tell me, is the prophecy as clear on the rebellion's end? Do we now face a triumphant age of Apocalypse unending? Granted, there's an inherent contradiction, but never mind that.'

'Raraku and Dryjhna are one,' Leoman said. 'As eternal as chaos and death. Your Malazan Empire is but a brief flare, already fading. We are born from darkness and to darkness we return. These are the truths you so fear, and in your fear discount.'

'I am no-one's marionette,' Felisin snapped.

Leoman's only reply to that was a soft laugh.

'If this is what becoming Sha'ik demands, then you'd better go back to that withered corpse at the gate and wait for someone else to show up.'

'Becoming Sha'ik shall not shatter your delusions of independence,' Leoman said, 'unless, of course, you will it.'

Listen to us. Too dark to see a thing. We are naught but three disembodied voices in futile counterpoint, here on this desert stage.

Holy Raraku mocks our flesh, makes of us no more than sounds at war with a vast silence.

Soft footfalls approached.

'Come and eat,' Leoman called out.

Something slapped wetly to the ground close to Felisin. The stench of raw meat wafted over her.

'A bear with white fur,' the Toblakai rumbled. 'For a moment, I dreamed I had returned to my home in Laederon. Nethaur, we call such beasts. But we fought on sand and rock, not snow and ice. I have brought its skin and its head and its claws, for the beast was twice as large as any I'd seen before.'

'Oh, I just can't wait for daylight,' Heboric said.

'The next dawn is the last before the oasis,' the giant savage said to Leoman. 'She must undertake the ritual.'

There was silence.

Heboric cleared his throat. 'Felisin—'

'Four voices,' she whispered. 'No bone, no flesh, just these feeble noises that claim their selves. Four points of view. The Toblakai is pure faith, yet he shall one day lose it all—'

'It has begun,' Leoman murmured.

'And Heboric, the rendered priest without faith, who shall one day discover it anew. Leoman, the master deceiver, who sees the world with eyes more cynical than Heboric in his fitting blindness, yet is ever searching the darkness . . . for hope.

'And finally, Felisin. Ah, now who is this woman in a child's raiment? Pleasures of the flesh devoid of pleasure. Selves surrendered one after another. Kindness yearned for behind every cruel word she utters. She believes in nothing. A crucible fired clean, empty. Heboric possesses hands unseen and what they now grasp is a power and a truth that he cannot yet sense. Felisin's hands . . . ah, they have grasped and touched, they have been slick and they have been soiled, and yet have held nothing. Life slips through them like a ghost.

'All was incomplete, Leoman, until Heboric and I came to you. You and your tragic child companion. The Book, Leoman.'

She heard him remove the clasps, heard the tome pulled free of its hide wrapping. 'Open it,' she told him.

'You must open it – nor is it dawn! The ritual—'

'Open it.'

'You—'

'Where is your faith, Leoman? You do not understand, do you? The test is not mine alone. The test is for each of us. Here. Now. Open the Book, Leoman.'

She heard his harsh breathing, heard it slow, heard it gentled by a fierce will. The skin cover crackled softly.

'What do you see, Leoman?'

He grunted. 'Nothing, of course. There is no light to see by.'

'Look again.'

She heard him and the others gasp. A glow the colour of spun gold had begun emanating from the Book of Dryjhna. On all sides came a distant whisper, then a roar. 'The Whirlwind awakens – but not here, not in the heart of Raraku. The Book, Leoman, what do you see?'

He reached down to touch the first page, peeled it back, then the next, then the one after that. 'But this is not possible – it is blank! Every page!'

'You see what you see, Leoman. Close the Book, give it to the Toblakai, now.'

The giant edged forward and crouched down, his massive, bloodstained hands accepting the Book. He did not hesitate.

A warm light bathed his face as he stared down at the first page. She saw tears fill his eyes and run crooked tracks down his scarred cheeks.

'Such beauty,' she whispered to him. 'And beauty makes you weep. Do you know why you feel such sorrow? No, not yet. One day . . . Close the Book, Toblakai.

'Heboric—'

'No.'

Leoman slid a dagger free, but was stilled by Felisin's hand.

'No,' the ex-priest repeated. 'My touch—'

'Aye,' she said. 'Your touch.'

'No.'

'You were tested before, Heboric, and you failed. Oh, how you failed. You fear you will fail again—'

'I do not, Felisin,' Heboric's tone was sharp, certain. 'That least of all. I shall not be part of this ritual, nor shall I risk laying hands on that cursed Book.'

'What matter if he opens the Book?' the Toblakai growled. 'He's as blind as an enkar'al. Let me kill him, Sha'ik Reborn. Let his blood seal this ritual.'

'Do it.'

The Toblakai moved in a blur, the wooden sword almost unseen as it slashed for Heboric's head. Had it struck it would have shattered the old man's skull, spraying bits of it for ten paces or more. Instead, Heboric's hands flared, one the hue of dried blood, the other bestial and fur-backed. They shot up to intercept the swing, each closing on one of the giant's wrists – and stopping the swing dead. The wooden sword flew out of the Toblakai's hands, vanishing into the darkness beyond the Book's pale glow.

The giant grunted in pain.

Heboric released the Toblakai's wrists, grasped the giant by his neck and belt, then, in a surge, threw him out into the darkness. There was a thud as he struck and the clay trembled beneath their feet.

Heboric staggered back, his face twisted in shock, and the blazing rage that entwined his hands winked out.

'We could see, then,' Felisin told him. 'Your hands. You were never forsaken, Heboric, no matter what the priests may have believed when they did what they did. You were simply being *prepared*.'

The old man fell to his knees.

'And so a man's faith is born anew. Know this: Fener would never risk investing you and you alone, Heboric Light Touch. Think on that, and be at ease . . .'

Out in the darkness, the Toblakai groaned.

Felisin rose to her feet. 'I shall have the Book now, Leoman. Come the dawn.' *Felisin, surrendering herself yet again. Remade. Reborn. Is this the last time? Oh no, it most certainly is not.*

With dawn an hour away, Icarium led the others to the edge of the warren. Hitching the stock of his crossbow on one hip, Fiddler handed Crokus the lantern, then glanced over at Mappo.

The Trell shrugged. 'The barrier is opaque – nothing of what lies beyond is visible.'

'They know nothing of what is to come,' Iskaral Pust whispered. 'An eternal flare of pain, but shall I waste words in an effort to prepare them? No, not at all, never. Words are too precious to be wasted, hence my coy silence while they hesitate in a fit of immobile ignorance.'

Fiddler gestured with the crossbow. 'You go first, Pust.'

The High Priest gaped. 'Me?' he squealed. 'Are you mad?' He ducked his head. 'They are deceived again, even that gnarled excuse for a soldier – oh, this is too easy!'

Hissing, Crokus stepped forward, raising the lantern high, then strode through the barrier, vanishing from the others. Icarium immediately followed.

With a growl, Fiddler gestured Iskaral Pust forward.

As the two disappeared, Mappo swung to Apsalar and her father. 'You two have been through once before,' he said. 'The warren's aura clings to you both.'

Rellock nodded. 'The false trail. We had to make sure of the D'ivers and Soletaken.'

The Trell swung his gaze to Apsalar. 'What warren is this?'

'I don't know. It has indeed been torn apart. There is little hope of determining its nature given the state it's now in. And my memories tell me nothing of such a warren so destroyed.'

Mappo sighed, rolling his shoulders to ease the tension binding his muscles. 'Ah, well, why assume that the Elder Warrens we know of – Tellann, Omtose Phellack, Kurald Galain – are the only ones that existed?'

The barrier was marked by a change in air pressure. Mappo swallowed and felt his ears pop. He blinked, his senses struggling to manage the flood that rushed upon them. The Trell stood with the others in a forest of towering trees, a mix of spruce, cedar and redwood all thickly braided in moss. Blue-tinged sunlight filtered down. The air smelled of decaying vegetation and insects buzzed. The scene's ethereal beauty descended on Mappo like a cooling balm.

'Don't know what I was expecting,' Fiddler muttered, 'but it wasn't this.'

A large dolomite boulder, taller than Icarium, rose from the mulch directly ahead. Sunlight bathed it in pale green, lifting into view the shadows of grooves, pits and other shapes carved into its surface.

'The sun never moves,' Apsalar said beside the Trell. 'The light is ever at that angle, the only angle that raises those carvings to our eyes.'

The base and sides of the boulder were a mass of hand and paw prints, every one the colour of blood.

The Path of Hands. Mappo turned to Iskaral Pust. 'More of your deceit, High Priest?'

'A lone boulder in a forest? Free of lichen and moss, bleached by another world's harsh sun? The Trell is dense beyond belief, but listen to this!' He offered Mappo a wide smile. 'Absolutely not! How could I move such an edifice? And look at those ancient carvings, those pits and whorls, how could such things be faked?'

Icarium had walked up to stand before the boulder. He followed the wending track of one of the grooves. 'No, these are real enough. Yet they are Tellann, the kind you would find at a site sacred to the T'lan Imass – the boulder typically surmounting a hilltop on a tundra or plain. I would not expect, of course, that the D'ivers and Soletaken could be aware of such an incongruity—'

'Of course not!' Iskaral burst out, then he frowned at the Jhag. 'Why do you stop?'

'How could I otherwise? You interrupted me—'

'A lie! But no, I must stuff my outrage into a bag, a bag such as the curious sack the Trell carries – such a curious sack, that! Is there another fragment trapped within it? The possibility is . . . possible. A likely likelihood, indeed, a certain certainty! I need but turn this ingenuous smile on the Jhag to show my benign patience at his foul insult, for I am a bigger man than he, oh yes. All his airs, his posturing, his poorly disguised asides – hark!' Iskaral Pust spun around, squinted into the forest beyond the boulder.

'Do you hear something, High Priest?' Icarium asked calmly.

'Hear, here?' Pust scowled. 'Why ask me that?'

Mappo asked Apsalar, 'How far into this wood have you gone?'

She shook her head. *Not far.*

'I'll take point,' Fiddler said. 'Straight ahead, I take it, past this rock?'

There were no alternative suggestions.

They set off, Fiddler ranging ahead, crossbow readied at hip-level, a Moranth quarrel set in the groove. Icarium followed, his bow still strapped on his back, sword sheathed. Pust, Apsalar and her father were next, with Crokus a few paces ahead of Mappo, who was the column's rearguard.

Mappo could not be sure of matching the Jhag's speed in responding to a threat, so he removed the bone mace from his sack. *Do I in truth carry a fragment of this warren within this tattered ruck? How fare my hapless victims, then? Perhaps I have sent them to paradise – a thought to ease my conscience . . .*

The Trell had travelled old forests before and this one was little different. The sounds of birds were few and far between, and apart from insects and the trees and plants themselves, there was no other indication of life. It would be easy enough to lose grip on imagination's reins in such a place, if one were so inclined, to fashion a brooding presence from the primeval atmosphere. *A place to ravel dark legends, to make us no more than children shivering to fraught tales . . . bah, what nonsense! The only brooding thing here is me.*

The roots were thick underfoot, a latticework revealing itself here and there through the humus, spreading out to bridge the gap between every tree. The air grew cooler as they journeyed on, abandoning its rich smells, and it eventually became apparent that the trees were thinning out, the spaces between them stretching from a few paces to half a dozen, then a dozen. Yet still the knotted roots remained thickly woven on the ground – too many to be explained by the forest itself. The sight of them triggered hints of a vaguely disturbing memory in Mappo, yet he could not track it down.

They could now see five hundred paces ahead, a vista of sentinel boles and damp air tinted blue under the strange sun's spectral light. Nothing moved. No-one spoke, and the only sound was their breathing, the rustle of clothing and armour, and the tread of their feet on the endless mat of entwined tree roots.

An hour later they reached the outer edge of the forest. Beyond it lay a dark, rolling plain.

Fiddler drew the company to a halt. 'Any thoughts on this?' he asked, staring out over the bare, undulating landscape that lay ahead.

The ground before them was a solid weave, a riotous

twisting of serpentine roots that stretched off into the distance.

Icarium crouched and laid a hand on one thick, coiled span of wood. He closed his eyes, then nodded. The Jhag straightened. 'The Azath,' he said.

'Tremorlor,' Fiddler muttered.

'I have never seen an Azath manifest itself in this way,' Mappo said. *No, not an Azath, but I have seen staves of wood . . .*

'I have,' Crokus said. 'In Darujhistan. The Azath House there grew from the ground, like the stump of a tree. I saw it with my own eyes. It rose to contain a Jaghut's Finnest.'

Mappo studied the youth for a long moment, then he turned to the Jhag. 'What else did you sense, Icarium?'

'Resistance. Pain. The Azath is under siege. This fragmented warren seeks to pull free of the House's grip. And now, an added threat . . .'

'The Soletaken and D'ivers.'

'Tremorlor is . . . aware . . . of those who seek it.'

Iskaral Pust cackled, then ducked at a glare from Crokus.

'Including us, I take it,' Fiddler said.

Icarium nodded. 'Aye.'

'And it means to defend itself,' the Trell said.

'If it can.'

Mappo scratched his jaw. *The responses of a living entity.*

'We should stop here,' Fiddler said. 'Get some sleep—'

'Oh no, you mustn't!' Iskaral Pust said. 'Urgency!'

'Whatever lies ahead,' the sapper growled, 'can wait. If we're not rested—'

'I agree with Fiddler,' Icarium said. 'A few hours . . .'

The camp was haphazard, bedrolls set out in silence, a scant meal shared. Mappo watched the others settling down until only he and Rellock remained awake. The Trell joined the old man as he prepared his own bedding.

Mappo spoke in a low voice, 'Why did you obey Iskaral's

commands, Rellock? To draw your daughter to this place . . . into these circumstances . . .'

The fisherman grimaced, visibly struggling towards a reply. 'I was gifted, sir, with this here arm. Our lives were spared—'

'As you said before, and you were delivered to Iskaral. To a fortress in a desert. Where you were made to draw your only child into danger . . . I am sorry if I offend, Rellock. I seek only to understand.'

'She ain't what she was. Not my little girl. No.' He hesitated, hands twitching where they rested on the bedroll. 'No,' he repeated, 'what's done is done, and there's no going back.' He looked up. 'Got to make the best of how things are. My girl knows things . . .' He glanced away, eyes narrowing as he stared at something only he could see. 'Terrible things. But, well, there's a child still there – I can see it. All that she knows . . . Well –' he fixed Mappo with a glare – 'knowing ain't enough. It ain't enough.' He scowled, then shook his head and looked away. 'I can't explain—'

'I am following you so far.'

With a sigh, Rellock resumed, 'She needs reasons. Reasons for everything. It's my feeling, anyway. I'm her father, and I say she's got more learning to do. It's no different from being out on the water – you learn no place safe. Not real learning. No place safe, Trell.' Shaking himself, he rose. 'Now you gone and made my head ache.'

'Forgive me,' Mappo said.

'If I'm lucky, she might do that for me one day.'

The Trell watched him finish laying out the bedroll. Mappo rose and headed to where he'd left his sack. *'We learn no place safe.' Whatever sea god looks down on you, old man, must surely fix an eye on his lost child now.*

Muffled in his bedrolls, unable to sleep, Mappo heard movement behind him, then Icarium's low voice.

'Best get back to sleep, lass.'

The Trell heard wry amusement in her reply. 'We're much alike, you and I.'

'How so?' Icarium asked.

She sighed. 'We each have our protectors – neither of whom is capable of protecting us. Especially not from ourselves. So they're dragged along, helpless, ever watchful, but so very helpless.'

Icarium's reply was measured and toneless. 'Mappo is a companion to me, a friend. Rellock is your father. I understand his notion of protection – what else is a father to do? But it is a different thing, Mappo and me.'

'Is it now?'

Mappo held his breath, ready to rise, to close this conversation now—

Apsalar continued after a moment. 'Perhaps you are right, Icarium. We are less alike than it first seemed. Tell me, what will you do with your memories once you find them?'

The Trell's silent relief was but momentary. Yet now he did not struggle with an urge to intervene; rather, he held himself very still, waiting to hear the reply to a question he had never dared ask Icarium.

'Your question . . . startles me, Apsalar. What do you do with yours?'

'They are not mine – most of them, anyway. I have a handful of images from my life as a fishergirl. Bargaining in a market for twine. Holding my father's hand over a cairn where cut flowers lay scattered on the weathered stones, a feel of lichen where once I touched skin. Loss, bewilderment – I must have been very young.

'Other memories belong to a wax witch, an old woman who sought to protect me during Cotillion's possession. She'd lost a husband, children, all sacrificed to Imperial glory. You'd think, wouldn't you, that bitterness would overwhelm all else within such a woman? But not so. Helpless to protect her loved ones, her instincts – so long bottled up – embraced me instead. And do so to this day, Icarium . . .'

'An extraordinary gift, lass . . .'

'Indeed. Finally, my last set of borrowed memories – the most confusing of all. An assassin's. Once mortal, then Ascendant. Assassins bow to the altar of efficiency, Icarium, and efficiency is brutal. It sacrifices mortal lives without a second thought, all for whatever is perceived as the greater need. At least it was so in the case of Dancer, who did not kill for coin, but for a cause that was less self-aggrandizing than you might think. In his mind, he was a man who fixed things. He viewed himself as honourable. A man of integrity, was Dancer. But efficiency is a cold-blooded master. And there's a final irony. A part of him, in defiance of his need to seek vengeance upon Laseen, actually . . . sympathizes. After all, she bowed to what she perceived as a greater need – one of Empire – and chose to sacrifice two men she called friends to answer that need.'

'Within you, then, is chaos.'

'Aye, Icarium. Such are memories in full flood. We are not simple creatures. You dream that with memories will come knowledge, and from knowledge, understanding. But for every answer you find, a thousand new questions arise. All that we were has led us to where we are, but tells us little of where we're going. Memories are a weight you can never shrug off.'

A stubborn tone was evident as Icarium muttered, 'A burden I would accept nonetheless.'

'Let me offer some advice. Do not say that to Mappo, unless you wish to further break his heart.'

The Trell's blood was a thunder coursing through him, his chest aching with a breath held overlong.

'I do not understand,' Icarium said quietly after a time, 'but I would never do that, lass.'

Mappo let the air loose, slowly, struggling to control himself. He felt tears run crooked tracks from the corners of his eyes.

'I do not understand.' This time, the words were a whisper.

'Yet you wish to.'

There was no reply to that. A minute passed, then there came to Mappo sounds of movement. 'Here, Icarium,' Apsalar said, 'dry those eyes. Jhag never weep.'

Sleep eluded Mappo and, he suspected, there were others among the group for whom rest offered no surcease from tortured thoughts. Only Iskaral Pust seemed at ease, if his groaning snores were any indication.

Before long, Mappo heard the sounds of movement once again, and Icarium spoke in a calm, measured voice. 'It is time.'

They broke camp swiftly. Mappo was still drawing the ties of his sack when Fiddler set out, a soldier approaching a battlefield, cautious yet determined. The High Priest of Shadow bounded after him. As Icarium prepared to follow, Mappo reached out and gripped the Jhag's arm.

'My friend, Azath Houses seek to imprison all who possess power – do you fathom what you risk?'

Icarium smiled. 'Not just me, Mappo. You ever underestimate yourself, what you have become after all these centuries. We must trust in the Azath understanding that we mean no harm, if we intend to continue onward.'

The others had all set out – Apsalar sparing one searching glance their way – leaving the two alone.

'How can we trust in something we cannot understand?' the Trell demanded. 'You said "aware". How? Precisely *what* is aware?'

'I have no idea. I sense a presence, that is all. And if I can sense it, then it in turn can sense me. Tremorlor suffers, Mappo. It fights alone, and its cause is just. I mean to help the

Azath, and so to Tremorlor lies the choice – to accept my help or not.'

The Trell struggled to disguise his distress. *Oh, my friend, you offer help without realizing how quickly that blade can turn. In your ignorance you are so pure, so noble. If Tremorlor knows you better than you know yourself, will it dare accept your offer?*

'What is wrong, friend?'

Bleak suspicion showed in the Jhag's eyes, and Mappo was forced to look away. *What is wrong? I would speak to warn you, my friend. Should Tremorlor take you, the world is freed of a vast threat, but I lose a friend. No, I betray you to eternal imprisonment. The Elders and the Nameless Ones who set upon me this task would command me with certainty. They would care nothing of love. Nor would the young Trell warrior who so freely made his vow hesitate – for he did not know the man he was to follow. Nor did he possess doubts. Not then, so long ago.* 'I beg you, Icarium, let us turn back now. The risk is too great, my friend.' He felt his eyes water as he stared out across the plain. *My friend. At last, dear Elders, I am revealed to you. You chose wrongly. I am a coward.*

'I wish,' Icarium said slowly, haltingly, 'I wish I could understand. The war I see within you breaks my heart, Mappo. You must realize by now . . .'

'Realize what?' the Trell croaked, still unable to meet the Jhag's eyes.

'That I would give my life for you, my only friend, my brother.'

Mappo wrapped his arms about himself. 'No,' he whispered. 'Do not say that.'

'Help me end your war. Please.'

The Trell drew a deep, ragged breath. 'The city of the First Empire, the one upon the old island . . .'

Icarium waited.

'Destroyed . . . by your hand, Icarium. Yours is a blind rage . . . a rage unequalled. It burns fierce, so fierce all your memory

688

of what you do is obliterated. I watch you – I have watched you stirring those cold ashes, ever seeking to discover who you are, yet there I stand, at your side, bound by a vow to prevent you ever committing such an act again. You have destroyed cities, entire peoples. Once you begin killing, you cannot stop, until all before you is . . . lifeless.'

The Jhag said nothing, nor could Mappo look at his friend. The Trell's arms ached with his own protective, helpless hug. His anguish was a storm within him, and he was holding it back with all his strength.

'And Tremorlor knows,' Icarium said, in a cold, flat voice. 'The Azath can do naught but take me.'

If it is able, and so sorely tested before the effort's even begun. In your anger you may destroy it – spirits below, what do we risk here?

'I believe this warren has shaped you, Icarium. After all this time, you have finally come home.'

'Where it began, it shall end. I go to Tremorlor.'

'Friend—'

'No. I cannot walk free with this knowledge – you must see that, Mappo. I cannot—'

'If Tremorlor takes you, you will not die, Icarium. Your imprisonment is eternal, yet you shall be . . . *aware*.'

'Aye, a worthy punishment for my crimes.'

The Trell cried out at that.

Icarium's hand fell on his shoulder. 'Walk with me to my prison, Mappo. Do what you must – what you clearly have done before – to prevent my rage. I must not be allowed to resist.'

Please—

'Do what a friend would do. And free yourself, if I am to be so presumptuous as to offer you a gift in return. We must end this.'

He shook his head, seeking to deny everything. *Coward! Strike him down now! Drag him away from here – far away – he will return to consciousness recalling none of this. I can lead him away, in some other direction, and we can be as we were, as we always have been—*

'Rise, please, the others await us.'

The Trell had not realized he was on the ground, curled tight. He tasted blood in his mouth.

'Rise, Mappo. One last task.'

Firm, strong hands helped him climb to his feet. He tottered as if drunk or fevered.

'Mappo, I cannot call you friend otherwise.'

'That,' the Trell gasped, 'was unfair—'

'Aye, it seems I must make you what I seem to be. Let anger be the iron of your resolve. Leave no room for doubt – you were ever too sentimental, Trell.'

Even your attacks with words are kindly said. Ah, gods, how can I do this?

'The others are deeply shaken by what they have seen – what shall we tell them?'

Mappo shook his head. *Still a child in so many ways, Icarium. They know.*

'Come along now. My home awaits this prodigal return.'

'It had to come,' Fiddler said as they arrived. Mappo studied each of them in turn and saw the knowledge plainly writ, in every hue. Iskaral Pust's wizened face was twisted in a febrile grin – fear, anticipation and a host of other emotions only he could explain, had he been willing. Apsalar seemed to have set aside whatever sympathy she felt, and now eyed Icarium as if gauging a potential opponent; her uncertainty at her own ability showed for the first time. There was resignation in Rellock's eyes, all too aware of the threat to his daughter. Crokus alone seemed immune to the knowledge, and Mappo once again wondered at the certainty the young man seemed to have discovered within himself. *As if the lad admires Icarium – but what part of the Jhag does he admire?*

They stood on a hill, the roots chaotic underfoot. *Some ancient creature lies imprisoned beneath us. All these hills . . .* Ahead, the landscape changed, the roots rising in narrow ridges to create thick walls, forming corridors in a sprawling, wild maze. Some of the roots within the walls seemed to be moving. Mappo's gaze narrowed as he studied that ceaseless motion.

'Make no efforts to save me,' Icarium announced, 'should Tremorlor seek to take me. Indeed, assist those efforts in any way you can—'

'Fool!' Iskaral Pust crowed. 'The Azath needs you first! Tremorlor risks a cast of the knuckles that even Oponn would quail at! Desperation! A thousand Soletaken and D'ivers are converging! My god has done all he can, as have I! And who will thank us? Who will acknowledge our sacrifice? You must not fail us now, horrid Jhag!'

Grimacing, Icarium turned to Mappo. 'I shall defend the Azath – tell me, can I fight without . . . without that burning rage?'

'You possess a threshold,' the Trell conceded. *But oh so near.*

'Hold yourself back,' Fiddler said, checking his crossbow. 'Until the rest of us have done all we can do.'

'Iskaral Pust,' Crokus snapped. 'That includes not just you, but your god—'

'Hah! You would command us? We have brought the players together – no more can be asked—'

The Daru closed on the High Priest, a knife-point flashing to rest lightly against Pust's neck. 'Not good enough,' he said. 'Call your god, damn you. We need more help!'

'The risks—'

'Are greater if you just stand back, dammit! *What if Icarium kills the Azath?*'

Mappo held his breath, astonished at how deeply Crokus understood the situation.

There was silence.

Icarium stepped back, shaken.

Oh yes, friend, you possess such power.

Iskaral Pust blinked, gaped, then shut his mouth with a snap. 'Unforeseen,' he finally whimpered. 'All that would be freed . . . oh, my! Release me now.'

Crokus stepped back, sheathing his knife.

'Shadowthrone . . . uh . . . my worthy Lord of Shadow . . . is thinking. Yes! Thinking furiously! Such is the vastness of his genius that he can outwit even himself!' The High Priest's eyes widened and he spun to face the forest behind them.

A distant howl sounded from the wood.

Iskaral Pust smiled.

'I'll be damned,' Apsalar muttered. 'I didn't think he had it in him.'

Five Hounds of Shadow emerged from the wood like a loping pack of wolves, though each was as tall as a pony. To mock all things natural, the pale, sightless Hound named Blind led the way. Her mate Baran ran behind and to her right. Gear and Shan followed in rough flanking positions. The pack's leader, Rood, sauntered in their wake.

Mappo shivered. 'I thought there were seven.'

'Anomander Rake killed two on the Rhivi Plain,' Apsalar said, 'when he demanded Cotillion cease possession of my body.'

Crokus spun in surprise. 'Rake? I didn't know that.'

Mappo raised an eyebrow at the Daru. 'You know Anomander Rake, Lord of Moon's Spawn?'

'We met but once,' Crokus said.

'I would hear that tale some day.'

The lad nodded, tight-lipped.

Mappo, you are the only fool here who believes we will survive this. He fixed his gaze once more on the approaching Hounds.

In all his travels with Icarium, they had never before crossed paths with the legendary creatures of Shadow, yet the Trell well knew their names and descriptions, and the Hound he feared most was Shan. She moved like fluid darkness, her eyes crimson slits. Where the others showed, in the scars tracked across their muscled bulk, the savage ferocity of brawlers, Shan's sleek approach was a true killer's, an assassin's. The Trell felt the hair rise on the back of his neck as those deadly eyes found and held him for the briefest of moments.

'They are not displeased,' Iskaral Pust crooned.

Mappo pulled his eyes away from the beasts and saw Fiddler staring at him. The knowledge that passed between them was instant and certain. The sapper's head tilted a fraction. The Trell sighed, slowly blinked, then turned to Icarium. 'My friend—'

'I welcome them,' the Jhag rumbled. 'We shall speak no more of it, Mappo.'

In silence the Hounds arrived, fanning out to encircle the company.

'Into the maze we go,' Iskaral Pust said, then cackled as a distant, uncanny scream reached them. The Hounds raised their heads at the sound, testing the motionless air, but seemed otherwise unexcited. There was around each beast an aura of dreadful competence, wrought with vast antiquity like threads of iron.

The High Priest of Shadow broke into another dance, brought to an abrupt halt by Baran's head and shoulder as the animal, with blurring speed, batted Iskaral Pust to the ground.

Fiddler grunted as he reached down to help the priest up. 'You've managed to irritate your god, Pust.'

'Nonsense,' the man gasped. 'Affection. The puppy was so pleased to see me it became overexcited.'

They set off towards the maze, beneath a sky the colour of polished iron.

Gesler strode to where Duiker, Bult and Captain Lull sat drinking weak herbal tea. The corporal's face was red and swollen around the fractured nose, his voice a rough whine. 'We can't pack no more aboard, so we're pulling out to catch the last of the tide.'

'How quickly can those undead oarsmen take you to Aren?' Lull asked.

'Won't be long. Three days at the most. Don't worry, we won't lose any of the wounded on the way, sir—'

'What makes you so certain of that, Corporal?'

'Things are kind of timeless on the *Silanda*, sir. All those heads still drip blood, only they ain't been attached to their bodies for months, years, maybe even decades. Nothing rots. Fener's tusk, we can't even grow beards when we're aboard, sir.'

Lull grunted.

It was an hour before dawn. The sounds of frenzied activity rising from Korbolo Dom's encampment had not ceased. Sorcerous wards prevented the Wickan warlocks from discovering the nature of that activity. The lack of knowing had stretched everyone's nerves taut.

'Fener guard you all,' Gesler said.

Duiker looked up to meet the man's eyes. 'Deliver our wounded, Corporal.'

'Aye, Historian, we'll do just that. And maybe we can even pry Nok's fleet out of the harbour, or shame Pormqual into marching. The captain of the City Garrison's a good man – Blistig – if he wasn't responsible for the protection of Aren, he'd be here by now. Anyway, maybe the two of us can put some iron into the High Fist's spine.'

'As you say,' Lull muttered. 'Get on with you now, Corporal, you're almost as ugly as me and it's turning my stomach.'

'Got more than a few spare Tiste Andii eyes if you'd like to try one out for a fitting, sir. Last chance.'

'I'll pass, Corporal, but thanks for the offer.'

'Don't mention it. Fare you well, Historian. Sorry we couldn't have done better with Kulp and Heboric.'

'You did better than anyone could have hoped for, Gesler.'

With a shrug, the man turned towards the waiting dory. Then he paused. 'Oh, Commander Bult.'

'Aye?'

'My apologies to the Fist for breaking his hand.'

'Sormo's managed to force-heal that, Corporal, but I'll pass your thoughts on.'

'You know, Commander,' Gesler said a moment before stepping into the boat, 'I just noticed – between you and the captain you got three eyes and three ears and almost a whole head of hair.'

Bult swung around to glare at the corporal. 'Your point?'

'Nothing. Just noticing, sir. See you all in Aren.'

Duiker watched the man row his way across the yellow sludge of the river. *See you all in Aren. That was feeble, Corporal Gesler, but well enough meant.*

'For the rest of my days,' Lull sighed, 'I'll know Gesler as the man who broke his nose to spite his face.'

Bult grinned, tossed the dregs of his tea onto the muddy ground and rose with a crackling of joints. 'Nephew will like that one, Captain.'

'Was it just a matter of mistrust, Uncle?' Duiker asked, looking up.

Bult stared down for a moment, then shrugged. 'Coltaine would tell you it was so, Historian.'

'But what do you think?'

'I'm too tired to think. If you are determined to know the Fist's thoughts on Korbolo Dom's offer, you might try asking him yourself.'

They watched the commander walk away.

Lull grunted. 'Can't wait to read your account of the Chain of

Dogs, old man. Too bad I didn't see you send a trunk full of scrolls with Gesler.'

Duiker climbed to his feet. 'It seems nobody wants to hold hands this night.'

'Might have better luck tomorrow night.'

'Might.'

'Thought you'd found a woman. A marine – what was her name?'

'I don't know. We shared one night . . .'

'Ah, sword too small for the sheath, eh?'

Duiker smiled. 'We decided it would not do to repeat that night. We each have enough losses to deal with . . .'

'You are both fools, then.'

'I imagine we are.'

Duiker set off through the restless, sleepless encampment. He heard few conversations, yet a bleak awareness roared around him, a sound only his bones could feel.

He found Coltaine outside his command tent, conferring with Sormo, Nil and Nether. The Fist's right hand was still swollen and mottled, and his pale, sweat-beaded face revealed the trauma of forced healing.

Sormo addressed the historian. 'Where is your Corporal List?'

Duiker blinked. 'I am not sure. Why?'

'He is possessed of visions.'

'Aye, he is.'

The warlock's gaunt face twisted in a grimace. 'We sense nothing of what lies ahead. A land so emptied is unnatural, Historian. It has been scoured, its soul destroyed. How?'

'List says there was a war once, out on the plain beyond the forest. So long ago that all memory of it has vanished. Yet an echo remains, sealed in the very bedrock.'

'Who fought this war, Historian?'

'Yet to be revealed, I'm afraid. A ghost guides List in his

696

dreams, but it will be no certain unveiling.' Duiker hesitated, then sighed. 'The ghost is Jaghut.'

Coltaine glanced east, seemed to study the paling skyline.

'Fist,' Duiker said after a moment, 'Korbolo Dom—'

There was a commotion nearby. They turned to see a nobleman rushing towards them. The historian frowned, then recognition came. 'Tumlit—'

The old man, squinting fiercely as he scanned each face, finally came to a halt before Coltaine. 'A most dreadful occurrence, Fist,' he gasped in his tremulous voice.

Duiker only now heard a restlessness rising from the refugee encampment stretched up the trader track. 'Tumlit, what has happened?'

'Another emissary, I'm afraid. Brought through in secret. Met with the Council – I sought to dissuade them but failed, alas. Pullyk and Nethpara have swayed the others. Fist, the refugees shall cross the river, under the benign protection of Korbolo Dom—'

Coltaine spun to his warlocks. 'To your clans. Send Bult and the captains to me.'

Shouts now sounded from the Wickans in the clearing as the mass of refugees surged forward, pushing through, down to the ford. The Fist found a nearby soldier. 'Have the clan war chiefs withdraw their warriors from their path – we cannot contest this.'

He's right – we won't be able to stop the fools.

Bult and the captains arrived in a rush and Coltaine snapped out his commands. Those orders made it clear to Duiker that the Fist was preparing for the worst. As the officers raced off, Coltaine faced the historian.

'Go to the sappers. By my command they are to join the refugee train, insignia and uniforms exchanged for mundane garb—'

'That won't be necessary, Fist – they all wear assorted rags and looted gear anyway. But I'll have them tie their helms to their belts.'

'Go.'

Duiker set off. The sky was lightening, and with that burgeoning glow the butterflies stirred on all sides, a silent shimmering that sent shivers through the historian for no obvious reason. He worked his way up the seething train, skirting one edge and pushing through the ranks of infantry who were standing back and watching the refugees without expression.

He spied a ragtag knot of soldiers seated well back from the trail, almost at the edge of the flanking picket line. The company ignored the refugees and seemed busy with the task of coiling ropes. A few glanced up as Duiker arrived.

'Coltaine commands you join the refugees,' the historian said. 'No arguments – take off your helms, now—'

'Who's arguing?' one squat, wide soldier muttered.

'What are you planning with the ropes?' Duiker demanded.

The sapper looked up, his eyes narrow slashes in his wide, battered face. 'We did some reconnoitring of our own, old man. Now if you'd shut up we can get ready, right?'

Three soldiers appeared from the forest side, approaching at a jog. One carried a severed head by its braid, trailing threads of blood. 'This one's done his last nod at post,' the man commented, dropping his prize to thud and roll on the ground. No-one else took notice, nor did the three sappers report to anyone.

The entire company seemed to complete their preparations all at once, ropes around one shoulder, helms strapped to belts, crossbows readied, then hidden beneath loose raincapes and telaban. In silence they rose and began making their way towards the mass of refugees.

Duiker hesitated. He turned to look down at the crossing. The head of the refugee column had pushed out into the ford, which was proving waist-deep, at least forty paces wide, its bottom thick, cloying mud. Butterflies swarmed above the mass of humanity in sunlit explosions of pallid yellow. A dozen Wickan horsewarriors had been sent ahead to guide the column. Behind them came the wagons of the noble blood – the only refugees staying dry and above the chaotic tumult. The historian glanced over at the surging train where the sappers had gone but they were nowhere to be seen, swallowed up in the crowds. From somewhere farther up the trader track came the terrible lowing of cattle being slaughtered.

The flanking infantry were readying weapons – Coltaine was clearly anticipating a rearguard defence of the landing.

Still the historian hesitated. If he joined the refugees and the worst came to pass, the ensuing panic would be as deadly as any slaughter visited upon them by Korbolo Dom's forces. *Hood's breath! We are now truly at that bastard's mercy.*

A hand closed on his arm and he spun around to see his nameless marine at his side.

'Come on,' she said. 'Into the mob – we're to support the sappers.'

'In what? Nothing has befallen the refugees yet – and they're near to halfway across—'

'Aye, and look at the heads turning to look downstream. The rebels have made a floating bridge – no, you can't see it from here, but it's there, packed with pikemen—'

'Pikemen? Doing what?'

'Watching. Waiting. Come on, lover, the nightmare's about to begin.'

They joined the mass of refugees, entered that human current as it poured down towards the landing. A sudden roar and muted clash of weapons announced that the rearguard had been struck. The tide's momentum increased. Packed within that jostling chaos, Duiker could see little to either side or behind – but the slope ahead was revealed, as was the River

Vathar itself, which they seemed to be sweeping towards with the swiftness of an avalanche. The entire ford was packed with refugees. Along the edges people were being pushed into deeper water – Duiker saw bobbing heads and arms struggling in the sludge, the current dragging them ever closer to the pikemen on the bridge.

A great cry of dismay rose from those on the river, faces now turning upstream to something the historian could not yet see.

The dozen horsewarriors gained the clearing on the opposite bank. He watched them frantically nocking arrows as they turned towards the line of trees farther up the bank. Then the Wickans were reeling, toppling from their mounts, feathered shafts jutting from their bodies. Horses screamed and went down.

The nobles' wagons clacked and clattered ashore, then stopped as the oxen pulling them sank down beneath a swarm of arrows.

The ford was blocked.

Panic now gripped the refugees, descending in a human wave down to the landing. Bellowing, Duiker was helpless as he was carried along into the yellow-smeared water. He caught a glimpse of what approached from upstream – another floating bridge, packed with pikemen and archers. Crews on both banks gripped ropes, guiding the bridge as the current drew it ever closer to the ford.

Arrows ripped through the clouds of whirling butterflies, descended on the mass of refugees. There was nowhere to hide, nowhere to go.

The historian found himself within a nightmare. All around him, unarmoured civilians died in that ghastly whisper and clatter. The mob surged in every direction now, caught in terrified, helpless eddies. Children vanished underfoot, trampled down into the turbid water.

A woman fell back against Duiker. He wrapped his arms

around her in an effort to keep her upright, then saw the arrow that had driven through the babe in her arms, then into her chest. He cried out in horror.

The marine appeared at his side, thrusting a reach of rope into his hands. 'Grab this!' she shouted. 'Hold on tight – we're through – don't let go!'

He twisted the rope around his wrists. Ahead of the marine, the strand stretched on, between the heaving bodies and out of sight. He felt it tighten, was pulled forward.

Arrows rained down ceaselessly. One grazed the historian's cheek, another bounced from the leather-sheathed chain protecting his shoulder. He wished to every god that he had donned his helm instead of tying it at his belt – from which it had long since been torn free and lost.

The pressure on the rope was steady, relentless, dragging him through the mob, over people and under them. More than once he was pulled down under the water, only to rise again half a dozen paces later, choking and coughing. At one point, as he went over the top of the seething press, he caught the flash of sorcery from somewhere ahead, a thundering wave, then he was yanked back down, twisting his shoulder to slide roughly between two screaming civilians.

The journey seemed unending, battering him with surreal glimpses until he was numb, feeling like a wraith being pulled through the whole of human history, an endless procession of pain, suffering and ignoble death. Fate's cast of chance was iron-barbed, sky-sent, or the oblivion of all that waited below. *There is no escape – another lesson of history. Mortality is a visitor never gone for long—*

Then he was being dragged over wet, muddy corpses and blood-slicked clay. The arrows no longer descended from the sky but sped low over the ground, striking wood and flesh on all sides. Duiker rolled through a deep, twisting rut, then came up against the spoked wheel of a wagon.

'Let go the rope!' the marine commanded. 'We're here, Duiker—'

Here.

He wiped the mud from his eyes, staying low as he looked around for the first time. Wickan horsewarriors, sappers and marines lay amidst dead and dying mounts, all so studded with arrows that the entire landing looked like a reed bed. The nobles' wagons had been cleared from the end of the ford and arrayed in a defensive crescent, although the fighting had pushed beyond them into the forest itself.

'Who?' Duiker gasped.

The woman lying beside him grunted. 'Just what's left of the sappers, the marines . . . and a few surviving Wickans.'

'That's it?'

'Can't get anyone else across – and besides, the Seventh and at least two of the clans are fighting in the rearguard. We're on our own, Duiker, and if we can't clear these woods . . .'

We will be annihilated.

She reached out to a nearby corpse, dragging it closer to remove the dead Wickan's helm. 'This one looks more your size than mine, old man. Here.'

'What are we fighting out there?'

'At least three companies. Mostly archers, though – I think Korbolo wasn't expecting any soldiers at the front of the column. The plan was to use the refugees to block our deployment and stop us from gaining this bank.'

'As if Korbolo knew Coltaine would reject the offer, but the nobles wouldn't.'

'Aye. The arrow fire's tailed off – those sappers are pushing them back – gods, they're mayhem! Let's find us some useful weapons and go join the fun.'

'Go ahead,' Duiker said. 'But here I stay – within sight of the river. I need to see . . .'

'You'll get yourself skewered, old man.'

'I'll risk it. Get going!'

She hesitated, then nodded and crawled off among the bodies.

The historian found a round shield and clambered up on the nearest wagon, where he almost stepped on a cowering figure. He stared down at the trembling man. 'Nethpara.'

'Save me, please!'

Ignoring the nobleborn, Duiker turned his attention back to the river.

The stream of refugees who reached the south bank could not go forward; they began spreading out along the shoreline. Duiker saw a mob of them discover the rope crew for the upstream bridge, and descend on them with a ferocity that disregarded their lack of armour and weapons. The crew were literally torn apart.

The slaughter had turned the river downstream into a pink mass of stained insects and bodies, and still the numbers grew. Another flaw in Korbolo's plan was revealed as the flights of arrows from the upstream bridge dwindled – the archers had already spent their supply. The floating platform upstream had been allowed to drift, closing the gap until the pikemen finally came into contact with the unarmed civilians on the ford. But they had not accounted for the roaring rage that met them. The refugees had been pushed past fear. Hands were slashed as they closed on the pikeheads, but they would not let go. Others clambered forward in a rush to get to the archers behind the wavering line of pikemen. The bridge sagged beneath the weight, then tilted. A moment later the river was solid with flailing, struggling figures – refugees and Korbolo's companies both – as the bridge tipped and broke apart.

And over it all, the butterflies swarmed, like a million yellow-petalled flowers dancing on swirling winds.

Another wave of sorcery erupted, and Duiker's head turned at the sound. He saw Sormo, out in the centre of the mass, astride his horse. The power that rolled from him tumbled towards the bridge downstream, striking the rebel soldiers with sparks that scythed like barbed wire. Blood sprayed into the air, and above the bridge the butterflies went from yellow to red and the stained clouds fell in a fluttering blanket.

But as Duiker watched, four arrows struck the warlock, one driving through his neck. Sormo's horse whipped its head around, screaming at the half-dozen arrows embedded in it. The animal staggered, slewing sideways to the edge of the shallows, then into deep water. Sormo reeled, then slowly slid from the saddle, vanishing beneath the sludge. The horse collapsed on top of him.

Duiker could not draw breath. Then he saw a thin, lean arm thrust skyward a dozen yards downstream.

Butterflies mobbed that straining, yearning reach, even as it slowly sank back down, then disappeared. The insects were converging, thousands, then hundreds of thousands. On all sides it seemed that the battle, the slaughter, paused and watched.

Hood's breath, they've come for him. For his soul. Not crows, not as it should be. Gods below!

A quavering voice rose from beneath the historian. 'What has happened? Have we won?'

The breath that Duiker pulled into his lungs was ragged. The mass of butterflies was a seething, frenzied mound on the spot where Sormo had appeared, a mound as high as a barrow and swelling with every moment that passed, with every staggering beat of the historian's heart.

'Have we won? Can you see Coltaine? Call him here – I would speak to him—'

The moment when all stood still and silent was broken as a thick flight of Wickan arrows struck the soldiers on the downstream bridge. What Sormo had begun, his clan kin completed: the last of the archers and pikemen went down.

Duiker saw three squares of infantry dog-trot down the north slope, pulled from the rearguard action to enforce order on the crossing. Wickan horsewarriors of the Weasel Clan rode out from the flanking woods, voicing their ululating victory cries.

Duiker swung about. He saw Malazan soldiers backing away from cover to cover – a handful of marines and less than thirty sappers. The arrow fire was intensifying, getting closer. *Gods, they've already done the impossible – do not demand more of them—*

The historian drew a breath, then climbed up onto the wagon's high bench. 'Everyone!' he shouted to the milling refugees crowding the bank. 'Every able hand! Find a weapon – to the forest, else the slaughter begins again! The archers are retur—'

He got no further, as the air shook with a savage, bestial roar. Duiker stared down, watching hundreds of civilians rush forward, caring nothing for weapons, intent only on closing with the companies of archers, on answering the day's carnage with a vengeance no less terrible.

We are all gripped in madness. I have never seen the like nor heard of such a thing – gods, what we have become . . .

The waves of refugees swept over the Malazan positions and, unwavering before frantic, devastating flights of arrows from the treeline, plunged into the forest. Shrieks and screams echoed eerily in the air.

Nethpara clambered into view. 'Where is Coltaine? I demand—'

Duiker reached down one-handed and gripped the silk scarf wound around the nobleman's neck. He dragged Nethpara closer. The man squealed, scratching uselessly at the historian's hand.

'Nethpara. He could have let you go. Let you cross. Alone. Under the shelter of Korbolo Dom's glorious *mercy*. How many

705

have died this day? How many of these soldiers, how many Wickans, have given their lives to protect your hide?'

'L-let go of me, you foul slave-spawn!'

A red mist blossomed before Duiker's eyes. He took the nobleman's flabby neck in both hands and began squeezing. He watched Nethpara's eyes bulge.

Someone battered at his head. Someone yanked at his wrists. Someone wrapped a forearm around his own neck and flexed iron-hard muscles across the throat. The mist dimmed, as if night was falling. The historian watched as hands pried his own from Nethpara's neck, watched as the man fell away, gasping.

Then dark's descent was done.

CHAPTER SEVENTEEN

> One who was many
> On the blood trail
> Came hunting his own voice
> Savage murder
> Sprites buzzing in the sun
> Came hunting his own voice
> But Hood's music is all
> He heard, the siren song
> Called silence.

> *Seglora's Account*
> Seglora

The captain had begun swaying, though not in time with the heaving ship. He poured wine all over the table as well as into the four goblets arrayed before him. 'Ordering thick-skulled sailors this way and that makes for a considerable thirst. I expect the food will be along shortly.'

Pormqual's treasurer, who did not consider the company worthy of knowing his name, raised painted eyebrows. 'But, Captain, we have already eaten.'

'Have we? That explains the mess, then, though the mess still has some explaining to do, because it must have been awful. You there,' he said to Kalam, 'you're as solid as any Fenn bear, was that palatable? Never mind, what would you know, anyway? I hear Seven Cities natives grow fruit just so they can eat the larvae in them. Gobble the worm and toss the apple, hey? If you want to know how you folk see the world, it's all there in that one custom. Now that we're all chums, what were we talking about?'

Salk Elan reached out and collected his goblet, sniffing cautiously before taking a swallow. 'The dear treasurer was surprising us with a complaint, Captain.'

'Was he now?' The captain leaned over the small table to stare at the treasurer. 'A complaint? Aboard my ship? You bring those to me, sir.'

'I just have,' the man replied, sneering.

'And deal with it I shall, as a captain must.' He leaned back with an air of satisfaction. 'Now, what else should we talk about?'

Salk Elan met Kalam's eye, winked. 'What if we were to touch on the small matter of those two privateers presently pursuing us?'

'They're not pursuing,' the captain said. He drained his goblet, smacked his lips, then refilled it from the webbed jug. 'They are keeping pace, sir, and that is entirely different, as you must surely grasp.'

'Well, I admit, I see the distinction less clearly than you do, Captain.'

'How unfortunate.'

'You might,' the treasurer rasped, 'endeavour to enlighten us.'

'What did you say? Lightendeavourus? Extraordinary, man!' He settled back in his seat, a contented expression on his face.

'They want a stronger wind,' Kalam ventured.

'Quickening,' the captain said. 'They want to dance around us, aye, the ale-pissing cowards. Toe to toe, that's how I'd like it, but no, they'd rather duck and dodge.' He swung surprisingly steady eyes on Kalam. 'That's why we'll take them unawares, come the dawn. Attack! Hard about! Marines prepare to board enemy vessel! I won't truck complaints aboard *Ragstopper*. Not a one, dammit. The next bleat I hear and the bleater loses a finger. Bleats again, loses another one. And so on. Each one nailed to the deck. Tap tap!'

Kalam closed his eyes. They had sailed four days now without an escort, the tradewinds pushing them along at a steady six knots. The sailors had run up every sheet of canvas they possessed and the ship sang a chorus of ominous creaks and groans, but the two pirate galleys could still sail circles around *Ragstopper*.

And the madman wants to attack.

'Did you say attack?' the treasurer whispered, his eyes wide. 'I forbid it!'

The captain blinked owlishly at the man. 'Why, sir,' he said in a calm voice, 'I looked into my tin mirror, did I not? It's lost its polish, on my word so it has. Between yesterday and today. I plan to take advantage of that.'

Since the voyage began, Kalam had managed to stay in his cabin for the most part, electing to emerge on deck only at the quietest hour, late in the last watch before dawn. Eating with the crew in the galley had also reduced the number of encounters with either Salk Elan or the treasurer. This night, however, the captain had insisted on his joining them at dinner. The appearance of the pirates at midday had made the assassin curious about how the captain would deal with the threat, so he had agreed.

It was clear that Salk Elan and the treasurer had established a truce of sorts as things never went beyond the occasional sardonic swipe. The exaggerated airs of civil discourse made their efforts at self-control obvious.

But it was the captain who was the true mystery aboard the *Ragstopper*. Kalam had heard enough talk in the galley and between the First and Second Mates to gauge that the man was viewed with both respect and some kind of twisted affection. *In the manner that you'd view a touchy dog. Pat once and the tail wags, pat twice and lose a hand.* He shifted roles with random alacrity, dismissive of propriety. He revealed a sense of humour that yanked taut comprehension. Too long in his company – especially when wine was the drink of choice – and the assassin's head ached with the effort of following the captain's wending ways. What was worse, Kalam sensed a thread of cool purpose within the scattered weave, as if the captain spoke two languages at once, one robust and divergent, the other silken with secrets. *I'd swear the bastard's trying to tell me something. Something vital.* He'd heard of a certain sorcery, from one of the less common warrens, that could lay a glamour upon a person's mind, a kind of mental block that the victim – in absolute, tortured awareness – could circle round but never manage to penetrate. *Ah, now I'm venturing into the absurd. Paranoia's the assassin's bedmate, and no rest comes in that clamouring serpent's nest. Would that I could speak with Quick Ben now—*

'—sleep with your eyes open, man?'

Kalam started, frowned at the captain.

'The master of this fine sailing ship was saying,' Salk Elan purred, 'that it's been a strange passing of days since we reached open water. It was an interrogative seeking your opinion, Kalam.'

'It's been four days since we left Aren Bay,' the assassin growled.

'Has it now?' the captain asked. 'Are you certain?'

'What do you mean?'

'Someone keeps knocking over the hisser, you see.'

'The what?' *Oh, the hissing of sand – I'd swear he's making up words as he goes along.* 'Are you suggesting you have but one hourglass on *Ragstopper?*'

'Official time is so kept by a single glass,' Elan said.

'While none of the others on board agree,' the captain

710

added, filling his goblet yet again. 'Four days . . . or fourteen?'

'Is this some kind of philosophic debate?' the treasurer demanded suspiciously.

'Hardly,' the captain managed to say during a belch. 'We left harbour with the first night of a quarter moon.'

Kalam tried to think back to the previous night. He'd stood on the forecastle, beneath a brilliantly clear sky. Had the moon already set? No, it rode the horizon, directly beneath the tip of the constellation known as the Dagger. *End of a three-quarter moon. But that's impossible.*

'Ten weevils a handful,' the captain went on. 'As good as a hisser in gauging passage. You'd have ten in close on a fortnight, unless the flour was foul from the start, only the cook swears otherwise—'

'Just as he'd swear he'd cooked us dinner here tonight,' Salk Elan said with a smile, 'though our bellies groan that what we've just eaten was anything but food. In any case, thank you for dispelling the confusion.'

'Well, sir, you've a point there, sharp enough to prick skin, though mine's thicker than most and I ain't anything if not stubborn.'

'For which I cannot help but admire you, Captain.'

What in Hood's name are these two talking about, or, rather, not talking about?

'A man gets so he can't even trust the beat of his own heart – mind you, I can't count past fourteen in any case, so's I could not help but lose track and tracking's what we're talking about here if I'm not mistaken.'

'Captain,' the treasurer said, 'you cause me great distress with your words.'

Salk Elan commented, 'You're not alone in that.'

'Do I offend you, sir?' The captain's face had reddened as he glared at the treasurer.

'Offend? No. Baffle. I dare say I am led to conclude that you

711

have lost the grip on your own mind. Thus, to ensure the safety of this ship, I have no choice—'

'No choice?' the captain erupted, rising from his seat. 'Words and grips like sand. What slips through your fingers can knock you over! I'll show you safety, you sweaty stream of lard!'

Kalam leaned back clear of the table as the captain went to the cabin door and began struggling with his cloak. Salk Elan had not moved from his seat, watching with a tight smile.

A moment later the captain flung open the cabin door and barrelled into the passageway, bellowing a call for his First Mate. His boots thumped like fists hammering a wall as he made for the galley.

The cabin's door creaked back and forth on its hinges.

The treasurer's mouth opened and closed, then opened again. 'What choice?' he whispered to no-one in particular.

'Not yours to make,' Elan drawled.

The noble swung to him. 'Not mine? And who else, if not the man entrusted with the Aren treasury—'

'Is that what it's officially called, then? How about Pormqual's ill-gotten loot? Those seals on the crates below have the High Fist's sigil on them, not the Imperial sceptre—'

And so you have been in the hold, Salk Elan? Interesting.

'To lay hands upon those crates is punishable by death,' the treasurer hissed.

Elan sneered his disgust. 'You're doing the dirty work of a thief, so what does that make you?'

The noble went white. In silence he rose and, using his hands to steady himself as the ship pitched, made his way across the small room, then out into the passageway.

Salk Elan glanced at Kalam. 'So, my reluctant friend, what do you make of this captain of ours?'

'Nothing I'd share with you,' Kalam rumbled.

'Your constant efforts to avoid me have been childish.'

'Well, it's either that or I kill you outright.'

'How unpleasant of you, Kalam, after all the efforts I have made on your behalf.'

The assassin rose. 'Rest assured I'll repay the debt, Salk Elan.'

'You could do that with your company alone – intelligent conversation aboard this ship is proving hard to come by.'

'I'll spare a thought in sympathy,' Kalam said, heading to the cabin door.

'You wrong me, Kalam. I am not your enemy. Indeed, we two are much alike.'

The assassin paused in the portalway. 'If you're seeking friendship between us, Salk Elan, you've just taken a long step back with that observation.' He stepped out into the passage and made his way forward.

He emerged onto the main deck and found himself in the midst of furious activity. Gear was being battened down, sailors checking the rigging and others taking in sail. It was past the tenth bell and the night sky was solid clouds, not a star showing.

The captain reeled down to Kalam's side. 'What did I tell you? Lost its polish!'

A squall was coming – the assassin could feel it in the wind that now swirled as if the air had nowhere to go.

'From the south,' the captain laughed, clapping Kalam on the shoulder. 'We'll turn on the hunters, aye, won't we just! Storm-jibbed and marines crowding the forecastle, we'll ram 'em down their throats! Hood take these smirking stalkers – we'll see how long their grins last with a short sword jabbing 'em in the face, hey?' He leaned close, the wine sour on his breath. 'Look to your daggers, man, it'll be a night for close work, aye, won't it just.' His face spasmed suddenly and he jerked away, began screaming at his crew.

The assassin stared after him. *Perhaps I'm not being paranoid, after all. The man's afflicted with something.*

The deck heeled as they came hard about. The storm's wind arrived at the same time, lifting *Ragstopper* to run before it on stiff, shortened sails. Lanterns shuttered and the crew settling into their tasks, they plunged on, northward.

A sea battle in a raging storm, and the captain expects the marines to board the enemy craft, to stand on a pitching, wave-whipped deck and take the fight to the pirates. This is beyond audacious.

Two large figures appeared from behind, flanking the assassin. Kalam grimaced. Both of the treasurer's bodyguards had been incapacitated by seasickness since the first day, and neither looked in any condition to be able to do anything except puke his guts out on the assassin's boots, yet they stood their ground, hands on weapons.

'Master wishes to speak with you,' one of them growled.

'Too bad,' Kalam growled back.

'Now.'

'Or what, you kill me with your breath? Master can speak with corpses, can he?'

'Master commands—'

'If he wants to talk, he can come here. Otherwise, like I said, too bad.'

The two tribesmen retreated.

Kalam moved forward, past the main mast, to where the two squads of marines crouched low before the forecastle. The assassin had weathered more than his share of squalls while serving in the Imperial campaigns, in galleys, transports and triremes, on three oceans and half a dozen seas. This storm was – thus far at least – comparatively tame. The marines were grim-faced, as would be expected before an engagement, but otherwise laconic as they readied their assault crossbows in the blunted glow of a shuttered lantern.

Kalam's gaze searched among them until he found the lieutenant. 'A word with you, sir—'

'Not now,' she snapped, donning her helmet and locking the cheek-guards in place. 'Get below.'

'He means to ram—'

'I know what he means to do. And when the crunch comes, the last thing we need is some Hood-damned civilian to watch out for.'

'Do you take the captain's orders . . . or the treasurer's?'

She looked up at that, eyes narrowing. The other marines paused. 'Get below,' she said.

Kalam sighed. 'I'm an Imperial veteran, Lieutenant—'

'Which army?'

He hesitated, then said, 'Second. Ninth Squad, Bridgeburners.'

As one, the marines sat back. All eyes were on him now.

The lieutenant scowled. 'Now how likely is that?'

Another marine, a grizzled veteran, barked out, 'Your sergeant? Let's hear some names, stranger.'

'Whiskeyjack. Other sergeants? Not many left. Antsy. Tormin.'

'You're Corporal Kalam, ain't you?'

The assassin studied the man. 'Who are you?'

'Nobody, sir, and been that way a long time.' He turned to his lieutenant and nodded.

'Can we count on you?' she asked Kalam.

'Not up front, but I'll be close by.'

She looked around. 'The treasurer's got an Imperial Writ – we're shackled to it, Corporal.'

'I don't think the treasurer trusts you, should it come down to making a choice between him and the captain.'

She made a face, as if tasting something bad. 'This attack's madness, but it's sharp madness.'

Kalam nodded, waited.

'I guess the treasurer's got reason.'

'If it comes to it,' the assassin said, 'leave the bodyguards to me.'

'Both of them?'

'Aye.'

The veteran spoke up. 'If we make the sharks sick in the gut with the treasurer, we'll hang for it.'

'Just be somewhere else when it happens – all of you.'

The lieutenant grinned. 'I think we can manage that.'

'Now,' Kalam said, loud enough to be heard by every marine, 'I'm just another one of those grease-faced civilians, right?'

'We never figured this outlawing stuff was for real,' a voice called out. 'Not Dujek Onearm. No way.'

Hood, for all I know you may be right, soldier. But he hid his uncertainty with a half-salute before making his way back down the length of the deck.

Ragstopper reminded Kalam of a bear crashing through thickets as it barrelled along – lumbering, broad and solid in the spraying high seas – *a spring bear, an hour out of the den, eyes red-rimmed with old sleep, miserable and gnawed with hunger deep in its belly. Somewhere ahead, two wolves slinking through the dark . . . they're in for a surprise . . .*

The captain was on the sterncastle, braced against the hand manning the tiller. His First Mate stood near him, one arm looped around the stern mast. Both were glaring ahead into the darkness, awaiting the first sighting of their quarry.

Kalam opened his mouth to speak, but a shout from the First Mate stopped him.

'A point to port, Captain! Beating three-quarters! Hood's breath, we're right on top of her!'

The pirate vessel, a low, single-masted raider barely visible in the gloom, was less than a hundred paces away, on a tack that would cut directly in front of *Ragstopper*. The positioning was breathtakingly perfect.

'All hands,' the captain bellowed through the howl of the storm, 'prepare to ram!'

The First Mate bolted ahead, shouting orders to his crew. Kalam saw the marines crouch low to the deck, readying for the impact. Faint screams reached the assassin from the pirate vessel. The taut square sail, storm-jibbed, billowed suddenly, the ship's prow pitching away as the pirate crew made a last, doomed effort to avoid the collision.

The gods were grinning down on the scene, but it was the rictus of a death's head. A swell lifted *Ragstopper* high just before the contact, then dropped the trader down onto the raider's low gunnels, just behind the peaked prow. Wood exploded, splintered and shuddered. Kalam was thrown forward, losing his grip on the starboard stern rail. He pitched from the sterncastle, struck the main deck with a tucked shoulder, rolling as the momentum carried him forward.

Masts snapped somewhere above him, sails whipping like ghost wings in the rain-tracked air.

Ragstopper settled, grinding, popping, canting heavily. Sailors were screaming, shrieking on all sides, but Kalam could see little of what was happening from where he lay. Groaning, he worked his way upright.

The last of the marines were plunging over the forward port rail, down and out of sight – presumably onto the raider's deck. *Or what's left of it.* The clash of weapons rose muted beneath the wailing wind.

The assassin turned, but the captain was nowhere in sight. Nor was there anyone at the tiller. The wreckage of a snapped spar cluttered the sterncastle.

Kalam made his way aft.

The locked ships had no steerage. Waves were pummelling *Ragstopper*'s starboard hull, flinging sheets of foaming water across the main deck. A body lay in that wash, face down and leaking blood that stretched weblike in the rolling water.

Reaching the man, Kalam turned him over. It was the First Mate, his forehead sharply caved in. The blood was coming from nose and throat; the water had washed clean the killing blow, and the assassin stared at the damage for half a dozen heartbeats before rising and stepping over the corpse.

Not so seasick after all.

He climbed to the sterncastle and began searching through the wreckage. The man at the tiller had lost most of his head, only a few twisted ropes of flesh and skin holding what was left of it to the body. He examined the slash across the neck. *Two-handed, a step behind and to the left. The spar crushed what was already dead.*

He found the captain and one of the treasurer's bodyguards beneath the sail. Splinters of wood jutted from the giant tribesman's chest and throat. He still gripped his two-handed tulwar. The captain's hands were shredded ribbons closed on the blade-end, blood pulsing from them to stain the swirling wash of seawater. A massive discolouring reached the span of the man's brow, but his breathing was steady.

Kalam pried the captain's fingers from the tulwar blade and dragged him free of the wreckage.

Ragstopper loosed its grip on the raider at the same time, dropping down into a trough, then pitching wildly as waves battered its hull. Figures appeared on the sterncastle, one taking the tiller, another crouching down beside the assassin.

Glancing up, Kalam found himself looking into Salk Elan's dripping face.

'He lives?'

'Aye.'

'We're not out of trouble yet,' Elan said.

'To Hood with that! We've got to get this man below.'

'We've sprung leaks up front – most of the marines are at the pumps.'

They lifted the captain between them. 'And the raider?'

'The one we hit? In pieces.'

'In other words,' the assassin said as they manhandled the captain down the slippery steps, 'not what the treasurer planned.'

Salk Elan stopped, his eyes sharpening. 'Seems we've slunk on the same path, you and I.'

'Where is the bastard?'

'He's taken command ... for now. Seems every officer's suffered an unlikely accident – anyway, we've got the other vessel closing on us, so, like I said, the fun's anything but over.'

'One thing at a time,' Kalam grunted.

They made their way down through the galley and into the passage. Water swirled ankle-deep, and the assassin could feel just how sluggish *Ragstopper* had become.

'You pulled rank on the marines, didn't you?' Elan asked as they reached the captain's door.

'I don't outrank the lieutenant.'

'Even so. Call it the power of notoriety, then – she's already had harsh words with the treasurer.'

'Why?'

'The bastard wants us to surrender, of course.'

They carried the captain to his cot. 'A transfer of cargo in this blow?'

'No, they'll wait it out.'

'Then we got time enough. Here, help me get him undressed.'

'His hands are bad.'

'Aye, we'll bandage them up next.'

Salk Elan stared down at the captain as the assassin pulled the blanket up around the man. 'Think he'll live?'

Kalam said nothing, pulling the captain's hands free to study the lacerations. 'He stopped a blow with these.'

'Now that's not an easy thing to do. Listen, Kalam, how are we in this?'

The assassin hesitated, then said, 'How did you put it? "Slunk the same path?" It seems neither one of us wants to end up in a shark's belly.'

'Meaning we'd better work together.'

'Aye, for now. Just don't expect me to kiss you good night, Elan.'

'Not even once?'

'You'd better get up top, find out what's going on. I can finish here.'

'Don't tarry, Kalam. Blood could spill fast.'

'Aye.'

Alone with the captain, the assassin found a sewing kit and began stitching flesh. He finished one hand and had started on the other when the captain groaned.

'Hood's breath,' Kalam muttered. 'Just another ten minutes, that's all I needed.'

'Doublecross,' the captain whispered, his eyes squeezed shut.

'We'd guessed as much,' the assassin said, continuing closing wounds. 'Now shut up and let me work.'

'Poor Pormqual's treasurer is crooked.'

'Like attracts like, as the saying goes.'

'You and that poncy skulker . . . two of a kind.'

'Thanks. So I keep hearing.'

'Up to you two, now.'

'And the lieutenant.'

The captain managed a smile, his eyes still closed. 'Good.'

Kalam sat back, reached for the bandages. 'Almost done.'

'Me too.'

'That bodyguard's dead, you'll be pleased to know.'

'Aye. Killed himself, the idiot. I ducked the first swing. The blade bit through the wrong ropes. Feel that, Kalam? We're rolling even – someone up top knows what we're doing, thank the gods. Still, way too heavy . . . but she'll hold together.'

'Got enough rags for that, then.'

720

'That we have.'

'All right, I'm done,' Kalam said, rising. 'Get some sleep, Captain. We need you hale. And fast.'

'Not likely. That other bodyguard will finish it first chance he gets. The treasurer needs me out of the way.'

'We'll take care of it, Captain.'

'Just like that?'

'Just like that.'

Closing the door behind him, Kalam paused, loosened the long-knife in its scabbard. *Just like that, Captain.*

The squall was spent, and the sky to the east was brightening, clean and gold. *Ragstopper* had come around as the tradewind returned. The mess on the sterncastle had been cleared away and the crew looked to have things in hand, although Kalam could see their tension.

The treasurer and his remaining bodyguard stood near the mainmast, the former staring steadily at the raider keeping pace to starboard, close enough to see figures on its deck, watching them in turn. The bodyguard's attention, however, was on Salk Elan, lounging near the forecastle steps. None of the crew seemed willing to cut across the ten paces separating the two men.

Kalam made his way to the treasurer's side. 'You have taken command, then?'

The man nodded sharply, his diffidence obvious as he avoided the assassin's eye. 'I intend to buy our way clear—'

'Take your cut, you mean. And how much would that be? Eighty, ninety per cent? With you along as hostage, of course.' He watched the blood leave the man's face.

'This is not your concern,' the treasurer said.

'You're right. But killing the captain and his officers is, because it jeopardizes this voyage. If the crew doesn't know for certain, you can rest assured it suspects.'

'We have the marines to deal with that. Back away and you'll survive intact. Step in and you'll be cut down.'

Kalam studied the raider. 'And what's their percentage? What's to stop them from slitting your throat and sailing off with the whole share?'

The treasurer smiled. 'I doubt my uncle and cousins would do that. Now, I suggest you go below – back to your cabin – and stay there.'

Ignoring that advice, Kalam went off to find the marines.

The engagement with the pirates had been fierce and short. Not only was the ship coming apart under them, but there was little fight left in the raider's panicked crew.

'More like a slaughter,' the lieutenant muttered as the assassin crouched down opposite her. The two squads sat in the forward hold, amidst streams of water running down the planks, busy stuffing rags into the breaches in the hull. 'We didn't even take a scratch.'

'What have you worked out thus far?' Kalam quietly asked.

She shrugged. 'As much as we need to, Corporal. What do you want us to do?'

'The treasurer will order you to stand down. The pirates will then relieve you of your weapons—'

'At which point they slit our throats and toss us overside – Imperial Writ or no, the man's committing treason.'

'Well, he's stealing from a thief, but I take your point.' Kalam rose. 'I'll talk with the crew and get back to you, Lieutenant.'

'Why don't we take down the treasurer and his bodyguard right now, Kalam?'

The assassin's eyes narrowed. 'Stick to the rules, Lieutenant. Leave murder to those whose souls are already stained.'

She bit her lip, studied him for a long time, then slowly nodded.

* * *

Kalam found the sailor he'd spoken with when the hold was being loaded at the Aren pier. The man was coiling ropes on the sterncastle with the air of someone needing to keep busy.

'Heard you saved the captain,' the sailor said.

'He's alive, but in bad shape.'

'Aye. Cook's standing outside his cabin door, sir. Wi' a cleaver and – ask any hog – the man can use it. Beru's blessing, I seen the man shave wi' it once, as clean as a virgin's tit.'

'Who is standing in for the officers?'

'If y' mean who's got things shipshape and all the hands at stations, that'd be me, sir, only our new commander ain't much interested in jawing wi' me. His swordsman's come over to tell me t' get ready to heave to, once the seas have settled some.'

'To transfer cargo.'

The man nodded.

'And then?'

'Well now, if the commander's true to his word, they'll let us go.'

Kalam grunted. 'And why would they be so kind?'

'Aye, I've been chewin' that one myself. We got sharp enough eyes – too sharp for them to breathe easy. Besides, there's what's been done to Captain. Got us a little peeved, that has.'

Boots thumped midships and the two men turned to see the bodyguard lead the marines onto the main deck. The lieutenant was looking none too happy.

'It's the gods' puke all round us now, sir,' the sailor muttered. 'Raider's closing.'

'So we've arrived,' Kalam said under his breath. He looked across to Salk Elan and found the man's eyes on him. The assassin gave a nod and Elan casually turned away, his hands hidden beneath his cloak.

'That raider's got a shipload of swords, sir. I make fifty or more, all gettin' ready.'

'Leave them to the marines. Your crew stays back – spread the word.'

The sailor moved off.

Kalam made his way to the main deck. The treasurer was facing off with the lieutenant.

'I said to surrender your weapons, Lieutenant!' the treasurer snapped.

'No, sir. We will not.'

The treasurer was trembling with rage. He gestured to his bodyguard.

The big tribesman did not get very far. He made a choking sound, hands reaching up to claw at the knife protruding from his throat. Then he fell to his knees, toppled.

Salk Elan stepped forward. 'Change of plans, my dear sir,' he said, bending to retrieve his knife.

The assassin moved behind the treasurer and pushed the point of his long-knife against the man's lower back. 'Not a word,' he growled, 'not a move.' He then turned to the marines. 'Lieutenant, prepare to repel boarders.'

'Aye, sir.'

The raider was coming alongside, the pirates jostling as they prepared to leap the distance between the ships. The difference in height meant that they had a climb to make – nor could those on deck see much of what awaited them on *Ragstopper*. A lone crewman on the raider had begun a lazy climb towards the lone mast's tiny crow's nest.

Too late, you fools.

The pirate captain – the treasurer's uncle, Kalam assumed – shouted a greeting across the distance.

'Say hello,' the assassin growled. 'Who knows, if your cousins are good enough, you might win the day yet.'

The treasurer raised a hand, called out his answer.

There was less than ten paces between the two ships now. Salk Elan approached those of the *Ragstopper*'s crew who stood near the marines. 'When she's close enough, use the grappling hooks. Make sure we're snug, lads, becuse if she gets away, she'll hound us from here to Falar.'

The pirate climbing the mast was halfway up, already swinging around to see if he could get a better look at the scene on *Ragstopper*'s main deck.

The raider's crew threw lines across. The ships closed.

A cry of warning from the lookout was cut short by a crossbow quarrel. The man toppled, landing amidst his fellows crowding the raider's deck. Angry shouts arose.

Kalam gripped the treasurer by the collar and dragged him back as the first of the pirates leapt the distance and swarmed up *Ragstopper*'s flank.

'You've made a terrible mistake,' the treasurer hissed.

The marines answered the assault with a murderous flight of quarrels. The first line of pirates pitched back.

Salk Elan shouted a warning that brought Kalam spinning around. Hovering just off the port side, directly behind the grouped marines, an apparition took form, its wings ten paces across, its shimmering scales bright yellow and blinding in the new day's light. The long reptilian head was a mass of fangs.

An enkar'al – this far from Raraku – Hood's breath!

'I warned you!' the treasurer laughed.

The creature was a blur as it plunged into the midst of the marines, talons crunching through chain and helms.

Kalam whirled again, drove his fist into the grinning treasurer's face. The man dropped to the deck unconscious, blood gushing from his nose and eyes.

'Kalam!' Salk Elan shouted. 'Leave the mage to me – help the marines!'

The assassin bolted forward. Enkar'al were mortal enough, just notoriously hard to kill, and rare even in their desert home – the assassin had never before faced one.

Seven marines were down. The creature's wings thundered

as it hung over the rest, its two taloned limbs darting downward, clashing against shields.

Pirates were streaming onto *Ragstopper*, opposed now by only half a dozen marines, the lieutenant among them.

Kalam had little time to think of what he planned, and none to gauge Salk Elan's progress. 'Stiffen shields!' he bellowed, then leapt forward, scrambling onto the shields. The enkar'al twisted around, razor claws lashing at his face. He ducked and drove his long-knife up between the creature's legs.

The point jammed against scale, snapping like a twig.

'Hood!'

Dropping the weapon, Kalam surged upward, clambering over the gnarled, scaly hide. Jaws snapped down at him but could not reach. The assassin swung around, onto the beast's back.

Sorcerous concussions reached his ears from the raider's deck.

Thrusting knife in one hand, his other arm looped around the enkar'al's sinuous neck, Kalam began slashing at the beating wings. The blade slipped through membrane, opening wide, spreading gaps. The enkar'al fell to the deck, into the midst of the surviving marines, who closed in around it, thrusting with their short swords.

The heavier weapons succeeded where long-knife failed, driving between scales. Blood sprayed. The creature screamed, thrashing about in its death throes.

There was fighting on all sides now, as pirates converged to cut down the last of the marines. Kalam clambered off the dying enkar'al, shifted the knife to his left hand and found a short sword lying beside a dead marine, barely in time to meet the charge of two pirates, their heavy scimitars slashing down on both sides.

The assassin leapt between the two men, inside their reach,

stabbed swiftly with both weapons, then pushed past, twisting his blades as he dragged them free.

His awareness blurred then, as Kalam surged through a crush of pirates, cutting, slashing and stabbing on all sides. He lost his knife as it jammed between ribs, used the freed hand to yank a helmet away from a collapsing warrior and jam it onto his head – the skullcap was too small, and a glancing blow from a wailing scimitar sent it flying even as he broke through the press, skidding on blood-slick decking as he spun around.

Half a dozen pirates wheeled to attack him.

Salk Elan struck the group from the side, a long-knife in either hand. Three pirates went down in the first attack. Kalam launched himself forward, batting aside a blade, then driving stiff fingers into its wielder's throat.

A moment later the clash of weapons had ceased. Figures were sprawled on all sides, some moaning, some shrieking and gibbering in pain, but most still and silent.

Kalam dropped to one knee, struggling to regain his breath.

'What a mess!' Salk Elan muttered, crouching to wipe his blades clean.

The assassin lifted his head and stared at him. Elan's fine clothes were scorched and soaked in blood. Half his face was bright red, flash-burned, the eyebrow on that side a smear of ash. He was breathing heavily, and every breath caused him obvious pain.

Kalam looked past the man. Not a single marine was standing. A handful of sailors moved among the bodies, pulling free those that still lived – they'd found but two thus far, neither one the lieutenant.

The acting First Mate came to the assassin's side. 'Cook wants to know.'

'What?'

'Is that big lizard tasty?'

Salk Elan's laugh became a cough.

'A delicacy,' Kalam muttered. 'A hundred jakatas a pound in Pan'potsun.'

'Permission to cross over to the raider, sir,' the sailor continued. 'We can resupply.'

The assassin nodded.

'I'll go with you,' Salk Elan managed.

'Appreciate that, sir.'

'Hey,' one of the sailors called, 'what should we do with the treasurer? The bastard's still alive.'

'Leave him to me,' Kalam said.

The treasurer was conscious as they loaded him down with sacks of coin, making noises behind his gag, his eyes wide. Kalam and Salk Elan carried the man between them to the side and pitched him over without ceremony.

Sharks converged on the splash the man made, but the effort of following him down proved too great for the already sated creatures.

The stripped-down raider was still burning beneath a column of smoke as it vanished beyond the horizon.

The Whirlwind lifted itself into a towering wall, higher than the eye could fathom and over a mile in width, around the Holy Desert Raraku. Within the wasteland's heart, all remained calm, the air refulgent with golden light.

Battered ridges of bedrock rose above the sands ahead, like blackened bones. Walking half a dozen paces in front, Leoman paused and turned. 'We must cross a place of spirits,' he said.

Felisin nodded. 'Older than this desert . . . they have risen and now watch us.'

'Do they mean us harm, Sha'ik Reborn?' the Toblakai asked, reaching for his weapon.

'No. They may be curious, but they are beyond caring.' She turned to Heboric. The ex-priest was still huddled within

728

himself, hidden beneath his tattoos. 'What do you sense?'

He flinched away from her voice, as if every word sent his way was a jagged dart. 'One needn't be an immortal ghost not to care,' he muttered.

She studied him. 'Fleeing from the joy of being reborn cannot last, Heboric. What you fear is becoming human once again—'

His laugh was bitter, sardonic.

'You do not expect to hear such thoughts from me,' she noted. 'For all that you disliked what I was, you are loath to relinquish that child.'

'You're still in that rush of power, Felisin, and it's deluded you into thinking it's delivered wisdom as well. There are gifts, and then there is that which must be earned.'

'He is as shackles about you, Sha'ik Reborn,' the Toblakai growled. 'Kill him.'

She shook her head, still eyeing Heboric. 'Since wisdom cannot be gifted to me, I would be gifted a wise man. His company, his words.'

The ex-priest looked up at that, eyes narrowing beneath the heavy shelf of his brow. 'I thought you'd left me no choice, Felisin.'

'Perhaps it only seemed that way, Heboric.'

She watched the struggle within him, the struggle that had always been there. *We have crossed a war-ravaged land, and all the while we were warring with ourselves. Dryjhna has but raised a mirror . . .* 'I have learned one thing from you, Heboric,' she said.

'And that is?'

'Patience.' She turned about, waved Leoman on.

They approached the folded, scarred outcroppings. There was little evidence that this place had once known sacred rites. The basaltic bedrock was impervious to the usual pitting and grooving that active hands often worked into the stone of holy sites, nor was there any pattern in the few boulders scattered about.

Yet Felisin could sense the presence of spirits, once strong, now but echoes, and their faint regard followed them with unseen eyes. Beyond the rise the desert swept out and down into an immense basin, where the dwindling sea of ancient times had finally died. Suspended dust cloaked the vast depression.

'The oasis lies near the centre,' Leoman said at her side.

She nodded.

'Less than seven leagues now.'

'Who carries Sha'ik's belongings?' she asked.

'I do.'

'I will take them.'

He was silent as he set down his pack, untied the flap and began removing items. Clothing, a scatter of a poor woman's rings, bracelets and earrings, a thin-bladed long-knife, its iron stained black except for the honed edge.

'Her sword awaits us at the encampment,' Leoman said when he'd done. 'She wore the bracelets on her left wrist only, the rings on her left hand.' He gestured down at some leather straps. 'She wound these around her right wrist and forearm.' He paused, looked up at her with hard eyes. 'It were best you matched the attire. Precisely.'

She smiled. 'To aid in the deceit, Leoman?'

He dropped his gaze. 'There may well be some . . . resistance. The High Mages—'

'Would bend the cause to their wills, create factions within the camp, then clash in a struggle to decide who will rule all. They have not yet done so, for they cannot determine if Sha'ik still lives. Yet they have prepared the ground.'

'Seer—'

'Ah, you accept that much at least.'

He bowed. 'None could deny the power that has come to you, yet . . .'

'Yet I did not myself open the Holy Book.'

He met her eyes. 'You did not.'

Felisin looked up. The Toblakai and Heboric stood a short distance away, watching, listening. 'What I shall open is not between those covers, but is within me. Now is not the time.' She faced Leoman again. 'You must trust in me.'

The skin tightened around the desert warrior's eyes.

'You never could easily yield that, could you, Leoman?'

'Who speaks?'

'We do.'

He was silent.

'Toblakai.'

'Yes, Sha'ik Reborn?'

'To a man who doubts you, you would use what?'

'My sword,' he replied.

Heboric snorted.

Felisin swung to him. 'And you? What would you use?'

'Nothing. I would be as I am, and if I prove worthy of trust, that man will come to it.'

'Unless . . . ?'

He scowled. 'Unless that man cannot trust himself, Felisin.'

She turned back to Leoman and waited.

Heboric cleared his throat. 'You cannot command someone to have faith, lass. Obedience, yes, but not belief itself.'

She said to Leoman, 'You've told me there is a man to the south. A man leading a battered remnant of an army and refugees numbering tens of thousands. They do as he bids, their trust is absolute – how has that man managed that?'

Leoman shook his head.

'Have you ever followed such a leader, Leoman?'

'No.'

'So you truly do not know.'

'I do not know, Seer.'

Dismissive of the eyes of three men, Felisin stripped

down and attired herself in Sha'ik's clothing. She donned the stained silver jewellery with an odd sense of long familiarity, then tossed aside the rags she had been wearing earlier. She studied the desert basin for a long moment, then said, 'Come, the High Mages have begun to lose their patience.'

'We're only a few days from Falar, according to the First Mate,' Kalam said. 'Everyone's talking about these tradewinds.'

'I bet they are,' the captain growled, looking as if he'd swallowed something sour.

The assassin refilled their tankards and leaned back. Whatever still afflicted the captain, keeping him to his cot for days now, went beyond the injuries he'd sustained at the hands of the bodyguard. *Mind you, head wounds can get complicated. Even so . . .* The captain trembled when he spoke, though his speech was in no way slurred or otherwise impaired. The struggle seemed to be in pushing the words out, in linking them into anything resembling a sentence. Yet in his eyes Kalam saw a mind no less sharp than it had been.

The assassin was baffled, yet he felt, on some instinctive level, that his presence gave strength to the captain's efforts. 'Lookout sighted a ship in our wake just before sunset yesterday – a Malazan fast trader, he thinks. If it was, it must have passed us without lights or hail in the night. No sign of it this morning.'

The captain grunted. 'Never made better time. Bet their eyes are wide, too, dropping headless cocks over the starboard side and into Beru's smiling maw at every blessed bell.'

Kalam took a mouthful of watered wine, studying the captain over the tankard's dented rim. 'We lost the last two marines last night. Left me wondering about that ship's healer of yours.'

'Been having a run of the Lord's push, he has. Not like him.'

'Well, he's passed out on pirates' ale right now.'

'Doesn't drink.'

'He does now.'

The look the captain gave him was like a bright, distant flare, a beacon warning of shoals ahead.

'All's not well, I take it,' the assassin quietly rumbled.

'Captain's head's askew, that's a fact. Tongue full of thorns, close by ears like acorns under the mulch, ready to hatch unseen. Hatch.'

'You'd tell me if you could.'

'Tell you what?' He reached a shaking hand towards the tankard. 'Can't hold what's not there, I always say. Can't hold in a blow, neither, lo, the acorn's rolled away, plumb away.'

'Your hands look well enough mended.'

'Aye, well enough.' The captain looked away, as if the effort of conversation had finally become too much.

The assassin hesitated, then said, 'I've heard of a warren . . .'

'Rabbits,' the captain muttered. 'Rats.'

'All right,' Kalam sighed, rising. 'We'll find you a proper healer, a Denul healer, when we get to Falar.'

'Getting there fast.'

'Aye, we are.'

'On the tradewinds.'

'Aye.'

'But there aren't any tradewinds, this close to Falar.'

Kalam emerged onto the deck, held his face to the sky for a moment, then made his way to the forecastle.

'How does he fare?' Salk Elan asked.

'Poorly.'

'Head injuries are like that. Get knocked wrong and you end up muttering marriage vows to your lapdog.'

'We'll see in Falar.'

'We'd be lucky to find a good healer in Bantra.'

'Bantra? Hood's breath, why Bantra when the main islands are but a few leagues farther along?'

Elan shrugged. '*Ragstopper*'s home berth, it seems. In case you haven't noticed, our acting First Mate lives in a tangle of superstition. He's a legion of neurotic sailors all rolled up in one, Kalam, and on this one you won't sway him – Hood knows I've tried.'

A shout from the lookout interrupted their conversation. 'Sails! Two pegs off the port bow! Six . . . seven . . . ten – Beru's blessing, a fleet!'

Kalam and Elan stepped over to the forecastle's portside rail. As yet, they could see nothing but waves.

The First Mate called up from the main deck. 'What's their bearing, Vole?'

'North, sir! And westerly. They'll cut across our wake, sir!'

'In about twelve hours,' Elan muttered, 'hard-tacking all the way.'

'A fleet,' Kalam said.

'Imperial. The Adjunct Tavore, friend.' The man turned and offered the assassin a tight smile. 'If you thought the blood had run thick enough over your homeland . . . well, thank the gods we're heading the other way.'

They could see the first of the sails now. *Tavore's fleet. Horse and troop transports, the usual league-long wake of garbage, sewage and corpses human and animal, the sharks and dhenrabi thrashing the waves. Any long journey by sea delivers an army foul of temper and eager to get to business. No doubt enough tales of atrocities have reached them to scorch mercy from their souls.*

'The serpent's head,' Elan said quietly, 'on that long, stretching Imperial neck. Tell me, Kalam, is there a part of you – an old soldier's – longing to be standing on a deck over there, noting with scant interest a lone, Falar-bound trader ship, while deep within you builds that quiet, deadly determination? On your way to deliver Laseen's punishment, what she's always

734

delivered, as an Empress must; a vengeance tenfold. Are you tugged between two tides right now, Kalam?'

'My thoughts are not yours to pillage, Elan, no matter how rampant your imagination. You do not know me, nor shall you ever know me.'

The man sighed. 'We've fought side by side, Kalam. We proved ourselves a deadly team. Our mutual friend in Ehrlitan had suspicions of what you intend – think of how much greater your chances with me at your side . . .'

Kalam slowly turned to face Elan. 'Chances of what?' he asked, his voice barely carrying.

Salk Elan's shrug was easy, careless. 'Whatever. You're not averse to partnerships, are you? There was Quick Ben and, before that, Porthal K'nastra – from your early pre-Imperial days in Karaschimesh. Hood knows, anyone looking at your history, Kalam, might well assert that you thrive on partnerships. Well, man, what do you say?'

The assassin responded with a slow blink of his lids. 'And what makes you think I am alone right now, Salk Elan?'

For the briefest yet most satisfying of moments, Kalam saw a flicker of uncertainty rattle Elan's face, before a smooth smile appeared. 'And where does he hide, up in the crow's nest with that dubiously named lookout?'

Kalam turned away. 'Where else?'

The assassin felt Salk Elan's eyes on his back as he strode away. *You've the arrogance common to every mage, friend. You'll have to excuse my pleasure in spreading cracks through it.*

CHAPTER EIGHTEEN

I stood in a place
where all shadows converged
the end of the Path of Hands
Soletaken and D'ivers
through the gates of truth
where from the darkness
all mysteries emerged.

The Path
Trout Sen'al'Bhok'arala

They came upon the four bodies at the edge of an upthrust of roots that seemed to mark the entrance to a vast maze. The figures were contorted, limbs shattered, their dark robes twisted and stiff with dried blood.

Recognition arrived dull and heavy in Mappo's mind, an answering of suspicions that came with little surprise. *Nameless Ones . . . Priests of the Azath, if such entities can have priests. How many cold hands have guided us here? Myself . . . Icarium . . . these two twisted roots . . . journeying to Tremorlor—*

With a grunt, Icarium stepped forward, his eyes on a broken staff lying beside one of the corpses. 'I have seen those before,' he said.

The Trell frowned at his friend. 'How? Where?'

'In a dream.'

'Dream?'

The Jhag gave him a half-smile. 'Oh yes, Mappo, I have dreams.' He faced the bodies again. 'It began as all such dreams begin. I am stumbling. In pain. Yet I bear no wounds, and my weapons are clean. No, the pain is within me, as of a knowledge once gained, then lost yet again.'

Mappo stared at his friend's back, struggling to comprehend his words.

'I arrive,' the Jhag continued in dry tones, 'at the outskirts of a town. A Trellish town on the plain. It has been destroyed. Scars of sorcery stain the ground . . . the air. Bodies rot in the streets, and Great Ravens have come to feed – their laughter is the voice of the stench.'

'Icarium—'

'And then a woman appears, dressed as are these here before us. A priestess. She holds a staff, from which fell power still bleeds.

' "What have you done?" I ask her.

' "Only what is necessary," is her soft reply. I see in her face a great fear as she looks upon me, and I am saddened by it. "Jhag, you must not wander alone."

'Her words seem to call up terrible memories. And images, faces – companions, countless in number. As if I have rarely been alone. Men and women have walked at my side, sometimes singly, sometimes in legion. These memories fill me with grief, as if in some way I have betrayed every one of those companions.' He paused, and Mappo saw his head slowly nod. 'Indeed, I understand this now. They were all guardians, like you, Mappo. And they all failed. Were, perhaps, killed by my own hand.'

He shook himself. 'The priestess sees what lies writ upon my face, for hers becomes its mirror. Then she nods. Her staff blossoms with sorcery . . . and I wander a lifeless plain, alone. The pain is gone – where it had lodged within me, there is now nothing. And, as I feel my memories drift apart . . . away . . . I sense I have but dreamed. And so awaken.' He turned then, offered Mappo a dreadful smile.

Impossible. A twisting of the truth. I saw the slaughter with my own eyes. I spoke with the priestess. You have been visited in your dreams, Icarium, with fickle malice.

Fiddler cleared his throat. 'Looks like they were guarding this entrance. Whatever found them proved too much.'

'They are known on the Jhag Odhan,' Mappo said, 'as the Nameless Ones.'

Icarium's eyes hardened on the Trell.

'That cult,' Apsalar muttered, 'is supposed to be extinct.'

The others looked at her. She shrugged. 'Dancer's knowledge.'

Iskaral sputtered. 'Hood take their rotting souls! Presumptuous bastards one and all – how dare they make such claims?'

'What claims?' Fiddler growled.

The High Priest hugged himself. 'Nothing. Speak nothing of it, yes. Servants of the Azath – pah! Are we naught but pieces on a gameboard? My master scoured them from the Empire, yes. A task for the Talons, as Dancer will tell you. A necessary cleansing, a plucking of a thorn from the Emperor's side. Slaughter and desecration. Merciless. Too many vulnerable secrets – corridors of power – oh, how they resented my master's entry into Deadhouse—'

'Iskaral!' Apsalar snapped.

The priest ducked as if cuffed.

Icarium faced the young woman. 'Who voiced that warning? Through your mouth – who spoke?'

She fixed cool eyes on him. 'Possessing these memories enforces a responsibility, Icarium, just as possessing none exculpates.'

The Jhag flinched.

Crokus had edged forward. 'Apsalar?'

She smiled. 'Or Cotillion? No, it is just me, Crokus. I am afraid I have grown weary of all these suspicions. As if I have no self unstained by the god who once possessed me. I was but a girl when I was taken. A fisherman's daughter. But I am no mere girl any more.'

Her father's sigh was loud. 'Daughter,' he rumbled, 'we ain't none of us what we once were, and there ain't nothing simple in what we've gone through to get here.' He scowled, as if struggling for words. 'But you ordered the High Priest to shut up, to protect secrets that Dancer – Cotillion – would want kept that way. So Icarium's suspicions were natural enough.'

'Yes,' she countered, 'I am not a slave to what I was. *I* decide what to do with the knowledge I possess. I choose my own causes, Father.'

Icarium spoke. 'I stand chastised, Apsalar.' He faced Mappo again. 'What more do you know of these Nameless Ones, friend?'

Mappo hesitated, then said, 'Our tribe welcomed them as guests, but their visits were rare. I believe, however, that indeed they view themselves as servants of the Azath. If Trell legends hold any truth, then the cult may well date from the time of the First Empire—'

'They have been eradicated!' Iskaral shrieked.

'Within the borders of the Malazan Empire, perhaps,' Mappo conceded.

'My friend,' Icarium said, 'you are withholding truths. I would hear them.'

The Trell sighed. 'They have taken it upon themselves to recruit your guardians, Icarium, and have done so since the beginning.'

'Why?'

'That I do not know. Now that you ask it—' He frowned. 'An interesting question. Dedication to noble vows? Protection of the Azath?' Mappo shrugged.

'Hood's stubby ankles!' Rellock growled. 'Might be guilt, for all we know.'

All eyes swung to him.

After a long, silent moment, Fiddler shook himself. 'Come on, then. Into the maze.'

Arms and limbs. What clawed at the binding roots, what stretched and twisted in a hopeless effort to pull free, what reached out in supplication, in silent appeal and in deadly offer from all sides, was an array of imprisoned life, and few among those horridly animate projections were human in origin.

Fiddler's imagination failed his compulsive desire to fashion likely bodies, heads and faces to such limbs, even as he knew that the reality of what lay hidden within the woven walls would pale his worst nightmares.

Tremorlor's gnarled gaol of roots held demons, ancient Ascendants and such a host of alien creatures that the sapper was left trembling in the realization of his insignificance and that of all his kind. Humans were but one tiny, frail leaf on a tree too massive even to comprehend. The shock of that unmanned him, mocking his audacity with an endless echo of ages and realms trapped within this mad, riotous prison.

They could hear battles raging on all sides, thus far mercifully in other branches of the tortured maze. The Azath was being assailed from all fronts. The sound of snapping, shattering wood cracked through the air. Bestial screams rent the iron-smeared air above them, voices lost from the throats that released them, voices the only thing that could escape this terrifying war.

The crossbow's stock was slick with sweat in Fiddler's hands as he edged forward, keeping to the centre of the path, beyond the reach of those grasping, unhuman hands. A sharp bend lay just ahead. The sapper crouched down, then glanced back at the others.

Only three Hounds remained. Shan and Gear had set off, taking divergent paths. Where they were now and what was happening to them Fiddler had no idea, but Baran, Blind and Rood did not seem perturbed at their absence. The sightless female padded at Icarium's side as if she was nothing more than a well-trained companion to the Jhag. Baran held back as rearguard, while Rood – pale, mottled, a solid mass of muscle – waited not five paces from Fiddler's position, motionless. Its eyes, a dark liquid brown, seemed fixed on the sapper.

He shivered, his gaze flicking once again to Blind. *At Icarium's side . . . so close . . .* He understood that proximity all too clearly, as did Mappo. If bargains could be struck with a House of the Azath, then Shadowthrone had managed it. The Hounds would not be taken – as much as Tremorlor would have yearned for such prizes, for the abrupt and absolute removal of these ancient killers – no, the deal involved a much greater prize . . .

Mappo stood on the Jhag's other side, the burnished longbone club raised before him. A surge of compassion flooded Fiddler. The Trell was being torn apart from within. He had more than just shapeshifters to guard against – there was, after all, the companion he loved as a brother.

Crokus and Apsalar, the former with his fighting knives out and held in admirably relaxed grips, flanked Servant. Pust slunk along a step behind them.

And this is what we are. This, and no more than this.

He had paused before the bend in response to an instinctive hesitation that seemed to wrap an implacable grip around his spine. *Go no farther. Wait.* The sapper sighed. *Wait for what?*

His eyes, still wandering over the group behind him, caught on something, focused.

Rood's hackles had begun a slow rise.

'*Hood!*'

Movement exploded all around him, a massive shape

741

barrelling into view directly ahead with a roar that turned Fiddler's marrow into spikes of ice. And above, a thudding flapping of leathery wings, huge talons darting down.

The charging Soletaken was a brown bear, as big as a noble-born's carriage, both flanks brushing the root walls of the maze, where arms were pulled, stretched, hands closed on thick fur. The sapper saw one unhuman limb torn from the trio of joints that formed its shoulder, spurting old, black blood. Ignoring these desperate efforts as if they were no more than burrs and thorns, the bear lunged forward.

Fiddler dropped to the root-bound floor – the bark hot and greasy with some kind of sweat – sparing no breath to shout even a warning. Not that it was needed.

The bear's underside swept over him in a blur, the fur pale and smeared in blood, then it was past, even as the sapper rolled to follow its attack.

The bear's attention was fixed exclusively on the blood-red enkar'al hovering before it – another Soletaken, shrieking with rage. The bear's paws lashed out, closing on empty air as the winged reptile darted backward – and into the reach of Mappo's club.

Fiddler could not fathom the strength behind the Trell's two-handed, full-shouldered swing. The weapon's tusked head struck the enkar'al's ridged chest and plunged inward with a snapping of bones. The enkar'al, itself the size of an ox, seemed literally to crumple and fold around that blow. Wing bones broke, neck and head were thrown forward, eyes and nostrils spraying blood.

The reptilian Soletaken was dead before it struck the root wall. Talons and hands received and held it.

'No!' Mappo roared.

Fiddler's gaze darted to Icarium – but the Jhag was not the cause of the Trell's cry, for the Hound Rood had attacked the massive bear, striking it from the side.

With a scream the Soletaken lurched sideways, up against the root wall. Few were the reaching limbs that could hold fast such a beast, yet one awaited it, one wrapped its green-skinned length around the bear's thick neck, and that one possessed a strength beyond even the Soletaken's.

Rood clamped a flailing paw in its jaws, crushing bones, then tore the appendage away with savage shakes of its head.

'Messremb!' the Trell bellowed, struggling in Icarium's restraining grip. 'An ally!'

'A Soletaken!' Iskaral Pust shrieked, dancing around.

Mappo sagged suddenly. 'A friend,' he whispered.

And Fiddler understood. *The first friend lost this day. The first . . .*

Tremorlor laid claim to both shapeshifters as roots snaked out, wrapping around the newcomers. The two beasts now faced each other on their respective walls – *their eternal resting places.* The Soletaken bear, blood gushing from the stump at the end of one limb, struggled on, but even its prodigious strength was useless against the otherworldly might of the Azath and the arm that held it, now tightening. Messremb's constricted throat struggled to find air. The red rims around its dark-brown eyes took on a bluish cast, the eyes bulging from their damp, streaked nests of fur.

Rood had pulled away and was placidly devouring the severed paw, bones and flesh and fur.

'Mappo,' Icarium said, 'see that stranger's arm crushing the life from him – do you understand? Not an eternal prison for Messremb. Hood will take him – death will take him, as it did the enkar'al . . .'

The entwining roots from the opposing walls reached out to each other, almost touching.

'The maze finds a new wall,' Crokus said.

'Quickly then,' Fiddler snapped, only now regaining his feet. 'Everyone to this side.'

They moved on, silent once again. Fiddler found his hands trembling incessantly now where they gripped his pitiful weapon. The strengths and savagery he had witnessed minutes earlier clashed with such alarm that it left his mind numb.

We cannot survive this. A hundred Hounds of Shadow would not be enough. Such shapeshifting creatures have arrived in their thousands, all here, all in Tremorlor's grounds – how many will reach the House? Only the strongest. The strongest . . . And what is it we dare? To step within the House, to find the gate that will take us to Malaz City, to the Deadhouse itself. Gods, we are but minor players . . . with one exception, a man we cannot afford to unleash, a man even the Azath fears.

Sounds of fierce battle assailed them from all sides. The other corridors of this infernal maze played host to a mayhem that Fiddler knew they themselves would soon be unable to avoid. Indeed, those terrible sounds had grown louder, closer. *We're getting nearer the House. We're all converging . . .*

He stopped, turning towards the others. He left his warning unspoken, for every face, every set of eyes that met his, bespoke the same knowledge.

Claws clattered ahead and the sapper whirled to see Shan arrive, slowing quickly from a frantic run. Her flanks were heaving, tracked in countless wounds.

Oh, Hood . . .

Another sound reached them, approaching from up the trail, from where the Hound had just come.

'He was warned!' Icarium cried. 'Gryllen! You were warned!'

Mappo had wrapped his arms around the Jhag. Icarium's sudden surge of anger stilled the air on all sides – as if an entire warren had drawn breath. The Jhag was motionless in that embrace, yet the sapper saw the Trell's arms strain, stretch to an unseen force. The sound that broke from Mappo was a thing of such pain, such distress and fear that Fiddler sagged, tears starting from his eyes.

The Hound Blind stepped away from Icarium's side, and the shock of seeing her tail dip jolted through the sapper.

Rood and Baran joined Shan, forming a nervous barrier – leaving Fiddler on the wrong side. He scrambled back, his limbs moving jerkily, as if weakened by a gallon of wine in his veins. His gaze held on Icarium, as the edge they now all tottered on finally revealed itself, promising horror.

All three Hounds flinched and jolted back a step. Fiddler spun about. The path ahead was closed into a new wall, a seething, swarming wall. *Oh, my, we meet again.*

The girl was no more than eleven or twelve, wearing a leather vest on which was stitched overlapping bronze scales – flattened coins, in fact – and the spear she held in her hands was heavy enough to waver as she resolutely maintained her guard stance.

Felisin glanced down at the basketful of braided flowers at the girl's bare, dusty feet. 'You've some skill with those,' she said.

The young sentry glanced again at Leoman, then the Toblakai.

'You may lower your weapon,' the desert warrior said.

The spear's trembling point dropped down to the sand.

The Toblakai's voice was hard, 'Kneel before Sha'ik Reborn!'

She was prostrate in an instant.

Felisin reached down and touched the girl's head. 'You may rise. What is your name?'

As she climbed hesitantly upright, she answered with a shake of her head.

'Likely one of the orphans,' Leoman said. 'None to speak for her in the naming rite. Thus, she has no name, yet she would give her life for you, Sha'ik Reborn.'

'If she would give her life for me, then she has earned a name. So with the other orphans.'

'As you wish – who then will speak for them?'

'I shall, Leoman.'

The edge of the oasis was marked by low, crumbling mud-brick walls and a thin scatter of palms under which sand crabs scuttled through dry fronds. A dozen white goats stood in nearby shade, light-grey eyes turned towards the newcomers.

Felisin reached down and collected one of the bracelets of braided flowers. She slipped it over her right wrist.

They continued on into the heart of the oasis. The air grew cooler; the pools of shadow they passed through were a shock after so long under unrelieved sunlight. The endless ruins revealed that a city had once stood here, a city of spacious gardens and courtyards, pools and fountains, all reduced to stumps and low ridges.

Corrals ringed the camp, the horses within them looking healthy and fit.

'How large is this oasis?' Heboric asked.

'Can you not enquire of the ghosts?' Felisin asked.

'I'd rather not. This city's destruction was anything but peaceful. Ancient invaders, crushing the last of the First Empire's island enclaves. The thin sky-blue potsherds under our feet are First Empire, the thick red ones are from the conquerors. From something delicate to something brutal, a pattern repeated through all of history. These truths weary me, down to my very soul.'

'The oasis is vast,' Leoman told the ex-priest. 'There are areas that hold true soil, and these we have planted with forage and crops. A few ancient cedar stands remain, amidst stumps that have turned to stone. There are pools and lakes, the water fresh and unending. Should we choose, we need never leave this place.'

'How many people?'

'Eleven tribes. Forty thousand of the best-trained cavalry this world has ever seen.'

Heboric grunted. 'And what can cavalry do against legions of infantry, Leoman?'

The desert warrior grinned. 'Only change the face of war, old man.'

'It's been tried before,' Heboric said. 'What has made the Malazan military so successful is its ability to adapt, to alter tactics – even on the field of battle. You think the Empire has not met horse cultures before, Leoman? Met, and subdued. A fine example would be the Wickans, or the Seti.'

'And how did the Empire succeed?'

'I am not the historian for such details – they never interested me. Had you a library with Imperial texts – works by Duiker and Tallobant – you could read for yourself. Assuming you can read Malazan, that is.'

'You define the limits of their region, the map of their seasonal rounds. You take and hold water sources, building forts and trading posts – for trade weakens your enemy's isolation, the very source of their power. And, depending on how patient you are, you either fire the grasslands and slaughter every animal on four legs, or you wait, and to every band of youths that rides into your settlements, you offer the glory of war and booty in foreign lands, with the promise to keep the group intact as a fighting unit. Such a lure plucks the flower from those tribes, until none but old men and old women mutter about the freedom that once existed,' Leoman replied.

'Ah, someone's done their reading, then.'

'Aye, we possess a library, Heboric. A vast one, at Sha'ik Elder's insistence. "Know your enemy better than they know themselves." So said Emperor Kellanved.'

'No doubt, though I dare say he wasn't the first.'

The mudbrick residences of the tribes appeared on all sides

as the group emerged from an avenue between horse pens. Children ran in the sandy streets, trader carts pulled by mules and oxen were slowly winding their way out from the centre, the market done for the day. Packs of dogs came forward to assuage their curiosity, then fled at the rank challenge of the stiff roll of white bear fur resting across the Toblakai's broad shoulders.

A crowd began to gather, following them as they made their way towards the settlement's heart. Felisin felt a thousand eyes on her, heard the uncertain murmuring. *Sha'ik, yet not Sha'ik. Yet Sha'ik, for look at her two favoured bodyguards, the Toblakai and Leoman of the Wastes, the great warriors thinned by their journey into the desert. The prophecy spoke of rebirth, a renewal. Sha'ik has returned. At long last, and she is reborn. Sha'ik Reborn—*

'Sha'ik Reborn!' The two words found a hissing cadence, a rhythm like waves, growing louder. The crowds burgeoned, word spreading with swift breath.

'I hope there's a clearing or amphitheatre at the centre,' Heboric muttered. He gave Felisin an ironic grin. 'When did we last travel a crowded street, lass?'

'Better from shame to triumph than the other way around, Heboric.'

'Aye, I'll not argue that.'

'There is a parade ground before the palace tent,' Leoman said.

'Palace tent? Ah, a message of impermanence, a symbol saluting tradition – the power of the old ways of life and all that.'

Leoman turned to Felisin. 'Your companion's lack of respect could prove problematic, Sha'ik Reborn. When we meet the High Mages—'

'He'll wisely keep his mouth shut.'

'He had better.'

'Cut out his tongue,' the Toblakai growled. 'Then we need not worry.'

'No?' Heboric laughed. 'You underestimate me still, oaf. I am blind, yet I see. Cut out my tongue and oh, how I shall speak! Relax, Felisin, I'm no fool.'

'You are if you continue using her old name,' Leoman warned.

Felisin left them to bicker, sensing that, at last, despite the sharp edges to the words they threw at one another, a bond was developing between the three men. Not something as simple as friendship – the Toblakai and Heboric had chains of hatred linking them, after all – but one of experiences shared. *My rebirth is what they share, even as they stand as points of a triangle, with Leoman the apex. Leoman, the man with no beliefs.* They were nearing the settlement's centre. She saw a platform to one side, a disc-shaped dais surrounding a fountain. 'There, to start.'

Leoman turned in surprise. 'What?'

'I would speak to these followers.'

'Now? Before we meet with the High Mages?'

'Yes.'

'You would make the three most powerful men in this camp wait?'

'Would that concern Sha'ik, Leoman? Does my rebirth require their blessing? Unfortunately they weren't there, were they?'

'But—'

'Time for you to shut your mouth, Leoman,' Heboric said, not unkindly.

'Clear a path for me, Toblakai,' Felisin said.

The giant swung abruptly, cutting directly for the platform. He said nothing, for nothing was needed. His presence alone split the mob, peeled it back on both sides in hushed silence.

They reached the dais. 'I shall need your lungs to start, Toblakai. Name me once I've ascended.'

'I shall, Chosen One.'

Heboric snorted softly. 'Now that's an apt title.'

A cascade of thoughts swept through Felisin as she climbed onto the stone platform. *Sha'ik Reborn, that dark cloak of Dryjhna descending. Felisin, nobleborn brat of Unta, whore of the mining pit. Open the Holy Book and thus complete the rite. That young woman has seen the face of the Abyss – that terrible journey behind her – and now comes the demand that she face the one before her. The young woman must relinquish her life. Opening the Holy Book – yet who would have thought the goddess so amenable to a deal? She knows my heart, and that grants her the confidence, it seems, of deferring her claim on it. The deal has been struck. Power granted – so many visions – yet Felisin remains, her rock-hard, scarred soul floats free in the vast Abyss.*

And Leoman knows . . .

'Kneel before Sha'ik Reborn!' The Toblakai's bellow was like thunder in the hot, motionless air. As one, thousands dropped down, heads bowed.

Felisin stepped past the giant. Dryjhna's power trickled into her – *ah, dear goddess, precious patroness, do you now hesitate in your gifts? Like this crowd, like Leoman, do you await the proof of my words? My intent?*

Yet the power was sufficient to make her quiet words a clear whisper in the ears of everyone present – including those of the three High Mages who now stood beneath the parade-ground archway – *who stood, who did not kneel.* 'Rise, my faithful ones.'

She felt the three distant men flinch at that, as they were meant to. *Oh yes, I know where you stand, you three . . .* 'The Holy Desert Raraku lies protected within the Whirlwind circle, ensuring the sanctity of my return. While beyond, the rebellion's claim to dominion – to rightful independence from the Malazan tyrants – continues its spreading tide of blood. My servants lead vast armies. All but one of the Seven Holy Cities have been liberated.' She was silent a moment, feeling the power building within her, yet when she spoke again it was in a low whisper. 'Our time of preparation is at an end. The time has come to march, to set forth from this oasis. The Empress, upon her distant throne, would punish us. A fleet approaches Seven Cities, an army commanded by her chosen Adjunct, a commander whose mind I hold as a map within my own – she possesses no secrets I do not know . . .'

The three High Mages had not moved. Felisin was gifted with knowing them, a sudden rush of knowledge that could only be Sha'ik Elder's. She could see their faces as if she stood but a pace from each of them, and she knew that they now shared that sense of sudden, precise proximity – and a part of her found admiration in their refusal to tremble. The eldest of the three was ancient, withered Bidithal, the one who had first found her, no more than a child, in answer to his own visions. His filmy eyes were fixed on her own. *Bidithal, remember that child? The one you used so brutally that first and only night, to scourge from her all pleasures of the flesh. You broke her within her own body, left scars that felt nothing, that were senseless. The child would not be distracted, no children of her own, no man at her side who could wrest loyalty away from the goddess. Bidithal, I have reserved a place for you in the fiery Abyss, as you well know. But for now, you serve me. Kneel.*

She saw with two visions, one close, the other from the distant vantage point of the platform, as the old man sank down, robes folding around him. She turned her attention to the next man. *Febryl, the most craven and conniving of my High Mages. Thrice you sought to poison me, and thrice Dryjhna's power burned the poison from my veins – yet not once did I condemn you. Did you believe me ignorant of your efforts? And your most ancient secret – your flight from Dassem Ultor before the final battle, your betrayal of the cause – did you think I knew nothing of this? Nonetheless, I have need of you, for you are the lodestone of dissent, of those who would betray me. On your knees, bastard!*

She added a surge of power to the command, which drove the man down to the ground as if with an invisible giant hand. He squirmed on the soft sand, whimpering.

Finally, we come to you, L'oric, my only true mystery. Your sorcerous arts are formidable, particularly in weaving an impervious barrier about you. The cast of your mind is unknown to me, even the breadth and depth of your loyalty. And though you seem faithless, I have found you the most reliable. For you are a pragmatist, L'oric. Like Leoman. Yet I am ever on your scales, my every decision, my every word. So, judge me now, High Mage, and decide.

He dropped to one knee, bowed his head.

Felisin smiled. *Half-measured. Very pragmatic, L'oric. I have missed you.*

She saw his wry answering smile there in the shadows cast by his hood.

Finished with the three men, Felisin's attention returned to the crowd awaiting her next pronouncement. Silence gripped the air. *What is left?* 'We must march, my children. Yet that alone is not enough. We must *announce* what we are about to do, for all to see.'

The goddess was ready.

Felisin – *Sha'ik Reborn* – raised her arms.

The golden dust twisted above her, corkscrewed into a column. It grew. The spout of raging wind and dust burgeoned, climbed skyward, drawing in the desert's gilded cloak, the breath clearing the vast dome on all sides, revealing a blue expanse that had not been seen for months.

And still the column grew, surging higher, ever higher.

The Whirlwind was naught but preparation for this. This, the raising of Dryjhna's standard, the spear that is the Apocalypse. A standard to tower over an entire continent, seen by all. Now, at last, the war begins. My war.

Her head tilted back, she let her sorcerous vision feast on

752

what was rising to the very edge of heaven's canopy. *Dear sister, see what you've made.*

The crossbow jolted in Fiddler's hands. A gout of fire bloomed in the heaving mass of rats, blackening and roasting scores of the creatures.

From point, the sapper had become rearguard, as the group retreated from Gryllen's nightmare pursuit. 'The D'ivers has stolen powerful lives,' said Apsalar, and Mappo, struggling to pull Icarium back, had nodded. 'Gryllen has never before shown such . . . capacity . . .'

Capacity. Fiddler grunted, chewing at the word. The last time he'd seen this D'ivers, the rats had been present in their hundreds. Now they were in their thousands, perhaps tens of thousands – he could only guess at their numbers.

The Hound Gear had rejoined them and now led their retreat down side tracks and narrow tunnels. They were seeking to circle around Gryllen – they could do naught else.

Until Icarium loses control, and gods, he's close. Far too close.

The sapper reached into his munitions, his fingers touching his last cusser, then brushing past, finding instead another flamer. No time to affix it to a quarrel, and he was running out of those anyway. The swarm's lead creatures, scampering towards him, were no more than half a dozen paces away. Fiddler's heart stuttered in his chest – *Have I let them get too close this time? Hood's breath!* He flung the grenado.

Roast rat.

Heaving bodies swallowed the liquid fire, rolled and tumbled towards him.

The sapper wheeled and ran.

He nearly plunged into Shan's blood-smeared jaws. Wailing, Fiddler dodged, spun, went sprawling among boots and moccasins. The group had come to a halt. He scrambled upright. 'We got to run!'

'Where?' The question came from Crokus, in a dry, heavy tone.

They were at a bend in the path, and at both ends swarmed a solid wall of rats.

Four Hounds attacked the far mob, only Shan remaining with the group – taking the place of Blind, perilously close to Icarium.

With a shriek of rage the Jhag threw Mappo from his shoulders with a seemingly effortless shrug. The Trell staggered, lost his balance and struck the root floor with a rattling thud.

'Everybody down!' Fiddler screamed, his hand blindly reaching into the munitions bag, closing on that large, smooth object within.

Keening, Icarium drew his sword. Wood snapped and recoiled in answer. The iron sky blushed crimson, began twisting into a vortex directly above them. Sap sprayed from the walls like sleet, spattering everyone.

Shan attacked Icarium but was batted aside, sent flying, the Jhag barely noticing.

Fiddler stared at Icarium a moment longer; then, pulling his cusser free, the sapper wheeled around and threw it at the D'ivers.

But it was not a cusser.

Eyes wide, Fiddler stared as the conch shell struck the root floor and shattered like glass.

He heard a savage crack behind him, but had no time to give it thought, and all further sounds vanished as a whispering voice rose from the ruined shell – *a Tano Spiritwalker's gift* – a whispering that soon filled the air, a song of bones, finding muscle as it swept outward.

The heaving mass of rats on both sides sought to retreat, but there was nowhere to flee – the sound enveloped all. The creatures began crumpling, the flesh withering, leaving only fur and bones. The song took that flesh, and so grew.

Gryllen's thousand-voiced scream was an anguished explosion of pain and terror. And it, too, was swallowed, devoured.

Fiddler clapped his hands to his ears as the song resonated within, insistent, a voice anything but human, anything but mortal. He twisted away, fell to his knees. His wide eyes stared, barely registering what he saw before him.

His companions were down, curling around themselves. The Hounds cowered, the massive beasts trembling, ears flat. Mappo crouched over the prone, motionless form of Icarium. In the Trell's hands was his bone club, the flat side of the head spattered with fresh blood and snagged strands of long reddish hair. Mappo finally dropped the weapon and slapped his hands over his ears.

Gods, this will kill us all – stop! Stop, dammit!

He realized he was going mad, his vision betraying him, for he now saw a wall, a wall of water, sleet grey and webbed with foam, rushing upon them down the path, building higher, escaping the root-walls and tumbling outward. And he found he could see into the wall now, as if it had turned to liquid glass. Wreckage, foundation stones softened by algae, the rotting remains of sunken ships, encrusted, shapeless hunks of oxidized metal, bones, skulls, casks and bronze-bound chests, splintered masts and fittings – the submerged memory of countless civilizations, an avalanche of tragic events, dissolution and decay.

The wave buried them, drove them all down with its immense weight, its relentless force.

Then was gone, leaving them dry as dust.

Silence filled the air, slowly broken by harsh gasps, bestial whimpers, the muted rustling of clothing and weapons.

Fiddler lifted his head, pushing himself to his hands and knees. Ghostly remnants of that flood seemed to stain him through and through, permeating him with ineffable sorrow.

Protective sorcery?

The Spiritwalker had smiled. *Of a sort.*

And I'd planned on selling the damned thing in G'danisban. My last cusser was a damned conch shell – I never checked, not once. Hood's breath!

He was slow to sense a new tension rising in the air. The sapper looked up. Mappo had retrieved his club and now stood over Icarium's unconscious form. Around him ranged the Hounds. Raised hackles on all sides.

Fiddler scrabbled for his crossbow. 'Iskaral Pust! Call off those Hounds, damn you!'

'The bargain! The Azath will take him!' the High Priest gasped, still staggering about in the stunned aftermath of the Tano's sorcery. 'Now's the time!'

'No,' growled the Trell.

Fiddler hesitated. *The deal, Mappo. Icarium made his wishes plain . . .* 'Call them off, Pust,' he said, moving towards the nervous stand-off. He plunged one hand into his munition bag and swung the leather sack around until he clutched it against his stomach. 'Got one last cusser, and those Hounds could be made of solid marble, it won't save 'em when I fall down on what I'm holding here.'

'Damned sappers! Who invented them? Madness!'

Fiddler grinned. 'Who invented them? Why, Kellanved, who else – who Ascended to become your god, Pust. I'd have thought you'd appreciate the irony, High Priest.'

'The bargain—'

'Will wait a while longer. Mappo, how hard did you hit him? How long will he be out?'

'As long as I wish, friend.'

Friend, and in that word: 'thank you.'

'All right then. Call the mutts off, Pust. Let's get to the House.'

The High Priest ceased his circling stagger; he paused,

slowly weaving back and forth. Glancing over at Apsalar, he offered her a wide grin.

'As the soldier says,' she said.

The grin vanished. 'The youth of today knows no loyalty. A shame, not at all how things used to be. Wouldn't you agree, Servant?'

Apsalar's father grimaced. 'You heard her.'

'Far too permissive, letting her get her way so. You've spoiled her, man! Betrayed by my own generation, alas! What next?'

'What's next is, we get going,' Fiddler said.

'And it won't be much farther,' Crokus said. He pointed down the path. 'There. I see the House. I see Tremorlor.'

The sapper watched Mappo sling his weapon over a shoulder, then gently lift Icarium. The Jhag hung limply within those massive arms. The scene was touched with such gentle caring that Fiddler had to look away.

CHAPTER NINETEEN

> The Day of Pure Blood
> was a gift of the Seven
> from their tombs of sand.
> Fortune was a river
> the glory a gift of the Seven
> that flowed yellow and crimson
> across the day.
>
> *Dog Chain*
> Thes'soran

In the local Can'eld dialect, it would come to be called Mesh'arn tho'ledann: the Day of Pure Blood. The River Vathar's mouth gushed blood and corpses into Dojal Hading Sea for close to a week after the slaughter, a tide that deepened from red to black amidst pallid, bloated bodies. To the fisherfolk plying those waters, that time was called the Season of Sharks, and more than one net was cut away before a ghastly harvest was pulled aboard.

Horror knew no sides, played no favourites. It spread like a stain outward, from tribe to tribe, from one city to the next. And from that revulsion was born fear among the natives of Seven Cities. A Malazan fleet was on its way, commanded by a woman hard as iron. What happened at

758

Vathar Crossing was a whetstone to hone her deadly edge.

Yet, Korbolo Dom was anything but finished.

The cedar forest south of the river rose on tiered steps of limestone, the trader track crazed with switchbacks and steep, difficult slopes. And the deeper into the wood the depleted train went, the more ancient, the more uncanny it became.

Duiker led his mare by the reins, stumbling as rocks turned underfoot. Alongside him clattered a wagon, sagging with wounded soldiers. Corporal List sat on the buckboard, his switch snapping the dusty, sweat-runnelled backs of the pair of oxen labouring at their yokes.

The losses at Vathar Crossing were a numb litany in the historian's mind. Over twenty thousand refugees, a disproportionate number of children among them. Less than five hundred able fighters remained in the Foolish Dog Clan, and the other two clans were almost as badly mauled. Seven hundred soldiers of the Seventh were dead, wounded or lost. A scant dozen engineers remained on their feet, and but a score of marines. Three noble families had been lost – an unacceptable attrition, this latter count, as far as the Council was concerned.

And Sormo E'nath. Within the one man, eight elder warlocks, a loss of not just power, but knowledge, experience and wisdom. A blow that had driven the Wickans to their knees.

Earlier that day, at a time when the train had ground to a temporary halt, Captain Lull had joined the historian to share some rations. Few words passed between them to start, as if the events at Vathar Crossing were something not to be talked about, even as they spread like a plague through every thought and echoed ghostlike behind every scene around them, every sound that rose from the camp.

Lull slowly put away the remnants of their meal. Then he paused, and Duiker saw the man studying his own hands, which had begun trembling. The historian looked away, surprised at the sudden shame that swept through him. He saw List, wrapped in sleep on the buckboard, trapped within his prison of dreams. *I could in mercy awaken the lad, yet the power for knowledge has mastered me. Cruelty comes easy these days.*

The captain sighed after a moment, hastily completing the task. 'Do you find the need to answer all this, Historian?' he asked. 'All those tomes you've read, those other thoughts from other men, other women. Other times. How does a mortal make answer to what his or her kind are capable of? Does each of us, soldier or no, reach a point when all that we've seen, survived, changes us inside? Irrevocably changes us. What do we become, then? Less human, or *more* human? Human enough, or too human?'

Duiker was silent for a long minute, his eyes on the rock-studded dirt that surrounded the boulder upon which he sat. Then he cleared his throat. 'Each of us has his own threshold, friend. Soldier or no, we can only take so much before we cross over . . . into something else. As if the world has shifted around us, though it's only our way of looking at it. A change of perspective, but there's no intelligence to it – you see but do not feel, or you weep yet look upon your own anguish as if from somewhere else, somewhere outside. It's not a place for answers, Lull, for every question has burned away. More human or less human – that's for you to decide.'

'Surely it has been written of, by scholars, priests . . . philosophers?'

Duiker smiled down at the dirt. 'Efforts have been made. But those who themselves have crossed that threshold . . . well, they have few words to describe the place they've found, and little inclination to attempt to explain it. As I said, it's a place without intelligence, a place where thoughts wander, formless, unlinked. Lost.'

'Lost,' the captain repeated. 'I am surely that.'

'Yet you and I, Lull, we are lost late in our lives. Look upon the children, and despair.'

'How to answer this? I must know, Duiker, else I go mad.'

'Sleight of hand,' the historian said.

'What?'

'Think of the sorcery we've seen in our lives, the vast, unbridled, deadly power we've witnessed unleashed. Driven to awe and horror. Then think of a trickster – those you saw as a child – the games of illusion and artifice they could play out with their hands, and so bring wonder to your eyes.'

The captain was silent, motionless. Then he rose. 'And there's my answer?'

'It's the only one I can think of, friend. Sorry if it's not enough.'

'No, old man, it's enough. It has to be, doesn't it?'

'Aye, that it does.'

'Sleight of hand.'

The historian nodded. 'Ask for nothing more, for the world – this world – won't give it.'

'But where will we find such a thing?'

'Unexpected places,' Duiker replied, also rising. Somewhere ahead, shouts rose and the convoy resumed its climb once more. 'If you fight both tears and a smile, you'll have found one.'

'Later, Historian.'

'Aye.'

He watched the captain set off back towards his company of soldiers, and wondered if all he'd said, all he'd offered to the man, was nothing but lies.

The possibility returned to him now, hours later as he trudged along on the trail. One of those random, unattached thoughts that were coming to characterize the blasted scape of his mind. Returned, lingered a moment, then drifted away and was gone.

The journey continued, beneath clouds of dust and a few remaining butterflies.

Korbolo Dom pursued, sniping at the train's mangled tail, content to await better ground before another major engagement. Perhaps even he quailed at what Vathar Forest had begun to reveal.

Among the tall cedars there were trees of some other species that had turned to stone. Gnarled and twisted, the petrified wood embraced objects that were themselves fossilized – the trees held offerings and had, long ago, grown around them. Duiker well recalled the last time he had seen such things, in what had been a holy place in the heart of an oasis, just north of Hissar. That site had revealed ram's horns locked in the wrapped crooks of branches, and there were plenty of those here as well, although they were the least disquieting of Vathar's offerings.

T'lan Imass. No room for doubt – their undead faces stare out at us, from all sides, skulls and withered faces peering out from wreaths of crystallized bark, the dark pits of their eyes tracking our passage. This is a burial ground, not of the flesh-and-blood forebears of the T'lan Imass, but of the deathless creatures themselves.

List's visions of ancient war – we see here its aftermath. Crumpled platforms were visible as well, stone latticework perched amidst branches that had once grown around them, closing up the assembled bones like the fingers of stone hands.

At the war's end, the survivors came here, carrying those comrades too shattered to continue, and made of this forest their eternal home. The souls of the T'lan Imass cannot join Hood, cannot even flee their prisons of bone and withered flesh. One does not bury such things – that sentence of earthen darkness offers no peace. Instead, let those remnants look out from their perches upon one another, upon the rare mortal passages on this trail . . .

Corporal List saw far too clearly, his visions delivering him deep into a history better left lost. Knowledge had beaten him down – *as it does us all, when delivered in too great a measure. Yet I hunger still.*

Cairns had begun appearing, heaps of boulders surmounted with totemic skulls. *Not barrows*, List had said. *Sites of engagement, the various clans, wherever the Jaghut turned from flight and lashed out.*

The day was drawing to a close when they reached the final height, a broad, jumbled basolith that seemed to have shed its limestone coat, the exposed bedrock deeply hued the colour of wine. Flat, treeless stretches were crowded with boulders set out in spirals, ellipses and corridors. Cedars were replaced by pines, and the number of petrified trees diminished.

Duiker and List had been travelling in the last third of the column, the wounded shielded by a battered rearguard of infantry. Once the last of the wagons and the few livestock that remained cleared the slope and made level ground, the footmen quickly gained the ridge, squads scattering to various vantage points and potential strongholds commanding the approach.

List halted his wagon and set the brake, then rose from the buckboard, stretched and looked down at Duiker with haunted eyes.

'Better lines of sight up here, anyway,' the historian offered.

'Always has been,' the corporal said. 'If we make for the head of the column, we'll come to the first of them.'

'The first of what?'

The blood leaving the lad's face bespoke another vision flooding his mind, a world and a time seen through unhuman eyes. After a moment he shuddered, wiping sweat from his face. 'I'll show you.'

They moved through the quiet press in silence. The efforts at making camp they saw on all sides looked wooden, refugees and soldiers alike moving as automatons. No-one bothered attempting to erect tents; they simply laid out their bedrolls on the flat rock. Children sat unmoving, watching with the eyes of old men and women.

The Wickan camps were no better. There was no escape from what had been, from the images and remembered scenes that rose again and again, remorselessly, before the mind's eye. Every frail, mundane gesture of normal life had shattered beneath the weight of knowledge.

Yet there was anger, white hot and buried deep, out of sight, as if mantled in peat. It had become the last fuel with any potency. *And so we move on, day after day, fighting every battle – those inside and those without – with an unyielding ferocity and determination. We are all in that place where Lull now lives, a place stripped of rational thought, trapped in a world without cohesion.*

Arriving at the vanguard, they came upon a scene. Coltaine, Bult and Captain Lull were present, and facing them in a ragged line ten paces away were the last of the Engineers.

The Fist turned as Duiker and List approached. 'Ah, this is well. I would have you witness this, Historian.'

'What have I missed?'

Bult grinned. 'Nothing; we've just managed the prodigious task of assembling the sappers – you'd think battles with Kamist Reloe were tactical nightmares. Anyway, here they are, looking like they're waiting to be ambushed, or worse.'

'And are they, Uncle?'

The commander's grin broadened. 'Maybe.'

Coltaine now stepped towards the assembled soldiers. 'Symbols of bravery and gestures of recognition can only ring hollow – this I know, yet what else is left to me? Three clan leaders have come to me, each begging to approach you men and women with an offer of formal adoption to their clan. Perhaps you are unaware of what such unprecedented requests reveal ... or perhaps, judging by your expressions, you know. I felt need to answer on your behalf, for I know more of you soldiers than do most Wickans, including those clan leaders, and they have each humbly withdrawn their requests.'

He was silent for a long moment.

'Nonetheless,' Coltaine finally continued, 'I would have you know, they meant to honour you.'

Ah, Coltaine, even you do not understand these soldiers well enough. Those scowls you see arrayed before you certainly look like disapproval, disgust even, but then, when have you ever seen them smile?

'So, I am left with the traditions of the Malazan Empire. There were enough witnesses at the Crossing to weave in detail the tapestry of your deeds, and among all of you, including your fallen comrades, the natural leadership of one was noted again and again. Without it, the day would have been truly lost.'

The sappers did not move, their scowls if anything deeper, more fierce.

Coltaine moved to stand before one man. Duiker recalled him well – a squat, hairless, immeasurably ugly sapper, his eyes thin slashes, his nose a flattened spread of angles and crooks. Audaciously, he wore fragments of armour that Duiker recognized as taken from a commander of the Apocalypse, though the helm tied to his belt was something that could have adorned an antique shop in Darujhistan. Another object that hung from his belt was difficult to identify, and it was a moment before the historian realized he was looking at the battered remnant of a shield: two reinforced grips behind a mangled plate-sized flap of bronze. A large, blackened crossbow hung from one shoulder, so covered and entwined with twigs, branches and other camouflage as to make it seem the man carried a bush.

'I believe the time has come,' Coltaine said, 'for a promotion. You are now a sergeant, soldier.'

The man said nothing, his eyes narrowing to the thinnest of slits.

'I think a salute would be appropriate,' Bult growled.

One of the other sappers cleared his throat and nervously yanked at his moustache.

Captain Lull rounded on the man. 'Got something to say about this, soldier?'

'Not much,' the man muttered.

'Out with it.'

The soldier shrugged. 'Well, only . . . he was a captain not two minutes ago, sir. The Fist's just demoted him. That's Captain Mincer, sir. Commands the Engineers. Or did.'

Mincer finally spoke. 'And since I'm now a sergeant, I suggest the captaincy go to this soldier.' He reached out and grabbed the woman beside him by the ear to drag her close. 'What used to be *my* sergeant. Name's Bungle.'

Coltaine stared a moment longer, then swung around and met Duiker's eyes with such comic pleasure that the historian's exhaustion was simply swept away, flashburned into oblivion. The Fist struggled to keep a straight face, and Duiker bit his lip in his own effort. His gaze caught on Lull, whose face showed the same struggle, even as the captain winked and mouthed three silent words.

Sleight of hand.

The question remained how Coltaine would now play it. Composing his face into stern regard, the Fist turned about again. He eyed Mincer, then the woman named Bungle. 'That will be fine, Sergeant,' he said. 'Captain Bungle, I would advise you to listen to your sergeant in all matters. Understood?'

The woman shook her head.

Mincer grimaced and said, 'She's no experience with that, Fist. I never asked *her* advice, I'm afraid.'

'From what I have gathered, you never asked *anyone's* advice when you were captain.'

'Aye, that's a fact.'

'Nor did you attend any staff briefings.'

'No, sir.'

'And why was that?'

Mincer shrugged.

Captain Bungle spoke. 'Beauty sleep, sir. That's what he always said.'

'Hood knows the man needs it,' Bult muttered.

Coltaine raised an eyebrow. 'And did he sleep, Captain? During those times?'

'Oh yes, sir. He sleeps when we march, too, sir. Sleeps while walking – I've never seen the like. Snoring away, sir, one foot in front of the other, a bag full of rocks on his back—'

'Rocks?'

'For when he breaks his sword, sir. He throws them, and there ain't a damned thing he can't hit.'

'Wrong,' Mincer growled. 'That lapdog . . .'

Bult seemed to choke, then spat in sympathy.

Coltaine had drawn his hands behind him, and Duiker saw them clench in a white-knuckled grip. As if sensing that attention, the Fist called out without turning, 'Historian!'

'I am here, Fist.'

'You will record this?'

'Oh, aye, sir. Every blessed word.'

'Excellent. Engineers, you are dismissed.'

The group wandered off, muttering. One man clapped Mincer on the shoulder and received a blistering glare in return.

Coltaine watched them leave, then strode to Duiker, Bult and Lull following.

'Spirits below!' Bult hissed.

Duiker smiled. 'Your soldiers, Commander.'

'Aye,' he said, suddenly beaming with pride. 'Aye.'

'I did not know what to do,' Coltaine confessed.

Lull grunted. 'You played it perfectly, Fist. That was

exquisite, no doubt already making the rounds as a Hood-damned full-blown legend. If they liked you before, they love you now, sir.'

The Wickan remained baffled. 'But why? I just demoted a man for unsurpassed bravery!'

'Returned him to the ranks, you mean. And that lifted every one of 'em up, don't you see that?'

'But Mincer—'

'Never had so much fun in his life, I'd bet. You can tell, when they get even uglier. Hood knows, I can't explain it – only sappers know a sapper's way of thinking and behaving, and sometimes not even them.'

'You've a captain named Bungle, now, nephew,' Bult said. 'Think she'll be there in polish and shine next briefing?'

'Not a chance,' Lull opined. 'She's probably packing her gear right now.'

Coltaine shook his head. 'They win,' he said, in evident wonder. 'I am defeated.'

Duiker watched the three men walk away, still discussing what had just happened. *Not lies after all. Tears and smiles, something so small, so absurd . . . the only possible answer . . .* The historian shook himself, and looked around until he found List. 'Corporal, I recall you had something to show me . . .'

'Yes, sir. Up ahead, not far, I think.'

They came to the ruined tower before reaching the forward outlying pickets. A squad of Wickans had commandeered the position, filling the ringed bedrock floor with supplies and leaving in attendance a lone, one-armed youth.

List laid a hand on one of the massive foundation stones. 'Jaghut,' he said. 'They lived apart, you know. No villages, no cities, just single, remote dwellings. Like this one.'

'Enjoyed their privacy, I take it.'

'They feared each other almost as much as they feared the T'lan Imass, sir.'

Duiker glanced over at the Wickan youth. The lad was fast asleep. *We're doing a lot of that these days. Just dropping off.* 'How old?' he asked the corporal.

'Not sure. A hundred, two, maybe even three.'

'Not years.'

'No. Millennia.'

'So, this is where the Jaghut lived.'

'The first tower. From here, pushed back, then again, then again. The final stand – the last tower – is in the heart of the plain beyond the forest.'

'Pushed back,' the historian repeated.

List nodded. 'Each siege lasted centuries, the losses among the T'lan Imass staggering. Jaghut were anything but wanderers. When they chose a place . . .' His voice fell off. He shrugged.

'Was this a typical war, Corporal?'

The young man hesitated, then shook his head. 'A strange bond, unique among the Jaghut. When the mother was in peril, the children returned, joined the battle. Then the father. Things . . . escalated.'

Duiker nodded, looked around. 'She must have been . . . special.'

Tight-lipped and pale, List pulled off his helm, ran a hand through his sweaty hair. 'Aye,' he finally whispered.

'Is she your guide?'

'No. Her mate.'

Something made the historian turn, as if in answer to a barely felt shiver of air. North, through the trees, then above them. His mind struggled to encompass what he saw: a column, a spear lit gold, rising . . . rising.

'Hood's breath!' List muttered. 'What is that?'

A lone word thundered through Duiker, flooding his mind,

driving out every thought, and he knew with utter certainty the truth of it, the single word that was answer to List's question.

'Sha'ik.'

Kalam sat in his gloomy cabin, inundated with the sound of hammering waves and shrieking wind. *Ragstopper* shuddered with every remorseless crash of the raging seas, the room around the assassin pitching in, it seemed, a dozen directions at once.

Somewhere in their wake, a fast trader battled the same storm, and her presence – announced by the lookout only minutes before the green and strangely luminescent cloud rolled over them – gnawed at Kalam, refusing to go away. *The same fast trader we'd seen before. Was the answer a simple one? While we squatted in that shithole of a home port, she'd been calmly shouldering the Imperial pier at Falar, no special rush in resupplying when you have a shore leave worth the name.*

But that did not explain the host of other details that plagued the assassin – details that, each on their own, rang a minor note of discord, yet together they created a cacophony of alarm in Kalam. Blurred passages of time, perhaps born of the man's driving aspiration to complete this voyage, at war with the interminable reality of day upon day, night upon night, the very sameness of such a journey.

But no, there's more than just a conflict of perspective. The hourglasses, the dwindled stores of food and fresh water, the captain's tortured hints of a world amiss aboard this damned ship.

And that fast trader, it should have sailed past us long ago . . .

Salk Elan. A mage – he stinks of it. Yet a sorcerer who could twist an entire crew's mind so thoroughly . . . that sorcerer would have to be a High Mage. Not impossible. Just highly unlikely among Mebra's covert circle of spies and agents.

There was no doubt in Kalam's mind that Elan had woven about himself a web of deceit, inasmuch as it was in such a man's nature to do so, whether necessary or not. Yet which strand should the assassin follow in his quest for the truth?

Time. How long has this journey been? Tradewinds where none should be, now a storm, driving us ever southeastward, a storm that had therefore not come from the ocean wastes – as the immutable laws of the sea would demand – but from the Falari Isles. In its dry season – a season of unbroken calm.

So, who plays with us here? And what role does Salk Elan have in this game, if any?

Growling, the assassin rose from his bunk, grabbing in mid-swing his satchel from its hook, then made his rocking way to the door.

The hold was like a siege tower under a ceaseless barrage of rocks. Mist filled the salty, close air and the keel was awash in shin-deep water. There was no-one about, every hand committed to the daunting task of holding *Ragstopper* together. Kalam cleared a space and dragged a chest free. He rummaged in his satchel until his hand found and closed on a small, misshapen lump of stone. He drew it out and set it on the chest-top.

It did not roll off; indeed, it did not move at all.

The assassin unsheathed a dagger, reversed his grip, then drove the iron pommel down on the stone. It shattered. A gust of hot, dry air washed over Kalam. He crouched lower.

'Quick! Quick Ben, you bastard, now's the time!'

No voice reached him through the storm's incessant roar.

I'm beginning to hate mages. 'Quick Ben, damn you!'

The air seemed to waver, like streams of heat rising from a desert floor. A familiar voice tickled the assassin's ears. 'Any idea the last time I've had a chance to sleep? It's all gone to Hood's shithole over here, Kalam – where are you and what do you want? And hurry up with it – this is killing me!'

'I thought you were my shaved knuckle in the hole, damn you!'

'You in Unta? The palace? I never figured—'

'Thanks for the vote of confidence,' the assassin cut in. 'No, I'm not in the Hood-cursed palace, you idiot. I'm at sea—'

'Aren't we all. You've just messed up, Kalam – I can't do this more than once.'

'I know. So I'm on my own when I get there. Fine, nothing new in that. Listen, what can you sense of where I am at this moment? Something's gone seriously awry on this ship, and I want to know what, and who's responsible.'

'Is that all? OK, OK, give me a minute . . .'

Kalam waited. The hair rose on his neck as he felt his friend's presence fill the air on all sides, a probing emanation that the assassin knew well. Then it was gone.

'Uh.'

'What does *that* mean, Quick?'

'You're in trouble, friend.'

'Laseen?'

'Not sure. Not directly – that ship stinks of a warren, Kalam, one of the rarest among mortals. Been confused lately, friend?'

'I was right, then! Who?'

'Someone, maybe on board, maybe not. Maybe sailing a craft within that warren, right alongside you, only you'll never see it. Anything valuable aboard?'

'You mean apart from my hide?'

'Yes, apart from your hide, of course.'

'Only a despot's ransom.'

'Ah, and someone wants it getting somewhere fast, and when it gets there that someone wants every damned person on board to forget where that place is. That's my guess, Kalam. I could be very wrong, though.'

'That's a comfort. You said you're in trouble over there? Whiskeyjack? Dujek, the squad?'

'Scraping through so far. How's Fiddler?'

'No idea. We decided on separate ways . . .'

'Oh no, Kalam!'

'Aye, Tremorlor. Hood's breath, it was your idea, Quick!'

'Assuming the House was . . . at peace. Sure, it should've

772

worked. Absolutely. I think. But something's gone bad there – every warren's lit up, Kalam. Chanced on a Deck of Dragons lately?'

'No.'

'Lucky you.'

Realization struck the assassin with a sharply drawn breath. 'The Path of Hands . . .'

'The Path . . . oh.' The mage's voice rose, 'Kalam! If you knew—'

'We didn't *know* a damned thing, Quick!'

'They might have a chance,' Quick Ben muttered a moment later. 'With Sorry—'

'Apsalar, you mean.'

'Whatever. Let me think, damn you.'

'Oh, terrific,' Kalam growled. 'More schemes . . .'

'I'm losing hold here, friend. Too tired . . . lost too much blood yesterday, I think. Mallet says . . .'

The voice trailed away. Cool mist seeped back in around the assassin. Quick Ben was gone. *And that's that. On my own in truth, now. Fiddler . . . oh, you bastard, we should have guessed, figured it out. Ancient gates . . . Tremorlor.*

He did not move for a long time. Finally he sighed, wiped the top of the chest, removing the last of the crushed rock from its damp surface, and rose.

The captain was awake, and he had company. Salk Elan grinned as Kalam entered the cramped room. 'We were just talking about you, partner,' Elan said. 'Knowing how set you get in your mind, and wondering how you'd take the news . . .'

'All right, I'll bite. What news?'

'This storm – we're being blown off course. A long way.'

'Meaning?'

'Seems we'll be making for a different port once it's spent.'

'Not Unta.'

'Oh, eventually, of course.'

The assassin's gaze fell to the captain. He looked unhappy, but resigned. Kalam conjured a map of Quon Tali in his mind, studied it a moment, then sighed. 'Malaz City. The island.'

'Never seen that legendary cesspool before,' Elan said. 'I can't wait. I trust you'll be generous enough to show me all the sights, friend.'

Kalam stared at the man, then smiled. 'Count on it, Salk Elan.'

They had paused for a rest, almost inured to the curdling cries and screams rising from other paths of the maze. Mappo lowered Icarium to the ground and knelt beside his unconscious friend. Tremorlor's desire for the Jhag was palpable. The Trell closed his eyes. *The Nameless Ones have guided us here, delivering Icarium to the Azath as they would a goat to a hill god. Yet it is not their hands that will be bloodied by the deed. I am the one who will be stained by this.*

He struggled to conjure the image of the destroyed town – his birthplace – but it was now haunted by shadows. Doubt had replaced conviction. He no longer believed his own memories. *Foolish! Icarium has taken countless lives. Whatever the truth behind my town's death . . .*

His hands clenched.

My tribe – the shoulder-women – would not betray me. What weight can be placed on Icarium's dreams? The Jhag remembers nothing. Nothing real. His equanimity softens truth, blurs the edges . . . smears every colour, until the memory is daubed anew. Thus. It is Icarium's kindness that has snared me . . .

Mappo's fists ached. He looked down at his companion, studied the expression of peaceful repose on the Jhag's blood-smeared face.

Tremorlor shall not have you. I am not to be so used. If the

Nameless Ones would deliver you, then they shall have to come for you themselves, and through me first.

He looked up, glared into the heart of the maze. *Tremorlor. Reach for him with your roots, and they shall feel the rage of a Trell warrior, his battle dream unleashed, ancient spirits riding his flesh in a dance of murder. This I promise, and so you are warned.*

'It's said,' Fiddler murmured beside him, 'that the Azath have taken gods.'

Mappo fixed the soldier with hooded eyes.

Fiddler squinted as he studied the riotous walls on all sides. 'What Elder gods – their names forgotten for millennia – are caged here? When did they last see light? When were they last able to move their limbs? Can you imagine an eternity thus endured?' He shifted the weight of the crossbow in his hands. 'If Tremorlor dies . . . imagine the madness unleashed upon the world.'

The Trell was silent for a moment, then he whispered, 'What are these darts that you fling at me?'

Fiddler's brows rose. 'Darts? None intended. This place sits on me like a cloak of vipers, that is all.'

'Tremorlor has no hunger for you, soldier.'

Fiddler's grin was crooked. 'Sometimes it pays being a nobody.'

'Now you mock in truth.'

The sapper's grin fell away. 'Widen your senses, Trell. Tremorlor's is not the only hunger here. Every prisoner in these walls of wood feels our passage. They might well flinch from you and Icarium, but no such fear constrains their regard for the rest of us.'

Mappo looked away. 'Forgive me. I've spared little thought for anyone else, as you have noted. Still, do not think I would hesitate in defending you if the need arose. I am not one to diminish the honour that is your companionship.'

Fiddler gave a sharp nod, straightened. 'A soldier's pragmatism. I had to know one way or the other.'

'I understand.'

'Sorry if I offended you.'

'Naught but a knife-tip's prod – you've stirred me to wakefulness.'

Iskaral Pust, squatting a few paces away, sputtered. 'Muddy the puddle, oh yes! Yank his loyalties this way and that – excellent! Witness the strategy of silence – while the intended victims unravel each other in pointless, divisive discourse. Oh yes, I have learned much from Tremorlor, and so assume a like strategy. Silence, a faint mocking smile suggesting I know more than I do, an air of mystery, yes, and fell knowledge. None could guess my confusion, my host of deluded illusions and elusive delusions! A mantle of marble hiding a crumbling core of sandstone. See how they stare at me, wondering – all wondering – at my secret wellspring of wisdom . . .'

'Let's kill him,' Crokus muttered, 'if only to put him out of our misery.'

'And sacrifice such entertainment?' Fiddler growled. He resumed his place at point. 'Time to go.'

'The blathering of secrets,' the High Priest of Shadow uttered in a wholly different voice, 'so they judge me ineffectual.'

The others spun to face him.

Iskaral Pust offered a beatific smile.

A swarm of wasps rose above the tangled root wall, sped over their heads and past – paying them no heed. Fiddler felt his heart thud back into place. He drew a shuddering breath. There were some D'ivers that he feared more than others. *Beasts are one thing, but insects . . .*

He glanced back at the others. Icarium hung limp in Mappo's arms. The Jhag's head was stained with blood. The Trell's gaze reached beyond the sapper to the edifice that awaited them. Mappo's expression was twisted with anguish, so thoroughly unmasked and vulnerable that the Trell's face was a child's face, with an attendant need that was all the more demanding for being wholly unconscious. A mute appeal that was difficult to resist.

Fiddler shook himself, pushing his attention past Mappo and his burden. Apsalar, her father and Crokus stood ranged behind the Trell in a protective cordon while beyond them were the Hounds and Iskaral Pust. Five pairs of bestial eyes and one human burned with intent – *dubious allies, our rearguard. Talk about a badly timed schism* – and that intent was fixed on the unconscious body in Mappo's arms.

Icarium himself wished it, and in so saying rendered the Trell's heart. The price of acquiescence is as nothing to the pain of refusal. Yet Mappo will surrender his life to this, and we're likely to do the same. None of us – not even Apsalar – is cold-hearted enough to stand back, to see the Jhag taken. Hood's breath, we are fools, and Mappo the greatest fool of us all . . .

'What's on your mind, Fid?' Crokus asked, his tone suggesting he had a pretty good idea.

'Sappers got a saying,' he muttered. 'Wide-eyed stupid.'

The Daru slowly nodded.

In other paths of the maze, the taking had begun. Shapeshifters – the most powerful of them, the survivors who'd made it this far – had begun their assault on the House of the Azath. A cacophony of screams echoed in the air, battering their senses. Tremorlor defended itself the only way it could, by devouring, by imprisoning – *but there are too many, coming too quickly* – wood snapped, woven cages shattered, the sound was of a forest being destroyed, branch by branch, tree by tree, an inexorable progression, closer, ever closer to the House itself.

'We're running out of time!' hissed Iskaral Pust, the Hounds moving in agitation around him. 'Things are coming up behind us. *Things!* How much clearer can I be?'

'We may still need him,' Fiddler said.

'Oh, aye!' the High Priest responded. 'The Trell can throw him like a sack of grain!'

'I can bring him around quickly enough,' Mappo growled. 'I still carry some of those Denul elixirs from your temple, Iskaral Pust.'

'Let's get moving,' the sapper said. Something was indeed coming up behind them, making the air redolent with sickly spice. The Hounds had pulled their attention from Mappo and Icarium and now faced the other way, revealing restless nerves as they shifted position. The trail made a sharp bend twenty paces from where the huge beasts stood.

A piercing scream ripped the air, coming from just beyond that bend, followed by the explosive sounds of battle. It ended abruptly.

'We've waited too long!' Pust hissed, cowering behind his god's Hounds. 'Now it comes!'

Fiddler swung his crossbow around, eyes fixed on the place where their pursuer would appear.

Instead, a small, nut-brown creature half flapped, half scampered into view. Tendrils of smoke drifted from it.

'Ai!' Pust shrieked. 'They plague me!'

Crokus bolted forward, pushing his way between Shan and Gear as if they were no more than a pair of mules. 'Moby?'

The familiar raced towards the Daru and leapt at the last moment to land in the lad's arms. Where it clung tenaciously, wings twitching. Crokus's head snapped back. 'Ugh, you stink like the Abyss!'

Moby, that damned familiar . . . Fiddler's gaze flicked to Mappo. The Trell was frowning.

'Bhok'aral!' The word came from Iskaral Pust as a curse. 'A pet? A *pet*? Madness!'

'My uncle's familiar,' Crokus said, approaching.

The Hounds shrank from his path.

Oh, lad, much more than that, it seems.

778

'An ally, then,' Mappo said.

Crokus nodded, though with obvious uncertainty. 'Hood knows how he found us. How he survived . . .'

'Dissembler!' Pust accused, creeping towards the Daru. 'A familiar? Shall we ask the opinion of that dead shapeshifter back there? Oh no, we can't, can we? *It's been torn to pieces!*'

Crokus said nothing.

'Never mind,' Apsalar said. 'We're wasting time. To the House—'

The High Priest wheeled on her. 'Never mind? What conniving deceit has arrived among us? What foul betrayal hangs over us? There, hanging from the lad's shirt—'

'Enough!' Fiddler snapped. 'Stay here then, Pust. You and your Hounds.' The sapper faced the House again. 'What do you think, Mappo? Nothing's got close to it yet – if we make a run for it . . .'

'We can but try.'

'Do you think the door will open for us?'

'I do not know.'

'Let's find out, then.'

The Trell nodded.

They had a clear view of Tremorlor. A low wall surrounded it, made of what appeared to be volcanic rock, jagged and sharp. The only visible break in that wall was a narrow gate, over which arched a weave of vines. The House itself was tawny in colour, probably built of limestone, its entrance recessed between a pair of squat, asymmetrical two-storey towers, neither of which possessed windows. A winding path of flagstones connected the gate with the shadow-swallowed door. Low, gnarled trees occupied the yard, each surmounting a hump.

A sister to Deadhouse in Malaz City. Little different from the one in Darujhistan. All of a kind. All Azath – though where that name came from and how long ago no-one knows or will ever know.

Mappo spoke in a low voice beside the sapper. 'It's said the Azath bridge the realms – every realm. It's said that even time itself ceases within their walls.'

'And those doors open to but a few, for reasons unknown.' Fiddler scowled at his own words.

Apsalar moved to the front, stepping past the sapper.

Startled, Fiddler grunted. 'In a hurry, lass?'

She looked back at him. 'The one who possessed me, Fiddler . . . an Azath welcomed him, once.'

True enough. And why does that make me so nervous now, and here? 'So, how's it done? Special knock? Key under the loose flagstone?'

Her answering smile was a balm to his agitation. 'No, something much simpler. Audacity.'

'Well, we've plenty of that. We're here, aren't we?'

'Aye, we are.'

She led the way, and all followed.

'That conch shell,' Mappo rumbled. 'Immense damage was delivered to the Soletaken and D'ivers, is still being delivered, it seems – for the Azath, it may be proving enough.'

'And you pray that is so.'

'Aye, I do.'

'So why didn't that deathly song destroy us as well?'

'You are asking me, Fiddler? The gift was given to you, was it not?'

'Yes. I saved a little girl – kin to the Spiritwalker.'

'Which Spiritwalker, Fiddler?'

'Kimloc.'

The Trell was silent for half a dozen paces, then a frustrated growl rose from him. 'A girl, you said. No matter how close a kin, Kimloc's reward far outweighed your gesture. More, it seemed precisely intended for its use – the sorcery in that song was aspected, Fiddler. Tell me, did Kimloc know you sought Tremorlor?'

'I certainly didn't tell him as much.'

'Did he touch you at any time – the brush of a finger against your arm, anything?'

'He asked to, as I recall. He wanted my story. I declined. But Hood's breath, Mappo, I truly cannot recall if there was some chance contact.'

'I think there must have been.'

'If so, I forgive him the indiscretion.'

'I imagine he anticipated that as well.'

Even as Tremorlor withstood the assault that raged from all sides, the battles were far from over, and in some places the sound of shattering wood was a seemingly unstoppable progression, coming ever closer.

Apsalar increased pace as one of those unseen, sundering avalanches drew near the group, driving for the arched gate. A moment later, amidst a rising roar, they all broke into a run.

'Where?' Fiddler demanded as he scrambled forward, head darting as he searched frantically in all directions. 'Where in Hood's name is it?'

The answer came in a sudden sleet of ice-cold water from above, the savage opening of a warren. Emerging from within that hovering, strangely suspended spray – not fifty paces behind them – the enormous head and maw of a dhenrabi lunged into view, wreathed in uprooted sea grasses, kelp and strange, skeletal branches.

A swarm of wasps rose before it and was devoured entire without pause.

Three more dhenrabi appeared from that torrential portal. The roiling spume of water that held them seemed to burn off wherever it descended upon the roots of the maze, yet the creatures remained suspended, riding the hissing maelstrom.

Images flashed through Fiddler within the span of a single heartbeat. *Kansu Sea. Not a Soletaken after all – not a single beast, but a pack. A D'ivers. And I'm out of cussers—*

A moment later, it became clear just how untested the Hounds of Shadow had been thus far. He *felt* the power emanate from the five beasts – so similar was it to that of dragons, it rolled like a breath, a surge of raw sorcery that preceded the Hounds as they sprang forward with blurring speed.

Shan was the first to reach the lead dhenrabi, the first to plunge into its gaping, serrated mouth – and vanish within that yawning darkness. The creature reared back lightning-quick, and if that massive, blunt visage could show surprise, it did so now.

Gear reached the next one, and the dhenrabi lunged, not to swallow, but to bite down, to flense with the thousand jagged plates of its teeth. The Hound's power buckled under those snapping jaws, but did not shatter. An instant later, Gear was through, past those teeth, burying itself within the creature – where it delivered mayhem.

The other Hounds made for the remaining two dhenrabi. Only Blind remained with the group.

The lead dhenrabi began thrashing now, whipping its enormous bulk as the torrent of its warren collapsed around it – crushing flat walls of the maze, where long-imprisoned victims stirred amidst the wreckage, withered limbs reaching skyward through mud-churned water, clutching air. The second dhenrabi fell into the same writhing tumult.

A hand clutched Fiddler's arm, pulling him hard around.

'Come on,' Crokus hissed. Moby was still clinging to his shirt. 'We've got more company, Fid.'

And now the sapper saw the object of the Daru's attention – off to his right, almost behind Tremorlor, still a thousand paces distant, yet fast approaching. A swarm like no other. Bloodflies, in a solid black cloud the size of a thunderhead, billowing, surging towards them.

Leaving the dhenrabi in the throes of violent death behind them, the group sprinted for the House.

As he passed beneath the leafless arch of vines, the sapper saw Apsalar reach the door, close her hands on the broad, heavy ring-latch and twist it. He saw the muscles rise on her forearms, straining. Straining.

Then she staggered back a step, as if dismissively, contemptuously shoved. As Fiddler, trailed by Crokus, Mappo with his charge, Apsalar's father, then Pust and Blind, reached the flat, paved landing, he saw her spin round, her expression one of shock and disbelief.

It won't open. Tremorlor has refused us.

The sapper skidded to a halt, whirled.

The sky was black, alive, and coming straight for them.

At Vathar's sparse, blistered edge, where the basolith of bedrock sank once more beneath its skin of limestone, and the land that stretched southward before and below their vantage point was nothing but studded stones in windswept, parched clay, they came upon the first of the Jaghut tombs.

Few among the outriders and the column's head paid it much attention. It looked like nothing more than a cairn marker, a huge, elongated slab of stone tilted upward at the southernmost end, as if pointing the way across the Nenoth Odhan to Aren or some other, more recent destination.

Corporal List had led the historian to it in silence while the others prepared rigging to assist in the task of guiding the wagons down the steep, winding descent to the plain's barren floor.

'The youngest son,' List said, staring down at the primitive tomb. His face was frightening to look at, for it wore a father's grief, as raw as if the child's death was but yesterday – a grief that had, if anything, grown with the tortured, unfathomable passage of two hundred thousand years.

He stands guard still, that Jaghut ghost. The statement, a silent utterance that was both simple and obvious, nevertheless took the historian's breath away. *How to comprehend this . . .*

'How old?' Duiker's voice was as parched as the Odhan that awaited them.

'Five. The T'lan Imass chose this place for him. The effort of killing him would have proved too costly, given that the rest of the family still awaited them. So they dragged the child here – shattered his bones, every one, as many times as they could on so small a frame – then pinned him beneath this rock.'

Duiker had thought himself beyond shock, beyond even despair, yet his throat closed up at List's toneless words. The historian's imagination was too sharp for this, raising images in his mind that seared him with overwhelming sorrow. He forced himself to look away, watched the activities among the soldiers and Wickans thirty paces distant. He realized that they worked mostly in silence, speaking only as their tasks required, and then in low, strangely subdued tones.

'Yes,' List said. 'The father's emotions are a pall unrelieved by time – so powerful, so rending, those emotions, that even the earth spirits had to flee. It was that or madness. Coltaine should be informed – we must move quickly across this land.'

'And ahead? On the Nenoth plain?'

'It gets worse. It was not just the children that the T'lan Imass pinned – still breathing, still aware – beneath rocks.'

'But why?' The question ripped from Duiker's throat.

'Pogroms need no reason, sir, none that can weather challenge, in any case. Difference in kind is the first recognition, the only one needed, in fact. Land, domination, pre-emptive attacks – all just excuses, mundane justifications that do nothing but disguise the simple distinction. They are not us. We are not them.'

'Did the Jaghut seek to reason with them, Corporal?'

'Many times, among those not thoroughly corrupted by power – the Tyrants – but you see, there was always an arrogance in the Jaghut, and it was a kind that could claw its way up your back when face to face. Each Jaghut's interest was with him or herself. Almost exclusively. They viewed the T'lan Imass no differently from the way they viewed ants underfoot, herds on the grasslands, or indeed the grass itself. Ubiquitous, a feature of the landscape. A powerful, emergent people, such as the T'lan Imass were, could not but be stung—'

'To the point of swearing a deathless vow?'

'I don't believe that, at first, the T'lan Imass realized how difficult the task of eradication would be. Jaghut were very different in another way – they did not flaunt their power. And many of their efforts in self-defence were . . . passive. Barriers of ice – glaciers – they swallowed the lands around them, even the seas, swallowed whole continents, making them impassable, unable to support the food the mortal Imass required.'

'So they created a ritual that would make them immortal—'

'Free to blow like the dust – and in the age of ice, there was plenty of dust.'

Duiker's gaze caught Coltaine standing near the edge of the trail. 'How far,' he asked the man beside him, 'until we leave this area of . . . of sorrow?'

'Two leagues, no more than that. Beyond are Nenoth's true grasslands, hills . . . tribes, each one very protective of what little water they possess.'

'I think I had better speak with Coltaine.'

'Aye, sir.'

The Dry March, as it came to be called, was its own testament to sorrow. Three vast, powerful tribes awaited them, two of them, the Tregyn and the Bhilard, striking at the beleaguered column like vipers. With the third, situated at the very western edge of the plains – the Khundryl – there was no immediate contact, though it was felt that that would not last.

The pathetic herd accompanying the Chain of Dogs died on

that march, animals simply collapsing, even as the Wickan cattle-dogs converged with fierce insistence that they rise – dead or no – and resume the journey. When butchered, these carcasses were little more than ropes of leathery flesh.

Starvation joined the terrible ravaging thirst, for the Wickans refused to slaughter their horses and attended them with eloquent fanaticism that no-one dared challenge. The warriors sacrificed of themselves to keep their mounts alive. One petition from Nethpara's Council, offering to purchase a hundred horses, was returned to the nobleborn leader smeared in human excrement.

The twin vipers struck again and again, contesting every league, the attacks increasing in ferocity and frequency, until it was clear that a major clash approached, only days away.

In the column's wake followed Korbolo Dom's army, a force that had grown with the addition of forces from Tarxian and other coastal settlements, and was now at least five times the size of Coltaine's Seventh and his Wickan clans. The renegade commander's measured pursuit – leaving engagement to the wild plains tribes – was ominous in itself.

He would be there for the imminent battle, without doubt, and was content to wait until then.

The Chain of Dogs – its numbers swollen by new refugees fleeing Bylan – crawled on, coming within sight of what the maps indicated was the Nenoth Odhan's end, where hills rose in a wall across the southern horizon. The trader track cut through the only substantial passage, a wide river valley between the Bylan'sh Hills to the east and the Saniphir Hills to the west, the track running for seven leagues, opening out on a plain that faced the ancient tel of Sanimon, then wrapped around it to encompass the Sanith Odhan and, beyond that, the Geleen Plain, the Dojal Odhan – and the city of Aren itself.

No relief army emerged from Sanimon Valley. A profound

sense of isolation descended like a shroud on the train, even as the valley's flanking hills began to reveal, in the day's dying light, twin encampments, both vast, of tribesmen – the main forces of the Tregyn and the Bhilard.

Here, then, at the mouth of the ancient valley . . . here it would be.

'We're dying,' Lull muttered as he came up alongside the historian on his way to the briefing. 'And I don't mean just figuratively, old man. I lost eleven soldiers today. Throats swollen so bad with thirst they couldn't draw breath.' He waved at a fly buzzing his face. 'Hood's breath, I'm swimming in this armour – by the time we're done, we'll all look like T'lan Imass.'

'I can't say I appreciate the analogy, Captain.'

'Wasn't expecting you to.'

'Horse piss. That's what the Wickans are drinking these days.'

'Aye, same for my crew. They're neighing in their sleep, and more than one's died from it.'

Three dogs loped past them, the huge one named Bent, a female, and the lapdog scrambling in their wake.

'They'll outlive us all,' Lull grumbled. 'Those damned beasts!'

The sky deepened overhead, the first stars pushing through the cerulean gauze.

'Gods, I'm tired.'

Duiker nodded. *Oh, indeed, we've travelled far, friend, and now stand face to face with Hood. He takes the weary as readily as the defiant. Offers the same welcoming grin.*

'Something in the air tonight, Historian. Can you feel it?'

'Yes.'

'Maybe Hood's Warren has drawn closer.'

'It has that feel, doesn't it?'

They arrived at the Fist's command tent, entered.

The usual faces were arrayed before them. Nil and Nether, the last remaining warlocks; Sulmar and Chenned, Bult and Coltaine himself. Each had become a desiccated mockery of the will and strength once present in their varied miens.

'Where's Bungle?' Lull asked, finding his usual camp-chair.

'Listening to her sergeant, I'd guess,' Bult said, with a ghost of a grin.

Coltaine had no time for idle talk. 'Something approaches, this night. The warlocks have sensed it, though that is all they can say. We are faced with preparing for it.'

Duiker looked to Nether. 'What kind of sense?'

She shrugged, then sighed. 'Vague. Troubled, even outrage – I don't know, Historian.'

'Sensed anything like it before? Even remotely?'

'No.'

Outrage.

'Draw the refugees close,' Coltaine commanded the captains. 'Double the pickets—'

'Fist,' Sulmar said, 'we face a battle tomorrow—'

'Aye, and rest is needed. I know.' The Wickan began pacing, but it was a slower pace than usual. It had lost its smoothness as well, its ease and elegance. 'And more, we are greatly weakened – the water casks are bone dry.'

Duiker winced. *Battle? No, tomorrow will see a slaughter. Soldiers unable to fight, unable to defend themselves.* The historian cleared his throat, made to speak, then stopped. *One word, yet even to voice it would be to offer the cruellest illusion. One word.*

Coltaine was staring at him. 'We cannot,' he said softly.

I know. For the rebellion's warriors as much as for us, the end to this must be with blood.

'The soldiers are beyond digging trenches,' Lull said into the heavy, all-too-aware silence.

'Holes, then.'

'Aye, sir.'

Holes. To break mounted charges, snap legs, send screaming beasts into the dust.

The briefing ended then, abruptly, as the air was suddenly charged, and whatever threatened to arrive now announced itself with a brittle crackle, a mist of something oily, like sweat clogging the air.

Coltaine led the group outside, to find the bristling atmosphere manifested tenfold beneath the night's sparkling canopy. Horses bucked. Cattle-dogs howled.

Soldiers were rising like spectres. Weapons rustled.

In the open space just beyond the foremost pickets, the air split asunder with a savage, ripping sound.

Three pale horses thundered from that rent, followed by three more, then another three, all harnessed, all screaming with terror. Behind them came a massive carriage, a fire-scorched, gaudily painted leviathan riding atop six spoked wheels that were taller than a man. Smoke trailed like thick strands of raw wool from the carriage, from the horses themselves, and from the three figures visible behind the last three chargers.

The white, screaming train was at full gallop – as if in head-long flight from whatever warren it had come from – and the carriage pitched wildly, alarmingly, as the beasts plunged straight for the pickets.

Wickans scattered to either side.

Staring with disbelief, Duiker saw all three figures sawing the reins, bellowing, flinging themselves against the backrest of their tottering perch.

The horses drove hooves into the earth, biting down on their momentum, the towering carriage slewing behind them, raising a cloud of smoke, dust and an emanation that the historian recognized with a jolt of alarm as *outrage*. The outrage, he now understood, of a warren – and its god.

Behind the lead carriage came another, then another, each pitching to one side or the other to avoid collision as they skidded to a halt.

As soon as the lead carriage ceased its headlong plunge, figures poured from it, armoured men and women, shouting, roaring commands that no-one seemed to pay any attention to, and waving blackened, smeared and dripping weapons.

A moment later, even as the other two carriages stopped, a loud bell clanged.

The frenzied, seemingly aimless activities of the figures promptly ceased. Weapons were lowered, and sudden silence filled the air behind the fading echo of the bell. Snorting and stamping, the lathered horses tossed their heads, ears twitching, nostrils wide.

The lead carriage was no more than fifteen paces from where Duiker and the others stood.

The historian saw a severed hand clinging to an ornate projection on one side of the carriage. After a moment it fell to the ground.

A tiny barred door opened and a man emerged, with difficulty squeezing his considerable bulk through the aperture. He was dressed in silks that were drenched in sweat. His round, glistening face revealed the passing echoes of some immense, all-consuming effort. In one hand he carried a stoppered bottle.

Stepping clear, he faced Coltaine and raised the bottle. 'You, sir,' he said in strangely accented Malazan, 'have much to answer for.' Then he grinned, displaying a row of gold-capped, diamond-studded teeth. 'Your exploits tremble the warrens! Your journey is wildfire in every street in Darujhistan, no doubt in every city, no matter how distant! Have you no notion how many beseech their gods on your behalf? Coffers overflow! Grandiose plans of salvation abound! Vast organizations have formed, their leaders coming to us, to the Trygalle Trade Guild, to pay for our fraught passage – though,' he added in a lower tone, '*all* the Guild's passages are fraught, which is what makes us so expensive.' He unstoppered the bottle. 'The great city of Darujhistan and its remarkable citizens – dismissing in an instant your Empire's voracious desires on it and on themselves – bring you this gift! By way of the shareholders –' he waved back at the various men and women behind him, now gathering into a group – 'of Trygalle – the foulest-tempered, greediest creatures imaginable, but that is neither here nor there, for here we are, are we not? Let it not be said of the citizens of Darujhistan that they are insensitive to the wondrous, and, dear sir, you are truly wondrous.'

The preposterous man stepped forward, suddenly solemn. He spoke softly. 'Alchemists, mages, sorcerers have all contributed, offering vessels with capacities belying their modest containers. Coltaine of Crow Clan, Chain of Dogs, I bring you food. I bring you water.'

Karpolan Demesand was one of the original founders of the Trygalle Trade Guild, a citizen of the small fortress city of the same name, situated south of the Lamatath Plain on the continent of Genabackis. Born of a dubious alliance between a handful of mages, Karpolan among them, and the city's benefactors – a motley collection of retired pirates and wreckers – the Guild came to specialize in expeditions so risk-laden as to make the average merchant pale. Each caravan was protected by a heavily armed company of shareholders – guards who possessed a direct stake in the venture, ensuring the fullest exploitation of their abilities. And such abilities were direly needed, for the caravans of the Trygalle Trade Guild – as was clear from the very outset – travelled the warrens.

'We knew we had a challenge on our hands,' Karpolan Demesand said with a beatific, glittering smile as they sat in Coltaine's command tent, with only the Fist and Duiker for company because everyone else was working outside, dispensing the caravan's life-giving supplies with all speed. 'That foul Warren of Hood is wrapped about you tighter than a funeral shroud on a corpse . . . if you'll forgive the image. The key is to ride fast, to stop for nothing, then get out as soon as humanly possible. In the lead wagon, I maintain the road, with every sorcerous talent at my command – a gruelling journey, granted, but then again, we don't come cheap.'

'I still find it hard to fathom,' Duiker said, 'that the citizens of Darujhistan, fifteen hundred leagues distant, should even know of what's happening here, much less care.'

Karpolan's eyes thinned. 'Ah, well, perhaps I exaggerated somewhat – the heat of the moment, I confess. You must understand – soldiers who not long ago were bent on conquering Darujhistan are now locked in a war with the Pannion Domin, a tyranny that would dearly love to swallow the Blue City if it could. Dujek Onearm, once Fist of the Empire and now outlaw to the same, has become an ally. And this, certain personages in Darujhistan know well, and appreciate . . .'

'But there is more to it,' Coltaine said quietly.

Karpolan smiled a second time. 'Is this water not sweet? Here, let me pour you another cup.'

They waited, watching the trader refill the three tin cups arrayed on the small table between them. When he was done, Karpolan sighed and sat back in the plush chair he had had removed from the carriage. 'Dujek Onearm.' The name was spoken half in benediction, half in wry dismay. 'He sends his greetings, Fist Coltaine. Our office in Darujhistan is small, newly opened, you understand. We do not advertise our services. Not openly, in any case. Frankly, those services include activities that are, on occasion, clandestine in nature. We trade not only in material goods but in information, the delivery of gifts, of people themselves . . . and other creatures.'

'Dujek Onearm was the force behind this mission,' Duiker said.

Karpolan nodded. 'With financial assistance from a certain cabal in Darujhistan, yes. His words were thus: "The Empress cannot lose such leaders as Coltaine of the Crow Clan."' The trader grinned. 'Extraordinary for an outlaw under a death sentence, wouldn't you say?' He leaned forward and held out a hand, palm up. Something shimmered into existence on it, a small oblong bottle of smoky grey glass on a silver chain. 'And, from an alarmingly mysterious mage among the Bridgeburners, this gift was fashioned.' He held it out to Coltaine. 'For you. Wear it. At all times, Fist.'

The Wickan scowled and made no move to accept it.

Karpolan's smile was wistful. 'Dujek is prepared to pull rank on this, friend—'

'An outlaw pulling rank?'

'Ah, well, I admit I voiced the same query. His reply was this: "Never underestimate the Empress."'

Silence descended, the meaning behind that statement slowly taking shape. *Locked in a war against an entire continent . . . stumbling onto a recognition of an even greater threat – the Pannion Domin . . . shall the Empire alone fight on behalf of a hostile land? Yet . . . how to fashion allies among enemies, how to unify against a greater threat with the minimum of fuss and mistrust? Outlaw your occupying army, so they've 'no choice' but to step free of Laseen's shadow. Dujek, ever loyal Dujek – even the ill-conceived plan of killing the last of the Old Guard – Tayschrenn's foolishness and misguided idea – insufficient to turn him. So now he has allies – those who were once his enemies – perhaps even Caladan Brood and Anomander Rake themselves . . .* Duiker turned to Coltaine and saw the same knowledge there in his drawn, stern visage.

The Wickan reached out and received the gift.

'The Empress *must not* lose you, Fist. Wear it, sir. Always.

And when the time comes, break it – against your own chest. Even if it's your last act, though I suggest you do not leave it until then. Such were its creator's frantic instructions.' Karpolan grinned again. 'And such a man, that creator! A dozen Ascendants would dearly love his head served up on a plate, his eyes pickled, his tongue skewered and roasted with peppers, his ears grilled—'

'Your point is made,' Duiker cut in.

Coltaine placed the chain around his neck and slipped the bottle beneath his buckskin shirt.

'A dire battle awaits you come dawn,' Karpolan said after a time. 'I cannot stay, will not stay. Though mage of the highest order, though merchant of ruthless cunning, I admit to a streak of sentimentality, gentlemen. I will not stand witness to this tragedy. More, we have one more delivery to make before we begin our return journey, and its achievement shall demand all of my skills, indeed, may exhaust them.'

'I had never before heard of your Guild, Karpolan,' Duiker said, 'but I would hear more of your adventures, some day.'

'Perhaps the opportunity will arise, Historian. For now, I hear my shareholders gathering, and I must see to reviving and quelling the horses – although, it must be said, they seem to have acquired a thirst for wild terror. No different from us, eh?' He rose.

'My thanks to you,' Coltaine growled, 'and your shareholders.'

'Have you a word for Dujek Onearm, Fist?'

The Wickan's response startled Duiker, slipping a rough blade of suspicion into him that would remain, nagging and fearful.

'No.'

Karpolan's eyes widened momentarily, then he nodded. 'We must be gone, alas. May your enemy pay dearly come the morrow, Fist.'

'They shall.'

Sudden bounty could not affect complete rejuvenation, but the army that rose with the dawn revealed a calm readiness that Duiker had not seen since Gelor Ridge.

The refugees remained tightly packed in a basin just north of the valley mouth. The Weasel and Foolish Dog clans guarded the position, situating themselves along a rise that faced the assembled forces of Korbolo Dom. More than thirty rebel soldiers stood ready to challenge each and every Wickan horsewarrior, and the inevitable outcome of that clash was so obvious, so brutally clear, that panic ripped through the massed refugees in waves, hopeless rippling surges this way and that, and wails of despair filled the dust-laden air above them.

Coltaine sought to drive through the tribesmen blocking the valley mouth, and do so quickly, and he thus concentrated his Crow Clan and most of the Seventh at the front. A fast, shattering breakthrough offered the only hope for the rear-guard clans, and indeed for the refugees themselves.

Duiker sat on his emaciated mare, positioned on a low rise sightly to the east of the main track where he could just make out the two Wickan clans to the north – Korbolo Dom's army somewhere unseen beyond them.

The carriages of the Trygalle Trade Guild had departed, vanishing with the last minutes of darkness before the eastern horizon began its pale awakening.

Corporal List rode up, reining in beside the historian. 'A fine morning, sir!' he said. 'The season is turning – change rides the air – can you feel it?'

Duiker eyed the man. 'One as young as you should not be so cheerful this day, Corporal.'

'Nor one as old as you so dour, sir.'

'Hood-damned upstart, is this what familiarity breeds?'

List grinned, which was answer enough.

Duiker's eyes narrowed. 'And what has your Jaghut ghost whispered to you, List?'

'Something he himself never possessed, Historian. Hope.'

'Hope? How, from where? Does Pormqual finally approach?'

'I don't know about that, sir. You think it's possible?'

'No, I do not.'

'Nor I, sir.'

'Then what in Fener's hairy balls are you going on about, List?'

'Not sure, sir. I simply awoke feeling . . .' he shrugged, 'feeling as if we'd just been blessed, god-touched, or something . . .'

'A fine enough way to meet our last dawn,' Duiker muttered, sighing.

The Tregyn and Bhilard tribes were readying themselves, but the sudden blaring of horns from the Seventh made it clear that Coltaine was not interested in the courtesy of awaiting them. The Crow lancers and mounted archers surged forward, up the gentle slope towards the eastern hill of the Bhilard.

'Historian!'

Something in the corporal's tone brought Duiker around. List was paying no attention to the Crow's advance – he faced the northwest, where another tribe's riders had just appeared, spreading out as they rode closer in numbers of appalling vastness.

'The Khundryl,' Duiker said. 'Said to be the most powerful tribe south of Vathar – as we can now acknowledge.'

Horse hooves thundered towards the rise and they turned to see Coltaine himself approach. The Fist's expression was impassive, almost calm as he stared northwestward.

Clashes had begun at the rearguard position – the day's first drawing of blood, most of it likely to be Wickan. Already the refugees had begun pushing southward, in the hope that will alone could see the valley prised open.

The Khundryl, in the tens of thousands, formed two distinct

masses, one directly west of Sanimon's mouth, the other farther to the north, on a flank of Korbolo Dom's army. Between these two was a small knot of war chiefs, who now rode directly towards the rise where sat Duiker, List and Coltaine.

'Looks like personal combat is desired, Fist,' Duiker said. 'We'd best ride back.'

'No.'

The historian's head turned. Coltaine had uncouched his lance and was readying his black-feathered round shield on his left forearm.

'Damn you, Fist – this is madness!'

'Watch your tongue, Historian,' the Wickan said distractedly.

Duiker's gaze fixed on the short stretch of silver chain visible around the man's neck. 'Whatever that gift is that you're wearing, it'll only work once. What you do now is what a war chief of the Wickans would, but not a Fist of the Empire.'

The man snapped around at that and the historian found the barbed point of the lance pricking his throat.

'And just when,' Coltaine rasped, 'can I choose to die in the manner I desire? You think I will use this cursed bauble?' Freeing his shield hand, he reached up and tore the chain from his neck. 'You wear it, Historian. All that we have done avails the world naught, unless the tale is told. Hood take Dujek Onearm! Hood take the Empress!' He flung the bottle at Duiker and it struck unerringly the palm of his right hand. Fingers closing around the object, he felt the serpentine slither of chain against calluses. The lance-point kissing his neck had not moved.

Their eyes locked.

'Excuse me, sirs,' List said. 'It appears this is not an instance of desired combat. If you would both observe . . .'

Coltaine pulled the weapon away, swung around.

The Khundryl war chiefs waited in a row before them, not thirty paces away. They wore, beneath skins and furs and fetishes, a strange greyish armour that looked almost reptilian. Long moustaches, knotted beards and spiked braids – all black – disguised most of their features, though what remained visible was sun-darkened and angular.

One nudged his pony a step closer and spoke in broken Malazan. 'Blackwing! How think you the odds this day?'

Coltaine twisted in his saddle, studied the dust clouds now both north and south, then settled back. 'I would make no wager.'

'We have long awaited this day,' the war chief said. He stood in his stirrups and gestured to the south hills. 'Tregyn and Bhilard both, this day.' He waved northward. 'And Can'eld, and Semk, aye, even Tithansi – what's left, that is. The great tribes of the south odhans, yet who among them all is the most powerful? The answer is with this day.'

'You'd better hurry,' Duiker said. *We're running out of soldiers for you to show your prowess on, you pompous bastard.*

Coltaine seemed to have similar thoughts, though his temper was cooler. 'The question belongs to you, nor do I care either way its answer.'

'Are such concerns beyond the Wickan clans, then? Are you not yourselves a tribe?'

Coltaine slowly settled the lance's butt in its socket. 'No, we are soldiers of the Malazan Empire.'

Hood's breath, I got through to him.

The war chief nodded, unperturbed by that answer. 'Then be watchful, Fist Coltaine, while you attend to this day.'

The riders wheeled about, parting to rejoin their clans.

'I believe,' Coltaine said, looking around, 'you have selected a good vantage, Historian, so here shall I remain.'

'Fist?'

A faint smile touched his lean features. 'For a short time.'

* * *

The Crow Clan and the Seventh gave it their all, but the forces holding the mouth of the valley – from their high ground to either side and farther down the valley's throat – did not yield. The Chain of Dogs contracted between the hammer of Korbolo Dom and the anvil of the Tregyn and Bhilard. It was only a matter of time.

The actions of the Khundryl clans changed all that. For they had come, not to join in the slaughter of Malazans, but to give answer to the one question demanded of their pride and honour. The south mass struck the Tregyn position like a vengeful god's scythe. The north was a spear thrusting deep into Korbolo Dom's flank. A third, hitherto unseen force swept up from the valley itself, behind the Bhilard. Within minutes of the perfectly timed contacts, the Malazan forces found themselves unopposed, while the chaos of battle reigned on all sides.

Korbolo Dom's army quickly recovered, reforming with as much precision as they could muster, and drove back the Khundryl after more than four hours of pitched battle. One aim had been achieved, however, and that was the shattering of the Semk, the Can'eld and whatever was left of the Tithansi. *Half an answer*, Coltaine had muttered at that point, in a tone of utter bewilderment.

The southern forces broke the Tregyn and Bhilard an hour later, and set off in pursuit of the fleeing remnants.

With dusk an hour away, a lone Khundryl war chief rode up to them at a slow canter, and as he neared they saw that it was the spokesman. He'd been in a scrap and was smeared in blood, at least half of it his own, yet he rode straight in his saddle.

He reined in ten paces from Coltaine.

The Fist spoke. 'You have your answer, it seems.'

'We have it, Blackwing.'

'The Khundryl.'

Surprise flitted on the warrior's battered face. 'You honour us, but no. We strove to break the one named Korbolo Dom, but failed. The answer is not the Khundryl.'

'Then you do honour to Korbolo Dom?'

The war chief spat at that, growled his disbelief. 'Spirits below! You cannot be such a fool! The answer this day . . .' The war chief yanked free his tulwar from its leather sheath, revealing a blade snapped ten inches above the hilt. He raised it over his head and bellowed, '*The Wickans! The Wickans! The Wickans!*'

CHAPTER TWENTY

> This path's a dire thing,
> the gate it leads to
> is like a corpse
> over which ten thousand
> nightmares bicker
> their fruitless claims.
>
> *The Path*
> Trout Sen'al' Bhok'arala

Seagulls wheeled above them, the first they'd seen in a long while. The horizon ahead, on their course bearing of south by southeast, revealed an uneven smudge that grew steadily even as the day prepared for its swift demise.

Not a single cloud marred the sky and the wind was brisk and steady.

Salk Elan joined Kalam on the forecastle. Both of them were wrapped in cloaks against the rhythmic spray kicked up by *Ragstopper*'s headlong plunge into the troughs. To the sailors manning stations on the main deck and aft, the sight of them standing there at the bow like a pair of Great Ravens was black-wrought with omens.

Oblivious to all this, Kalam's gaze held on the island that awaited them.

'By midnight,' Salk Elan said with a loud sigh. 'Ancient birthplace of the Malazan Empire—'

The assassin snorted. 'Ancient? How old do you think the Empire is? Hood's breath!'

'All right, too romantic by far. I was but seeking a mood—'

'Why?' Kalam barked.

Elan shrugged. 'No particular reason, except perhaps this brooding atmosphere of anticipation, nay, impatience, even.'

'What's to brood about?'

'You tell me, friend.'

Kalam grimaced, said nothing.

'Malaz City,' Elan resumed. 'What should I expect?'

'Imagine a pigsty by the sea and that'll do. A rotten, festering bug-ridden swamp—'

'All right, all right! Sorry I asked!'

'The captain?'

'No change, alas.'

Why am I not surprised? Sorcery – gods, how I hate sorcery!

Salk Elan rested long-fingered hands on the rail, revealing once again his love of green-hued gems set in gaudy rings. 'A fast ship could take us across to Unta in a day and a half . . .'

'And how would you know that?'

'I asked a sailor, Kalam, how else? That salt-crusted friend of yours pretending to be in charge, what's his name again?'

'I don't recall asking.'

'It's a true, admirable talent, that.'

'What is?'

'Your ability to crush your own curiosity, Kalam. Highly practical in some ways, dreadfully risky in others. You're a hard man to know, harder even to predict—'

'That's right, Elan.'

'Yet you like me.'

'I do?'

'Aye, you do. And I'm glad, because it's important to me—'

'Go find a sailor if you're that way, Elan.'

The other man smiled. 'That is not what I meant, but of course you're well aware of that, you just can't help flinging darts. What I'm saying is, I enjoy being liked by someone I admire—'

Kalam spun around. 'What do you find so admirable, Salk Elan? In all your vague suppositions, have you discovered a belief that I'm susceptible to flattery? Why are you eager for a partnership?'

'Killing the Empress won't be easy,' the man replied. 'But just imagine succeeding! Achieving what all thought to be impossible! Oh yes, I want to be part of that, Kalam Mekhar! Right there alongside you, driving blades into the heart of the most powerful Empire in the world!'

'You've lost your mind,' Kalam said in a quiet voice, barely audible above the seas. 'Kill the Empress? Am I to join you in this madness? Not a chance, Salk Elan.'

'Spare me the dissembling,' he sneered.

'What sorcery holds this ship?'

Salk Elan's eyes widened involuntarily. Then he shook his head. 'Beyond my abilities, Kalam, and Hood knows I've tried. I've searched every inch of Pormqual's loot, and nothing.'

'The ship herself?'

'Not that I could determine. Look, Kalam, we're being tracked by someone in a warren – that's my guess. Someone who wants to make certain of that cargo. A theory only, but it's all I've got. Thus, friend, all my secrets unveiled.'

Kalam was silent a long moment, then he shook himself. 'I have contacts in Malaz City – an unexpected converging well ahead of schedule, but there it is.'

'Contacts, excellent – we'll need them. Where?'

'There's a black heart in Malaz City, the blackest. The one thing every denizen avoids mention of, wilfully ignores – and there, if all goes well, we will await our allies.'

'Let me guess: the infamous tavern called Smiley's, once owned by the man who would one day become an Emperor – the sailors tell me the food is quite awful.'

Kalam stared at the man in wonder. *Hood alone knows, either breathtakingly sardonic or . . . or what, by the Abyss?* 'No, a place called the Deadhouse. And not inside it, but at the gates, though by all means, Salk Elan, feel free to explore its yard.'

The man leaned both arms on the rail, squinting out at the dull lights of Malaz City. 'Assuming a long wait for your friends, perhaps I shall, perhaps I shall at that.'

It was unlikely he noticed Kalam's feral grin.

Iskaral Pust gripped the latch with both hands, his feet planted against the door, and, gibbering his terror, pulled frantically – to no avail. With a growl, Mappo stepped over Icarium where he lay at the foot of Tremorlor's entrance, and prised the High Priest from the unyielding barrier.

Fiddler heard the Trell straining at the latch, but the sapper's attention was fixed on the swarm of bloodflies. Tremorlor was resisting them, but the advance was inexorable. Blind stood at his side, head lifted, hackles raised. The four other Hounds had reappeared on the trail and were charging towards the yard's vine-wreathed gate. The shadow cast down by the D'ivers swept over them like black water.

'It either opens at the touch,' Apsalar said in a startlingly calm voice, 'or it does not open at all. Stand back, Mappo, let us all try.'

'Icarium stirs!' Crokus cried out.

'It's the threat,' the Trell answered. 'Gods below, not here, not now!'

'No better time!' Iskaral Pust shrieked.

Apsalar spoke again. 'Crokus, you're the last to try but Fiddler. Come here, quickly.'

The silence that followed told Fiddler all he needed to

know. He risked a glance back to where Mappo crouched over Icarium. 'Awaken him,' he said, 'or all is lost.'

The Trell lifted his face and the sapper saw the anguished indecision writ there. 'This close to Tremorlor – the risk, Fiddler—'

'What—'

But he got no further.

As if speared by lightning, the Jhag's body jolted, a high-pitched keening rising from him. The sound buffeted the others and sent them tumbling. Fresh blood streaming from the wound on his head and his eyes struggling to open, Icarium surged to his feet. The ancient single-edged long sword slipped free, the blade a strange, shivering blur.

The Hounds and the D'ivers swarm reached the yard simultaneously. The grounds and ragged trees erupted, chaotic webs of root and branch twisting skyward like black sails, billowing, spreading wide. Other roots snapped out for the Hounds – the beasts screamed. Blind was gone from Fiddler's side, down among her kin.

At that moment, in the midst of all he saw, Fiddler grinned inwardly. *Not just Shadowthrone for treachery – how could an Azath resist the Hounds of Shadow?*

A hand gripped his shoulder.

'The latch!' Apsalar hissed. 'Try the door, Fid!'

The D'ivers struck Tremorlor's last, desperate defence. Wood exploded.

The sapper was pushed against the door by a pair of hands on his back, catching a momentary glimpse of Mappo, his arms wrapped around a still mostly unaware Icarium, holding the Jhag back even as that keening sound rose and with it an overwhelming, inexorable power burgeoned. The pressure slapped Fiddler against the door's sweaty, dark wood and held him there in effortless contempt, whispering its promise of annihilation. He struggled to work his arm towards

805

the latch, straining every muscle to that single task.

Hounds howled from the farthest reaches of the yard, a triumphant, outraged sound that rose towards fear as Icarium's own rage swallowed all else. Fiddler felt the wood tremble, felt that tremble spread through the House.

His sweat mingling with Tremorlor's, the sapper gave one last surge of all his strength, willing success, willing the achievement of moving his arm, closing a hand on the latch.

And failed.

Behind him another blood-curdling noise reached through, that of the bloodflies, breaking through the wooden nets, coming ever closer, only moments from clashing with Icarium's deadly anger – *the Jhag will awaken then. No other choice – and our deaths will be the least of it. The Azath, the maze and all its prisoners . . . oh, be very thorough in your rage, Icarium, for the sake of this world and every other—*

Stabbing pain lanced the back of Fiddler's hand – *Bloodflies!* – but there was a weight behind it. Not stings, but the grip of small claws. The sapper cocked his head and found himself staring into Moby's fanged grin.

The familiar made its way down the length of his arm, claws puncturing skin. The creature seemed to be shifting in and out of focus before Fiddler's eyes, and with each blur the weight on his arm was suddenly immense. He realized he was screaming.

Moby clambered beyond the sapper's hand onto the door itself, reached out a tiny, wrinkled hand to the latch, touched it.

Fiddler tumbled onto damp, warm flagstones. He heard shouts behind him, the scrabbling of boots, while the House groaned on all sides. He rolled onto his back, and in the process came down on something that snapped and crackled beneath his weight, lifting to him a bitter smell of dust.

Then Icarium's deathly keening was among them.

Tremorlor shook.

Fiddler twisted into a sitting position.

They were in a hallway, the limestone walls shedding a dull yellow, throbbing light. Mappo still held Icarium and as the sapper watched, the Trell struggled to retain his embrace. A moment later the Jhag subsided, slumping once again in the Trell's arms. The golden light steadied, the walls themselves stilled. Icarium's rage was gone.

Mappo sagged to the floor, head hanging over the insensate body of his friend.

Fiddler slowly looked around to see if they'd lost anyone. Apsalar crouched beside her father, their backs to the now shut door. Crokus had dragged a cowering Iskaral Pust in with him, and the High Priest looked up, blinking as if in disbelief.

Fiddler's voice was a croak. 'The Hounds, Iskaral Pust?'

'Escaped! And yet, even in the midst of betrayal, they threw their power against the D'ivers!' He paused, sniffed the dank air. 'Can you smell it? Tremorlor's satisfaction – the D'ivers has been taken.'

'That betrayal might have been instinctive, High Priest,' Apsalar said. 'Five Ascendants in the House's yard – the vast risk to Tremorlor itself, given Shadow's own penchant for treachery—'

'Lies! We played true!'

'A first time for everything,' Crokus muttered. He looked across to Fiddler. 'Glad it opened to you, Fid.'

The sapper started, searched the hallway. 'It didn't. Moby opened the door and ripped my arm to shreds in the process – where is that damned runt? It's in here somewhere—'

'You're sitting on a corpse,' Apsalar's father observed.

Fiddler glanced down to find himself on a nest of bones and rotted clothing. He clambered clear, cursing.

'I don't see him,' Crokus said. 'You sure he made it inside, Fid?'

'Aye, I'm sure.'

'He must have gone deeper into the House—'

'He seeks the gate!' Pust squealed. 'The Path of Hands!'

'Moby's a famil—'

'More lies! That disgusting bhok'aral is a Soletaken, you fool!'

'Relax. There is no gate in here that offers a shapeshifter anything,' Apsalar said, slowly rising, her eyes on the withered corpse behind Fiddler. 'That would have been the Keeper – each Azath has a guardian. I'd always assumed they were immortal . . .' She stepped forward, kicked at the bones. She grunted. 'Not human – those limbs are too long, and look at the joints – too many of them. This thing could bend every which way.'

Mappo lifted his head. 'Forkrul Assail.'

'The least known of the Elder Races, then. Not even hinted of in any Seven Cities legend I've heard.' She swung her attention to the hallway.

Five paces from the door the passage opened on a T-intersection, with double doors directly opposite the entrance.

'The layout's almost identical,' Apsalar whispered.

'To what?' Crokus asked.

'Deadhouse, Malaz City.'

Pattering feet approached the intersection, and a moment later Moby scampered into view. The creature flapped up and into the Daru's arms.

'He's shaking,' Crokus said, hugging the familiar.

'Oh, great,' Fiddler muttered.

'The Jhag,' Pust hissed from where he knelt a few paces from Mappo and Icarium. 'I saw you crushing him in your arms – is he dead?'

The Trell shook his head. 'Unconscious. I don't think he'll awaken for some time—'

'Then let the Azath take him! Now! We are within Tremorlor. Our need for him has ended!'

'No.'

'Fool!'

A bell clanged somewhere outside. They all looked at each other in disbelief.

'Did we hear that?' Fiddler wondered. 'A *merchant's* bell?'

'Why a merchant?' Pust growled, eyes darting suspiciously.

But Crokus was nodding. 'A merchant's bell. In Darujhistan, that is.'

The sapper went to the door. From within, the latch moved smoothly under his hand, and he swung the door back.

Thin sheets of tangled root now rose from the yard, towering over the House itself in a clash of angles and planes. Humped earth steamed on all sides. Waiting just outside the arched gate were three huge, ornate carriages, each drawn by nine white horses. A roundish figure stood beneath the arch, wearing silks. The figure raised a hand towards Fiddler and called out in Daru, 'Alas, I can go no farther! I assure you, all is calm out here. I seek the one named Fiddler.'

'Why?' the sapper barked.

'I deliver a gift. Gathered in great haste and at vast expense, I might add. I suggest we complete the transaction as quickly as possible, all things considered.'

Crokus now stood beside Fiddler. The Daru was frowning at the carriages. 'I know the maker of those,' he said quietly. 'Bernuk's, just back of Lakefront. But I've never seen them that big before – gods, I've been away too long.'

Fiddler sighed. 'Darujhistan.'

'I'm certain of it,' Crokus said, shaking his head.

Fiddler stepped outside and studied the surroundings. Things seemed, as the merchant had said, calm. Quiescent. Still uneasy, the sapper made his way down the path. He halted two paces from the archway and eyed the merchant warily.

'Karpolan Demesand, sir, of the Trygalle Trade Guild, and this is a run that I and my shareholders shall never regret, yet hope never to repeat.' The man's exhaustion was very evident, and his silks hung soaked in sweat. He gestured and an armoured woman with a deathly pale face stepped past him, carrying a small crate. Karpolan continued, 'Compliments of a certain mage of the Bridgeburners, who was advised – in timely fashion – of your situation in a general way, by the corporal you share.'

Fiddler accepted the box, now grinning. 'The efforts of this delivery surpass me, sir,' he said.

'Me as well, I assure you. Now we must flee – ah, a rude bluntness – I meant "depart", of course. We must depart.' He sighed, looking around. 'Forgive me, I am weary, beyond even achieving the expected courtesies of civil discourse.'

'No need for apologies,' Fiddler said. 'While I have no idea how you got here and no idea how you'll get back to Darujhistan, I wish you a safe and swift journey. One last question, however: did the mage say anything about where the contents of this crate came from?'

'Oh, indeed he did, sir. From the Blue City's streets. An obscure reference you are clearly fortunate to understand in an instant, I see.'

'Did the mage give you any warning as to the handling of this package, Karpolan?'

The merchant grimaced. 'He said we were not to jostle too much. However, this last stretch of our journey was somewhat . . . rough. I regret to say that some of the crate's contents may well be broken.'

Fiddler smiled. 'I am pleased to inform you that they have survived.'

Karpolan Demesand frowned. 'You have not yet examined the contents – how can you tell?'

'You'll just have to trust me on that one, sir.'

Crokus closed the door once Fiddler had carried the crate inside. The sapper gingerly set the container down and prised open the lid. 'Ah, Quick Ben,' he whispered, eyes scanning the objects nestled within, 'one day I shall raise a temple in your name.' He counted seven cussers, thirteen masonry crackers and four flamers.

'But how did that merchant get here?' Crokus asked. 'From Darujhistan! Hood's breath, Fid!'

'Don't I know it.' He straightened, glanced at the others. 'I'm feeling good, comrades. Very good indeed.'

'Optimism!' Pust snarled in a tone close to bursting with disgust. The High Priest yanked at the wispy remnants of his hair. 'While that foul monkey pisses terror into the lad's lap! *Optimism!*'

Crokus now held the familiar out from him and stared disbelieving at the stream pouring down to splash the flagstones. 'Moby?' The creature was grinning sheepishly.

'Soletaken, you mean!'

'A momentary lapse,' Apsalar said, eyeing the squirming creature. 'The realization of what has come about. That, or an odd sense of humour.'

'What are you babbling about?' Pust demanded, eyes narrowing.

'He thought he'd found the Path, thought that what called him here was the ancient promise of Ascendancy – and in a way, Moby was right in thinking that. The bhok'aral there in your hands, Crokus, is demonic. In true form, it could hold you as you now hold it.'

Mappo grunted. 'Ah, I see now.'

'Then why not enlighten us?' Crokus snapped.

Apsalar nudged the corpse at her feet. 'Tremorlor needed a new guardian. Need I be any clearer?'

Crokus blinked, looking again at Moby, the trembling creature in his hands. 'My uncle's familiar?'

'A demon, at the moment somewhat intimidated by expectation, we might assume. But I'm sure the creature will grow into the role.'

811

Fiddler had been packing the Moranth munitions into his leather sack while this had been going on. Now he rose and gingerly swung the bag over a shoulder. 'Quick Ben believed we'd find a portal somewhere in here, a warren's gate—'

'Linking the Houses!' Pust crowed. 'Outrageous audacity – this cunning mage of yours has charmed me, soldier. He should have been a servant of Shadow!'

He was, but never mind that. If your god's of a mind to, he'll tell you – though I wouldn't hold my breath . . . 'It's time to find that portal—'

'To the T-intersection, down the left passage to the two doors. The one to the left takes us into the tower. Top floor.' Apsalar smiled.

Fiddler stared at her a moment, then nodded. *Your borrowed memories* . . .

Moby led the way, revealing a return of nerve, and something like possessive pride. Just beyond the intersection, in the left-hand passage, there was an alcove set in the wall, on which hung resplendent scale armour suited to a wearer over ten foot tall and of massive girth. Two double-bladed axes leaned against the niche walls, one to either side. Moby paused there to play a tiny, loving hand over one iron-sheathed boot, before wistfully moving on. Crokus stumbled in passing as it momentarily gripped his full attention.

Upon opening the door, they entered the tower's ground floor. A stone staircase spiralled up from its centre. At the foot of the saddlebacked steps lay another body, a young, dark-skinned woman who looked as if she had been placed there but an hour before. She was dressed in what were clearly underclothes, though the armour that had once covered them was nowhere to be seen. Vicious wounds crisscrossed her slight form.

Apsalar approached, crouched down and rested a hand on the girl's shoulder. 'I know her,' she whispered.

'Eh?' Rellock growled.

'The memory of the one who possessed me, Father,' she said. 'His mortal memory—'

'Dancer,' Fiddler said.

She nodded. 'This is Dassem Ultor's daughter. The First Sword recovered her after Hood was done using her, and brought her here, it seems.'

'Before breaking his vow to Hood—'

'Aye, before Dassem cursed the god he once served.'

'That was years ago, Apsalar,' Fiddler said.

'I know.'

They were silent, all studying the frail young woman lying at the foot of the stairs. Mappo shifted Icarium's weight in his arms, as if uneasy with the echo he knew he had become, even though it was understood that he would not do with his burden what Dassem Ultor had done.

Apsalar straightened and cast her eyes up the staircase. 'If Dancer's memory serves, the portal awaits.'

Fiddler swung to the others. 'Mappo? You will join us?'

'Aye, though perhaps not all the way – assuming there's a means to leave that warren when one so chooses—'

'Quite an assumption,' the sapper said.

The Trell simply shrugged.

'Iskaral Pust?'

'Oh, aye. Of course, of course! Why not, why ever not? To walk the maze back out? Insanity! Iskaral Pust is anything but insane, as you all well know. Aye, I shall accompany you . . . and silently add to naught but myself: perhaps an opportunity for betrayal will yet arise! Betray what? Betray whom? Does it matter? It is not the goal that brings pleasure, but the journey taken to achieve it!'

Fiddler met Crokus's sharp gaze. 'Watch him,' he said.

'I shall.'

The sapper then glanced down to Moby. The familiar squatted by the doorway, quietly playing with its own tail. 'How does one say goodbye to a bhok'aral?'

'With a boot in the backside, how else?' Pust offered.

'Care to try that with this one?' Fiddler asked.

The High Priest scowled, made no move.

'He was out there when we travelled the storms, wasn't he?' Crokus said, approaching the tiny wizened creature. 'Recall those battles we could not see? He was protecting us . . . all along.'

'Aye,' the sapper said.

'Ulterior motives!' Pust hissed.

'Nonetheless.'

'Gods, he'll be lonely!' Crokus gathered the bhok'aral into his arms. There was no shame to the tears in the lad's eyes.

Blinking, Fiddler turned away, grimacing as he studied the staircase. 'It'll do you no good to draw it out, Crokus,' he said.

'I'll find a way to visit,' the Daru whispered.

'Think on what you see, Crokus,' Apsalar said. 'He looks content enough. As for being alone, how do you know that will be the case? There are other Houses, other guardians . . .'

The lad nodded. Slowly he released his grip on the familiar and set it down. 'With luck, there won't be any crockery lying around.'

'What?'

Crokus smiled. 'Moby always had bad luck around crockery, or should I say it the other way around?' He rested a hand on the creature's blunt, hairless head, then rose. 'Let's go.'

The bhok'aral watched the group ascend the stairs. A moment later there was a midnight flash from above, and they were gone. The creature listened carefully, cocking its tiny head, but there was no more sound from the chamber above.

It sat unmoving for a few more minutes, idly plucking at its own tail, then swung about and scampered into the hallway, coming to a stop before the suit of armour.

The massive, closed great helm tilted with a soft creak, and a ragged voice came from it. 'I am pleased my solitude is at an end, little one. Tremorlor welcomes you with all its heart . . . even if you have made a mess on the hallway floor.'

Dust and gravel sprayed, rapping against Duiker's shield, as the Wickan horsewarrior struck the ground and rolled, coming to a stop at the historian's feet. No more than a lad, the Crow looked almost peaceful, eyes closed as if in gentle sleep. But for him, all dreams had ended.

Duiker stepped over the body and stood for a moment in the dust it had raised. The short sword in his right hand was glued there by blood, announcing every shift of his grip with a thick, sobbing sound.

Riders wheeled across the hoof-churned space before the historian. Arrows sped out from the gaps between them, hummed like tigerflies through the air. He jerked his shield around to catch one darting for his face, and grunted at the solid whack that drove the hide-covered rim against mouth and chin, splitting both.

Tarxian cavalry had broken through and was only moments away from severing the dozen remaining squads from the rest of the company. The Crow counterattack had been savage and furious, but costly. Worst of all, Duiker saw as he moved warily forward, it might well have failed.

The infantry squads had been broken apart and had reformed into four groups – only one of them substantial – which now struggled to re-knit. Less than a score of Crow horsewarriors remained upright, each one surrounded by Tarxians hacking at them with their broad-bladed tulwars. Everywhere horses writhed and screamed on the ground, kicking out in their pain.

The back end of a cavalry horse nearly knocked him over. Stepping around, Duiker closed in and thrust the point of his sword into a Tarxian's leather-clad thigh. The light armour resisted a moment, until the historian threw all his weight behind the stab, feeling the point pierce flesh, sink deep and grate against bone. He twisted the blade.

A tulwar slashed down, biting solidly into Duiker's shield. He bent low, pulling the snagged weapon with him. Fresh blood drenched his sword hand as he yanked his blade free. The historian hacked and chopped at the man's hip until the horse sidestepped, carrying the rider beyond his reach.

He pushed his helm rim clear of his eyes, blinked away grit and sweat, then moved forward again, towards the largest knot of infantry.

Three days since Sanimon Valley and the bloody reprieve granted them by the Khundryl tribe. Their unexpected allies had closed that battle pursuing the remnants of their rival tribes into the hours of dusk, before slipping off to return, presumably, to their own lands. They had not been seen since.

The mauling had driven Korbolo Dom into a rage – that much was patently clear – for the attacks were now incessant, a running battle over forty hours long and with no sign that it would relent any time soon.

The beleaguered Chain of Dogs was struck again and again, from the flanks, from behind, at times from two or three directions at once. What vengeful blades, lances and arrows did not achieve, exhaustion was completing. Soldiers were simply falling to the ground, their armour in tatters, countless minor wounds slowly draining the last of their reserves. Hearts failed, major blood vessels burst beneath skin to blossom into bruises that were deep black, as if some dreadful plague now ran amok through the troops.

The scenes Duiker had witnessed were beyond horror, beyond his ability to comprehend.

He reached the infantry even as the other groups managed to close and link up, wheeling into a bladed wheel formation that no horse – no matter how well trained – would challenge.

Within the ring, a swordsman began beating sword on shield, bellowing to add his voice to the rhythm of blows. The wheel spun, each soldier stepping in time, spun, crossing the ground, spun, slowly returning to where the remaining company still held the line on this, the west flank of the Chain.

Duiker moved with them, part of the outer ring, delivering killing blows to whatever wounded enemy soldier the wheel trampled. Five Crow riders kept pace. They were the last survivors of the counterattack and, of those, two would not fight again.

A few moments later the wheel reached the line, broke apart and melted into it. The Wickans dug spurs into their lathered horses to race southward. Duiker pushed his way through the ranks until he stumbled into the clear. He lowered his quivering arms, spat blood onto the ground, then slowly raised his head.

The mass of refugees marched before him, a procession grinding past the spot where he stood. Wreathed in dust, hundreds of faces were turned in his direction, watching that thin cordon of infantry behind him – all that lay between them and slaughter – as it surged, buckled and grew ever thinner with each minute that passed. The faces were expressionless, driven to a place beyond thought and beyond emotion. They were part of a tidal flow where no ebb was possible, where to drop back too far was fatal, and so they stumbled on, clutching the last and most precious of their possessions: their children.

Two figures approached Duiker, coming down alongside the stream of refugees from the vanguard position. The historian stared at them blankly, sensing that he should recognize the two – but every face had become a stranger's face.

'Historian!'

The voice jarred him out of his fugue. His split lip stung as he said, 'Captain Lull.'

A webbed jug was thrust at him. Duiker forced his short sword back into its scabbard and accepted the jug. The cool water filled his mouth with pain but he ignored it, drinking deep.

'We've reached Geleen Plain,' Lull said.

The other person was Duiker's nameless marine. She wavered where she stood, and the historian saw a vicious puncture wound in her left shoulder, where a lance-point had slipped over her shield. Broken rings from her armour glittered in the gaping hole.

Their eyes met. Duiker saw nothing still alive in those once beautiful light-grey eyes, yet the alarm he felt within him came not from what he saw, but from his own lack of shock, the frightening absence of all feeling – even dismay.

'Coltaine wants you,' Lull said.

'He's still breathing, is he?'

'Aye.'

'I imagine he wants this.' Duiker pulled free the small glass bottle on its silver chain. 'Here—'

'No,' Lull said, frowning. 'Wants you, Historian. We've run into a tribe of the Sanith Odhan – so far they're just watching.'

'Seems the rebellion's a less certain thing down here,' Duiker muttered.

Sounds of battle along the flanking line diminished. Another pause, a few heartbeats in which to recover, to repair armour, quench bleeding.

The captain gestured and they began walking alongside the refugees.

'What tribe, then?' the historian asked after a moment. 'And, more importantly, what's it got to do with me?'

'The Fist has reached a decision,' Lull said.

Something in those words chilled Duiker. He thought to

probe for more, yet dismissed the notion. The details of that decision belonged to Coltaine. *The man leads an army that refuses to die. We've not lost a refugee to enemy action in thirty hours. Five thousand soldiers . . . spitting in the face of every god . . .*

'What do you know of the tribes this close to the city?' Lull asked as they continued on.

'They've no love of Aren,' Duiker said.

'Worse for them under the Empire?'

The historian grunted, seeing the direction the captain pursued in his questions. 'No, better. The Malazan Empire understands borderlands, the different needs of those living in the countryside – vast territories in the Empire, after all, remain nomadic, and the tribute demanded is never exorbitant. More, payment for passage across tribal lands is always generous and prompt. Coltaine should know this well enough, Captain.'

'I imagine he does – I'm the one that needs convincing.'

Duiker glanced at the refugees on their left, scanning the row upon row of faces, young and old, within the ever-present shroud of dust. Thoughts pushed past weariness, and Duiker felt himself tottering on an edge, beyond which – he could now clearly see – waited Coltaine's desperate gamble.

The Fist has reached a decision.

And his officers balk, flinch back overwhelmed with uncertainty. Has Coltaine succumbed to despair? Or does he see all too well?

Five thousand soldiers . . .

'What can I say to you, Lull?' Duiker asked.

'That there's no choice left.'

'You can answer that yourself.'

'I dare not.' The man grimaced, his scarred face twisting, his lone eye narrowing amidst a nest of wrinkles. 'It's the children, you see. It's what they have left – the last thing they have left. Duiker—'

The historian's abrupt nod cut out the need to say anything more – a swiftly granted mercy. He'd seen those faces, had come close to studying them – as if, he'd thought at the time, seeking to find the youth that belonged there, the freedom and innocence – but that was not what he sought, nor what he found. Lull had led him to the word itself. Simple, immutable, thus far still sacrosanct.

Five thousand soldiers will give their lives for it. But is this some kind of romantic foolishness – do I yearn for recognition among these simple soldiers? Is any soldier truly simple – simple in the sense of having a spare, pragmatic way of seeing the world and his place in it? And does such a view preclude the profound awareness I now believe exists in these battered, footsore men and women?

Duiker swung his gaze to his nameless marine, and found himself meeting those remarkable eyes, as if she had but waited for him – his thoughts, doubts and fears – to come around, to seek her.

She shrugged. 'Are we so blind that we cannot see it, Duiker? We defend their *dignity*. There, simple as that. More, it is our strength. Is this what you wished to hear?'

I'll accept that minor castigation. Never underestimate a soldier.

Sanimon itself was a massive tel, a flat-topped hill half a mile across and over thirty arm-spans high, its jumbled plateau barren and windswept. In the Sanith Odhan immediately south of it, where the Chain now struggled, two ancient raised roads remained from the time when the tel had been a thriving city. Both roads ran straight as spears on solid cut-stone foundations; the one to the west – now unused as it led to another tel in hills bone dry and nowhere else – was called Painesan'm. The other, Sanijhe'm, stretched southwest and still provided an overland route to the inland sea called Clatar. At a height of fifteen arm-spans, the roads had become causeways.

Coltaine's Crow Clan commanded Sanijhe'm near the tel,

manning it as if it was a wall. The southern third of Sanimon itself was now a Wickan strongpoint, with warriors and archers of the Foolish Dog and Weasel clans. As the refugees were led along the east edge of Sanimon, the tel's high cliff wall obviated the need for a flanking guard on that side. Troops moved to support the rearguard and the eastern flank. Korbolo Dom's forces, which had been engaged in a running battle with both elements, had their noses bloodied once again. The Seventh was still something to behold, despite its diminished numbers, soldiers among it pitching dead to the ground without a visible wound on them, others wailing and weeping even as they slayed their foes. The arrival of mounted Wickan archers completed the rout, and the time had come once more for rest.

Fist Coltaine stood waiting, alone, facing the odhan to the south. His feather cloak fluttered in the wind, its ragged edges shivering in the air's breath. Lining a ridge of hills in that direction, two thousand paces distant, another tribe sat their horses, barbaric war standards motionless against the pale-blue sky.

Duiker's gaze held on the man as they approached. He tried to put himself inside Coltaine's skin, to find the place where the Fist now lived – and flinched back in his mind. *No, not a failure of imagination on my part. An unwillingness. I can carry no-one else's burden – not even for a moment. We are all pulled inside ourselves now, each alone . . .*

Coltaine spoke without turning. 'The Kherahn Dhobri – or so they are named on the map.'

'Aren's reluctant neighbours,' Duiker said.

The Fist turned at that, his eyes sharp. 'We have ever held to our treaties,' he said.

'Aye, Fist, we have – to the outrage of many Aren natives.'

Coltaine faced the distant tribe again, silent for a long minute.

The historian glanced at his nameless marine. 'You should seek out a cutter,' he said.

'I can still hold a shield—'

'No doubt, but it's the risk of infection . . .'

Her eyes widened and Duiker was felled mute, a rush of sorrow flooding him. He broke the gaze. *You're a fool, old man.*

Coltaine spoke. 'Captain Lull.'

'Fist.'

'Are the wagons ready?'

'Aye, sir. Coming up now.'

Coltaine nodded. 'Historian.'

'Fist?'

The Wickan slowly turned round to face Duiker. 'I give you Nil and Nether, a troop from the three clans. Captain, has Commander Bult informed the wounded?'

'Aye, sir, and they have refused you.'

The skin tightened around Coltaine's eyes, but then he slowly nodded.

'As has,' Lull continued, looking at Duiker, 'Corporal List.'

'I admit,' the Fist sighed, 'those I selected from my own people are none too pleased – yet they will not disobey their warleader. Historian, you shall command as you see fit. Your responsibility, however, is singular. Deliver the refugees to Aren.'

And so we come to this. 'Fist—'

'You are Malazan,' Coltaine cut in. 'Follow the prescribed procedures—'

'And if we are betrayed?'

The Wickan smiled. 'Then we all join Hood, here in one place. If there must be an end to this, let it be fitting.'

'Hold on as long as you can,' Duiker whispered. 'I'll skin Pormqual's face and give the order through his lips if I have to—'

'Leave the High Fist to the Empress – and her Adjunct.'

822

The historian reached for the glass bottle around his neck.

Coltaine shook his head. 'This tale is yours, Historian, and right now, no-one is more important than you. And if you one day see Dujek, tell him this: it is not the Empire's soldiers the Empress cannot afford to lose, it is its memory.'

A troop of Wickans rode towards them, leading spare mounts – including Duiker's faithful mare. Beyond them, the lead wagons of the refugees emerged from the dust, and off to one side waited three additional wagons, guarded – Duiker could see – by Nil and Nether.

The historian drew a deep breath. 'About Corporal List—'

'He will not be swayed,' Captain Lull cut in. 'He asked that I pass on his words of farewell, Duiker. I believe he muttered something about a ghost at his shoulder, whatever that means, then he said: "Tell the historian that I have found my war."'

Coltaine looked away as if those words had struck through to him where all other words could not. 'Captain, inform the companies: we attack within the hour.'

Attack. Hood's breath! Duiker felt awkward in his own body, his hands like leaden lumps at his sides, as if the question of what to do with his own flesh and bone – what to do in the next moment – had driven him to a crisis.

Lull's voice broke through. 'Your horse has arrived, Historian.'

Duiker released a shaky breath. Facing the captain, he slowly shook his head. 'Historian? No, perhaps I shall return to being a historian a week from now. But at this moment, and for what's to come . . .' He shook his head a second time. 'I have no word for what I should be called right now.' He smiled. 'I think "old man" suffices—'

Lull seemed rattled by Duiker's smile. The captain faced Coltaine. 'Fist, this man feels he has no title. He's chosen "old man".'

'A poor choice,' the Wickan growled. 'Old men are wise –

not fools.' He scowled at Duiker. 'There is not one among your acquaintances who struggles with who and what you are. We know you as a soldier. Does that title insult you, sir?'

Duiker's eyes narrowed. 'No. At least, I don't think so.'

'Lead the refugees to safety, soldier.'

'Yes, Fist.'

The nameless marine spoke. 'I have something for you, Duiker.'

Lull grunted. 'What, here?'

She handed him a tatter of cloth. 'Wait a while before you read what's on it. Please.'

He could only nod as he tucked the scrap in his belt. He looked at the three figures before him, wishing Bult and List had been present for this, but there would be no staged good-byes, no comfort of roles to step into. Like everything else, the moment was messy, awkward and incomplete.

'Get on that scrawny beast of yours,' Lull said. 'And stay in Hood's blindside, friend.'

'I wish the same for you, all of you.'

Coltaine hissed, wheeling to face north. He bared his teeth. 'Not a chance of that, Duiker. We intend to carve a bloody path . . . right down the bastard's throat.'

Flanked by Nil and Nether, Duiker rode at the head of the refugee train, heading towards the tribe on the ridge. The Wickan outriders and those guarding the selected wagons that trundled directly ahead were all very young – boys and girls still with their first weapons. Their collective outrage at having been sent from their clans was a silent storm.

Yet, if Coltaine has erred in this gamble, they will wield those weapons one more time . . . one last time.

'Two riders,' Nil said.

'Good sign,' Duiker grunted, eyes focusing on the Kherahn pair that now approached at a canter. Both were elders, a man

824

and a woman, lean and weathered, their skin the same hue as the buckskins that clothed them. Hook-bladed swords were slung under their left arms and ornate iron helmets covered their heads; their eyes were framed in robust cheek-plates.

'Stay here, Nil,' Duiker said. 'Nether, with me, please.' He nudged his mare forward.

They met just beyond the lead wagons, reining in to face each other with a few paces between them.

Duiker was the first to speak. 'These are Kherahn Dhobri lands, recognized by treaty. The Malazan Empire honours all such treaties. We seek passage—'

The woman, her eyes on the wagons, snapped in un-accented Malazan, 'How much?'

'A collection from all the soldiers of the Seventh,' Duiker said. 'In Imperial coin, a worth totalling forty-one thousand silver jakatas—'

'A full-strength Malazan army's annual wages,' the woman said, scowling. 'This was no "collection". Do your soldiers know you have stolen their wages to buy passage?'

Duiker blinked, then said softly, 'The soldiers insisted, Elder. This was in truth a collection.'

Nether then spoke. 'From the three Wickan clans, an additional payment: jewellery, cookware, skins, bolts of felt, horseshoes, tack and leather, and an assortment of coins looted in the course of our long journey from Hissar, in an amount approaching seventy-three thousand silver jakatas. All given freely.'

The woman was silent for a long moment, then her companion said something to her in their own tongue. She shook her head in reply, her flat, dun eyes finding the historian again. 'And with this offer, you seek passage for these refugees, and for the Wickan clans, and for the Seventh.'

'No, Elder. For the refugees alone – and this small guard you see here.'

'We reject your offer.'

Lull was right to dread this moment. Dammit—

'It is too much,' the woman said. 'The treaty with the Empress is specific.'

At a loss, Duiker could only shrug. 'Then a portion thereof—'

'With the remainder entering Aren, where it shall be hoarded uselessly until such time as Korbolo Dom breaches the gates, and so you end up paying him for the privilege of slaughtering you.'

'Then,' Nether said, 'with that remainder, we would hire you as escort.'

Duiker's heart stuttered.

'To the city's gates? Too far. We shall escort you to Balahn village, and the beginning of the road known as Aren Way. This, however, leaves a portion remaining. We shall sell you food, and what healing may prove necessary and within the abilities of our horsewives.'

'Horsewives?' Nether asked, her brows rising.

The elder nodded.

Nether smiled. 'The Wickans are pleased to know the Kherahn Dhobri.'

'Come forward, then, with your people.'

The two rode back to their kin. Duiker watched them for a moment, then he wheeled his horse and stood in his stirrups. Far to the north, over Sanimon, hung a dust cloud. 'Nether, can you send Coltaine a message?'

'I can offer him a knowing, yes.'

'Do so. Tell him: he was right.'

The sense rose slowly, as if from a body all had believed cold, a corpse in truth, the realization rising, filling the air, the spaces in between. Faces took on a cast of disbelief, a numbness that was reluctant to yield its protective barriers. Dusk arrived, clothing an encampment of thirty thousand refugees in the joining of two silences – one from the land and the night sky with its crushed-glass stars, the other from the people themselves. Dour-faced Kherahnal moved among them, their gifts and gestures belying their expressions and reserve. And to each place they went, it was as if they brought, in their touch, a release.

Sitting beneath that glittering night sky, surrounded by thick grasses, Duiker listened to the cries that cut through the darkness, wrenching at his heart. Joy wrought with dark, blistering anguish, wordless screams, uncontrolled wailing. A stranger would have believed that some horror stalked the camp, a stranger would not have understood the release that the historian heard, the sounds that his own soul answered with burning pain, making him blink at the stars that blurred and swam overhead.

The release born of salvation was nevertheless tortured, and Duiker well knew why, well knew what was reaching down from the north – a host of inescapable truths. Somewhere out there in the darkness stood a wall of human flesh, clothed in shattered armour, which still defied Korbolo Dom, which had purchased and was still purchasing this dread salvation. There was no escape from that knowledge.

Grasses whispered near him and he sensed a familiar presence crouch down beside him.

'How fares Coltaine?' Duiker asked.

Nether sighed. 'The linkage is broken,' she said.

The historian stiffened. After a long moment he released a shaky breath. 'Gone, then?'

'We do not know. Nil continues with the effort, but I fear in our weariness our blood ties are insufficient. We sensed no death cry, and we most surely would, Duiker.'

'Perhaps he's been captured.'

'Perhaps. Historian, if Korbolo Dom arrives on the morrow,

these Kherahn will pay dearly for this contract. Nor may they prove sufficient in . . . in—'

'Nether?'

She hung her head. 'I am sorry, I cannot stop my ears – they may be deluding themselves. Even if we make it to Balahn, to Aren Way, it is still three leagues to the city itself.'

'I share your misgivings. But out there, well, it's the gestures of kindness, don't you see? We none of us have any defence against them.'

'The release is too soon, Duiker!'

'Possibly, but there's not a damned thing we can do about it.'

They turned at the sound of voices. A group of figures approached from the encampment. A hissing argument was under way, quickly quelled as the group neared.

Duiker slowly rose, Nether doing the same beside him.

'I trust we are not interrupting anything untoward,' Nethpara called out, the words dripping.

'I would suggest,' the historian said, 'that the Council retire for the night. A long day of marching awaits us all tomorrow—'

'And that,' Pullyk Alar said hastily, 'is precisely why we are here.'

'Those of us retaining a measure of wealth,' Nethpara explained, 'have succeeded in purchasing from the Kherahn fresh horses for our carriages.'

'We wish to leave now,' Pullyk added. 'Our small group, that is, and make with all haste for Aren—'

'Where we shall insist the High Fist despatch a force to provide guard for the rest of you,' Nethpara said.

Duiker stared at the two men, then at the dozen figures behind them. 'Where is Tumlit?' he asked.

'Alas, he fell ill three days ago and is no longer among the living. We all deeply mourn his passing.'

No doubt. 'Your suggestion has merit, but is rejected.'

'But—'

'Nethpara, if you start moving now, you'll incite panic, and that is something none of us can afford. No, you travel with the rest of us, and must be content with being the first of the refugees to pass beneath the city gates at the head of the train.'

'This is an outrage!'

'Get out of my sight, Nethpara, before I finish what I began at Vathar Crossing.'

'Oh, do not for a moment believe I have forgotten, Historian!'

'An additional reason for rejecting your request. Return to your carriages, get some sleep – we'll be pushing hard tomorrow.'

'A certainty!' Pullyk hissed. 'Korbolo Dom is hardly finished with us! Now that Coltaine's dead and his army with him, we are to trust our lives to these stinking nomads? And when the escort ends? Three leagues from Aren! You send us all to our deaths!'

'Aye,' Duiker growled. 'All, or none. Now I'm done speaking. Leave.'

'Oh, are you now that Wickan dog reborn?' He reached for the rapier at his belt. 'I hereby challenge you to a duel—'

The historian's sword was a blur, the flat of the blade cracking Pullyk Alar's temple. The nobleborn dropped to the ground unconscious.

'Coltaine reborn?' Duiker whispered. 'No, just a soldier.'

Nether spoke, her eyes on the prone body. 'Your Council will have to pay dearly to have that healed, Nethpara.'

'I suppose I could have swung harder and saved you the coin,' Duiker muttered. 'Get out of my sight, all of you.'

The Council retreated, carrying their fallen spokesman with them.

'Nether, have the Wickans watch them.'

'Aye, sir.'

* * *

Balahn village was a squalid collection of low mudbrick houses, home to perhaps forty residents, all of whom had fled days earlier. The only structure less than a century old was the Malazan arched gate that marked the beginning of the Aren Way, a broad, raised military road that had been constructed at Dassem Ultor's command early in the conquest.

Deep ditches flanked the Aren Way, and beyond them were high, flat-topped earthen banks on which grew for the entire ten-mile stretch and in two precise rows, tall cedars that had been transplanted from Geleen on the Clatar Sea.

The Kherahn spokeswoman joined Duiker and the two warlocks in the wide concourse before the Way's gate. 'Payment has been received and all agreements between us honoured.'

'We thank you, Elder,' the historian said.

She shrugged. 'A simple transaction, soldier. No words of thanks are necessary.'

'True. Not necessary, but given in any case.'

'Then you are welcome.'

'The Empress will hear of this, Elder, in the most respectful of terms.'

Her steady eyes darted away at this. She hesitated, then said, 'Soldier, a large force approaches from the north – our rearguard has seen the dust. They come swiftly.'

'Ah, I see.'

'Perhaps some of you will make it.'

'We'll better that if we can.'

'Soldier?'

'Aye, Elder?'

'Are you certain Aren's gates will open to you?'

Duiker's laugh was harsh. 'I'll worry about that when we get there, I think.'

'There's wisdom in that.' She nodded, then gathered her reins. 'Goodbye, soldier.'

'Farewell.'

The Kherahn Dhobri departed, a task that took no more than five minutes, the wagons under heavy escort. Duiker eyed what he could see of the refugee train, their presence overwhelming the small village's ragged boundaries.

He'd set a difficult, gruelling pace, a day and a night with but the briefest pauses for rest, and the message had clearly reached them, one and all, that safety would be assured only once they were within Aren's massively fortified walls.

Three leagues left – it'll take us until dawn to achieve that. Each league I push them hard slows those that follow. Yet what choice do I have? 'Nil, inform your Wickans – I want the entire train through this gate before the sun's set. Your warriors are to use every means possible to achieve that, short of killing or maiming. The refugees may have forgotten their terror of you – remind them.'

'There are but thirty in the troop,' Nether reminded him. 'And all youths at that—'

'Angry youths, you mean. Well, let's offer them an outlet.'

Aren Way accommodated them in their efforts, for the first third, locally known as Ramp, was a gentle downward slope towards the plain on which the city sat. Cone-shaped hills kept pace with them to the east, and would do so to within a thousand paces of Aren's north wall. The hills were not natural: they were mass graves, scores of them, from the misguided slaughter of the city's residents by the T'lan Imass in Kellanved's time. The hill nearest Aren was among the largest, and was home to the city's ruling families and the Holy Protector and Falah'dan.

Duiker left Nil to lead the vanguard and rode at the very rear of the train, where he, Nether and three Wickans shouted themselves hoarse in an effort to hasten the weakest and slowest among the refugees. It was a heartbreaking task, and they passed more than one body that had given out at the pace. There was no time for burial, nor the strength to carry them.

To the north and slightly east, the clouds of dust grew steadily closer.

'They're not taking the road,' Nether gasped, wheeling her mount around to glare at the dust. 'They come overland – slower, much slower—'

'But a shorter route on the map,' Duiker said.

'The hills aren't marked, are they?'

'No, non-Imperial maps show it as a plain – the barrows are too recent an addition, I'd guess.'

'You'd think Korbolo would have a Malazan version—'

'It appears not – and that alone may save us, lass . . .'

Yet he could hear the false ring in his own words. The enemy was too close – less than a third of a league away, he judged. Even with the burial mounds, mounted troops could cover that distance in a few-score minutes.

Faint Wickan warcries from the vanguard reached them.

'They've sighted Aren,' Nether said. 'Nil shows me through his eyes—'

'The gates?'

She frowned. 'Closed.'

Duiker cursed. He rode his mare among the stragglers. 'The city's been sighted!' he shouted. 'Not much more! *Move!*'

From some hidden, unexpected place, reserves of energy rose in answer to the historian's words. He sensed, then saw, a ripple run through the masses, a faint quickening of pace, of anticipation – and of fear. The historian twisted in his saddle.

The cloud loomed above the cone-shaped mounds. Closer, yet not as close as it should have been.

'Nether! Are there soldiers on Aren's walls?'

'Aye, not an inch to spare—'

'The gates?'

'No.'

'How close are we up there?'

'A thousand paces – people are running now—'

'*What in Hood's name is wrong with them?*'

He stared again at the dust cloud. 'Fener's hoof! Nether, take your Wickans – ride for Aren!'

'What about you?'

'To Hood with me, damn you! Go! Save your children!'

She hesitated, then spun her horse around. 'You three!' she barked at the Wickan youths. 'With me!'

He watched them drive their weary horses forward along one edge of the Way, sweeping past the stumbling, pitching refugees.

The train had stretched out, those fleeter of foot slipping ever farther ahead. The elderly surrounded the historian, each step a tortured struggle. Many simply stopped and sat down on the road to await the inevitable. Duiker screamed at them, threatened them, but it was no use. He saw a child, no more than eighteen months old, wandering lost, arms outstretched, dry-eyed and appallingly silent.

Duiker rode close, leaned over in his saddle and swept the child into one arm. Tiny hands gripped the torn fragments of his shirt.

A last row of mounds now separated him and the tail end of the train from the pursuing army.

The flight had not slowed and that was the only evidence the historian had that the gates had, at last, opened to receive the refugees. *Either that or they're spreading out in frantic, hopeless waves along the wall – but no, that would be a betrayal beyond sanity—*

And now he could see, a thousand paces away: Aren. The north gates, flanked by solid towers, yawned for three-quarters of their height – the last, lowest quarter was a seething mass of figures, pushing, crowding, clambering over each other in their panic. But the tide's strength was too great, too inexorable to stopper that passageway. Like a giant maw, Aren was swallowing the refugees. The Wickans rode at either side, desperately trying to contain the human river, and Duiker could now see among them soldiers in the uniform of the Aren City Garrison joining in the effort.

And the army itself? The High Fist's army?

They stood on the walls. They watched. Row upon row of faces, figures jostling for a vantage point along the north wall's entire length. Resplendently dressed individuals occupied the platforms atop the towers flanking the gates, looking down at the starved, bedraggled, screaming mob that thronged the city entrance.

City Garrison Guards were suddenly among the last of those refugees still moving. On all sides around Duiker, he saw grim-faced soldiers pick people up and carry them at a half-jog towards the gates. Spotting one guardsman bearing the insignia of a captain, the historian rode up to him. 'You! Take this child!'

The man reached up to close his hands around the silent, wide-eyed toddler. 'Are you Duiker?' the captain asked.

'Aye.'

'You're to report to the High Fist immediately, sir – there, on the left-hand tower—'

'That bastard will have to wait,' Duiker growled. 'I will see every damned refugee through first! Now run, Captain, but tell me your name, for there may well be a mother or father still alive for that child.'

'Keneb, sir, and I will take care of the lass until then, I swear it.' The man then hesitated, freed one hand and gripped Duiker's wrist. 'Sir . . .'

'What?'

'I'm – I'm sorry, sir.'

'Your loyalty's to the city you've sworn to defend, Captain—'

'I know sir, but those soldiers on the walls, sir – well, they're as close as they're allowed to get, if you understand me. And they're not happy about it.'

'They're not alone in that. Now get going, Captain Keneb.'

Duiker was the last. When the gate finally emptied, not a single breathing refugee remained outside the walls, barring those he could see well down the road, still seated on the cobbles, unable to move, drawing their last breaths – too far away to retrieve, and it was clear that the Aren soldiers had been given strict orders about how far beyond the gate they were permitted.

Thirty paces from the gate and with the array of guards standing in the gap watching him, Duiker wheeled his horse around one final time. He stared northward, first to the dust cloud now ascending the last, largest barrow, then beyond it, to the glittering spear that was the Whirlwind. His mind's eye took him farther still, north and east, across rivers, across plains and steppes, to a city on a different coast. Yet the effort availed him little. Too much to comprehend, too swift, too immediate this end to that extraordinary, soul-scarring journey.

A chain of corpses, hundreds of leagues long. No, it is all beyond me, beyond, I now believe, any of us . . .

He swung his horse around, eyes fixing on that yawning gate and the guards gathered there. They parted to form a path. Duiker tapped his heels into the mare's flanks.

He ignored the soldiers on the wall, even when the triumphant cry burst from them like a beast unchained.

Shadows flowed in silent waves over the barren hills. Apt's glittering eye scanned the horizon for a moment longer, then the demon dipped her elongated head to look down on the boy crouched beside her forelimb.

He too was studying Shadow Realm's eerie landscape, his own single, multifaceted eye glistening beneath the jutting brow ridge.

After a long moment he lifted his head and met her gaze. 'Mother,' he asked, 'is this home?'

A voice spoke from a dozen paces away. 'My colleague ever underestimates this realm's natural inhabitants. Ah, there is the child.'

The boy turned and watched the tall, black-clad man approach. 'Aptorian,' the stranger continued, 'your generous shaping of this lad – no matter how well-meant – will do naught but scar him within, in the years to come.'

Apt clicked and hissed a reply.

'Ah, but you have achieved the opposite, Lady,' the man said. 'For he now belongs to neither.'

The demon spoke again.

The man cocked his head, regarded her for a long moment, then half-smiled. 'Presumptuous of you.' His gaze fell to the boy. 'Very well.' He crouched. 'Hello.'

The boy returned the greeting shyly.

Casting a last irritated glance at Apt, the man offered the child his hand. 'I'm . . . Uncle Cotillion—'

'You can't be,' the boy said.

'Oh, and why not?'

'Your eyes – they're different – so small, two fighting to see as one. I think they must be weak. When you approached, you walked through a stone wall and then the trees, rippling the ghost world as if ignorant of its right to dwell here.'

Cotillion's eyes widened. 'Wall? Trees?' He glanced up at Apt. 'Has his mind fled?'

The demon answered at length.

Cotillion paled. 'Hood's breath!' he finally muttered, and when he turned back to the child it was with an expression of awe. 'What is your name, lad?'

'Panek.'

'You possess one, then. Tell me, what else – apart from your name – do you recall of your . . . other world?'

'I remember being punished. I was told to stay close to Father—'

'And what did he look like?'

'I don't remember. I don't remember any of their faces. We were waiting to see what they'd do with us. But then we were led away – the children – away. Soldiers pushed my father, dragged him in the opposite direction. I was supposed to stay close, but I went with the children. They punished me – punished all of the children – for not doing what we were told.'

Cotillion's eyes narrowed. 'I don't think your father had much choice, Panek.'

'But the enemy were fathers too, you see. And mothers and grandmothers – they were all so angry with us. They took our clothes. Our sandals. They took everything from us, they were so angry. Then they punished us.'

'And how did they do that?'

'They nailed us to crosses.'

Cotillion said nothing for a long moment. When he finally spoke, his voice was strangely flat. 'You remember that, then.'

'Yes. And I promise to do as I'm told. From now on. Whatever Mother says. I promise.'

'Panek. Listen carefully to your uncle. You weren't punished for not doing what you were told. Listen – this is hard, I know, but try to understand. They hurt you because they could, because there was no-one there who was capable of stopping them. Your father would have tried – I'm sure he did. But, like you, he was helpless. We're here now, with you – your mother and Uncle Cotillion – we're here to make sure you'll never be helpless again. Do you understand?'

Panek looked up at his mother. She clicked softly.

'All right,' the boy said.

'We'll teach each other, lad.'

Panek frowned. 'What can I teach you?'

Cotillion grimaced. 'Teach me what you see . . . here, in this realm. Your ghost world, the Shadow Hold that was, the old places that remain—'

'What you walk through unseeing.'

'Aye. I've often wondered why the Hounds never run straight.'

'Hounds?'

'You'll meet them sooner or later, Panek. Cuddly mutts, one and all.'

Panek smiled, revealing sharp fangs. 'I like dogs.'

With a slight flinch, Cotillion said, 'I'm sure they'll like you in turn.' He straightened, faced Apt. 'You're right, you can't do this alone. Let us think on it, Ammanas and I.' He faced the lad again. 'Your mother has other tasks now. Debts to pay. Will you go with her or come with me?'

'Where do you go, Uncle?'

'The other children have been deposited nearby. Would you like to help me get them settled?'

Panek hesitated, then replied, 'I would like to see them again, but not right away. I will go with Mother. The man who asked her to save us needs to be looked after – she explained that. I would like to meet him. Mother says he dreams of me, of when he first saw me.'

'I'm sure he does,' Cotillion muttered. 'Like me, he is haunted by helplessness. Very well, until we meet again.' He shifted his attention one last time, stared long into Apt's eye. 'When I Ascended, Lady, it was to escape the nightmares of feeling . . .' He grimaced. 'Imagine my surprise that I now thank you for such chains.'

Panek broke in. 'Uncle, do you have any children?'

He winced, looked away. 'A daughter. Of sorts.' He sighed, then smiled wryly. 'We had a falling-out, I'm afraid.'

'You must forgive her.'

'Damned upstart!'

'You said we must teach each other, Uncle.'

Cotillion's eyes widened on the lad, then he shook his head. 'The forgiveness is the other way around, alas.'

'Then I must meet her.'

'Well, anything is possible—'

Apt spoke.

Cotillion scowled. 'That, Lady, was uncalled-for.' He turned away, wrapping his cloak about himself.

After half a dozen strides he paused, glancing back. 'Give Kalam my regards.' A moment later shadows engulfed him.

Panek continued staring. 'Does he imagine,' he asked his mother, 'that he now walks unseen?'

The greased anchor chain rattled smoothly, slipping down into the black, oily water, and *Ragstopper* came to a rest in Malaz Harbour, a hundred yards from the docks. A scatter of dull yellow lights marked the lower quarter's front street, where ancient warehouses interspersed by ramshackle taverns, inns and tenement houses faced the piers. To the north was the ridge that was home to the city's merchants and nobles – the larger estates abutting the cliff wall and its switchback stairs that ascended to Mock's Hold. Few lights were visible in that old bastion, though Kalam could see a pennant flapping heavily in a high wind – too dark to make out its colours.

A shiver of presentiment ran through him at the sight of that pennant. *Someone's here . . . someone important.*

The crew were settling down behind him, grumbling about the late hour of arrival which would prevent them from immediately disembarking into the harbour streets. The Harbourmaster would wait until the morrow before rowing out to inspect the craft and ensure that the sailors were hale – free of infections and the like.

The midnight bell had sounded its atonal note only minutes earlier. *Salk Elan judged rightly, damn him.*

It had never been part of the plan, this stop in Malaz City.

839

Kalam had originally intended to await Fiddler in Unta, where they would finalize the details. Quick Ben had insisted that the sapper could come through via Deadhouse, though the mage was typically evasive about specifics. Kalam had begun to view the Deadhouse option as more of a potential escape route if things went wrong than anything else, and even then as a last recourse. He'd never liked the Azath, had no faith in anything that appeared so benign. Friendly traps were always far deadlier than openly belligerent ones.

There was silence behind him now, and the assassin briefly wondered at how swiftly sleep had come to the men sprawled on the main deck. *Ragstopper* was motionless, cordage and hull murmuring their usual natural noises. Kalam leaned on the forecastle rail, eyes on the city before him, on the dark bulks of ships resting in their berths. The Imperial Pier was off to his right, where the cliff face reached down to the sea. No craft was visible there.

He thought to glance back up at the pennant's dark wing above the Hold, but the effort seemed too much – too dark in any case – and his imagination was ever fuelled by thinking the worse of all he could not know.

And now came sounds from farther out in the bay. Another ship, edging its way through the darkness, another late arrival.

The assassin glanced down at his hands where they rested on the rail. They felt like someone else's, that polished, dark-brown hue of his skin, the pale scars that crossed it here and there – not his own, but the victims of someone else's will.

He shook off the sensation.

The island city's smells drifted out to him. The usual stench of a harbour: sewage warring with rot, brackish water of the sea mixing with a pungent whiff from the sluggish river that emptied into the bay. His eyes focused again on the dark, snag-toothed grin of the harbourfront buildings. A few streets in, he knew, occupying one squalid corner amidst tenement blocks and fish-stalls, stood the Deadhouse. Unmentioned and avoided by all denizens of the city, and to all outward appearances completely abandoned, its yard overgrown, its black, rough stones smothered in vines. No lights from the gaping windows in the twin towers.

If anyone can make it, it's Fiddler. The bastard's always been charmed. A sapper all his life, it seems, with a sapper's extra sense. What would he say if he stood here beside me right now? 'Don't like it, Kal. Something's awry all right. Move those hands of yours . . .'

Kalam frowned, glanced back down at his hands, willing them to lift clear of the rail.

Nothing.

He attempted to step back, but his muscles refused, deaf to his command. Sweat sprang out beneath his clothes, beading the backs of his hands.

A soft voice spoke beside him. 'There's such irony in this, my friend. You see, it's your mind that's betrayed you. The formidable, deadly mind of the assassin Kalam Mekhar.' Salk Elan leaned on the rail beside him, studying the city. 'I've admired you for so long, you know. You're a damned legend, the finest killer the Claw ever had – and lost. Ah, and it's that loss that rankles the most. Had you the will for it, Kalam, you could now be in command of the entire organization – oh, Topper might disagree, and I'll grant you, in some ways he's your superior by far. He would have killed me on the first day, no matter how uncertain he was of whatever risk I might have presented. Even so,' Salk Elan continued after a moment, 'knife to knife, you're his better, friend.

'Another irony for you, Kalam. I was not in Seven Cities to find you – indeed, we knew nothing of your presence there. Until I came across a certain Red Blade who did, that is. She'd been following you since Erhlitan, before you delivered the Book to Sha'ik – did you know you led the Red Blades directly to that witch? Did you know that they succeeded in assassinating her? That Red Blade would have been here with me, in fact, if not for an unfortunate incident in Aren. But I prefer working alone.

'Salk Elan, a name I admit to being proud of. But here and now, of course, my vanity insists that you know my true name, which is Pearl.' He paused, looked around, sighed. 'You threw me but once, with that sly hint that maybe Quick Ben was hiding in your baggage. I almost panicked then, until I realized if that were true, I'd already be dead – sniffed out and fed to the sharks.

'You should never have left the Claw, Kalam. We don't deal with rejection very well. The Empress wants you, you know, wants a conversation with you, in fact. Before skinning you alive, I imagine. Alas, things aren't so simple, are they?

'And so, here we are . . .'

In his peripheral vision, Kalam saw the man draw forth a dagger. 'It's those immutable laws within the Claw, you see. One in particular, which I'm sure you well know . . .'

The blade sank deep into Kalam's side with a dull, distant pain. Pearl withdrew the weapon. 'Oh, not fatal, just lots of blood. A weakening, if you will. Malaz City is quiet tonight, don't you think? Not surprising – there's something in the air – every cutpurse, guttersnipe and thug can feel it, and they're one and all keeping their heads low. Three Hands await you, Kalam, eager for the hunt to start. That immutable law, Kalam . . . in the Claw, we deal with our own.'

Hands gripped the assassin. 'You'll awaken once you hit the water, friend. Granted, it's something of a swim, especially with the armour you're wearing. And the blood won't help – this bay's notorious for sharks, isn't it. But I've great confidence in you, Kalam. I know you'll make it to dry land. That far, at least. After that, well . . .'

He felt himself being lifted, edged over the rail. He stared down at the black water below.

'A damned shame,' Pearl gasped close to his ear, 'about the captain and this crew, but I've no choice, as I'm sure you understand. Farewell, Kalam Mekhar.'

The assassin struck the water with a soft splash. Pearl stared down as the disturbance settled. His confidence in Kalam wavered. The man was in chain armour, after all. Then he shrugged, drew forth a pair of throat-stickers and swung to face the motionless figures lying on the main deck. 'A good man's work is never done, alas,' he said, stepping forward.

The shape that emerged from the shadows to face him was huge, angular, black-limbed. A single eye gleamed from the long-snouted head, and hovering dimly behind that head was a rider, his face a mockery of his mount's.

Pearl stepped back, offered a smile. 'Ah, an opportunity to thank you for your efforts against the Semk. I knew not where you came from then, nor how you've come to be here now, or why, but please accept my gratitude—'

'Kalam,' the rider whispered. 'He was here but a moment ago.'

Pearl's eyes narrowed. 'Ah, now I understand. You weren't following *me*, were you? No, of course not. How silly of me! Well, to answer your question, child, Kalam has gone into the city—'

The demon's lunge interrupted him. Pearl ducked beneath the snapping jaws – and directly into the sweeping foreclaw. The impact threw the Claw twenty feet, crashing him up against a battened-down dory. His shoulder dislocated with a stab of pain. Pearl rolled, forcing himself into a sitting position. He watched the demon stalk towards him.

'I see I've met my match,' Pearl whispered. 'Very well.' He reached under his shirt. 'Try this one, then.'

The tiny bottle shattered on the deck between them. Smoke billowed, began coalescing.

'The Kenryll'ah looks eager, wouldn't you say? Well –' he

843

struggled to his feet – 'I think I'll leave you two to it. There's a certain tavern in Malaz City I've been dying to see.'

He gestured and a warren opened, swept over him, and when it closed, Pearl was gone.

Apt watched the Imperial demon acquire its form, a creature twice its weight, hulking and bestial.

The child reached down and patted Apt's lone shoulder. 'Let's be quick with this one, shall we?'

A chorus of shudders and explosions of wood awoke the captain. He blinked in the darkness as *Ragstopper* pitched wildly about him. Voices screamed on deck. Groaning, the captain pushed himself off the bed, sensing a clarity in his mind that he'd not known in months, a freedom of action and thought that told unequivocally that Pearl's influence was gone.

He clambered to his cabin door, limbs weak with disuse, and made his way into the passage.

Emerging on deck, he found himself in a crowd of cowering sailors. Two horrific creatures were battling directly in front of them, the larger of the two a mass of shredded flesh, unable to match its opponent's lightning speed. Its wild flailing with a massive double-bladed axe had reduced the deck and the rails to pulp. An earlier swing had chopped through the mast, and though it remained upright, snagged in cordage somewhere high above them, it leaned precariously, its weight canting the ship hard over.

'Captain!'

'Have the lads drag the surviving dories clear, Palet, and back up astern – we'll lower 'em from there.'

'Aye, sir!' The acting First Mate snapped out the commands, then swung back to offer the captain a grin. 'Glad you're back, Carther—'

'Shut your face, Palet – that's Malaz City out there and I

844

drowned years ago, remember?' He squinted at the warring demons. '*Ragstopper*'s not going to survive this—'

'But the loot—'

'To Hood with that! We can always raise her – but we need to be alive to do it. Now, let's lend a hand with those dories – we're taking on water and going down fast.'

'Beru fend! The sea's crawling with sharks!'

Fifty yards farther out, the captain of the fast trader stood with his First Mate, both of them straining to make out the source of the commotion ahead.

'Back oars,' the captain said. 'Full stop.'

'Aye, sir.'

'That ship's going down. Assemble rescue crews, lower the boats—'

Horse hooves clomped on the main deck behind them. Both men turned. The First Mate stepped forward. 'You there! What in Mael's name do you think you're doing? How did you get that damned animal on deck?'

The woman tightened the girth-strap another notch, then swung up into the saddle. 'I'm sorry,' she said. 'But I cannot wait.'

Sailors and marines scattered as she drove the horse forward. The creature cleared the side rail and leapt out into darkness. A loud splash followed a moment later.

The First Mate turned back to his captain, jaw hanging.

'Get Ship's Mage and a goat,' the captain snapped.

'Sir?'

'Anyone brave and stupid enough to do what she just did has earned our every assistance. Have Ship's Mage clear a path through the sharks and whatever else might await her. Be quick about it!'

CHAPTER TWENTY-ONE

Every throne is an arrow-butt.

Kellanved

Beneath the whirlwind's towering spire was a lower billowing of dust as the massive army decamped. Borne on wayward gusts, the ochre clouds spread out from the oasis, settling here and there among the weathered folds of ruins. The air was lit gold on all sides, as if the desert had at last unveiled its memories of wealth and glory, only to reveal them for what they truly were.

Sha'ik stood on the flat roof of a wooden watchtower near the palace concourse, the scurrying efforts of an entire city beneath her almost unnoticed as she stared into the opaqueness to the south. The young girl she had adopted kneeled close by, watching her new mother with sharp, steady eyes.

The ladder below creaked incessantly to someone's laboured ascent, Sha'ik slowly realized, and as she turned she saw Heboric's head and shoulders emerge through the trap. The ex-priest clambered onto the platform and laid an invisible hand on the girl's head before turning to squint at Sha'ik.

'L'oric's the one to watch,' Heboric said. 'The other two think they're subtle, but they're anything but.'

'L'oric,' she murmured, returning her gaze to the south. 'What is your sense of him?'

'You've knowledge that surpasses mine, lass—'

'Nevertheless.'

'I think he senses the bargain.'

'Bargain?'

Heboric moved to stand beside her and leaned his tattooed forearms on the thin wooden railing. 'The one the goddess made with you. The one that proves that a rebirth did not in truth occur—'

'Did it not, Heboric?'

'No. No child chooses to be born, no child has any say in the matter. You had both. Sha'ik has not been reborn, she has been re-*made*. L'oric may well seize on this, believing it to be a gap in your armour.'

'He risks the wrath of the goddess, then.'

'Aye, and I don't think he's ignorant of that, lass, which is why he needs to be watched. Carefully.'

They were silent for a time, both staring out into the south's impenetrable shroud. Eventually Heboric cleared his throat. 'Perhaps, with your new gifts, you can answer some questions.'

'Such as?'

'When did Dryjhna choose you?'

'What do you mean?'

'When did the manipulation begin? Here in Raraku? Skullcup? Or on a distant continent? When did the goddess first cast her gaze upon you, lass?'

'She never did.'

Heboric started. 'That seems—'

'Unlikely? Yes, but it is the truth. The journey was mine, and mine alone. You must understand, even goddesses cannot foresee unexpected deaths, those twists of mortality, decisions taken, paths followed or not followed. Sha'ik Elder had the gift of prophecy, but such a gift, when given, is no more than a seed. It grows in the freedom of a human soul. Dryjhna was greatly disturbed by Sha'ik's visions. Visions that made no sense. A hint of peril, but nothing certain, nothing at all. Besides,' she added with a shrug, 'strategy and tactics are anathema to the Apocalypse.'

Heboric grimaced. 'That doesn't bode well.'

'Wrong. We are free to devise our own.'

'Even if the goddess did not guide you, someone or something did. Else Sha'ik would never have been given those visions.'

'Now you speak of fate. Argue that with your fellow scholars, Heboric. Not every mystery can be unravelled, much as you believe otherwise. Sorry if that pains you . . .'

'Not half as sorry as I am. But it occurs to me that even as mortals are but pieces on a gameboard, so too are the gods.'

' "Elemental forces in opposition," ' she said, smiling.

Heboric's brows rose, then he scowled. 'A quote. A familiar one—'

'It should be. It's carved into the Imperial Gate in Unta, after all. Kellanved's own words, as a means to justify the balance of destruction with creation – the expansion of the Empire, in all its hungry glory.'

'Hood's breath!' the old man hissed.

'Have I sent your mind spinning in other directions, Heboric?'

'Aye.'

'Well, save your breath. The subject of your next treatise – no doubt that handful of obscure old fools will dance in excitement.'

'Old fools?'

'Your fellow scholars. Your readers, Heboric.'

'Ah.'

They were silent again for some time, until the ex-priest spoke once more. 'What will you do?' he asked softly.

'With what has happened out there?'

'With what's still happening. Korbolo Dom reaping sense-less slaughter in your name—'

'In the name of the goddess,' she corrected, hearing the brittle anger in her own voice. She'd already exchanged sharp words with Leoman on this subject.

'Word of the "rebirth" has probably reached him—'

'No, it has not. I have sealed Raraku, Heboric. The storm raised around us can scour flesh from bones. Not even a T'lan Imass could survive the passage.'

'Yet you have made an announcement,' the old man said. 'The Whirlwind.'

'Which has raised in Korbolo Dom doubts. And fears. He is very eager to complete the task he's chosen. He's still unfettered, and so is free to answer his obsessions—'

'And so, what will you do? Aye, we can march, but it will take months to reach the Aren Plain, and by then Korbolo will have given Tavore all the justification she needs to deliver a ruthless punishment. The rebellion was bloody, but your sister will make what's already happened seem like a scratch on the backside.'

'You assume she is my superior, Heboric, don't you? In tactics—'

'There's precedent for how far your sister will go in cruelty, lass,' he growled. 'Witness you standing here . . .'

'And there lies my greatest advantage, old man. Tavore believes she will face a desert witch whom she has never met. Ignorance will not sway her contempt for such a creature. Yet I am not ignorant of *my* enemy . . .'

A subtle change had come to the distant roar of the Whirlwind towering behind them. Sha'ik smiled. Heboric's sense of that change came moments later. He turned. 'What is happening?'

'It will not take us months to reach Aren, Heboric. Have you not wondered what the Whirlwind is?'

The ex-priest's blind eyes widened as he faced that pillar of dust and wind. Sha'ik wondered how the man's preternatural senses perceived the phenomenon, but his next words made it clear that whatever he saw was true. 'By the gods, it's *toppling*!'

'Dryjhna's Warren, Heboric, our whirling road to the south.'

'Will it take us there in time, Fel— Sha'ik? In time to stop Korbolo Dom's madness?'

She did not answer, for it was already too late.

As Duiker rode in through the gates, gauntleted hands reached out to grasp the halter and reins, dragging his mare to a stuttering halt. A smaller hand closed on the historian's wrist, tugging with something like desperation. He looked down, and saw in Nether's face a sickly dread that poured ice into his veins.

'To the tower,' she pleaded. 'Quickly!'

A strange murmuring was building from Aren's walls, a sound of darkness that filled the dusty air. Sliding down from the saddle, Duiker felt his heart begin to thunder. Nether's hand pulled him through the crowd of Garrison Guards and refugees. He felt other hands reach out, touch lightly as if seeking a blessing or conferring one, then slip past.

An arched doorway suddenly yawned before him, leading to a gloomy landing with stone steps rising along the inside of the tower wall. The sound from the city walls was building to a roar, a wordless cry of outrage, horror and anguish. It echoed with mad intent within the tower, and rose in timbre with each step that the warlock and the historian climbed.

On the middle landing she swept him past the T-shaped arrow slits, edging them both behind the pair of bowmen pressed against the narrow windows, then on, up the worn stairs. Neither archer even so much as noticed them.

As they neared the shaft of bright light directly beneath the roof hatch, a quavering voice reached down.

'There's too many . . . I can do nothing, no, the gods forgive me – too many, too many . . .'

850

Nether ascended the shaft of light, Duiker following. They emerged onto the broad platform. Three figures stood at the outer wall. The one on the left Duiker recognized as Mallick Rel – the adviser he had last seen in Hissar – his silks billowing in the hot wind. The man beside him was probably High Fist Pormqual, tall, wiry, slope-shouldered and wearing clothes that would beggar a king, his pale hands skittering across the top of the battlement like trapped birds. To his right stood a soldier in functional armour, a torc on his left arm denoting his commander's rank. He held his burly arms wrapped around himself, as if trying to crush his own bones. The stress bound within him seemed about to explode.

Near the hatch sat Nil, a disarrayed jumble of limbs. The young warlock swung a grey, aged face towards Duiker. Nether swept down to wrap her brother in a fierce hug that she seemed unwilling or unable to relax.

The soldiers lining the walls to either side were screaming now, a sound that cut the air like Hood's own scythe.

The historian went to the wall beside the commander. Duiker's hands reached out to grip the sun-baked stone of the merlon. Following the rapt gaze of the others, he could barely draw breath. Panic surged through him as his eyes took in the scene on the slope of the closest burial mound.

Coltaine.

Above a contracting mass of less than four hundred soldiers, three standards waved: the Seventh's; the polished, articulated dog skeleton of the Foolish Dog Clan; the Crow's black wings surmounting a bronze disc that flashed in the sunlight. Defiant and proud, the bearers continued to hold them high.

On all sides, pressing in with bestial frenzy, were Korbolo Dom's thousands, a mass of footsoldiers devoid of all discipline, interested only in slaughter. Mounted companies rode past them along both visible edges, surging into the gap between the city's walls and the mound – though not riding close enough to come within bow range from Aren's archers. Korbolo Dom's own guard and, no doubt, the renegade Fist himself had moved into position atop the mound behind the last one, and a platform was being raised, as if to ensure a clear view of the events playing out on the nearer barrow.

The distance was not enough to grant mercy to the witnesses on the tower or along the city's wall. Duiker saw Coltaine there, amidst a knot of Mincer's engineers and a handful of Lull's marines, his round shield a shattered mess on his left arm, his lone long-knife snapped to the length of a short sword in his right hand, his feather cloak glistening as if brushed with tar. The historian saw Commander Bult, guiding the retreat towards the hill's summit. Cattle-dogs surged and leapt around the Wickan veteran like a frantic bodyguard, even as arrows swept through them in waves. Among the creatures one stood out, huge, seemingly indomitable, pin-cushioned with arrows, yet fighting on.

The horses were gone. The Weasel Clan was gone. The Foolish Dog warriors were but a score in number, surrounding half a dozen old men and horsewives – the very last of a dwindled, cut-away heart. Of the Crow, it was clear that Coltaine and Bult were the last.

Soldiers of the Seventh, few with any armour left, held themselves in a solid ring around the others. Many of them no longer raised weapons, yet stood their ground even as they were cut to pieces. No quarter was given, every soldier who fell with wounds was summarily butchered – their helmets torn off, their forearms shattered as they sought to ward off the attacks, their skulls crumpling to multiple blows.

The stone beneath Duiker's hands had gone slick, sticky. Iron lances of pain shot up his arms. He barely noticed.

With a wrenching effort, the historian pulled back, reaching out red fingers to grip Pormqual—

The garrison commander blocked him, held him back.

The High Fist saw Duiker, flinched away. 'You do not understand!' he screamed. 'I cannot save them! Too many! Too many!'

'You can, you bastard! A sortie can drive right to that mound – a cordon, damn you!'

'No! We'll be crushed! I must not!'

The commander's low growl reached Duiker. 'You're right, Historian. But he won't do it. The High Fist won't let us save them—'

Duiker struggled to free himself of the man's grip but was pushed back.

'For Hood's sake!' the commander snapped. 'We've tried – we've all tried—'

Mallick Rel stepped close, said softly, 'My heart weeps, Historian. The High Fist cannot be swayed—'

'This is murder!'

'For which Korbolo Dom shall pay, and dearly.'

Duiker spun around, lurched back to the wall.

They were dying. There, almost within reach – no, within a *soldier's* reach. Anguish closed a black fist in the historian's gut. *I cannot watch.*

Yet I must.

He saw fewer than a hundred soldiers still upright, but it had become a slaughter – the only battle that remained was among Korbolo's forces for the chance of delivering fatal blows and raising grisly trophies with triumphant shrieks. The Seventh were falling, and falling, using naught but flesh and bone to shield their leaders – the ones who had led them across a continent, to die now, almost within the shadow of Aren's high walls.

And on those walls was ranged an army, ten thousand fellow soldiers to witness this, the greatest crime ever committed by a Malazan High Fist.

How Coltaine had managed to get this far was beyond

Duiker's ability to comprehend. He was seeing the end of a battle that must have run without cessation for days – a battle that had ensured the survival of the refugees – *and this is why that dust cloud was so slow to approach.*

The last of the Seventh vanished beneath swarming bodies. Bult stood with his back to the standard bearer, a Dhobri tulwar in each hand. A mob closed on him and drove lances into the veteran, sticking him as they would a cornered boar. Even then he tried to rise up, slashing out with a tulwar to chop into the leg of a man – who reeled back howling. But the lances stabbed deep, pushed the Wickan back, pinned him to the ground. Blades flashed down on him, hacking him to death.

The standard bearer left his position – the standard itself propped up between corpses – and leapt forward in a desperate effort to reach his commander. A blade neatly decapitated him, sending his head toppling back to join the bloody jumble at the standard's base, and thus did Corporal List die, having experienced countless mock deaths all those months ago at Hissar.

The Foolish Dog's position vanished beneath a press of bodies, the standard toppling moments later. Bloody scalps were lifted and waved about, the trophies spraying red rain.

Surrounded by the last of the engineers and marines, Coltaine fought on. His defiance lasted but a moment longer before Korbolo Dom's warriors killed the last defender, then swallowed up Coltaine himself, burying him in their mindless frenzy.

A huge arrow-studded cattle-dog darted to where Coltaine had gone down, but then a lance speared the beast, raising it high. It writhed as it slid down the shaft, and even then the creature delivered one final death to the enemy gripping the weapon, by tearing out the soldier's throat.

Then it too was gone.

The Crow standard wavered, leaned to one side, then pitched down, vanishing in the press.

Duiker stood unmoving, disbelieving.

Coltaine.

A high-pitched wail rose behind the historian. He slowly turned. Nether still held Nil as if he were a babe, but her head was tilted back, raised heavenward, her eyes wide.

A shadow swept over them.

Crows.

And to Sormo the Elder warlock, there on the wall of Unta, there came eleven crows – eleven – to take the great man's soul, for no single creature could hold it all. Eleven.

The sky above Aren was filled with crows, a black sea of wings, closing from all sides.

Nether's wail grew louder and louder still, as if her own soul was being ripped out through her throat.

Shock jolted through Duiker. *It's not done – it's not over—* He spun round, saw the cross being raised, saw the still living man nailed to it.

'*They'll not free him!*' Nether screamed. She was suddenly at his side and staring out at the barrow. She tore at her hair, clawed at her own scalp, until blood streamed down her face. Duiker grasped her wrists – so thin, so childlike in his hands – and pulled them away before she could reach her own eyes.

Kamist Reloe stood on the platform, Korbolo Dom at his side. Sorcery blossomed – a virulent, wild wave that surged up and crashed against the approaching crows. Black shapes spun and tumbled from the sky—

'*No!*' Nether shrieked, writhing in Duiker's arms, seeking to fling herself over the wall.

The cloud of crows scattered, reformed, sought to approach once again.

Kamist Reloe obliterated hundreds more.

'Release his soul! From the flesh! *Release it!*'

Beside them, the garrison commander turned and called to one of his aides in a voice of ice, 'Get me Squint, Corporal. Now!'

The aide did not bother darting down the stairs – he simply went to the far wall, leaned out and screamed, 'Squint! Up here, damn you!'

Another wave of sorcery swept more crows from the sky. In silence, they regrouped once again.

The roar from Aren's walls had stilled. Now only silence held the air.

Nether had collapsed against the historian, a child in his arms. Duiker could see Nil curled and motionless on the platform near the hatch – either unconscious or dead. He had wet himself, the puddle spreading out around him.

Boots thumped on the stairs.

The aide said to the commander, 'He's been helping the refugees, sir. I don't think he has any idea what's going on . . .'

Duiker turned again to look out at the lone figure nailed to the cross. He still lived – they would not let him die, would not free his soul, and Kamist Reloe knew precisely what he was doing, knew the full horror of his crime, as he methodically destroyed the vessels for that soul. On all sides, screaming warriors pressed close, seething on the barrow like insects.

Objects started striking the figure on the cross, leaving red stains. *Pieces of flesh, gods – pieces of flesh – what's left of the army –* this was a level of cruelty that left Duiker cowering inside.

'Over here, Squint!' he heard the commander growl. A figure pushed to Duiker's side, short, squat, grey-haired. His eyes, buried in a nest of wrinkles, were fixed on that distant figure. 'Mercy,' he whispered.

'Well?' the commander demanded.

'That's half a thousand paces, Blistig—'

'I know.'

'Might take more than one shot, sir.'

'Then get started, damn you.'

The old soldier, wearing a uniform that looked as if it had not been washed or repaired in decades, unslung the longbow from one shoulder. He gathered the string, stepped into the bow's plane, bent it hard over one thigh. His limbs shook as he edged the string's loop into its niche. Then he straightened up and studied the arrows in the quiver strapped to his hip.

Another wave of sorcery struck the crows.

After a long moment, Squint selected an arrow. 'I'll try for the chest. Biggest target, sir, and enough good hits and that'll do the poor soul.'

'Another word, Squint,' Blistig whispered, 'and I'll have your tongue.'

The soldier nocked the arrow. 'Clear me some space, then.'

Nether was limp in Duiker's arms as he dragged her back a step.

The man's bow, even strung, was as tall as he was. His forearms as he drew the string back were like hemp ropes, bundled and twisted and taut. The string brushed his stubbled jawline as he completed the draw, then locked it in place with a slow, even exhalation.

Duiker saw the man tremble suddenly, and his eyes widened, revealing themselves for the first time – black, small marbles in red-streaked nests.

Raw fear edged Blistig's voice. 'Squint—'

'That's got to be Coltaine, sir!' the old man gasped. 'You want me to kill Coltaine—'

'Squint!'

Nether raised her head and reached out one bloody hand in supplication. 'Release him. *Please*.'

The old man studied her a moment. Tears streamed down his face. The trembling stilled – the bow itself had not moved an inch.

'Hood's breath!' Duiker hissed. *He's weeping. He can't aim – the bastard can't aim—*

The bowstring thrummed. The long shaft cut through the sky.

'Oh, gods!' Squint moaned. 'Too high – too high!'

It rose, swept through the massed crows untouched and unwavering, began arcing down.

Duiker could have sworn that Coltaine looked up then, lifted his gaze to greet that gift, as the iron head impacted his forehead, shattered the bone, sank deep into his brain and killed him instantly. His head snapped back between the spars of wood, then the arrow was through.

The warriors on the barrow's slopes flinched back.

The crows shook the air with their eerie cries and plunged down towards the sagging figure on the cross, sweeping over the warriors crowding the slopes. The sorcery that battered at them was shunted aside, scattered by whatever force – *Coltaine's soul?* – now rose to join the birds.

The cloud descended on Coltaine, swallowing him entire and covering the cross itself – at that distance they were to Duiker like flies swarming a piece of flesh.

And when they rose, exploding skyward, the warleader of the Crow Clan was gone.

Duiker staggered, leaned hard against the stone wall. Nether slipped down through his motionless arms, her blood-matted hair hiding her face as she curled around his feet.

'I killed him,' Squint moaned. 'I killed Coltaine. Who took that man's life? A broken old soldier of the High Fist's army – he killed Coltaine . . . Oh, Beru, have mercy on my soul . . .'

Duiker wrapped the old man in his arms and held him fiercely. The bow clattered on the platform's wooden slats. The historian felt the man crumpling against him as if his bones had turned to dust, as if centuries stole into him with each ragged breath.

Commander Blistig gripped the bowman by the back of the collar and yanked him upright. 'Before the day's through, you bastard,' he hissed, 'ten thousand soldiers will be voicing your name.' The words shook. 'Like a prayer, Squint, like a Hood-damned prayer.'

The historian squeezed his eyes shut. It had become a day to hold in his arms broken figures.

But who will hold me?

Duiker opened his eyes, raised his head. High Fist Pormqual's mouth was moving, as if in a silent plea for forgiveness. Shock was written on the man's thin, oiled face and, as he met the historian's gaze, a flash of raw fear.

Out on the barrow Korbolo Dom's army was stirring, like reeds in eddies, a restless, meaningless motion. The aftermath was now upon them. Voices rose, wordless cries, but they were too few to break the dreadful silence and its growing power.

The crows were gone, the crossed spars of wood stood empty, rising above the masses with their blood-streaked shafts.

Overhead, the sky had begun to die.

Duiker's gaze returned to Pormqual. The High Fist seemed to shrink into Mallick Rel's shadow. He shook his head as if to deny the day.

Thrice denied, High Fist.

Coltaine is dead. They are all dead.

CHAPTER TWENTY-TWO

I saw the sun's bolt
arc an unerring path
to the man's forehead.
As it struck, the crows
converged like night
drawing breath.

Dog Chain
Seglora

Faint ripples licked the garbage-studded mud beneath the docks. Night insects danced just beyond the water's reach, and the bank itself seethed in the egg-laying frenzy of some kind of eels. In their thousands, black and gleaming, the small creatures writhed beneath the dancing insects. This silent breaching of the harbour's shore had for generations passed almost unnoticed by human eyes – a mercy granted only because the eels were wholly unpalatable.

From the darkness beyond came the sound of cascading water. The ripples that reached shore from that commotion were larger, more agitated, the only indication that a stranger had arrived to disturb the scene.

Kalam stumbled ashore, collapsing onto mud that swarmed beneath him. Warm blood still leaked between the fingers of his right hand where it pressed against the knife wound. The assassin wore no shirt, and his chain armour was even now settling somewhere in the mud bottom of Malaz Bay behind him, leaving him with only buckskin leggings and moccasins.

In clambering out of the armour during his sudden plunge into the deep, he had been forced to pull off his belt and knife harness. In his desperate need to return to the surface, to draw air into his lungs, he'd let everything slip from his grasp.

Leaving him now unarmed.

Somewhere out in the bay a ship was being torn apart, the savage noises drifting across the water. Kalam wondered at that, but only briefly. He had other things on his mind.

Faint nips told him that the eels were resenting his intrusion. Struggling to slow his breathing, he squirmed farther up the slimy bank. Broken crockery dug into his flesh as he made his way onto the first of the stone breakwaters. He rolled onto his back and stared up at the seaweed-bearded underside of the pier. A moment later he closed his eyes, began concentrating.

The bleeding in his side slowed to a thin trickle, then ceased.

A few minutes later he sat up and began pulling off the eels that clung like leeches, flinging them out into the darkness where he could hear the skittering of the harbour's rats. The creatures were closing in, and the assassin had heard enough whispered tales to know he was anything but safe from the fearless hordes in this underworld.

Kalam could wait no longer. He pushed himself up into a crouch, eyeing the ragged piles that rose beyond the breakwater. If the tide had been in, the massive bronze rings bolted three-quarters of the way up those wooden boles would have been within reach. Black pitch coated the piles except where ships had been thrown against them, leaving gaping dents of raw, water-soaked wood.

Only one way up, then . . .

The assassin made his way along the base of the barrier until he stood opposite a merchant trader. The wide-bellied ship lay canted on its side in the mud. A thick hemp rope stretched from its bow to one of the brass rings high on the pile.

Under normal circumstances the climb would have been a simple one, but even with the inner discipline that was part of a Claw's training, Kalam could not prevent fresh blood welling from the wound in his side as he made his way up the rope. He felt himself weakening as he worked his way closer to the ring, and when he reached it he paused, limbs shaking, while he sought to recover his strength.

There had been no time for thought since Salk Elan had pitched him over the side, and none now. Cursing his own stupidity was a waste of time. Killers awaited him in Malaz City's dark, narrow streets and alleys. His next few hours would, in all likelihood, be his last this side of Hood's Gates.

Kalam had no intention of being easy prey.

Crouched against the huge ring, he worked to slow his breathing once more, to still the seep of blood from his side and the countless leech-wounds.

Eyes on the warehouse roofs with sorcery-enhanced vision, and I've not even a shirt to hide my body's heat. They know I'm wounded, a challenge to the higher disciplines – I doubt even Surly in her prime could manage a cooling of flesh in these straits. Can I?

Once more he closed his eyes. *Draw the blood from the surface, draw it down to hide within muscle, close to bone. Every breath must be ice, every touch upon cobble and stone a matching of temperature. No residue in passage, no bloom in movement. What will they expect of a wounded man?*

Not this.

He opened his eyes, released one hand from the ring and pressed his forearm against the pitted metal. It felt warm.

Time to move.

The top of the pile was within easy reach. Kalam

straightened, slowly pulling himself onto the guano-crusted surface. Front Street stretched out before him. Cargo carts crowded the locked warehouse doors facing onto the street, the nearest one less than twenty paces away.

To run would be to invite death, because his body could not adjust to changes in temperature fast enough and the bloom would be unmissable.

One of those eels has crawled too far, and is about to crawl farther still. Flat on his belly, Kalam edged forward onto the damp cobblestones, his face against them as he sent his breath down beneath him.

Sorcery makes a hunter lazy, tuned only to what they expect will be obvious, given their enhanced senses. They forget the game of shadows, the play of darkness, the most subtle telltale signs . . . I hope.

He could not look up, but he knew that he was in truth completely exposed, like a worm crossing a flagstone path. A part of his mind threatened to shriek its panic, but the assassin crushed it down. Higher discipline was a ruthless master – of his own mind, his own body, his own soul.

His greatest dread was a break in the overcast sky above the city. The moon had become his enemy, and should it awaken, even the laziest of watchers could not fail to see the shadow Kalam would throw across the cobbles.

Minutes passed as he slid his agonizingly slow way across the street. The city beyond was silent, unnaturally so. A hunters' maze, prepared for him should he manage to reach it. A thought slipped through – *I've been spotted already, but why spoil the game? This hunt's to be a protracted pleasure, something to satisfy the brotherhood's thirst for vengeance. After all, why prepare a maze if you kill your victim before he can even reach it?*

The bitter logic of that was like a hot dagger in his chest, threatening to shatter his camouflage more thoroughly than anything else could. Yet he managed to slow his rise from the street, drawing and holding his breath before looking up.

He was beneath the cart, the top of his head brushing the flatbed's underside.

He paused. They were expecting a contest of subtlety, but sleight of hand was only one of Kalam's talents. *Always an advantage, those other, unexpected ones . . .* The assassin slipped forward, cleared the first wagon, then the next three before coming to the warehouse doors.

The cargo entrance was of course huge, two sliding palisade-like panels, now chained together with a massive padlock. To one side of them, however, was a smaller side door, also padlocked.

Kalam darted to it and flattened himself against the weathered wood. Both hands closed on the padlock.

There was nothing subtle in the brute strength the assassin possessed. While the padlock itself resisted the twisting force he delivered, the fittings that held it could not. His body pressing against the lock and latch muffled the splintering sounds.

Lock and fittings came away in his hands. Cradling them, Kalam reached out and pulled the door back just enough to let him slip through into the darkness beyond.

A rapid search through the main chamber led him to a large tool rack. He collected a pair of pick-tongs, a hatchet, a burlap sack of cloth-tacks, and a barely serviceable work-knife, its tip broken and its edge heavily nicked. He found a blacksmith's leather workshirt and slipped it on. In the backroom, he discovered a door that opened onto the alley behind the warehouse.

The Deadhouse, he judged, was about six streets away. *But Salk Elan knows – and they'll be waiting for me. I'd have to be an idiot to make straight for it – and they know that, as well.*

Slipping his various makeshift weapons into the shirt's tool-loops, Kalam unlatched the door, edged it open a crack and peered out. Seeing no movement, he pushed it open a few inches more, scanning the nearest rooftops, then the sky.

No-one, and the clouds were a solid cloak. Faint light bled from a few shuttered windows, which had the effect of deepening the gloom everywhere else. Somewhere in the distance a dog barked.

He stepped outside and padded down one edge of the crate-littered alley.

A pool of deeper darkness occupied an alcove near the alley mouth ahead. Kalam's eyes found it, locked on it. He pulled out his knife and hatchet and without pause swept straight for it.

The darkness poured its sorcery over him as he plunged into the alcove, his attack so sudden, so unexpected, that the two figures within had no time to draw weapons. The brutal blade of the work-knife tore out one man's throat. The hatchet chopped down to crush a clavicle and snap ribs. He released that weapon and slapped the palm of his left hand over the man's mouth as he drove the head back to crunch against the wall. The other Claw – a woman – slid down with a wet gurgling sound.

A moment later Kalam was searching their bodies, collecting throwing stars, throwing knives, two braces of short, wide-bladed stickers, a garrotte and the most cherished prize of all, a ribless Claw crossbow, screw-loaded, compact and deadly – if only at close range. Eight quarrels accompanied it, each one with an iron head that glistened with the poison called White Paralt.

Kalam appropriated the thin, black cloak from the man's corpse, pulling up its hood with its gauze vents positioned over his ears. The projecting cowl was also of gauze, ensuring peripheral vision.

The sorcery was fading as he completed his accoutrements, revealing that at least one of his victims had been a mage. *Damned sloppy – Topper's letting them get soft.*

865

He emerged from the alcove, raised his head and sniffed the air. A Hand's link had been broken – they would know that trouble had arrived, and would even now be slowly, cautiously closing in.

Kalam smiled. *You wanted a quarry on the run. Sorry to disappoint you.*

He set out into the night, hunting Claw.

The Hand's leader cocked his head, then stepped into the clear. A moment later two figures emerged from the alley and closed to confer.

'Blood's been spilled,' the leader murmured. 'Topper shall be—'

A soft clicking made him turn. 'Ah, now we learn the details,' the man said, watching their cloaked companion approach.

'The killer has arrived,' the newcomer growled.

'I am about to pluck Topper's strand—'

'Good, it's time he understood.'

'What—'

Both of the leader's companions fell to the cobbles. An enormous fist connected with the leader's face. Bone and cartilage crunched. The leader blinked unseeing eyes that filled with blood. With septum lodged in his forebrain, he crumpled.

Kalam crouched down to whisper in the dead man's ear. 'I know you can hear me, Topper. Two Hands left. Run and hide – I'll still find you.'

He straightened, retrieved his weapons.

The corpse at his feet gurgled a wet laugh and the assassin looked down as a spectral voice emerged from the dead man's lips. 'Welcome back, Kalam. Two Hands, you said? Not any more, old friend—'

'Scared you, did I?'

'Salk Elan appears to have let you off too easily. I shall not be as kind, I'm afraid—'

'I know where you are, Topper, and I'm coming for you.'

There was a long silence, then the corpse spoke one last time. 'By all means, my friend.'

The Imperial Warren was holed like cheesecloth that night, as Hand after Hand of Claw pushed through into the city. One such portal opened directly in a lone man's path – and the five figures announced their arrival with gasping breaths and splashed blood, the swift and as swiftly done noises of dying. Not one had managed more than a step onto the slick cobbles of Malaz City before their flesh began cooling in the gentle night.

Screams echoed down streets and alleys as denizens foolish enough to brave the open paid for their temerity with their lives. The Claw took no more chances.

The game that Kalam had turned, turned yet again.

The mosaic at their feet was endless, the multicoloured stones creating a pattern that defied comprehension, the strange floor stretching away to every horizon. The echo of their boots was muted and faintly sonorous.

Fiddler hitched his crossbow over one shoulder, with a shrug. 'We'd see trouble from a league away,' he said.

'You are all betraying the Azath,' Iskaral Pust hissed, pacing in circles around the group. 'The Jhag belongs beneath a root-webbed mound. That was the deal, the agreement, the scheme . . .' His voice fell away briefly, then resumed in a different tone. 'What agreement? Did Shadowthrone receive any answers to his query? Did the Azath reveal its ancient, stony face? No. Silence was the reply – to all. My master could have pronounced his intention to defecate on the House's portal and still the reply would not have changed. Silence.

Well, it certainly *seemed* there was a consensus. No objections were voiced, were they? No, not at all. Certain assumptions were necessary, oh yes, very necessary. And in the end, there was a sort of victory, was there not? All but for that Jhag there in the Trell's arms.' He stopped, panting as he regained his breath. 'Gods, we are walking for ever!'

'We should begin our journey,' Apsalar said.

'I'm for that,' Fiddler muttered. 'Only, which direction?'

Rellock had knelt down to study the mosaic tiles. They were the only source of light – overhead was pitch black. Each tile was no larger than a hand's width. The glow they cast pulsed in a slow but steady rhythm. The old fisherman now grunted.

'Father?'

'The pattern here—' He pointed to one tile in particular. 'That mottled line . . .'

Fiddler crouched down and studied the floor. 'If that's a track or something, it's a crooked one.'

'A track?' The fisherman looked up. 'No, here, along this side. That's the Kanese coastline.'

'What?'

The man ran one blunt fingertip down the ragged line. 'Starts on the Quon coast, down to Kan, then up to Cawn Vor – and there, that's Kartool Island, and southeast, there, in the tile's centre, that's Malaz Island.'

'You're trying to tell me that here, on this one tile at our feet, is mapped most of the Quon Tali continent?' Yet even as he asked, the pattern resolved itself, and before him was indeed what Apsalar's father had claimed. 'Then what,' he asked softly, 'is on the rest of them?'

'Well, they ain't consistent, if that's what you're wondering. There's breaks – other maps of other places, I guess. It's all jumbled, but I'd say the scale was the same on all of them.'

Fiddler slowly straightened. 'But that means . . .' His voice trailed into silence, as he looked out upon this endless floor, stretching for leagues in every direction. *Every god in the Abyss! Are these all the realms? Every world – every place home to a House of the Azath? Queen of Dreams, what power is this?*

'Within the warren of the Azath,' Mappo said, his tone one of awe, 'you could go . . . *anywhere.*'

'Are you sure of that?' Crokus asked. 'Here are the maps, yes, but –' he pointed down at the tile displaying the continent of Quon Tali – 'where's the gate? The way in?'

No-one spoke for a long moment, then Fiddler cleared his throat. 'You got an idea, lad?'

The Daru shrugged. 'Maps are maps – this one could be sitting on a tabletop, if you see my point.'

'So what do you suggest?'

'Ignore it. The only thing these tiles signify is that every House, in every place, is part of a pattern, a grand design. But even knowing that doesn't mean we can actually make sense of it. The Azath is beyond even the gods. We can end up getting lost in suppositions, in a mental game that takes us nowhere.'

'That's true enough,' the sapper grunted. 'And we're nowhere closer to figuring out which direction to walk in.'

'Perhaps Iskaral Pust has the right idea,' Apsalar said. Her boots grated on the tiles as she turned. 'Alas, he seems to have disappeared.'

Crokus spun around. 'Damn that bastard!'

The High Priest of Shadow, who had been ceaselessly circling them, was indeed nowhere to be seen. Fiddler grimaced. 'So he figured it out and didn't bother explaining before taking his leave—'

'Wait!' Mappo said. He set Icarium down, then took a dozen paces. 'Here,' he said. 'Hard to make out at first but now I see it clearly.'

The Trell seemed to be staring at something at his feet. 'What have you found?' Fiddler asked.

'Come closer – almost impossible to see otherwise, though that makes little sense . . .'

The others approached.

A gaping hole yawned, a ragged gap where Iskaral Pust had simply fallen through and vanished. Fiddler knelt, edging closer to the hole. 'Hood's breath!' he groaned. The tiles were no more than an inch thick. Beneath them was not solid ground. Beneath them there was . . . nothing.

'Is that the way out, do you think?' Mappo asked behind him.

The sapper edged back, the slick tiles suddenly feeling like the thinnest ice. 'Damned if I know, but I don't plan on jumping in and finding out.'

'I share your caution,' the Trell rumbled. He turned back to where Icarium lay and gathered his companion once again in his arms.

'That hole might spread,' Crokus said. 'I suggest we get moving. Any direction, just away from here.'

Apsalar hesitated. 'And Iskaral Pust? Perhaps he's lying unconscious on a ledge or something?'

'Not a chance,' Fiddler replied. 'From what I saw, the poor man's still falling. One look and every bone in me screamed *oblivion*. I think I'll trust my instincts on this one, lass.'

'A sad demise,' she said. 'I had grown almost fond of him.'

Fiddler nodded. 'Our very own pet scorpion, aye.'

Crokus took the lead as they moved away from the hole. Had they waited a few minutes longer, they would have seen a dull yellow mist rise from the gaping darkness, thickening until it was opaque. The mist remained for a time, then it began to dissipate, and when it finally vanished, so too had the hole – as if it had never been. The mosaic was complete once more.

Deadhouse. Malaz City, the heart of the Malazan Empire. There is nothing for us there. More, an explanation that made sense would challenge even my experienced inventiveness. We must, I fear, take our leave.

Somehow.

But this is far beyond me – this warren – and worse, my crimes are like wounds that refuse to close. I cannot escape my cowardice. In the end – and all here know it, though they do not speak of it – my selfish desires made a mockery of my integrity, my vows. I had a chance to see the threat ended, ended for ever.

How can friendship defeat such an opportunity? How can the comfort of familiarity rise up like a god, as if change itself had become something demonic? I am a coward – the offer of freedom, the sighing end to a lifetime's vow, proved the greatest terror of all.

And so, the simple truth . . . the tracks we have walked in for so long become our lives, in themselves a prison—

Apsalar leapt forward, her fingertips touching shoulder, then braids, then nothing. Her momentum took her forward, into the place where Mappo and Icarium had been a moment earlier. She fell towards a yawning darkness.

Crying out, Crokus grasped her ankles. He was pulled momentarily along the tiles towards the gaping hole before a fisherman's strong hands closed on him and anchored him down.

Together, the two men dragged Apsalar from the pit's edge. A dozen paces beyond it stood Fiddler – the Daru's cry had been the first intimation of trouble.

'They're gone!' Crokus shouted. 'They fell through – there was no warning, Fid! Nothing at all!'

The sapper softly cursed, lowering himself into an uneasy crouch. *We're intruders here . . .* He'd heard rumours of warrens that were airless, that were instant death to mortals who dared enter them. There was an arrogance in assuming that every realm in existence bowed to human needs. *Intruders – this place cares nothing for us, nor are there any laws demanding that it accommodate us.*

Mind you, the same could be said for any world.

He hissed, slowly straightened, fighting against the sudden welling of grief at the loss of two men he had come to consider friends. *And which of us is next?* 'To me,' he growled. 'All three of you – carefully.' He unslung his pack, set it down and rummaged inside until he found a coiled length of rope. 'We're tying ourselves together – if one goes, either we save him or her, or we all go. Agreed?'

Relieved nods answered him.

Aye, the thought of wandering alone in this warren is not a pleasant one.

They quickly attached the rope between them.

The four travellers had walked another thousand paces when the air stirred – the first wind they had felt since entering the warren – and they ducked as one beneath the passage of something enormous directly overhead.

Scrabbling for his crossbow, Fiddler twisted around to look skyward. 'Hood's breath!'

But the three dragons were already past, ignoring the humans entirely. They flew in triangular formation like a flight of geese, and were of a kind, ochre-scaled, their wing-spans as far across as five wagons end to end. Long, sinuous tails stretched back behind them.

'Foolish to think,' Apsalar muttered, 'that we're the only ones to make use of this realm.'

Crokus grunted. 'I've seen bigger . . .'

A faint grin cracked Fiddler's features. 'Aye, lad, I know you have.'

The dragons were almost at the edge of their vision when they banked as one, plunged down towards the ground and broke through the tiles, vanishing from sight.

No-one spoke for a long minute, then Apsalar's father cleared his throat and said, 'I think that just told us something.'

The sapper nodded. 'Aye.' *You go through when you get to where you're going – even if you don't exactly plan on it.* He thought back to Mappo and Icarium. The Trell would have had no reason to accompany them all the way to Malaz City. After all, Mappo had a friend to heal, to coax back to consciousness. He'd be looking for a safe place to do that. As for Iskaral Pust . . . *Probably at the cliff's foot right now, screaming up at the bhok'arala for a rope . . .*

'All right,' Fiddler said, straightening. 'Seems we've just got to keep moving . . . until the time and place arrives.'

'Mappo and Icarium are not lost, not dead,' Crokus said in obvious relief as they began walking again.

'Nor is the High Priest,' Apsalar added.

'Well,' the Daru muttered, 'I suppose we have to take the bad with the good.'

Fiddler briefly wondered about those three dragons – where they had gone, what tasks awaited them – then he shrugged. Their appearance, their departure and, in between and most importantly, their *indifference* to the four mortals below was a sobering reminder that the world was far bigger than that defined by their own lives, their own desires and goals. The seemingly headlong plunge this journey had become was in truth but the smallest succession of steps, of no greater import than the struggles of a termite.

The worlds live on, beyond us, countless unravelling tales.

In his mind's eye he saw his horizons stretch out on all sides, and as they grew ever vaster he in turn saw himself as ever smaller, ever more insignificant.

We are all lone souls. It pays to know humility, lest the delusion of control, of mastery, overwhelms. And indeed, we seem a species prone to that delusion, again and ever again . . .

Korbolo Dom's warriors celebrated their triumph through the hours of darkness after the Fall of Coltaine. The sounds of that

873

revelry drifted over Aren's walls and brought a coldness to the air that had little to do with the physical reality of the sultry night.

Within the city, facing the north gates, was a broad concourse, generally used as a caravan staging area. This open space was now packed with refugees. The task of billeting would have to await the more pressing needs of food, water and medical attention.

Commander Blistig had set his garrison to those efforts, and his soldiers worked tirelessly, displaying extraordinary compassion, as if answering their own need to respond to the enemy's triumph beyond the walls. Coltaine, his Wickans and the Seventh had given their lives for those the guard now tended. Solicitude was fast becoming an overwhelming gesture.

Yet other tensions rode the air.

The final sacrifice was unnecessary. We could have saved them, if not for the coward commanding us. Two powerful honours had clashed – the raw duty to save the lives of fellow soldiers, and the discipline of the Malazan command structure – and from that collision ten thousand living, breathing, highly trained soldiers now stood broken.

Down in the concourse, Duiker wandered aimlessly through the crowds. Figures loomed before him every now and then, blurred faces murmuring meaningless words, offering information that they each believed – hoped – would soothe him. The Wickan youths had claimed Nil and Nether and now protected them with a fierceness that none dared challenge. Countless refugees had been retrieved from the very edge of Hood's Gates, each one a source of savage defiance – a pleasure revealed in glittering eyes and bared teeth. Those few for whom the final flight – and perhaps the release of salvation itself – had proved too much for their broken, riven flesh, were fought for in unyielding desperation. Hood had to reach for those failing souls, reach for, grasp and drag them into oblivion, with the healers employing every skill they possessed to defeat the effort.

Duiker had found his own oblivion deep inside himself, and he had no desire to leave its numbing comfort. Within that place, pain could do naught but gnaw at the very edges, and those edges seemed to be growing ever more distant.

Words occasionally seeped through, as various officers and soldiers delivered details of things they clearly felt the historian should know. The caution in their voices was not necessary, for the information was absorbed stripped of feeling. Duiker was beyond hurting.

The *Silanda*, with its load of wounded soldiers, had not arrived, he learned from a Wickan youth named Temul. Adjunct Tavore's fleet was less than a week away. Korbolo Dom was likely to begin a siege, for Sha'ik was on her way from Raraku, leading an army twice the size of the renegade Fist's own force. Mallick Rel had led High Fist Pormqual back to the palace. A plan was now in the air, a plan to reap vengeance, and it was but hours away—

Blinking, Duiker tried to focus on the face before him, the face telling him this news in an urgent tone. But the first brush of recognition sent the historian reeling back in his mind. Too much pain was embedded in the memories that were so closely chained to that recognition. He stepped back.

The figure reached out a strong hand that closed on Duiker's ragged shirt and pulled the historian closer once again. The bearded mouth was moving, shaping words, demanding, angry words.

'—through to you, Historian! It's the assumptions, don't you see? Our only reports have come from that nobleman, Nethpara. But we need a soldier's assessment – do you understand? Damn you, it's almost dawn!'

'What? What are you talking about?'

Blistig's face twisted. 'Mallick Rel has got through to Pormqual. Hood knows how, but he has! We're going to strike Korbolo's army – in less than an hour's time, when they're still drunk, still exhausted. We're marching out, Duiker! Do you understand me?'

Cruel . . . so cruel—

'How many are out there? We need reliable estimates—'

'Thousands. Tens of thousands. Hundreds—'

'Think, damn you! If we can knock these bastards out . . . before Sha'ik arrives—'

'I don't know, Blistig! That army grew with every Hood-cursed league!'

'Nethpara judges just under ten thousand—'

'The man's a fool.'

'He's also laying the deaths of thousands of innocent refugees at Coltaine's feet—'

'W— What?' The historian staggered, and if not for Blistig's grip would have fallen.

'Don't you see? Without you, Duiker, that version of what happened out there will win the day. It's already spread through the ranks and it's damned troubling. Certainty's crumbling – the desire for vengeance is weakening—'

It was enough. The historian felt a jolt. Eyes widening, he straightened. 'Where is he? Nethpara! Where—'

'He's been in with Pormqual and Mallick Rel for the past two bells.'

'Take me there.'

A succession of horns echoed behind them, the call for assembly. Duiker's gaze swept past the commander to the ranks contracting into formation. He stared skyward, saw the stars dimming in a lightening sky.

'Fener's tusk,' Blistig growled. 'It might be too late—'

'Take me to Pormqual – to Mallick Rel—'

'Follow me, then.'

The refugees were stirring as garrison soldiers moved among them, beginning the task of clearing the concourse to allow room for the High Fist's army.

Blistig pushed through the crowd, Duiker a step behind him. 'Pormqual's ordered my garrison out with them,' the commander said over his shoulder. 'Rearguard. That's in defiance of my responsibility. My task is to defend this city, yet the High Fist has been conscripting from my own soldiers, bleeding the companies. I'm down to three hundred now, barely enough to hold the walls. Especially with all the Red Blades under arrest—'

'Under arrest! Why?'

'Seven Cities blood – Pormqual doesn't trust them.'

'The fool! They're the most loyal soldiers of the Empire I've ever known—'

'I agree, Historian, but my opinion is worthless—'

'Mine had better not be,' Duiker said.

Blistig paused, turning. 'Do you support the High Fist's decision to attack?'

'Hood, no!'

'Why?'

'Because we don't know how many are out there. Wiser to wait for Tavore, wiser still to let Korbolo fling his warriors against these walls—'

Blistig nodded. 'We'd cut them to pieces. The question is, can you convince Pormqual of all you've just said?'

'You know him,' Duiker retorted. 'I don't.'

The commander grimaced. 'Let's go.'

The standards of the High Fist's army flanked a knot of mounted figures near the mouth of the main avenue leading off from the concourse. Blistig led the historian directly for them.

Duiker saw Pormqual seated atop a magnificent warhorse. The High Fist's armour was ornate, more decorative than functional. The jewelled hilt of a Grisian broadsword jutted from one hip; the helm bore a gold-threaded sunburst on the polished iron skullcap. His face looked sickly and bloodless.

Mallick Rel sat on a white horse beside the High Fist, silk-cloaked and weaponless, a sea-blue cloth wrapped about his head. Various officers, both mounted and on foot, surrounded them, and among that group Duiker saw Nethpara and Pullyk Alar.

A red mist descended on the scene as Duiker's stare fixed on the two noblemen. Increasing his pace, he pushed past Blistig, who snapped a hand out to drag the historian back.

'Leave that till later, man. You've got a more immediate responsibility to deal with first.'

Trembling, Duiker forced his rage back. He managed a nod.

'Come on, the High Fist has seen us.'

Pormqual's expression was cold as he looked down on Duiker. His voice was shrill as he said, 'Historian, your arrival is timely. We have two tasks before us this day, both of which require your presence—'

'High Fist—'

'Silence! Interrupt me again and I'll have your tongue cut out!' He paused, settled, then resumed his statement. 'First of all, you shall yourself accompany us in the battle to come. To witness the proper means of dealing with that rabble. The selling of the lives of innocent refugees is not a bargain I shall make – there shall be no repetition of earlier tragedies, earlier crimes of treason! The fools out there have only now settled to sleep – and they shall pay for that stupidity, I assure you.

'Then, when the renegades have been slaughtered, we shall attend to other responsibilities, primarily your arrest and that of the warlocks known as Nil and Nether – the last remaining "officers" of Coltaine's horrific command. And I assure you, the punishment following your conviction shall match the severity of your crimes.' He gestured and an aide led Duiker's mare forward. 'Alas, your beast is hardly fit for the company, but it shall suffice.

'Commander Blistig, prepare your soldiers for marching. We wish our rearguard to be no more and no less than three hundred paces behind us. I trust that is within your capabilities – if not, inform me now, and I shall happily place someone else in command of the garrison.'

'Aye, High Fist, the task is within my capabilities.'

Duiker's gaze swung to Mallick Rel, and the historian wondered at the satisfied flush in the priest's face, but only for a moment. *Ah, of course, past slights. Not a man to cross, are you, Rel?*

In silence, the historian walked to his horse and climbed into the saddle. He laid a hand on the mare's thin, ungroomed neck, then gathered the reins.

The lead companies of medium cavalry were assembled at the gate. Once out of the city, little time would be wasted, as the horsewarriors would immediately part in a sweeping manoeuvre intended to surround Korbolo's encampment, while the infantry poured out from the gate to assemble into solid phalanxes before marching on the enemy position.

Blistig had departed the scene without a backward glance. Duiker stared at the distant gate, scanned the troops gathered there.

'Historian.'

He turned his head, looked down at Nethpara.

The nobleman was smiling. 'You should have treated me with more respect. I suppose you see that now, although it's come too late for you.'

Nethpara did not notice Duiker slip his boot from the stirrup.

'For the insults you have committed upon my person . . . for the laying of hands on me, Historian, you shall suffer—'

'No doubt,' Duiker cut in. 'And here's one last insult.' He kicked out, the toe of his boot driving into the nobleman's flabby throat, then up. Trachea crumpled inward, head snapped back with a crunching, popping sound, Nethpara pitched backward, thumped heavily on the cobblestones. His eyes stared up unseeing at the pale sky.

Pullyk Alar shrieked.

Soldiers closed in around the historian, weapons out.

'By all means,' Duiker said, 'I shall welcome an end to this—'

'You shall not be so fortunate!' Pormqual hissed, white with rage.

Duiker sneered at the man. 'You've already convicted me as an executioner. What's one more, you craven pile of dung?' He shifted his gaze to Mallick Rel. 'And as for you, Jhistal, come closer – my life's still incomplete.'

The historian did not notice – nor did anyone else – the arrival of a captain of Blistig's garrison. The man had been about to speak with Duiker, to inform him of the safe delivery of a child to a grandfather. But at the word 'Jhistal' he stiffened, then, eyes widening, he took a step back.

The gates opened just then, and the troops of cavalry poured through. Motion rippled through the legions of infantry as weapons were readied.

Keneb took another step back, that lone word echoing in his mind. He knew it from somewhere, but full awareness eluded him, even as alarms rang in his mind. A voice within was shouting that he needed to find Blistig – he did not yet know why, but it was imperative—

But he had run out of time.

Keneb stared out as the army surged towards the gate. The orders had been given, and the momentum was unstoppable.

The captain took another step back, his words to Duiker forgotten. He stumbled over Nethpara's body unnoticing, then spun about. And ran.

Sixty paces on, Keneb's mind was suddenly flooded with the memory of when he had last heard the word 'Jhistal'.

* * *

Duiker rode with the mounted officers out onto the plain.

Korbolo Dom's army looked to be in full panicked flight, though the historian noted that they still held on to their weapons even as they fled back over the mound and its facing slope. The High Fist's cavalry rode hard to either side, quickly outpacing the footsoldiers as they pushed to complete the encirclement. Both wings rode beyond line of sight, into the evenly distributed hills of the burial ground.

The High Fist's legions moved at double time, silent and determined. They had no hope of catching the fleeing army until the cavalry had completed the encirclement, closing off all avenues of escape.

'As you predicted, High Fist!' Mallick Rel shouted to Pormqual as they cantered along. 'They are routed!'

'But they shall not escape, shall they?' Pormqual laughed, pitching unevenly in his saddle.

Gods below, the High Fist can't even ride.

The pursuit took them up and over the first barrow, and they rode among the corpses of the Seventh and the Wickans. Those looted bodies spread northward in a wide swath, mapping the route of Coltaine's running battle, over the next barrow, then around the base of the one beyond. Duiker struggled to keep from scanning those corpses, seeking familiar faces in their unfamiliar expressions of death. He stared forward, studying the fleeing renegades.

Pormqual periodically slowed their pace to keep within the midst of the infantry. The wings of cavalry were somewhere ahead, and had not reappeared. In the meantime, the thousands of fleeing soldiers stayed ahead of the phalanxes, sweeping around the barrows, leaving booty behind as they went.

The High Fist and his army doggedly pursued, down into a vast basin, packed with the routed enemy who began pouring up the gently sloping sides. Dust ringed the crest to the east and west, and directly ahead.

'The encirclement is complete!' Pormqual cried. 'See the dust!'

Duiker frowned at that dust. Faintly, he heard the sounds of battle. A moment later those sounds began to diminish, while the rising dust thickened, deepened.

The infantry marched down into the basin.

Something's wrong . . .

The fleeing soldiers had reached the crests now on all sides but the south, but instead of continuing their panicked pace, they slowed, readied their weapons and turned about.

The curtain of dust climbed higher behind those warriors, then mounted figures appeared – not Pormqual's cavalry, but tribal riders. A moment later the ring of footsoldiers thickened, as rank after rank joined them.

Duiker spun in his saddle. Seven Cities cavalry lined the south skylines, closing the back door.

And so we ride into the simplest of traps. Leaving Aren defenceless . . .

'Mallick!' Pormqual shrieked, reining in. 'What is happening! What has happened?'

The priest's head was jerking in all directions, his jaw dropping. 'Treachery!' he hissed. He swung his white horse around, eyes fixing on Duiker. 'This is your doing, Historian! Part of the bargain Nethpara hinted at! More, I see the sorcery around you now – you have been communicating with Korbolo Dom! Gods, we were fools!'

Duiker ignored the man, his eyes squinting as he studied the scene to the south, and the tag-end elements of Pormqual's army as they wheeled about to face the threat now behind them. Clearly, the High Fist's cavalry wings had been annihilated.

'We are surrounded! They are in the tens of thousands! We shall be slaughtered!' The High Fist jabbed a finger at the historian. 'Kill him! Kill him now!'

'Wait!' Mallick Rel shouted. He turned to Pormqual. 'Please, High Fist, leave that to me, I beg you! Be assured that I shall exact a worthy punishment!'

'As you say, then, but—' Pormqual glared about. 'What shall we do, Mallick?'

The priest pointed to the north. 'There, riders approach under a white flag – let us see what Korbolo Dom proposes, High Fist! What have we to lose?'

'I cannot speak with them!' Pormqual gibbered. 'I cannot think! Mallick – please!'

'Very well,' the Jhistal priest acceded. He swung his mount around, jabbed spurred heels into the beast's flanks and rode through the milling ranks of the High Fist's trapped army.

Midway up the distant north slope, the converging riders met. The parley lasted less than a minute, then Mallick wheeled and rode back.

'If we push back we can break the elements to the south,' Duiker quietly said to the High Fist. 'A fighting withdrawal back to the city's gates—'

'Not another word from you, traitor!'

Mallick Rel arrived, his expression filled with hope. 'Korbolo Dom has had enough of bloodshed, High Fist! Yesterday's slaughter has left him sickened!'

'What does he propose, then?' Pormqual demanded, leaning forward.

'Our only hope, High Fist. You must command your army to lay down its arms – to pass them out to the edges, then withdraw into a compact mass in the centre of this basin. They shall be prisoners of war, and therefore treated with mercy. As for you and me, we shall be made hostages. When Tavore arrives, arrangements will be made for our honourable return. High Fist, we have no choice in the matter . . .'

A strange lassitude seeped into Duiker as he listened. He knew he could say nothing to sway the High Fist. He slowly dismounted, reached under his mare and unhitched the girth.

'What are you doing, traitor?' Mallick Rel demanded.

'I'm freeing my horse,' the historian said reasonably. 'The enemy won't bother with her – too worn out to be of any use. She'll head back to Aren – it's the least I can do for her.' He removed the saddle, dropped it to the ground to one side, then pulled the bit from the mare's mouth.

The priest stared for a moment longer, a slight frown on his face, then he turned back to the High Fist. 'They await our reply.'

Duiker stepped close to his horse's head and laid a hand on the soft muzzle. 'Take care,' he whispered. Then he stepped back, gave the animal a slap on the rump. The mare sprang away, wheeled, then trotted southward – as Duiker knew she would.

'What choice?' Pormqual whispered. 'Unlike Coltaine, I must consider my soldiers . . . their lives are worth everything . . . peace will return to this land, sooner or later . . .'

'Thousands of husbands, wives, and fathers and mothers will bless your name, High Fist. To fight now, to seek out that bitter, pointless end, ah, they will curse your name for all eternity.'

'I cannot have that,' Pormqual agreed. He faced his officers. 'Lay down arms. Deliver the orders – all weapons to go to the edges and left there, the ranks to withdraw to the centre of the basin.'

Duiker stared at the four captains who listened in silence to the High Fist's commands. A long moment passed, then the officers saluted and rode off.

Duiker turned away.

The disarmament took close to an hour, the Malazan soldiers yielding their weapons in silence. Those weapons were piled on the ground just beyond the phalanxes, then the soldiers made their way inward, forming up in tight, restless ranks in the basin's centre.

Tribal horsewarriors then rode down and collected the arms. Twenty minutes later an army of ten thousand Malazans crowded the basin, weaponless, helpless.

Korbolo Dom's vanguard detached from the forces on the north ridge and rode down towards the High Fist's position.

Duiker stared at the approaching group. He saw Kamist Reloe, a handful of war chiefs, two unarmed women who were in all likelihood mages, and Korbolo Dom himself, a squat half-Napan, all hair shaved from his body, revealing scars in tangled webs. He was smiling as he reined in with his companions before the High Fist, Mallick Rel and the other officers.

'Well done,' he growled, his eyes on the priest.

The Jhistal dismounted, stepped forward and bowed. 'I deliver to you High Fist Pormqual and his ten thousand. More, I deliver to you the city Aren, in Sha'ik's name—'

'Wrong,' Duiker chuckled.

Mallick Rel faced him.

'You've not delivered Aren, Jhistal.'

'What claims do you make now, old man?'

'I'm surprised you didn't notice,' the historian said. 'Too busy gloating, I guess. Take a close look at the companies around you, especially those to the south . . .'

Mallick's eyes narrowed as he scanned the gathered legions. Then he paled. 'Blistig!'

'Seems the commander and his garrison decided to stay behind after all. Granted, they're only two or three hundred, but we both know that that will be enough – for the week or so until Tavore arrives. Aren's walls are high, well impregnated these days with Otataral, I believe – proof against any sorcery. Thinking on it, I would predict that there are Red Blades lining those walls now, as well as the garrison. You have failed in your betrayal, Jhistal. Failed.'

The priest jerked forward, the back of his hand cracking against Duiker's face. The historian was spun around by the savage blow, and the rings on the man's hand raking through the flesh of one cheek burst the barely healed splits in his lips and chin. He fell hard to the ground and felt something shatter against his sternum.

He pushed himself up, the blood streaming down his lacerated face. Looking down at the ground beneath him, he expected to see tiny fragments of broken glass, but there were none. The leather thong around his neck now had nothing on it at all.

Hands pulled him roughly to his feet and dragged him around to face Mallick Rel once more.

The priest was trembling still. 'Your death shall be—'

'Silence!' Korbolo snapped. He eyed Duiker. 'You are the historian who rode with Coltaine.'

The historian faced him. 'I am.'

'You are a soldier.'

'As you say.'

'I do, and so you shall die with these soldiers, in a manner no different—'

'You mean to slaughter ten thousand unarmed men and women, Korbolo Dom?'

'I mean to cripple Tavore before she even sets foot on this continent. I mean to make her too furious to think. I mean to crack that façade so she dreams of vengeance day and night, poisoning her every decision.'

'You always fashioned yourself as the Empire's harshest Fist, didn't you, Korbolo Dom? As if cruelty's a virtue . . .'

The pale-blue-skinned commander simply shrugged. 'Best join the others now, Duiker – a soldier of Coltaine's army deserves that much.' Korbolo then turned to Mallick. 'My mercy, however, does not extend to that one soldier whose arrow stole Coltaine from our pleasure. Where is he, Priest?'

'He went missing, alas. Last seen an hour after the deed – Blistig had his soldiers search everywhere, without success. Even if he has now found him, he is with the garrison, afraid to say.'

The renegade Fist scowled. 'There have been disappointments this day, Mallick Rel.'

'Korbolo Dom, sir!' Pormqual said, still bearing an expression of disbelief. 'I do not understand—'

'Clearly you do not,' the commander agreed, his face twisting in disgust. 'Jhistal, have you any particular fate in mind for this fool?'

'None. He is yours.'

'I cannot grant him the dignified sacrifice I have in mind for his soldiers. That would leave too bitter a taste in my mouth, I'm afraid.' Korbolo Dom hesitated, then sighed and made a slight gesture with one hand.

A war chief's tulwar flashed behind the High Fist, lifted the man's head clean from his shoulders and sent it spinning. The warhorse bolted in alarm and broke through the ring of soldiers. The beautiful beast galloped down among the unarmed soldiers, carrying its headless burden into their midst. The High Fist's corpse, Duiker saw, rode in the saddle with a grace not matched in life, weaving this way and that before hands reached up to slow the frightened horse, and Pormqual's body slid to one side, falling into waiting arms.

It may have been his imagination, but Duiker thought he could hear the harsh laughter of a god.

There was no shortage of spikes, yet it took a day and a half before the last screaming prisoner was nailed to the last crowded cedar lining Aren Way.

Ten thousand dead and dying Malazans stared down on that wide, exquisitely engineered Imperial road – eyes unseeing or eyes uncomprehending – it made little difference.

Duiker was the last, the rusty iron spikes driven through his wrists and upper arms to hold him in place high on the tree's blood-streaked bole. More spikes were hammered through his ankles and the muscles of his outer thighs.

The pain was unlike anything the historian had ever known before. Yet even worse was the knowledge that that pain would accompany his entire final journey down into eventual unconsciousness, and with it – an added trauma – were the images burned into him: almost forty hours of being driven on foot up Aren Way, watching each and every one of those ten thousand soldiers joined to the mass crucifixion in a chain of suffering stretching over three leagues, each link scores of men and women nailed to every tree, to every available space on those tall, broad trunks.

The historian was well beyond shock when his turn finally came, as the last soldier to close the human chain, and he was dragged to the tree, up the scaffolding, pushed against the ridged bark, arms forced outward, feeling the cold bite of the iron spikes pressed against his skin, and then, when the mallets swung, the explosion of pain that loosed his bowels, leaving him stained and writhing. The greatest pain arrived when the scaffolding dropped from under him, and his full weight fell onto the pinning spikes. Until that moment, he had truly believed he had gone as far into agony as was humanly possible.

He was wrong.

After what seemed like an eternity when the ceaseless shrieking of his sundered flesh had drowned out all else within him, a cool, calm clarity emerged, and thoughts, scattered and wandering, rose into his fading awareness.

The Jaghut ghost . . . why do I think of him now? Of that eternity of grief? What is he to me? What is anyone or anything to me, now? I await Hood's Gate at last – the time for memories, for regrets and comprehensions is past. You must see that now, old man. Your nameless marine awaits you, and Bult and Corporal List, and Lull and Sulwar and Mincer. Kulp and Heboric, too, most likely. You leave a place of strangers now, and go to a place of companions, of friends.

So claim the priests of Hood.

It's the last gift. I am done with this world, for I am alone in it. Alone.

A ghostly, tusked face rose before his mind's eye, and though he had never before seen it, he knew that the Jaghut had found him. The gravest compassion filled that creature's unhuman eyes, a compassion that Duiker could not understand.

Why grieve, Jaghut? I shall not haunt eternity as you have done. I shall not return to this place, nor suffer again the losses a mortal suffers in life, and in living. Hood is about to bless me, Jaghut – no need to grieve . . .

Those thoughts echoed only a moment longer, as the Jaghut's ravaged face faded and darkness closed in around the historian, closed in until it swallowed him.

And with it, awareness ceased.

CHAPTER TWENTY-THREE

> Laseen sent Tavore
> Rushing across the seas
> to clasp Coltaine's hand
> And closing her fingers
> She held crow-picked bones.
>
> *The Sha'ik Uprising*
> Wu

Kalam threw himself into the shadows at the base of a low, battered wall, then dragged the still-warm corpse half over him. He ducked his head down, then lay still, battling to slow his breathing.

A few moments later, light footfalls sounded on the street's cobbles. A voice hissed an angry halt.

'They pursued,' another hunter whispered. 'And he ambushed them – here. Gods! What kind of man is he?'

A third Claw spoke, a woman. 'He can't be far away—'

'Of course he's close,' snapped the leader who had first called the halt. 'He doesn't have wings, does he? He's not immortal, he's not immune to the charms of our blades – no more such mutterings, do you two hear me? Now spread out – you, up that side, and you, up the other.' Sorcery cast its cold breath. 'I'll stay in the middle,' the leader said.

Aye, and unseen, meaning you're first, bastard.

Kalam listened as the other two headed off. He knew the pattern they would assume, the two flankers moving ahead, the leader – hidden in sorcery – hanging back, eyes flicking between the two hunters, scanning alley mouths, rooftops, a rib-less crossbow in each hand. Kalam waited a moment longer, then slowly, silently slipped free of the corpse and rose into a crouch.

He padded into the street, his bare feet making no sound. To someone who knew what to look for, the bloom of darkness edging forward twenty paces ahead was just discernible. Not an easy spell to maintain, it was inevitably weaker to the rear, and Kalam could make out a hint of the figure moving within it.

He closed the distance like a charging leopard. One of Kalam's elbows connected with the base of the leader's skull, killing him instantly. He caught one of the crossbows before it struck the cobbles, but the other eluded him, clattering and skittering on the street. Silently cursing, the assassin continued his charge, angling right, towards an alley mouth twenty paces behind the flanker on that side.

He dived at the muted snap of a crossbow and felt the quarrel rip through his cloak. Then he was rolling into the alley's narrow confines, sliding on rotted vegetables. Rats scattered from his path as he regained his feet and darted into deeper shadows.

An alcove loomed on his left and he spun, backed into its gloom and pulled free his own crossbow. Doubly armed, he waited.

A figure edged into view and paused opposite him, no more than six feet away.

The woman ducked and twisted even as Kalam fired – and the assassin knew he had missed. Her dagger, however, did not. The blade, flashing out from her hand, thudded as it struck him just beneath his right clavicle. A second thrown weapon – an iron star – embedded itself in the alcove's wooden door beside Kalam's face.

He pressed the release on the second crossbow. The quarrel took her low in the belly. She tumbled back and was dead of the White Paralt before she stopped moving.

Kalam was not – the weapon jutting from his chest must be clean. He sank down, laying the two crossbows on the ground, then reached up and withdrew the knife, reversing grip.

He'd already used up his other weapons, although he still retained the tongs and the small sack of cloth-tacks.

The last hunter was close, waiting for Kalam to make another break – and the man knew precisely where he hid. The body lying opposite was the clearest indication of that.

Now what?

The right-hand side of his shirt was wet and sticky, and he could feel the heat of the blood streaming down his body on that side. It was his third minor wound of the night – a throwing star had found his back during the next-to-last skirmish. Such weapons were never poisoned – too risky for the thrower, even when gloved. The heavy apron had absorbed most of the impact, and he'd scraped the star off against a wall.

His mental discipline in slowing the flow of blood from the various wounds was close to tatters. He was weakening. Fast.

Kalam looked straight up. The underside of a wooden balcony was directly overhead, the two paint-chipped braces about seven and a half feet above the ground. A jump might allow him to reach one, but that would be a noisy affair, and success would leave him helpless.

He drew the tongs from their loop. Gripping the bloody knife in his teeth, he slowly straightened, reaching up with the tongs. They closed over the brace.

Now, will the damned thing hold my weight?

Gripping the handles hard, he cautiously tensed his shoulders, drew himself up an inch, then another. The brace did not so much as groan – and he realized that the wooden beam in all likelihood extended into a deep socket in the stone wall itself. He continued pulling himself upward.

The challenge was maintaining silence, for any rustle or whisper of noise would alert his hunter. Arms and shoulders trembling, Kalam drew his legs up, a fraction at a time, tucked his right leg even higher, then edged it, foot first, through the triangular gap above the brace.

He hooked that leg, pulled, and was finally able to ease the strain on his arms and shoulders.

Kalam hung there, motionless, for a long minute.

Claws liked waiting games. They excelled in contests of patience. His hunter had evidently concluded that this was one of those games, and he intended to win it.

Well, stranger, I don't play by your rules.

He slipped the tongs free, held them out and lifted them towards the balcony's floor. This was the greatest risk, since he had no idea what occupied that floor above him. He probed with the tongs in minute increments until he could reach no farther, then he lowered the tool down and left it there.

The knife stayed clenched between his teeth, filling his mouth with the taste of his own blood. With both hands freed, Kalam gripped the balcony's ledge, slowly pulled his weight away from the brace and drew himself up. Hands climbing the railings, he swung a leg over and, a moment later, crouched on the balcony floor, the tongs at his feet.

He scanned the area. Clay pots housing various herbs, a moulded bread oven on a foundation of bricks occupying one end, the heat radiating from it reaching the assassin's sweat-cooled face.

A barred hatch that a person would have to crawl to get through offered the only way into the room beyond.

His scan ended upon meeting the eyes of a small dog crouched at the end opposite the bread oven. Black-haired, compactly muscled and with a foxlike snout and ears, the creature was chewing on half a rat, and as it chewed it watched Kalam's every move with those sharp, black eyes.

Kalam released a very soft sigh. *Another dubious claim to fame for Malaz City: the Malazan ratter, bred for its fearless insanity.* There was no predicting what the dog would do once it had decided its meal was done. It might lick his hand. It might bite his nose off.

He watched it sniff at the mangled meat between its paws, then gobble it up, chewing overlong as it considered Kalam. Then it ate the rat's tail, choking briefly – the sound barely a whisper – before managing to swallow its length.

The ratter licked its forepaws, rose into a sitting position, ducked its head to lick elsewhere, then stood facing the bleeding assassin.

The barking exploded in the night air, a frenzy that had the ratter bouncing around with the effort.

Kalam leapt up onto the balcony rail. A blur of motion darted beneath him, down in the alley. He plunged straight for it, the throwing knife in his left hand.

Even as he dropped through the air, he was sure he was finished. His lone hunter had found allies – another entire Hand.

Sorcery flared upward to strike Kalam like a massive fist. The knife flew from nerveless fingers. Twisting, his trajectory knocked awry by the mage's attack, he missed his target and struck the cobbles hard on his left side.

The maniacal barking overhead continued unabated.

Kalam's intended target charged him, blades flashing. He drew his legs up and kicked out, but the man slipped past with a deft motion. The knife blade scored against Kalam's ribs on either side. The hunter's forehead cracked against his nose. Light exploded behind the assassin's eyes.

A moment later, as the hunter reared back, straddling Kalam, and raised both knives, a snarling black bundle landed on the man's head. He shrieked as razorlike, overlong canines ripped open one side of his face.

Kalam caught one wrist, snapped it and pulled the knife from the spasming hand.

The hunter was desperately stabbing at the ratter with the other knife, without much luck, then he threw the weapon away and reached for the writhing dog.

Kalam sank his knife into the hunter's heart.

Pushing the body aside, he staggered upright – to find himself surrounded.

'You can call your dog off, Kalam,' a woman said.

He glanced down at the animal – it hadn't slowed. Blood spattered the cobbles around the corpse's head and neck.

'Alas,' Kalam growled. 'Not mine . . . though I wish I had a hundred of the beasts.' The pain of his shattered nose throbbed. Tears streamed from his eyes, joining the flow of blood dripping from his lips and chin.

'Oh, for Hood's sake!' The woman turned to one of her hunters. 'Kill the damned thing—'

'Not necessary,' Kalam said, stepping over. He reached down, grabbed the creature by its scruff and lobbed it back towards the balcony. The ratter yelped, just clearing the rail, then vanished from sight. A wild skitter of claws announced its landing.

A wavering voice reached down from the balcony's hatch. 'Flower, darling, settle down now, there's a good boy.'

Kalam eyed the leader. 'All right, then,' he said. 'Finish it.'

'With pleasure—'

The quarrel's impact threw her into Kalam's arms, almost skewering him on the great barbed point jutting from her chest. The four remaining hunters dived for cover, not knowing what had arrived, as horse hooves crashed in the alley.

Kalam gaped to see his stallion charging for him and,

crouched low over the saddle and swinging back the clawfoot on the Marine-issue crossbow, Minala.

The assassin stepped aside a split second before being trampled, grasped an edge of the saddle and let the animal's momentum swing him up behind Minala. She thrust the crossbow into his hands. 'Cover us!'

Twisting, he saw four shapes in pursuit. Kalam fired. The hunters pitched down to the ground as one. The quarrel careened off a wall and skittered away into the darkness.

The alley opened onto a street. Minala wheeled the stallion to the left. Hooves skidded, spraying sparks. Righting itself, the horse bolted forward.

Malaz City's harbour district was a tangle of narrow, twisting streets and alleys, seemingly impossible for a horse at full gallop, in the dead of night. The next few minutes marked the wildest ride Kalam had ever known. Minala's skill was breathtaking.

After a short while, Kalam leaned close to her. 'Where in Hood's name are you taking us? The whole city's crawling with Claws, woman—'

'I know, damn you!'

She guided the stallion across a wooden bridge. Looking up, the assassin saw the upper district and, beyond it, a looming black shape: the cliff – and Mock's Hold.

'Minala!'

'You wanted the Empress, right? Well, you bastard, she's right there – in Mock's Hold!'

Oh, Hood's shadow!

The tiles gave way without a sound. Cold blackness swallowed the four travellers.

The drop ended abruptly, in a bone-jarring impact with smooth, polished flagstones.

Groaning, Fiddler sat up, the sack of munitions still strapped to his shoulders. He'd injured his barely healed ankle in the fall and the pain was excruciating. Teeth clenched, he looked around. The others were all in one piece, it seemed, slowly clambering to their feet.

They were in a round room, a perfect match to the one they had left in Tremorlor. For a moment, the sapper feared they had simply returned there, but then he smelled salt in the air.

'We're here,' he said. 'Deadhouse.'

'What makes you so sure?' Crokus demanded.

Fiddler crawled over to a wall and levered himself upright. He tested the leg, winced. 'I smell Malaz Bay – and feel how damp the air is. This ain't Tremorlor, lad.'

'But we might be in any House, in any place beside a bay—'

'We might,' the sapper conceded.

'It's simply a matter of finding out,' Apsalar said reasonably. 'You've hurt your ankle again, Fiddler.'

'Aye. I wish Mappo was here with his elixirs . . .'

'Can you walk?' Crokus asked.

'Not much choice.'

Apsalar's father approached the stair, looked down. 'Someone's home,' he said. 'I see lantern light.'

'Oh, that's just wonderful,' Crokus muttered, unsheathing his knives.

'Put 'em away,' Fiddler said. 'Either we're guests or we're dead. Let's go introduce ourselves, shall we?'

Descending to the main floor – with Fiddler leaning hard on the Daru – they passed through an open door into the hallway. Lanterns glowed in niches along its length, and the flicker of firelight issued from the open double doors opposite the entranceway.

As at Tremorlor, a massive suit of armour filled an alcove halfway down the hall's length, and this one had seen serious battle.

The group paused to regard it briefly, in silence, before continuing on to the opened doors.

Apsalar leading, they entered the main chamber. The flames in the stone fireplace seemed to be burning without fuel, and a strange blackness around its edges revealed it as a small portal, opened onto a warren of ceaseless fire.

A figure, its back to them, stood staring into those flames. Dressed in faded ochre robes, the man was solid, broadshouldered and at least seven feet tall. A long, iron-hued ponytail swept down between his shoulders, bound just above the small of his back with a dull length of chain.

Without turning, the guardian spoke in a low, rumbling voice. 'Your failure in taking Icarium has been noted.'

Fiddler grunted. 'In the end, it was not up to us. Mappo—'

'Oh yes, Mappo,' the guardian cut in. 'The Trell. He has walked at Icarium's side too long, it seems. There are duties that surpass friendship. The Elders scarred him deep when they destroyed an entire settlement and laid the blame at Icarium's feet. They imagined that would suffice. A Watcher was needed, desperately. The one who had held that responsibility before had taken his own life. For months Icarium walked the land alone, and the threat was too great.'

The words reached into Fiddler, tore at his insides. *No, Mappo believes Icarium destroyed his home, murdered his family, everyone he knew. No, how could you have done that?*

'The Azath has worked towards this taking for a long time, mortals.' The man turned then. Huge tusks framed his thin mouth, jutting from his lower lip. The greenish cast of his weathered skin made him look ghostly, despite the hearth's warm light. Eyes the colour of dirty ice regarded them.

Fiddler stared, seeing what he could not believe – the resemblance was unmistakeable, every feature an echo. His mind reeled.

'My son must be stopped – his rage is a poison,' the Jaghut

said. 'Some responsibilities surpass friendship, surpass even blood.'

'We are sorry,' Apsalar said quietly after a long moment, 'but the task was ever beyond us, beyond those you see here.'

The cold, unhuman eyes studied her. 'Perhaps you are right. It is my turn to apologize. I had such . . . hopes.'

'Why?' Fiddler whispered. 'Why is Icarium so cursed?'

The Jaghut cocked his head, then abruptly swung back to the fire. 'Wounded warrens are a dangerous thing. *Wounding* one is far more so. My son sought a way to free me from the Azath. He failed. And was . . . damaged. He did not understand – and now he never will – that I am content here. There are few places in all the realms that offer a Jaghut peace, or, rather, such peace as we are capable of achieving. Unlike your kind, we yearn for solitude, for that is our only safety.'

He faced them again. 'For Icarium, of course, there is another irony. Without memory, he knows nothing of what once motivated him. He knows nothing of wounded warrens or the secrets of the Azath.' The Jaghut's sudden smile was a thing of pain. 'He knows nothing of me, either.'

Apsalar lifted her head suddenly, 'You are Gothos, aren't you?'

He did not answer.

Fiddler's gaze was drawn to a bench against the near wall. He hobbled to it and sat down. Leaning his head against the warm stone wall, he closed his eyes. *Gods, our struggles are as nothing, our inner scars naught but scratches. Bless you, Hood, for your gift of mortality. I could not live as these Ascendants do – I could not so torture my soul . . .*

'It is time for you to leave,' the Jaghut rumbled. 'If you are ailing with wounds, you shall find a bucket of water near the front door – the water has healing properties. This night is rife with unpleasantries in the streets beyond, so tread with care.'

Apsalar turned, meeting Fiddler's eyes as he blinked them

open and struggled to focus through his tears. *Oh, Mappo, Icarium . . . so entwined . . .*

'We must go,' she said.

He nodded, pushed himself to his feet. 'I could do with a drink of water,' he muttered.

Crokus was taking a last look around, at the faded tapestries, the ornate bench, the pieces of stone and wood placed on ledges, finally at the numerous scrolls stacked on a desktop against the wall opposite the double doors. With a sigh he backed away. Apsalar's father followed.

They returned to the hall and approached the entranceway. The bucket stood to one side, a wooden ladle hanging from a hook above it.

Apsalar took the ladle, dipped it into the water, offered it to Fiddler.

He drank deep, then barked in pain as an appallingly swift mending gripped his ankle. A moment later it passed. He sagged, suddenly covered in sweat. The others eyed him. 'For Hood's sake,' the sapper panted, 'don't drink unless you truly need it.'

Apsalar replaced the ladle.

The door opened at a touch, revealing a night sky and a shambles of a yard. A flagstone path wound its way to an arched gate. The entire grounds were enclosed by a low stone wall. Tenement houses rose beyond, every shutter closed.

'Well?' Crokus asked, turning to Fiddler.

'Aye. Malaz City.'

'Damned ugly.'

'Indeed.'

Testing his ankle and finding not a single tremor of pain, Fiddler walked down the path to the arched gate. In the dark pool of its shadow, he looked out onto the street.

No movement. No sound.

'I don't like this at all.'

'Sorcery has touched this city,' Apsalar pronounced. 'And I know its taste.'

Fiddler eyes narrowed on her. 'Claw?'

She nodded.

The sapper swung his pack around to reach beneath the flap. 'That means close-up scuffles, maybe.'

'If we're unlucky.'

He withdrew two sharpers. 'Yeah.'

'Where to?' Crokus whispered.

Damned if I know. 'Let's try Smiley's – it's a tavern both Kalam and I know well . . .'

They stepped out from the gate.

A huge shadow unfolded before them, revealing a hulking, ungainly shape.

Apsalar's hand shot out and stilled Fiddler's arm even as he prepared to throw. 'No, wait.'

The demon tilted a long-snouted head their way, regarding them with one silver eye. Then a figure astride its shoulder leaned into view. A youth, stained in old blood, his face a human version of the beast's.

'Aptorian,' Apsalar said in greeting.

The youth's fanged mouth opened and a rasping voice emerged. 'You seek Kalam Mekhar.'

'Yes,' Apsalar answered.

'He approaches the keep on the cliff—'

Fiddler started. 'Mock's Hold? Why?'

The rider cocked his head. 'He wishes to see the Empress?'

The sapper spun, eyes straining towards the towering bastion. A dark pennant flapped from the weathervane. 'Hood take us, she's *here*!'

'We shall guide you,' the rider said, offering a ghastly smile. 'Through Shadow – safe from the Claw.'

Apsalar smiled in return. 'Lead on, then.'

* * *

There was no slowing of pace as they rode towards the foot of wide stone stairs leading up the cliff face.

Kalam gripped Minala's arm. 'You'd better slow—'

'Just hold tight,' she growled. 'They aren't so steep.'

They aren't so steep? Fener's—

Muscles surged beneath them as the stallion plunged forward. Before the beast's hooves struck the stones, however, the world shifted into formless grey. The stallion screamed and reared back, but too late. The warren swallowed them.

Hooves skidded wildly beneath them. Kalam was thrown to one side, met a wall and was scraped off. A polished floor rose up to meet him, punched the air from his lungs. The crossbow flew from his hands and skittered away. Gasping, the assassin slowly rolled over.

They had arrived in a musty hallway, and the stallion was anything but pleased. The ceiling was high and arched, with an arm's reach to spare above the rearing animal. Somehow Minala had stayed in the saddle. She struggled to calm the stallion, and a moment later succeeded, leaning forward to rest one hand lightly just behind its flaring nostrils.

With a groan, Kalam climbed to his feet.

'Where are we?' Minala hissed, staring up and down the long, empty hall.

'If I'm correct, Mock's Hold,' the assassin muttered, retrieving the crossbow. 'The Empress knows we're coming – seems she's grown impatient . . .'

'If that's the case, Kalam, we're as good as dead.'

He was not inclined to disagree, but said nothing, stepping past the horse and eyeing the doors at the far end. 'I think we're in the Old Keep.'

'That explains the dust – even so, it smells like a stable.'

'Not surprising – half this building's been converted into just that. The Main Hall remains, though.' He nodded towards the doors. 'Through there.'

'No other approaches?'

He shook his head. 'None surviving. Her back door will be a warren, in any case.'

Minala grunted and climbed down from the saddle. 'Do you think she's been watching?'

'Magically? Maybe – you're wondering if she knows about you.' He hesitated, then handed her the crossbow. 'Let's pretend she doesn't. Hold back – I'll lead the stallion through.'

She nodded, cocking the weapon.

He looked at her. 'How in Hood's name did you get here?'

'The Imperial transport that left a day after *Ragstopper*. This horse wasn't out of place among Pormqual's breeders. We, too, were caught in that cursed storm, but the only real trouble came when we had to disembark from the bay. That's a swim I don't want to repeat. Ever.'

The assassin's eyes widened. 'Hood's breath, woman!' He looked away, then back. 'Why?'

She bared her teeth. 'Can you really be that dense, Kalam? In any case, was I wrong?'

There were some barriers the assassin had never expected to be breached. Their swift crumble left him breathless. 'All right,' he finally said, 'but I'll have you know, I'm anything but subtle.'

Her brows arched. 'You could have fooled me.'

Kalam faced the doors once again. He was armed with a single knife and had lost too much blood. *Hardly what you'd call properly equipped to assassinate an Empress, but it will have to do* . . . Without another word to Minala, he slipped forward, gathering the stallion's reins. The animal's hooves clopped loudly as they approached the old double doors.

He laid a hand against the wood. The dark-stained planks were sweating. *There's sorcery on the other side. Powerful sorcery.* He stepped back, met Minala's eyes where she stood ten paces back, and slowly shook his head.

She shrugged, lifting the crossbow in her hands.

He faced the doors again and gripped the latch of the one to his left. It lifted silently.

Kalam pushed the door open.

Inky darkness flowed out, bitter cold.

'Step within, Kalam Mekhar,' a woman's voice invited.

He saw little option. He had come for this, though the final shaping was not as he would have liked. The assassin strode into the dark, the stallion following.

'That is close enough. Unlike Topper and his Claw, I do not underestimate you.'

He could see nothing, and the voice seemed to be coming from everywhere at once. The door behind him – slightly ajar – offered a slight lessening of the gloom, but that reached but a pace or two before the blackness absorbed it entirely.

'You've come to kill me, Bridgeburner,' Empress Laseen said in a cool, dry voice. 'All this way. Why?'

The question startled him.

There was wry amusement in her voice as she continued, 'I cannot believe that you must struggle to find your answer, Kalam.'

'The deliberate murder of the Bridgeburners,' the assassin growled. 'The outlawing of Dujek Onearm. The attempted murders of Whiskeyjack, myself and the rest of the Ninth Squad. Old disappearances. A possible hand in Dassem Ultor's death. The assassination of Dancer and the Emperor. Incompetence, ignorance, betrayal . . .' He let his litany fall away.

Empress Laseen was silent for a long time, then she said in a low tone, 'And you are to be my judge. And executioner.'

'That's about right.'

'Am I permitted a defence?'

He bared his teeth. The voice was coming from everywhere – everywhere but one place, he now realized, the corner off to

904

his left, a corner that he estimated was no more than four strides away. 'You can try, Empress.' *Hood's breath, I can barely stand upright, and she's most likely got wards. As Quick Ben says, when you've got nothing, bluff . . .*

Laseen's tone hardened. 'High Mage Tayschrenn's efforts in Genabackis were misguided. The decimation of the Bridgeburners was not a part of my intentions. Within your squad was a young woman, possessed by a god that sought to kill me. Adjunct Lorn was sent to deal with her—'

'I know about that, Empress. You're wasting time.'

'I do not see it as a waste, given that time may be all I shall enjoy here in the mortal realm. Now, to continue answering your charges. The outlawing of Dujek is a temporary measure, a ruse, in fact. We perceived the threat that was the Pannion Domin. Dujek, however, was of the opinion that he could not deal with it on his own. We needed to fashion allies of enemies, Kalam. We needed Darujhistan's resources, we needed Caladan Brood and his Rhivi and Barghast, we needed Anomander Rake and his Tiste Andii. And we needed the Crimson Guard off our backs. Now, none of those formidable forces are strangers to pragmatism – one and all they could see the threat represented by the Pannion Seer and his rising empire. But the question of trust remained problematic. I agreed to Dujek's plan to cut him and his Host loose. As outlaws, they are, in effect, distanced from the Malazan Empire and its desires – our answer, if you will, to the issue of trust.'

Kalam's eyes narrowed in thought. 'And who knows of this ruse?'

'Only Dujek and Tayschrenn.'

After a moment he grunted. 'And what of the High Mage? What's his role in all this?'

He heard the smile as she said, 'Ah, well, he remains in the background, out of sight, but there for Dujek should Onearm need him. Tayschrenn is Dujek's – how do you soldiers say it – his *shaved knuckle in the hole.*'

Kalam was silent for a long minute. The only sounds in the chamber were his breathing and the slow but steady drip of his blood onto the flagstones. Then he said, 'There are older crimes that remain . . .' The assassin frowned. *The only sounds . . .*

'Assassinating Kellanved and Dancer? Aye, I ended their rule of the Malazan Empire. Usurped the throne. A most vicious betrayal, in truth. An empire is greater than any lone mortal—'

'Including you.'

'Including me. An empire enforces its own necessities, makes demands in the name of duty – and that particular burden is something you, as a soldier, most certainly understand. I knew those two men very well, Kalam – a claim you cannot make. I answered a necessity I could not avoid, with reluctance, with anguish. Since that time, I have made grievous errors in judgement – and I must live with those—'

'Dassem Ultor—'

'Was a rival. An ambitious man, sworn to Hood. I would not risk civil war, so I struck first. I averted that civil war, and so have no regrets on that.'

'It seems,' the assassin murmured dryly, 'you've prepared for this.' *Oh, haven't you just.*

After a moment she went on. 'So, if Dassem Ultor was sitting here right now, instead of me – tell me, Kalam, do you think he would have let you get this close? Do you think he would have sought to reason with you?' She was silent for a few more breaths, then continued, 'It seems clear that my efforts to disguise the direction of my voice have failed, for you face me directly. Three, perhaps four strides, Kalam, and you can end the reign of Empress Laseen. What do you choose?'

Smiling, Kalam shifted the grip of the knife in his right hand. *Very well, I'll play along.* 'Seven Cities—'

'Will be answered in kind,' she snapped.

Despite himself, the assassin's eyes widened at the anger he heard there. *Well, what do you know? Empress, you did not need your illusions after all. Thus, the hunt ends here.* He sheathed the knife.

And smiled in admiration when she gasped.

'Empress,' he rumbled.

'I – I admit to some confusion . . .'

I'd not thought acting one of your fortes, Laseen . . . 'You could have begged for your life. You could have given more reasons, made more justifications. Instead, you spoke, not with your voice, but with an empire's.' He turned away. 'Your hiding place is safe. I will leave your . . . presence—'

'Wait!'

He paused, brows raised at the sudden uncertainty in her voice. 'Empress?'

'The Claw – I can do nothing – I cannot recall them.'

'I know. They deal with their own.'

'Where will you go?'

He smiled in the darkness. 'Your confidence in me is flattering, Empress.' He swung the stallion around, strode to the doorway, then turned back one last time. 'If you meant to ask, will I come for you again? The answer is no.'

Minala was covering the entrance from a few paces away. She slowly straightened as Kalam stepped into the hallway. The crossbow held steady as the assassin pulled the stallion into view, then went around and shut the door.

'Well?' she demanded in a hiss.

'Well, what?'

'I heard voices – murmuring, garbled – is she dead? Did you kill the Empress?'

I killed a ghost, perhaps. No, a scarecrow I made in Laseen's guise. An assassin should never see the face behind the victim's mask. 'Naught but mocking echoes in that chamber. We're done here, Minala.'

Her eyes flashed. 'After all this . . . *mocking echoes*? You've crossed three continents to do this!'

He shrugged. 'It's our nature, isn't it? Again and again, we cling to the foolish belief that simple solutions exist. Aye, I anticipated a dramatic, satisfying confrontation – the flash of sorcery, the spray of blood. I wanted a sworn enemy dead by my hand. Instead –' he rumbled a laugh – 'I had an audience with a mortal woman, more or less . . .' He shook himself. 'In any case, we've the Claw's gauntlet ahead of us.'

'Terrific. What do we do now, then?'

He grinned. 'Simple – straight down their Hood-damned throat.'

'A foolish belief if ever I've heard one . . .'

'Aye. Come on.'

Leading the stallion, they went down the hallway.

The unnatural darkness slowly dissipated in the old Main Hall. Revealed in one corner was a chair on which was seated a withered corpse. Wisps of hair fluttered lightly in a faint draught, the lips were peeled back, the eye sockets two depthless voids.

A warren opened near the back wall and a tall, lean man draped in a dark-green cloak stepped through. He paused in the centre of the chamber, cocked his head towards the double doors opposite, then turned to the corpse on the chair. 'Well?'

Empress Laseen's voice emerged from those lifeless lips. 'No longer a threat.'

'Are you sure, Empress?'

'At some point in our conversation, Kalam realized that I was not here in the flesh, that he would have to resume his hunt. It seemed, however, that my words had an effect. He is not an unreasonable man, after all. Now, if you would kindly call off your hunters.'

'We have been over this – you know that is impossible.'

908

'I would not lose him, Topper.'

His laugh was a bark. 'I said I cannot call off my hunters, Empress – do you take that to mean you actually expect them to *succeed*? Hood's breath, Dancer himself would have hesitated before taking on Kalam Mekhar. No, better to view this disastrous night as a long-overdue winnowing of the brotherhood's weaker elements . . .'

'Generous of you, indeed.'

His smile was wry. 'We have learned lessons in killing this night, Empress. Much to ponder. Besides, I have a victim on which to vent my frustration.'

'Pearl, your favoured lieutenant.'

'Favoured no longer.'

A hint of warning entered Laseen's tone. 'I trust he will recover from your attentions, Topper.'

He sighed. 'Aye, but for the moment I will leave him to sweat . . . and consider Kalam's most pointed lesson. A certain measure of humility does a man good, I always say. Would you not agree, Empress?

'Empress?'

I have been talking to a corpse. Ah, Laseen, that is what I love most about you – your extraordinary ability to make one eat one's own words . . .

The captain of the Guard literally stumbled on them as they edged their way alongside the old keep's outer wall. Minala raised the crossbow and the man cautiously held his hands out to the sides. Kalam stepped forward and dragged him into the shadows, then quickly disarmed him.

'All right, Captain,' the assassin hissed. 'Tell me where the Hold's unwelcome guests are hiding.'

'I take it you don't mean yourselves,' the man said, sighing. 'Well, the gatehouse guard's been muttering about figures on the stairs – of course, the old bastard's half blind. But in the grounds here . . . nothing.'

'You can do better than that, Captain . . . ?'

The man scowled. 'Aragan. And here I am only days away from a new posting . . .'

'And that doesn't have to change, with a little co-operation.'

'I've just done the rounds – everything's quiet, as far as I can tell. Mind you, that doesn't mean a thing, does it?'

Minala glanced pointedly up at the pennant flapping from the weathervane above the Hold. 'And your official guest? No bodyguards?'

Captain Aragan grinned. 'Oh, the Empress, you mean.' Something in his tone hinted at great amusement. 'She's not aged well, has she?'

Inky blackness billowed in the courtyard. Minala shouted a warning even as the crossbow bucked in her hands. A voice shouted in pain.

Kalam straight-armed the captain, sending him sprawling to one side, then spun, knife flashing in his hand.

Four Hands of the Claw had appeared – twenty killers were converging on them. Throwing stars hissed through the darkness. Minala cried out, the crossbow flying from her grip as she staggered back. A bucking wave of sorcery rolled over the cobbles – and vanished.

Shadows swirled in the midst of the Hands, adding to the confusion. When something huge and ungainly stepped into view, Kalam's eyes widened with recognition. *Apt!* The demon lashed out. Bodies flew in all directions. The Hand most distant turned as one to meet this new threat. A rock-sized object flew towards them. The five hunters scattered – but too late, as the sharper struck the flagstones.

The explosion sent shards of iron scything through them.

A lone hunter closed with Kalam. Two thin-bladed knives darted forward in a blur. One struck the assassin in his right shoulder, the other missed his face by inches. Kalam's knife fell from nerveless fingers and he reeled back. The hunter leapt at him.

The sack of cloth-tacks intercepted the path of the man's head with a sickening crunch. The hunter dropped to writhe on the ground.

Another sharper detonated nearby. More screams rang through the courtyard.

Hands gripped Kalam's tattered apron, dragged him into the shadows. The assassin weakly struggled. 'Minala!'

A familiar voice whispered close to him. 'We've got her – and Crokus has the stallion—'

Kalam blinked. 'Sorry?'

'It's Apsalar these days, Corporal.'

The shadows closed on all sides. Sounds faded.

'You're full of holes,' Apsalar observed. 'Busy night, I take it.'

He grunted as the knife was slowly withdrawn from his shoulder, and he felt the blood welling in the blade's wake. A face leaned into his view, a grey-streaked red snarl of beard, a battered soldier's visage that now grinned.

'Hood's breath!' Kalam muttered. 'That's a damned ugly face you've got there, Fid.'

The grin broadened. 'Funny,' Fiddler said, 'I was just thinking the same – and that's what I don't get, what with you finding this flash lady for company—'

'Her wounds—'

'Minor,' Apsalar said from close by.

'Did you get her?' Fiddler asked. 'Did you kill the Empress?'

'No. I changed my mind—'

'Damn, we could – you *what*?'

'She's a sweet sack of bones after all, Fid – remind me to tell you the whole tale some time, provided you repay in kind, since I gather you managed to use the Azath gates.'

'Aye, we did.'

'Any problems?'

'Nothing to it.'

'Glad to hear one of us had it easy.' Kalam struggled to sit up. 'Where are we?'

A new voice spoke, sibilant and wry. 'The Realm of Shadow . . . My realm!'

Fiddler groaned, looked up. 'Shadowthrone is it now? Kellanved, more like it! We ain't fooled, y' got that? You can hide in those fancy shadows all you like, but you're still just the damned Emperor!'

'Ai, I quail!' The insubstantial figure giggled suddenly, edging back. 'And you, are you not a soldier of the Malazan Empire? Did you not take a vow? Did you not swear allegiance . . . to *me*?'

'To the Empire, you mean!'

'Why quibble about such minor distinctions? The truth remains that the aptorian has delivered you . . . to me, to me, to me!'

Sudden clicking, buzzing sounds made the god shift around to face the demon. When the strange noises coming from Apt ceased, Shadowthrone faced the group once again. 'Clever bitch! But we knew that, didn't we? She and that ugly child riding her, agh! Corporal Kalam of the Bridgeburners, it seems you've found a woman – oh, look at her eyes! Such fury! I am impressed, most impressed. And now you wish to settle down, yes? I wish to reward you all!' He gestured with both hands as if delivering blessings. 'Loyal subjects that you all are!'

Apsalar spoke in her cool, detached way. 'I do not seek any reward, nor does my father. We would have our associations severed – with you, with Cotillion, and with every other Ascendant. We would leave this warren, Ammanas, and return to the Kanese coast—'

'And I with them,' Crokus said.

'Oh, wonderful!' the god crooned. 'Synchronous elegance,

this fullest of full circles! To the Kanese coast indeed! To the very road where first we met, oh yes. Go, then! I send you with the smoothest of gestures. Go!' He raised an arm and caressed the air with his long, ghostly fingers.

Shadows swept over the three figures, and when they cleared, Apsalar, her father and Crokus had vanished.

The god giggled again. 'Cotillion will be so pleased, won't he just. Now, what of you, soldier? My magnanimity is rarely seen – I have so little of it! Quickly, before I tire of all this amusement.'

'Corporal?' Fiddler asked, crouching beside the assassin. 'Kalam, I ain't too thrilled with a god making offers, if you know what I mean—'

'Well, we haven't heard much of those offers yet, have we? Kell— Shadowthrone, I could do with a rest, if that's what you've in mind.' He glanced across and met Minala's eyes. She nodded. 'Some place safe—'

'Safe! Nowhere safer! Apt shall be at your side, as vigilant as ever! And comfort, oh yes, much comfort—'

'Ugh,' Fiddler said. 'Sounds dull as death. Count me out.'

The god seemed to cock its head. 'In truth, I owe you nothing, sapper. Only Apt speaks for you. Alas, she's acquired a certain . . . leverage. And oh, yes, you were a loyal enough soldier, I suppose. You wish to return to the Bridgeburners?'

'No.'

Kalam turned in surprise, to see his friend frowning.

'On our way up to Mock's Hold,' the sapper explained, 'we listened in on a group of guards during a shift-change – seems there's a last detachment of recruits holed up in Malaz Harbour on their way to join Tavore.' He met Kalam's eyes. 'Sorry, Corporal, but I'm for getting involved in putting down that rebellion in your homeland. So, I'll enlist . . . again.'

Kalam reached out a blood-smeared hand. 'Just stay alive, then, that's all I ask.'

The sapper nodded.

Shadowthrone sighed. 'And with such soldiers, it is no wonder we conquered half a world – no, Fiddler, I do not mock. This once, I do not mock. Though Laseen does not deserve such as you. Nonetheless, when these mists clear, you will find yourself in the alley back of Smiley's Tavern.'

'That will do me fine, Kellanved. I appreciate it.'

A moment later the sapper was gone.

The assassin turned a jaded eye on Shadowthrone. 'You understand, don't you, that I won't try to kill Laseen – my hunt's over. In fact, I'm tempted to warn you and Cotillion off her – leave the Empire to the Empress. You've got your own, right here—'

'Tempted to warn us, you said?' The god swept closer. 'Bite it back, Kalam, lest you come to regret it.' The shadow-wrapped form withdrew again. 'We do as we please. Never forget that, mortal.'

Minala edged to Kalam's side and laid a trembling hand on his uninjured shoulder. 'Gifts from gods make me nervous,' she whispered. 'Especially this one.'

He nodded, in full agreement.

'Oh,' Shadowthrone said, 'don't be like that! My offer stands. Sanctuary, a true opportunity to settle down. Husband and wife, hee hee! No, mother and father! And, best of all, there's no need to wait for children of your own – Apt has found some for you!'

The mists surrounding them suddenly cleared, and they saw, beyond Apt and her charge, a ragtag encampment sprawled over the summit of a low hill. Small figures wandered among the tent rows. Woodsmoke rose from countless fires.

'You wished for their lives,' Shadowthrone hissed in glee. 'Or so Apt claims. Now you have them. Your children await you, Kalam Mekhar and Minala Eltroeb – all thirteen hundred of them!'

CHAPTER TWENTY-FOUR

The priest of Elder Mael
dreams rising seas . . .

Dusk
Sethand

The whirlwind's spinning tunnel opened out onto the plain in an explosion of airborne dust. Wiry, strangely black grasses lay before Sha'ik as she led her train forward. After a moment she slowed her mount. What she had first thought to be humped stones stretching out in all directions she now realized were corpses, rotting under the sun. They had come upon a battlefield, one of the last engagements between Korbolo Dom and Coltaine.

The grasses were black with dried blood. Capemoths fluttered here and there across the scene. Flies buzzed the heat-swollen bodies. The stench was overpowering.

'Souls in tatters,' Heboric said beside her.

She glanced at the old man, then gestured Leoman forward to her other side. 'Take a scouting party,' she told the desert warrior. 'See what lies ahead.'

'Death lies ahead,' Heboric said, shivering despite the heat.

Leoman grunted. 'We are already in its midst.'

'No. This – this is nothing.' The ex-priest swung his sightless eyes towards Sha'ik. 'Korbolo Dom – *what has he done?*'

'We shall discover that soon enough,' she snapped, waving Leoman and his troop forward.

The army of the Apocalypse marched out from the Whirlwind Warren. Sha'ik had attached each of her three mages to a battalion – she preferred them apart, and distanced from her. They had been none too pleased by the order of march, and she now sensed the three sorcerers questing ahead with enhanced sensitivities – questing, then flinching back, L'oric first, then Bidithal and finally Febryl. From three sources came echoes of appalled horror.

And, should I choose it, I could do the same: Reach ahead with unseen fingers to touch what lies before us. Yet she would not.

'There is trepidation in you, lass,' Heboric murmured. 'Do you now finally regret the choices you have made?'

Regret? Oh, yes. Many regrets, beginning with a vicious argument with my sister, back in Unta, a sisterly spat that went too far. A hurt child . . . accusing her sister of killing their parents. One, then the other. Father. Mother. A hurt child, who had lost all reasons to smile. 'I have a daughter now.'

She sensed his attention suddenly focusing on her, the old man wondering at this strange turn of thought, wondering, then slowly – in anguish – coming to understand.

Sha'ik went on, 'And I have named her.'

'I've yet to hear it,' the ex-priest said, as if each word edged forward on thinnest ice.

She nodded. Leoman and his scouts had disappeared beyond the next rise. A faint haze of smoke awaited them there, and she wondered at the portent. 'She rarely speaks. Yet when she does . . . a gift with words, Heboric. A poet's eye. In some ways, as I might have become, given the freedom . . .'

'A gift with words, you say. A gift for you, but it may well be a curse for her, one that has little to do with freedom. Some people invite awe whether they like it or not. Such people come to be very lonely. Lonely in themselves, Sha'ik.'

Leoman reappeared, reining in on the crest. He did not wave them to a quicker pace – he simply watched as Sha'ik guided her army forward.

A moment later another party of riders arrived at the desert warrior's side. Tribal standards on display – strangers. Two of the newcomers drew Sha'ik's attention. They were still too distant to make out their features, but she knew them anyway: Kamist Reloe and Korbolo Dom.

'She will not be lonely,' she told Heboric.

'Then feel no awe,' he replied. 'Her inclination will be to observe, rather than participate. Mystery lends itself to such remoteness.'

'I can feel no awe, Heboric,' Sha'ik said, smiling to herself.

They approached the waiting riders. The ex-priest's attention stayed on her as they guided their horses up the gentle slope.

'And,' she continued, 'I understand remoteness. Quite well.'

'You have named her Felisin, haven't you?'

'I have.' She turned her head, stared into his sightless eyes. 'It's a fine name, is it not? It holds such . . . promise. A fresh innocence, such as that which parents would see in their child, those bright, eager eyes—'

'I wouldn't know,' he said.

She watched the tears roll down his weathered, tattooed cheeks, feeling detached from their significance, yet understanding that his observation was not meant as a condemnation. *Only loss.* 'Oh, Heboric,' she said. 'It's not worthy of grief.'

Had she thought a moment longer before speaking those words, she would have realized that they, beyond any others, would break the old man. He seemed to crumple inward before her eyes, his body shuddering. She reached out a hand he could not see, almost touched him, then withdrew it – and even as she did so, she knew that a moment of healing had been lost.

Regrets? Many. Unending.

'Sha'ik! I see the goddess in your eyes!' The triumphant claim was Kamist Reloe's, his face bright even as it seemed twisted with tension. Ignoring the mage, she fixed her gaze on Korbolo Dom. *Half-Napan – he reminds me of my old tutor, even down to the cool disdain in his expression. Well, this man has nothing to teach me.* Clustered around the two men were the warleaders of the various tribes loyal to the cause. There was something like shock in their faces, intimations of horror. Another rider was now visible, seated with equanimity on a mule, wearing the silken robes of a priest. He alone seemed untroubled, and Sha'ik felt a shiver of unease.

Leoman sat his horse slightly apart from the group. Sha'ik already sensed a dark turmoil swirling between the desert warrior and Korbolo Dom, the renegade Fist.

With Heboric at her side, she reached the crest and saw what lay beyond. In the immediate foreground was a ruined village – a scattering of smouldering houses and buildings, dead horses, dead soldiers. The stone-built entrance to the Aren Way was blackened with smoke.

The road stretched away in an even declination southward. The trees lining it to either side . . .

Sha'ik nudged her horse forward. Heboric matched her, silent and hunched, shivering in the heat. Leoman rode to flank her on the other side. They approached the Aren Gate.

The group wheeled to follow, in silence.

Kamist Reloe spoke, the faintest quaver in his voice. 'See what has been made of this proud gate? The Malazan Empire's Aren Gate is now Hood's Gate, Seer. Do you see the significance? Do you—'

'Silence!' Korbolo Dom growled.

Aye, silence. Let silence tell this tale.

They passed beneath the gate's cool shadow and came to the

first of the trees, the first of the bloated, rotting bodies nailed to them. Sha'ik halted.

Leoman's scouts were approaching at a fast canter. Moments later they arrived, reined in.

'Report,' Leoman snapped.

Four pale faces regarded them, then one said, 'It does not change, sir. More than three leagues – as far as we could see. There are – there are *thousands*.'

Heboric pulled his horse to one side, nudged it closer to the nearest tree and squinted up at the closest corpse.

Sha'ik was silent for a long minute, then, without turning, she said, 'Where is your army, Korbolo Dom?'

'Camped within sight of the city—'

'You failed to take Aren, then.'

'Aye, Seer, we failed.'

'And Adjunct Tavore?'

'The fleet has reached the bay, Seer.'

What will you make of this, sister?

'The fools surrendered,' Korbolo Dom said, his voice betraying his own disbelief. 'At High Fist Pormqual's command. And that is the Empire's new weakness – what used to be a strength: those soldiers obeyed the command. The Empire has lost its great leaders—'

'Has it now?' She finally faced him.

'Coltaine was the last of them, Seer,' the renegade Fist asserted. 'This new Adjunct is untested – a nobleborn, for Hood's sake. Who awaits her in Aren? Who will advise her? The Seventh is gone. Pormqual's army is gone. Tavore has an army of recruits. About to face veteran forces three times their number. The Empress has lost her mind, Seer, to think that this pureblood upstart will reconquer Seven Cities.'

She turned away from him and stared down the Aren Way. 'Withdraw your army, Korbolo Dom. Link up with my forces here.'

'Seer?'

'The Apocalypse has but one commander, Korbolo Dom. Do as I say.'

And silence once again tells its tale.

'Of course, Seer,' the renegade Fist finally grated.

'Leoman.'

'Seer?'

'Encamp our own people. Have them bury the dead on the plain.'

Korbolo Dom cleared his throat. 'And once we've regrouped – what do you propose to do then?'

Propose? 'We shall meet Tavore. But the time and place shall be of my choosing, not hers.' She paused, then said, 'We return to Raraku.'

She ignored the shouts of surprise and dismay, ignored the questions flung at her, even as they rose into demands. *Raraku – the heart of my newfound power. I shall need that embrace . . . if I am to defeat this fear – this terror – of my sister. Oh, Goddess, guide me now . . .*

The protests, eliciting no responses, slowly died away. A wind had picked up, moaned through the gate behind them.

Heboric's voice rose above it. 'Who is this? I can see nothing – can sense nothing. Who is this man?'

The corpulent, silk-clad priest finally spoke. 'An old man, Unhanded One. A soldier, no more than that. One among ten thousand.'

'Do – do you . . .' Heboric slowly turned, his milky eyes glistening. 'Do you hear a god's laughter? Does anyone hear a god's laughter?'

The Jhistal priest cocked his head. 'Alas, I hear only the wind.'

Sha'ik frowned at Heboric. He looked suddenly so . . . small.

After a moment she wheeled her horse around. 'It is time to leave. You have your orders.'

Heboric was the last, sitting helpless on his horse, staring up at a corpse that told him nothing. There was no end to the laughter in his head, the laughter that rode the wind sweeping through Aren Gate at his back.

What am I not meant to see? Is it you who have truly blinded me now, Fener? Or is it that stranger of jade who flows silent within me? Is this a cruel joke . . . or some kind of mercy?

See what has become of your wayward son, Fener, and know – most assuredly know – that I wish to come home.

I wish to come home.

Commander Blistig stood at the parapet, watching the Adjunct and her retinue ascend the broad limestone steps that led to the palace gate directly beneath him. She was not as old as he would have liked, but even at this distance he sensed something of the rumoured hardness in her. An attractive younger woman walked at her side – Tavore's aide and lover, it was said – but Blistig could not recall if he'd ever heard her name. On the Adjunct's other flank strode the captain of her family's own house guard, a man named Gimlet. He had the look of a veteran, and that was reassuring.

Captain Keneb arrived. 'No luck, Commander.'

Blistig frowned, then sighed. The scorched ship's crew had disappeared almost immediately after docking and offloading the wounded soldiers from Coltaine's Seventh. The garrison commander had wanted them present for the Adjunct's arrival – he suspected Tavore would desire to question them – *and Hood knows, those irreverent bastards could do with a blistering . . .*

'The Seventh's survivors have been assembled for her inspection, sir,' Keneb said.

'Including the Wickans?'

'Aye, and both warlocks among them.'

Blistig shivered despite the sultry heat. They were a

frightening pair. So cold, so silent. *Two children who are not.*

And Squint was still missing – the commander well knew that it was unlikely he would ever see that man again. Heroism and murder in a single gesture would be a hard thing for any person to live with. He only hoped that they wouldn't find the old bowman floating face down in the harbour.

Keneb cleared his throat. 'Those survivors, sir . . .'

'I know, Keneb, I know.' *They're broken. Queen's mercy, so broken. Mended flesh can do only so much. Mind you, I've got my own troubles with the garrison – I've never seen a company so . . . brittle.*

'We should make our way below, sir – she's almost at the gate.'

Blistig sighed. 'Aye, let's go meet this Adjunct Tavore.'

Mappo gently laid Icarium down in the soft sand of the sink-hole. He'd rigged a tarp over his unconscious friend, sufficient for shade, but there was little he could do about the stench of putrefaction that hung heavy in the motionless air. It was not the best of smells for the Jhag to awaken to . . .

The ruined village was behind them now, the black gate's shadow unable to reach to where Mappo had laid out the camp beside the road and its ghastly sentinels. The Azath warren had spat them out ten leagues to the north, days ago now. The Trell had carried Icarium in his arms all that way, seeking a place free of death – he'd hoped to have found it by now. Instead, the horror had worsened.

Mappo straightened at the sound of wagon wheels clattering on the road. He squinted against the glare. A lone ox pulled a flatbed cart up Aren Way. A man sat hunched on the buck-board seat, and there was motion behind him – two more men crouched down on the bed, bent to some unseen task.

Their progress was slow, as the driver stopped the cart at every tree, the man spending a minute or so staring up at the bodies nailed to it, before moving on to the next one.

Picking up his sack, Mappo made his way towards them.

On seeing him, the driver drew the cart to a halt and set the brake. He casually reached over the back of the seat and lifted into view a massive flint sword, which he settled sideways across his thighs.

'If you mean trouble, Trell,' the driver growled, 'back away now or you'll regret it.'

The other two men straightened up at this, both armed with crossbows.

Mappo set down his sack and held out both hands. All three men were strangely hued, and the Trell sensed a latent power in them that made him uneasy. 'The very opposite of trouble, I assure you. For days now I've walked among the dead – you're the first living people I've seen in that time. Seeing you has been a relief, for I had feared I was lost in one of Hood's nightmares . . .'

The driver scratched his red-bearded jaw. 'I'd say you are at that.' He set his sword down, twisted around. 'Reckon it's all right, Corporal – besides, maybe he has some bandages we can barter from him or something.'

The older of the two men on the flatbed swung down to the ground and approached Mappo.

The Trell said, 'You have injured soldiers? I've some skill in healing.'

The corporal's smile was taut, pained. 'I doubt you'd want to waste your skills. We ain't got hurt people in the wagon – we got a pair of dogs.'

'Dogs?'

'Aye. We found them at the Fall. Seems Hood didn't want 'em . . . not right away, anyway. Personally, I can't figure out why they're still alive – they're so full of holes and chopped up . . .' He shook his head.

The driver had climbed down as well, and was making his

923

way up to the end of the road, studying each and every corpse before moving on.

Mappo gestured the driver's way. 'You're looking for someone.'

The corporal nodded. 'We are, but the bodies are pretty far gone, it's kind of hard to tell for sure. Still, Stormy says he'll know him when he sees him, if he's here.'

Mappo's gaze flicked from the corporal, travelled down Aren Way. 'How far does this go?'

'The whole way, Trell. Ten thousand soldiers, give or take.'

'And you've . . .'

'We've checked them all.' The corporal's eyes narrowed. 'Well, Stormy's up to the last few, anyway. You know, even if we wasn't looking for someone particular . . . well, at the very least . . .' He shrugged.

Mappo looked away, his own face tightening. 'Your friend mentioned something called the Fall. What is that?'

'The place where Coltaine and the Seventh went down. The dogs were the only survivors. Coltaine guided thirty thousand refugees from Hissar to Aren. It was impossible, but that's what he did. He saved those ungrateful bastards and his reward was to get butchered not five hundred paces from the city's gate. No-one helped him, Trell.' The corporal's eyes searched Mappo's. 'Can you imagine that?'

'I am afraid I know nothing of the events you describe.'

'So I guessed. Hood knows where you've been hiding lately.'

Mappo nodded. After a moment he sighed. 'I'll take a look at your dogs, if you like.'

'All right, but we don't hold out much hope. Thing is, the lad's gone and taken to 'em, if you know what I mean.'

The Trell walked to the cart and clambered aboard.

He found the lad hunched down over a mass of red, torn flesh and bone, feebly waving flies from the flesh.

'Hood's mercy,' Mappo whispered, studying what had once been a cattle-dog. 'Where's the other one?'

The youth pulled back a piece of cloth, revealing a lapdog of some kind. All four legs had been deliberately broken. Pus crusted the breaks and the creature shook with fever.

'That little one,' the youth said. 'It was left lying on this one.' His tone was filled with pain and bewilderment.

'Neither one will make it, lad,' Mappo said. 'That big one should have died long ago – it may well be dead now—'

'No. No, he's alive. I can feel his heart, but it's slowing. It's slowing, and we can't do nothing. Gesler says we should help it along, that slowing, we should end its pain, but maybe . . . maybe . . .'

Mappo watched the lad fuss over the hapless creatures, his long-fingered, almost delicate hands daubing the wounds with a blood-soaked piece of cloth. After a moment, the Trell straightened, slowly turning to stare down the long road. He heard a shout behind him, close to the gate, then heard the corporal named Gesler running to join Stormy.

Ah, Icarium. Soon you will awaken, and still I shall grieve, and so lead you to wonder . . . My grief begins with you, friend, for your loss of memories – memories not of horror, but of gifts given so freely . . . Too many dead . . . how to answer this? How would you answer this, Icarium?

He stared for a long time down Aren Way. Behind him the lad crouched over the cattle-dog's body, while the crunch of boots approached slowly from up the road. The cart pitched as Stormy clambered up to take his seat. Gesler swung himself into the flat-bed, expressionless.

The youth looked up. 'You find him, Gesler? Did Stormy find him?'

'No. Thought for a minute . . . but no. He ain't here, lad. Time to head back to Aren.'

'Queen's blessing,' the youth said. 'Then there's always a chance.'

'Aye, who can say, Truth, who can say.'

The lad, Truth, returned his attention to the cattle-dog.

Mappo slowly turned, met the corporal's eyes and saw the lie writ plain. The Trell nodded.

'Thanks for taking a look at the dogs, anyway,' Gesler said. 'I know, they're finished. I guess we wanted . . . well, we would have liked . . .' His voice fell away, then he shrugged. 'Want a ride back to Aren?'

Mappo shook his head and climbed down to stand at the roadside. 'Thank you for the offer, Corporal. My kind aren't welcome in Aren, so I'll pass.'

'As you like.'

He watched them turn the cart around.

How would you answer this . . .

They were thirty paces down the road when the Trell shouted. They halted, Gesler and Truth straightening to watch as Mappo jogged forward, rummaging in his pack as he did so.

Iskaral Pust padded down the rock-strewn, dusty path. He paused to scratch vigorously beneath his tattered robes, first one place, then another, then another. A moment later he shrieked and began tearing at his clothes.

Spiders. Hundreds of them, spinning away, falling to the ground, scattering into cracks and crevices as the High Priest thrashed about.

'I knew it!' Iskaral screamed. 'I knew it! Show yourself! I dare you!'

The spiders reappeared, racing over the sun-baked ground.

Gasping, the High Priest staggered back, watching as the D'ivers sembled into human form. He found himself facing a wiry, black-haired woman. Though she was an inch shorter than him, her frame and features bore a startling resemblance to his own. Iskaral Pust scowled.

'You thought you had me fooled? You thought I didn't know you were lurking about!'

The woman sneered. 'I *did* have you fooled! Oh, how you hunted! Thick-skulled idiot! Just like every Dal Honese man I've ever met! A thick-skulled idiot!'

'Only a Dal Honese woman would say that—'

'Aye, and who would know better!'

'What is your name, D'ivers?'

'Mogora, and I've been with you for months. Months! I saw you lay the false trail – I saw you painting those hand and paw marks on the rocks! I saw you move that stone to the forest's edge! My kin may be idiots, but I am not!'

'You'll never get to the real gate!' Iskaral Pust shrieked. 'Never!'

'I – don't – want – to!'

His eyes narrowed on her sharp-featured face. He began circling her. 'Indeed,' he crooned, 'and why is that?'

Twisting to keep him in front of her, she crossed her arms and regarded him down the length of her nose. 'I escaped Dal Hon to be rid of idiots. Why would I become Ascendant just to rule over *other* idiots?'

'You are a true Dal Honese hag, aren't you? Spiteful, condescending, a sneering bitch in every way!'

'And you are a Dal Honese oaf – conniving, untrustworthy, shifty—'

'Those are all words for the same thing!'

'And I've plenty more!'

'Let's hear them, then.'

They began down the trail, Mogora resuming her litany. 'Lying, deceitful, thieving, shifty—'

'You said that one already!'

'So what? *Shift*y, slimy, slippery . . .'

The enormous undead dragon rose silently from its perch on the mesa's summit, wings spreading to glow with the sun's light, even as the membrane dimmed the colour that reached through. Black, flat eyes glanced down at the two figures scrambling towards the cliff face.

The attention was momentary. Then an ancient warren opened before the soaring creature, swallowed it whole, then vanished.

Iskaral Pust and Mogora stared at the spot in the sky for a moment longer. A half-grin twitched on the High Priest's features. 'Ah, *you* weren't fooled, were you? You came here to guard the true gate. Ever mindful of your duties, you T'lan Imass. You Bonecasters with your secrets that drive me mad!'

'You were born mad,' Mogora muttered.

Ignoring her, he continued addressing the now vanished dragon. 'Well, the crisis is past, isn't it? Could you have held? Against all those children of yours? Not without Iskaral Pust, oh no! Not without me!'

Mogora barked a contemptuous laugh.

He threw her a glare, then scampered ahead.

Stopping beneath the lone, gaping window high in the cliff tower, he screamed, 'I'm home! I'm home!' The words echoed forlornly, then faded.

The High Priest of Shadow began dancing in place, too agitated to remain still, and he kept dancing as a minute passed, then another. Mogora watched him, one eyebrow raised.

Finally a small, brown head emerged from the window and peered down.

The bared fangs might have been a smile, but Iskaral Pust could not be sure of that. He could never be sure of that.

'Oh, look,' Mogora murmured, 'one of your fawning worshippers.'

'Aren't you funny.'

'What I am is hungry. Who's going to prepare meals now that Servant's gone?'

'You are, of course.'

She flew into a spitting rage. Iskaral Pust watched her antics with a small smile on his face. *Ah, glad to see I've not lost my charm . . .*

The enormous, ornate wagon stood in a cloud of dust well away from the road, the horses slow to lose their terror, stamping, tossing their heads.

Two knee-high creatures scampered from the wagon and padded on bandy legs towards the road, their long arms held out to the sides. Outwardly, they resembled bhok'arala, their small, wizened faces corkscrewing as they squinted in the harsh sunlight.

Yet they were speaking Daru.

'Are you sure?' the shorter of the pair said.

The other snarled in frustration. 'I'm the one who's linked, right? Not you, Irp, not you. Baruk would never be such a fool as to task you with anything – except grunt work.'

'You got that right, Rudd. Grunt work. I'm good at that, ain't I? Grunt work. Grunt, grunt, grunt – you sure about this? Really sure?'

They made their way up the bank and approached the last tree lining the road. Both creatures squatted down before it, staring up in silence at the withered corpse nailed to the bole.

'I don't see nothing,' Irp muttered. 'I think you're wrong. I think you've lost it, Rudd, and you won't admit it. I think—'

'I'm one word away from killing you, Irp, I swear it.'

'Fine. I die good, you know. Grunt, gasp, grunt, sigh . . . grunt.'

Rudd ambled to the tree's base, the few stiff hairs of his hackles the only sign of his simmering temper. He clambered upward, pulled himself onto the chest of the corpse and rummaged with one hand beneath the rotted shirt. He plucked loose a tattered, soiled piece of cloth. Unfolding it, he frowned.

Irp's voice rose from below. 'What is it?'

'A name's written on here.'

'Whose?'

Rudd shrugged. '"Sa'yless Lorthal."'

'That's a woman's name. He's not a woman, is he?'

'Of course not!' Rudd snapped. A moment later he tucked the cloth back under the shirt. 'Mortals are strange,' he muttered, as he began searching beneath the shirt again. He quickly found what he sought, and drew forth a small bottle of smoky glass.

'Well?' Irp demanded.

'It broke all right,' Rudd said with satisfaction. 'I can see the cracks.' He leaned forward and bit through the thong, then, clutching the bottle in one hand, scrambled back down. Crouched at the base, he held the bottle to the sun and squinted through it.

Irp grunted.

Rudd then held the bottle against one pointed ear and shook it. 'Ah! He's in there all right!'

'Good, let's go—'

'Not yet. The body comes with us. Mortals are particular that way – he won't want another. So, go get it, Irp.'

'There's nothing left of the damned thing!' Irp squawked.

'Right, then it won't weigh much, will it?'

Grumbling, Irp climbed the tree and began pulling out the spikes.

Rudd listened to his grunts with satisfaction, then he shivered. 'Hurry up, damn you! It's eerie around here.'

The Jhag's eyes fluttered open and slowly focused on the wide, bestial face looking down on him. Puzzled recognition followed. 'Mappo Trell. My friend.'

'How do you feel, Icarium?'

He moved slightly, winced. 'I – I am injured.'

930

'Aye. I'm afraid I gave away my last two elixirs, and so could not properly heal you.'

Icarium managed a smile. 'I am certain, as always, that the need was great.'

'You may not think so, I'm afraid. I saved the lives of two dogs.'

Icarium's smile broadened. 'They must have been worthy beasts. I look forward to that tale. Help me up, please.'

'Are you certain?'

'Yes.'

Mappo supported Icarium as he struggled to his feet. The Jhag tottered, then found his balance. He raised his head and looked around. 'Where – where are we?'

'What do you remember?'

'I – I remember nothing. No, wait. We'd sighted a demon – an aptorian, it was, and decided to follow it. Yes, that I recall. That.'

'Ah, well, we are far to the south, now, Icarium. Cast out from a warren. Your head struck a rock and you lost consciousness. Following that aptorian was a mistake.'

'Evidently. How – how long?'

'A day, Icarium. Just a day.'

The Jhag had steadied, visibly regaining strength until Mappo felt it safe to step away, though one hand remained on Icarium's shoulder.

'West of here lies the Jhag Odhan,' the Trell said.

'Yes, a good direction. I admit, Mappo, I feel close this time. Very close.'

The Trell nodded.

'It's dawn? Have you packed up our camp?'

'Aye, though I suggest we walk but a short distance today – until you're fully recovered.'

'Yes, a wise decision.'

It was another hour before they were ready to leave, for

Icarium needed to oil his bow and set a whetstone to his sword. Mappo waited patiently, seated on a boulder, until the Jhag finally straightened and turned to him, then nodded.

They set off, westward.

After a time, as they walked on the plain, Icarium glanced at Mappo. 'What would I do without you, my friend?'

The nest of lines framing the Trell's eyes flinched, then he smiled ruefully as he considered his reply. 'Perish the thought.'

As it reached into the wasteland known as the Jhag Odhan, the plain stretched before them, unbroken.

EPILOGUE

Hood's sprites are revealed
the disordered host
Whispering of deaths
in wing-flap chorus

Dour music has its own
beauty, for the song of ruin
is most fertile.

Wickan Dirge
Fisher

The young widow, a small clay flask clutched in her hands, left the horsewife's yurt and walked out into the grassland beyond the camp. The sky overhead was empty and, for the woman, lifeless. Her bare feet stepped heavily, toes snagging in the yellowed grass.

When she'd gone thirty paces she stopped and lowered herself to her knees. She faced the vast Wickan plain, her hands resting on her swollen belly, the horsewife's flask smooth, polished and warm beneath the calluses.

The searching was complete, the conclusions inescapable. The child within her was ... *empty*. A thing without a soul. The vision of the horsewife's pale, sweat-beaded face rose to hover before the young woman, her words whispering like the wind. *Even a warlock must ride a soul – the children they claimed were no different from children they did not claim. Do you understand? What grows within you possesses . . . nothing. It has been cursed – for reasons only the spirits know.*

The child within you must be returned to the earth.

She unstoppered the flask. There would be pain, at least to begin with, then a cooling numbness. No-one from the camp would watch, all eyes averted from this time of shame.

A storm cloud hung on the north horizon. She had not noticed it before. It swelled, rolled closer, towering and dark.

The widow raised the flask to her lips.

A hand swept over her shoulder and clamped onto her wrist. The young woman cried out and twisted around to see the horsewife, her breath coming in gasps, her eyes wide as she stared at the storm cloud. The flask fell to the ground. Figures from the camp were now running towards the two women.

The widow searched the old woman's weathered face, seeing fear and . . . *hope*? 'What? What is it?'

The horsewife seemed unable to speak. She continued staring northward.

The storm cloud darkened the rolling hills. The widow turned and gasped. The cloud was not a cloud. It was a swarm, a seething mass of black, striding like a giant towards them, tendrils spinning off, then coming around again to rejoin the main body.

Terror gripped the widow. Pain shot up her arm from where the horsewife still clutched her wrist, a hold that threatened to snap bones.

Flies! Oh, spirits below – flies . . .

The swarm grew closer, a flapping, tumbling nightmare.

The horsewife screamed in wordless anguish, as if giving voice to a thousand grieving souls. Releasing the widow's wrist, she fell to her knees.

The young woman's heart hammered with sudden realization.

No, not flies. Crows. Crows, so many crows—

Deep within her, the child stirred.

This ends the Second Tale of the Malazan Book of the Fallen

GLOSSARY

Tribes of the Seven Cities Subcontinent

Arak: Pan'potsun Odhan
Bhilard: east of Nenoth Odhan
Can'eld: northeast of Ubaryd
Debrahl: north regions
Dhis'bahl: Omari and Nahal Hills
Gral: Ehrlitan foothills down to Pan'potsun
Kherahn Dhobri: Geleen Plain
Khundryl: west of Nenoth Odhan
Pardu: north of Geleen Grasslands
Semk: Karas Hills and Steppes
Tithan: south of Sialk
Tregyn: west of Sanimon

Seven Cities (Bisbrha and Debrahl) Language (Selected Words)

bhok'arala: a squall of cliff-dwelling winged monkeys (common)
(**bhok'aral**: singular)
bloodfly: a biting insect

chigger fleas: windborne fleas of the desert
dhenrabi: a large marine carnivore
Dryjhna: the Apocalypse
durhang: an opiate
emrag: an edible cactus favoured by Trell
emulor: a poison derived from flowers
enkar'al: a winged reptile equivalent in size to a horse (very rare)
esanthan'el: a dog-sized winged reptile
guldindha: a broad-leafed tree
jegura: a medicinal cactus
kethra knife: a fighting weapon
Marrok: dry-season siesta
Mezla: vaguely pejorative name for Malazans
odhan: plains, wastelands
rhizan: a squirrel-sized winged lizard (common)
sawr'ak: a thin light beer served cold
sepah: unleavened bread
She'gai: a hot wind of the dry season
simharal: a seller of children
tapu: a food-hawker
tapuharal: a seller of goat meat (cooked)
tapusepah: a seller of bread
taputasr: a seller of pastries
tasr: sepah with honey
telaba: a sea cloak of the Dosii (Dosin Pali)
tralb: a poison derived from mushrooms
White Paralt: a poison derived from spiders

Place Names

Aren: Holy City and site of Imperial Headquarters
Balahn (Battle of)

Bat'rol: a small village near Hissar

Caron Tepasi: an inland city

Chain of Dogs Coltaine's train of soldiers and refugees journeying from Hissar to Aren

Dojal Spring (Battle of)

Dosin Pali: a city on the south coast of Otataral Island

Ehrlitan: Holy City

G'danisban: a city near Pan'potsun

Geleen: a city on the coast of the Clatar Sea

Gelor Ridge (Battle of Gelor)

Guran: an inland city

Hissar: a city on the east coast

Holy Desert Raraku: a region west of the Pan'potsun Odhan

Karakarang: a Holy City on Otataral Island

Nenoth (Battle of)

Pan'potsun: Holy City

Rutu Jelba: a port city on north Otataral Island

Sanimon (Battle of)

Sekala Plain (Battle of)

Sialk: a city on the east coast

The Path of Hands: a Soletaken and D'ivers path to Ascendancy

Tremorlor (the Azath House in the Wastes, also Odhanhouse)

Ubaryd: a Holy City on the south coast

Vathar Crossing (Coltaine's Crossing, the Vathar Massacre): the Day of Pure Blood, Mesh'arn tho'ledann

Vin'til Basin: southwest of Hissar

The World of Sorcery

The Warrens (the Paths – those Warrens accessible to humans)

Denul: the Path of Healing
D'riss: the Path of Stone
Hood's Path: the Path of Death
Meanas: the Path of Shadow and Illusion
Ruse: the Path of the Sea
Rashan: the Path of Darkness
Serc: the Path of the Sky
Tennes: the Path of the Land
Thyr: the Path of Light

The Elder Warrens

Kurald Galain: the Tiste Andii Warren of Darkness
Kurald Emurlahn: the Tiste Edur Warren
Tellann: the T'lan Imass Warren
Omtose Phellack: the Jaghut Warren
Starvald Demelain: the Tiam Warren, the First Warren

Titles and Groups

First Sword of Empire: Malazan and T'lan Imass, a title denoting an Imperial champion
Fist: a military governor in the Malazan Empire
High Fist: a commander of armies in a Malazan Campaign
Kron T'lan Imass: the name of the clans under the command of Kron
Logros T'lan Imass: the name of the clans under the command of Logros

The Bridgeburners: a legendary élite division in the Malaz 2nd Army
The Pannion Seer: a mysterious prophet ruling the lands south of Darujhistan
The Warlord: the name for Caladan Brood
The Claw: the covert organization of the Malazan Empire

Peoples (human and non-human)

Barghast (non-human): pastoral nomadic warrior society
Forkrul Assail (non-human): extinct mythical people (one of the Four Founding Races)
Jaghut (non-human): extinct mythical people (one of the Four Founding Races)
Moranth (non-human): highly regimented civilization centred in Cloud Forest
T'lan Imass: one of the Four Founding Races, now immortal
Tiste Andii (non-human): an Elder Race
Tiste Edur (non-human): an Elder Race
Trell (non-human): pastoral nomadic warrior society

The Deck of Dragons – The Fatid (and associated Ascendants)

High House Life
King
Queen (Queen of Dreams)
Champion
Priest
Herald
Soldier
Weaver

Mason
Virgin

High House Death
King (Hood)
Queen
Knight (once Dassem Ultor)
Magi
Herald
Soldier
Spinner
Mason
Virgin

High House Light
King
Queen
Champion
Priest
Captain
Soldier
Seamstress
Builder
Maiden

High House Dark
King
Queen
Knight (Son of Darkness)
Magi
Captain
Soldier
Weaver
Mason
Wife

High House Shadow
King (Shadowthrone/Ammanas)
Queen
Assassin (the Rope/Cotillion)
Magi
Hound

Unaligned
Oponn (the Jesters of Chance)
Obelisk (Burn)
Crown
Sceptre
Orb
Throne

Bonecaster: a shaman of the T'lan Imass
D'ivers: a higher order of shapeshifting
Otataral: a magic-negating reddish ore mined from the Tanno
Hills, Seven Cities
Soletaken: an order of shape-shifting
Warrens of Chaos: the miasmic paths between the Warrens

Ascendants

Apsalar, Lady of Thieves
Beru, Lord of Storms
Burn, Lady of the Earth, the Sleeping Goddess
Caladan Brood, the Warlord
Cotillion/The Rope (the Assassin of High House Shadow)
Dessembrae, Lord of Tragedy
D'rek, the Worm of Autumn (sometimes the Queen of Disease,
see Poliel)

Fanderay, She-Wolf of Winter
Fener, the Boar (*see also* Tennerock)
Gedderone, Lady of Spring and Rebirth
Great Ravens, ravens sustained by magic
Hood (King of High House Death)
Jhess, Queen of Weaving
Kallor, the High King
K'rul, Elder God
Mael, Elder God
Mowri, Lady of Beggars, Slaves and Serfs
Nerruse, Lady of Calm Seas and Fair Wind
Oponn, Twin Jesters of Chance
Osserc, Lord of the Sky
Poliel, Mistress of Pestilence
Queen of Dreams (Queen of High House Life)
Shadowthrone/Ammanas (King of High House Shadow)
Shedenul/Soliel, Lady of Health
Soliel, Mistress of Healing
Tennerock/Fener, the Boar of Five Tusks
The Crippled God, King of Chains
The Hounds (of High House Shadow)
Togg (*see* Fanderay), the Wolf of Winter
Trake/Treach, the Tiger of Summer and Battle
Son of Darkness/Moon's lord/Anomander Rake (Knight of High House Dark)
Treach, First Hero

Steven Erikson's epic fantasy sequence
continues in *Memories of Ice*, now
available in Bantam Press trade paperback.
Here is the Prologue as a taster . . .

The ancient wars of the T'lan Imass and the Jaghut
saw the world torn asunder. Vast armies contended
on the ravaged lands, the dead piled high, their bone
the bones of hills, their spilled blood the blood of seas.
Sorceries raged until the sky itself was fire . . .

> Kinick Karbar'n *Ancient Histories, Vol. I*

Maeth'ki Im (Pogrom of the Rotted Flower), the 33rd Jaghut War
298,665 years before Burn's Sleep

Swallows darted through the clouds of midges dancing over
the mudflats. The sky above the marsh remained grey, but it
had lost its mercurial wintry gleam, and the warm wind sighing through the air above the ravaged land held the scent of healing.

What had once been the inland freshwater sea the T'lan called Jaghra Til – born from the shattering of the Jaghut ice-fields – was now in its own death-throes. The pallid overcast was reflected in dwindling pools and stretches of knee-deep water for as far south as the eye could scan, but nonetheless, newly birthed land dominated the vista.

The breaking of the sorcery that had raised the glacial age had returned to the region the old, natural seasons, but the memories

944

of mountain-high ice lingered. The exposed bedrock to the north was gouged and scraped, its basins filled with boulders. The heavy silts that had formed the floor of the inland sea still bubbled with escaping gases, as the land, freed of the enormous weight with the glacier's passing eight years ago, slowly rose.

Jaghra Til's life had been short, yet the silts that had settled on its bottom were thick. And treacherous.

Pran Chole, Bonecaster of Cannig Tol's clan among the Kron T'lan, sat motionless atop a mostly buried boulder along an ancient beach ridge. The descent before him was snarled in low, wiry grasses and withered driftwood. Twelve paces beyond, the land dropped slightly, then stretched out into a broad basin of mud. Three ranag had become trapped in a boggy sinkhole twenty paces into the basin. A bull male, his mate and their calf, ranged in a pathetic defensive circle. Mired and vulnerable, they must have seemed easy kills for the pack of ay that found them. But the land was treacherous indeed. The large tundra wolves had succumbed to the same fate as the ranag. Pran Chole counted six ay, including a yearling. Tracks indicated that another yearling had circled the sinkhold dozens of times before wandering westward, doomed no doubt to die in solitude.

How long ago had this drama occurred? There was no way to tell. The mud had hardened on ranag and ay alike, forming cloaks of clay latticed with cracks. Spots of bright green showed where windborn seeds had germinated, and the Bonecaster was reminded of his visions when spiritwalking – a host of mundane details twisted into something unreal. For the beasts, the struggle had become eternal, hunter and hunted locked together for all time.

Someone padded to his side, crouched down beside him. Pran Chole's tawny eyes remained fixed on the frozen tableau. The rhythm of footsteps told the Bonecaster the identity of his companion, and now came the warm-blooded smells that were as much a signature as resting eyes upon the man's face.

Cannig Tol spoke. 'What lies beneath the clay, Bonecaster?'

'Only that which has shaped the clay itself, Clan Leader.'

'You see no omen in these beasts?'

Pran Chole smiled. 'Do you?'

Cannig Tol considered for a time, then said, 'Ranag are gone from these lands. So too the ay. We see before us an ancient battle.

These statements have depth, for they stir my soul.'

'Mine as well,' the Bonecaster conceded.

'We hunted the ranag until they were no more, and this brought starvation to the ay, for we had also hunted the tenag until they were no more too. The agkor who walk with the bhederin would not share with the ay, and now the tundra is empty. From this, I conclude that we were wasteful and thoughtless in our hunting.'

'Yet the need to feed our own young—'

'The need for more young was great.'

'It remains so, Clan Leader.'

Cannig Tol grunted. 'The Jaghut are powerful in these lands, Bonecaster. They did not flee – not at first. You know the cost in Imass blood.'

'And the land yields its bounty to answer that cost.'

'To serve our war.'

'Thus, the depths are stirred.'

The Clan Leader nodded and was silent. Pran Chole waited. In their shared words they still tracked the skin of things. Revelation of the muscle and bone was yet to come. But Cannig Tol was no fool, and the wait was not long.

'We are as those beasts.'

The Bonecaster's eyes shifted to the south horizon, tightened.

Cannig Tol continued. 'We are the clay, and our endless war against the Jaghut is the struggling beast beneath. The surface is shaped by what lies beneath.' He gestured with one hand. 'And before us now, in these creatures slowly turning to stone, is the curse of eternity.' There was still more. Pran Chole said nothing. 'Ranag and ay,' Cannig Tol resumed. 'Almost gone from the mortal realm. Hunter and hunted both.'

'To the very bones,' the Bonecaster whispered.

'Would that you had seen an omen,' the Clan Leader muttered, rising.

Pran Chole also straightened. 'Would that I had,' he agreed in a tone that only faintly echoed Cannig Tol's wry, sardonic utterance.

'Are we close, Bonecaster?'

Pran Chole glanced down at his shadow, studied the antlered silhouette, the figure hinted at within the furred cape, ragged

946

hides and headdress. The sun's angle made him seem tall – almost as tall as a Jaghut. 'Tomorrow,' he said. 'They are weakening. A night of travel will weaken them yet more.'

'Good. Then the clan shall camp here tonight.'

The Bonecaster listened as Cannig Tol made his way back down to where the others waited. With darkness, Pran Chole would spiritwalk into the whispering earth, seeking those of his own kind. While their quarry was weakening, Cannig Tol's clan was yet weaker. Less than a dozen adults remained. When pursuing Jaghut, the distinction of hunter and hunted had little meaning.

He lifted his head and sniffed the crepuscular air. Another Bonecaster wandered this land. The taint was unmistakable. He wondered who it was, wondered why it travelled alone, bereft of clan and kin. And, knowing that even as Pran had sensed its presence so it in turn had sensed his, he wondered why it had not yet sought them out.

She pulled herself clear of the mud and dropped down onto the sandy bank, her breath coming in harsh, laboured gasps. Her son and daughter squirmed free of her leaden arms, crawled further onto the island's modest hump. The Jaghut mother lowered her head until her brow rested against the cool, damp sand. Grit pressed into the skin of her forehead with raw insistence. The burns there were too recent to have healed, nor were they likely to. She was defeated, and death had only to await the arrival of her hunters.

They were mercifully competent, at least. These T'lan Imass cared nothing for torture. A swift killing blow. For her, then for her children. And with them – this meagre, tattered family – the last of the Jaghut would vanish from this continent. Mercy arrived in many guises. Had they not joined in chaining Raest, they would all – Imass and Jaghut both – have found themselves kneeling before the Tyrant. A temporary truce of expedience. She'd known enough to flee once the chaining was done; she'd known, even then, that the Imass clan would resume the pursuit. The mother felt no bitterness, but that made her no less desperate.

Sensing a new presence on the small island, her head snapped up. Her children had frozen in place, staring up in terror at the Imass woman who now stood before them. The mother's grey eyes

947

narrowed. 'Clever, Bonecaster. My senses were tuned only to those behind us. Very well, be done with it.'

The young, black-haired woman smiled. 'No bargains, Jaghut? You always seek bargains to spare the lives of your children. Have you broken the kin-threads with these two, then? They seem young for that.'

'Bargains are pointless. Your kind never agree to them.'

'No, yet still *your* kind try.'

'I shall not. Kill us, then. Swiftly.'

The Imass was wearing the skin of a panther. Her eyes were as black and seemed to match its shimmer in the dying light. She looked well-fed, her large, swollen breasts indicating that she had recently birthed. The Jaghut mother could not read the woman's expression, only that it lacked the typical grim certainty she usually associated with the strange, rounded faces of the T'lan Imass.

The Bonecaster spoke. 'I have enough Jaghut blood on my hands. I leave you to the Kron clan that shall find you tomorrow.'

'To me,' the mother growled, 'it matters naught which of you kills us, only that you kill us.'

The woman's broad mouth quirked. 'I can see your point.'

Weariness threatened to overwhelm the Jaghut mother, but she managed to pull herself into a sitting position. 'What,' she asked between gasps, 'do you want?'

'To offer you a bargain.'

Breath catching, the Jaghut mother stared into the Bonecaster's dark eyes, and saw nothing of mockery. Her gaze then dropped, for the briefest of moments, on her son and daughter, then back up to hold steady on the woman's own.

The T'lan Imass nodded slowly.

The earth had cracked some time in the past, a wound of such depth as to birth a molten river wide enough to stretch from horizon to horizon. Vast and black, the river of stone and ash reached southwestward, down to the distant sea. Only the smallest of plants had managed to find purchase, and the Bonecaster's passage – a Jaghut child in the crook of each arm – raised sultry clouds of dust that hung motionless in her wake.

She judged the boy at perhaps five years of age; his sister

perhaps four. Neither seemed entirely aware, and clearly neither had understood their mother when she'd hugged them goodbye. The long flight down the L'Amath and across the Jaghra Til had driven them both into shock. No doubt witnessing the ghastly death of their father had not helped matters. They clung to her with their small, grubby hands, grim reminders of the child she had but recently lost. Before long, both began suckling at her breasts, evincing desperate hunger. Some time later, the children slept.

The lava flow thinned as she approached the coast. A range of hills rose into distant mountains on her right. A level plain stretched directly before her, ending at a ridge half a league distant. Though she could not see it, she knew that on the other side of the ridge, the land slumped down to the sea. The plain itself was marked by regular humps, the mounds were arrayed in concentric circles, and at the centre was a larger dome – all covered in a mantle of lava and ash. The rotted tooth of a ruined tower rose from the plain's edge, at the base of the first line of hills. Those hills, as she had noted the first time she had visited this place, were themselves far too evenly spaced to be natural.

The Bonecaster lifted her head. The mingled scents were unmistakable, one ancient and dead, the other . . . less so. The boy stirred in her clasp, but remained asleep.

'Ah,' she murmured, 'you sense it as well.'

Skirting the plain, she walked towards the blackened tower.

The gate was just beyond the ragged edifice, suspended in the air at about six times her height. She saw it as a red welt, a thing damaged, but no longer bleeding. She could not recognize the warren – the old damage obscured the portal's characteristics. Unease rippled faintly through her.

The Bonecaster set the children down by the tower, then sat on a block of tumbled masonry. Her gaze fell to the two young Jaghut, still curled in sleep, lying on their beds of ash. 'What choice?' she whispered. 'It must be Omtose Phellack. It certainly isn't Tellann. Starvald Demelain? Unlikely.' Her eyes were pulled to the plain, narrowing on the mound rings. 'Who dwelt here? Who else was in the habit of building in stone?' She fell silent for a long moment, then swung her attention back to the ruin. 'This tower is the final proof, for it is naught else but Jaghut, and such a structure would

949

not be raised this close to an inimical warren. No, the gate is Omtose Phellack. It must be so.'

Still, there were additional risks. An adult Jaghut in the warren beyond, coming upon two children not of its own blood, might as easily kill them as adopt them. 'Then their deaths stain another's hands, a Jaghut's.' Scant comfort, that distinction. *It matters not which of you kills us, only that you kill us.* The breath hissed between the woman's teeth. 'What choice?' she asked again.

She would let them sleep a little longer. Then, she would send them through the gate. A word to the boy – *take care of your sister. The journey shall not be long.* And to them both – *your mother waits beyond.* A lie, but they would need courage. *If she cannot find you, then one of her kin will. Go then, to safety, to salvation.*

After all, what could be worse than death?

She rose as they approached. Pran Chole tested the air, frowned. The Jaghut had not unveiled her warren. Even more disconcerting, where were her children?

'She greets us with calm,' Cannig Tol muttered.

'She does,' the Bonecaster agreed.

'I've no trust in that – we should kill her immediately.'

'She would speak with us,' Pran Chole said.

'A deadly risk, to appease her desire.'

'I cannot disagree, Clan Leader. Yet . . . what has she done with her children?'

'Can you not sense them?'

Pran Chole shook his head. 'Prepare your spearmen,' he said, stepping forward.

There was peace in her eyes, so clear an acceptance of her own imminent death that the Bonecaster was shaken. He walked through shin-deep water, then stepped onto the island's sandy bank to stand face to face with the Jaghut. 'What have you done with them?' he demanded.

The mother smiled, the skin peeling back to reveal her tusks. 'Gone.'

'Where?'

'Beyond your reach, Bonecaster.'

Pran Chole's frown deepened. 'These are our lands. There is no place here that is beyond our reach. Have you slain them with your own hands?'

The Jaghut cocked her head, studied the T'lan Imass. 'I had always believed you were united in your hatred of our kind. I had always believed that such concepts as compassion and mercy were alien to your natures.'

The Bonecaster stared at the woman, then his gaze dropped away, past her, and scanned the soft clay ground. 'A T'lan Imass has been here,' he said. 'A woman. The Bonecaster—' *The one I could not find in my spiritwalk. The one who chose not to be found.* 'What has she done?'

'She has explored this land,' the Jaghut replied. 'She has found a gate far to the south. It is Omtose Phellack.'

'I am glad,' Pran Chole said, 'I am not a mother.' *And you, woman, should be glad I am not cruel.* He gestured. Heavy spears flashed past the Bonecaster. Six long, fluted heads of flint punched through the skin covering the Jaghut's chest. She staggered, then folded to the ground in a clatter of spearshafts.

Thus ended the 33rd Jaghut War.

Pran Chole whirled. 'We've no time for a pyre. We must strike southwards. Quickly.'

Cannig Tol stepped forward as his warriors went to retrieve their weapons. The Clan Leader's eyes narrowed on the Bonecaster. 'What distresses you?'

'A renegade Bonecaster has taken the children.'

'South?'

'To Morn.'

The Clan Leader's brows knitted.

'The renegade believes the Rent to be Omtose Phellack.'

Pran Chole watched the blood leave Cannig Tol's face. 'Go to Morn, Bonecaster,' he whispered. 'We are not cruel. Go now.'

Pran Chole bowed. The Tellann warren engulfed him.

The faintest release of her power sent the two Jaghut children upward, into the gate's maw. The girl cried out a moment before reaching it, a longing wail for her mother, whom she imagined waited beyond. Then the two small figures vanished within.

The Bonecaster sighed and continued to stare upward, seeking any evidence that the passage had gone awry. It seemed, however, that no wound had reopened, no gush of wild power from the portal. Did it look different? She could not be sure. This was new land for her; she had nothing of the bone-bred sensitivity that she had known all her life among the lands of the Tarad clan, in the heart of the First Empire.

The Tellann warren opened behind her. The woman spun around, moments from veering into her Soletaken form. An arctic fox bounded into view, slowed upon seeing her, then sembled back into its Imass form. She saw before her a young man, wearing the skin of his totem animal across his shoulders, and a battered antler headdress. His expression was twisted with fear, his eyes not on her, but on the portal beyond.

The woman smiled. 'I greet you, fellow Bonecaster. Yes, I have sent them through. They are beyond the reach of your vengeance, and this pleases me.'

His tawny eyes fixed on her. 'Who are you? What clan?'

'I have left my clan, but I was once counted among the Logros. I am named Kilava.'

'You should have let me find you last night,' Pran Chole said. 'I would then have been able to convince you that a swift death was the greater mercy for those children than what you have done here, Kilava.'

'They are young enough to be adopted—'

'You have come to the place called Morn,' Pran Chole interjected, his voice cold. 'To the ruins of an ancient city—'

'Jaghut—'

'Not Jaghut! This tower, yes, but it was built long afterwards, in the time between the city's destruction and the T'ol Ara'd, which but buried something already dead.' He raised a hand, pointed towards the suspended gate. 'It was this – this wounding – that destroyed the city, Kilava. The warren beyond – do you not understand? It is *not* Omtose Phellack! Tell me this – how are such wounds sealed? You know the answer, Bonecaster!'

The woman slowly turned, studied the Rent. 'If a soul sealed that wound, then it should have been freed . . . when the children arrived—'

'Freed,' Pran Chole hissed, '*in exchange!*'

Trembling, Kilava faced him again. 'Then where is it? Why has it not appeared?'

Pran Chole turned to study the central mound on the plain.

'Oh,' he whispered, 'but it has.' He glanced back at his fellow Bonecaster. 'Tell me, will you in turn give up your life for those children? They are trapped now, in an eternal nightmare of pain. Does your compassion extend to sacrificing yourself in yet another exchange?' He sighed. 'I thought not, so wipe away those tears, Kilava. Hypocrisy ill suits a Bonecaster.'

'What . . .' the woman managed after a time, 'what has been freed?'

Pran Chole shook his head. He studied the mound again. 'I am not sure, but we shall have to do something about it, sooner or later, Kilava. I suspect we have plenty of time. The creature must now free itself of its tomb, and that has been thoroughly warded. More, there is the T'ol Ara'd's mantle of stone still clothing the barrow.' After a moment, he added, 'but time we shall have.'

'What do you mean?'

'The Gathering has been called. The Ritual of Tellann awaits us, Bonecaster.'

She spat. 'You are all insane. To choose immortality for the sake of a war – madness. I shall defy the call, Bonecaster.'

He nodded. 'Yet the Ritual shall be done. I have spiritwalked into the future, Kilava. I have seen my withered face of two hundred thousand and more years hence. We shall have our eternal war.'

Bitterness filled Kilava's voice. 'My brother shall be pleased.'

'Who is your brother?'

'Onos T'oolan, the First Sword.'

Pran Chole turned at this. 'You are the Defier. You slaughtered your clan – your kin—'

'To break the link and thus achieve freedom, yes. Alas, my eldest brother's skills more than matched mine. Yet now we are *both* free, though what I celebrate, Onos T'oolan curses.' She wrapped her arms around herself, and Pran Chole saw upon her layers and layers of pain. Hers was a freedom he did not envy. She spoke again. 'This city, then. Who built it?'

'K'Chain Che'Malle.'

'I know the name, but little else of them.'

Pran Chole nodded. 'We shall, I expect, learn.'

* * *

Korelri and Jacuruku, in the Time of Dying
119,736 Years before Burn's Sleep (three years after the Fall of the
Crippled God)

The Fall had shattered a continent. Forests had burned, the firestorms lighting the horizon in every direction, bathing crimson the heaving ash-filled clouds blanketing the sky. The conflagration had seemed unending, world-devouring, and through it all could be heard the screams of a god.

Pain gave birth to rage. Rage to poison, an infection sparing no-one.

Scattered survivors remained, reduced to savagery, wandering a landscape pocked with huge craters now filled with murky, lifeless water, the sky churning endlessly above them. Kinship had been dismembered, love had proved a burden too costly to carry. They ate what they could, often each other, and scanned the ravaged world around them with rapacious intent.

One figure walked alone. Wrapped in rotting rags, he was of average height, his features blunt and unprepossessing. There was a dark cast to his face, a heavy inflexibility in his eyes. He walked as if gathering suffering unto himself, unmindful of its vast weight, walked as if incapable of yielding, of denying the gifts of his own spirit.

In the distance, ragged bands eyed the figure as he strode, step by step, across what was left of the continent that would one day be called Korelri. Hunger might have driven them closer, but there were no fools left among the survivors of the Fall, and so they maintained a watchful distance, their curiosity dulled by fear. For the man was an ancient god, and he walked among them.

Beyond the suffering he absorbed, K'rul would have willingly embraced their broken souls, yet he had fed – was feeding – on the blood spilled onto this land, and the truth was this: the power born of that would be needed.

In K'rul's wake, men and women killed men, killed women, killed chidren. Dark slaughter was the river the Elder God rode.

Elder Gods embodied a host of harsh unpleasantries.

The foreign god had been torn apart in his descent to earth. He

954

had come down in pieces, in streaks of flame. His pain was fire, screams and thunder, a voice that had been heard by half the world. Pain, and outrage. And, K'rul reflected, grief. It would be a long time before the foreign god could begin to reclaim the remaining fragments of its life, and so begin to unveil its nature. K'rul feared that day's arrival. From such a shattering could only come madness.

The summoners were dead, destroyed by what they had called down upon them. There was no point in hating them, no need to conjure up images of what they in truth deserved by way of punishment. They had, after all, been desperate. Desperate enough to part the fabric of chaos, to open a way into an alien, remote realm; to then lure a curious god of that realm closer, ever closer to the trap they had prepared. The summoners sought power.

All to destroy one man.

The Elder God has crossed the ruined continent, had looked upon the still-living flesh of the Fallen God, had seen the unearthly maggots that crawled forth from that rotting, pulsing meat and broken bone. Had seen what those maggots flowered into. Even now, as he reached the battered shoreline of Jacuruku, the ancient sister continent to Korelri, they wheeled above him on their broad, black wings. Sensing the power within him, they were hungry for its taste. But a strong god could ignore the scavengers that trailed in his wake, and K'rul was a strong god. Temples had been raised in his name. Blood had for generations soaked countless altars. The nascent cities were wreathed in the smoke of forges, pyres, the red glow of humanity's dawn. The First Empire had risen, on a continent half a world away from where K'rul now walked. An empire of humans, born from the legacy of the T'lan Imass.

But it had not been alone for long. Here, on Jacuruku, in the shadow of long-dead K'Chain Che'Malle ruins, another empire had emerged. Brutal, a devourer of souls, its ruler was a warrior without equal. K'rul had come to destroy him, had come to snap the chains of twelve million slaves – even the Jaghut Tyrants had not commanded such heartless mastery over their subjects. No, it took a mortal human to achieve this level of tyranny over his kin.

Two other Elder Gods were converging on the Kallorian

Empire. The decision had been made. The three – last of the Elders – would bring to a close this High King's despotic rule. K'rul could sense his companions. Both were close; both had been comrades once, but they all, K'rul included, had changed, had drifted far apart. This would mark the first conjoining in millennia.

He could sense a fourth presence as well, a savage, ancient beast following his spoor. A beast of the earth, of winter's frozen breath, a beast with white fur bloodied, wounded almost unto death by the Fall. A beast with but one surviving eye to look upon the destroyed land that had once been its home long before the empire's rise. Trailing, but coming no closer. And, K'rul well knew, it would remain a distant observer to all that was about to occur. The Elder god could spare it no sorrow, yet was not indifferent to its pain.

We each survive as we must, and when time comes to die, we find our places of solitude . . .

The Kallorian Empire had spread to every shoreline of Jacuruku, yet K'rul saw no-one as he took his first steps inland. Lifeless wastes stretched out on all sides. The air was grey with ash and dust, the skies overhead churning like lead in a smith's cauldron. The Elder God experienced the first breath of unease, sidling chill across his soul. Above him the god-spawned scavengers cackled as they wheeled.

A familiar voice spoke in K'rul's mind. *Brother, I am upon the north shore.*

'And I the west.'

Are you troubled?

'I am. All is . . . dead.'

Incinerated. The heat remains deep beneath the beds of ash. Ash . . . and bone.

A third voice spoke. *Brothers, I am come from the south, where once dwelt the cities. All destroyed. The echoes of a continent's death-cry still linger. Are we deceived? Is this illusion?*

K'rul addressed the first Elder who had spoken in his mind. 'Draconus, I too feel that death-cry. Such pain . . . indeed, more dreadful in its aspect than that of the Fallen One. If not a deception as our sister suggests, what has he done?'

We have stepped onto this land, and so all share what you sense, K'rul, Draconus replied. *I, too, am not certain of its truth. Sister, do you approach the High King's abode?*

The third voice spoke. *I do, brother Draconus. Would you and brother K'rul join me now, that we may confront this mortal as one?*

'We shall.'

Warrens opened, one to the far north, the other directly before K'rul.

The two elder Gods joined their sister upon a ragged hilltop where wind swirled through the ashes, spinning funereal wreathes skyward. Directly before them, on a heap of burnt bones, was a throne.

The man seated upon it was smiling. 'As you can see,' he rasped after a moment of scornful regard, 'I have . . . prepared for your arrival. Oh yes, I knew you were coming. Draconus, of Tiam's kin. K'rul, Opener of the Paths.' His grey eyes swung to the third Elder. 'And *you*. My dear, I was under the impression that you had abandoned your . . . old self. Walking among the mortals, playing the role of middling sorceress – such a deadly risk, though perhaps this is what entices you so to the mortal game. You've stood on fields of battles, woman. One stray arrow . . .' He slowly shook his head.

'We have come, Kallor,' K'rul said, 'to end your reign of terror.'

The man's brows rose. 'You would take from me all that I have worked so hard to achieve? Fifty years, dear rivals, to conquer an entire continent. Oh, perhaps Ardatha still held out – always late in sending me my rightful tribute – but I ignored such petty gestures. She has fled, did you know? The bitch. Do you imagine yourselves the first to challenge me? The Circle brought down a foreign god. Aye, the effort went awry, thus sparing me the task of killing the fools with my own hand. And the Fallen One? Well, he'll not recover for some time, and even then, do you truly imagine he will accede to anyone's bidding? I would have—'

'Enough,' Draconus growled. 'Your prattling grows wearisome, Kallor.'

'Very well,' the High King sighed. He leaned forward. 'You've come to liberate my people from my tyrannical rule. Alas, I am not one to relinquish such things. Not to you, not to anyone.' He settled back, waved a languid hand. 'Thus, what you would refuse me, I now refuse you.'

Though the truth was before K'rul's eyes, he could not believe it. 'What have—'

'Are you blind?' Kallor shrieked, clutching at the arms of his throne. 'It is gone! *They* are gone! Break the chains, will you? Go ahead – no, I surrender them! Here, all about you, is *now free*! Dust! Bones! All free!'

'You have in truth incinerated an entire continent?' the sister Elder whispered. 'Jacuruku—'

'It is more, and never again shall be. What I have unleashed will never heal. Do you understand me? Never. And it is all your fault. Yours. Paved in bone and ash, this noble road you chose to walk. *Your* road.'

'We cannot allow this—'

'It is done, you foolish woman!'

K'rul spoke within the minds of his kin. *It must done. I will fashion a . . . a place for this. Within myself.*

A warren to hold all this? Draconus asked in horror. *My brother—*

No, it must be done. Join with me now, this shaping will not be easy—

It will break you, K'rul, his sister said. *There must be another way.*

None. To leave this continent as it is . . . no, this world is young. To carry such a scar . . .

What of Kallor? Draconus inquired. *What of this . . . this creature?*

We mark him, K'rul replied. *We know his deepest desire, do we not? And the span of his life?*

Long, my friends.

Agreed.

K'rul blinked, fixed his dark, heavy eyes on the High King. 'For this crime, Kallor, we deliver appropriate punishment. Know this: you, Kallor Eiderann Tes'thesula, shall know mortal life unending. Mortal, in the ravages of age, in the pain of wounds and the anguish of despair. In dreams brought to ruin. In love withered. In the shadow of Death's spectre, ever a threat to end what you will not relinquish.'

Draconus spoke. 'Kallor Eiderann Tes'thesula, you shall never ascend.'

Their sister said, 'Kallor Eiderann Tes'thesula, each time you rise, you shall then fall. All that you achieve shall turn to dust in your hands. As you have wilfully done here, so it shall be in turn visited upon all that you do.'

'Three voices curse you,' K'rul intoned. 'It is done.'

The man on the throne trembled. His lips drew back in a rictus snarl. 'I shall break you. Each of you. I swear this upon the bones of twelve million sacrifices. K'rul, you shall fade from the world, you shall be forgotten. Draconus, what you create shall be turned upon you. And as for you, woman, unhuman hands shall tear your body into pieces, upon a field of battle, yet you shall know no respite – thus, my curse upon you, Sister of Cold Nights. Kallor Eiderann Tes'thesula, one voice, has spoken three curses. Thus.'

They left Kallor upon his throne, upon its heap of bones. They merged their power to draw chains around a continent of slaughter, then pulled it into a warren created for that sole purpose, leaving the land itself bared. To heal.

The effort left K'rul broken, bearing wounds he knew he would carry for all his existence. More, he could already feel the twilight of his worship, the blight of Kallor's curse. To his surprise, the loss pained him less than he would have imagined.

The three stood at the portal of the nascent, eternally lifeless realm, and looked upon their handiwork.

Then Draconus spoke. 'I am forging a sword.'

K'rul and the Sister of Cold Nights nodded, for this was known to them both.

'The power I have invested possesses a . . . a finality.'

'Then,' K'rul whispered, 'you must make alterations in the final shaping.'

'So it seems. I shall need to think long on this.'

After a long moment, K'rul and his brother turned to their sister.

She shrugged. 'I shall endeavour to guard myself. When my destruction comes, it will be through betrayal and naught else. There can be no precaution against such a thing, lest my life become its own nightmare of suspicion and mistrust. To this, I shall not surrender. Until that moment, I shall continue to play the mortal game.'

'Careful, then,' K'rul murmured, 'whom you choose to fight for.'

'Find a companion,' Draconus advised. 'A worthy one.'

'Wise words from you both. I thank you.'

There was nothing more to be said. The three had come

together, with an intent they had now achieved. Perhaps not in the manner they would have wished, but it was done. And the price had been paid. Willingly. Three lives and one, each destroyed. For the one, the beginning of eternal hatred. For the three, a fair exchange.

Elder Gods, it has been said, embodied a host of unpleasantries.

In the distance, the beast watched the three figures part ways. Riven with pain, white fur stained and dripping blood, the gouged pit of its lost eye glittering wet, it held its hulking mass on trembling legs. It longed for death, but death would not come. It longed for vengeance, but those who had wounded it were dead. There but remained the man seated on the throne, the one who had laid waste to the beast's home. Time enough for the settling of that score.

A final longing filled the creature's ravaged soul. Somewhere, amidst the conflagration of the Fall and the chaos that followed, it had lost its mate and was now alone. Perhaps she still lived. Perhaps she wandered, wounded as he was, searching the broken wastes for a sign of him. Or, perhaps she had fled, in pain and terror, to the warren that had given fire to her spirit. Wherever she had gone – assuming she still lived – he would find her.

The three distant figures unveiled warrens, each vanishing into their Elder realms. The beast elected to follow none of them. They were young entities as far as he and his mate were concerned, and the warren she might have fled to was, in comparison to those of the Elder Gods, ancient. The path that awaited him was perilous, and he knew fear in his labouring heart. The portal that opened before him revealed a grey-streaked, swirling storm of power. The beast hesitated, then strode into it.

And was gone.